THE AGATHA CHRISTIE
COMPANION

The three books in this volume are reproduced
by arrangement with William Collins Sons & Co. Ltd.
This edition published 1980 by Book Club Associates

Printed in Great Britain
by W & J Mackay Limited, Chatham

THE THIRD AGATHA CHRISTIE COMPANION

Dumb Witness

Murder in Mesopotamia

Mrs McGinty's Dead

BOOK CLUB ASSOCIATES LONDON

CONTENTS

Dumb Witness

AGATHA
CHRISTIE

TO
DEAR PETER,
MOST FAITHFUL OF FRIENDS
AND DEAREST OF COMPANIONS,
A DOG IN A THOUSAND

Contents

1 . The Mistress of Littlegreen House

MISS ARUNDELL died on May 1st. Though her illness was short her death did not occasion much surprise in the little country town of Market Basing where she had lived since she was a girl of sixteen. For Emily Arundell was well over seventy, the last of a family of five, and she had been known to be in delicate health for many years and had indeed nearly died of a similar attack to the one that killed her some eighteen months before.

But though Miss Arundell's death surprised no one, something else did. The provisions of her will gave rise to varying emotions, astonishment, pleasurable excitement, deep condemnation, fury, despair, anger and general gossip. For weeks and even months Market Basing was to talk of nothing else! Every one had their own contribution to make to the subject from Mr Jones the grocer, who held that "blood was thicker than water," to Mrs Lamphrey at the post office, who repeated *ad nauseam* that "there's something behind it, depend upon it! You mark my words."

What added zest to the speculations on the subject was the fact that the will had been made as lately as April 21st. Add to this the further fact that Emily Arundell's near relations had been staying with her just before that date over Easter Bank Holiday and it will be realised that the most scandalous theories could be propounded, pleasurably relieving the monotony of everyday life in Market Basing.

There was one person who was shrewdly suspected of knowing more about the matter than she was willing to admit. That was Miss Wilhelmina Lawson, Miss Arundell's companion. Miss Lawson, however, professed herself just as much in the dark as every one else. She, too, she declared, had been dumbfounded when the will was read out.

A lot of people, of course, did not believe this. Nevertheless, whether Miss Lawson was or was not as ignorant as she declared herself to be, only one person really knew the true facts. That person was the dead woman herself. Emily Arundell had kept her own counsel as she was in the habit of doing. Even to her lawyer she had said nothing of the motives underlying her action. She was content with making her wishes clear.

In that reticence could be found the keynote of Emily Arundell's character. She was, in every respect, a typical product of her generation. She had both its virtues and its vices. She was autocratic and often overbearing, but she was also intensely warm-hearted. Her tongue was sharp but her actions were kind. She was outwardly sentimental but inwardly shrewd. She had a succession of companions whom she bullied unmercifully, but treated with great generosity. She had a great sense of family obligation.

On the Friday before Easter Emily Arundell was standing in the hall of Littlegreen House giving various directions to Miss Lawson.

Emily Arundell had been a handsome girl and she was now a well-preserved, handsome old lady with a straight back and a brisk manner. A faint yellowness in her skin was a warning that she could not eat rich food with impunity.

Miss Arundell was saying:

"Now then, Minnie, where have you put them all?"

"Well, I thought—I hope I've done right—Dr and Mrs Tanios in the Oak room and Theresa in the Blue room and Mr Charles in the Old Nursery——"

Miss Arundell interrupted:

"Theresa can have the Old Nursery and Charles will have the Blue room."

"Oh, yes—I'm sorry—I thought the Old Nursery being rather more inconvenient——"

"It will do very nicely for Theresa."

In Miss Arundell's day, women took second place. Men were the important members of society.

"I'm so sorry the dear little children aren't coming," murmured Miss Lawson, sentimentally.

She loved children and was quite incapable of managing them.

"Four visitors will be quite enough," said Miss Arundell. "In any case, Bella spoils her children abominably. They never dream of doing what they are told."

Minnie Lawson murmured:

"Mrs Tanios is a very devoted mother."

Miss Arundell said with grave approval:

"Bella is a good woman."

Miss Lawson sighed and said:

"It must be very hard for her sometimes—living in an outlandish place like Smyrna."

Emily Arundell replied:

"She has made her bed and she must lie on it."

And having uttered this final Victorian pronouncement she went on:

"I am going to the village now to speak about the orders for the week-end."

"Oh, Miss Arundell, do let me. I mean——"

"Nonsense. I prefer to go myself. Rogers needs a sharp word. The trouble with you is, Minnie, that you're not *emphatic* enough. Bob! Bob! Where *is* the dog?"

A wire-haired terrier came tearing down the stairs. He circled round and round his mistress uttering short staccato barks of delight and expectation.

Together mistress and dog passed out of the front door and down the short path to the gate.

Miss Lawson stood in the doorway smiling rather foolishly after them, her mouth a little open. Behind her a voice said tartly:

"Them pillowcases you gave me, miss, isn't a pair."

"What? How stupid of me. . . ."

Minnie Lawson plunged once more into household routine.

Emily Arundell, attended by Bob, made a royal progress down the main street of Market Basing.

It was very much of a royal progress. In each shop she entered the proprietor always hurried forward to attend to her.

She was Miss Arundell of Littlegreen House. She was "one of our oldest customers." She was "one of the old school. Not many about like her nowadays."

"Good-morning, miss. What can I have the pleasure of doing

for you—Not tender? Well, I'm sorry to hear that. I thought myself it was as nice a little saddle—Yes, of course, Miss Arundell. If you say so, it is so—No, indeed, I wouldn't think of sending Canterbury to *you*, Miss Arundell—Yes, I'll see to it myself, Miss Arundell."

Bob and Spot, the butcher's dog, circled slowly round each other, hackles raised, growling gently. Spot was a stout dog of nondescript breed. He knew that he must not fight with customers' dogs, but he permitted himself to tell them, by subtle indication, just exactly what mincemeat he would make of them were he free to do so.

Bob, a dog of spirit, replied in kind.

Emily Arundell said "Bob!" sharply and passed on.

In the greengrocer's there was a meeting of heavenly bodies. Another old lady, spherical in outline, but equally distinguished by that air of royalty, said:

"Mornin', Emily."

"Good-morning, Caroline."

Caroline Peabody said:

"Expecting any of your young people down?"

"Yes, all of them. Theresa, Charles and Bella."

"So Bella's home, is she? Husband too?"

"Yes."

It was a simple monosyllable, but underlying it was knowledge common to both ladies.

For Bella Biggs, Emily Arundell's niece, had married a Greek. And Emily Arundell's people, who were what is known as "all service people," simply did not marry Greeks.

By way of being obscurely comforting (for of course such a matter could not be referred to openly) Miss Peabody said:

"Bella's husband's got brains. *And* charming manners!"

"His manners are delightful," agreed Miss Arundell.

Moving out into the street Miss Peabody asked:

"What's this about Theresa being engaged to young Donaldson?"

Miss Arundell shrugged her shoulders.

"Young people are so casual nowadays. I'm afraid it will have to be a rather long engagement—that is, if anything comes of it. He has no money."

"Of course Theresa has her own money," said Miss Peabody.

Miss Arundell said stiffly:

"A man could not possibly wish to live on his wife's money."

Miss Peabody gave a rich, throaty chuckle.

"They don't seem to mind doing it, nowadays. You and I are out of date, Emily. What I can't understand is what the child *sees* in him. Of all the namby-pamby young men!"

"He's a clever doctor, I believe."

"Those *pince-nez*—and that stiff way of talking! In my young days we'd have called him a poor stick!"

There was a pause while Miss Peabody's memory, diving into the past, conjured up visions of dashing, bewhiskered young men. . . .

She said with a sigh:

"Send that young dog Charles along to see me—if he'll come."

"Of course. I'll tell him."

The two ladies parted.

They had known each other for considerably over fifty years. Miss Peabody knew of certain regrettable lapses in the life of General Arundell, Emily's father. She knew just precisely what a shock Thomas Arundell's marriage had been to his sisters. She had a very shrewd idea of certain troubles connected with the younger generation.

But no word had ever passed between the two ladies on any of these subjects. They were both upholders of family dignity, family solidarity, and complex reticence on family matters.

Miss Arundell walked home, Bob trotting sedately at her heels. To herself, Emily Arundell admitted what she would never have admitted to another human being, her dissatisfaction with the younger generation of her family.

Theresa, for instance. She had no control over Theresa since the latter had come into her own money at the age of twenty-one. Since then the girl had achieved a certain notoriety. Her picture was often in the papers. She belonged to a young, bright, go-ahead set in London—a set that had freak parties and occasionally ended up in the police courts. It was not the kind of notoriety that Emily Arundell approved of for an Arundell. In fact, she disapproved very much of Theresa's way of living. As

regards the girl's engagement, her feelings were slightly confused. On the one hand she did not consider an upstart Dr
Donaldson good enough for an Arundell. On the other she was
uneasily conscious that Theresa was a most unsuitable wife for a
quiet country doctor.

With a sigh her thoughts passed on to Bella. There was no fault
to find with Bella. She was a good woman—a devoted wife and
mother, quite exemplary in behaviour—and extremely dull!
But even Bella could not be regarded with complete approval.
For Bella had married a foreigner—and not only a foreigner—
but a Greek. In Miss Arundell's prejudiced mind a Greek was
almost as bad as an Argentine or a Turk. The fact that Dr Tanios
had a charming manner and was said to be extremely able in his
profession only prejudiced the old lady slightly more against
him. She distrusted charm and easy compliments. For this
reason, too, she found it difficult to be fond of the two children.
They had both taken after their father in looks—there was really
nothing English about them.

And then Charles. . . .

Yes, Charles. . . .

It was no use blinding one's eyes to facts. Charles, charming
though he was, was not to be trusted. . . .

Emily Arundell sighed. She felt suddenly tired, old, depressed. . . .

She supposed that she couldn't last much longer. . . .

Her mind reverted to the will she had made some years ago.

Legacies to the servants—to charities—and the main bulk of
her considerable fortune to be divided equally between these,
her three surviving relations. . . .

It still seemed to her that she had done the right and equitable
thing. It just crossed her mind to wonder whether there might
not be some way of securing Bella's share of the money so that
her husband could not touch it . . . She must ask Mr Purvis.

She turned in at the gate of Littlegreen House.

Charles and Theresa Arundell arrived by car—the Tanios, by
train.

The brother and sister arrived first. Charles, tall and good-
looking with his slightly mocking manner, said:

"Hullo, Aunt Emily, how's the girl? You look fine."

And he kissed her.

Theresa put an indifferent young cheek against her withered one.

"How are you, Aunt Emily?"

Theresa, her aunt thought, was looking far from well. Her face, beneath its plentiful make-up, was slightly haggard and there were lines round her eyes.

They had tea in the drawing-room. Bella Tanios, her hair inclined to straggle in wisps from below the fashionable hat that she wore at the wrong angle, stared at her cousin Theresa with a pathetic eagerness to assimilate and memorise her clothes. It was poor Bella's fate in life to be passionately fond of clothes without having any clothes sense. Theresa's clothes were expensive, slightly bizarre, and she herself had an exquisite figure.

Bella, when she arrived in England from Smyrna, had tried earnestly to copy Theresa's elegance at an inferior price and cut.

Dr Tanios, who was a big bearded jolly looking man, was talking to Miss Arundell. His voice was warm and full—an attractive voice that charmed a listener almost against his or her will. Almost in spite of herself, it charmed Miss Arundell.

Miss Lawson was fidgeting a good deal. She jumped up and down, handing plates, fussing over the tea-table. Charles, whose manners were excellent, rose more than once to help her, but she expressed no gratitude.

When, after tea, the party went out to make a tour of the garden Charles murmured to his sister:

"Lawson doesn't like me. Odd, isn't it?"

Theresa said, mockingly.

"Very odd. So there *is* one person who can withstand your fatal fascination?"

Charles grinned—an engaging grin and said:

"Lucky it's only Lawson. . . ."

In the garden Miss Lawson walked with Mrs Tanios and asked her questions about the children. Bella Tanios' rather drab face lighted up. She forgot to watch Theresa. She talked eagerly and animatedly. Mary had said such a *quaint* thing on the boat. . . .

She found Minnie Lawson a most sympathetic listener.

17

Presently a fair-haired young man with a solemn face and pince-nez was shown into the garden from the house. He looked rather embarrassed. Miss Arundell greeted him politely.

Theresa said:

"Hullo, Rex!"

She slipped an arm through his. They wandered away.

Charles made a face. He slipped away to have a word with the gardener, an ally of his from old days.

When Miss Arundell re-entered the house Charles was playing with Bob. The dog stood at the top of the stairs, his ball in his mouth, his tail gently wagging.

"Come on, old man," said Charles.

Bob sank down on his haunches, nosed his ball slowly and slowly nearer the edge. As he finally bunted it over he sprang to his feet in great excitement. The ball bumped slowly down the stairs. Charles caught it and tossed it up to him. Bob caught it neatly in his mouth. The performance was repeated.

"Regular game of his, this," said Charles.

Emily Arundell smiled.

"He'll go on for hours," she said.

She turned into the drawing-room and Charles followed her. Bob gave a disappointed bark.

Glancing through the window Charles said:

"Look at Theresa and her young man. They *are* an odd couple!"

"You think Theresa is really serious over this?"

"Oh, she's crazy about him!" said Charles with confidence. "Odd taste, but there it is. I think it must be the way he looks at her as though she were a scientific specimen and not a live woman. That's rather a novelty for Theresa. Pity the fellow's so poor. Theresa's got expensive tastes."

Miss Arundell said drily:

"I've no doubt she can change her way of living—if she wants to! And after all she has her own income."

"Eh? Oh yes, yes, of course."

Charles shot an almost guilty look at her.

That evening, as the others were assembled in the drawing-room waiting to go in to dinner, there was a scurry and a burst of profanity on the stairs. Charles entered with his face rather red.

"Sorry, Aunt Emily, am I late? The dog of yours nearly made me take the most frightful toss. He'd left that ball of his on the top of the stairs."

"Careless little doggie," cried Miss Lawson, bending down to Bob.

Bob looked at her contemptuously and turned his head away.

"I know," said Miss Arundell. "It's most dangerous. Minnie, fetch the ball and put it away."

Miss Lawson hurried out.

Dr Tanios monopolised the conversation at the dinner-table most of the time. He told amusing stories of his life in Smyrna.

The party went to bed early. Miss Lawson carrying wool, spectacles, a large velvet bag and a book accompanied her employer to her bedroom chattering happily.

"Really *most* amusing, Dr Tanios. He is such *good* company! Not that I should quite care for that kind of life myself . . . One would have to boil the water, I expect . . . And goat's milk, perhaps—such a disagreeable taste——"

Miss Arundell snapped:

"Don't be a fool, Minnie. You told Ellen to call me at half-past six?"

"Oh, yes, Miss Arundell. I said no tea, but don't you think it might be wiser—You know, the vicar at Southbridge—a most conscientious man, told me distinctly that there was no obligation to come fasting——"

Once more Miss Arundell cut her short.

"I've never yet taken anything before Early Service and I'm not going to begin now. *You* can do as you like."

"Oh, no—I didn't mean—I'm sure——"

Miss Lawson was flustered and upset.

"Take Bob's collar off," said Miss Arundell.

The slave hastened to obey.

Still trying to please she said:

"Such a *pleasant* evening. They all seem so *pleased* to be here."

"Hmph," said Emily Arundell. "All here for what they can get."

"Oh, dear Miss Arundell——"

"My good Minnie, I'm not a fool whatever else I am! I just wonder which of them will open the subject first."

She was not long left in doubt on that point. She and Miss Lawson returned from attending Early Service just after nine. Dr and Mrs Tanios were in the dining-room, but there were no signs of the two Arundells. After breakfast, when the others had left, Miss Arundell sat on, entering up some accounts in a little book.

Charles entered the room about ten.

"Sorry I'm late, Aunt Emily. But Theresa's worse. She's not unclosed an eyelid yet."

"At half-past ten breakfast will be cleared away," said Miss Arundell. "I know it is the fashion not to consider servants nowadays, but that is not the case in *my* house."

"Good. That's the true diehard spirit!"

Charles helped himself to kidneys and sat down beside her.

His grin, as always, was very attractive. Emily Arundell soon found herself smiling indulgently at him. Emboldened by this sign of favour, Charles plunged.

"Look here, Aunt Emily, sorry to bother you, but I'm in the devil of a hole. Can you possibly help me out? A hundred would do it."

His aunt's face was not encouraging. A certain grimness showed itself in her expression.

Emily Arundell was not afraid of speaking her mind. She spoke it.

Miss Lawson bustling across the hall almost collided with Charles as he left the dining-room. She glanced at him curiously. She entered the dining-room to find Miss Arundell sitting very upright with a flushed face.

2. The Relations

CHARLES RAN LIGHTLY up the stairs and tapped on his sister's door. Her answering "Come in" came promptly and he entered.

Theresa was sitting up in bed yawning.

Charles took a seat on the bed.

"What a decorative female you are, Theresa," he remarked appreciatively.

Theresa said sharply.

"What's the matter?"

Charles grinned.

"Sharp, aren't you? Well, I stole a march on you, my girl! Thought I'd make my touch before *you* got to work."

"Well?"

Charles spread his hands downwards in negation.

"Nothing doing! Aunt Emily ticked me off good and proper. She intimated that she was under no illusions as to why her affectionate family had gathered round her! And she also intimated that the said affectionate family would be disappointed. Nothing being handed out but affection—and not so much of that."

"You might have waited a bit," said Theresa, drily.

Charles grinned again.

"I was afraid you or Tanios might get in ahead of me. I'm sadly afraid, Theresa my sweet, that there'll be nothing doing this time. Old Emily is by no means a fool."

"I never thought she was."

"I even tried to put the wind up her."

"What d'you mean?" asked his sister sharply.

"Told her she was going about it the right way to get bumped off. After all she can't take the dibs to heaven with her. Why not loosen up a bit?"

"Charles, you are a fool!"

"No, I'm not. I'm a bit of a psychologist in my way. It's never a bit of good sucking up to the old girl. She much prefers you to stand up to her. And after all, I was only talking sense. We get the money when she dies—she might just as well part with a little beforehand! Otherwise the temptation to help her out of the way might become overwhelming."

"Did she see your point?" asked Theresa, her delicate mouth curling up scornfully.

"I'm not sure. She didn't admit it. Just thanked me rather nastily for my advice and said she was perfectly capable of taking care of herself. 'Well,' I said, 'I've warned you.' 'I'll remember it,' she said."

Theresa said angrily:

"Really, Charles, you are an utter fool."

"Damn it all, Theresa, I was a bit ratty myself! The old girl's rolling—simply rolling. I bet she doesn't spend a tenth part of her income—what has she got to spend it on, anyway? And here we are—young, able to enjoy life—and to spite us she's capable of living to a hundred . . . I want my fun now . . . So do you. . . ."

Theresa nodded.

She said in a low, breathless voice:

"They don't understand—old people don't . . . they can't . . . They don't know what it is to *live*!"

Brother and sister were silent for some minutes.

Charles got up.

"Well, my love, I wish you better success than I've had. But I rather doubt it."

Theresa said:

"I'm rather counting on Rex to do the trick. If I can make old Emily realise how brilliant he is, and how it matters terrifically that he should have his chance and not have to sink into a rut as a general practioner. . . . Oh, Charles, a few thousands of capital just at this minute would make all the difference in the world to our lives!"

"Hope you get it, but I don't think you will. You've got through a bit too much capital in riotous living in your time. I say, Theresa, you don't think the dreary Bella or the dubious Tanios will get anything, do you?"

"I don't see that money would be any good to Bella. She goes about looking like a rag-bag and her tastes are purely domestic."

"Oh, well," said Charles, vaguely. "I expect she wants things for those unprepossessing children of hers, schools, and plates for their front teeth and music lessons. And anyway it isn't Bella—it's Tanios. I bet *he's* got a nose for money all right! Trust a Greek for that. You know he's got through most of Bella's? Speculated with it and lost it all."

"Do you think he'll get something out of old Emily?"

"He won't if I can prevent him," said Charles, grimly.

He left the room and wandered downstairs. Bob was in the hall. He fussed up to Charles agreeably. Dogs liked Charles.

He ran towards the drawing-room door and looked back at Charles.

"What's the matter?" said Charles, strolling after him.

Bob hurried into the drawing-room and sat down expectantly by a small bureau.

Charles strolled over to him.

"What's it all about?"

Bob wagged his tail, looked hard at the drawers of the bureau and uttered an appealing squeak.

"Want something that's in here?"

Charles pulled open the top drawer. His eyebrows rose.

"Dear, dear," he said.

At one side of the drawer was a little pile of treasury notes.

Charles picked up the bundle and counted them. With a grin he removed three one pound notes and two ten shilling ones and put them in his pocket. He replaced the rest of the notes carefully in the drawer where he had found them.

"That was a good idea, Bob," he said. "Your Uncle Charles will be able at any rate to cover expenses. A little ready cash always comes in handy."

Bob uttered a faint reproachful bark as Charles shut the drawer.

"Sorry old man," Charles apologised. He opened the next drawer. Bob's ball was in the corner of it. He took it out.

"Here you are. Enjoy yourself with it."

Bob caught the ball, trotted out of the room and presently bump, bump, bump, was heard down the stairs.

Charles strolled out into the garden. It was a fine sunny morning with a scent of lilac.

Miss Arundell had Dr Tanios by her side. He was speaking of the advantage of an English education—a good education—for children and how deeply he regretted that he could not afford such a luxury for his own children.

Charles smiled with satisfied malice. He joined in the conversation in a light-hearted manner, turning it adroitly into entirely different channels.

Emily Arundell smiled at him quite amiably. He even fancied that she was amused by his tactics and was subtly encouraging them.

Charles' spirits rose. Perhaps, after all, before he left——

Charles was an incurable optimist.

Dr Donaldson called for Theresa in his car that afternoon and drove her to Worthem Abbey, one of the local beauty spots. They wandered away from the Abbey itself into the woods.

There Rex Donaldson told Theresa at length about his theories and some of his recent experiments. She understood very little but listened in a spellbound manner, thinking to herself:

"How clever Rex is—and how absolutely adorable!"

Her fiancé paused once and said rather doubtfully:

"I'm afraid this is dull stuff for you, Theresa."

"Darling, it's too thrilling," said Theresa, firmly. "Go on. You take some of the blood of the infected rabbit——?"

Dr Donaldson went on.

Presently Theresa said with a sigh.

"Your work means a terrible lot to you, my sweet."

"Naturally," said Dr Donaldson.

It did not seem at all natural to Theresa. Very few of her friends did any work at all, and if they did they made extremely heavy weather about it.

She thought, as she had thought once or twice before, how singularly unsuitable it was that she should have fallen in love with Rex Donaldson. Why did these things, these ludicrous and amazing madnesses, happen to one? A profitless question. This had happened to her.

She frowned, wondering at herself. Her crowd had been so gay—so cynical. Love affairs were necessary to life, of course, but why take them seriously? One loved and passed on.

But this feeling of hers for Rex Donaldson was different, it went deeper. She felt instinctively that here there would be no passing on . . . Her need of him was simple and profound. Everything about him fascinated her. His calmness and detachment, so different from her own hectic, grasping life, the clear, logical coldness of his scientific mind, and something else, imperfectly understood, a secret force in the man masked by his unassuming slightly pedantic manner, but which she nevertheless felt and sensed instinctively.

In Rex Donaldson there was genius—and the fact that his profession was the main preoccupation of his life and that she was only a part—though a necessary part—of existence to him only heightened his attraction for her. She found herself for the first time in her selfish pleasure-loving life content to take second place. The prospect fascinated her. For Rex she would do anything—anything!

"What a damned nuisance money is," she said, petulantly. "If only Aunt Emily were to die we could get married at once, and you could come to London and have a laboratory full of test tubes and guinea pigs, and never bother any more about children with mumps and old ladies with livers."

Donaldson said:

"There's no reason why your aunt shouldn't live for many years to come—if she's careful."

Theresa said despondently:

"I know that. . . ."

In the big double-bedded room with the old-fashioned oak furniture, Dr Tanios said to his wife:

"I think that I have prepared the ground sufficiently. It is now your turn, my dear."

He was pouring water from the old-fashioned copper can into the rose-patterned china basin.

Bella Tanios sat in front of the dressing-table wondering why, when she combed her hair as Theresa did, it should not look like Theresa's!

There was a moment before she replied. Then she said:

"I don't think I want—to ask Aunt Emily for money."

"It's not for yourself, Bella, it's for the sake of the children. Our investments have been so unlucky."

His back was turned, he did not see the swift glance she gave him—a furtive, shrinking glance.

She said with mild obstinacy.

"All the same, I think I'd rather not . . . Aunt Emily is rather difficult. She can be generous but she doesn't like being asked."

Drying his hands, Tanios came across from the wash-stand.

"Really, Bella, it isn't like you to be so obstinate. After all, what have we come down here for?"

She murmured:

"I didn't—I never meant—it wasn't to ask for money. . . ."

"Yet you agreed that the only hope if we are to educate the children properly is for your aunt to come to the rescue."

Bella Tanios did not answer. She moved uneasily.

But her face bore the mild, mulish look that many clever husbands of stupid wives know to their cost.

She said:

"Perhaps Aunt Emily herself may suggest——"

"It is possible, but I've seen no signs of it so far."

Bella said:

"If we could have brought the children with us. Aunt Emily couldn't have helped loving Mary. And Edward is *so* intelligent."

Tanios said, drily:

"I don't think your aunt is a great child lover. It is probably just as well the children aren't here."

"Oh, Jacob, but——"

"Yes, yes, my dear. I know your feelings. But these desiccated English spinsters—bah, they are not human. We want to do the best we can, do we not, for our Mary and our Edward? To help us a little would involve no hardship to Miss Arundell."

Mrs Tanios turned, there was a flush in her cheeks.

"Oh, please, please, Jacob, not this time. I'm sure it would be unwise. I would so very very much rather not."

Tanios stood close behind her, his arm encircled her shoulders. She trembled a little and then was still—almost rigid.

26

He said and his voice was still pleasant:

"All the same, Bella, I think—I think you will do what I ask . . . You usually do, you know—in the end . . . Yes, I think you will do what I say. . . ."

3. The Accident

It was Tuesday afternoon. The side door to the garden was open. Miss Arundell stood on the threshold and threw Bob's ball the length of the garden path. The terrier rushed after it.

"Just one more, Bob," said Emily Arundell. "A good one."

Once again the ball sped along the ground with Bob racing at full speed in pursuit.

Miss Arundell stooped down, picked up the ball from where Bob laid it at her feet and went into the house, Bob following her closely. She shut the side door, went into the drawing-room, Bob still at her heels, and put the ball away in a drawer.

She glanced at the clock on the mantelpiece. It was half-past six.

"A little rest before dinner, I think, Bob."

She ascended the stairs to her bedroom. Bob accompanied her. Lying on the big chintz-covered couch with Bob at her feet, Miss Arundell sighed. She was glad that it was Tuesday and that her guests would be going to-morrow. It was not that this week-end had disclosed anything to her that she had not known before. It was more the fact that it had not permitted her to forget her own knowledge.

She said to herself:

"I'm getting old, I suppose. . . ." And then, with a little shock of surprise: "I *am* old. . . ."

She lay with her eyes closed for half an hour, then the elderly house-parlourmaid, Ellen, brought hot water and she rose and prepared for dinner.

Dr Donaldson was to dine with them that night. Emily Arundell wished to have an opportunity of studying him at close quarters. It still seemed to her a little incredible that the exotic Theresa should want to marry this rather stiff and pedantic young man. It also seemed a little odd that this stiff and pedantic young man should want to marry Theresa.

She did not feel as the evening progressed that she was getting to know Dr Donaldson any better. He was very polite, very formal and, to her mind, intensely boring. In her own mind she agreed with Miss Peabody's judgment. The thought flashed across her brain, "Better stuff in our young days."

Dr Donaldson did not stay late. He rose to go at ten o'clock. After he had taken his departure Emily Arundell herself announced that she was going to bed. She went upstairs and her young relations went up also. They all seemed somewhat subdued to-night. Miss Lawson remained downstairs performing her final duties, letting Bob out for his run, poking down the fire, putting the guard up and rolling back the hearthrug in case of fire.

She arrived rather breathless in her employer's room about five minutes later.

"I think I've got everything," she said, putting down wool, work-bag, and a library book. "I do hope the book will be all right. She hadn't got any of the ones on your list but she said she was sure you'd like this one."

"That girl's a fool," said Emily Arundell. "Her taste in books is the worst I've ever come across."

"Oh, dear. I'm so sorry—Perhaps I ought——"

"Nonsense, it's not your fault." Emily Arundell added kindly. "I hope you enjoyed yourself this afternoon."

Miss Lawson's face lighted up. She looked eager and almost youthful.

"Oh, yes, thank you very much. So *kind* of you to spare me. I had the most interesting time. We had the Planchette and really—it wrote the most *interesting* things. There were several messages . . . Of course it's not *quite* the same thing as the sittings . . . Julia Tripp has been having a lot of success with the automatic writing. Several messages from Those who have Passed Over. It—it really makes one feel so grateful—that such things should be permitted. . . ."

Miss Arundell said with a slight smile:

"Better not let the vicar hear you."

"Oh, but indeed, dear Miss Arundell, I am convinced—quite convinced—there can be *nothing* wrong about it. I only wish dear Mr Lonsdale would *examine* the subject. It seems to me so

29

narrow-minded to condemn a thing that you have not even *investigated*. Both Julia and Isabel Tripp are such truly *spiritual* women."

"Almost too spiritual to be alive," said Miss Arundell.

She did not care much for Julia and Isabel Tripp. She thought their clothes ridiculous, their vegetarian and uncooked fruit meals absurd, and their manner affected. They were women of no traditions, no roots—in fact—no breeding! But she got a certain amount of amusement out of their earnestness and she was at bottom kind-hearted enough not to grudge the pleasure that their friendship obviously gave to poor Minnie.

Poor Minnie! Emily Arundell looked at her companion with mingled affection and contempt. She had had so many of these foolish, middle-aged women to minister to her—all much the same, kind, fussy, subservient and almost entirely mindless.

Really poor Minnie was looking quite excited to-night. Her eyes were shining. She fussed about the room vaguely touching things here and there without the least idea of what she was doing, her eyes all bright and shining.

She stammered out rather nervously:

"I—I do wish you'd been there . . . I feel, you know, that you're not quite a believer yet. But to-night there was a message— for E.A., the initials came *quite* definitely. It was from a man who had passed over many years ago—a very good-looking military man—Isabel saw him quite distinctly. It must have been dear General Arundell. Such a beautiful message, so full of love and comfort, and how through patience all could be attained."

"Those sentiments sound very unlike papa," said Miss Arundell.

"Oh, but our Dear Ones change so—on the other side. Everything is love and understanding. And then the Planchette spelt out something about a *key*—I think it was the key of the Boule cabinet—could that be it?"

"The key of the Boule cabinet?" Emily Arundell's voice sounded sharp and interested.

"I think that was it. I thought perhaps it might be important papers—something of the kind. There was a well authenticated case where a message came to look in a certain piece of furniture and actually a *will* was discovered there."

"There wasn't a will in the Boule cabinet," said Miss Arundell. She added abruptly: "Go to bed, Minnie. You're tired. So am I. We'll ask the Tripps in for an evening soon."

"Oh, that *will* be nice! Good-night, dear. Sure you've got everything? I hope you haven't been tired with so many people here. I must tell Ellen to air the drawing-room *very well* to-morrow, and shake out the curtains—all this smoking leaves such a smell. I must say I think it's very good of you to let them all smoke in the drawing-room!"

"I must make some concessions to modernity," said Emily Arundell. "Good-night, Minnie."

As the other woman left the room, Emily Arundell wondered if this spiritualistic business was really good for Minnie. Her eyes had been popping out of her head, and she had looked so restless and excited.

Odd about the Boule cabinet, thought Emily Arundell as she got into bed. She smiled grimly as she remembered the scene of long ago. The key that had come to light after papa's death, and the cascade of empty brandy bottles that had tumbled out when the cabinet had been unlocked! It was little things like that, things that surely neither Minnie Lawson nor Isabel and Julia Tripp could possibly know, which made one wonder whether, after all, there wasn't something in this spiritualistic business. . . .

She felt wakeful lying on her big four-poster bed. Nowadays she found it increasingly difficult to sleep. But she scorned Dr Grainger's tentative suggestion of a sleeping draught. Sleeping draughts were for weaklings, for people who couldn't bear a finger-ache, or a little toothache, or the tedium of a sleepless night.

Often she would get up and wander noiselessly round the house, picking up a book, fingering an ornament, rearranging a vase of flowers, writing a letter or two. In those midnight hours she had a feeling of the equal liveliness of the house through which she wandered. They were not disagreeable, those nocturnal wanderings. It was as though ghosts walked beside her, the ghosts of her sisters, Arabella, Matilda and Agnes, the ghost of her brother Thomas, the dear fellow as he was before That Woman got hold of him! Even the ghost of General Charles

31

Laverton Arundell, that domestic tyrant with the charming manners who shouted and bullied his daughters but who nevertheless was an object of pride to them with his experiences in the Indian Mutiny and his knowledge of the world. What if there were days when he was "not quite so well" as his daughters put it evasively?

Her mind reverting to her niece's fiancé, Miss Arundell thought, "I don't suppose *he'll* ever take to drink! Calls himself a *man* and drank *barley water* this evening! Barley water! And I opened papa's special port."

Charles had done justice to the port all right. Oh! if only Charles were to be trusted. If only one didn't know that with him——

Her thoughts broke off . . . Her mind ranged over the events of the week-end. . . .

Everything seemed vaguely disquieting. . . .

She tried to put worrying thoughts out of her mind.

It was no good.

She raised herself on her elbow and by the light of the night-light that always burned in a little saucer she looked at the time.

One o'clock and she had never felt less like sleep.

She got out of bed and put on her slippers and her warm dressing-gown. She would go downstairs and just check over the weekly books ready for the paying of them the following morning.

Like a shadow she slipped from her room and along the corridor where one small electric bulb was allowed to burn all night.

She came to the head of the stairs, stretched out one hand to the baluster rail and then, unaccountably, she stumbled, tried to recover her balance, failed and went headlong down the stairs.

The sound of her fall, the cry she gave, stirred the sleeping house to wakefulness. Doors opened, lights flashed on.

Miss Lawson popped out of her room at the head of the staircase.

Uttering little cries of distress she pattered down the stairs. one by one the others arrived—Charles, yawning, in a resplendent dressing-gown. Theresa, wrapped in dark silk. Bella in a navy-blue kimono, her hair bristling with combs to "set the wave."

Dazed and confused Emily Arundell lay in a crushed heap. Her shoulder hurt her and her ankle—her whole body was a confused mass of pain. She was conscious of people standing over her, of that fool Minnie Lawson crying and making ineffectual gestures with her hands, of Theresa with a startled look in her dark eyes, of Bella standing with her mouth open looking expectant, of the voice of Charles saying from somewhere—very far away so it seemed——

"It's that damned dog's ball! He must have left it here and she tripped over it. See? Here it is!"

And then she was conscious of authority, putting the others aside, kneeling beside her, touching her with hands that did not fumble but *knew*.

A feeling of relief swept over her. It would be all right now.

Dr Tanios was saying in firm, reassuring tones:

"No, it's all right. No bones broken . . . Just badly shaken and bruised—and of course she's had a bad shock. But she's been very lucky that it's no worse."

Then he had cleared the others off a little and picked her up quite easily and carried her up to her bedroom, where he had held her wrist for a minute, counting, then nodded his head, sent Minnie (who was still crying and being generally a nuisance) out of the room to fetch brandy and to heat water for a hot bottle.

Confused, shaken, and racked with pain, she felt acutely grateful to Jacob Tanios in that moment. The relief of feeling oneself in capable hands. He gave you just that feeling of assurance—of confidence—that a doctor ought to give.

There was something—something she couldn't quite get hold of—something vaguely disquieting—but she wouldn't think of it now. She would drink this and go to sleep as they told her.

But surely there was something missing—some one.

Oh, well, she wouldn't think . . . Her shoulder hurt her— She drank down what she was given.

She heard Dr Tanios say—and in what a comfortable assured voice—"She'll be all right, now."

She closed her eyes.

*

She awoke to a sound that she knew—a soft, muffled bark. She was wide awake in a minute.

Bob—naughty Bob! He was barking outside the front door—his own particular "out all night very ashamed of myself" bark, pitched in a subdued key but repeated hopefully.

Miss Arundell strained her ears. Ah, yes, that was all right. She could hear Minnie going down to let him in. She heard the dreak of the opening front door, a confused low murmur—Minnie's futile reproaches—"Oh, you naughty little doggie—a very naughty little Bobsie——" She heard the pantry door open. Bob's bed was under the pantry table.

And at that moment Emily realised what it was she had subconsciously missed at the moment of her accident. It was Bob! All that commotion—her fall, people running—normally Bob would have responded by a crescendo of barking from inside the pantry.

So *that* was what had been worrying her at the back of her mind. But it was explained now—Bob, when he had been let out last night, had shamelessly and deliberately gone off on pleasure bent. From time to time he had these lapses from virtue—though his apologies afterwards were always all that could be desired.

So that was all right. But was it? What else was there worrying her, nagging at the back of her head. Her accident—something to do with her accident.

Ah, yes, somebody had said—Charles—that she had slipped on Bob's ball which he had left on the top of the stairs. . . .

The ball had been there—he had held it up in his hand. . . .

Emily Arundell's head ached. Her shoulder throbbed. Her bruised body suffered. . . .

But in the midst of her suffering her mind was clear and lucid. She was no longer confused by shock. Her memory was perfectly clear.

She went over in her mind all the events from six o'clock yesterday evening. . . . She retraced every step . . . till she came to the moment when she arrived at the stairhead and started to descend the stairs. . . .

A thrill of incredulous horror shot through her. . . .

Surely—surely, she must be mistaken. . . . One often had

queer fancies after an event had happened. She tried—earnestly she tried—to recall the slippery roundness of Bob's ball under her foot. . . .

But she could recall nothing of the kind.

Instead——

"Sheer nerves," said Emily Arundell. "Ridiculous fancies."

But her sensible, shrewd, Victorian mind would not admit that for a moment. There was no foolish optimism about the Victorians. They could believe the worst with the utmost ease.

Emily Arundell believed the worst.

4. Miss Arundell Writes a Letter

IT WAS Friday.

The relations had left.

They left on the Wednesday as originally planned. One and all, they had offered to stay on. One and all they had been steadfastly refused. Miss Arundell explained that she preferred to be "quite quiet."

During the two days that had elapsed since their departure, Emily Arundel had been alarmingly meditative. Often she did not hear what Minnie Lawson said to her. She would stare at her and curtly order her to begin all over again.

"It's the *shock*, poor dear," said Miss Lawson.

And she added with the kind of gloomy relish in disaster which brightens so many otherwise drab lives:

"I dare say she'll never be quite herself again."

Dr Grainger, on the other hand, rallied her heartily.

He told her that she'd be downstairs again by the end of the week, that it was a positive disgrace she had no bones broken, and what kind of a patient was she for a struggling medical man? If all his patients were like her, he might as well take down his plate straight away.

Emily Arundell replied with spirit—she and old Dr Granger were allies of long standing. He bullied and she defied—they always got a good deal of pleasure out of each other's company!

But now, after the doctor had stumped away, the old lady lay with a frown on her face, thinking—thinking—responding absent-mindedly to Minnie Lawson's well-meant fussing—and then suddenly coming back to consciousness and rending her with a vitriolic tongue.

"Poor little Bobsie," twittered Miss Lawson, bending over Bob who had a rug spread on the corner of his mistress's bed.

36

"Wouldn't little Bobsie be unhappy if he knew what he'd done to his poor, poor Missus?"

Miss Arundell snapped:

"Don't be idiotic, Minnie. And where's your English sense of justice? Don't you know that every one in this country is accounted innocent until he or she is proved guilty?"

"Oh, but we do know——"

Emily snapped

"We don't know anything at all. Do stop fidgeting, Minnie. Pulling this and pulling that. Haven't you any idea how to behave in a sick-room? Go away and send Ellen to me."

Meekly Miss Lawson crept away.

Emily Arundell looked after her with a slight feeling of self-reproach. Maddening as Minnie was, she did her best.

Then the frown settled down again on her face.

She was desperately unhappy. She had all a vigorous strong-minded old lady's dislike of inaction in any given situation. But in this particular situation she could not decide upon her line of action.

There were moments when she distrusted her own faculties, her own memory of events. And there was no one, absolutely no one in whom she could confide.

Half an hour later, when Miss Lawson tiptoed creakingly into the room, carrying a cup of beef-tea, and then paused irresolute at the view of her employer lying with closed eyes, Emily Arundell suddenly spoke two words with such force and decision that Miss Lawson nearly dropped the cup.

"Mary Fox," said Miss Arundell.

"A box, dear?" said Miss Lawson. "Did you say you wanted a box?"

"You're getting deaf, Minnie. I didn't say anything about a box. I said Mary Fox. The woman I met at Cheltenham last year. She was the sister of one of the Canons of Exeter Cathedral. Give me that cup. You've spilt it into the saucer. And don't tiptoe when you come into a room. You don't know how irritating it is. Now go downstairs and get me the London telephone book."

"Can I find the number for you, dear? Or the address?"

"If I'd wanted you to do that I'd have told you so. Do what I

37

tell you. Bring it here, and put my writing things by the bed."

Miss Lawson obeyed orders.

As she was going out of the room after having done everything required of her, Emily Arundell said unexpectedly:

"You're a good, faithful creature, Minnie. Don't mind my bark. It's a good deal worse than my bite. You're very patient and good to me."

Miss Lawson went out of the room with her face pink and incoherent words burbling from her lips.

Sitting up in bed, Miss Arundell wrote a letter. She wrote it slowly and carefully, with numerous pauses for thought and copious underlining. She crossed and recrossed the page—for she had been brought up in a school that was taught never to waste notepaper. Finally, with a sigh of satisfaction, she signed her name and put it into an envelope. She wrote a name upon the envelope. Then she took a fresh sheet of paper. This time she made a rough draft and after having reread it and made certain alterations and erasures, she wrote out a fair copy. She read the whole thing through very carefully, then satisfied that she had expressed her meaning she enclosed it in an envelope and addressed it to William Purvis, Esq., Messrs. Purvis, Purvis, Charlesworth and Purvis, Solicitors, Harchester.

She took up the first envelope again, which was addressed to M. Hercule Poirot, and opened the telephone directory. Having found the address she added it.

A tap sounded at the door.

Miss Arundell hastily thrust the letter she had just finished addressing—the letter to Hercule Poirot—inside the flap of her writing-case.

She had no intention of rousing Minnie's curiosity. Minnie was a great deal too inquisitive.

She called "Come in" and lay back on her pillows with a sigh of relief.

She had taken steps to deal with the situation.

5. Hercule Poirot Receives a Letter

THE EVENTS which I have just narrated were not, of course, known to me until a long time afterwards. But by questioning various members of the family in detail, I have, I think, set them down accurately enough.

Poirot and I were only drawn into the affair when we received Miss Arundell's letter.

I remember the day well. It was a hot, airless morning towards the end of June.

Poirot had a particular routine when opening his morning correspondence. He picked up each letter, scrutinised it carefully and neatly slit the envelope open with his paper-cutter. Its contents were perused and then placed in one of four piles beyond the chocolate-pot. (Poirot always drank chocolate for breakfast—a revolting habit.) All this with a machine-like regularity!

So much was this the case that the least interruption of the rhythm attracted one's attention.

I was sitting by the window, looking out at the passing traffic. I had recently returned from the Argentine and there was something particularly exciting to me in being once more in the roar of London.

Turning my head, I said with a smile:

"Poirot, I—the humble Watson—am going to hazard a deduction."

"Enchanted, my friend. What is it?"

I struck an attitude and said pompously:

"You have received this morning *one* letter of particular interest!"

"You are indeed the Sherlock Holmes! Yes, you are perfectly right."

I laughed.

"You see, *I know your methods*, Poirot. If you read a letter through twice it must mean that it is of special interest."

"You shall judge for yourself, Hastings."

With a smile my friend tendered me the letter in question.

I took it with no little interest, but immediately made a slight grimace. It was written in one of those old-fashioned spidery handwritings, and it was, moreover, crossed on two pages.

"Must I read this, Poirot?" I complained.

"Ah, no, there is no compulsion. Assuredly not."

"Can't you tell me what it says?"

"I would prefer you to form your own judgment. But do not trouble if it bores you."

"No, no, I want to know what it's all about," I protested.

My friend remarked dryly:

"You can hardly do *that*. In effect, the letter says nothing at all."

Taking this as an exaggeration I plunged without more ado into the letter.

M. Hercule Poirot.

   Dear Sir,

      After much doubt and indecision, I am writing (the last word was crossed out and the letter went on) *I am emboldened to write to you in the hope that you may be able to assist me in a matter of a strictly private nature.* (The words *strictly private* were underlined three times.) *I may say that your name is not unknown to me. It was mentioned to me by a Miss Fox of Exeter, and although Miss Fox was not herself acquainted with you, she mentioned that her brother-in-law's sister (whose name I cannot, I am sorry to say, recall) had spoken of your kindness and discretion in the highest terms* (*highest terms* underlined once). *I did not inquire, of course, as to the nature* (*nature* underlined) *of the inquiry you had conducted on her behalf, but I understood from Miss Fox that it was of a painful and confidential nature* (last four words underlined heavily).

I broke off my difficult task of spelling out the spidery words.

"Poirot," I said. "Must I go on? Does she ever get to the point?"

"Continue, my friend. Patience."

"Patience!" I grumbled. "It's exactly as though a spider had got into an inkpot and was walking over a sheet of notepaper! I remember my Great-Aunt Mary's writing used to be much the same!"

Once more I plunged into the epistle.

In my present dilemma, it occurs to me that you might undertake the necessary investigations on my behalf. The matter is such, as you will readily understand, as calls for the utmost discretion and I may, in fact—and I need hardly say how sincerely I hope and pray (pray underlined twice) *that this may be the case—I may, in fact, be completely mistaken. One is apt sometimes to attribute too much significance to facts capable of a natural explanation.*

"I haven't left out a sheet?" I murmured in some perplexity.

Poirot chuckled.

"No, no."

"Because this doesn't seem to make sense. What is it she is talking about?"

"*Continuez toujours.*"

"*The matter is such, as you will readily understand*—No, I'd got past that. Oh! here we are. *In the circumstances as I am sure you will be the first to appreciate, it is quite impossible for me to consult any one in Market Basing* (I glanced back at the heading of the letter. Littlegreen House, Market Basing, Berks), *but at the same time you will naturally understand that I feel uneasy (uneasy* under-lined). *During the last few days I have reproached myself with being unduly fanciful (fanciful* underlined three times) *but have only felt increasingly perturbed. I may be attaching undue importance to what is, after all, a trifle (trifle* underlined twice) *but my uneasiness remains. I feel definitely that my mind must be set at rest on the matter. It is actually preying on my mind and affecting my health, and naturally I am in a difficult position as I can say nothing to any one (nothing to any one* underlined with heavy lines). *In your wisdom you may say, of course, that the whole thing is nothing but a mare's nest. The facts may be capable of a perfectly innocent ex-planation (innocent* underlined). *Nevertheless, however trivial it may seem, ever since the incident of the dog's ball, I have felt increasingly doubtful and alarmed. I should therefore welcome your views and counsel on the matter. It would, I feel sure, take a great weight off my mind. Perhaps you would kindly let me know what your fees are and what you advise me to do in the matter?*

I must impress on you again that nobody here knows anything at all. The facts are, I know, very trivial and unimportant, but my health is not too good and my nerves (nerves underlined three times) are not what they used to be. Worry of this kind, I am convinced, is very bad for me, and the more I think over the matter, the more I am convinced that I was quite right and no mistake was possible. Of course, I shall not dream of saying anything (underlined) to any one (underlined).

Hoping to have your advice in the matter at an early date.

I remain, Yours faithfully,

Emily Arundell."

I turned the letter over and scanned each page closely.

"But, Poirot," I expostulated, "what is it all *about?*"

My friend shrugged his shoulders.

"What indeed?"

I tapped the sheets with some impatience.

"What a woman! Why can't Mrs—or Miss Arundell——"

"Miss, I think. It is typically the letter of a spinster."

"Yes," I said. "A real, fussy old maid. Why can't she say what she's talking about?"

Poirot sighed.

"As you say—a regrettable failure to employ order and method in the mental processes, and without order and method, Hastings——"

"Quite so," I interrupted hastily. "Little grey cells practically non-existent."

"I would not say that, my friend."

"I would! What's the *sense* of writing a letter like that?"

"Very little—that is true," Poirot admitted.

"A very long rigmarole all about nothing," I went on. "Probably some upset to her fat lapdog—an asthmatic pug or a yapping Pekingese!" I looked at my friend curiously. "And yet you read that letter through twice. I do not understand you, Poirot."

Poirot smiled.

'You, Hastings, you would have put it straight in the waste-paper basket?'

"I'm afraid I should." I frowned down on the letter. "I suppose I'm being dense, as usual, but *I* can't see anything of interest in this letter!"

"Yet there is one point in it of great interest—a point that struck me at once."

"Wait," I cried. "Don't tell me. Let me see if I can't discover it for myself."

It was childish of me, perhaps. I examined the letter very thoroughly. Then I shook my head.

"No, I don't see it. The old lady's got the wind up, I realise that—but then, old ladies often do! It may be about nothing—it may conceivably be about something, but I don't see that you can tell that that is so. Unless your instinct——"

Poirot raised an offended hand.

"Instinct! You know how I dislike that word. 'Something seems to tell me'—that is what you infer. *Jamais de la vie!* Me, I *reason*. I employ the little grey cells. There is one interesting point about that letter which you have overlooked utterly, Hastings."

"Oh, well," I said wearily. "I'll buy it."

"Buy it? Buy what?"

"An expression. Meaning that I will permit you to enjoy yourself by telling me just where I have been a fool."

"Not a fool, Hastings, merely unobservant."

"Well, out with it. What's the interesting point? I suppose, like the 'incident of the dog in the nighttime,' the point *is* that there is no interesting point!"

Poirot disregarded this sally on my part. He said quietly and calmly:

"The interesting point is the *date*."

"The date?"

I picked up the letter. On the top left-hand corner was written April 17th.

"Yes," I said slowly. "That *is* odd. April 17th."

"And we are to-day June 28th. *C'est curieux, n'est ce pas?* Over two months ago."

I shook my head doubtfully.

"It probably doesn't mean anything. A slip. She meant to put June and wrote April instead."

"Even then it would be ten or eleven days old—an odd fact. But actually you are in error. Look at the colour of the ink. That letter was written more than ten or eleven days ago. No, April 17th is the date assuredly. But why was the letter not sent?"

I shrugged my shoulders.

"That's easy. The old pussy changed her mind."

"Then why did she not destroy the letter? Why keep it over two months and post it now?"

I had to admit that that was harder to answer. In fact I couldn't think of a really satisfactory answer. I merely shook my head and said nothing.

Poirot nodded.

"You see—it is a point! Yes, decidedly a curious point."

He went over to his writing-table and took up a pen.

"You are answering the letter?" I asked.

"Oui, mon ami."

The room was silent except for the scratching of Poirot's pen. It was a hot, airless morning. A smell of dust and tar came in through the window.

Poirot rose from his desk, the completed letter in his hand. He opened a drawer and drew out a little square box. From this he took out a stamp. Moistening this with a little sponge he prepared to affix it to the letter.

Then suddenly he paused, stamp in hand, shaking his head with vigour.

"Non!" he exclaimed. "That is the wrong thing I do." He tore the letter across and threw it into the waste-paper basket.

"Not so must we tackle this matter! We will *go*, my friend."

"You mean to go down to Market Basing?"

"Precisely. Why not? Does not one stifle in London to-day? Would not the country air be agreeable?"

"Well, if you put it like that," I said. "Shall we go in the car?" I had acquired a second-hand Austin.

"Excellent. A very pleasant day for motoring. One will hardly need the muffler. A light overcoat, a silk scarf——"

"My dear fellow, you're not going to the North Pole!" I protested.

"One must be careful of catching the chill," said Poirot sententiously.

"On a day like this?"

Disregarding my protests, Poirot proceeded to don a fawn-coloured overcoat and wrap his neck up with a white silk handkerchief. Having carefully placed the wetted stamp face downwards on the blotting-paper to dry, we left the room together.

6. We Go to Littlegreen House

I DON'T know what Poirot felt like in his coat and muffler but I myself felt roasted before we got out of London. An open car in traffic is far from being a refreshing place on a hot summer's day.

Once we were outside London, however, and getting a bit of pace on the Great West Road my spirits rose.

Our drive took us about an hour and a half, and it was close upon twelve o'clock when we came into the little town of Market Basing. Originally on the main road, a modern by-pass now left it some three miles to the north of the main stream of traffic and in consequence it had kept an air of old-fashioned dignity and quietude about it. Its one wide street and ample market square seemed to say, "I was a place of importance once and to any person of sense and breeding I am still the same. Let this modern speeding world dash along their new-fangled road; I was built to endure in a day when solidarity and beauty went hand in hand."

There was a parking area in the middle of the big square, though there were only a few cars occupying it. I duly parked the Austin, Poirot divested himself of his superfluous garments, assured himself that his moustaches were in their proper condition of symmetrical flamboyance and we were then ready to proceed.

For once in a way our first tentative inquiry did not meet with the usual response, "Sorry, but I'm a stranger in these parts." It would seem indeed probable that there were no strangers in Market Basing! It had that effect! Already, I felt, Poirot and myself (and especially Poirot) were somewhat noticeable. We tended to stick out from the mellow background of an English market town secure in its traditions.

"Littlegreen House?" The man, a burly, ox-eyed fellow

looked us over thoughtfully. "You go straight up the High Street and you can't miss it. On your left. There's no name on the gate, but it's the first big house after the bank." He repeated again, "You can't miss it."

His eyes followed us as we started on our course.

"Dear me," I complained. "There is something about this place that makes me feel extremely conspicuous. As for you, Poirot, you look positively exotic."

"You think it is noticed that I am a foreigner—yes?"

"The fact cries aloud to heaven," I assured him.

"And yet my clothes are made by an English tailor," mused Poirot.

"Clothes are not everything," I said. "It cannot be denied, Poirot, that you have a noticeable personality. I have often wondered that it has not hindered you in your career."

Poirot sighed.

"That is because you have the mistaken idea implanted in your head that a detective is necessarily a man who puts on a false beard and hides behind a pillar! The false beard, it is *vieux jeu*, and shadowing is only done by the lowest branch of my profession. The Hercule Poirots, my friend, need only to sit back in a chair and think."

"Which explains why we are walking along this exceedingly hot street on an exceedingly hot morning."

"That is very neatly replied, Hastings. For once, I admit, you have made the score off me."

We found Littlegreen House easily enough, but a shock awaited us—a house-agent's board.

As we were staring at it, a dog's bark attracted my attention.

The bushes were thin at that point and the dog could be easily seen. He was a wire-haired terrier, somewhat shaggy as to coat. His feet were planted wide apart, slightly to one side, and he barked with an obvious enjoyment of his own performance that showed him to be actuated by the most amiable motives.

"Good watchdog, aren't I?" he seemed to be saying. "Don't mind me! This is just my fun! My duty too, of course. Just have to let 'em know there's a dog about the place! Deadly dull morning. Quite a blessing to have something to do. Coming into

47

our place? Hope so. It's durned dull. I could do with a little conversation."

"Hullo, old man," I said and shoved forward a fist.

Craning his neck through the railings he sniffed suspiciously, then gently wagged his tail, uttering a few short, staccato barks.

"Not been properly introduced, of course, have to keep this up! But I see you know the proper advances to make."

"Good old boy," I said.

"Wuff," said the terrier amiably.

"Well, Poirot?" I said, desisting from this conversation and turning to my friend.

There was an odd expression on his face—one that I could not quite fathom. A kind of deliberately suppressed excitement seems to describe it best.

"The Incident of the Dog's Ball," he murmured. "Well, at least, we have here a dog."

"Wuff," observed our new friend. Then he sat down, yawned widely and looked at us hopefully.

"What next?" I asked.

The dog seemed to be asking the same question.

"*Parbleu*, to Messrs.—what is it—Messrs. Gabler and Stretcher."

"That does seem indicated," I agreed.

We turned and retraced our steps, our canine acquaintance sending a few disgusted barks after us.

The premises of Messrs. Gabler and Stretcher were situated in the Market Square. We entered a dim outer officer where we were received by a young woman with adenoids and a lack-lustre eye.

"Good-morning," said Poirot politely.

The young woman was at the moment speaking into a telephone but she indicated a chair and Poirot sat down. I found another and brought it forward.

"I couldn't say, I'm sure," said the young woman into the telephone vacantly. "No, I don't know what the rates would be. . . . Pardon? Oh, main water, I think, but, of course, I couldn't be certain . . . I'm very sorry, I'm sure . . . No, he's out. . . . No, I couldn't say. . . . Yes, of course I'll ask him. . . . Yes . . . 8135? I'm afraid I haven't quite go it. Oh . . . 8935 . . .

48

39 . . . Oh, 5135. . . . Yes, I'll ask him to ring you . . . after six.
. . . Oh, pardon, before six. . . . Thank you so much."

She replaced the receiver, scribbled 5139 on the blotting-pad and turned a mildly inquiring but uninterested gaze on Poirot.

Poirot began briskly.

"I observe that there is a house to be sold just on the outskirts of this town. Littlegreen House, I think is the name."

"Pardon?"

"A house to be let or sold," said Poirot slowly and distinctly. "Littlegreen House."

"Oh, Littlegreen House," said the young woman vaguely. "*Littlegreen* House, did you say?"

"That is what I said."

"Littlegreen *House*," said the young woman, making a tremendous mental effort. "Oh, well, I expect Mr Gabler would know about that."

"Can I see Mr Gabler?"

"He's out," said the young woman with a kind of faint, anæmic satisfaction as of one who says, "A point to me."

"Do you know when he will be in?"

"I couldn't say, I'm sure," said the young woman.

"You comprehend, I am looking for a house in this neighbourhood," said Poirot.

"Oh, yes," said the young woman, uninterested.

"And Littlegreen House seems to me just what I am looking for. Can you give me particulars?"

"Particulars?" The young woman seemed startled.

"Particulars of Littlegreen House."

Unwillingly she opened a drawer and took out an untidy file of papers.

Then she called, "John."

A lanky youth sitting in a corner looked up.

"Yes, miss."

"Have we got any particulars of—what did you say?"

"Littlegreen House," said Poirot distinctly.

"You've got a large bill of it here," I remarked, pointing to the wall.

She looked at me coldly. Two to one, she seemed to think,

49

was an unfair way of playing the game. She called up her own reinforcements.

"You don't know anything about Littlegreen House, do you, John?"

"No, miss. Should be in the file."

"I'm sorry," said the young woman without looking so in the least. "I rather fancy we must have sent all the particulars out."

"*C'est domage.*"

"Pardon?"

"A pity."

"We've a nice bungalow at Hemel End, two bed., one sitt."

She spoke without enthusiasm, but with the air of one willing to do her duty by her employer.

"I thank you, no."

"And a semi-detached with small conservatory. I could give you particulars of that."

"No, thank you. I desired to know what rent you were asking for Littlegreen House."

"It's not to be rented," said the young woman, abandoning her position of complete ignorance of anything to do with Littlegreen House in the pleasure of scoring a point. "Only to be sold outright."

"The board says, 'To be Let or Sold.'"

"I couldn't say as to that, but it's for sale only."

At this stage in the battle the door opened and a grey-haired, middle-aged man entered with a rush. His eye, a militant one, swept over us with a gleam. His eyebrows asked a question of his employee.

"This is Mr Gabler," said the young woman.

Mr Gabler opened the door of an inner sanctum with a flourish.

"Step in here, gentlemen." He ushered us in, an ample gesture swept us into chairs and he himself was facing us across a flat-topped desk.

"And now what can I do for you?"

Poirot began again perseveringly.

"I desired a few particulars of Littlegreen House——"

He got no further. Mr Gabler took command.

"Ah! Littlegreen House—*there's* a property! An absolute

bargain. Only just come into the market. I can tell you, gentlemen, we don't often get a house of that class going at the price.
Taste's swinging round. People are fed up with jerry-building.
They want sound stuff. Good, honest building. A beautiful
property—character—feeling—Georgian throughout. That's
what people want nowadays—there's a feeling for period houses
if you understand what I mean. Ah, yes, Littlegreen House
won't be long in the market. It'll be snapped up. Snapped up! A
member of parliament came to look at it only last Saturday.
Liked it so much he's coming down again this week-end. And
there's a stock exchange gentleman after it too. People want
quiet nowadays when they come to the country, want to be well
away from main roads. That's all very well for some people, but
we attract class here. And that's what that house has got. Class!
You've got to admit, they knew how to build for gentlemen in
those days. Yes, we shan't have Littlegreen long on our books."

Mr Gabler, who, it occurred to me, lived up to his name very
happily, paused for breath.

"Has it changed hands often in the last few years?" inquired
Poirot.

"On the contrary. Been in one family over fifty years. Name
of Arundell. Very much respected in the town. Ladies of the old
school."

He shot up, opened the door and called:

"Particulars of Littlegreen House, Miss Jenkins. Quickly
now."

He returned to the desk.

"I require a house about this distance from London," said
Poirot. "In the country, but not in the dead country, if you
understand me——"

"Perfectly—perfectly. Too much in the country doesn't do.
Servants don't like it for one thing. Here, you have the advantages of the country but not the disadvantages." Miss Jenkins
flitted in with a typewritten sheet of paper which she placed in
front of her employer who dismissed her with a nod.

"Here we are," said Mr Gabler, reading with practised
rapidity. "Period House of character: four recep., eight bed and
dressing, usual offices, commodious kitchen premises, ample
outbuildings, stables, etc. Main water, old-world gardens,

inexpensive upkeep, amounting in all the three acres, two summer-houses, etc., etc. Price £2,850 or near offer."

"You can give me an order to view?"

"Certainly, my dear sir." Mr Gabler began writing in a flourishing fashion. "Your name and address?"

Slightly to my surprise, Poirot gave his name as Mr Parotti.

"We have one or two other properties on our books which might interest you," Mr Gabler went on.

Poirot allowed him to add two further additions.

"Littlegreen House can be viewed any time?" he inquired.

"Certainly, my dear sir. There are servants in residence. I might perhaps ring up to make certain. You will be going there immediately? Or after lunch?"

"Perhaps after lunch would be better."

"Certainly—certainly. I'll ring up and tell them to expect you about two o'clock—eh? Is that right?"

"Thank you. Did you say the owner of the house—a Miss Arundell, I think you said?"

"Lawson. Miss Lawson. That is the name of the present owner. Miss Arundell, I am sorry to say, died a short time ago. That is how the place has come into the market. And I can assure you it will be snapped up. Not a doubt of it. Between you and me, just in confidence, if you do think of making an offer I should make it quickly. As I've told you, there are two gentlemen after it already, and I shouldn't be surprised to get an offer for it any day from one or other of them. Each of them knows the other's after it, you see. And there's no doubt that competition spurs a man on. Ha, ha! I shouldn't like you to be disappointed."

"Miss Lawson is anxious to sell, I gather."

Mr Gabler lowered his voice confidentially.

"That's just it. The place is larger than she wants—one middle-aged lady living by herself. She wants to get rid of this and take a house in London. Quite understandable. That's why the place is going so ridiculously cheap."

"She would be open, perhaps, to an offer?"

"That's the idea, sir. Make an offer and set the ball rolling. But you can take it from me that there will be no difficulty in getting a price very near the figure named. Why, it's ridiculous!

To build a house like that nowadays would cost every penny of six thousand, let alone the land value and the valuable frontages."

"Miss Arundell died very suddenly, didn't she?"

"Oh, I wouldn't say that. Anno domini—anno domini. She had passed her three-score years and ten some time ago. And she'd been ailing for a long time. The last of her family—you know something about the family, perhaps?"

"I know some people of the same name who have relations in this part of the world. I fancy it must be the same family".

"Very likely. Four sisters there were. One married fairly late in life and the other three lived on here. Ladies of the old school. Miss Emily was the last of them. Very highly thought of in the town."

He leant forward and handed Poirot the orders.

"You'll drop in again and let me know what you think of it, eh? Of course, it may need a little modernising here and there. That's only to be expected. But I always say, 'What's a bathroom or two? That's easily done.'"

We took our leave and the last thing we heard was the vacant voice of Miss Jenkins saying:

"Mrs Samuels rang up, sir. She'd like you to ring her—Holland 5391."

As far as I could remember that was neither the number Miss Jenkins had scribbled on her pad nor the number finally arrived at through the telephone.

I felt convinced that Miss Jenkins was having her revenge for having been forced to find the particulars of Littlegreen House.

7 . *Lunch at the George*

As WE emerged into the market square, I remarked that Mr Gabler lived up to his name! Poirot assented with a smile.

"He'll be rather disappointed when you don't return," I said. "I think he feels he has as good as sold you that house already."

"Indeed, yes, I fear there is a deception in store for him."

"I suppose we might as well have lunch here before returning to London, or shall we lunch at some more likely spot on our way back?"

"My dear Hastings, I am not proposing to leave Market Basing so quickly. We have not yet accomplished that which we came to do."

I stared.

"Do you mean—but, my dear fellow, that's all a wash-out. The old lady is dead."

"Exactly."

The tone of that one word made me stare at him harder than ever. It was evident that he had some bee in his bonnet over this incoherent letter.

"But if she's dead, Poirot," I said gently, "what's the use? She can't tell you anything now. Whatever the trouble was, it's over and finished with."

"How lightly and easily you put the matter aside! Let me tell you that *no* matter is finished with until Hercule Poirot ceases to concern himself with it!"

I should have known from experience that to argue with Poirot is quite useless. Unwearily I proceeded.

"But since she is dead——"

"Exactly, Hastings. Exactly—exactly—exactly. . . . You keep repeating the significant point with a magnificently obtuse disregard of its significance. Do you not see the importance of the point? Miss Arundell is *dead*."

"But, my dear Poirot, her death was perfectly natural and ordinary! There wasn't anything odd or unexplained about it. We have old Gabler's word for that."

"We have his word that Littlegreen House is a bargain at £2,850. Do you accept that as gospel also?"

"No, indeed. It struck me that Gabler was all out to get the place sold—it probably needs modernising from top to toe. I'd swear he—or rather his client—will be willing to accept a very much lower figure than that. These large Georgian houses fronting right on the street must be the devil to get rid of."

"*Eh bien*, then," said Poirot. "Do not say, 'But Gabler says so!' as though he were an inspired prophet who could not lie."

I was about to protest further, but at this minute we passed the threshold of The George and with an emphatic "Chut!" Poirot put a damper on further conversation.

We were directed to the coffee-room, a room of fine proportions, tightly-shut windows and an odour of stale food. An elderly waiter attended to us, a slow, heavy-breathing man. We appeared to be the only lunchers. We had some excellent mutton, large slabs of watery cabbage and some dispirited potatoes. Some rather tasteless stewed fruit and custard followed. After gorgonzola and biscuits the waiter brought us two cups of a doubtful fluid called coffee.

At this point Poirot produced his orders to view and invited the waiter's aid.

"Yes, sir, I know where most of these are. Hemel Down is three miles away—on the Much Benham road—quite a little place. Naylor's Farm is about a mile away. There's a kind of lane goes off to it not long after the King's Head. Bissett Grange? No, I've never heard of that. Littlegreen House is just close by, not more than a few minutes' walk."

"Ah, I think I have already seen it from the outside. That is the most possible one, I think. It is in good repair—yes?"

"Oh, yes, sir. It's in good condition—roof and drains and all that. Old-fashioned, of course. It's never been modernised in any way. The gardens are a picture. Very fond of her garden Miss Arundell was."

"It belongs, I see, to a Miss Lawson."

"That's right, sir. Miss Lawson, she was Miss Arundell's

companion and when the old lady died everything was left to her—house and all.'

"Indeed? I suppose she had no relations to whom to leave it."

"Well, it was not quite like that, sir. She *had* nieces and nephews living. But, of course, Miss Lawson was with her all the time. And, of course, she was an old lady and—well—that's how it was."

"In any case I suppose there was just the house and not much money?"

I have often had occasion to notice how, where a direct question would fail to elicit a response, a false assumption brings instant information in the form of a contradiction.

"Very far from that, sir. Very far indeed. Every one was surprised at the amount the old lady left. The will was in the paper and the amount and everything. It seems she hadn't lived up to her income for many a long year. Something like three or four hundred thousand pounds she left."

"You astonish me," cried Poirot. "It is like a fairy tale—eh? The poor companion suddenly becomes unbelievably wealthy. Is she still young, this Miss Lawson? Can she enjoy her new-found wealth?"

"Oh, no, sir, she's a middle-aged person, sir."

His enunciation of the word person was quite an artistic performance. It was clear that Miss Lawson, ex-companion, had cut no kind of a figure in Market Basing.

"It must have been disappointing for the nephews and nieces," mused Poirot.

"Yes, sir, I believe it came as somewhat of a shock to them. Very unexpected. There's been feeling over it here in Market Basing. There are those who hold it isn't right to leave things away from your own flesh and blood. But, of course, there's others as hold that every one's got a right to do as they like with their own. There's something to be said for both points of view, of course."

"Miss Arundell had lived for many years here, had she not?"

"Yes, sir. She and her sisters and old General Arundell, their father, before them. Not that I remember him, naturally, but I believe he was quite a character. Was in the Indian Mutiny."

"There were several daughters?"

"Three of them that I remember, and I believe there was one that married. Yes, Miss Matilda, Miss Agnes, and Miss Emily. Miss Matilda, she died first, and then Miss Agnes, and finally Miss Emily."

"That was quite recently?"

"Beginning of May—or it may have been the end of April."

"Had she been ill some time?"

"On and off—on and off. She was on the sickly side. Nearly went off a year ago with that there jaundice. Yellow as an orange she was for some time after. Yes, she'd had poor health for the last five years of her life."

"I suppose you have some good doctors down here?"

"Well, there's Dr Grainger. Been here close on forty years, he has, and folks mostly go to him. He's a bit crotchety and he has his fancies but he's a good doctor, none better. He's got a young partner, Dr Donaldson. He's more the new-fangled kind. Some folk prefer him. Then, of course, there's Dr Harding, but he doesn't do much."

"Dr Grainger was Miss Arundell's doctor, I suppose?"

"Oh, yes. He'd pulled her through many a bad turn. He's the kind that fair bullies you into living whether you want to or not."

Poirot nodded.

"One should learn a little about a place before one comes to settle in it," he remarked. "A good doctor is one of the most important people."

"That's very true, sir."

Poirot then asked for his bill to which he added a substantial tip.

"Thank you, sir. Thank you very much, sir. I'm sure I hope you'll settle here, sir."

"I hope so, too," said Poirot mendaciously.

We set forth from The George.

"Satisfied yet, Poirot?" I asked as we emerged into the street.

"Not in the least, my friend."

He turned in an unexpected direction.

"Where are you off to now, Poirot?"

"The church, my friend. It may be interesting. Some brasses —an old monument."

57

I shook my head doubtfully.

Poirot's scrutiny of the interior of the church was brief. Though an attractive specimen of what the guidebook calls Early Perp. it had been so conscientiously restored in Victorian vandal days that little of interest remained.

Poirot next wandered seemingly aimlessly about the churchyard reading some of the epitaphs, commenting on the number of deaths in certain families, occasionally exclaiming over the quaintness of a name.

I was not surprised, however, when he finally halted before what I was pretty sure had been his objective from the beginning.

An imposing marble slab bore a partly-effaced inscription:

SACRED

TO THE MEMORY OF

JOHN LAVERTON ARUNDELL

GENERAL 24TH SIKHS

WHO FELL ASLEEP IN CHRIST MAY 19TH 1888

AGED 69

"FIGHT THE GOOD FIGHT WITH ALL THY MIGHT"

ALSO OF

MATILDA ANN ARUNDELL

DIED MARCH 10TH 1912

"I WILL ARISE AND GO TO MY FATHER"

ALSO OF

AGNES GEORGINA MARY ARUNDELL

DIED NOVEMBER 20TH 1921

"ASK AND YE SHALL RECEIVE"

Then came a brand new piece of lettering, evidently just done:

ALSO OF

EMILY HARRIET LAVERTON ARUNDELL

DIED MAY 1ST 1936

"THY WILL BE DONE"

Poirot stood looking for some time.

He murmured softly:

"May 1st. . . . May 1st. . . . And to-day, June 28th, I receive her letter. You see, do you not, Hastings, that that fact has got to be explained?"

I saw that it had.

That is to say, I saw that Poirot was determined that it should be explained.

8. Interior of Littlegreen House

ON LEAVING the churchyard, Poirot led the way briskly in the direction of Littlegreen House. I gathered that his rôle was still that of the prospective purchaser. Carefully holding the various orders to view in his hand with the Littlegreen House one uppermost, he pushed open the gate and walked up the path to the front door.

On this occasion our friend the terrier was not to be seen, but the sound of barking could be heard inside the house, though at some distance—I guessed in the kitchen quarters.

Presently we heard footsteps crossing the hall and the door was opened by a pleasant-faced woman of between fifty and sixty, clearly the old-fashioned type of servant seldom seen nowadays.

Poirot presented his credentials.

"Yes, sir, the house-agent telephoned. Will you step this way, sir?"

The shutters which I had noticed were closed on our first visit to spy out the land, were now all thrown open in preparation for our visit. Everything, I observed, was spotlessly clean and well kept. Clearly our guide was a thoroughly conscientious woman.

"This is the morning-room, sir."

I glanced round approvingly. A pleasant room with its long windows giving on the street. It was furnished with good, solid, old-fashioned furniture, mostly Victorian, but there was a Chippendale bookcase and a set of attractive Hepplewhite chairs.

Poirot and I behaved in the customary fashion of people being shown over houses. We stood stock still, looking a little ill at ease, murmuring remarks such as "Very nice." "A very pleasant room." "The morning-room, you say?"

The maid conducted us across the hall and into the corresponding room on the other side. This was much larger.

"The dining-room, sir."

This room was definitely Victorian. A heavy mahogany dining-table, a massive sideboard of almost purplish mahogany with great clusters of carved fruit, solid leather-covered dining-room chairs. On the wall hung what were obviously family portraits.

The terrier had continued to bark in some sequestered spot. Now the sound suddenly increased in volume. With a crescendo of barking he could be heard galloping across the hall.

"*Who's* come into the house? *I'll* tear him limb from limb," was clearly the "burden of his song."

He arrived in the doorway, sniffing violently.

"Oh, Bob, you naughty dog," exclaimed our conductress. "Don't you mind him, sir. He won't do you no harm."

Bob, indeed, having discovered the intruders, completely changed his manner. He fussed in and introduced himself to us in an agreeable manner.

"Pleased to meet you, I'm sure," he observed as he sniffed round our ankles. "Excuse the noise, won't you, but I have my job to do. Got to be careful who we let in, you know. But it's a dull life and I'm really quite pleased to see a visitor. Dogs of your own, I fancy?"

This last was addressed to me as I stooped and patted him.

"Nice little fellow," I said to the woman. "Needs plucking a bit, though."

"Yes, sir, he's usually plucked three times a year."

"Is he an old dog?"

"Oh, no, sir. Bob's not more than six. And sometimes he behaves just like a puppy. Gets hold of cook's slippers and prances about with them. And he's very gentle though you wouldn't believe it to hear the noise he makes sometimes. The only person he goes for is the postman. Downright scared of him the postman is."

Bob was now investigating the legs of Poirot's trousers. Having learned all he could he gave vent to a prolonged sniff ("H'm, not too bad, but not really a doggy person") and returned to me cocking his head on one side and looking at me expectantly.

"I don't know why dogs always go for postmen, I'm sure," continued our guide.

"It's a matter of reasoning," said Poirot. "The dog, he argues from reason. He is intelligent, he makes his deductions according to his point of view. There are people who may enter a house and there are people who may not—that a dog soon learns. *Eh bien*, who is the person who most persistently tries to gain admission, rattling on the door twice or three times a day—and who is never by any chance admitted? The postman. Clearly, then, an undesirable guest from the point of view of the master of the house. He is always sent about his business, but he persistently returns and tries again. Then a dog's duty is clear, to aid in driving this undesirable man away, and to bite him if possible. A most reasonable proceeding."

He beamed on Bob.

"And a most intelligent person, I fancy."

"Oh, he is, sir. He's almost human, Bob is."

She flung open another door.

"The drawing-room, sir."

The drawing-room conjured up memories of the past. A faint fragrance of potpourri hung about it. The chintzes were worn, their pattern faded garlands of roses. On the walls were prints and water-colour drawings. There was a good deal of china— fragile shepherds and shepherdesses. There were cushions worked in crewel stitch. There were faded photographs in handsome silver frames. There were many inlaid work-boxes and tea caddies. Most fascinating of all to me were two exquisitely cut tissue-paper ladies under glass stands. One with a spinning-wheel, one with a cat on her knee.

The atmosphere of a bygone day, a day of leisure, of refinement, of "ladies and gentlemen" closed round me. This was indeed a "withdrawing-room." Here ladies sat and did their fancy-work, and if a cigarette was ever smoked by a favoured member of the male sex, what a shaking out of curtains and general airing of the room there would be afterwards!

My attention was drawn by Bob. He was sitting in an attitude of rapt attention close beside an elegant little table with two drawers in it.

As he saw that I was noticing him, he gave a short, plaintive yelp, looking from me to the table.

"What does he want?" I asked.

Our interest in Bob was clearly pleasing to the maid, who obviously was very fond of him.

"It's his ball, sir. It was always kept in that drawer. That's why he sits there and asks."

Her voice changed. She addressed Bob in a high falsetto.

"It isn't there any longer, beautiful. Bob's ball is in the kitchen. In the kitchen, Bobsie."

Bob shifted his gaze impatiently to Poirot.

"This woman's a fool," he seemed to be saying. "You look a brainy sort of chap. Balls are kept in certain places—this drawer is one of those places. There always has been a ball here. Therefore there should be a ball there now. That's obvious dog-logic, isn't it?"

"It's not there now, boy," I said.

He looked at me doubtfully. Then, as we went out of the room he followed slowly in an unconvinced manner.

We were shown various cupboards, a downstairs cloakroom, and a small pantry place, "where the mistress used to do the flowers, sir."

"You were with your mistress a long time?" asked Poirot.

"Twenty-two years, sir."

"You are alone here caretaking?"

"Me and cook, sir."

"She was also a long time with Miss Arundell?"

"Four years, sir. The old cook died."

"Supposing I were to buy the house, would you be prepared to stay on?"

She blushed a little.

"It's very kind of you, sir, I'm sure, but I'm going to retire from service. The mistress left me a nice little sum, you see, and I'm going to my brother. I'm only remaining here as a convenience to Miss Lawson until the place is sold—to look after everything."

Poirot nodded.

In the momentary silence a new sound was heard.

"Bump, bump, BUMP."

A monotonous sound increasing in volume and seeming to descend from above.

"It's Bob, sir." She was smiling. "He's got hold of his ball and he's bumping it down the stairs. It's a little game of his."

63

As we reached the bottom of the stairs a black rubber ball arrived with a thud on the last step. I caught it and looked up. Bob was lying on the top step, his paws splayed out, his tail gently wagging. I threw it up to him. He caught it neatly, chewed it for a minute or two with evident relish, then laid it between his paws and gently edged it forward with his nose till he finally bunted it over and it bumped once more down the stairs, Bob wagging his tail furiously as he watched its progress.

"He'll stay like that for hours, sir. Regular game of his. He'd go on all day at it. That'll do now, Bob. The gentlemen have got something else to do than play with you."

A dog is a great promoter of friendly intercourse. Our interest and liking for Bob had quite broken down the natural stiffness of the good servant. As we went up to the bedroom floors, our guide was talking quite garrulously as she gave us accounts of Bob's wonderful sagacity. The ball had been left at the foot of the stairs. As we passed him, Bob gave us a look of deep disgust and stalked down in a dignified fashion to retrieve it. As we turned to the right I saw him slowly coming up again with it in his mouth, his gait that of an extremely old man forced by unthinking persons to exert himself unduly.

As we went round the bedrooms, Poirot began gradually to draw our conductress out.

"There were four Miss Arundells lived here, did they not?" he asked.

"Originally, yes, sir, but that was before my time. There was only Miss Agnes and Miss Emily when I came and Miss Agnes died soon afterwards. She was the youngest of the family. It seemed odd she should go before her sister."

"I suppose she was not so strong as her sister?"

"No, sir, it's odd that. My Miss Arundell, Miss Emily, she was always the delicate one. She'd had a lot to do with doctors all her life. Miss Agnes was always strong and robust and yet she went first and Miss Emily who'd been delicate from a child outlived all the family. Very odd the way things happen."

"Astonishing how often that is the case."

Poirot plunged into (I feel sure) a wholly mendacious story of an invalid uncle which I will not trouble to repeat here. It suffices to say that it had its effect. Discussions of death and such matters do more to unlock the human tongue than any other subject. Poirot was in a position to ask questions that would have been regarded with suspicious hostility twenty minutes earlier.

"Was Miss Arundell's illness a long and painful one?"

"No, I wouldn't say that, sir. She'd been ailing, if you know what I mean, for a long time—ever since two winters before. Very bad she was then—this here jaundice. Yellow in the face they go and the whites of their eyes——"

"Ah, yes, indeed——" (Anecdote of Poirot's cousin who appeared to have been the Yellow Peril in person.)

"That's right—just as you say, sir. Terribly ill she was, poor dear. Couldn't keep anything down. If you ask me, Dr Grainger hardly thought she'd pull through. But he'd a wonderful way with her—bullying, you know. 'Made up your mind to lie back and order your tombstone?' he'd say. And she'd say, 'I've a bit of fight in me still, doctor,' and he'd say. 'That's right–that's what I like to hear.' A hospital nurse we had, and she made up her mind that it was all over—even said to the doctor once that she supposed she'd better not worry the old lady too much by forcing her to take food—but the doctor rounded on her. 'Nonsense', he said. 'Worry her? You've got to bully her into taking nourishment.' Valentine's beef juice at such and such a time, Brand's essence—teaspoonfuls of brandy. And at the end he said something that I've never forgotten. 'You're young, my girl,' he said to her. 'You don't realise what fine fighting material there is in age. It's young people who turn up their toes and die because they're not interested enough to live. You show me any one who's lived to over seventy and you show me a fighter— some one who's got the will to live.' And it's true sir—we're always saying how wonderful old people are—their vitality and the way they've kept their faculties—but as the doctor put it that's just *why* they've lived so long and got to be so old."

"But it is profound what you say there—very profound! And Miss Arundell was like that? Very alive? Very interested in life?"

"Oh, yes, indeed, sir. Her health was poor, but her brain was as keen as anything. And as I was saying, she got over that illness of hers—surprised the nurse, it did. A stuck up young thing she was, all starched collars and cuffs and the waiting on she had to have and tea at all hours."

"A fine recovery."

"Yes, indeed, sir. Of course, the mistress had to be very careful as to diet at first, everything boiled and steamed, no grease in the cooking, and she wasn't allowed to eat eggs either. Very monotonous it was for her."

"Still the main thing is she got well."

"Yes, sir. Of course, she had her little turns. What I'd call bilious attacks. She wasn't always very careful about her food after a time—but still they weren't very serious until the last attack."

"Was it like her illness of two years before?"

"Yes, just the same sort of thing, sir. That nasty jaundice—an awful yellow colour again—and the terrible sickness and all the rest of it. Brought it on herself I'm afraid she did, poor dear. Ate a lot of things she shouldn't have done. That very evening she was took bad she'd had curry for supper and as you know, sir, curry's rich and a bit oily."

"Her illness came on suddenly, did it?"

"Well, it seemed so, sir, but Dr Grainger he said it had been working up for some time. A chill—the weather had been very changeable—and too rich feeding."

"Surely her companion—Miss Lawson was her companion, was she not—could have dissuaded her from rich dishes?"

"Oh, I don't think Miss Lawson would have much say. Miss Arundell wasn't one to take orders from any one."

"Had Miss Lawson been with her during her previous illness?"

"No, she came after that. She'd been with her about a year."

"I suppose she'd had companions before that?"

"Oh, quite a number, sir."

"Her companions didn't stay as long as her servants," said Poirot, smiling.

The woman flushed.

"Well, you see, sir, it was different. Miss Arundell didn't get out much and what with one thing and another——" she paused.

Poirot eyed her for a minute then he said:

66

"I understand a little the mentality of elderly ladies. They crave, do they not, for novelty. They get, perhaps, to the end of a person."

"Well now, that's very clever of you, sir. You've hit it exactly. When a new lady came Miss Arundell was always interested to start with—about her life and her childhood and where she'd been and what she thought about things, and then, when she knew all about her, well, she'd get—well, I suppose bored is the real word."

"Exactly. And between you and me, these ladies who go as companions, they are not usually very interesting—very amusing, eh?"

"No, indeed, sir. They're poor-spirited creatures, most of them. Downright foolish, now and then. Miss Arundell soon got through with them, so to speak. And then she'd make a change and have some one else."

"She must have been unusually attached to Miss Lawson, though."

"Oh, I don't think so, sir."

"Miss Lawson was not in any way a remarkable woman?"

"I shouldn't have said so, sir. Quite an ordinary person."

"You liked her, yes?"

The woman shrugged her shoulders slightly.

"There wasn't anything to like or dislike. Fussy she was—a regular old maid and full of this nonsense about spirits."

"*Spirits?*" Poirot looked alert.

"Yes, sir, spirits. Sitting in the dark round a table and dead people came back and spoke to you. Downright irreligious I call it—as if we didn't know departed souls had their rightful place and aren't likely to leave it."

"So Miss Lawson was a spiritualist! Was Miss Arundell a believer too?"

"Miss Lawson would have liked her to be!" snapped the other. There was a spice of satisfied malice in her tone.

"But she wasn't?" Poirot persisted.

"The mistress had too much sense." She snorted. "Mind you, I don't say it didn't *amuse* her. 'I'm willing to be convinced,' she'd say. But she'd often look at Miss Lawson as much as to say, 'My poor dear, what a fool you are to be so taken in!'"

"I comprehend. She did not believe in it, but it was a source of amusement to her."

"That's right, sir. I sometimes wondered if she didn't—well have a bit of quiet fun, so to speak, pushing the table and that sort of thing. And the others all as serious as death."

"The others?"

"Miss Lawson and the two Miss Tripps."

"Miss Lawson was a very convinced spiritualist?"

"Took it all for gospel, sir."

"And Miss Arundell was very attached to Miss Lawson, of course."

It was the second time Poirot had made this certain remark and he got the same response.

"Well, hardly that, sir."

"But surely," said Poirot. "If she left her everything. She did, did she not?"

The change was immediate. The human being vanished. The correct maid-servant returned. The woman drew herself up and said in a colourless voice that held reproof for familiarity in it:

"The way the mistress left her money is hardly my business, sir."

I felt that Poirot had bungled the job. Having got the woman in a friendly mood, he was now proceeding to throw away his advantage. He was wise enough to make no immediate attempt to recover lost ground. After a commonplace remark about the size and number of the bedrooms he went towards the head of the stairs.

Bob had disappeared, but as I came to the stair-head, I stumbled and nearly fell. Catching at the baluster to steady myself I looked down and saw that I had inadvertently placed my foot on Bob's ball which he had left lying on the top of the stairs.

The woman apologised quickly.

"I'm sorry, sir. It's Bob's fault. He leaves his ball there. And you can't see it against the dark carpet. Death of some one some day it'll be. The poor mistress had a nasty fall through it. Might easily have been the death of her."

Poirot stopped suddenly on the stairs.

"She had an accident, you say?"

68

"Yes, sir. Bob left his ball there, as he often did, and the mistress came out of her room and fell over it and went right down the stairs. Might have been killed."

"Was she much hurt?"

"Not as much as you'd think. Very lucky she was, Dr Grainger said. Cut her head a little, and strained her back, and of course there were bruises and it was a nasty shock. She was in bed for about a week, but it wasn't serious."

"Was this long ago?"

"Just a week or two before she died."

Poirot stooped to recover something he had dropped.

"Pardon—my fountain pen—ah, yes, there it is."

He stood up again.

"He is careless, this Master Bob," he observed.

"Ah well, he don't know no better, sir," said the woman in an indulgent voice. "Nearly human he may be, but you can't have everything. The mistress, you see, usedn't to sleep well at nights and often she'd get up and wander downstairs and round and about the house."

"She did that often?"

"Most nights. But she wouldn't have Miss Lawson or any one fussing after her."

Poirot had turned into the drawing-room again.

"A beautiful room this," he observed. "I wonder, would there be space in this recess for my bookcase? What do you think, Hastings?"

Quite fogged I remarked cautiously that it would be difficult to say.

"Yes, sizes are so deceptive. Take, I pray you, my little rule and measure the width of it and I will write it down."

Obediently I took the folding rule that Poirot handed me and took various measurements under his direction whilst he wrote on the back of an envelope.

I was just wondering why he adopted such an untidy and uncharacteristic method of making a neat entry in his little pocket-book when he handed the envelope to me, saying:

"That is right, is it not? Perhaps you had better verify it."

There were no figures on the envelope. Instead was written: 'When we go upstairs again, pretend to remember an appointment and ask if you can telephone. Let the woman come with you and delay her as long as you can."

"That's all right," I said, pocketing the envelope. "I should say both bookcases would go in perfectly."

"It is as well to be sure, though. I think, if it is not too much trouble, I would like to look at the principal bedroom again. I am not quite sure of the wall space there."

"Certainly, sir. It's no trouble."

We went up again. Poirot measured a portion of wall, and was just commenting aloud on the respective possible positions of bed, wardrobe and writing table, when I looked my watch, gave a somewhat exaggerated start and exclaimed:

"By Jove, do you know it's three o'clock already? What will Anderson think? I ought to telephone to him." I turned to the woman. "I wonder if I might use your telephone if you have one."

"Why, certainly, sir. It's in the little room off the hall. I'll show you."

She bustled down with me, indicating the instrument, and then I got her to help me in finding a number in the telephone directory. In the end I made a call—to a Mr Anderson in the neighbouring town of Harchester. Fortunately he was out and I was able to leave a message saying it was unimportant and that I would ring up later!

When I emerged Poirot had descended the staircase and was standing in the hall. His eyes had a slightly green tinge. I had no clue to his excitement but I realised that he *was* excited.

Poirot said:

"That fall from the top of the stairs must have given your mistress a great shock. Did she seem perturbed about Bob and his ball after it?"

"It's funny your saying that, sir. It worried her a lot. Why, just as she was dying, she was delirious and she rambled on a lot about Bob and his ball and something about a picture that was ajar."

"A picture that was ajar," said Poirot, thoughtfully.

"Of course, it didn't make sense, sir, but she was rambling, you see."

"One moment—I must just go into the drawing-room once more."

70

He wandered round the room examining the ornaments. In especial, one big jar with a lid on it seemed to attract him. It was not, I fancy, a particularly good bit of china. A piece of Victorian humour—it had on it a rather crude picture of a bulldog sitting outside a front door with a mournful expression on its face. Below was written: *Out all night and no key.*

Poirot, whose taste I have always been convinced, is hopelessly bourgeois, seemed lost in admiration.

"Out all night and no key," he murmured. "It is amusing, that! Is that true of our Master Bob? Does he sometimes stay out all night?"

"Very occasional, sir. Oh, very occasional. He's a very good dog, Bob is."

"I am sure he is. But even the best of dogs——"

"Oh, it's quite true, sir. Once or twice he's gone off and come home perhaps at four in the morning. Then he sits down on the step and barks till he's let in."

"Who lets him in—Miss Lawson?"

"Well, any one who hears him, sir. It was Miss Lawson, sir, last time. It was the night of the mistress's accident. And Bob came home about five. Miss Lawson hurried down to let him in before he could make a noise. She was afraid of waking up the mistress and hadn't told her Bob was missing for fear of worrying her."

"I see. She thought it was better Miss Arundell shouldn't be told?"

"That's what she said, sir. She said, 'He's sure to come back. He always does, but she might worry and that would never do.' So we didn't say anything."

"Was Bob fond of Miss Lawson?"

"Well, he was rather contemptuous of her if you know what I mean, sir. Dogs can be. She was kind to him. Called him a good doggie and a nice doggie, but he used to look at her kind of scornful like and he didn't pay any attention at all to what she told him to do."

Poirot nodded. "I see," he said.

Suddenly he did something which startled me.

He pulled a letter from his pocket—the letter he had received this morning.

"Ellen," he said, "do you know anything about this?"

The change that came over Ellen's face was remarkable.

Her jaw dropped and she stared at Poirot with an almost comical expression of bewilderment.

"Well," she ejaculated. "I never did!"

The observation lacked coherency, perhaps, but it left no doubt of Ellen's meaning.

Gathering her wits about her she said slowly:

"Are you the gentleman that letter was written to then?"

"I am. I am Hercule Poirot."

Like most people, Ellen had not glanced at the name on the order Poirot had held out to her on his arrival. She nodded her head slowly.

"That was it," she said. "Hercules Poirot." She added an S to the Christian name and sounded the T of the surname.

"My word!" she exclaimed. "Cook *will* be surprised."

Poirot said, quickly:

"Would it not be advisable, perhaps, for us to go to the kitchen and there in company with your friend, we could talk the matter over?"

"Well—if you don't mind, sir."

Ellen sounded just a little doubtful. This particular social dilemma was clearly new to her. But Poirot's matter of fact manner reassured her and we departed forthwith to the kitchen, Ellen elucidating the situation to a large, pleasant-faced woman who was just lifting a kettle from a gas ring.

"You'll never believe it, Annie. This is actually the gentleman that letter was to. You know, the one I found in the blotter."

"You must remember I am in the dark," said Poirot. "Perhaps you will tell me how the letter came to be posted so late in the day?"

"Well, sir, to tell the truth I didn't know what to do. Neither of us did, did we?"

"Indeed, we didn't," the cook confirmed.

"You see, sir, when Miss Lawson was turning out things after the mistress's death a good lot of things were given away or thrown away. Among them was a little papier-mâché, I think they call it, blotter. Very pretty it was, with a lily of the valley on it. The mistress always used it when she wrote in bed. Well,

72

Miss Lawson didn't want it so she gave it to me along with a lot of other little odds and ends that had belonged to the mistress. I put it away in a drawer, and it wasn't till yesterday that I took it out. I was going to put some new blotting-paper in it so that it was ready for me to use. There was a sort of pocket inside and I just slipped my hand in it when what should I find but a letter in the mistress's handwriting, tucked away.

"Well, as I say I didn't know rightly what to do about it. It was the mistress's hand all right, and I saw as she'd written it and slipped it in there waiting to post it the next day and then she'd forgot, which is the kind of thing she did many a time, poor dear. Once it was a dividend warrant to her bank and no one could think where it had got to, and at last it was found pushed right back in the pigeon-holes of the desk."

"Was she untidy?"

"Oh, no, sir, just the opposite. She was always putting things away and clearing them up. That was half the trouble. If she'd left things about it would really have been better. It was their being tidied away and then forgotten that was always happening."

"Things like Bob's ball, for instance?" asked Poirot with a smile.

The sagacious terrier had just trotted in from outdoors and greeted us anew in a very friendly manner.

"Yes, indeed, sir. As soon as Bob finished playing with his ball she'd put it away. But that was all right because it had its own place—in the drawer I showed you."

"I see. But I interrupted you. Pray go on. You discovered the letter in the blotter?"

"Yes, sir, that was the way of it, and I asked Annie what she thought I'd better do. I didn't like to put it in the fire—and of course, I couldn't take upon myself to open it, and neither Annie nor I could see that it was any business of Miss Lawson's, so after we'd talked it over a bit, I just put a stamp on it and ran out to the post box and posted it."

Poirot turned slightly to me.

"*Voilà*," he murmured.

I could not help saying, maliciously:

"Amazing how simple an explanation can be!"

I thought he looked a little crestfallen, and rather wished I hadn't been so quick to try and rub it in.

He turned again to Ellen.

"As my friend says: How simple an explanation can be! You understand when I received a letter dated over two months ago I was somewhat surprised."

"Yes, I suppose you must have been, sir. We didn't think of that."

"Also——" Poirot coughed. "I am in a little dilemma. That letter, you see—it was a commission with which Miss Arundell wished to entrust me. A matter of somewhat private character." He cleared his throat importantly. "Now that Miss Arundell is dead I am in some doubt how to act. Would Miss Arundell have wished me to undertake the commission in these circumstances or not? It is difficult—very difficult."

Both women were looking at him respectfully.

"I shall have, I think, to consult Miss Arundell's lawyer. She had a lawyer, did she not?"

Ellen answered, quickly.

"Oh, yes, sir. Mr Purvis from Harchester."

"He knew all her affairs?"

"I think so, sir. He's done everything for her ever since I can remember. It was him she sent for after the fall she had."

"The fall down the stairs?"

"Yes, sir."

"Now let me see when was that exactly?"

The cook broke in.

"Day after Bank Holiday it was. I remember that well. I stayed in to oblige on Bank Holiday seeing she had all those people staying and I had the day on Wednesday instead."

Poirot had whipped out his pocket almanac.

"Precisely—precisely. Easter Bank Holiday, I see, fell on the thirteenth this year. Then Miss Arundell had her accident on the fourteenth. This letter to me was written three days later. A pity that it was never sent. However it may still not be too late——" he paused. "I rather fancy that the—er—commission she wished me to perform was connected with one of the —er—guests you mentioned just now."

This remark, which could only have been a pure shot in the

dark, met with immediate response. A quick look of intelligence passed across Ellen's face. She turned to the cook who gave her back an answering glance.

"That'll be Mr Charles," she said.

"If you would tell me just who was there ——" Poirot suggested.

"Dr Tanios and his wife, Miss Bella that was, and Miss Theresa and Mr Charles."

"They were all nephews and nieces?"

"That's right, sir. Dr Tanios, of course, is no relation. In fact he's a foreigner, a Greek or something of the sort, I believe. He married Miss Bella, Miss Arundell's niece, her sister's child. Mr Charles and Miss Theresa are brother and sister."

"Ah, yes, I see. A family party. And when did they leave?"

"On the Wednesday morning, sir. And Dr Tanios and Miss Bella came down again the next week-end because they were worried about Miss Arundell."

"And Mr Charles and Miss Theresa?"

"They came the week-end after. The week-end before she died."

Poirot's curiosity, I felt, was quite insatiable. I could see no point in these continued questions. He got the explanation of his mystery, and in my opinion the sooner he retired with dignity the better.

The thought seemed to go from my brain to his.

"*Eh bien*," he said. "This information you have given me is very helpful. I must consult this Mr Purvis, I think you said? Thank you very much for all your help."

He stooped and patted Bob.

"*Brave chien, va!* You loved your mistress."

Bob responded amiably to these overtures and, hopeful of a little play, went and fetched a large piece of coal. For this he was reproved and the coal removed from him. He sent me a glance in search of sympathy.

"These women," it seemed to say. "Generous with the food, but not really sportsmen!"

9. *Reconstruction of the Dog's Ball Incident*

"WELL, POIROT," I said, as the gate of Littlegreen House closed behind us. "You are satisfied now, I hope!"

"Yes, my friend. I am satisfied."

"Thank heaven for that! All the mysteries explained! The Wicked Companion and the Rich Old Lady myth exploded. The delayed letter and even the famous incident of the dog's ball shown in their true colours. Everything settled satisfactorily and according to Cocker!"

Poirot gave a dry little cough and said:

"I would not use the word *satisfactorily*, Hastings."

"You did a minute ago."

"No, no. I did not say the matter was *satisfactory*. I said that, personally, my curiosity was *satisfied*. I know the truth of the Dog's Ball incident."

"And very simple it was too!"

"Not quite so simple as you think." He nodded his head several times. Then he went on: "You see, I know one little thing which you do not."

"And what is that?" I asked somewhat sceptically.

"*I know that there is a nail driven into the skirting board at the top of the stairs.*"

I stared at him. His face was quite grave.

"Well," I said after a minute or two. "Why shouldn't there be?"

"The question is, Hastings, why should there be."

"How do I know. Some household reason, perhaps. Does it matter?"

"Certainly it matters. And I can think of no household reason for a nail to be driven in at the top of the skirting board in that particular place. It was carefully varnished, too, so as not to show."

"What are you driving at, Poirot? Do *you* know the reason?"

"I can imagine it quite easily. If you wanted to stretch a piece of strong thread or wire across the top of the stairs about a foot from the ground, you could tie it one side to the balusters, but on the inner wall side you would need something like a nail to attach the thread to."

"Poirot!" I cried. "What on earth are you driving at?"

"*Mon cher ami*, I am reconstructing *the incident of the Dog's Ball!* Would you like to hear my reconstruction?"

"Go ahead."

"*Eh bien*, here it is. Some one had noticed the habit Bob had of leaving his ball at the top of the stairs. A dangerous thing to do—it might lead to an accident." Poirot paused a minute, then said in a slightly different tone. "If you wished to kill some one, Hastings, how would you set about it?"

"I—well really—I don't know. Fake up some *alibi* or something, I suppose."

"A proceeding, I assure you, both difficult and dangerous. But then you are not the type of a cold-blooded cautious murderer. Does it not strike you that the *easiest* way of removing some one you want to remove from your path is to take advantage of *accident*? Accidents are happening all the time. And sometimes—Hastings—*they can be helped to happen!*"

He paused a minute then went on:

"I think the dog's ball left so fortuitously at the top of the stairs gave our murderer an idea. Miss Arundell was in the habit of coming out of her room in the night and wandering about—her eyesight was not good, it was quite within the bounds of probability that she might stumble over it and fall headlong down those stairs. But a careful murderer does not leave things to chance. A *thread* stretched across the top of the stairs would be a much better way. It would send her pitching head foremost. Then, when the household come rushing out—there, plain to see, is the *cause* of the accident—*Bob's ball!*"

"How horrible!" I cried.

Poirot said, gravely:

"Yes, it was horrible. . . . It was also unsuccessful. . . . Miss Arundell was very little hurt though she might easily have broken her neck. Very disappointing for our unknown friend!

But Miss Arundell was a sharp-witted old lady. Every one told her she had slipped on the ball, and there the ball was as evidence, but she herself recalling the happening felt that the accident had arisen differently. She had *not* slipped on the ball. And in addition she remembered something else. *She remembered hearing Bob barking for admission at five o'clock the next morning.*

"This, I admit, is something in the way of guess-work but I believe I am right. *Miss Arundell had put away Bob's ball herself* the evening before in its drawer. After that he went out *and did not return.* In that case *it was not Bob* who put that ball on the top of the stairs."

"That is pure guess-work, Poirot," I objected.

He demurred.

"Not quite, my friend. There are the significant words uttered by Miss Arundell when she was delirious—something about Bob's ball and a 'picture ajar.' You see the point, do you not?"

"Not in the least."

"Curious. I know your language well enough to realise that one does not talk of a picture being *ajar*. A *door* is *ajar*. A picture is *awry*."

"Or simply crooked."

"Or simply crooked, as you say. So I realised at once that Ellen has mistaken the meaning of the words she heard. It is not ajar—but a or the jar that was meant. Now in the drawing-room there is a rather noticeable china jar. There is, I have already observed, a picture of a dog on it. With the remembrance of these delirious ravings in my mind I go up and examine it more closely. I find that it deals with the subject of *a dog who has been out all night.* You see the trend of the feverish woman's thoughts? Bob was like the dog in the picture on the jar—out all night—*so it was not he who left the ball on the stairs.*"

I cried out, feeling some admiration in spite of myself.

"You're an ingenious devil, Poirot! How you think of these things beats me!"

"I do not 'think of them.' They are *there*—plain—for any one to see. *Eh bien*, you realise the position? Miss Arundell, lying in bed after her fall, becomes suspicious. That suspicion she feels is perhaps fanciful and absurd but there it is. '*Since the incident of the Dog's Ball I have been increasingly uneasy.'* And so—and so she writes to me, and by a piece of bad luck her letter does not reach me until over two months have gone by. Tell me, does her letter not fit in *perfectly* with these facts?"

"Yes," I admitted. "It does."

Poirot went on:

"There is another point worthy of consideration. Miss Lawson was exceedingly anxious that the fact of Bob's being out all night should not get to Miss Arundell's ears."

"You think that she——"

"I think that the fact should be noted very carefully."

I turned the thing over in my mind for a minute or two.

"Well," I said at last with a sigh. "It's all very interesting—as a mental exercise that is. And I take off my hat to you. It's been a masterful piece of reconstruction. It's almost a pity really that the old lady has died."

"A pity—yes. She wrote to me that some one had attempted to murder her (that is what it amounts to, after all) and a very short time after, she was dead."

"Yes," I said. "And it's a grand disappointment to you that she died a natural death, isn't it? Come, admit it."

Poirot shrugged his shoulders.

"Or perhaps you think she was poisoned," I said maliciously.

Poirot shook his head somewhat despondently.

"It certainly seems," he admitted, "as though Miss Arundell died from natural causes."

"And therefore," I said, "we return to London with our tail between our legs."

"*Pardon*, my friend, but we do *not* return to London."

"What do you mean, Poirot?" I cried.

"If you show the dog the rabbit, my friend, does he return to London. No, he goes into the rabbit hole."

"What do you mean?"

"The dog hunts rabbits. Hercule Poirot hunts murderers. We have here a murderer—a murderer whose crime failed, yes, perhaps, but nevertheless a murderer. And I, my friend, am going into the burrow after him—or her as the case may be."

He turned sharply in at the gate.

"Where are you off to, Poirot?"

"Into the burrow, my friend. This is the house of Dr Grainger who attended Miss Arundell in her last illness."

Dr Grainger was a man of sixty odd. His face was thin and bony with an aggressive chin, bushy eyebrows, and a pair of very shrewd grey eyes. He looked keenly from me to Poirot.

"Well, what can I do for you?" he asked abruptly.

Poirot swept into speech in the most flamboyant manner.

"I must apologise, Dr Grainger, for this intrusion. I must confess straightaway that I do not come to consult you professionally."

Dr Grainger said drily:

"Glad to hear it. You look healthy enough!"

"I must explain the purpose of my visit," went on Poirot. "The truth of the matter is that I am writing a book—the life of the late General Arundell who I understand lived in Market Basing for some years before his death."

The doctor looked rather surprised.

"Yes, General Arundell lived here till his death. At Little-green House—just up the road past the Bank—you've been there, perhaps?" Poirot nodded assent. "But you understand that was a good bit before my time. I came here in 1919."

"You knew his daughter, however, the late Miss Arundell?"

"I knew Emily Arundell well."

"You comprehend, it has been a severe blow to me to find that Miss Arundell has recently died."

"End of April."

"So I discovered. I counted, you see, on her giving me various personal details and reminiscences of her father."

"Quite—quite. But I don't see what I can do about it."

Poirot asked:

"General Arundell has no other sons or daughters living?"

"No. All dead, the lot of them."

"How many were there?"

"Five. Four daughters, one son."

"And in the next generation?"

"Charles Arundell and his sister Theresa. You could get on to them. I doubt, though, if it would be much use to you. The younger generation doesn't take much interest in its grand-fathers. And there's a Mrs Tanios, but I doubt if you'd get much there either."

80

"They might have family papers—documents?"

"They might have. Doubt it, though. A lot of stuff was cleared out and burnt after Miss Emily's death, I know."

Poirot uttered a groan of anguish.

Grainger looked at him curiously.

"What's the interest in old Arundell? I never heard he was a big pot in any way?"

"My dear sir." Poirot's eyes gleamed with the excitement of the fanatic. "Is there not a saying that History knows nothing of its greatest men? Recently certain papers have come to light which throw an entirely different light on the whole subject of the Indian Mutiny. There is secret history there. And in that secret history John Arundell played a big part. The whole thing is fascinating—fascinating! And let me tell you, my dear sir, it is of especial interest at the present time. India—the English policy in regard to it—is the burning question of the hour."

"H'm" said the doctor. "I have heard that old General Arundell used to hold forth a good deal on the subject of the Mutiny. As a matter of fact, he was considered a prize bore on the subject."

"Who told you that?"

"A Miss Peabody. You might call on her, by the way. She's our oldest inhabitant—knew the Arundells intimately. And gossip is her chief recreation. She's worth seeing for her own sake—a character."

"Thank you. That is an excellent idea. Perhaps, too, you would give me the address of young Mr Arundell, the grandson of the late General Arundell."

"Charles? Yes, I can put you on to him. But he's an irreverent young devil. Family history means nothing to him."

"He is quite young?"

"He's what an old fogy like me calls young," said the doctor with a twinkle. "Early thirties. The kind of young man that's born to be a trouble and responsibility to their families. Charm of personality and nothing else. He's been shipped about all over the world and done no good anywhere."

"His aunt was doubtless fond of him?" ventured Poirot. "It is often that way."

"H'm—I don't know. Emily Arundell was no fool. As far as I know he never succeeded in getting any money out of her. Bit of a tartar that old lady. I liked her. Respected her too. An old soldier every inch of her."

"Was her death sudden?"

"Yes, in a way. Mind you, she'd been in poor health for some years. But she'd pulled through some narrow squeaks."

"There was some story—I apologise for repeating gossip——" Poirot spread out his hands deprecatingly—"that she had quarrelled with her family?"

"She didn't exactly *quarrel* with them," said Dr Grainger, slowly. "No, there was no open quarrel as far as I know."

"I beg your pardon. I am, perhaps, being indiscreet."

"No, no. After all, the information's public property."

"She left her money away from her family, I understand?"

"Yes, left it all to a frightened, fluttering hen of a companion. Odd thing to do. Can't understand it myself. Not like her."

"Ah, well," said Poirot thoughtfully. "One can imagine such a thing happening. An old lady, frail and in ill-health. Very dependent on the person who attends and cares for her. A clever woman with a certain amount of personality could gain a great ascendency that way."

The word ascendency seemed to act like a red rag to a bull.

Dr Grainger snorted out:

"Ascendency? Ascendency? Nothing of the kind! Emily Arendell treated Minnie Lawson worse than a dog. Characteristic of that generation! Anyway, women who earn their living as companions are usually fools. If they've got brains they're earning a better living some other way. Emily Arundell didn't suffer fools gladly. She usually wore out one poor devil a year. Ascendency? Nothing of the sort!"

Poirot hastened off the treacherous ground.

"It is possible, perhaps," he suggested, "that there are old family letters and documents in this Miss—er—Lawson's possession?"

"Might be," agreed Grainger. "Usually are a lot of things tucked away in an old maid's house. I don't suppose Miss Lawson's been through half of it yet."

82

Poirot rose.

"Thank you very much, Dr Grainger. You have been most kind."

"Don't thank me," said the doctor. "Sorry I can't do anything helpful. Miss Peabody's your best chance. Lives at Morton Manor—about a mile out."

Poirot was sniffing at a large bouquet of roses on the doctor's table.

"Delicious," he murmured.

"Yes, I suppose so. Can't smell 'em myself. Lost my sense of smell when I had flu four years ago. Nice admission for a doctor, eh? 'Physician, heal thyself.' Damned nuisance. Can't enjoy a smoke as I used to."

"Unfortunate, yes. By the way, you *will* give me young Arundell's address?"

"I can get it for you, yes." He ushered us out into the hall and called "Donaldson."

"My partner," he explained. "He should have it all right. He's by way of being engaged to Charles's sister, Theresa."

He called again: "Donaldson."

A young man came out from a room at the back of the house. He was of medium height and of rather colourless appearance. His manner was precise. A greater contrast to Dr Grainger could not be imagined.

The latter explained what he wanted.

Dr Donaldson's eyes, very pale blue eyes slightly prominent, swept over us appraisingly. When he spoke it was in a dry, precise manner.

"I don't know exactly where Charles is to be found," he said. "I can give you Miss Theresa Arundell's address. Doubtless she will be able to put you in touch with her brother."

Poirot assured him that that would do perfectly.

The doctor wrote down an address on a page in his notebook, tore it out and handed it to Poirot.

Poirot thanked him and said good-bye to both doctors. As we went out of the door I was conscious of Dr Donaldson standing in the hall peering after us with a slightly startled look on his face.

10. Visit to Miss Peabody

"Is it really necessary to tell such elaborate lies, Poirot?" I asked as we walked away.

Poirot shrugged his shoulders.

"If one is going to tell a lie at all—and I notice, by the way, that your nature is very much averse to lying—now, me, it does not trouble me at all——"

"So I've noticed," I interjected.

"——As I was remarking, *if* one is going to tell a lie at all, it might as well be an artistic lie, a romantic lie, a convincing lie!"

"Do you consider this a convincing lie? Do you think Dr Donaldson was convinced?"

"That young man is of a sceptical nature," admitted Poirot, thoughtfully.

"He looked definitely suspicious to me."

"I do not see why he should be so. Imbeciles are writing the lives of other imbeciles every day. It is as you say, done."

"First time I've heard you call yourself an imbecile," I said, grinning.

"I can adopt a rôle, I hope, as well as any one," said Poirot coldly. "I am sorry you do not think my little fiction well imagined. I was rather pleased with it myself."

I changed the subject.

"What do we do next?"

"That is easy. We get into your car and pay a visit to Morton Manor."

Morton Manor proved to be an ugly substantial house of the Victorian period. A decrepit butler received us somewhat doubtfully and presently returned to ask if "we had an appointment."

"Please tell Miss Peabody that we come from Dr Grainger," said Poirot.

After a wait of a few minutes the door opened and a short, fat woman waddled into the room. Her sparse, white hair was neatly parted in the middle. She wore a black velvet dress, the nap of which was completely rubbed off in various places, and some really beautiful fine point lace was fastened at her neck with a large cameo brooch.

She came across the room peering at us shortsightedly. Her first words were somewhat of a surprise.

"Got anything to sell?"

"Nothing, madame," said Poirot.

"Sure?"

"But absolutely."

"No vacuum cleaners?"

"No."

"No stockings?"

"No."

"No rugs?"

"No."

"Oh, well," said Miss Peabody, settling herself in a chair, "I suppose it's all right. You'd better sit down then."

We sat obediently.

"You'll excuse my asking," said Miss Peabody with a trace of apology in her manner. "Got to be careful. You wouldn't believe the people who come along. Servants are no good. They can't tell. Can't blame 'em either. Right voices, right clothes, right names. How are they to tell? Commander Ridgeway, Mr Scot Edgerton, Captain d'Arcy Fitzherbert. Nice looking fellows, some of 'em. But before you know where you are they've shoved a cream making machine under your nose."

Poirot said earnestly:

"I assure you, madame, that we have nothing whatever of that kind."

"Well, you should know," said Miss Peabody.

Poirot plunged into his story. Miss Peabody heard him out without comment, blinking once or twice out of her small eyes. At the end she said:

"Goin' to write a book, eh?"

"Yes."

"In English?"

"Certainly—in English."

"But you're a foreigner. Eh? Come now, you're a foreigner, aren't you?"

"That is true."

She transferred her gaze to me.

"You are his secretary, I suppose?"

"Er—yes," I said doubtfully.

"Can you write decent English?"

"I hope so."

"H'm—where did you go to school?"

"Eton."

"Then you can't."

I was forced to let this sweeping charge against an old and venerable centre of education pass unchallenged as Miss Peabody turned her attention once more to Poirot.

"Goin' to write a life of General Arundell, eh?"

"Yes. You knew him, I think."

"Yes, I knew John Arundell. He drank."

There was a momentary pause. Then Miss Peabody went on musingly:

"Indian Mutiny, eh? Seems a bit like flogging a dead horse to me. But that's your business."

"You know, madame, there is a fashion in these things. At the moment India is the mode."

"Something in that. Things do come round. Look at sleeves."

We maintained a respectful silence.

"Leg o' muttons were always ugly," said Miss Peabody. "But I always looked well in Bishops." She fixed a bright eye on Poirot. "Now then, what do you want to know?"

Poirot spread out his hands.

"Anything! Family history. Gossip. Home life."

"Can't tell you anything about India," said Miss Peabody. "Truth is, I didn't listen. Rather boring these old men and their anecdotes. He was a very stupid man—but I dare say none the worse General for that. I've always heard that intelligence didn't get you far in the army. Pay attention to your Colonel's wife and listen respectfully to your superior officers and you'll get on— that's what my father used to say."

Treating this dictum respectfully, Poirot allowed a moment or two to elapse before he said:

"You knew the Arundell family intimately, did you not?"

"Knew 'em all," said Miss Peabody. "Matilda, she was the eldest. A spotty girl. Used to teach in Sunday School. Was sweet on one of the curates. Then there was Emily. Good seat on a horse, she had. She was the only one who could do anything with her father when he had one of his bouts on. Cartloads of bottles used to be taken out of that house. Buried them at night, they did. Then, let me see, who came next, Arabella or Thomas? Thomas, I think. Always felt sorry for Thomas. One man and four women. Makes a man look a fool. He was a bit of an old woman himself, Thomas was. Nobody thought he'd ever marry. Bit of a shock when he did."

She chuckled—a rich Victorian fruity chuckle.

It was clear that Miss Peabody was enjoying herself. As an audience we were almost forgotten. Miss Peabody was well away in the past.

"Then came Arabella. Plain girl. Face like a scone. She married all right though, even if she were the plainest of the family. Professor at Cambridge. Quite an old man. Must have been sixty if he was a day. He gave a series of lectures here—on the wonders of Modern Chemistry I think it was. I went to 'em. He mumbled, I remember. Had a beard. Couldn't hear much of what he said. Arabella used to stay behind and ask questions. She wasn't a chicken herself. Must have been getting on for forty. Ah well, they're both dead now. Quite a happy marriage it was. There's something to be said for marrying a plain woman—you know the worst at once and she's not so likely to be flighty. Then there was Agnes. She was the youngest—the pretty one. Rather gay we used to think her. Almost fast! Odd, you'd think if any of them had married it would have been Agnes, but she didn't. She died not long after the war."

Poirot murmured:

"You said that Mr Thomas's marriage was rather unexpected."

Again Miss Peabody produced that rich, throaty chuckle.

"Unexpected? I should say it was! Made a nine days scandal. You'd never have thought it of him—such a quiet, timid, retiring man and devoted to his sisters."

She paused a minute.

"Remember a case that made rather a stir in the late nineties? Mrs Varley? Supposed to have poisoned her husband with arsenic. Good-looking woman. Made a big to do, that case. She was acquitted. Well, Thomas Arundell quite lost his head. Used to get all the papers and read about the case and cut out the photographs of Mrs Varley. And would you believe it, when the trial was over, off he went to London and asked her to marry him? Thomas! Quiet, stay at home Thomas! Never can tell with men, can you? They're always liable to break out."

"And what happened?"

"Oh, she married him all right."

"It was a great shock to his sisters?"

"I should think so! They wouldn't receive her. I don't know that I blame them, all things considered. Thomas was mortally offended. He went off to live in the Channel Islands and nobody heard any more of him. Don't know whether his wife poisoned her first husband. She didn't poison Thomas. He survived her by three years. There were two children, boy and girl. Good-looking pair—took after their mother."

"I suppose they came here to their aunt a good deal?"

"Not till after their parents died. They were at school and almost grown-up by then. They used to come for holidays. Emily was alone in the world then and they and Bella Biggs were the only kith and kin she had."

"Biggs?"

"Arabella's daughter. Dull girl—some years older than Theresa. Made a fool of herself, though. Married some Dago who was over at the University. A Greek doctor. Dreadful looking man—got rather a charming manner, though, I must admit. Well, I don't suppose poor Bella had many chances. Spent her time helping her father or holding wool for her mother. This fellow was exotic. It appealed to her."

"Has it been a happy marriage?"

Miss Peabody snapped out:

"I wouldn't like to say for certain about *any* marriage! They *seem* quite happy. Two rather yellow-looking children. They live in Smyrna."

"But they are now in England, are they not?"

"Yes, they came over in March. I rather fancy they'll be going back soon."

"Was Miss Emily Arundell fond of her niece?"

"Fond of Bella? Oh, quite. She's a dull woman—wrapped up in her children and that sort of thing."

"Did she approve of the husband?"

Miss Peabody chuckled.

"She didn't *approve* of him, but I think she rather liked the rascal. He's got brains, you know. If you ask me, he was jockeying her along very nicely. Got a nose for money that man."

Poirot coughed.

"I understand Miss Arundell died a rich woman?" he murmured.

Miss Peabody settled herself more comfortably in her chair.

"Yes, that's what made all the pother! Nobody dreamed she was quite as well off as she was. How it came about was this way. Old General Arundell left quite a nice little income—divided equally among his son and daughters. Some of it was reinvested, and I think every investment has done well. There were some original shares of Mortauld. Now, of course, Thomas and Arabella took their shares with them when they married. The other three sisters lived here, and they didn't spend a tenth part of their joint income, it all went back and was reinvested. When Matilda died, she left her money to be divided between Emily and Agnes, and when Agnes died she left hers to Emily. And Emily still went on spending very little. Result, she died a rich woman—and the Lawson woman gets it all!"

Miss Peabody brought out the last sentence as a kind of triumphal climax.

"Did that come as a surprise to you, Miss Peabody?"

"To tell you the truth, it did! Emily had always given out quite openly that at her death her money was to be divided between her nieces and her nephew. And as a matter of fact that was the way it was in the original will. Legacies to the servants and so on and then to be divided between Theresa, Charles and Bella. My goodness, there *was* a to do when, after her death, it was found she'd made a new will leaving it all to poor Miss Lawson!"

"Was the will made just before her death!"

Miss Peabody directed a sharp glance at him.

"Thinking of undue influence. No, I'm afraid that's no use. And I shouldn't think poor Lawson had the brains or the nerve to attempt anything of the sort. To tell you the truth, she seemed as much surprised as anybody—or said she was!"

Poirot smiled at the addition.

"The will was made about ten days before her death," went on Miss Peabody. "Lawyer says it's all right. Well—it may be."

"You mean——" Poirot leaned forward.

"Hanky panky, that's what I say," said Miss Peabody. "Something fishy somewhere."

"Just what exactly is your idea?"

"Haven't got one? How should I know where the hanky panky comes in? I'm not a lawyer. But there's something queer about it, mark my words."

Poirot said, slowly:

"Has there been any question of contesting the will?"

"Theresa's taken counsel's opinion, I believe. A lot of good that'll do her! What's a lawyer's opinion nine times out of ten? 'Don't!' Five lawyers advised me once against bringing an action. What did I do? Paid no attention. Won my case too. They had me in the witness-box and a clever young whippersnapper from London tried to make me contradict myself. But he didn't manage it. 'You can hardly identify these furs positively, Miss Peabody,' he said. 'There is no furrier's mark on them.'"

"'That may be,' I said. 'But there's a darn on the lining and if any one can do a darn like that nowadays I'll eat my umbrella.' Collapsed utterly, he did."

Miss Peabody chuckled heartily.

"I suppose," said Poirot cautiously, "that—er—feeling—runs rather high between Miss Lawson and members of Miss Arundell's family?"

"What do you expect? You know what human nature is. Always trouble after a death, anyway. A man or woman is hardly cold in their coffin before most of the mourners are scratching each other's eyes out."

Poirot sighed.

"Too true."

"That's human nature," said Miss Peabody tolerantly.

Poirot changed to another subject.

"Is it true that Miss Arundell dabbled in spiritualism?"

Miss Peabody's penetrating eye observed him very acutely.

"If you think," she said, "that the spirit of John Arundell came back and ordered Emily to leave her money to Minnie Lawson and that Emily obeyed, I can tell you that you're very much mistaken. Emily wouldn't be that kind of fool. If you ask me, she found spiritualism one degree better than playing patience or cribbage. Seen the Tripps?"

"No."

"If you had, you'd realise just the sort of silliness it was. Irritating women. Always giving you messages from one or other of your relations—and always totally incongruous ones. They believe it all. So did Minnie Lawson. Oh, well, one way of passing your evenings is as good as another, I suppose."

Poirot tried yet another tack.

"You know young Charles Arundell, I presume? What kind of a person is he?"

"He's no good. Charmin' fellow. Always hard up—always in debt—always returning like a bad penny from all over the world. Knows how to get round women all right." She chuckled. "I've seen too many like him to be taken in! Funny son for Thomas to have had, I must say. He was a staid old fogy if you like. Model of rectitude. Ah, well, bad blood somewhere. Mind you, I *like* the rascal—but he's the kind who would murder his grandmother for a shilling or two quite cheerfully. No moral sense. Odd the way some people seem to be born without it."

"And his sister?"

"Theresa?" Miss Peabody shook her head and said slowly. "I don't know. She's an exotic creature. Not usual. She's engaged to that namby-pamy doctor down here. You've seen him, perhaps?"

"Dr Donaldson."

"Yes. Clever in his profession, they say. But he's a poor stick in other ways. Not the sort of young man I'd fancy if I were a young girl. Well, Theresa should know her mind. She's had her experiences, I'll be bound."

"Dr Donaldson did not attend Miss Arundell?"

"He used to when Grainger was away on holiday."

"But not in her last illness."

"Don't think so."

Poirot said, smiling:

"I gather, Miss Peabody, that you don't think much of him as a doctor?"

"Never said so. As a matter of fact you're wrong. He's sharp enough, and clever in his way—but it's not *my* way. Take an instance. In the old days when a child ate too many green apples it had a bilious attack and the doctor called it a bilious attack and went home and sent you along a few pills from the surgery. Nowadays, you're told the child suffers from pronounced acidosis, that its diet must be supervised and you get the same medicine, only it's in nice little white tablets put up by manufacturing chemists and costs you about three times as much! Donaldson belongs to that school, and mind you, most young mothers prefer it. It *sounds* better. Not that that young man will be in this place long ministering to measles and bilious attacks. He's got his eye on London. He's ambitious. He means to specialise."

"In any particular line?"

"Serum therapeutics. I think I've got it right. The idea being that you get one of these nasty hypodermic needles stuck into you no matter how well you feel, just in case you should catch something. I don't hold with all these messy injections myself."

"Is Dr Donaldson experimenting with any particular disease?"

"Don't ask me. All I know is a G.P.'s practice isn't good enough for him. He wants to set up in London. But to do that he's got to have money and he's as poor as a church mouse, whatever a church mouse may be."

Poirot murmured:

"Sad that real ability is so often baulked by lack of money. And yet there are people who do not spend a quarter of their incomes."

"Emily Arundell didn't," said Miss Peabody. "It was quite a surprise to some people when that will was read. The amount, I mean, not the way it was left."

"Was it a surprise, do you think, to the members of her own family?"

"That's telling," said Miss Peabody screwing up her eyes with a good deal of enjoyment. "I wouldn't say yes, and I wouldn't say no. One of 'em had a pretty shrewd idea."

"Which one?"

"Master Charles. He'd done a bit of calculation on his own account. He's no fool, Charles."

"But a little bit of a rogue, eh?"

"At any rate, he isn't a namby-pamby stick," said Miss Peabody viciously.

She paused a minute and then asked:

"Going to get in touch with him?"

"That was my intention." Poirot went on solemnly. "It seems to me possible that he might have certain family papers relating to his grandfather?"

"More likely to have made a bonfire of them. No respect for his elders, that young man."

"One must try all avenues," said Poirot sententiously.

"So it seems," said Miss Peabody dryly.

There was a momentary glint in her blue eye that seemed to affect Poirot disagreeably. He rose.

"I must not trespass any longer on your time, madame. I am most grateful for what you have been able to tell me."

"I've done my best," said Miss Peabody. "Seem to have got rather a long way from the Indian Mutiny, don't we?"

She shook hands with us both.

"Let me know when the book comes out," was her parting remark. "I shall be *so* interested."

And the last thing we heard as we left the room was a rich, throaty chuckle.

11. *Visit to the Misses Tripp*

"AND NOW," said Poirot as we re-entered the car. "What do we do next?"

Warned by experience I did not this time suggest a return to town. After all, if Poirot was enjoying himself in his own fashion why should I object?

I suggested some tea.

"Tea, Hastings? What an idea! Regard the time."

"I have regarded it—looked at it, I mean. It's half-past five. Tea is clearly indicated."

Poirot sighed.

"Always the afternoon tea with you English! No, *mon ami*, no tea for us. In a book of etiquette I read the other day that one must not make the afternoon call after six o'clock. To do so is to commit the solecism. We have, therefore, but half an hour in which to accomplish our purpose."

"How social you are to-day, Poirot! On whom are we calling now?"

"Les demoiselles Tripp."

"Are you writing a book on spiritualism now? Or is it still the life of General Arundell?"

"It will be simpler than that, my friend. But we must inquire where these ladies live."

Directions were forthcoming readily enough, but of a somewhat confused nature involving as they did a series of lanes. The abode of the Misses Tripp turned out to be a picturesque cottage—so extremely old-world and picturesque that it looked as though it might collapse any minute.

A child of fourteen or thereabouts opened the door and with difficulty squeezed herself against the wall sufficiently to allow us to pass inside.

The interior was very rich in old oak beams—there was a big

open fireplace and such very small windows that it was difficult to see clearly. All the furniture was of pseudo simplicity—ye olde oake for ye cottage dweller—there was a good deal of fruit in wooden bowls and large numbers of photographs—most of them, I noticed, of the same two people represented in different poses—usually with bunches of flowers clasped to their breasts or clutching large leghorn picture-hats.

The child who had admitted us had murmured something and disappeared, but her voice was clearly audible in an upper storey.

"Two gentlemen to see you, miss."

A sort of twitter of female voices arose and presently with a good deal of creaking and rustling a lady descended the staircase and came graciously towards us.

She was nearer fifty than forty, her hair was parted in the middle in Madonna fashion, her eyes were brown and slightly prominent. She wore a sprigged muslin dress that conveyed an odd suggestion of fancy dress.

Poirot stepped forward and started the conversation in his most flourishing manner.

"I must apologise for intruding upon you, mademoiselle, but I am in somewhat of a predicament. I came here to find a certain lady, but she has left Market Basing and I was told that you would certainly have her address."

"Really? Who was that?"

"Miss Lawson."

"Oh, Minnie Lawson. Of *course!* We are the *greatest* friends. Do sit down, Mr—er—?"

"Parotti—my friend, Captain Hastings."

Miss Tripp acknowledged the introductions and began to fuss a little.

"Sit here, won't you—no, please—really, I always prefer an *upright* chair myself. Now, are you sure you are comfortable there? Dear Minnie Lawson—oh, here is my sister."

More creaking and rustling and we were joined by a second lady, dressed in green gingham that would have been suitable for a girl of sixteen.

"My sister Isabel—Mr—er—Parrot—and—er—Captain Hawkins. Isabel dear, these gentlemen are friends of Minnie Lawson's."

95

Miss Isabel Tripp was less buxom than her sister. She might indeed have been described as scraggy. She had very fair hair done up into a large quantity of rather messy curls. She cultivated a girlish manner and was easily recognisable as the subject of most of the flower poses in photography. She clasped her hands now in girlish excitement.

"How delightful! Dear Minnie! You have seen her lately?"

"Not for some years," explained Poirot. "We have quite lost touch with each other. I have been travelling. That is why I was so astonished and delighted to hear of the good fortune that had befallen my old friend."

"Yes, indeed. And so *well* deserved! Minnie is such a rare soul. So simple—so earnest."

"Julia," cried Isabel.

"Yes, Isabel?"

"How remarkable. *P*. You remember the planchette distinctly insisted on *P*. last night. A visitor from over the water and the initial *P*."

"So it did," agreed Julia.

Both ladies looked at Poirot in rapt and delighted surprise.

"It never lies," said Miss Julia softly.

"Are you interested at all in the occult, Mr Parrot?"

"I have little experience, mademoiselle, but—like any one who has travelled much in the East, I am bound to admit that there is much one does not understand and that cannot be explained by natural means."

"So true," said Julia. "Profoundly true."

"The East," murmured Isabel. "The home of mysticism and the occult."

Poirot's travellings in the East, as far as I knew, consisted of one journey to Syria extended to Iraq, and which occupied perhaps a few weeks. To judge by his present conversation one would swear that he had spent most of his time in jungles and bazaars and in intimate converse with fakirs, dervishes, and mahatmas.

As far as I could make out the Misses Tripp were vegetarians, theosophists, British Israelites, Christian-scientists, spiritualists and enthusiastic amateur photographers.

"One sometimes feels," said Julia with a sigh, "that Market

Basing is an impossible place to live. There is no beauty here—no *soul*. One must have soul, don't you think so, Captain Hawkins?"

"Quite," I said, slightly embarrassed. "Oh, quite."

"*Where there is no vision the people perish*," quoted Isabel with a sigh. "I have often tried to discuss things with the vicar, but find him painfully *narrow*. Don't you think, Mr Parrot, that any definite creed is bound to be *narrowing*?"

"And everything is so simple, really," put in her sister. "As we know so well, everything is joy and love!"

"And you say, as you say," said Poirot. "What a pity it seems that misunderstandings and quarrels should arise—especially over money."

"Money is so sordid," sighed Julia.

"I gather that the late Miss Arundell was one of your converts?" said Poirot.

The two sisters looked at each other.

"I wonder," said Isabel.

"We were never quite sure," breathed Julia. "One minute she seemed to be convinced and then she would say something—so—so ribald."

"Ah, but you remember that last manifestation," said Julia. "That was really most remarkable." She turned to Poirot. "It was the night dear Miss Arundell was taken ill. My sister and I went round after dinner and we had a sitting—just the four of us. And you know we saw—we all three saw—*most* distinctly, a kind of *halo* round Miss Arundell's head."

"*Comment?*"

"Yes. It was a kind of luminous haze." She turned to her sister. "Isn't that how you would describe it, Isabel?"

"Yes. Yes, just that. A luminous haze gradually surrounding Miss Arundell's head—an aureole of faint light. It was a *sign*—we know that now—a sign that she was about to pass over to the other side."

"Remarkable," said Poirot in a suitably impressed voice. "it was dark in the room, yes?"

"Oh, yes, we always get better results in the dark, and it was quite a warm evening so we didn't even have the fire on."

"A most interesting spirit spoke to us," said Isabel. "Fatima, her name was. She told us she had passed over in the time of the Crusades. She gave us a most beautiful message."

"She actually spoke to you?"

"No, not direct voice. She rapped it out. Love. Hope. Life. Beautiful words."

"And Miss Arundell was actually taken ill at the séance?"

"It was just after. Some sandwiches and port wine were brought in, and dear Miss Arundell said she wouldn't have any as she wasn't feeling very well. That was the beginning of her illness. Mercifully, she did not have to endure much suffering."

"She passed over four days later," said Isabel.

"And we have already had messages from her," said Julia eagerly. "Saying that she is very happy and that everything is beautiful and that she hopes that there is love and peace among all her dear ones."

Poirot coughed.

"That—er—is hardly the case, I fear?"

"The relations have behaved *disgracefully* to poor Minnie," said Isabel. Her face flushed with indignation.

"Minnie is the most *unworldly* soul," chimed in Julia.

"People have gone about saying the *unkindest* things—that she *schemed* for this money to be left her!"

"When really it was the *greatest* surprise to her——"

"She could hardly belive her *ears* when the lawyer read the will——"

"She told us so herself. 'Julia,' she said to me. 'My dear, you could have knocked me over with a feather. Jut a few bequests to the servants and then Littlegreen House and the residue of my estate to Wilhelmina Lawson.' She was so flabbergasted she could hardly speak. And when she could she asked how much it would be—thinking perhaps it would be a few thousand pounds—and Mr Purvis, after humming and hawing and talking about confusing things like gross and net personalities, said it would be in the neighbourhood of three hundred and seventy-five thousand pounds. Poor Minnie nearly fainted, she told us."

"She had no *idea*," the other sister reiterated. "She never thought of such a thing happening!"

"That is what she told you, yes?"

"Oh, yes, she repeated it several times. And that's what

makes it so *wicked* of the Arundell family to go on as they have done—cold-shouldering her and treating her with suspicion. After all, this is a free country——"

"English people seem to labour under that misapprehenson," murmured Poirot.

"And I should hope *any one* can leave their money exactly as they choose! *I* think Miss Arundell acted very *wisely*. Obviously she *mistrusted* her own relatives and I dare say she had her reasons."

"Ah?" Poirot leant forward with interest. "Indeed?"

This flattering attention encouraged Isabel to proceed.

"Yes, indeed. Mr Charles Arundell, her nephew, is a thoroughly bad lot. That's well known! I believe he's even wanted by the police in some foreign country. Not at all a desirable character. As for his sister, well, I've not actually *spoken* to her, but she's a very queer-looking girl. Ultra modern, of course, and terribly made-up. Really, the sight of her mouth made me quite *ill*. It looked like *blood*. And I rather suspect she takes drugs—her manner was so *odd* sometimes. She's by way of being engaged to that nice young Dr Donaldson, but I fancy even *he* looked a little disgusted sometimes. Of course, she is atractive in her way, but I hope that he will come to his senses in time and marry some nice English girl who is fond of country life and outdoor pursuits."

"And the other relations?"

"Well, there you are again. Very undesirable. Not that I've anything to say against Mrs Tanios—she's quite a nice woman—but absolutely stupid and completely under her husband's thumb. Of course, he's really a Turk, I believe—rather dreadful for an English girl to marry a *Turk*, I think, don't you? It shows a certain lack of *fastidiousness*. Of course, Mrs Tanios is a very good mother, though the children are singularly unattractive, poor little things."

"So altogether you think Miss Lawson was a more worthy recipient of Miss Arundell's fortune?"

Julia said serenely:

"Minnie Lawson is a thoroughly *good* woman. And so *unworldly*. It isn't as though she had ever *thought* about money. She was *never* grasping."

"Still, she has never thought of refusing to accept the legacy?"

Isabel drew back a little.

"Oh, well—one would hardly do *that*."

Poirot smiled.

"No, perhaps not. . . ."

"You see, Mr Parrot," put in Julia. "She regards it as a *trust*—a sacred *trust*."

"And she is quite willing to do something for Mrs Tanios or for the Tanios children," went on Isabel. "Only she doesn't want *him* to get hold of it."

"She even said she would consider making Theresa an allowance."

"And that, I think, was very generous of her—considering the off-hand way that girl has always treated her."

"Indeed, Mr Parrot, Minnie is the most *generous* of creatures. But there now, you know her, of course!"

"Yes," said Poirot. "I know her. But I still do not know—her address."

"Of course! How stupid of me! Shall I write it down for you?"

"I can write it down."

Poirot produced the invariable notebook.

"17, Clanroyden Mansions, W.2. Not very far from Whiteleys. You'll give her our love, won't you? We haven't heard from her just lately."

Poirot rose and I followed suit.

"I have to thank you both very much," he declared, "for a most charming talk as well as for your kindness in supplying me with my friend's address."

"I wounder they didn't give it to you at the house," exclaimed Isabel. "It must be that Ellen! Servants are so *jealous* and *so small minded*. They used to be quite rude to Minnie sometimes."

Julia shook hands in a *grande dame* manner.

"We have enjoyed your visit," she declared graciously. "I wonder——"

She flashed a glance of inquiry at her sister.

"You would, perhaps——" Isabel flushed a little, "Would you, that is to say, stay and share our evening meal? A very simple one—some shredded raw vegetables, brown bread and butter, fruit."

"It sounds delicious," Poirot said hastily. "But alas! my friend and I have to return to London."

With renewed handshaking and messages to be delivered to Miss Lawson, we at last made our exit.

12. Poirot Discusses the Case

"THANK GOODNESS, Poirot," I said with fervour, "you got us out of those raw carrots! What awful women!"

"Pour nous, un bon bifteck—with the fried potatoes—and a good bottle of wine. What should we have had to drink there, I wonder?"

"Well, water, I should think," I replied with a shudder. "Or non-alcoholic cider. It was that kind of place! I bet there's no bath and no sanitation except an E.C. in the garden!"

"Strange how women enjoy living an uncomfortable life," said Poirot thoughtfully. "It is not always poverty, though they are good at making the best of straitened circumstances."

"What orders for the chauffeur now?" I asked, as I negotiated the last bend of the winding lanes, and we emerged on to the road to Market Basing. "On what local light do we call next? Or do we return to *The George* and interrogate the asthmatic waiter once more?"

"You will be glad to hear, Hastings, that we have finished with Market Basing——"

"Splendid."

"For the moment only. I shall return!"

"Still on the track of your unsuccessful murderer?"

"Exactly."

"Did you learn anything from the fandango of nonsense we've just been listening to?"

Poirot said precisely:

"There were certain points deserving of attention. The various characters in our drama begin to emerge more clearly. In some ways it resembles, does it not, a novelette of olden days? The humble companion, once despised, is raised to affluence and now plays the part of lady bountiful."

"I should imagine that such a patronage must be very galling to people who regard themselves as the rightful heirs!"

"As you say, Hastings. Yes, that is very true."

We drove on in silence for some minutes. We had passed through Market Basing and were now once more on the main road. I hummed to myself softly the tune of "Little Man, You've had a Busy Day."

"Enjoyed yourself, Poirot?" I asked at last.

Poirot said coldly:

"I do not know quite what you mean by 'enjoyed myself', Hastings."

"Well," I said, "it seemed to me you've been treating yourself to a busman's holiday!"

"You do not think that I am serious?"

"Oh, you're *serious* enough. But this business seems to be of the academic kind. You're tackling it for your own mental satisfaction. What I mean is—it's not *real*."

"*Au contaire*, it is intensely real."

"I express myself badly. What I mean is, if there were a question of *helping* our old lady, of protecting her against further attack—well, there would be some excitement then. But as it is, I can't help feeling that as she is dead, why worry?"

"In that case, *mon ami*, one would not investigate a murder case at all!"

"No, no, no. That's quite different. I mean, then you have a *body*. . . . Oh, dash it all!"

"Do not enrage yourself. I comprehend perfectly. You make a distinction between a *body* and a mere *decease*. Supposing, for instance, that Miss Arundell had died with sudden and alarming violence instead of respectably of a long-standing illness—then you would not remain indifferent to my efforts to discover the truth?"

"Of course I wouldn't."

"But all the same, some one did attempt to murder her?"

"Yes, but they didn't *succeed*. That makes all the difference."

"It does not intrigue you at all to know *who* attempted to kill her?"

"Well, yes, it does in a way."

"We have a very restricted circle," said Poirot musingly. "That thread——"

"The thread which you merely deduce from a nail in the

skirting-board!" I interrupted. "Why, that nail may have been there for years!"

"No. The varnish was quite fresh."

"Well, I still think there might be all sorts of explanations of it."

"Give me one."

At the moment I could not think of anything sufficiently plausible. Poirot took advantage of my silence to sweep on with his discourse.

"Yes, a restricted circle. That thread could only have been stretched across the top of the stairs after every one had gone to bed. Therefore we have *only the occupants of the house to consider*. That is to say, the guilt lies between seven people. Dr Tanios. Mrs Tanios. Theresa Arundell. Charles Arundell. Miss Lawson. Ellen. Cook."

"Surely you can leave the servants out of it."

"They received legacies, *mon cher*. And there *might* have been other reasons—spite—a quarrel—dishonesty—one cannot be *certain*."

"It seems to me very unlikely."

"Unlikely, I agree. But one must take all possibilities into consideration."

"In that case, you must allow for eight people, not seven."

"How so?"

I felt I was about to score a point.

"You must include *Miss Arundell* herself. How do you know she may not have stretched that thread across the stairs in order to trip up some other member of the house-party?"

Poirot shrugged his shoulders.

"It is a *bêtise* you say there, my friend. If Miss Arundell laid a trap, she would be careful not to fall into it herself. It was *she* who fell down the stairs, remember."

I retired crestfallen.

Poirot went on in a thoughtful voice:

"The sequence of events is quite clear—the fall—the letter to me—the visit of the lawyer—but there is one doubtful point. Did Miss Arundell deliberately hold back the letter to me, hesitating to post it? Or did she, once having written it, assume it *was* posted?"

"That we can't possibly tell," I said.

"No. We can only *guess*. Personally, I fancy that she assumed it had been posted. She must have been surprised at getting no reply. . . ."

My thoughts had been busy in another direction.

"Do you think this spiritualistic nonsense counted at all?" I asked. "I mean, do you think, in spite of Miss Peabody's ridiculing of the suggestion, that a command was given at one of these *séances* that she should alter her will and leave her money to the Lawson woman?"

Poirot shook his head doubtfully.

"That does not seem to fit in with the general impression I have formed of Miss Arundell's character."

"The Tripp women say that Miss Lawson was completely taken aback when the will was read," I said thoughtfully.

"That is what she told them, yes," agreed Poirot.

"But you don't believe it?"

"*Mon ami*—you know my suspicious nature! I believe nothing that any one says unless it can be confirmed or corroborated."

"That's right, old boy," I said affectionately. "A thoroughly nice, trustful nature."

"'He says,' 'she says,' 'they say'—Bah! what does that mean? Nothing at all. It may be absolute truth. It may be useful falsehood. Me, I deal only with *facts*."

"And the facts are?"

"Miss Arundell had a fall. That, nobody disputes. The fall was not a natural one—it was contrived."

"The evidence for that being that Hercule Poirot says so!"

"Not at all. There is the evidence of the nail. The evidence of Miss Arundell's letter to me. The evidence of the dog having been out that night. The evidence of Miss Arundell's words about the jar and the picture and Bob's ball. All these things are *facts*."

"And the next fact, please?"

"The next fact is the answer to our usual question. Who benefits by Miss Arundell's death? Answer—Miss Lawson."

"The wicked companion! On the other hand, the others thought they were going to benefit. And at the time of the accident they *would* have benefited."

"Exactly, Hastings. That is why they all lie equally under suspicion. There is also the little fact that Miss Lawson took pains to prevent Miss Arundell learning that Bob had been out all night."

"You call that suspicious?"

"Not at all. I merely note it. It may have been natural concern for the old lady's peace of mind. That is by far the most likely explanation."

I looked at Poirot sideways. He is so confoundedly slippery.

"Miss Peabody expressed the opinion that there was 'hanky-panky' about the will," I said. "What do you suppose she meant by that?"

"It was, I think, her way of expressing various nebulous and unformulated suspicions."

"Undue influence, it seems, can be washed out," I said. thoughtfully. "And it certainly looks as though Emily Arundell was much too sensible to believe in any tomfoolery like spiritualism."

"What makes you say that spiritualism is tomfoolery, Hastings?"

I stared at him in astonishment.

"My dear Poirot—those appalling women——"

He smiled.

"I quite agree with your estimate of the Misses Tripp. But the mere fact that the Misses Tripp have adopted with enthusiasm Christian Science, vegetarianism, theosophy and spiritualism does not really constitute a damning indictment of those subjects! Because a foolish woman will tell you a lot of nonsense about a fake scarab which she has bought from a rascally dealer, that does not necessarily bring discredit on the general subject of Egyptology!"

"Do you mean you *believe* in spiritualism, Poirot?"

"I have an open mind on the subject. I have never studied any of its manifestations myself, but it must be accepted that many men of science and learning have pronounced themselves satisfied that there are phenomena which cannot be accounted for by—shall we say the credulity of a Miss Tripp?"

"Then you believe in this rigmarole of an aureole of light surrounding Miss Arundell's head?"

Poirot waved a hand.

"I was speaking generally—rebuking your attitude of quite unreasoning scepticism. I may say that, having formed a certain opinion of Miss Tripp and her sister, I should examine very carefully any fact they presented for my notice. Foolish women, *mon ami*, are foolish women, whether they are talking about spiritualism or politics or the relation of the sexes or the tenets of the Buddhist faith."

"Yet you listened to what they had to say very carefully."

"That has been my task to-day—to listen. To hear what every one has got to tell me about these seven people—and mainly, of course, the five people primarily concerned. Already we know certain aspects of these people. Take Miss Lawson. From the Misses Tripp we learn she was devoted, unselfish, unworldly and altogether a beautiful character. From Miss Peabody we learn that she was credulous, stupid, without the nerve or the brains to attempt anything criminal. From Dr Grainger we learn that she was downtrodden, that her position was precarious, and that she was a poor 'frightened, fluttering hen,' were, I think, the words he used. From our waiter we learned that Miss Lawson was 'a person,' and from Ellen that Bob, the dog, despised her! Every one, you see, saw her from a slightly different angle. That is the same with the others. Nobody's opinion of Charles Arundell's morals seems to have been high, but nevertheless they vary in their manner of speaking of him. Dr Grainger calls him indulgently 'an irreverent young devil.' Miss Peabody says he would murder his grandmother for twopence but clearly prefers a rascal to a 'stick.' Miss Tripp hints not only that he would do a criminal action but that he has done one—or more. These sidelights are all very useful and interesting. They lead to the next thing."

"Which is?"

"To see for ourselves, my friend."

13 . Theresa Arundell

ON THE FOLLOWING morning we made our way to the address given us by Dr Donaldson.

I suggested to Poirot that a visit to the lawyer, Mr Purvis, might be a good thing, but Poirot negatived the idea strongly.

"No, indeed, my friend. What could we say—what reason could we advance for seeking information?"

"You're usually pretty ready with reasons, Poirot! Any old lie would do, wouldn't it?"

"On the contrary, my friend, 'any old lie,' as you put it, would *not* do. Not with a lawyer. We should be—how do you say it—thrown out with the flea upon the ear."

"Oh, well," I said. "Don't let us risk *that!*"

So, as I have said, we set out for the flat occupied by Theresa Arundell.

The flat in question was situated in a block at Chelsea overlooking the river. It was furnished expensively in the modern style, with gleaming chromium and thick rugs with geometric designs upon them.

We were kept waiting a few minutes and then a girl entered the room and looked at us inquiringly.

Theresa Arundell looked about twenty-eight or nine. She was tall and very slender, and she looked rather like an exaggerated drawing in black and white. Her hair was jet black—her face heavily made-up, dead pale. Her eyebrows, freakishly plucked, gave her an air of mocking irony. Her lips were the only spot of colour, a brilliant gash of scarlet in a white face. She also conveyed the impression—how I do not quite know, for her manner was almost wearily indifferent—of being at least twice as much alive as most people. There hung about her the restrained energy of a whip lash.

With an air of cool inquiry she looked from me to Poirot.

Wearied (I hoped) of deceit, Poirot had on this occasion sent in his own card. She was holding it now in her fingers, twirling it to and fro.

"I suppose," she said, "you're M. Poirot?"

Poirot bowed in his best manner.

"At your service, mademoiselle. You permit me to trespass for a few moments of your valuable time?"

With a faint imitation of Poirot's manner, she replied:

"Enchanted, M. Poirot. Pray sit down."

Poirot sat, rather gingerly, on a low square easy-chair. I took an upright one of webbing and chromium. Theresa sat negligently on a low stool in front of the fireplace. She offered us both cigarettes. We refused and she lighted one herself.

"You know my name perhaps, mademoiselle?"

She nodded.

"Little friend of Scotland Yard. That's right, isn't it?"

Poirot, I think, did not much relish this description. He said with some importance:

"I concern myself with problems of crime, mademoiselle."

"How frightfully thrilling," said Theresa Arundell in a bored voice. "And to think I've lost my autograph book!"

"The matter with which I concern myself is this," continued Poirot. "Yesterday I received a letter from your aunt."

Her eyes—very long, almond-shaped eyes—opened a little. She puffed smoke in a cloud.

"From my *aunt*, M. Poirot?"

"That is what I said, mademoiselle."

She murmured:

"I'm sorry if I'm spoiling sport in any way, but really, you know, there isn't any such person! All my aunts are mercifully dead. The last died two months ago."

"Miss Emily Arundell?"

"Yes, Miss Emily Arundell. You don't receive letters from corpses, do you, M. Poirot?"

"Sometimes I do, mademoiselle."

"How *macabre!*"

But there was a new note in her voice—a note suddenly alert and watchful.

"And what did my aunt say, M. Poirot?"

"That, mademoiselle, I can hardly tell you just at present. It was, you see, a somewhat"—he coughed—"delicate matter."

There was silence for a minute or two. Theresa Arundell smoked. Then she said:

"It all sounds delightfully hush-hush. But where exactly do I come in?"

"I hoped, mademoiselle, that you might consent to answer a few questions."

"Questions? What about?"

"Questions of a family nature."

Again I saw her eyes widen.

"That sounds rather pompous! Supposing you give me a specimen."

"Certainly. Can you tell me the present address of your brother Charles?"

The eyes narrowed again. Her latent energy was less apparent. It was as though she withdrew into a shell.

"I'm afraid I can't. We don't correspond much. I rather think he has left England."

"I see."

Poirot was silent for a minute or two.

"Was that all you wanted to know?"

"Oh, I have other questions. For one—are you satisfied with the way in which your aunt disposed of her fortune? For another—how long have you been engaged to Dr Donaldson?"

"You do jump about, don't you?"

"Eh bien?"

"Eh bien—since we are so foreign!—my answer to both those questions is that they are none of your business! *Ça ne vous regarde pas, M. Hercule Poirot.*"

Poirot studied her for a moment or two attentively. Then, with no trace of disappointment, he got up.

"So it is like that! Ah, well, perhaps it is not surprising. Allow me, mademoiselle, to congratulate you upon your French accent. And to wish you a very good morning. Come, Hastings."

We had reached the door when the girl spoke. The simile of a whip-lash came again into my mind. She did not move from her position, but the two words were like the flick of a whip.

"Come back!" she said.

Poirot obeyed slowly. He sat down again and looked at her inquiringly.

"Let's stop playing the fool," she said. "It's just possible that you might be useful to me, M. Hercule Poirot."

"Delighted, mademoiselle—and how?"

Between two puffs of cigarette smoke she said very quietly and evenly:

"Tell me how to break that will."

"Surely a lawyer——"

"Yes, a lawyer, perhaps—if I knew the right lawyer. But the only lawyers I know are respectable men! Their advice is that the will holds good in law and that any attempt to contest it will be useless expense."

"But you do not believe them."

"I believe there is always a way to do things—if you don't mind being unscrupulous and are prepared to pay. Well, *I am prepared to pay*."

"And you take it for granted that I am prepared to be unscrupulous if I am paid?"

"I've found that to be true of most people! I don't see why you should be an exception. People always protest about their honesty and their rectitude to begin with, of course."

"Just so, that is part of the game, eh? But what, given that I was prepared to be—unscrupulous—do you think I could do?"

"I don't know. But you're a clever man. Every one knows that. You could think out some scheme."

"Such as?"

Theresa Arundell shrugged her shoulders.

"That's your business. Steal the will and substitute a forgery. . . . Kidnap the Lawson and frighten her into saying she bullied Aunt Emily into making it. Produce a later will made on old Emily's deathbed."

"Your fertile imagination takes my breath away, mademoiselle!"

"Well, what is your answer? I've been frank enough. If it's righteous refusal, there's the door."

"It is not righteous refusal—yet——" said Poirot.

Theresa Arundell laughed. She looked at me.

"Your friend," she observed, "looks shocked. Shall we send him out to chase himself round the block?"

Poirot addressed himself to me with some slight irritation.

"Control, I pray of you, your beautiful and upright nature, Hastings. I demand pardon for my friend, mademoiselle. He is, as you have perceived, honest. But he is also faithful. His loyalty to myself is absolute. In any case, let me emphasise this point"— he looked at her very hard—"whatever we are about to do will be strictly within the law."

She raised her eyebrows slightly.

"The law," said Poirot thoughtfully, "has a lot of latitude."

"I see," she smiled faintly. "All right, we'll let that be understood. Do you want to discuss your share of the booty—if there turns out to be any booty?"

"That, also, can be understood. Some nice little pickings— that is all I ask?"

"Done," said Theresa.

Poirot leant forward.

"Now listen, mademoiselle, usually—in ninety-nine cases out of a hundred cases, shall we say, I am on the side of the law. The hundredth—well, the hundredth is different. For one thing, it is usually much more lucrative. . . . But it has to be done very quietly, you understand—very, very quietly. My reputation, it must not suffer. I have to be careful."

Thereas Arundell nodded.

"And I must have *all* the facts of the case! I must have the truth! You comprehend that once one knows the truth it is an easier matter to know just what lies to tell!"

"That seems eminently reasonable."

"Very well then. Now, on what date was this will made?"

"On April 21st."

"And the previous will?"

"Aunt Emily made a will five years ago."

"Its provisions being——?"

"After a legacy to Ellen and one to a former cook, all her property was to be divided between the children of her brother Thomas and the children of her sister Arabella."

"Was this money left in trust?"

"No, it was left to us absolutely."

"Now be careful. Did you all know the provisions of this will?"

"Oh, yes. Charles and I knew—and Bella knew too. Aunt Emily made no secret of it. In fact, if any of us asked for a loan she would usually say, 'You'll have all my money when I'm dead and gone. Be content with that fact.'"

"Would she have refused a loan if there had been a case of illness or any dire necessity?"

"No, I don't think she would," said Theresa slowly.

"But she considered you all had enough to live on?"

"She considered so—yes."

There was bitterness in that voice.

"But you—did not?"

Theresa waited a minute or two before speaking. Then she said:

"My father left us thirty thousand pounds each. The interest on that, safely invested, amounts to about twelve hundred a year. Income-tax takes another wedge off it. A nice little income on which one can manage very prettily. But I—" her voice changed, her slim body straightened, her head went back—all that wonderful aliveness I had sensed in her came to the fore— "But I want something better than that out of life! I want the best! The best food, the best clothes—something with line to it—beauty—not just suitable covering in the prevailing fashion. I want to live and enjoy—to go to the Mediterranean and lie in the warm summer sea—to sit round a table and play with exciting wads of money—to give parties—wild, absurd, extravagant parties—I want everything that's going in this rotten world—and I don't want it some day—I want it now!"

Her voice was wonderfully exciting, warm, exhilarating, intoxicating.

Poirot was studying her intently.

"And you have, I fancy, had it now?"

"Yes, Hercule—I've had it!"

"And how much of the thirty thousand is left?"

She laughed suddenly.

"Two hundred and twenty-one pounds, fourteen and sevenpence. That's the exact balance. So you see, little man, you've got to be paid by results. No results—no fees."

"In that case," said Poirot in a matter of fact manner, "there will certainly be results."

"You're a great little man, Hercule. I'm glad we got together."

Poirot went on in a business-like way:

"There are a few things that are actually necessary that I should know. Do you drug?"

"No, never."

"Drink?"

"Quite heavily——but not for the love of it. My crowd drinks and I drink with them, but I could give it up to-morrow."

"That is very satisfactory."

She laughed.

"I shan't give the show away in my cups, Hercule."

Poirot proceeded:

"Love affairs?"

"Plenty in the past."

"And the present?"

"Only Rex."

"That is Dr Donaldson?"

"Yes."

"He seems, somehow, very alien from the life you mention."

"Oh, he is."

"And yet you care for him. Why, I wonder?"

"Oh, what are reasons? Why did Juliet fall for Romeo?"

"Well, for one thing, with all due deference to Shakespeare, he happened to be the first man she had seen."

Theresa said slowly:

"Rex wasn't the first man I saw—not by a long way." She added in a lower voice, "But I think—I feel—he'll be the last man I'll ever see."

"And he is a poor man, mademoiselle."

She nodded.

"And he, too, needs money?"

"Desperately. Oh, not for the reasons I did. He doesn't want luxury—or beauty—or excitement—or any of these things. He'd wear the same suit until it went into holes—and eat a congealed chop every day for lunch quite happily, and wash in a cracked tin bath. If he had money it would all go on test-tubes

114

and a laboratory and all the rest of it. He's ambitious. His profession means everything to him. It means more to him than—I do."

"He knew that you would come into money when Miss Arundell died?"

"I told him so. Oh! after we were engaged. He isn't really marrying me for my money if that is what you are getting at."

"You are still engaged?"

"Of course we are."

Poirot did not reply. His silence seemed to disquiet her.

"Of course we are," she repeated sharply. And then she added, "You—have you seen him?"

"I saw him yesterday—at Market Basing."

"Why? What did you say to him?"

"I said nothing. I only asked him for your brother's address."

"Charles?" Her voice was sharp again. "What did you want with Charles?"

"Charles? Who wants Charles?"

It was a new voice—a delightful, man's voice.

A bronzed-faced young man with an agreeable grin strolled into the room.

"Who is talking about me?" he asked. "I heard my name in the hall, but I didn't eavesdrop. They were very particular about eavesdropping at Borstal. Now then, Theresa my girl, what's all this? Spill the beans."

14. Charles Arundell

I MUST CONFESS that from the moment I set eyes on him I
entertained a sneaking liking for Charles Arundell. There was
something so debonair and carefree about him. His eyes had an
agreeable and humorous twinkle and his grin was one of the
most disarming I have ever encountered.

He came across the room and sat down on the arm of one of
the massive, upholstered chairs.

"What's it all about, old girl?" he asked.

"This is M. Hercule Poirot, Charles. He is prepared to—er—
do some dirty work for us in return for a small consideration."

"I protest," cried Poirot. "*Not* dirty work—shall we say a
little harmless deception of some kind—so that the original
intention of the testator is carried out? Let us put it that way."

"Put it any way you like," said Charles agreeably. "What
made Theresa think of you, I wonder?"

"She did not," said Poirot quickly. "I came here of my own
accord."

"Offering your services?"

"Not quite that. I was asking for you. Your sister told me you
had gone abroad."

"Theresa," said Charles, "is a very careful sister. She hardly
ever makes a mistake. In fact, she's suspicious as the devil."

He smiled at her affectionately but she did not smile back.
She looked worried and thoughtful.

"Surely", said Charles, "we've got things the wrong way
round? Isn't M. Poirot famous for tracking down criminals?
Surely not for aiding and abetting them?"

"We're not criminals," said Theresa sharply.

"But we're willing to be," said Charles affably. "I'd thought
of a spot of forgery myself—that's rather my line. I got sent
down from Oxford because of a little misunderstanding about a

116

cheque. That was childishly simple, though—merely a question of adding a nought. Then there was another little *fracas* with Aunt Emily and the local bank. Foolish on my part, of course. I ought to have realised the old lady was sharp as needles. However, all these incidents have been very small fry—fivers or tenners—that class. A death-bed will would be admittedly risky. One would have to get hold of the stiff and starched Ellen and—is suborn the word?—anyway, induce her to say she had witnessed it. It would take some doing, I fear. I might even marry her and then she wouldn't be able to give evidence against me afterwards."

He grinned amiably at Poirot.

"I feel sure you've installed a secret dictaphone and Scotland Yard is listening in," he said.

"Your problem interests me," said Poirot with a touch of reproof in his manner. "Naturally I could not connive at anything against the law. But there are more ways than one——" he stopped significantly.

Charles Arundell shrugged his graceful shoulders.

"I've no doubt there's an equal choice of devious ways inside the law," he said agreeably. "You should know."

"By whom was the will witnessed? I mean the one made on April 21st?"

"Purvis brought down his clerk and the second witness was the gardener."

"It was signed then in Mr Purvis's presence?"

"It was."

"And Mr Purvis, I fancy, is a man of the highest respectability?"

"Purvis, Purvis, Charlesworth and once more Purvis are just about as respectable and impeccable as the Bank of England," said Charles.

"He didn't like making the will," said Theresa. "In an ultra-correct fashion I believe he even tried to dissuade Aunt Emily from making it."

Charles said sharply:

"Did he tell you that, Theresa?"

"Yes. I went to see him again yesterday."

"It's no good, my sweet—you ought to realise that. Only piles up the six and eightpences."

Theresa shrugged her shoulders.

Poirot said:

"I will ask of you to give me as much information as you can about the last weeks of Miss Arundell's life. Now, to begin with, I understand that you and your brother and also Dr Tanios and his wife stayed there for Easter?"

"Yes, we did."

"Did anything happen of significance during that week-end?"

"I don't think so."

"Nothing? But I thought——"

Charles broke in.

"What a self-centred creature you are, Theresa. Nothing of significance happened to *you!* Wrapped in love's young dream! Let me tell you, M. Poirot, that Theresa has a blue-eyed boy in Market Basing. One of the local sawbones. She's got rather a faulty sense of proportion in consequence. As a matter of fact, my revered aunt took a header down the stairs and nearly passed out. Wish she had. It would have saved all this fuss."

"She fell down the stairs?"

"Yes, tripped over the dog's ball. Intelligent little brute left it at the top of the stairs and she took a header over it in the night."

"This was—when?"

"Let me see—Tuesday—the evening before we left."

"Your aunt was seriously injured?"

"Unfortunately she didn't fall on her head. If she had we might have pleaded softening of the brain—or whatever it's called scientifically. No, she was hardly hurt at all."

Poirot said dryly:

"Very disappointing for you!"

"Eh? Oh, I see what you mean. Yes, as you say, very disappointing. Tough nuts, these old ladies."

"And you all left on the Wednesday morning?"

"That's right."

"That was Wednesday, the fifteenth. When did you next see your aunt?"

"Well, it wasn't the next week-end. It was the week-end after that."

"That would be—let me see—the twenty-fifth, would it not?"

"Yes, I think that was the date."

"And your aunt died—when?"

"The following Friday."

"Having been taken ill on the Monday night?"

"Yes."

"That was the Monday that you left?"

"Yes."

"You did not return during her illness?"

"Not until the Friday. We didn't realise she was really bad."

"You got there in time to see her alive?"

"No, she died before we arrived."

Poirot shifted his glance to Theresa Arundell.

"You accompanied your brother on both these occasions?"

"Yes."

"And nothing was said during that second week-end about a new will having been made?"

"Nothing," said Theresa.

Charles, however, had answered at the same moment.

"Oh, yes," he said. "It was."

He spoke airly as ever, but there was something a little constrained as though the airiness were more artificial than usual.

"It *was?*" said Poirot.

"Charles!" cried Theresa.

Charles seemed anxious not to meet his sister's eye.

He spoke to her without looking at her.

"Surely you remember, old girl? I told you. Aunt Emily made a kind of ultimatum of it. Sat there like a judge in court. Made a kind of speech. Said she thoroughly disapproved of all her relations—that is to say, of me and Theresa. Bella, she allowed, she had nothing against, but on the other hand she disliked and distrusted her husband. Buy British was ever Aunt Emily's motto. If Bella were to inherit any considerable sum of money she said she was convinced that Tanios would somehow or other get possession of it. Trust a Greek to do that! 'She's safer as she is,' she went on to say. Then she said that neither I nor Theresa were fit people to be trusted with money. We would only gamble and squander it away. Therefore, she finished up, she had made a new will and had left the entire estate to Miss Lawson. 'She is a fool,' said Aunt Emily, 'but she is a faithful soul. And I really believe she is devoted to me. She cannot help her lack of brains. I have thought it fairer to tell you this, Charles, as you may as well realise that it will not be possible for you to raise money on your expectations from me.' Rather a nasty one, that. Just what I'd been trying to do."

"Why didn't you tell me, Charles?" demanded Theresa fiercely.

"Thought I did." Charles avoided her eye.

Poirot asked:

"And what did you say, Mr Arundell?"

"I?" said Charles airily. "Oh, I just laughed. No good cutting up rough. That's not the way. 'Just as you please, Aunt Emily,' I said. 'Bit of a blow, perhaps, but after all, it's your own money and you can do what you like with it.'"

"And your aunt's reaction to that?"

"Oh, it went down well—very well indeed. She said, 'Well, I will say you're a sportsman, Charles.' And I said, 'Got to take the rough with the smooth. As a matter of fact, if I've no expectations what about giving me a tenner now?' And she said I was an impudent boy and actually parted with a fiver."

"You concealed your feelings very cleverly."

"Well, as a matter of fact, I didn't take it very seriously."

"You didn't?"

"No. I thought it was what you might call a gesture on the old bean's part. She wanted to frighten us all. I'd a pretty shrewd suspicion that after a few weeks or perhaps months she'd tear that will up. She was pretty hot on family, Aunt Emily. And, as a matter of fact, I believe that's what she *would* have done if she hadn't died so confoundedly suddenly."

"Ah!" said Poirot. "It is an interesting idea that."

He remained silent for a minute or two then went on:

"Could any one, Miss Lawson, for instance, have overheard your conversation?"

"Rather. We weren't speaking any too low. As a matter of fact, the Lawson bird was hovering about outside the door when I went out. Been doing a bit of snooping in my opinion."

Poirot turned a thoughtful glance on Theresa.

"And you knew nothing of this?"

Before she could answer, Charles broke in.

"Theresa, old girl, I'm sure I told you—or hinted to you?"

There was a queer sort of pause. Charles was looking fixedly at Theresa, and there was an anxiety, a fixity, about his gaze that seemed out of all proportion to the subject matter.

Theresa said slowly:

"If you had told me—I don't think—I could have forgotten, do you, M. Poirot?"

Her long, dark eyes turned to him.

Poirot said slowly:

"No, I don't think you could have forgotten, Miss Arundell."

Then he turned sharply to Charles.

"Let me be quite clear on one point. Did Miss Arundell tell you she was about to alter her will, or did she tell you specifically that she *had* altered it?"

Charles said quickly:

"Oh, she was quite definite. As a matter of fact she showed me the will."

Poirot leaned forward. His eyes opened wide.

"This is very important. You say that Miss Arundell actually showed you the will?"

Charles gave a sudden schoolboy wriggle—a rather disarming action. Poirot's gravity made him quite uncomfortable.

"Yes," he said. "She showed it to me."

"You can swear definitely to that?"

"Of course I can." Charles looked nervously at Poirot. "I don't see what is so significant about that."

There was a sudden brusque movement from Theresa. She had risen and was standing by the mantelpiece. She quickly lit another cigarette.

"And you, mademoiselle?" Poirot whirled suddenly round on her. "Did your aunt say nothing of importance to you during that week-end?"

"I don't think so. She was—quite amiable. That is, as amiable as she usually was. Lectured me a bit about my way of life and all that. But then, she always did. She seemed perhaps a bit more jumpy than usual."

Poirot said, smiling:

"I suppose, mademoiselle, that you were more taken up with your fiancé?"

121

Theresa said sharply:

"He wasn't there. He was away, he'd gone to some medical congress."

"You had not seen him then since the Easter week-end? Was that the last time you had seen him?"

"Yes—on the evening before we left he came to dinner."

"You had not—excuse me—had any quarrel with him then?"

"Certainly not."

"I only thought seeing that he was away on your second visit——"

Charles broke in:

"Ah, but you see, that second week-end was rather unpremeditated. We went down on the spur of the moment."

"Really?"

"Oh, let's have the truth," said Theresa wearily. "You see, Bella and her husband were down the week-end before—fussing over Aunt Emily because of her accident. We thought they might steal a march on us——"

"We thought," said Charles with a grin, "that we'd better show a little concern for Aunt Emily's health too. Really, though, the old lady was much too sharp to be taken in by the dutiful attention stunt. She knew very well how much it was worth. No fool, Aunt Emily."

Theresa laughed suddenly.

"It's a pretty story, isn't it? All of us with our tongues hanging out for money."

"Was that the case with your cousin and her husband?"

"Oh, yes, Bella's always hard up. Rather pathetic the way she tries to copy all my clothes at about an eighth of the price. Tanios speculated with her money, I believe. They're hard put to it to make both ends meet. They've got two children and want to educate them in England."

"Can you perhaps give me their address?" said Poirot.

"They're staying at the Durham Hotel in Bloomsbury."

"What is she like, your cousin?"

"Bella? Well, she's a dreary woman. Eh, Charles?"

"Oh, definitely a dreary woman. Rather like an earwig. She's a devoted mother. So are earwigs, I believe."

"And her husband?"

"Tanios? Well, he looks a bit odd, but he's really a thoroughly nice fellow. Clever, amusing and a thorough good sport."

"You agree, mademoiselle?"

"Well, I must admit I prefer him to Bella. He's a damned clever doctor, I believe. All the same, I wouldn't trust him very far."

"Theresa," said Charles, "doesn't trust anybody."

He put an arm round her.

"She doesn't trust me."

"Any one who trusted you, my sweet, would be mentally deficient," said Theresa kindly.

The brother and sister moved apart and looked at Poirot.

Poirot bowed and moved to the door.

"I am—as you say—on the job! It is difficult, but mademoiselle is right. There is always a way. Ah, by the way, this Miss Lawson, is she the kind that might conceivably lose her head under cross-examination in court?"

Charles and Theresa exchanged glances.

"I should say," said Charles, "that a really bully K.C. could make her say black was white!"

"That," said Poirot, "may be very useful."

He skipped out of the room and I followed him. In the hall he picked up his hat, moved to the front door, opened it and shut it again quickly with a bang. Then he tiptoed to the door of the sitting-room and unblushingly applied his ear to the crack. At whatever school Poirot was educated, there were clearly no unwritten rules about eavesdropping. I was horrified but powerless. I made urgent signs to Poirot but he took no notice.

And then, clearly, in Theresa Arundell's deep, vibrant voice, there came two words:

"You fool!"

There was the noise of footsteps along the passage and Poirot quickly seized me by the arm, opened the front door and passed through, closing it noiselessly behind him.

15. Miss Lawson

"POIROT," I said. "Have we *got* to listen at doors?"

"Calm yourself, my friend. It was only I who listened! It was not you who put your ear to the crack. On the contrary, you stood bolt upright like a soldier."

"But I heard just the same."

"True. Mademoiselle was hardly whispering."

"Because she thought that we had left the flat."

"Yes, we practised a little deception there."

"I don't like that sort of thing."

"Your moral attitude is irreproachable! But let us not repeat ourselves. This conversation has occurred on previous occasions. You are about to say that it is not playing the game. And my reply is that murder is not a game."

"But there is no question of murder here."

"Do not be sure of that."

"The *intention*, yes, perhaps. But after all, murder, and *attempted* murder are not the same thing."

"Morally they are exactly the same thing. But what I meant was, are you so sure that it is only *attempted* murder that occupies our attention?"

I stared at him.

"But old Miss Arundell died a perfectly natural death."

"I repeat again—*are you so sure?*"

"Every one says so!"

"Every one? Oh, *là là!*"

"The doctor says so," I pointed out. "Dr Grainger. He ought to know."

"Yes, he ought to know." Poirot's voice was dissatisfied. "But remember, Hastings, again and again a body is exhumed —and in each case a certificate has been signed in all good faith by the doctor attending the case."

"Yes, but in this case, Miss Arundell died of a long-standing complaint."

"It seems so—yes."

Poirot's voice was still dissatisfied. I looked at him keenly.

"Poirot," I said, "I'll begin a sentence with Are you sure! Are you sure *you* are not being carried away by professional zeal? You *want* it to be murder and so you think it *must* be murder."

The shadow on his brow deepened. He nodded his head slowly.

"It is clever what you say there, Hastings. It is a weak spot on which you put your finger. Murder is my business. I am like a great surgeon who specialises in—say—appendicitis or some rarer operation. A patient comes to him and he regards that patient solely from the standpoint of his own specialised subject. Is there any possible reason for thinking this man suffers from so and so . . . ? Me, I am like that, too. I say to myself always, 'Can this possibly be murder?' And you see, my friend, there is nearly always a possibility."

"I shouldn't say there was much possibility here," I remarked.

"But she died, Hastings! You cannot get away from that fact. She *died!*"

"She was in poor health. She was past seventy. It all seems perfectly natural to me."

"And does it also seem natural to you that Theresa Arundell should call her brother a fool with that degree of intensity?"

"What has that got to do with it?"

"Everything! Tell me, what did you think of that statement of Mr Charles Arundell's—that his aunt had shown him her new will?"

I looked at Poirot, warily.

"What do *you* make of it?" I asked.

Why should Poirot always be the one to ask the questions.

"I call it very interesting—very interesting indeed. So was Miss Theresa Arundell's reaction to it. Their passage of arms was suggestive—very suggestive."

"H'm," I said, in oracular fashion.

"It opens up two distinct lines of inquiry."

"They seem a nice pair of crooks," I remarked. "Ready for

anything. The girl's amazingly good-looking. As for young Charles, he's certainly an attractive scoundrel."

Poirot was just hailing a taxi. It drew into the kerb and Poirot gave an address to the driver.

"17 Clanroyden Mansions, Bayswater."

"So it's Lawson next," I commented. "And after that—the Tanios?"

"Quite right, Hastings."

"What rôle are you adopting here?" I inquired as the taxi drew up at Clanroyden Mansions. "The biographer of General Arundell, a prospective tenant of Littlegreen House, or something more subtle still?"

"I shall present myself simply as Hercule Poirot."

"How very disappointing," I gibed

Poirot merely threw me a glance and paid off the taxi.

No. 17 was on the second floor. A pert-looking maid opened the door and showed us into a room that really struck a ludicrous note after the one we had just left.

Theresa Arundell's flat had been bare to the point of emptiness. Miss Lawson's on the other hand was so crammed with furniture and odds and ends that one could hardly move about without the fear of knocking something over.

The door opened and a rather stout, middle-aged lady came in. Miss Lawson was very much as I had pictured her. She had an eager, rather foolish face, untidy greyish hair and pince-nez perched a little askew on her nose. Her style of conversation was spasmodic and consisted of gasps.

"Good-morning—er—I don't think——"

"Miss Wilhelmina Lawson?"

"Yes—yes—that *is* my name. . . ."

"My name is Poirot—Hercule Poirot. Yesterday I was looking over Littlegreen House."

"Oh, yes?"

Miss Lawson's mouth fell a little wider open and she made some inefficient dabs at her untidy hair.

"Won't you sit down?" She went on. "Sit here, won't you? Oh, dear, I'm afraid that table is in your way. I'm just a leetle bit crowded here. So difficult! These flats! Just a teeny bit on the small side. But *so* central! And I do like being central. Don't you?"

With a gasp she sat down on an uncomfortable looking Victorian chair and, her pince-nez still awry, leaned forward breathlessly and looked at Poirot hopefully.

"I went to Littlegreen House in the guise of a purchaser," went on Poirot. "But I should like to say at once—this is in the strictest confidence——"

"Oh, yes," breathed Miss Lawson, apparently pleasurably excited.

"The very strictest confidence," continued Poirot, "that I went there with another object . . . You may or you may not be aware that shortly before she died Miss Arundell wrote to me——"

He paused and then went on.

"I am a well-known private detective."

A variety of expressions chased themselves over Miss Lawson's slightly flushed countenance. I wondered which one Poirot would single out as relevant to his inquiry. Alarm, excitement, surprise, puzzlement. . . .

"Oh," she said. Then after a pause, "Oh," again.

And then, quite unexpectedly, she asked:

"Was it about the money?"

Poirot, even, was slightly taken aback. He said tentatively:

"You mean the money that was——"

"Yes, yes. The money that was taken from the drawer?"

Poirot said, quietly:

"Miss Arundell didn't tell you she had written to me on the subject of that money?"

"No, indeed. I had no idea—Well, really, I must say I'm very surprised——"

"You thought she would not have mentioned it to any one?"

"I certainly didn't think so. You see, she had a very good idea——"

She stopped again. Poirot said, quickly.

"She had a very good idea who took it. That is what you would say, is it not?"

Miss Lawson nodded and continued breathlessly:

"And I shouldn't have thought she would have wanted—well, I mean she said—that is, she seemed to feel——"

Again Poirot cut in neatly into the midst of these incoherencies.

"It was a family matter?"

"Exactly."

"But me," said Poirot, "I specialise in family matters. I am you see, very, very discreet."

Miss Lawson nodded vigorously.

"Oh! of course—that makes a difference. It's not like the *police*."

"No, no. I am not at all like the police. That would not have done at all."

"Oh, no. Dear Miss Arundell was such a *proud* woman. Of course, there had been trouble before with Charles, but it was always hushed up. Once, I believe, he had to go to Australia!"

"Just so," said Poirot. "Now the facts of the case were as follows, were they not? Miss Arundell had a sum of money in a drawer——"

He paused. Miss Lawson hastened to confirm his statement.

"Yes—from the Bank. For the wages, you know, and the books."

"And how much was missing exactly?"

"Four pound notes. No, no, I am wrong, three pound notes and two ten-shilling notes. One must be exact, I know, very exact, in such matters." Miss Lawson looked at him earnestly and absent-mindedly knocked her pince-nez a little further awry. Her rather prominent eyes seemed to goggle at him.

"Thank you, Miss Lawson. I see you have an excellent business sense."

Miss Lawson bridled a little and uttered a deprecatory laugh.

"Miss Arundell suspected, no doubt with reason, that her nephew Charles was responsible for this theft," went on Poirot.

"Yes."

"Although there was no particular evidence to show who actually took the money?"

"Oh, but it must have been Charles! Mrs Tanios wouldn't do such a thing, and her husband was quite a stranger and wouldn't have known where the money was kept—neither of them would. And I don't think Theresa Arundell would dream of such a thing. She's got plenty of money and always so beautifully dressed."

"It might have been one of the servants," Poirot suggested.

Miss Lawson seemed horrified by the idea.

"Oh, no, indeed, neither Ellen nor Annie would have *dreamed* of such a thing. They are both *most* superior women and *absolutely honest* I am sure."

Poirot waited a minute or two. Then he said:

"I wonder if you can give me any idea—I am sure you can, for if any one possessed Miss Arundell's confidence you did——"

Miss Lawson murmured confusedly:

"Oh, I don't know about that, I'm sure——" but she was clearly flattered.

"I feel that you will be able to help me."

"Oh, I'm sure, if I can—anything I can do——"

Poirot went on:

"This is in confidence——"

A sort of owlish expression appeared on Miss Lawson's face. The magical words "in confidence" seemed to be a kind of Open Sesame.

"Have you any idea of the reason which caused Miss Arundell to alter her will?"

"Her will? Oh—her will?"

Miss Lawson seemed slightly taken aback.

Poirot said, watching her closely:

"It is true, is it not, that she made a new will shortly before her death, leaving all her fortune to you?"

"Yes, but I knew nothing about it. Nothing at all!" Miss Lawson was shrill in protest. "It was the *greatest* surprise to me! A *wonderful* surprise, of course! So *good* of dear Miss Arundell. And she never even gave me a *hint*. Not the smallest hint! I was so taken aback when Mr Purvis read it out, I didn't know where to look, or whether to laugh or cry! I assure you, M. Poirot, the *shock* of it—the *shock*, you know. The *kindness*—the wonderful kindness of dear Miss Arundell. Of course, I'd hoped, perhaps, for just a little something—perhaps just a teeny, teeny legacy— though of course, there was no *reason* she should have left me even that. I'd not been with her so very long. But this—it was like—it was like a fairy story! Even now I can't quite believe in it, if you know what I mean. And sometimes—well sometimes —I don't feel altogether comfortable about it. I mean—well, I mean——"

She knocked off her pince-nez, picked them up, fumbled with them and went on even more incoherently.

"Sometimes I feel that—well, flesh and blood is flesh and blood after all, and I don't feel quite comfortable at Miss Arundell's leaving all her money away from her family. I mean, it doesn't seem *right*, does it? Not *all* of it. Such a *large* fortune, too! Nobody had any *idea*! But—well—it does make one feel uncomfortable—and every one saying things, you know—and I'm sure I've never been an *ill-natured* woman! I mean I wouldn't have dreamed of influencing Miss Arundell in any way! And it's not as though I could, either. Truth to tell, I was always just a teeny weeny bit afraid of her! She was so *sharp*, you know, so inclined to *jump* on you. And quite rude sometimes! 'Don't be a downright fool,' she'd snap. And really, after all, I had my feelings and sometimes I'd feel quite upset . . . And then to find out that all the time she'd really been fond of me—well, it was very wonderful, wasn't it? Only of course, as I say, there's been a lot of *unkindness*, and really in some ways one feels—I mean, well, it does seem a little *hard*, doesn't it, on some people?"

"You mean that you would prefer to relinquish the money?" asked Poirot.

Just for a moment I fancied a flicker of some quite different expression showed itself in Miss Lawson's dull, pale blue eyes. I imagined that, just for a moment, a shrewd, intelligent woman sat there instead of an amiable, foolish one.

She said with a little laugh.

"Well—of course, there is the other side of it too . . . I mean there are two sides to every question. What I say is, Miss Arundell meant me to have the money. I mean if I didn't take it I should be going against her *wishes*. And that wouldn't be right either, would it?"

"It is a difficult question," said Poirot, shaking his head.

"Yes, indeed, I have worried over it a great deal. Mrs Tanios— Bella—she is such a nice woman—and those dear little childen! I mean, I feel sure Miss Arundell wouldn't have wanted her to—I feel, you see, that dear Miss Arundell intended me to use my *discretion*. She didn't want to leave any money *outright* to Bella because she was afraid that man would get hold of it."

"What man?"

'Her husband. You know, Mr Poirot, the poor girl is *quite* under his thumb. She does *anything* he tells her. I dare say she'd *murder* some one if he told her to! And she's afraid of him. I'm quite sure she's afraid of him. I've seen her look simply *terrified* once or twice. Now that isn't right, Mr Poirot—you can't say that's right."

Poirot did not say so. Instead he inquired:

"What sort of man is Dr Tanios?"

"Well," said Miss Lawson, hesitatingly, "he's a very pleasant man."

She stopped, doubtfully.

"But you don't trust him?"

"Well—no, I don't. I don't know," went on Miss Lawson doubtfully, "that I'd trust *any* man very much! Such *dreadful* things one hears! And all their *poor* wives go through! It's really terrible! Of course, Dr Tanios pretends to be very fond of his wife and he's quite charming to her. His manners are really *delightful*. But I don't trust foreigners. They're so *artful!* And I'm quite sure dear Miss Arundell didn't want her money to get into *his* hands!"

"It is hard on Miss Theresa Arundell and Mr Charles Arundell also to be deprived of their inheritance," Poirot suggested.

A spot of colour came into Miss Lawson's face.

"I think Theresa has quite as much money as is good for her!" she said sharply. "She spends hundreds of pounds on her cloths alone. And her underclothing—it's wicked! When one thinks of so many nice, well-bred girls who have to earn their own living——"

Poirot, gently completed the sentence.

"You think it would do no harm for her to earn hers for a bit?"

Miss Lawson looked at him solemnly.

"It might do her a lot of *good*," she said. "It might bring her to her senses. Adversity teaches us many things."

Poirot nodded slowly. He was watching her intently.

"And Charles?"

"Charles doesn't deserve a penny," said Miss Lawson, sharply.

"If Miss Arundell cut him out of her will, it was for a very good cause—after his wicked threats."

"Threats?" Poirot's eyebrows rose.

"Yes, threats."

"What threats? When did he threaten her?"

"Let me see, it was—yes, of course, it was at Easter. Actually on *Easter Sunday*—which made it even worse!"

"What did he say?"

"He asked her for money and she refused to give it him! And then he told her that it wasn't wise of her. He said if she kept up that attitude he would—now what was the phrase—a very vulgar American one—oh, yes, he said he would bump her off!"

"He threatened to bump her off?"

"Yes."

"And what did Miss Arundell say?"

"She said: 'I think you'll find, Charles, that I can look after myself.'"

"You were in the room at the time?"

"Not exactly in the room," said Miss Lawson after a momentary pause.

"Quite, quite," said Poirot, hastily. "And Charles, what did he say to that?"

"He said: 'Don't be too sure.'"

Poirot said slowly:

"Did Miss Arundell take this threat seriously?"

"Well, I don't know . . . She didn't say anything to me about it . . . But then she wouldn't do that, any way."

Poirot said quietly:

"You knew, of course, that Miss Arundell was making a new will?"

"No, no. I've told you, it was a complete surprise. I never dreamt——"

Poirot interrupted.

"You did not know the *contents*. But you knew the *fact*—that there *was* a will being made?"

"Well—I suspected—I mean her sending for the lawyer when she was laid up——"

"Exactly. That was after she had a fall, was it not?"

"Yes, Bob—Bob was the dog—he had left his ball at the top of the stairs—and she tripped over it and fell."

"A nasty accident."

132

"Oh, yes, why, she might easily have broken her leg or her arm. The doctor said so."

"She might quite easily have been killed."

"Yes, indeed."

Her answer seemed quite natural and frank.

Poirot said, smiling:

"I think I saw Master Bob at Littlegreen House."

"Oh, yes, I expect you did. He's a dear little doggie."

Nothing annoys me more than to hear a sporting terrier called a dear little doggie. No wonder, I thought, that Bob despised Miss Lawson and refused to do anything she told him.

"And he is very intelligent?" went on Poirot.

"Oh, yes, very."

"How upset he'd be if he knew he had nearly killed his mistress?"

Miss Lawson did not answer. She merely shook her head and sighed.

Poirot asked:

"Do you think it possible that that fall influenced Miss Arundell to remake her will?"

We were getting perilously near the bone here, I thought, but Miss Lawson seemed to find the question quite natural.

"You know," she said, "I shouldn't wonder if you weren't right. It gave her a *shock*—I'm sure of that. Old people never like to think there's any chance of their dying. But an accident like that makes one *think*. Or perhaps she might have had a *premonition* that her death wasn't far off."

Poirot said casually:

"She was in fairly good health, was she not?"

"Oh, yes. Very well, indeed."

"Her illness must have come on very suddenly?"

"Oh, it did. It was quite a shock. We had had some friends that evening——" Miss Lawson paused.

"Your friends, the Misses Tripp. I have met those ladies. They are quite charming."

Miss Lawson's face flushed with pleasure.

"Yes, aren't they? Such *cultured* women! Such wide interests! And so very *spiritual!* They told you, perhaps—about our sittings? I expect you are a sceptic—but indeed, I wish I could tell you the inexpressible joy of getting into touch with those who've passed over!"

"I am sure of it. I am sure of it."

"Do you know, Mr Poirot, my mother has spoken to me—more than once. It is such a joy to know that one's dear ones are still thinking of one and watching over one."

"Yes, yes, I can well understand that," said Poirot, gently. "And was Miss Arundell also a believer?"

Miss Lawson's face clouded over a little.

"She was willing to be convinced," she said, doubtfully. "But I do not think she always approached the matter in the right frame of mind. She was sceptical and unbelieving—and once or twice her attitude attracted a most *undesirable* type of spirit! There were some very ribald messages—all due, I am *convinced*, to Miss Arundell's attitude."

"I should think very likely due to Miss Arundell," agreed Poirot.

"But on that last evening——" continued Miss Lawson, "perhaps Isabel and Julia told you?—there were distinct phenomena. Actually the beginning of a materialisation. Ecto-plasm—you know what ectoplasm is perhaps?"

"Yes, yes, I am acquainted with its nature."

"It proceeds, you know, from the medium's mouth in the form of a *ribbon* and builds itself up into a *form*. Now I am *convinced*, Mr Poirot, that *unknown to herself* Miss Arundell was a *medium*. On that evening I distinctly saw a *luminous ribbon* issuing from dear Miss Arundell's mouth! Then her head became enveloped in a luminous mist."

"Most interesting!"

"And then, unfortunately, Miss Arundell was suddenly taken ill and we had to break up the *séance*."

"You sent for the doctor—when?"

"First thing the following morning."

"Did he think the matter grave?"

"Well, he sent in a hospital nurse the following evening, but I think he hoped she would pull through."

"The—excuse me—the relatives were not sent for?"

Miss Lawson flushed.

"They were notified as soon as possible—that is to say, when Dr Grainger pronounced her to be in danger."

"What was the cause of the attack? Something she had eaten?"

"No, I don't think there was anything in particular. Dr Grainger said she hadn't been quite as careful in diet as she should have been. I think he thought the attack was probably brought on by a chill. The weather had been very treacherous."

"Theresa and Charles Arundell had been down that week-end, had they not?"

Miss Lawson pursed her lips together.

"They had."

"The visit was not a success," Poirot suggested, watching her.

"It was not." She added quite spitefully. "Miss Arundell knew what they'd come for!"

"Which was?" asked Poirot, watching her.

"Money!" snapped Miss Lawson. "And they didn't get it."

"No?" said Poirot.

"And I believe that's what Dr Tanios was after too," she went on.

"Dr Tanios. He was not down that same week-end, was he?"

"Yes, he came down on the Sunday. He only stayed about an hour."

"Every one seems to have been after poor Miss Arundell's money," hazarded Poirot.

"I know, it is not very nice to think of, is it?"

"No, indeed," said Poirot. "it must have been a shock to Charles and Theresa Arundell that week-end when they learned that Miss Arundell had definitely disinherited them!"

Miss Lawson stared at him.

Poirot said:

"Is that not so? Did she not specifically inform them of the fact?"

"As to that, I couldn't say. *I* didn't hear anything about it! There wasn't any *fuss*, or anything, as far as I know. Both Charles and his sister seemed to go away *quite* cheerful."

"Ah! possibly I have been misinformed. Miss Arundell actually kept her will in the house, did she not?"

Miss Lawson dropped her pince-nez and stooped to pick them up.

135

"I really couldn't say. No, I think it was with Mr Purvis."

"Who was the executor?"

"Mr Purvis was."

"After the death did he come over and look through her papers?"

"Yes, he did."

Poirot looked at her keenly and asked her an unexpected question.

"Do you like Mr Purvis?"

Miss Lawson was fluttered.

"Like Mr Purvis? Well, really, that's difficult to say, isn't it? I mean, I'm sure he's a very *clever* man—that is a clever lawyer, I mean. But rather a brusque *manner*! I mean, it's not very pleasant always, to have some one speaking to you as though—well, really I can't explain what I mean—he was quite civil and yet at the same time, almost *rude* if you know what I mean."

"A difficult situation for you," said Poirot, sympathetically.

"Yes, indeed it was."

Miss Lawson sighed and shook her head.

Poirot rose to his feet.

"Thank you very much, mademoiselle, for all your kindness and help."

Miss Lawson rose too. She sounded slightly flustered.

"I'm sure there's nothing to thank *me* for—nothing at all! So glad if I've been able to do anything—if there's anything more I *can* do——"

Poirot came back from the door. He lowered his voice.

"I think, Miss Lawson, that there is something you ought to be told. Charles and Theresa Arundell are hoping to upset this will."

A sharp flush of colour came into Miss Lawson's cheeks.

"They can't do that," she said, sharply. "My lawyer says so."

"Ah," said Poirot. "You have consulted a lawyer, then?"

"Certainly. Why shouldn't I?"

"No reason at all. A very wise proceeding. Good-day to you, mademoiselle."

When he emerged from Clanroyden Mansions into the street Poirot drew a deep breath.

"Hastings, *mon ami*, that woman is either exactly what she seems or else she is a very good actress."

"She doesn't believe Miss Arundell's death was anything but natural. You can see that," I said.

Poirot did not answer. There are moments when he is conveniently deaf. He hailed a taxi.

"Durham Hotel, Bloomsbury," he told the driver.

18. Mrs Tanois

"GENTLEMAN TO SEE YOU, madam."

The woman who was sitting writing at one of the tables in the writing-room of the Durham Hotel turned her head and then rose, coming towards us uncertainly.

Mrs Tanios might have been any age over thirty. She was a tall, thin woman with dark hair, rather prominent light "boiled gooseberry" eyes and a worried face. A fashionable hat was perched on her head at an unfashionable angle and she wore a rather depressed-looking cotton frock.

"I don't think——" she began vaguely.

Poirot bowed.

"I have just come from your cousin, Miss Theresa Arundell."

"Oh! from Theresa? Yes?"

"Perhaps I could have a few minutes private conversation?"

Mrs Tanios looked about her rather vacantly. Poirot suggested a leather sofa at the far end of the room.

As we made our way there a high voice squeaked out.

"Mother, where are you going?"

"I shall be just over here. Go on with your letter, darling."

The child, a thin, peaky-looking girl of about seven, settled down again to what was evidently a laborious task. Her tongue showed through her parted lips in the effort of composition.

The far end of the room was quite deserted. Mrs Tanios sat down, we did the same. She looked inquiringly at Poirot.

He began:

"It is in reference to the death of your aunt, the late Miss Emily Arundell."

Was I beginning to fancy things, or did a look of alarm spring up suddenly in those pale, prominent eyes.

"Yes?"

"Miss Arundell," said Poirot, "altered her will a very short time before she died. By the new will everything was left to Miss Wilhelmina Lawson. What I want to know, Mrs Tanios, is whether you will join with your cousins, Miss Theresa and Mr Charles Arundell, in trying to contest that will?"

"Oh!" Mrs Tanios drew a deep breath. "But I don't think that's possible, is it? I mean, my husband consulted a lawyer and he seemed to think that it was better not to attempt it."

"Lawyers, madame, are cautious people. Their advice is usually to avoid litigation at all costs—and no doubt they are usually right. But there are times when it pays to take a risk. I am not a lawyer myself and therefore I look at the matter rather differently. Miss Arundell—Miss Theresa Arundell, I mean—is prepared to fight. What about you?"

"I—Oh! I really don't know." She twisted her fingers nervously together: "I should have to consult my husband."

"Certainly, you must consult your husband before anything definite is undertaken. But what is your *own* feeling in the matter?"

"Well, really, I don't know." Mrs Tanios looked more worried than ever. "It depends so much on my husband."

"But you *yourself*, what do you think, madame?"

Mrs Tanios frowned, then she said slowly:

"I don't think I like the idea very much. It seems—it seems rather indecent, doesn't it?"

"Does it, madame?"

"Yes—after all if Aunt Emily chose to leave her money away from her family, I suppose we must put up with it."

"You do not feel aggrieved in the matter, then?"

"Oh, yes, I do." A quick flush showed in her cheeks. "I think it was most unfair! *Most* unfair! And so unexpected. It was so unlike Aunt Emily. And so very unfair on the children."

"You think it is very unlike Miss Emily Arundell?"

"I think it was extraordinary of her!"

"Then isn't it possible that she was not acting of her own free will? Don't you think that perhaps she was being unduly influenced?"

Mrs Tanios frowned again. Then she said almost unwillingly.

"The difficult thing is that I can't see Aunt Emily being influenced by *anybody*! She was such a decided old lady."

Poirot nodded approvingly.

"Yes, what you say is true. And Miss Lawson is hardly what one would describe as a strong character."

"No, she's a nice creature really—rather foolish, perhaps—but very, very kind. That's partly why I feel——"

"Yes, madame?" said Poirot as she paused.

Mrs Tanios twisted her fingers nervously again as she answered:

"Well, that it would be mean to try and upset the will. I feel certain that it wasn't in any way Miss Lawson's doing—I'm sure she'd be quite incapable of scheming and intriguing——"

"Again, I agree with you, madame."

"And that's why I feel that to go to law would be—well, would be undignified and spiteful, and besides it would be very expensive, wouldn't it?"

"It would be expensive, yes."

"And probably useless, too. But you must speak to my husband about it. He's got a much better head for business than I have."

Poirot waited a minute or two, then he said:

"What reason do you think lay behind the making of that will?"

A quick colour rose in Mrs Tanios' cheeks as she murmured:

"I haven't the least idea."

"Madame, I have told you I am not a lawyer. But you have not asked me what my profession is."

She looked at him inquiringly.

"I am a detective. And, a short time before she died, Miss Emily Arundell wrote me a letter."

Mrs Tanios leaned forward, her hands pressed themselves together.

"A letter?" she asked, abruptly. "About my husband?"

Poirot watched her for a minute or two, then he said, slowly:

"I am afraid I am not at liberty to answer that question."

"Then it *was* about my husband." Her voice rose slightly. "What did she say? I can assure you, Mr—er—I don't know your name."

"Poirot is my name. Hercule Poirot."

"I can assure you, Mr Poirot, that if anything was said in that letter against my husband, it was entirely untrue! I know, too, who will have inspired that letter! And that is another reason why I would rather have nothing to do with *any* action undertaken by Theresa and Charles! Theresa has never liked my husband. She has said things! I know she has said things! Aunt Emily was prejudiced against my husband because he was not an Englishman, and she may therefore have believed things that Theresa said about him. But they are *not true*, Mr Poirot, you can take my word for that!"

"Mother—I've finished my letter."

Mrs Tanios turned quickly. With an affectionate smile she took the letter the little girl held out to her.

"That's very nice, darling, very nice, indeed. And that's a beautiful drawing of Mickey Mouse."

"What shall I do now, Mother?"

"Would you like to get a nice postcard with a picture on it. Here's the money. You go to the gentleman in the hall and choose one and then you can send it to Selim."

The child moved away. I remembered what Charles Arundell had said. Mrs Tanios was evidently a devoted wife and mother. She was also, as he had said, a little like an earwig.

"That is your only child, madame?"

"No, I have a little boy also. He is out with his father at the moment."

"They did not accompany you to Littlegreen House on your visits?"

"Oh, yes, sometimes, but you see, my aunt was rather old and children were inclined to worry her. But she was very kind and always sent them out nice presents at Christmas."

"Let me see, when did you last see Miss Emily Arundell?"

"I think it was just about ten days before she died."

"You and your husband and your two cousins were all down there together, were you not?"

"Oh, no, that was the week-end before—at Easter."

"And you and your husband were down there the week-end after Easter as well?"

"Yes."

"And Miss Arundell was in good health and spirits then?"

"Yes, she seemed much as usual."

"She was not ill in bed?"

"She was laid up with a fall she had had, but she came downstairs again while we were there."

"Did she say anything to you about having made a new will?"

"No, nothing at all."

"And her manner to you was quite unchanged?"

A slightly longer pause this time before Mrs Tanios said: "Yes."

I feel sure that at that moment Poirot and I had the same conviction.

Mrs Tanios was lying!

Poirot paused a minute and then said:

"Perhaps I should explain that when I asked if Miss Arundell's manner to you was unchanged, I was not using the 'you' plural. I referred to *you personally*."

Mrs Tanios replied quickly.

"Oh! I see. Aunt Emily was very nice to me. She gave me a little pearl and diamond brooch and she sent ten shillings to each of the children."

There was no constraint in her manner now. The words came freely with a rush.

"And as regards your husband—was there no change in her manner to him?"

The constraint had returned. Mrs Tanios did not meet Poirot's eye as she replied:

"No, of course not—why should there be?"

"But since you suggest that your cousin Theresa Arundell might have tried to poison your aunt's mind——"

"She did! I'm sure she did!" Mrs Tanios leant forward eagerly. "You are quite right. There *was* a change! Aunt Emily was suddenly far more distant to him. And she behaved very oddly. There was a special digestive mixture he recommended—even went to the trouble of getting her some—going to the chemist and having it made up. She thanked him and all that—but rather stiffly, and later I actually saw her pouring the bottle down the sink!"

Her indignation was quite fierce.

Poirot's eyes flickered.

"A very odd procedure," he said. His voice was carefully unexcited.

"I thought it *most* ungrateful," said Dr Tanios' wife hotly.

"As you say, elderly ladies distrust foreigners sometimes," said Poirot. "I am sure they think that English doctors are the only doctors in the world. Insularity accounts for a lot."

"Yes, I suppose it does." Mrs Tanios looked slightly mollified.

"When do you return to Smyrna, madame?"

"In a few weeks time. My husband—ah! here is my husband and Edward with him."

17. Dr Tanois

I MUST say that my first sight of Dr Tanios was rather a shock. I had been imbuing him in my mind with all sorts of sinister attributes. I had been picturing to myself a dark bearded foreigner with a swarthy aspect and a sinister cast of countenance.

Instead, I saw a rotund, jolly, brown-haired, brown-eyed man. And though it is true he had a beard, it was a modest brown affair that made him look more like an artist.

He spoke English perfectly. His voice had a pleasant timbre and matched the cheerful good-humour of his face.

"Here we are," he said, smiling to his wife. "Edward has been passionately thrilled by his first ride in the tube. He has always been in buses until to-day."

Edward was not unlike his father in appearance, but both he and his little sister had a definitely foreign-looking appearance and I understood what Miss Peabody had meant when she described them as rather yellow looking children.

The presence of her husband seemed to make Mrs Tanios nervous. Stammering a little she introduced Poirot to him. Me, she ignored.

Dr Tanios took up the name sharply.

"Poirot? Monsieur Hercule Poirot? But I know that name well! And what brings you to us, M. Poirot?"

"It is the affair of a lady lately deceased. Miss Emily Arundell," replied Poirot.

"My wife's aunt? Yes—what of her?"

Poirot said slowly:

"Certain matters have arisen in connection with her death——"

Mrs Tanios broke in suddenly.

"It's about the will, Jacob. M. Poirot has been conferring with Theresa and Charles."

Some of the tensity went out of Dr Tanios' attitude. He dropped into a chair.

"Ah, the will! An iniquitous will—but there, it is not my business, I suppose."

Poirot sketched an account of his interview with the two Arundells (hardly a truthful one, I may say) and cautiously hinted at a fighting chance of upsetting the will.

"You interest me, M. Poirot, very much. I may say I am of your opinion. Something could be done. I actually went as far as to consult a lawyer on the subject, but his advice was not encouraging. Therefore——" he shrugged his shoulders.

"Lawyers, as I have told your wife, are cautious people. They do not like taking chances. But me, I am different! And you?"

Dr Tanios laughed—a rich rollicking laugh.

"Oh, I'd take a chance all right! Often have, haven't I, Bella, old girl?" He smiled across at her, and she smiled back at him—but in a rather mechanical manner, I thought.

He turned his attention back to Poirot.

"I am not a lawyer," he said. "But in my opinion it is perfectly clear that that will was made when the old lady was not responsible for what she was doing. That Lawson woman is both clever and cunning."

Mrs Tanios moved uneasily. Poirot looked at her quickly.

"You do not agree, madame?"

She said rather weakly:

"She has always been very kind. I shouldn't call her clever."

"She's been kind to you," said Dr Tanios, "because she had nothing to fear from you, my dear Bella. You're easily taken in!"

He spoke quite good-humouredly, but his wife flushed.

"With me it was different," he went on. "She didn't like me. And she made no bones about showing it! I'll give you an instance. The old lady had a fall down the stairs when we were staying there. I insisted on coming back the following week-end to see how she was. Miss Lawson did her utmost to prevent us. She didn't succeed, but she was annoyed about it, I could see. The reason was clear. *She wanted the old lady to herself.*"

Again Poirot turned to the wife.

"You agree, madame?"

Her husband did not give her time to answer.

145

"Bella's too kind-hearted," he said. "You won't get her to impute bad motives to anybody. But I'm quite sure I was right. I'll tell you another thing, M. Poirot. The secret of her ascendency over old Miss Arundell was spiritualism! That's how it was done, depend upon it!"

"You think so?"

"Sure of it, my dear fellow. I've seen a lot of that sort of thing. It gets hold of people. You'd be amazed! Especially any one of Miss Arundell's age. I'd be prepared to bet that that's how the suggestion came. Some spirit—possibly her dead father—ordered her to alter her will and leave her money to the Lawson woman. She was in bad health—credulous——"

There was a very faint movement from Mrs Tanios. Poirot turned to her.

"You think it possible—yes?"

"Speak up, Bella," said Dr Tanios. "Tell us your views?"

He looked at her encouragingly. Her quick look back at him was an odd one. She hesitated, then said:

"I know so little about these things. I dare say you're right, Jacob."

"Depend upon it I'm right, eh, M. Poirot?"

Poirot nodded his head.

"It may be—yes." Then he said, "You were down at Market Basing, I think, the week-end before Miss Arundell's death?"

"We were down at Easter and again the week-end after—that is right."

"No, no, I meant the week-end after that—on the *26th*. You were there on the Sunday, I think?"

"Oh Jacob, were you?" Mrs Tanios looked at him wide-eyed.

He turned quickly.

"Yes, you remember? I just ran down in the afternoon. I told you about it."

Both Poirot and I were looking at her. Nervously she pushed her hat a little further back on her head.

"Surely you remember, Bella," her husband continued. "What a terrible memory you've got."

"Of course!" she apologised, a thin smile on her face. "It's quite true, I have a shocking memory. And it's nearly two months ago now."

"Miss Theresa Arundell and Mr Charles Arundell were there then, I believe?" said Poirot.

"They may have been," said Tanios easily. "I didn't see them."

"You were not there very long then?"

"Oh, no—just half an hour or so."

Poirot's inquiring gaze seemed to make him a little uneasy.

"Might as well confess," he said with a twinkle. "I hoped to get a loan—but I didn't get it. I'm afraid my wife's aunt didn't take to me as much as she might. Pity, because I liked her. She was a sporting old lady."

"May I ask you a frank question, Dr Tanios?"

Was there or was there not a momentary apprehension in Tanios' eye?

"Certainly, M. Poirot."

"What is your opinion of Charles and Theresa Arundell?"

The doctor looked slightly relieved.

"Charles and Theresa?" he looked at his wife with an affectionate smile. "Bella, my dear, I don't suppose you mind my being frank about your family?"

She shook her head, smiling faintly.

"Then it's my opinion they're rotten to the core, both of them! Funnily enough I like Charles the best. He's a rogue but he's a likable rogue. He's no moral sense but he can't help that. People are born that way."

"And Theresa?"

He hesitated.

"I don't know. She's an amazingly attractive young woman. But she's quite ruthless, I should say. She'd murder any one in cold blood if it suited her book. At least that's my fancy. You may have heard, perhaps, that her mother was tried for murder?"

"And acquitted," said Poirot.

"As you say and acquitted," said Tanios quickly. "But all the same, it makes one—wonder sometimes."

"You met the young man to whom she is engaged?"

"Donaldson? Yes, he came to supper one night."

"What do you think of him?"

"A very clever fellow. I fancy he'll go far—if he gets the chance. It takes money to specialise."

147

"You mean that he is clever in his profession."

"That is what I mean, yes. A first-class brain." He smiled. "Not quite a shining light in society yet. A little precise and prim in manner. He and Theresa make a comic pair. The attraction of opposites. She's a social butterfly and he's a recluse."

The two children were bombarding their mother.

"Mother, can't we go in to lunch? I'm so hungry. We'll be late."

Poirot looked at his watch and gave an exclamation.

"A thousand pardons! I delay your lunch hour."

Glancing at her husband Mrs Tanios said, uncertainly:

"Perhaps we can offer you——"

Poirot said quickly:

"You are most amiable, madame, but I have a luncheon engagement for which I am already late."

He shook hands with both the Tanios and with the children. I did the same.

We delayed for a minute or two in the hall. Poirot wanted to put through a telephone call. I waited for him by the hall porter's desk. I was standing there when I saw Mrs Tanios come out into the hall and look searchingly around. She had a hunted, harried look. She saw me and came swiftly across to me.

"Your friend—M. Poirot—I suppose he has gone?"

"No, he is in the telephone box."

"Oh."

"You wanted to speak to him?"

She nodded. Her air of nervousness increased.

Poirot came out of the box at that moment and saw us standing together. He came quickly across to us.

"M. Poirot," she began quickly in a low, hurried voice. "There is something that I would like to say—that I *must* tell you——"

"Yes, madame."

"It is important—very important. You see——"

She stopped. Dr Tanios and the two children had just emerged from the writing-room. He came across and joined us.

"Having a few last words with M. Poirot, Bella?"

His tone was good-humoured, the smile on his face pleasantness itself.

148

"Yes——" She hesitated, then said. "Well, that is really all, M. Poirot. I just wanted you to tell Theresa that we will back her up in anything she decides to do. I quite see that the family *must* stand together."

She nodded brightly to us, then taking her husband's arm she moved off in the direction of the dining-room.

I caught Poirot by the shoulder.

"That wasn't what she started to say, Poirot!"

He shook his head slowly, watching the retreating couple.

"She changed her mind," I went on.

"Yes, *mon ami*, she changed her mind."

"Why?"

"I wish I knew," he murmured.

"She will tell us some other time," I said hopefully.

"I wonder. I rather fear—she may not. . . . "

18. "A Nigger in the Woodpile"

WE HAD LUNCH at a small restaurant not far away. I was eager to learn what he made of the various members of the Arundell family.

"Well, Poirot?" I asked impatiently.

With a look of reproof Poirot turned his whole attention to the menu. When he had ordered he leaned back in his chair, broke his roll of bread in half and said with a slightly mocking intonation:

"Well, Hastings?"

"What do you think of them now you've seen them all?"

Poirot replied slowly.

"*Ma foi*, I think they are an interesting lot! Really, this case is an enchanting study! It is, how do you say, the box of surprises? Look how each time I say, 'I got a letter from Miss Arundell before she died,' something crops up. From Miss Lawson I learn about the missing money. Mrs Tanios says at once, 'About my husband?' Why about her husband? Why should Miss Arundell write to me, Hercule Poirot, about Dr Tanios?"

"That woman has something on her mind," I said.

"Yes, she knows something. But *what?* Miss Peabody tells us that Charles Arundell would murder his grandmother for two-pence. Miss Lawson says that Mrs Tanios would murder any one if her husband told her to do so. Dr Tanios says that Charles and Theresa are rotten to the core, and he hints that their mother was a murderess and says apparently carelessly that Theresa is capable of murdering any one in cold blood.

"They have a pretty opinion of each other, all these people! Dr Tanios thinks, or *says* he thinks, that there was undue influence. His wife, before he came in, evidently did *not* think so. She does not want to contest the will at first. Later she veers round. See you, Hastings—it is a pot that boils and seethes and every now and then a significant fact comes to the surface and can be seen. There is *something* in the depths there—yes, there is *something*! I swear it, by my faith as Hercule Poirot, I swear it!"

I was impressed in spite of myself by his earnestness.

After a minute or two I said:

"Perhaps you are right, but it seems so vague—so nebulous."

"But you agree with me that there is *something*?"

"Yes," I said hesitatingly. "I believe I do."

Poirot leaned across the table. His eyes bored into mine.

"Yes—you have changed. You are no longer amused, superior —indulging me in my academic pleasures. But what is it that has convinced you? It is not my excellent reasoning—*non, ce n'est pas ça!* But *something*—something quite independent—has produced an effect on you. Tell me, my friend, what it is that has suddenly induced you to take this matter seriously?"

"I think," I said slowly, "it was Mrs Tanios. She looked—she looked—*afraid*. . . ."

"Afraid of me?"

"No—no, not of you. It was something else. She spoke so quietly and sensibly to begin with—a natural resentment at the terms of the will, perhaps, but otherwise she seemed so resigned and willing to leave things as they are. It seemed the natural attitude of a well-bred but rather apathetic woman. And then that sudden change—the eagerness with which she came over to Dr Tanios' point of view. The way she came out into the hall after us—the—almost *furtive* way——"

Poirot nodded encouragingly.

"And another little thing which you may not have noticed——"

"I notice everything!"

"I mean the point about her husband's visit to Littlegreen House on that last Sunday. I could swear she knew nothing of it—that it was the most complete surprise to her—and yet she took her cue so quickly—agreed that he had told her about it and that she had forgotten. I—I didn't like it, Poirot."

"You are quite right, Hastings—it was significant—that."

"It left an ugly impression of—of fear on me."

Poirot nodded his head slowly.

"You felt the same?" I asked.

"Yes—that impression was very definitely in the air." He

paused and then went on. "And yet you liked Tanios, did you not? You found him an agreeable man, open-hearted, good-natured, genial. Attractive in spite of your insular prejudice against the Argentines, the Portuguese and the Greeks—a thoroughly congenial personality?"

"Yes," I admitted. "I did."

In the silence that ensued, I watched Poirot. Presently I said: "What are you thinking of, Poirot?"

"I am reflecting on various people, handsome young Norman Gale, bluff, hearty Evelyn Howard, the pleasant Dr Sheppard, the quiet, reliable Knighton."

For a moment I did not understand these references to people who had figured in past cases.

"What of them?" I asked.

"They were all delightful personalities. . . . "

"My goodness, Poirot, do you really think that Tanios——"

"No, no. Do not jump to conclusions, Hastings. I am only pointing out that one's own personal reactions to people are singularly unsafe guides. One must go not by one's feelings but by facts."

"H'm," I said. "Facts are not our strong suit. No, no, Poirot, don't go over it all again!"

"I will be brief, my friend, do not fear. To begin with, we have quite certainly a case of attempted murder. You admit that, do you not?"

"Yes," I said slowly. "I do."

I had, up to now, been a little sceptical over Poirot's (as I thought) somewhat fanciful reconstruction of the events on the night of Easter Tuesday. I was forced to admit, however, that his deductions were perfectly logical.

"*Très bien*. Now one cannot have attempted murder without a murderer. One of the people present on that evening was a murderer—in intention if not in fact."

"Granted."

"Then that is our starting point—a murderer. We make a few inquiries—we, as you would say—stir the mud—and what do we get—several very interesting accusations uttered apparently casually in the course of conversations."

"You think they were not casual?"

"Impossible to tell at the moment! Miss Lawson's innocent seeming way of bringing out the fact that Charles threatened his aunt may have been quite innocent or it may not. Dr Tanios' remarks about Theresa Arundell may have absolutely no malice behind them, but be merely a physician's genuine opinion. Miss Peabody, on the other hand, is probably quite genuine in her opinion of Charles Arundell's proclivities—but it is, after all, merely an opinion. So it goes on. There is a saying, is there not, a nigger in the woodpile. *Eh bien*, that is just what I find here. There is—not a nigger—but a murderer in our woodpile."

"What I'd like to know is, what you yourself really think, Poirot?"

"Hastings—Hastings—I do not permit myself to 'think'—not, that is, in the sense that you are using the word. At the moment I only make certain reflections."

"Such as?"

"I consider the question of motive. What are the likely *motives* for Miss Arundell's death? Clearly the most obvious one is *gain*. Who would have gained by Miss Arundell's death—if she had died on Easter Tuesday?"

"Every one—with the exception of Miss Lawson."

"Precisely."

"Well, at any rate, one person is automatically cleared."

"Yes," said Poirot thoughtfully. "It would seem so. But the interesting thing is that the person who would have gained nothing if death had occurred on Easter Tuesday, gains everything when death occurs two weeks later."

"What are you getting at, Poirot?" I said, slightly puzzled.

"Cause and effect, my friend, cause and effect."

I looked at him doubtfully.

He went on:

"Proceed logically! What exactly happened—after the accident?"

I hate Poirot in this mood. Whatever one says is bound to be wrong! I proceeded with intense caution.

"Miss Arundell was laid up in bed."

"Exactly. With plenty of time to think. What next?"

"She wrote to you."

Poirot nodded.

"Yes, she wrote to me. And the letter was not posted. A thousand pities, that."

"Do you suspect that there was something fishy about that letter not being posted?"

Poirot frowned.

"There, Hastings, I have to confess that I do not know. I think—in view of everything I am almost sure—that the letter was genuinely mislaid. I believe—but I cannot be sure—that the fact that such a letter was written was unsuspected by anybody. Continue—what happened next?"

I reflected.

"The lawyer's visit," I suggested.

"Yes—she sent for her lawyer and in due course he arrived."

"And she made a new will," I continued.

"Precisely. She made a new and very unexpected will. Now, in view of that will we have to consider very carefully a statement made to us by Ellen. Ellen said, if you remember, that Miss Lawson was particularly anxious that the news that Bob had been out all night should not get to Miss Arundell's ears."

"But—oh, I see—no, I don't. Or do I begin to see what you are hinting at. . . ?"

"I doubt it!" said Poirot. "But if you do, you realise, I hope, the *supreme importance* of that statement."

He fixed me with a fierce eye.

"Of course. Of course," I said hurriedly.

"And then," continued Poirot, "various other things happen. Charles and Theresa come for the week-end, and Miss Arundell shows the new will to Charles—or so he *says*."

"Don't you believe him?"

"I only believe statements that are *checked*. Miss Arundell does not show it to Theresa."

"Because she thought Charles would tell her."

"But he doesn't. *Why* doesn't he?"

"According to Charles himself he *did* tell her."

"Theresa said quite positively that he *didn't*—a very interesting and suggestive little clash. And when we depart she calls him a fool."

"I'm getting fogged, Poirot," I said plaintively.

"Let us return to the sequence of events. Dr Tanios comes

154

down on Sunday—possibly without the knowledge of his wife."

"I should say certainly without her knowledge."

"Let us say *probably*. To proceed! Charles and Theresa leave on the Monday. Miss Arundell is in good health and spirits. She eats a good dinner and sits in the dark with the Tripps and the Lawson. Towards the end of the séance she is taken ill. She retires to bed and dies four days later and Miss Lawson inherits all her money, and Captain Hastings says she died a natural death!"

"Whereas Hercule Poirot says she was given poison in her dinner on no evidence at all!"

"I have *some* evidence, Hastings. Think over our conversation with the Misses Tripp. And also one statement that stood out from Miss Lawson's somewhat rambling conversation."

"Do you mean the fact that she had curry for dinner? Curry would mask the taste of a drug. Is that what you meant?"

Poirot said slowly:

"Yes, the curry has a certain significance, perhaps."

"But," I said, "if what you advance (in defiance of all the medical evidence) is true, only Miss Lawson or one of the maids could have killed her."

"I wonder."

"Or the Tripp women? Nonsense. I can't believe that! All these people are palpably innocent."

Poirot shrugged his shoulders.

"Remember this, Hastings, stupidity—or even silliness, for that matter—can go hand in hand with intense cunning. And do not forget the original attempt at murder. That was not the handiwork of a particularly clever or complex brain. It was a very *simple* little murder, suggested by Bob and his habit of leaving the ball at the top of the stairs. The thought of putting a thread across the stairs was quite simple and easy—a child could have thought of it!"

I frowned.

"You mean——"

"I mean that what we are seeking to find here is just one thing—the wish to kill. Nothing more than that."

"But the poison must have been a very skilful one to leave no trace," I argued. "Something that the ordinary person would have difficulty in getting hold of. Oh, damn it all, Poirot, I simply can't believe it now. You can't *know*! It's all pure hypothesis."

"You are wrong, my friend. As the result of our various conversations this morning I have now something definite to go upon. Certain faint but unmistakable indications. The only thing is—I am afraid."

"Afraid? Of what?"

He said gravely:

"Of disturbing the dogs that sleep. That is one of your proverbs, is it not? To let the sleeping dogs lie! That is what our murderer does at present—sleeps happily in the sun. . . . Do we not know, you and I Hastings, how often a murderer, his confidence disturbed, turns and kills a second—or even a *third* time!"

"You are afraid of that happening?"

He nodded.

"Yes. *If* there is a murderer in the woodpile—and I think there is, Hastings. Yes, I think there is. . . ."

19. Visit to Mr Purvis

Poirot called for his bill and paid it.

"What do we do next?" I asked.

"We are going to do what you suggested earlier in the morning. We are going to Harchester to interview Mr Purvis. That is why I telephoned from the Durham Hotel."

"You telephoned to Purvis?"

"No, to Theresa Arundell. I asked her to write me a letter of introduction to him. To approach him with any chance of success we must be accredited by the family. She promised to send it round to my flat by hand. It should be awaiting us there now."

We found not only the letter but Charles Arundell who had brought it round in person.

"Nice place you have here, M. Poirot," he remarked, glancing round the sitting-room of the flat.

At that moment my eye was caught by an imperfectly shut drawer in the desk. A small slip of paper was preventing it from shutting.

Now if there was one thing absolutely incredible it was that Poirot should shut a drawer in such a fashion! I looked thoughtfully at Charles. He had been alone in this room awaiting our arrival. I had no doubt that he had been passing the time by snooping among Poirot's papers. What a young crook the fellow was! I felt myself burning with indignation.

Charles himself was in a most cheerful mood.

"Here we are," he remarked, presenting a letter. "All present and correct—and I hope you'll have more luck with old Purvis than we did."

"He held out very little hope, I suppose?"

"Definitely discouraging. . . . In his opinion the Lawson bird had clearly got away with the doings."

"You and your sister have never considered an appeal to the lady's feelings?"

Charles grinned.

"I considered it—yes. But there seemed to be nothing doing. My eloquence was in vain. The pathetic picture of the disinherited black sheep—and a sheep not so black as he was painted—(or so I endeavoured to suggest)—failed to move the woman! You know, she definitely seems to dislike me! I don't know why." He laughed. "Most old women fall for me quite easily. They think I've never been properly understood and that I've never had a fair chance!"

"A useful point of view."

"Oh, it's been extremely useful before now. But, as I say, with the Lawson, nothing doing. I think she's rather anti-man. Probably used to chain herself to railings and wave a suffragette flag in good old pre-war days."

"Ah, well," said Poirot, shaking his head. "If simpler methods fail——"

"We must take to crime," said Charles cheerfully.

"Aha," said Poirot. "Now, speaking of crime, young man, is it true that you threatened your aunt—that you said that you would 'bump her off,' or words to that effect?"

Charles sat down in a chair, stretched his legs out in front of him and stared hard at Poirot.

"Now who told you that?" he said.

"No matter. Is it true?"

"Well, there are elements of truth about it."

"Come, come, let me hear the true story—the *true* story, mind."

"Oh, you can have it, sir. There was nothing melodramatic about it. I'd been attempting a touch—if you gather what I mean."

"I comprehend."

"Well, that didn't go according to plan. Aunt Emily intimated that any efforts to separate her and her money would be quite unavailing! Well, I didn't lose my temper, but I put it to her plainly. 'Now look here, Aunt Emily,' I said, 'you know, you're going about things in such a way that you'll end by getting bumped off!' She said, rather sniffily, what did I mean. 'Just that,' I said. 'Here are your friends and relations all hanging around with their mouths open, all as poor as church mice—whatever church mice may be—all hoping. And what do you do? Sit down on the dibs and refuse to part. That's the way people get themselves murdered. Take it from me, if you're bumped off, you'll only have yourself to blame.'

"She looked at me then, over the top of her spectacles in a way she had. Looked at me rather nastily. 'Oh,' she said dryly enough, 'so that's your opinion, is it?' 'It is,' I said. 'You loosen up a bit, that's my advice to you.' 'Thank you, Charles,' she said, 'for your well-meant advice. But I think you'll find I'm well able to take care of myself.' 'Please yourself, Aunt Emily', I said. I was grinning all over my face—and I fancy she wasn't as grim as she tried to look. 'Don't say I didn't warn you.' 'I'll remember it,' she said."

He paused.

"That's all there was to it."

"And so," said Poirot, "you contented yourself with a few pound notes you found in a drawer."

Charles stared at him, then burst out laughing.

"I take off my hat to you," he said. "You're some sleuth! How did you get hold of *that*?"

"It is true, then?"

"Oh, it's true enough! I was damned hard up. Had to get money somehow. Found a nice little wad of notes in a drawer and helped myself to a few. I was very modest—didn't think my little subtraction would be noticed. Even then, they'd probably think it was the servants."

Poirot said dryly:

"It would be very serious for the servants if such an idea had been entertained."

Charles shrugged his shoulders.

"Every one for himself," he murmured.

"And *le diable* takes the hindermost," said Poirot. "That is your creed, is it?"

Charles was looking at him curiously.

"I didn't know the old lady had ever spotted it. How did you come to know about it—and about the bumping-off conversation?"

"Miss Lawson told me."

"The sly old pussy cat!" He looked, I thought, just a shade disturbed. "She doesn't like me and she doesn't like Theresa," he said presently. "You don't think—she's got anything more up her sleeve?"

"What could she have?"

"Oh, I don't know. It's just that she strikes me as a malicious old devil." He paused. "She hates Theresa . . . " he added.

"Did you know, Mr Arundell, that Dr Tanios came down to see your aunt on the Sunday before she died?"

"What—on the Sunday that we were there?"

"Yes. You did not see him?"

"No. We were out for a walk in the afternoon. I supose he must have come then. Funny that Aunt Emily didn't mention his visit. Who told you?"

"Miss Lawson."

"Lawson again? She seems to be a mine of information."

He paused and then said:

"You know, Tanios is a nice fellow. I like him. Such a jolly, smiling chap."

"He has an attractive personality, yes," said Poirot.

Charles rose to his feet.

"If I'd been him I'd have murdered the dreary Bella years ago! Doesn't she strike you as the type of woman who is marked out by fate to be a victim? You know, I should never be surprised if bits of her turned up in a trunk at Margate or somewhere!"

"It is not a pretty action that you attribute there to her husband the good doctor," said Poirot severely.

"No," said Charles meditatively. "And I don't think really that Tanios would hurt a fly. He's much too kind-hearted."

"And what about you? Would you do murder if it were made worth your while?"

Charles laughed—a ringing, genuine laugh.

"Thinking about a spot of blackmail, M. Poirot? Nothing doing. I can assure you that I didn't put——" he stopped suddenly and then went on—"strychnine in Aunt Emily's soup."

With a careless wave of his hand he departed.

"Were you trying to frighten him, Poirot?" I asked. "If so, I don't think you succeeded. He showed no guilty reactions whatsoever."

"No?"

"No. He seemed quite unruffled."

"Curious that pause he made," said Poirot.

"A pause?"

"Yes. A pause before the word strychnine. Almost as though he had been about to say something else and thought better of it."

I shrugged my shoulders.

"He was probably thinking of a good, venomous-sounding poison."

"It is possible. It is possible. But let us set off. We will, I think, stay the night at the George in Market Basing."

Ten minutes later saw us speeding through London, bound once more for the country.

We arrived in Harchester about four o'clock and made our way straight to the offices of Purvis, Purvis, Charlesworth and Purvis.

Mr Purvis was a big, solidly-built man with white hair and a rosy complexion. He had a little the look of a country squire. His manner was courteous but reserved.

He read the letter we had brought and then looked at us across the top of his desk. It was a shrewd look and a somewhat searching one.

"I know you by name, of course, M. Poirot," he said politely. "Miss Arundell and her brother have, I gather, engaged your services in this matter, but exactly in what capacity you propose to be of use to them I am at a loss to imagine."

"Shall we say, Mr Purvis, a fuller investigation of all the circumstances?"

The lawyer said dryly:

"Miss Arundell and her brother have already had my opinion as to the legal position. The circumstances were perfectly clear and admit of no misrepresentation."

"Perfectly, perfectly," said Poirot quickly. "But you will not, I am sure, object to just repeating them so that I can envisage the situation clearly."

The lawyer bowed his head.

"I am at your service."

Poirot began:

"Miss Arundell wrote to you giving you instructions on the seventeenth of April, I believe?"

Mr Purvis consulted some papers on the table before him.

"Yes, that is correct."

"Can you tell me what she said?"

"She asked me to draw up a will. There were to be legacies to two servants and to three or four charities. The rest of her estate was to pass to Wilhelmina Lawson absolutely."

"You will pardon me, Mr Purvis, but you were surprised?"

"I will admit that—yes, I was surprised."

"Miss Arundell had made a will previously?"

"Yes, she had made a will five years ago."

"That will, after certain small legacies, left her property to her nephew and nieces?"

"The bulk of her estate was to be divided equally between the children of her brother Thomas and the daughter of Arabella Biggs, her sister."

"What has happened to that will?"

"At Miss Arundell's request I brought it with me when I visited her at Littlegreen House on April 21st."

"I should be much obliged to you, Mr Purvis, if you would give me a full description of everything that occurred on that occasion."

The lawyer paused for a minute or two. Then he said, very precisely:

"I arrived at Littlegreen House at three o'clock in the afternoon. One of my clerks accompanied me. Miss Arundell received me in the drawing-room."

"How did she look to you?"

"She seemed to me in good health in spite of the fact that she was walking with a stick. That, I understand, was on account of a fall she had had recently. Her general health, as I say, seemed good. She struck me as slightly nervous and over-excited in manner."

"Was Miss Lawson with her?"

"She was with her when I arrived. But she left us immediately."

"And then?"

"Miss Arundell asked me if I had done what she had asked me to do, and if I had brought the new will with me for her to sign.

"I said I had done so. I——er——" he hesitated for a minute or two, then went on stiffly. "I may as well say that, as far as it was proper for me to do so, I remonstrated with Miss Arundell. I pointed out to her that this new will might be regarded as grossly unfair to her family who were, after all, her own flesh and blood."

"And her answer?"

"She asked me if the money was or was not her own to do with as she liked. I replied that certainly that was the case. 'Very well then,' she said. I reminded her that she had known this Miss Lawson a very short time, and I asked her if she was quite sure that the injustice she was doing to her own family was legitimate. Her reply was, 'My dear friend, I know perfectly what I am doing.'"

"Her manner was excited, you say."

"I think I can definitely say that it was, but understand me, M. Poirot, she was in full possession of her faculties. She was in every sense of the word fully competent to manage her own affairs. Though my sympathies are entirely with Miss Arundell's family, I should be obliged to maintain that in any court of law."

"That is quite understood. Proceed, I pray of you."

"Miss Arundell read through her existing will. Then she stretched out her hand for the one I had had drawn up. I may say that I would have preferred to submit a draft first but she had impressed upon me that the will must be brought her ready to sign. That presented no difficulties as its provisions were so simple. She read it through, nodded her head, and said she would sign it straightaway. I felt it my duty to enter one last protest. She heard me out quite patiently, but said that her mind was quite made up. I called in my clerk and he and the gardener acted as witnesses to her signature. The servants, of course, were ineligible owing to the fact that they were beneficiaries under the will."

"And afterwards, did she entrust the will to you for safe keeping?"

"No, she placed it in a drawer of her desk, which drawer she locked."

"What was done with the original will? Did she destroy it?"

"No, she locked it away with the other."

"After her death, where was the will found?"

"In that same drawer. As executor I had her keys and went through her papers and business documents."

"Were both wills in the drawer?"

"Yes, exactly as she had placed them there."

"Did you question her at all as to the motive for this rather surprising action?"

"I did. But I got no satisfactory answer. She merely assured me that 'she knew what she was doing.'"

"Nevertheless you were surprised at the proceeding?"

"Very surprised. Miss Arundell, I should say, had always shown herself to have a strong sense of family feeling."

Poirot was silent a minute, then he asked:

"You did not, I suppose, have any conversation with Miss Lawson on the subject?"

"Certainly not. Such a proceeding would have been highly improper."

Mr Purvis looked scandalised at the mere suggestion.

"Did Miss Arundell say anything to indicate that Miss Lawson knew that a will was being drawn in her favour?"

"On the contrary. I asked her if Miss Lawson was aware of what was being done, and Miss Arundell snapped out that she knew nothing about it.

"It was advisable, I thought, that Miss Lawson should not be aware of what had happened. I endeavoured to hint as much and Miss Arundell seemed quite of my opinion."

"Just why did you stress that point, Mr Purvis?"

The old gentleman returned his glance with dignity.

"Such things, in my opinion, are best undiscussed. Also it might have led to future disappointment."

"Ah," Poirot drew a long breath. "I take it that *you thought it probable that Miss Arundell might change her mind in the near future?*"

The lawyer bowed his head.

"That is so. I fancied that Miss Arundell had had some violent altercation with her family. I thought it probable that when she cooled down, she would repent of her rash decision."

"In which case she would have done—what?"

"She would have given me instructions to prepare a new will."

"She might have taken the simpler course of merely destroying the will lately made, in which case the older will would have been good?"

"That is a somewhat debatable point. All earlier wills, you understand, had been definitely revoked by the testator."

"But Miss Arundell would not have had the legal knowledge to appreciate that point. She may have thought that by destroying the later will, the earlier one would stand."

"It is quite possible"

"Actually, if she died intestate, her money would pass to her family?"

"Yes. One half to Mrs Tanios, one half divisible between Charles and Theresa Arundell. But the fact remains, however, that she did *not* change her mind! She died with her decision unchanged."

"But that," said Poirot, "is where I come in."

The lawyer looked at him inquiringly.

Poirot leaned forward.

"Supposing," he said, "that Miss Arundell, on her deathbed, *wished to destroy that will.* Supposing that she believed that she *had* destroyed it—but that, in reality, she only destroyed the *first* will."

Mr Purvis shook his head.

"No, *both* wills were intact."

"Then supposing she destroyed a *dummy* will—*under the impression that she was destroying the genuine document.* She was very ill, remember, it would be easy to deceive her."

"You would have to bring evidence to that effect," said the lawyer sharply.

"Oh! undoubtedly—undoubtedly. . . ."

"Is there—may I ask—is there any reason to believe something of the kind happened?"

Poirot drew back a little.

"I should not like to commit myself at this stage——"

"Naturally, naturally," said Mr Purvis, agreeing with a phrase that was familiar to him.

"But I may say, strictly in confidence, that there are some curious features about this business!"

"Really? You don't say so?"

Mr Purvis rubbed his hands together with a kind of pleasurable anticipation.

"What I wanted from you and what I have got," continued Poirot, "is your opinion that Miss Arundell would, sooner or later, have changed her mind and relented towards her family."

"That is only my personal opinion, of course," the lawyer pointed out.

"My dear sir, I quite understand. You do not, I believe, act for Miss Lawson?"

"I advised Miss Lawson to consult an independent solicitor," said Mr Purvis.

His tone was wooden.

Poirot shook hands with him, thanking him for his kindness and the information he had given us.

20. Second Visit to Littlegreen House

On our way from Harchester to Market Basing, a matter of some ten miles, we discussed the situation.

"Have you any grounds at all, Poirot, for that suggestion you threw out?"

"You mean that Miss Arundell may have believed that that particular will was destroyed? No, *mon ami*—frankly, no. But it was incumbent upon me—you must perceive that—to make *some* sort of suggestion! Mr Purvis is a shrewd man. Unless I threw out some hint of the kind I did, he would ask himself what I could be doing in this affair."

"Do you know what you remind me of, Poirot?" I said.

"No, *mon ami*."

"Of a juggler juggling with a lot of different coloured balls! They are all in the air at once."

"The different coloured balls are the different lies I tell—eh?"

"That's about the size of it."

"And some day, you think, there will come the grand crash?"

"You can't keep it up for ever," I pointed out.

"That is true. There will come the grand moment when I catch the balls one by one, make my bow, and walk off the stage."

"To the sound of thunderous applause from the audience."

Poirot looked at me rather suspiciously.

"That well may be, yes."

"We didn't learn very much from Mr Purvis," I remarked, edging away from the danger-point.

"No, except that it confirmed our general ideas."

"And it confirmed Miss Lawson's statement that she knew nothing about the will until after the old lady's death."

"Me, I do not see that it confirmed anything of the sort."

"Purvis advised Miss Arundell not to tell her, and Miss Arundell replied that she had no intention of doing so."

"Yes, that is all very nice and clear. But there are keyholes, my friend, and keys that unlock locked drawers."

"Do you really think that Miss Lawson would eavesdrop and poke and pry around?" I asked rather shocked.

Poirot smiled.

"Miss Lawson—she is not an old school tie, *mon cher*. We know that she overheard *one* conversation which she was not supposed to have heard—I refer to the one in which Charles and his aunt discussed the question of bumping-off miserly relatives."

I admitted the truth of that.

"So you see, Hastings, she may easily have overheard some of the conversation between Mr Purvis and Miss Arundell. He has a good, resonant voice."

"As for poking and prying," went on Poirot. "More people do it than you would suppose. Timid and easily frightened people such as Miss Lawson often acquire a number of mildly dishonourable habits which are a great solace and recreation to them."

"Really, Poirot!" I protested.

He nodded his head a good many times.

"But yes, it is so, it is so."

We arrived at the George and took a couple of rooms. Then we strolled off in the direction of Littlegreen House.

When we rang the bell, Bob immediately answered the challenge. Dashing across the hall, barking furiously, he flung himself against the front door.

"I'll have your liver and your lights!" he snarled. "I'll tear you limb from limb! I'll teach you to try and get into *this* house! Just wait until I get my teeth into you."

A soothing murmur added itself to the clamour.

"Now then, boy. Now then, there's a good doggie. Come in here."

Bob, dragged by the collar, was immured in the morning-room much against his will.

"Always spoiling a fellow's sport," he grumbled. "First chance I've had of giving any one a really good fright for ever so long. Just aching to get my teeth into a trouser leg. You be careful of yourself without me to protect you."

The door of the morning-room was shut on him, and Ellen drew back bolts and bars and opened the front door.

"Oh, it's you, sir," she exclaimed.

She drew the door right back. A look of highly pleasurable excitement spread over her face.

"Come in, sir, if you please, sir."

We entered the hall. From beneath the door on the left, loud snuffling sounds proceeded, interspersed with growls. Bob was endeavouring to "place" us correctly.

"You can let him out," I suggested.

"I will, sir. He's quite all right, really, but he makes such a noise and rushes at people so it frightens them. He's a splendid watchdog though."

She opened the morning-room door, and Bob shot through like a suddenly projected cannon-ball.

Who is it? Where are they? Oh, there you are. Dear me, don't I seem to remember——" sniff—sniff—sniff—prolonged snort. "Of course! We *have* met!"

"Hullo, old man," I said. "How goes it?"

Bob wagged his tail perfunctorily.

"Nicely, thank you. Let me just see——" he resumed his researches. "Been talking to a spaniel lately, I smell. Foolish dogs, I think. What's this? A cat? That is interesting. Wish we had her here. We'd have rare sport. H'm—not a bad bull-terrier."

Having correctly diagnosed a visit I had lately paid to some doggy friends, he transferred his attentions to Poirot, inhaled a noseful of benzine and walked away reproachfully.

"Bob," I called.

He threw me a look over his shoulder.

"It's all right. I know what I'm doing. I'll be back in jiffy."

"The house is all shut up. I hope you'll excuse——" Ellen hurried into the morning-room and began to unfasten the shutters.

"Excellent, this is excellent," said Poirot, following her in and sitting down. As I was about to join him, Bob reappeared from some mysterious region, ball in mouth. He dashed up the stairs and sprawled himself on the top step, his ball between his paws. His tail wagged slowly.

"Come on," he said. "Come on. Let's have a game."

My interest in detection momentarily eclipsed, we played for some minutes, then with a feeling of guilt I hurried into the morning-room.

Poirot and Ellen seemed to be well away on the subject of illness and medicines.

"Some little white pills, sir, that's all she used to take. Two or three after every meal. That was Dr Grainger's orders. Oh, yes, she was very good about it. Tiny little things they were. And then there was some stuff Miss Lawson swore by. Capsules, they were, Dr Loughbarrow's liver capsules. You can see advertisements of them on all the hoardings."

"She took those too?"

"Yes. Miss Lawson got her them to begin with, and she thought they did her good."

"Did Dr Grainger know?"

"Oh, sir, he didn't mind. 'You take 'em if you think they do you good,' he'd say to her. And she said, 'Well, you may laugh, but they *do* do me good. A lot better than any of *your* physic.' And Dr Grainger, he laughed, and said faith was worth all the drugs ever invented."

"She didn't take anything else?"

"No. Miss Bella's husband, the foreign doctor, he went out and got her a bottle of something, but although she thanked him very politely she poured it away and that I know for a fact! And I think she was right. You don't know where you are with these foreign things."

"Mrs Tanios saw her pouring it away, didn't she?"

"Yes, and I'm afraid she was rather hurt about it, poor lady. I'm sorry, too, for no doubt it was kindly meant on the doctor's part."

"No doubt. No doubt. I suppose any medicines that were left in the house were thrown away when Miss Arundell died?"

Ellen looked a little surprised at the question.

"Oh, yes, sir. The nurse threw away some and Miss Lawson got rid of all the old lot in the medicine-cupboard in the bathroom."

"Is that where the—er—Dr Loughbarrow's Liver Capsules were kept?"

"No, they were kept in the corner-cupboard in the dining-room so as to be handy for taking after meals as directed."

"What nurse attended Miss Arundell? Can you give me her name and address?"

Ellen could supply that at once and did.

Poirot continued to ask questions about Miss Arundell's last illness.

Ellen gave details with relish, describing the sickness, the pain, the onset of jaundice, and the final delirium. I don't know whether Poirot got any satisfaction out of the catalogue. He listened patiently enough and occasionally interpolated some pertinent little question, usually about Miss Lawson and the amount of time she spent in the sickroom. He was also exceedingly interested in the diet administered to the ill woman, comparing it with that administered to some dead relative (non-existent) of his own.

Seeing that they were enjoying themselves so much, I stole out in the hall again. Bob had gone to sleep on the landing, his ball lying under his chin.

I whistled to him and he sprang up, alert at once. This time, however, doubtless out of offended dignity, he made a protracted business of despatching the ball down to me, several time catching it back at the last minute.

"Disappointed, aren't you? Well, perhaps I *will* let you have it this time."

When I next went back to the morning-room, Poirot was talking about Dr Tanios' surprise visit on the Sunday before the old lady's death.

"Yes, sir, Mr Charles and Miss Theresa were out for a walk. Dr Tanios wasn't expected, I know. The mistress was lying down and she was very surprised when I told her who it was. 'Dr Tanios?' she said. 'Is Mrs Tanios with him?' I told her no, the gentleman had come alone. So she said to tell him she'd be down in a minute."

"Did he stay long?"

"Not above an hour, sir. He didn't look too pleased when he went away."

"Have you any idea of the—er—purpose of his visit?"

"I couldn't say, I'm sure, sir."

"You did not happen to hear anything?"

Ellen's face flushed suddenly.

"No, I did *not*, sir! I've never been one to listen at doors, no matter what *some* people will do—and people who ought to know better!"

"Oh, but you misunderstand me." Poirot was eager, apologetic. "It just occurred to me that perhaps you might have brought in tea while the gentleman was there and if so, you could hardly have helped hearing what he and your mistress were talking about."

Ellen was mollified.

"I'm sorry, sir, I misunderstood you. No, Dr Tanios didn't stay for tea."

Poirot looked up at her and twinkled a little.

"And if I want to know what he came down for—well, it is possible that Miss Lawson might be in a position to know? Is that it?"

"Well, if she doesn't know, sir, nobody does," said Ellen with a sniff.

"Let me see," Poirot frowned as though trying to remember. "Miss Lawson's bedroom—was it next to Miss Arundell's?"

"No, sir. Miss Lawson's room is right at the top of the staircase. I can show you, sir."

Poirot accepted the offer. As he went up the stairs he kept close to the wall side, and just as he reached the top uttered an exclamation and stooped to his trouser-leg.

"Ah—I have just caught a thread—ah, yes, there is a nail here in the skirting-board."

"Yes, there is, sir. I think it must have worked loose or something. I've caught my dress on it once or twice."

"Has it been like that long?"

"Well, some time, I'm afraid, sir. I noticed it first when the mistress was laid up—after her accident, that was, sir—I tried to pull it out but I couldn't."

"It has had a thread round it some time, I think."

"That's right, sir, there was a little loop of thread, I remember. I can't think what for, I'm sure."

But there was no suspicion in Ellen's voice. To her it was just one of the things that occur in houses and which one does not bother to explain!

Poirot had stepped into the room at the top of the stairs. It was

172

of moderate size. There were two windows directly facing us. There was a dressing-table across one corner and between the windows was a wardrobe with a long mirror. The bed was to the right behind the door facing the windows. On the left-hand wall of the room was a big mahogany chest of drawers and a marble-topped washstand.

Poirot looked round the room thoughtfully and then came out again on the landing. He went along the passage, passing two other bedrooms and then came to the large bedchamber which had belonged to Emily Arundell.

"The nurse had the little room next door," Ellen explained.

Poirot nodded thoughfully.

As we descended the stairs, he asked if he might walk round the garden.

"Oh, yes, sir, certainly. It looks lovely just now."

"The gardener is still employed?"

"Angus? Oh, yes, Angus is still here. Miss Lawson wants everything kept nice because she thinks it will sell better that way."

"I think she is wise. To let a place run to seed is not the good policy."

The garden was very peaceful and beautiful. The wide borders were full of lupins and delphiniums and great scarlet poppies. The peonies were in bud. Wandering along we came presently to a potting-shed where a big, rugged old man was busy. He saluted us respectfully and Poirot engaged him in conversation.

A mention that we had seen Mr Charles that day thawed the old man and he became quite garrulous.

"Always a one, he was! I've known him come out here with half a gooseberry pie and the cook hunting high and low for it! And he'd go back with such an innocent face that durned if they wouldn't say it must have been the cat, though I've never known a cat eat a gooseberry pie! Oh, he's a one, Mr Charles is!"

"He was down here in April, wasn't he?"

"Yes, down here two week-ends. Just before the missus died, it was."

"Did you see much of him?"

"A good bit, I did. There wasn't much for a young gentleman to do down here, and that's a fact. Used to stroll up to the George and have one. And then he'd potter round here, asking me questions about one thing and another."

"About flowers?"

"Yes—flowers—and weeds too." The old man chuckled.

"Weeds?"

Poirot's voice held a sudden, tentative note. He turned his head and looked searchingly along the shelves. His eye stopped at a tin.

"Perhaps he wanted to know how you got rid of them?"

"He did that!"

"I suppose this is the stuff you use."

Poirot turned the tin gently round and read the label.

"That's it," said Angus. "Very handy stuff it is."

"Dangerous stuff?"

"Not if you use it right. It's arsenic, of course. Had a bit of a joke about that, Mr Charles and I did. Said as how when he had a wife and didn't like her, he'd come to me and get a little of that stuff to put her away with! Maybe, I sez, *she*'ll be the one that wants to do away with *you!* Ah, that made him laugh proper, that did! It was a good one, that!"

We laughed as in duty bound. Poirot prised up the lid of the tin.

"Nearly empty," he murmured.

The old man had a look.

"Aye, there's more gone than I thought. No idea I'd used that much. I'll be having to order some more."

"Yes," said Poirot smiling. "I'm afraid there's hardly enough for you to spare me some for *my* wife!"

We all had another good laugh over this witticism.

"You're not married, I take it, mister?"

"No."

"Ah! it's always them as isn't that can afford to joke about it. Those that isn't married don't know what trouble is!"

"I gather that your wife——?" Poirot paused delicately.

"She's alive all right—very much so."

Angus seemed a little depressed about it.

Complimenting him on his garden, we bade him farewell.

174

21 . The Chemist—The Nurse— The Doctor

THE TIN OF weed-killer had started a new train of thought in my mind. It was the first definite suspicious circumstance that I had encountered. Charles' interest in it, the old gardener's obvious surprise at finding the tin almost empty—it all seemed to point in the right direction.

Poirot was, as usual when I am excited, very non-committal.

"Even if some of the weed-killer *has* been taken, there is as yet no evidence that Charles was the person to take it, Hastings."

"But he talked so much to the gardener about it!"

"Not a very wise procedure if he was going to help himself to some."

Then he went on:

"What is the first and simplest poison to come into your mind if you were asked to name one quickly?"

"Arsenic, I suppose."

"Yes. You understand then, that very marked pause before the word strychnine when Charles was talking to us to-day."

"You mean——?"

"That he was about to say 'arsenic in the soup,' and stopped himself."

"Ah!" I said, "and why did he stop himself?"

"Exactly. *Why?* I may say, Hastings, that it was to find the answer to that particular 'why?' which made me go out into the garden in search of any likely source of weed-killer."

"And you found it!"

"And I found it."

I shook my head.

"It begins to look rather bad for young Charles. You had a good talk with Ellen over the old lady's illness. Did her symptoms resemble those of arsenic poisoning?"

Poirot rubbed his nose.

175

"It is difficult to say. There was abdominal pain—sickness."

'Of course—that's it!"

"H'm, I am not so sure."

"What poison did it resemble?"

"*Eh bien*, my friend, it resembled not so much poison as disease of the liver and death from that cause!"

"Oh, Poirot," I cried. "It *can't* be natural death! It's *got* to be murder!"

"Oh, *là là*, we seem to have changed places, you and I."

He turned abruptly into a chemist's shop. After a long discussion of Poirot's particular internal troubles, he purchased a small box of indigestion lozenges. Then, when his purchase was wrapped up and he was about to leave the shop, his attention was taken by an attractively-wrapped package of Dr Loughbarrow's Liver Capsules.

"Yes, sir, a very good preparation." The chemist was a middle-aged man of a chatty disposition. "You'll find them very efficacious."

"Miss Arundell used to take them, I remember. Miss Emily Arundell."

"Indeed she did, sir. Miss Arundell of Littlegreen House. A fine old lady, one of the old school. I used to serve her."

"Did she take many patent medicines?"

"Not really, sir. Not so many as some elderly ladies I could name. Miss Lawson, now, her companion, the one that's come into all the money——"

Poirot nodded.

"She was a one for this, that, and the other. Pills, lozenges, dyspepsia tablets, digestive mixtures, blood mixtures. Really enjoyed herself among the bottles." He smiled ruefully. "I wish there were more like her. People nowadays don't take to medicines as they used. Still, we sell a lot of toilet preparations to make up for it."

"Did Miss Arundell take these Liver Capsules regularly?"

"Yes, she'd been taking them for three months, I think, before she died."

"A relative of hers, a Dr Tanios, came in to have a mixture made up one day, didn't he?"

"Yes, of course, the Greek gentleman that married Miss

Arundell's niece. Yes, a very interesting mixture it was. One I've not previously become acquainted with."

The man spoke as of a rare botanical trophy.

"It makes a change, sir, when you get something new. Very interesting combination of drugs, I remember. Of course, the gentleman is a doctor. Very nice he was—a pleasant way with him."

"Did his wife do any shopping here?"

"Did she now? I don't recall. Oh, yes, came in for a sleeping-draught—chloral it was, I remember. A double quantity the prescription was for. It's always a little difficult for us with hypnotic drugs. You see, most doctors don't prescribe much at a time."

"Whose prescription was it?"

"Her husband's, I think. Oh, of course, it was quite all *right*—but, you know, we have to be careful nowadays. Perhaps you don't know the fact, but if a doctor makes a mistake in a prescription and we make it up in all good faith and anything goes wrong it's we who have to take the blame—not the doctor."

"That seems very unfair!"

"It's worrying, I'll admit. Ah, well, I can't complain. No trouble has come *my* way—touching wood."

He rapped the counter sharply with his knuckles.

Poirot decided to buy a package of Dr Loughbarrow's Liver Capsules.

"Thank you, sir. Which size? 25, 50, 100?"

"I suppose the larger ones are better value—but still——"

"Have the 50, sir. That's the size Miss Arundell had. Eight and six."

Poirot agreed, paid over eight and six and received the parcel. Then we left the shop.

"So Mrs Tanios bought a sleeping-draught," I exclaimed as we got out into the street. "An overdose of that would kill any one, wouldn't it?"

"With the greatest of ease."

"Do you think old Miss Arundell——"

I was remembering Miss Lawson's words, "*I dare say she'd murder some one if he told her to!*"

Poirot shook his head.

177

"Chloral is a narcotic, and a hypnotic. Used to alleviate pain and as a sleeping-draught. It can also become a habit."

"Do you think Mrs Tanios had acquired the habit?"

Poirot shook his head perplexedly.

"No, I hardly think so. But it is curious. I can think of one explanation. But that would mean——"

He broke off and looked at his watch.

"Come, let us see if we can find this Nurse Carruthers who was with Miss Arundell in her last illness."

Nurse Carruthers proved to be a sensible-looking, middle-aged woman.

Poirot now apeared in yet another rôle and with one more fictitious relative. This time he had an aged mother for whom he was anxious to find a sympathetic hospital nurse.

"You comprehend—I am going to speak to you quite frankly. My mother, she is difficult. We have had some excellent nurses, young women, fully competent, but the very fact that they are young has been against them. My mother dislikes young women, she insults them, she is rude and fractious, she fights against open windows and modern hygiene. It is very difficult."

He signed mournfully.

"I know," said Nurse Carruthers sympathetically. "It's very trying sometimes. One has to use a lot of tact. It's no use upsetting a patient. Better to give in to them as far as you can. And once they feel you're not trying to force things on them, they very often relax and give in like lambs."

"Ah, I see that you would be ideal in the part. You understand old ladies."

"I've had to do with a few in my time," said Nurse Carruthers with a laugh. "You can do a lot with patience and good-humour."

"That is so wise. You nursed Miss Arundell, I believe. Now, she could not have been an easy old lady."

"Oh, I don't know. She was strong willed, but I didn't find her difficult at all. Of course, I wasn't there any length of time. She died on the fourth day."

"I was talking to her niece, Miss Theresa Arundell, only yesterday."

"Really. Fancy that now! What I always say is—the world's a small place!"

178

"You know her, I expect?"

"Well, of course, she came down after her aunt's death and she was here for the funeral. And, of course, I've seen her about before when she's been staying down here. A very handsome girl."

"Yes, indeed—but too thin—definitely too thin."

Nurse Carruthers, conscious of her own comfortable plumpness, preened herself slightly.

"Of course," she said, "one shouldn't be *too* thin."

"Poor girl," continued Poirot. "I am sorry for her. *Entre nous*," he leaned forward confidentially, "her aunt's will was a great blow."

"I suppose it must have been," said Nurse Carruthers. "I know it caused a good deal of *talk*."

"I cannot imagine what induced Miss Arundell to disinherit all her family. It seems an extraordinary procedure."

"Most extraordinary. I agree with you. And, of course, people say there must have been something behind it all."

"Did you ever get any idea of the *reason*? Did old Miss Arundell say anything?"

"No. Not to me—that is."

"But to somebody else?"

"Well, I rather fancy she mentioned *something* to Miss Lawson because I heard Miss Lawson say, 'Yes, dear, but you see it's at the lawyer's.' And Miss Arundell said, 'I'm sure it's in the drawer downstairs.' And Miss Lawson said, 'No, you sent it to Mr Purvis. Don't you remember?' And then my patient had an attack of nausea again and Miss Lawson went away while I saw to her, but I've often wondered if it was the will they were talking about."

"It certainly seems probable."

Nurse Carruthers went on:

"If so, I expect Miss Arundell was worried and perhaps wanted to alter it—but there, she was so ill, poor dear, after that—that she was past thinking of anything."

"Did Miss Lawson take part in the nursing at all?" asked Poirot.

"Oh, dear no, she was no manner of good! Too fussy, you know. She only irritated my patient."

"Did you, then, do all the nursing yourself? *C'est formidable ça*."

"The maid—what was her name—Ellen, helped me. Ellen was very good. She was used to illness and used to looking after the old lady. We managed pretty well between us. As a matter of fact, Dr Grainger was sending in a night nurse on the Friday, but Miss Arundell died before the night nurse arrived."

"Perhaps Miss Lawson helped to prepare some of the invalid's food?"

"No, she didn't do anything at all. There wasn't really anything to prepare. I had the Valentine and the brandy—and the Brand's and glucose and all that. All Miss Lawson did was to go about the house crying and getting in every one's way."

The nurse's tone held distinct acrimony.

"I can see," said Poirot smiling, "that you have not a very high opinion of Miss Lawson's usefulness."

"Companions are usually a poor lot, in my opinion. They're not *trained*, you see, in any way. Just *amateurs*. And usually they're women who wouldn't be any good at anything else."

"Do you think Miss Lawson was very attached to Miss Arundell?"

"She seemed to be. Very upset and took on terribly when the old lady died. More than the relatives did, in *my* opinion," Nurse Carruthers finished with a sniff.

"Perhaps, then," said Poirot nodding his head sagely, "Miss Arundell knew what she was doing when she left her money as she did."

"She was a very shrewd old lady," said the nurse. "There wasn't much *she* didn't take in and know about, I must say!"

"Did she mention the dog, Bob, at all?"

"It's funny you should say that! She talked about him a lot—when she was delirious. Something about his ball and a fall she'd had. A nice dog, Bob was—I'm very fond of dogs. Poor fellow, he was very miserable when she died. Wonderful, aren't they? Quite human."

And on the note of the humanity of dogs, we parted.

"There is one who has clearly no suspicions," remarked Poirot after we had left.

He sounded slightly discouraged.

We had a bad dinner at the George—Poirot groaning a good deal, especially over the soup.

"And it is so easy, Hastings, to make good soup. *Le pot au feu*——"

I avoided a disquisition on cookery with some difficulty.

After dinner we had a surprise.

We were sitting in the "lounge" which we had to ourselves. There had been one other man at dinner—a commercial traveller by his appearance—but he had gone out. I was just idly turning over the pages of an antiquated *Stock-Breeder's Gazette* or some such periodical when I suddenly heard Poirot's name being mentioned.

The voice in question was somewhere outside.

"Where is he? In here? Right—I can find him."

The door was flung violently open, and Dr Grainger, his face rather red, his eyebrows working irritably, strode into the room. He paused to closed the door and then advanced upon us in no uncertain fashion.

"Oh, here you are! Now then, M. Hercule Poirot, what the devil do you mean by coming round to see me and telling me a pack of lies?"

"One of the juggler's balls?" I murmured maliciously.

Poirot said in his oiliest voice:

"My dear doctor, you must allow me to explain——"

"Allow you? Allow you? Damn it, I'll *force* you to explain! You're a detective, that's what you are! A nosing, prying detective! Coming round to me and feeding me up with a pack of lies about writing old General Arundell's biography! More fool me to be taken in by such a damn fool story."

"Who told you of my identity?" asked Poirot.

"Who told me? Miss Peabody told me. *She* saw through you all right!"

"Miss Peabody—yes." Poirot sounded reflective. "I rather thought——"

Dr Grainger cut in angrily.

"Now then, sir, I'm waiting for your explanation!"

"Certainly. My explanation is very simple. *Attempted murder*."

"What? What's that?"

Poirot said quietly:

"Miss Arundell had a fall, did she not? A fall down the stairs shortly before her death?"

"Yes, what of it? She slipped on that damned dog's ball."

Poirot shook his head.

"No, doctor, *she did not*. A *thread* was fastened across the top of the stairs so as to trip her up."

Dr Grainger stared.

"Then why didn't she tell me so?" he demanded. "Never said a word to me about it."

"That is perhaps understandable—if it were *a member of her own family* who placed that thread there!"

"H'm—I see." Grainger cast a sharp glance at Poirot, then threw himself into a chair. "Well?" he said. "How did you come to be mixed up in this affair?"

"Miss Arundell wrote to me, stressing the utmost secrecy. Unfortunately the letter was delayed."

Poirot proceeded to give certain carefully-edited details and explained the finding of the nail driven into the skirting-board.

The doctor listened with a grave face. His anger had abated.

"You can comprehend my position was a difficult one," Poirot finished. "I was employed, you see, by a dead woman. But I counted the obligation none the less strong for that."

Dr Grainger's brows were drawn together in thought.

"And you've no idea who it was stretched that thread across the head of the stairs?" he asked.

"I have no *evidence* as to who it was. I will not say I have no *idea*."

"It's a nasty story," said Grainger, his face grim.

"Yes. You can understand, can you not, that to begin with I was uncertain whether there had or had not been a sequel?"

"Eh? What's that?"

"To all intents and purposes Miss Arundell died a natural death, but could one be sure of that? There had been *one* attempt on her life. How could I be sure that there had not been a second? And this time a successful one!"

Grainger nodded thoughtfully.

"I suppose you are *sure*, Dr Grainger—please do not get angry—that Miss Arundell's death *was* a natural one? I have come across certain evidence today——"

182

He detailed the conversation he had had with old Angus, Charles Arundell's interest in the weed-killer, and finally the old man's surprise at the emptiness of the tin.

Grainger listened with keen attention. When Poirot had finished he said, quietly:

"I see your point. Many a case of arsenical poisoning has been diagnosed as acute gastro enteritis and a certificate given—especially when there are no suspicious contributing circumstances. In any case, arsenical poisoning presents certain difficulties—it has so many different forms. It may be acute, subacute, nervous or chronic. There may be vomiting and abdominal pain—these symptoms may be entirely absent—the person may fall suddenly to the ground and expire shortly afterwards—there may be narcotism and paralysis. The symptoms vary widely."

Poirot said:

"*Eh bien*, taking the facts into account, what is your opinion?"

Dr Grainger was silent for a minute or two. Then he said slowly:

"Taking everything into account, and without any bias whatever, I am of the opinion that no form of arsenical poisoning could account for the symptoms in Miss Arundell's case. She died, I am quite convinced, of yellow atrophy of the liver. I have, as you know, attended her for many years, and she has suffered previously from attacks similar to that which caused her death. That is my considered opinion, M. Poirot."

And there, perforce, the matter had to rest.

It seemed rather an anti-climax when, somewhat apologetically, Poirot produced the package of Liver Capsules he had bought at the chemists.

"Miss Arundell took these, I believe?" he said. "I suppose they could not be injurious in any way?"

"That stuff? No harm in it. *Aloes—podophyllin*—all quite mild and harmless," said Grainger. "She liked trying the stuff. I didn't mind."

He got up.

"You dispensed certain medicines for her yourself?" asked Poirot.

"Yes—a mild liver pill to be taken after food." His eyes

twinkled. "She could have taken a boxful without hurting herself. I'm not given to poisoning my patients, M. Poirot."

Then, with a smile, he shook hands with us both and departed.

Poirot undid the package he had purchased at the chemists. The medicament consisted of transparent capsules, three-quarters full of a dark brown powder.

"They look like a seasick remedy I once took," I remarked.

Poirot opened a capsule, examined its contents and tasted it gingerly with his tongue. He made a grimace.

"Well," I said, throwing myself back in my chair and yawning. "Everything seems harmless enough. Dr Loughbarrow's specialities, and Dr Grainger's pills! And Dr Grainger seems definitely to negative the arsenic theory. Are you convinced at last, my stubborn Poirot."

"It is true that I am pig-headed—that is your expression, I think?—Yes, definitely I have the head of the pig," said my friend, meditatively.

"Then, in spite of having the chemist, the nurse and the doctor against you, you still think that Miss Arundell was murdered?"

Poirot said, quietly:

"That is what I believe. No—more than believe. I am *sure* of it, Hastings."

"There's one way of proving it, I suppose," I said slowly. "Exhumation."

Poirot nodded.

"Is that the next step?"

"My friend, I have to go carefully."

"Why?"

"Because," his voice dropped, "I am afraid of a second tragedy."

"You mean——?"

"I am afraid, Hastings, I am afraid. Let us leave it at that."

22. The Woman on the Stairs

ON THE FOLLOWING morning a note arrived by hand. It was in a rather weak, uncertain handwriting slanting very much uphill.

DEAR M. POIROT,

I hear from Ellen that you were at Littlegreen House yesterday. I shall be much obliged if you could call and see me some time to-day.

Yours truly,
WILHELMINA LAWSON.

"So *she's* down here," I remarked.

"Yes."

"Why has she come, I wonder?"

Poirot smiled.

"I do not suppose there is any sinister reason. After all, the house belongs to her."

"Yes, that's true, of course. You know, Poirot, that's the worst of this game of ours. Every single little thing that any one does is open to the most sinister constructions."

"It is true that I myself have enjoined upon you the motto, 'suspect every one.'"

"Are you still in that state yourself?"

"No—for me it has boiled down to this. I suspect one particular person."

"Which one?"

"Since, at the moment, it is only suspicion and there is no definite proof, I think I must leave you to draw your own deductions, Hastings. And do not neglect the psychology—that is important. The character of the murder—implying as it does a certain temperament in the murderer—that is an essential clue to the crime."

"I can't consider the character of the murderer if I don't know who the murderer is!"

"No, no, you have not paid attention to what I have just said. If you reflect sufficiently on the character—the necessary character of the *murder—then* you will realise *who* the murderer is!"

"Do you really know, Poirot?" I asked, curiously.

"I cannot say I *know* because I have no proofs. That is why I cannot say more at the present. But I am quite sure—yes, my friend, in my own mind I am very sure."

"Well," I said, laughing, "Mind he doesn't get *you!* That *would* be a tragedy!"

Poirot started a little. He did not take the matter as a joke. Instead he murmured: "You are right. I must be careful—extremely careful."

"You ought to wear a coat of chain mail," I said, chaffingly. "And employ a taster in case of poison! In fact, you ought to have a regular band of gunmen to protect you!"

"*Merci*, Hastings, I shall rely on my wits."

He then wrote a note to Miss Lawson saying that he would call at Littlegreen House at eleven o'clock.

After that we breakfasted and then strolled out into the Square. It was about a quarter past ten and a hot sleepy morning.

I was looking into the window of the antique shop at a very nice set of Hepplewhite chairs when I received a highly painful lunge in the ribs, and a sharp, penetrating voice said: "Hi!"

I spun round indignantly to find myself face to face with Miss Peabody. In her hand (the instrument of her assault upon me) was a large and powerful umbrella with a spiked point.

Apparently completely callous to the severe pain she had inflicted, she observed in a satisfied voice:

"Ha! Thought it was you. Don't often make a mistake."

I said rather coldly:

"Er—Good-morning. Can I do anything for you?"

"You can tell me how that friend of yours is getting on with his book—Life of General Arundell?"

"He hasn't actually started to write it yet," I said.

Miss Peabody indulged in a little silent but apparently satisfying laughter. She shook like a jelly. Recovering from that attack, she remarked:

"No, I don't suppose he will be starting to write it."

I said, smiling:

"So you saw through our little fiction?"

"What d'you take me for—a fool?" asked Miss Peabody. "I saw soon enough what your downy friend was after! Wanted me to talk! Well, *I* didn't mind. I like talking. Hard to get any one to listen nowadays. Quite enjoyed myself that afternoon."

She cocked a shrewd eye at me.

"What's it all about, eh? What's it all about?"

I was hesitating what exactly to reply when Poirot joined us. He bowed with *empressement* to Miss Peabody.

"Good-morning, mademoiselle. Enchanted to encounter you."

"Good-mornin'," said Miss Peabody. "What are you this morning, Parotti or Poirot—eh?"

"It was very clever of you to pierce my disguise so rapidly," said Poirot, smiling.

"Wasn't much disguise to pierce! Not many like you about, are there? Don't know if that's a good thing or a bad one. Difficult to say."

"I prefer, mademoiselle, to be unique."

"You've got your wish, I should say," said Miss Peabody, drily. "Now then, Mr Poirot, I gave you all the gossip you wanted the other day. Now it's my turn to ask questions. What's it all about? Eh? What's it all about?"

"Are you not asking a question to which you already know the answer?"

"I wonder." She shot a sharp glance at him. "Something fishy about that will? Or is it something else? Going to dig Emily up? Is that it?"

Poirot did not answer.

Miss Peabody nodded her head slowly and thoughtfully as though she had received a reply.

"Often wondered," she said inconsequently, "what it would feel like . . . Readin' the papers, you know—wondered if any one would ever be dug up in Market Basing . . . Didn't think it would be Emily Arundell. . . ."

She gave him a sudden, piercing look.

"She wouldn't have liked it, you know. I suppose you've thought of that—hey?"

"Yes, I have thought of it."

"I suppose you would do—you're not a fool! Don't think you're particularly officious either."

Poirot bowed.

"Thank you, mademoiselle."

"And that's more than most people would say—looking at your moustache. Why d'you have a moustache like that? D'you like it?"

I turned away convulsed with laughter.

"In England the cult of the moustache is lamentably neglected," said Poirot. His hand surreptitiously caressed the hirsute adornment.

"Oh, I see! Funny," said Miss Peabody. "Knew a woman once who had a goitre and was proud of it! Wouldn't believe that, but it's true! Well, what I say is, it's lucky when you're pleased with what the Lord has given you. It's usually the other way about."

She shook her head and sighed.

"Never thought there would be a murder in this out of the world spot." Again she shot a sudden, piercing look at Poirot. "Which of 'em did it?"

"Am I to shout that to you here in the street?"

"Probably means you don't know. Or do you? Oh, well—bad blood—bad blood. I'd like to know whether that Varley woman poisoned her husband or not. Makes a difference."

"You believe in heredity?"

Miss Peabody said, suddenly:

"I'd rather it was Tanios. An outsider! But wishes ain't horses, worse luck. Well, I'll be getting along. I can see you're not goin' to tell me anything . . . Who are you actin' for, by the way?"

Poirot said, gravely:

"I am acting for the dead, mademoiselle."

I am sorry to say that Miss Peabody received this remark with a sudden shriek of laughter. Quickly subduing her mirth she said:

"Excuse me. It sounded like Isabel Tripp—that's all! What an awful woman! Julia's worse, I think. So painfully girlish. Never did like mutton dressed lamb fashion. Well, good-bye. Seen Dr Grainger at all?"

"Mademoiselle, I have the bone to pick with you. You betrayed my secret."

Miss Peabody indulged in her peculiar throaty chuckle.

"Men are simple! He'd swallowed that preposterous tissue of lies you told him. Wasn't he mad when I told him? Went away snorting with rage! He's looking for you."

"He found me last night."

"Oh! I wish I'd been there."

"I wish you had, mademoiselle," said Poirot, gallantly.

Miss Peabody laughed and prepared to waddle away. She addressed me over her shoulder.

"Good-bye, young man. Don't you go buying those chairs. They're a fake."

She moved off, chuckling.

"That," said Poirot, "is a very clever old woman."

"Even although she did not admire your moustaches?"

"Taste is one thing," said Poirot coldly. "Brains are another."

We passed into the shop and spent a pleasant twenty minutes looking round. We emerged unscathed in pocket and proceeded in the direction of Littlegreen House.

Ellen, rather redder in the face than usual, admitted us and showed us into the drawing-room. Presently footsteps were heard descending the stairs and Miss Lawson came in. She seemed somewhat out of breath and flustered. Her hair was pinned up in a silk handkerchief.

"I hope you'll excuse my coming in like this, M. Poirot. I've been going through some locked-up cupboards—so many things—old people are inclined to *hoard* a little, I'm afraid—dear Miss Arundell was no exception—and one gets so much dust in one's *hair*—astonishing, you know, the things people collect—if you can believe me, two dozen needlebooks—actually, two dozen."

'You mean that Miss Arundell had bought two dozen needlebooks?"

"Yes, and put them away and forgot about them—and, of course, now the needles are all rusty—such a pity. She used to give them to the maids as Christmas presents."

"She was very forgetful—yes?"

'Oh, *very*. Especially in the way of putting things away. Like a dog with a bone, you know. That's what we used to call it between us. "Now don't go and dog and bone it," I used to say to her."

She laughed and then producing a small handkerchief from her pocket suddenly began to sniff.

"Oh, dear," she said tearfully. "It seems so dreadful of me to be laughing here."

"You have too much sensibility," said Poirot. "You feel things too much."

"That's what my mother always used to say to me, M. Poirot. 'You take things to heart too much, Minnie,' she used to say. It's a great drawback, M. Poirot, to be so sensitive. Especially when one has one's living to get."

"Ah, yes, indeed, but that is all a thing of the past. You are now your own mistress. You can enjoy yourself—travel—you have absolutely no worries or anxieties."

"I suppose that's true," said Miss Lawson, rather doubtfully.

"Assuredly it is true. Now talking of Miss Arundell's forgetfulness I see how it was that her letter to me never reached me for so long a time."

He explained the circumstances of the finding of the letter. A red spot showed in Miss Lawson's cheek. She said sharply:

"Ellen should have told *me*! To send that letter off to you without a word was great impertinence! She should have consulted me first. *Great* impertinence, I call it! Not one word did I hear about the whole thing. Disgraceful!"

"Oh, my dear lady, I am sure it was done in all good faith."

"Well, I think it was very *peculiar* myself! *Very* peculiar! Servants really do the oddest things. Ellen should have remembered that I am the mistress of the house now."

She drew herself up, importantly.

"Ellen was very devoted to her mistress, was she not?" said Poirot.

"Yes, I dare say, but that makes no difference. I should have been *told*!"

"The important thing is—that I received the letter," said Poirot.

"Oh, I agree that it's no good making a fuss after things have happened, but all the same I think Ellen ought to be told that she mustn't take it upon herself to do things without asking first!"

She stopped, a red spot on each cheekbone.

Poirot was silent for a minute, then he said:

"You wanted to see me to-day? In what way can I be of service to you?"

Miss Lawson's annoyance subsided as promptly as it had arisen. She began to be flustered and incoherent again.

"Well, really—you see, I just *wondered* . . . Well, to tell the truth, M. Poirot, I arrived down here yesterday and, of course, Ellen told me you had been here, and I just wondered—well, as you hadn't *mentioned* to me that you were coming—Well, it seemed rather *odd*—and I couldn't see——"

"You could not see what I was doing down here?" Poirot finished for her.

"I—well—no, that's exactly it. I couldn't."

She looked at him, flushed but inquiring.

"I must make a little confession to you," said Poirot. "I have permitted you to remain under a misapprehension, I am afraid. You assumed that the letter I received from Miss Arundell concerned itself with the question of a small sum of money abstracted by—in all possibility—Mr Charles Arundell."

Miss Lawson nodded.

"But that, you see, was not the case . . . In fact, the first I heard of the stolen money was from you . . . Miss Arundell wrote to me on the subject of her accident."

"Her accident?"

"Yes, she had a fall down the stairs, I understand."

"Oh, quite—quite——" Miss Lawson looked bewildered. She stared vacantly at Poirot. She went on. "But—I'm sorry—I'm sure it's very stupid of me—but why should she write to *you*? I understand—in fact, I think you said so—that you are a detective. You're not a—a doctor, too? Or a faith healer, perhaps?"

"No, I am not a doctor—nor a faith healer. But, like the doctor, I concern myself sometimes with so-called accidental deaths."

"With accidental deaths?"

"With *so-called* accidental deaths, I said. It is true that Miss Arundell did not *die*—but she might have died!"

"Oh, dear me, yes, the doctor said so, but I don't understand——"

Miss Lawson sounded still bewildered.

"The cause of the accident was supposed to be the ball of the little Bob, was it not?"

"Yes, yes, that was it. It was Bob's ball."

"Oh, no, it was not Bob's ball."

"But, excuse me, Mr Poirot, I saw it there myself—as we all ran down."

"You saw it—yes, perhaps. But *it was not the cause of the accident. The cause of the accident, Miss Lawson, was a dark-coloured thread stretched about a foot above the top of the stairs!*"

"But—but a dog couldn't——"

"Exactly," said Poirot quickly. "A dog could not do that—he is not sufficiently intelligent—or, if you like, he is not sufficiently *evil* . . . A *human being* put that thread in position. . . ."

Miss Lawson's face had gone deadly white. She raised a shaking hand to her face.

"Oh, Mr Poirot—I can't believe it—you don't mean—but that is awful—really awful. You mean it was done on *purpose?*"

"Yes, it was done on purpose."

"But that's dreadful. It's almost like—like killing a person."

"If it had succeeded it *would* have been killing a person! In other words—it would have been murder!"

Miss Lawson gave a little shrill cry.

Poirot went on in the same grave tone.

"A nail was driven into the skirting board so that the thread could be attached. That nail was varnished so as not to show. Tell me, do you ever remember a smell of varnish that you could not account for?"

Miss Lawson gave a cry.

"Oh, how extraordinary! To think of that! Why, of course! And to think I never thought—never dreamed—but then, how could I? And yet it did seem odd to me at the time."

Poirot leant forward.

"So—you can help us, mademoiselle. Once again you can help us. *C'est épatant!*"

"To think that was it! Oh, well, it all fits in."

"Tell me, I pray of you. You smelt varnish—yes?"

"Yes. Of course, I didn't know what it was. I thought—dear me—is it paint—no, it's more like floor stain, and then, of course, I thought I must have *imagined* it."

"When was this?"

"Now let me see—when was it?"

"Was it during that Easter week-end when the house was full of guests?"

"Yes, that was the time—but I'm trying to recall just which day it was . . . Now, let me see, it wasn't Sunday. No, and it wasn't on Tuesday—that was the night Dr Donaldson came to dinner. And on the Wednesday they had all left. No, of course, it was the *Monday*—Bank Holiday. I'd been lying awake—rather worried, you know. I always think Bank Holiday is such a worrying day! There had been only just enough cold beef to go round at supper and I was afraid Miss Arundell might be annoyed about it. You see *I'd* ordered the joint on the Saturday, and of course I ought to have said seven pounds but I thought five pounds would do nicely, but Miss Arundell was always so vexed if there was any shortage—she was so hospitable——"

Miss Lawson paused to draw a deep breath and then rushed on.

"And so I was lying awake and wondering whether she'd say anything about it to-morrow, and what with one thing and another I was a long time dropping off—and then just as I was going off something seemed to wake me up—a sort of rap or tap—and I sat up in bed, and then I sniffed. Of course, I'm always terrified of fire—sometimes I think I smell fire two or three times a night—(so awful wouldn't it be if one were *trapped*?) Anyway there was a smell, and I sniffed hard but it wasn't smoke or anything like that. And I said to myself it's more like paint or floor stain—but of course, one wouldn't smell that in the middle of the night. But it was quite strong and I sat up sniffing and sniffing, and then I saw her in the glass——"

"Saw *her*? Saw whom?"

"In my looking-glass, you know, it's really most convenient. I left my door open a little always, so as to hear Miss Arundell if she were to call, and if she went up and down stairs I could see her. The one light was always left switched on in the passage. That's how I came to see her kneeling on the stairs—Theresa, I mean. She was kneeling on about the third step with her head bent down over something and I was just thinking, 'How odd, I wonder if she's *ill?*' when she got up and went away, so I supposed she'd just slipped or something. Or perhaps was stooping to pick something up. But, of course, I never thought about it again one way or another."

"The tap that aroused you would be the tap of the hammer on the nail," mused Poirot.

"Yes, I suppose it would. But oh, M. Poirot, how *dreadful*—how truly dreadful. I've always felt Theresa was, perhaps, a little *wild*, but to do a thing like that."

"You are sure it was Theresa?"

"Oh, dear me, yes."

"It couldn't have been Mrs Tanios or one of the maids, for instance?"

"Oh, no, it was Theresa."

Miss Lawson shook her head and murmured to herself.

"Oh, dear, Oh, dear," several times.

Poirot was staring at her in a way I found it hard to understand.

"Permit me," he said suddenly, "to make an experiment. Let us go upstairs and endeavour to reconstruct this little scene."

"Reconstruct? Oh, really—I don't know—I mean I don't quite see——"

"I will show you," said Poirot, cutting in upon these doubts in an authoritative manner.

Somewhat flustered, Miss Lawson led the way upstairs.

"I hope the room's tidy—so much to do—what with one thing and another——" she tailed off incoherently.

The room was indeed somewhat heavily littered with miscellaneous articles, obviously the result of Miss Lawson's turning out of cupboards. With her usual incoherence Miss Lawson managed to indicate her own position and Poirot was able to verify for himself the fact that a portion of the staircase was reflected in the wall-mirror.

"And now, mademoiselle," he suggested, "if you will be so good as to go out and reproduce the actions that you saw."

Miss Lawson, still murmuring, "Oh, dear——" bustled out to fulfil her part. Poirot acted the part of observer.

The performance concluded, he went out on the landing and asked which electric light had been left switched on.

"This one—this one along here. Just outside Miss Arundell's door."

Poirot reached up, detached the bulb and examined it.

"A forty watt lamp, I see. Not very powerful."

"No, it was just so that the passage shouldn't be quite dark."

Poirot retraced his steps to the top of the stairs.

"You will pardon me, mademoiselle, but with the light being fairly dim and the way that shadow falls it is hardly possible that you can have seen very clearly. Can you be positive it was Miss Theresa Arundell and not just an indeterminate female figure in a dressing-gown?"

Miss Lawson was indignant.

"No, indeed, M. Poirot! I'm *perfectly* sure! I know Theresa well enough, I should hope! Oh, it was her all right. Her dark dressing-gown and that big shining brooch she wears with the initials—I saw that plainly."

"So that there is no possible doubt. You saw the initials?"

"Yes, T.A. I know the brooch. Theresa often wore it. Oh, yes, I could swear to its being Theresa—and I will swear to it if necessary!"

There was a firmness and decision in those last two sentences that was quite at variance with her usual manner.

Poirot looked at her. Again there was something curious in his glance. It was aloof, appraising—and had also a queer appearance of finality about it.

"You would swear to that, yes?" he said.

"If—if—it's necessary. But I suppose it—will it be necessary?"

Again Poirot turned that appraising glance upon her.

"That will depend on the result of the exhumation," he said.

"Ex—exhumation?"

Poirot put out a restraining hand. In her excitement Miss Lawson very nearly went headlong down the stairs.

"It may possibly be a question of exhumation," he said.

"Oh, but surely—how *very* unpleasant! But I mean, I'm sure the family would oppose the idea very strongly—very strongly indeed."

"Probably they will."

"I'm quite sure they won't hear of such a thing!"

"Ah, but if it is as an order from the Home Office."

"But M. Poirot—*why*? I mean it's not as though—not as though——"

"Not as though what?"

"Not as though there were anything—*wrong*."

"You think not?"

"No, of course not. Why, there *couldn't* be! I mean the doctor and the nurse and everything——"

"Do not upset yourself," said Poirot calmly and soothingly.

"Oh, but I can't help it! Poor dear Miss Arundell! It's not even as though Theresa had been here in the house when she died."

"No, she left on the Monday before she was taken ill, did she not?"

"Quite early in the morning. So you see, *she* can't have had anything to do with it!"

"Let us hope not," said Poirot.

"Oh, dear." Miss Lawson clasped her hands together. "I've never known *anything* so dreadful as all this! Really, I don't know whether I'm on my head or my heels."

Poirot glanced at his watch.

"We must depart. We are returning to London. And you, mademoiselle, you are remaining down here some little time?"

"No—no . . . I have really no settled plans. Actually I'm going back myself to-day . . . I only came down just for a night to—to settle things a little."

"I see. Well, good-bye, mademoiselle, and forgive me if I have upset you at all."

"Oh, M. Poirot. *Upset* me? I feel quite *ill*! Oh, dear—Oh dear. It's such a *wicked* world! Such a dreadfully wicked world."

Poirot cut short her lamentations by taking her hand firmly in his.

"Quite so. And you are still ready to swear *that you saw Theresa Arundell kneeling on the stairs on the night of Easter Bank Holiday?*"

"Oh, yes, I can swear to that."

"And you can also swear that you saw a halo of light round Miss Arundell's head during the *séance*?"

Miss Lawson's mouth fell open.

"Oh, M. Poirot, don't—don't joke about these things."

"I am not joking. I am perfectly serious."

Miss Lawson said with dignity:

"It wasn't exactly a halo. It was more like the beginning of a manifestation. A ribbon of some luminous material. I think it was beginning to form into a face."

"Extremely interesting. *Au revoir*, mademoiselle, and please keep all this to yourself."

"Oh, of course—of course. I shouldn't dream of doing anything else. . . ."

The last we saw of Miss Lawson was her rather sheeplike face gazing after us from the front door step.

23. Dr Tanios Calls on Us

NO SOONER had we left the house than Poirot's manner changed. His face was grim and set.

"*Dépêchons nous*, Hastings," he said. "We must get back to London as soon as possible."

"I'm willing." I quickened my pace to suit his. I stole a look at his grave face.

"Who do you suspect, Poirot?" I asked. "I wish you'd tell me. Do you believe it was Theresa Arundell on the stairs or not?"

Poirot did not reply to my question. Instead he asked a question of his own.

"Did it strike you—reflect before you answer—did it strike you that there was something *wrong* with that statement of Miss Lawson's?"

"How do you mean—wrong with it?"

"If I knew that I should not be asking you!"

"Yes, but wrong in what way?"

"That is just it. I cannot be precise. But as she was talking I had, somehow, a feeling of unreality . . . as though there was something—some small point that was wrong—that was, yes, that was the feeling—something that was *impossible* . . . ."

"She seemed quite positive it was Theresa!"

"Yes, yes."

"But after all, the light couldn't have been very good. I don't see how she can be quite so sure."

"No, no, Hastings, you are not helping me. It was some small point—something connected with—yes, I am sure of it—with the bedroom."

"With the bedroom?" I repeated, trying to recall the details of the room. "No," I said at last. "I can't help you."

Poirot shook his head, vexedly.

"Why did you bring up that spiritualistic business again?" I asked.

"Because it is important."

"What is important? Miss Lawson's luminous 'ribbon development'?"

"You remember the Misses Tripp's description of the *séance*?"

"I know they saw a halo round the old lady's head." I laughed in spite of myself. "*I* shouldn't think she was a saint by all accounts! Miss Lawson seems to have been terrified by her. I felt quite sorry for the poor woman when she described how she lay awake, worried to death because she might get into trouble over ordering too small a sirloin of beef."

"Yes, it was an interesting touch that."

"What are we going to do when we get to London?" I asked as we turned into the George and Poirot asked for the bill.

"We must go and see Theresa Arundell immediately."

"And find out the truth? But won't she deny the whole thing anyway?"

"*Mon cher*, it is not a criminal offence to kneel upon a flight of stairs! She may have been picking up a pin to bring her luck— something of that sort!"

"And the smell of varnish?"

We could say no more just then, as the waiter arrived with the bill.

On the way to London we talked very little. I am not fond of talking and driving, and Poirot was so busy protecting his moustaches with his muffler from the disastrous effects of wind and dust that speech was quite beyond him.

We arrived at the flat at about twenty to two.

George, Poirot's immaculate and extremely English manservant, opened the door.

"A Dr Tanios is waiting to see you, sir. He has been here for half an hour."

"Dr Tanios? Where is he?"

"In the sitting-room, sir. A lady also called to see you, sir. She seemed very distressed to find you were absent from home. It was before I received your telephone message, sir, so I could not tell her when you would be returning to London."

"Describe this lady."

"She was about five foot seven, sir, with dark hair and light blue eyes. She was wearing a grey coat and skirt and a hat worn very much to the back of the head instead of over the right eye."

"Mrs Tanios," I ejaculated in a low voice.

"She seemed in a condition of great nervous excitement, sir. Said it was of the utmost importance she should find you quickly."

"What time was this?"

"About half-past ten, sir."

Poirot shook his head as he passed on towards the sitting-room.

"That is the second time I have missed hearing what Mrs Tanios has to say. What would you say, Hastings? Is there a fate in it?"

"Third time lucky," I said consolingly.

Poirot shook his head doubtfully.

"Will there be a third time? I wonder. Come, let us hear what the husband has to say."

Dr Tanios was sitting in an arm-chair reading one of Poirot's books on psychology. He sprang up and greeted us.

"You must forgive this intrusion. I hope you don't mind my forcing my way in and waiting for you like this."

"*Du tout, du tout.* Pray sit down. Permit me to offer you a glass of sherry."

"Thank you. As a matter of fact I have an excuse. M. Poirot, I am worried, terribly worried, about my wife."

"About your wife? I'm very sorry. What's the matter?"

Tanios said:

"You have seen her perhaps, lately?"

It seemed quite a natural question, but the quick look that accompanied it was not so natural.

Poirot replied in the most matter of fact manner.

"No, not since I saw her at the hotel with you yesterday."

"Ah—I thought perhaps she might have called upon you."

Poirot was busy pouring out three glasses of sherry.

He said in a slightly abstracted voice:

"No. Was there any—reason for her calling on me?"

"No, no." Dr Tanios accepted his sherry. "Thank you. Thank you very much. No, there was no exact *reason*, but to be frank I am very much concerned about my wife's state of health."

"Ah, she is not strong?"

"Her bodily health," said Tanios slowly, "is good. I wish I could say the same for her mind."

"Ah?"

"I fear, M. Poirot, that she is on the verge of a complete nervous breakdown."

"My dear Dr Tanios, I am extremely sorry to hear this."

"This condition has been growing for some time. During the last two months her manner towards me has completely changed. She is nervous, easily startled, and she has the oddest fancies— actually they are more than fancies—they are *delusions*!

"Really?"

"Yes. She is suffering from what is commonly known as persecution mania—a fairly well-known condition."

Poirot made a sympathetic noise with his tongue.

"You can understand my anxiety!"

"Naturally. Naturally. But what I do not quite understand is why you have come to me. How can I help you?"

Dr Tanios seemed a little embarrassed.

"It occurred to me that my wife might have—or may yet— come to you with some extraordinary tale. She may conceivably say that she is in danger from me—something of that kind."

"But why should she come to *me*?"

Dr Tanios smiled—it was a charming smile—genial yet wistful.

"You are a celebrated detective, M. Poirot. I saw—I could see at once—that my wife was very impressed at meeting you yesterday. The mere fact of meeting a detective would make a powerful impression on her in her present state. It seems to me highly probable that she might seek you out and—and—well, confide in you. That is the way these nervous affections go! There is a tendency to turn against those nearest and dearest to you."

"Very distressing."

"Yes, indeed. I am very fond of my wife." There was a rich tenderness in his voice. "I always feel it was so brave of her to marry me—a man of another race—to come out to a far country —to leave all her own friends and surroundings. For the last few days I have been really distraught . . . I can see only one thing for it. . . ."

"Yes?"

"Perfect rest and quiet—and suitable psychological treatment. There is a splendid home I know of run by a first-class man. I want to take her down there—it is in Norfolk—straightaway. Perfect rest and isolation from outside influence—that is what is needed. I feel convinced that once she has been there a month or two under skilled treatment there will be a change for the better."

"I see," said Poirot.

He uttered the words in a matter of fact manner without any clue to the feelings that prompted him.

Tanios again shot a quick glance at him.

"That is why, if she should come to you, I should be obliged if you will let me know at once."

"But certainly. I will telephone you. You are at the Durham Hotel still?"

"Yes. I am going back there now."

"And your wife is not there?"

"She went out directly after breakfast."

"Without telling you where she was going?"

"Without saying a word. That is most unlike her."

"And the children?"

"She took them with her."

"I see."

Tanios got up.

"Thank you so much, M. Poirot. I need hardly say that if she does tell you any high-flown stories of intimidation and persecution pay no attention to them. It is, unfortunately, a part of her malady."

"Most distressing," said Poirot with sympathy.

"It is indeed. Although one knows, medically speaking, that it is part of a recognised mental disease, yet one cannot help being hurt when a person very near and dear to you turns against you and all their affection changes to dislike."

"You have my deepest sympathy," said Poirot as he shook hands with his guest.

"By the way——" Poirot's voice recalled Tanios just as he was at the door.

"Yes?"

"Do you ever prescribe chloral for your wife?"

"I—no—at least I may have done. But not lately. She seems to have taken an aversion to any form of sleeping draught."

"Ah! I suppose because she does not trust you?"

"M. Poirot!"

Tanios came striding forward angrily.

"That would be part of the disease," said Poirot smoothly.

Tanios stopped.

"Yes, yes, of course."

"She is probably highly suspicious of anything you give her to eat or drink. Probably suspects you of wanting to poison her?"

"Dear me, M. Poirot, you are quite right. You know something of such cases, then?"

"One comes across them now and then in my profession, naturally. But do not let me detain you. You may find her waiting for you at the hotel."

"True. I hope I shall. I feel terribly anxious."

He hurried out of the room.

Poirot went swiftly to the telephone. He flicked over the pages of the telephone directory and asked for a number.

"Allo—Allo—is that the Durham Hotel. Can you tell me if Mrs Tanios is in? What? TANIOS. Yes, that is right. Yes? Yes? Oh, I see."

He replaced the receiver.

"Mrs Tanios left the hotel this morning early. She returned at eleven, waited in the taxi whilst her luggage was brought down and drove away with it."

"Does Tanios know she took away her luggage?"

"I think not as yet."

"Where has she gone?"

"Impossible to tell."

"Do you think she will come back here?"

"Possibly. I cannot tell."

"Perhaps she will write."

"Perhaps."

"What can we do?"

Poirot shook his head. He looked worried and distressed.

"Nothing at the moment. A hasty lunch and then we will go and see Theresa Arundell."

"Do you believe it *was* her on the stairs?"

"Impossible to tell. One thing I made sure of—Miss Lawson could not have seen her face. She saw a tall figure in a dark dressing gown, that is all."

"And the brooch."

"My dear friend, a brooch is not part of a person's anatomy! It can be detached from that person. It can be lost—or borrowed—or even stolen."

"In other words you don't want to believe Theresa Arundell guilty."

"I want to hear what she has to say on the matter."

"And if Mrs Tanios comes back?"

"I will arrange for that."

George brought in an omelette.

"Listen, George," said Poirot. "If that lady comes back, you will ask her to wait. If Dr Tanios comes while she is here on no account let him in. If he asks if his wife is here, you will tell him she is not. You understand?"

"Perfectly, sir."

Poirot attacked the omelette.

"This business complicates itself," he said. "We must step very carefully. If not—the murderer will strike again."

"If he did you might get him."

"Quite possibly, but I prefer the life of the innocent to the conviction of the guilty. We must go very, very carefully."

24. Theresa's Denial

WE FOUND Theresa Arundell just preparing to go out.

She was looking extraordinarily attractive. A small hat of the most outrageous fashion descended rakishly over one eye. I recognised with momentary amusement that Bella Tanios had worn a cheap imitation of such a hat yesterday and had worn it—as George had put it—on the back of the head instead of over the right eye. I remembered well how she had pushed it farther and farther back on her untidy hair.

Poirot said, politely.

"Can I have just a minute or two, mademoiselle, or will it delay you too much?"

Theresa laughed.

"Oh, it doesn't matter. I'm always three-quarters of an hour late for everything. I might just as well make it an hour."

She led him into the sitting-room. To my surprise Dr Donaldson rose from a chair by the window.

"You've met M. Poirot already, Rex, haven't you?"

"We met at Market Basing," said Donaldson, stiffly.

"You were pretending to write the life of my drunken grandfather, I understand," said Theresa. "Rex, my angel, will you leave us?"

"Thank you, Theresa, but I think that from every point of view it would be advisable for me to be present at this interview."

There was a brief duel of eyes. Theresa's were commanding. Donaldson's were impervious. She showed a quick flash of anger.

"All right, stay then, damn you!"

Dr Donaldson seemed unperturbed.

He seated himself again in the chair by the window, laying down his book on the arm of it. It was a book on the pituitary gland, I noticed.

Theresa sat down on her favourite low stool and looked impatiently at Poirot.

"Well, you've seen Purvis? What about it?"

Poirot said in a non-committal voice:

"There are—possibilities, mademoiselle."

She looked at him thoughtfully. Then she sent a very faint glance in the direction of the doctor. It was, I think, intended as a warning to Poirot.

"But it would be well, I think," went on Poirot, "for me to report later when my plans are more advanced."

A faint smile showed for a minute on Theresa's face.

Poirot continued:

"I have to-day come from Market Basing and while there I have talked to Miss Lawson. Tell me, mademoiselle, did you on the night of April 13th (that was the night of the Easter Bank Holiday) kneel upon the stairs after every one had gone to bed?"

"My dear Hercule Poirot, what an extraordinary question. Why should I?"

"The question, mademoiselle, is not why you *should*, but whether you *did*."

"I'm sure I don't know. I should think it most unlikely."

"You comprehend, mademoiselle, Miss Lawson *says you did*."

Theresa shrugged her attractive shoulders.

"Does it matter?"

"It matters very much."

She stared at him. In a perfectly amiable fashion. Poirot stared back.

"Loopy!" said Theresa.

"*Pardon?*"

"Definitely loopy!" said Theresa. "Don't you think so, Rex?"

Dr Donaldson coughed.

"Excuse me, M. Poirot, but what is the point of the question?"

My friend spread out his hands.

"It is most simple! Some one drove in a nail in a convenient position at the head of the stairs. The nail was just touched with brown varnish to match the skirting board."

"Is this a new kind of witchcraft?" asked Theresa.

"No, mademoiselle, it is much more homely and simple than that. On the following evening, the Tuesday, *some one* attached a string or thread from the nail to the balusters with the result that when Miss Arundell came out of her room she caught her foot in it and went headlong down the stairs."

Theresa drew in her breath sharply.

"That was Bob's ball!"

"*Pardon*, it was not."

There was a pause. It was broken by Donaldson who said in his quiet, precise voice.

"Excuse me, but what evidence have you in support of this statement?"

Poirot said quietly:

"The evidence of the nail, the evidence of Miss Arundell's own written words, and finally the evidence of Miss Lawson's eyes."

Theresa found her voice.

"She says *I* did it, does she?"

Poirot did not answer except by bending his head a little.

"Well, it's a lie! I had nothing to do with it!"

"You were kneeling on the stairs for quite another reason?"

"I wasn't kneeling on the stairs at all!"

"Be careful, mademoiselle."

"I wasn't there! I never came out of my room after I went to bed on any evening I was there."

"Miss Lawson recognised you."

"It was probably Bella Tanios or one of the maids she saw."

"She says it was you."

"She's a damned liar!"

"She recognised your dressing-gown and a brooch you wear."

"A brooch—what brooch?"

"A brooch with your initials."

"Oh, I know the one! What a circumstantial liar she is!"

"You still deny that it was you she saw?"

"If it's my word against hers——"

"You are a better liar than she is—eh?"

Theresa said, calmly:

"That's probably quite true. But in this case I'm speaking the truth. I wasn't preparing a booby trap, or saying my prayers, or picking up gold or silver, or doing anything at all on the stairs."

"Have you this brooch that was mentioned?"

"Probably. Do you want to see it?"

"If you please, mademoiselle."

Theresa got up and left the room. There was an awkward silence. Dr Donaldson looked at Poirot much as I imagined he might have looked at an anatomical specimen.

Theresa returned.

"Here it is."

She almost flung the ornament at Poirot. It was a large rather showy chromium or stainless steel brooch with T.A. enclosed in a circle. I had to admit that it was large enough and showy enough to be easily seen in Miss Lawson's mirror.

"I never wear it now. I'm tired of it," said Theresa. "London's been flooded with them. Every little skivvy wears one."

"But it was expensive when you bought it?"

"Oh, yes. They were quite exclusive to begin with."

"When was that?"

"Last Christmas, I think it was. Yes, about then."

"Have you ever lent it to any one?"

"No."

"You had it with you at Littlegreen House?"

"I suppose I did. Yes, I did. I remember."

"Did you leave it about at all? Was it out of your possession while you were there?"

"No, it wasn't. I wore it on a green jumper, I remember. And I wore the same jumper every day."

"And at night?"

"It was still in the jumper."

"And the jumper?"

"Oh, hell, the jumper was sitting on a chair."

"You are sure no one removed the brooch and put it back again the next day?"

"We'll say so in court if you like—if you think that's the best lie to tell! Actually I'm *quite sure* that nothing like that happened! It's a pretty idea that somebody framed me—but I don't think it's true."

Poirot frowned. Then he got up, attached the brooch carefully to his coat lapel and approached a mirror on a table at the other end of the room. He stood in front of it and then moved slowly backward, getting an effect of distance.

Then he uttered a grunt.

"Imbecile that I am! Of course!"

He came back and handed the brooch to Theresa with a bow.

"You are quite right, mademoiselle. The brooch did *not* leave your possession! I have been regrettably dense."

"I do like modesty," said Theresa, pinning the brooch on carelessly.

She looked up at him.

"Anything more? I ought to be going."

"Nothing that cannot be discussed later."

Theresa moved towards the door. Poirot went on in a quiet voice:

"There is a question of exhumation, it is true——"

Theresa stopped dead. The brooch fell from her hand to the ground.

"What's that?"

Poirot said clearly:

"It is possible that the body of Miss Emily Arundell may be exhumed."

Theresa stood still, her hands clenched. She said in a low, angry voice:

"Is this *your* doing? It can't be done without an application from the family!"

"You are wrong, mademoiselle. It can be done on an order from the Home Office."

"My God!" said Theresa.

She turned and walked swiftly up and down.

Donaldson said quietly:

"I really don't see that there is any need to be so upset, Tessa. I dare say that to an outsider the idea is not very pleasant, but——"

She interrupted him.

"Don't be a fool, Rex!"

Poirot asked.:

"The idea disturbs you, mademoiselle?"

"Of course it does! It isn't decent. Poor old Aunt Emily. Why the devil *should* she be exhumed?"

"I presume," said Donaldson, "that there is some doubt as to the cause of death?" He looked inquiringly at Poirot. He went on. "I confess that I am surprised. I think that there is no doubt that Miss Arundell died a natural death from a disease of long standing."

"You told me something about a rabbit and liver trouble once," said Theresa. "I've forgotten it now, but you infect a rabbit with blood from a person with yellow atrophy of the liver, and then you inject that rabbit's blood into another rabbit, and then that second rabbit's blood into a person and the person gets a diseased liver. Something like that."

"That was merely an illustration of serum therapeutics," said Donaldson patiently.

"Pity there are so many rabbits in the story!" said Theresa with a reckless laugh. "None of us keep rabbits." She turned on Poirot and her voice altered.

"M. Poirot, is this *true*?" she asked.

"It is true enough, but—there are ways of avoiding such a contingency, mademoiselle."

"Then avoid it!" Her voice sank almost to a whisper. It was urgent, compelling. "Avoid it *at all costs!*"

Poirot rose to his feet.

"Those are your instructions?" His voice was formal.

"Those are my instructions."

"But, Tessa——" Donaldson interrupted.

She whirled round on her fiancé.

"Be quiet! She was *my* aunt, wasn't she? Why should *my* aunt be dug up? Don't you know there will be paragraphs in the papers and gossip and general unpleasantness?" She swung round again on Poirot.

"You must stop it! I give you *carte blanche*. Do anything you like, but *stop it!*"

Poirot bowed formally.

"I will do what I can. *Au revoir, mademoiselle, au revoir, doctor.*"

"Oh, go away!" cried Theresa. "And take St Leonards with you. I wish I'd never set eyes on either of you."

We left the room. Poirot did not this time deliberately place his ear to the crack, but he dallied—yes, he dallied.

And not in vain. Theresa's voice rose clear and defiant:

"Don't look at me like that, Rex."

And then suddenly, with a break in her voice—"Darling."

Dr Donaldson's precise voice answered her.

He said very clearly:

"That man means mischief."

Poirot grinned suddenly. He drew me through the front door.

"Come, St Leonards," he said. *"C'est drôle, ça!"*

Personally I thought the joke a particularly stupid one.

25. I Lie Back and Reflect

No, I THOUGHT, as I hurried after Poirot, there was no doubt about it now. Miss Arundell had been murdered and Theresa knew it. But was she herself the criminal or was there another explanation?

She was afraid—yes. But was she afraid for herself or for some one else? Could that some one be the quiet, precise young doctor with the calm, aloof manner?

Had the old lady died of genuine disease *artificially induced*?

Up to a point it all fitted in—Donaldson's ambitions, his belief that Theresa would inherit money at her aunt's death. Even the fact that he had been at dinner there on the evening of the accident. How easy to leave a convenient window open and return in the dead of night to tie the murderous thread across the staircase. But then, what about the placing of the nail in position?

No, Theresa must have done that. Theresa, his fiancée and accomplice. With the two of them working in together, the whole thing seemed clear enough. In that case it was probably Theresa who had actually placed the thread in position. The *first* crime, the crime that failed, had been *her* work. The second crime, the crime that had succeeded was Donaldson's more scientific masterpiece.

Yes—it all fitted in.

Yet even now there were loose strands. Why had Theresa blurted out those facts about inducing liver disease in human beings? It was almost as though she did not realise the truth. . . .
But in that case—and I felt my mind growing bewildered, and I interrupted my speculations to ask:

"Where are we going, Poirot?"

"Back to my flat. It is possible that we may find Mrs Tanios there."

My thoughts switched off on a different track.

Mrs Tanios! That was another mystery! If Donaldson and Theresa were guilty, where did Mrs Tanios and her smiling husband come in? What did the woman want to tell Poirot and what was Tanios' anxiety to prevent her doing so?

"Poirot," I said humbly. "I'm getting rather muddled. They're not *all* in it, are they?"

"Murder by a syndicate? A family syndicate? No, not this time. There is the mark of one brain and one brain only in this. The psychology is very clear."

"You mean that either Theresa or Donaldson did it—but not *both* of them? Did he get her to hammer that nail in on some entirely innocent pretext, then?"

"My dear friend, from the moment I heard Miss Lawson's story I realised that there were three possibilities. (1) That Miss Lawson was telling the exact truth. (2) That Miss Lawson had invented the story for reasons of her own. (3) That Miss Lawson actually believed her own story, but that her identification rested upon the brooch—and as I have already pointed out to you—a brooch is easily detachable from its owner."

"Yes, but Theresa insists that the brooch did not leave her possession."

"And she is perfectly right. I had overlooked a small but intensely significant fact."

"Very unlike you, Poirot," I said solemnly.

"*N'est ce pas?* But one has one's lapses."

"Age will tell!"

"Age has nothing to do with it," said Poirot coldly.

"Well, what is the significant fact?" I asked as we turned in at the entrance of the Mansions.

"I will show you."

We had just reached the flat.

George opened the door to us. In reply to Poirot's anxious question he shook his head.

"No, sir, Mrs Tanios has not called. Neither has she telephoned."

Poirot went into the sitting-room. He paced up and down for a few moments. Then he picked up the telephone. He got first on to the Durham Hotel.

"Yes—yes, please. Ah, Dr Tanios, this is Hercule Poirot

speaking. Your wife has returned? Oh, not returned. Dear me.
. . . Taken her luggage, you say. . . . And the children. . . .
You have no idea where she has gone. . . . Yes, quite. . . . Oh,
perfectly. . . . If my professional services are of any use to you? I
have a certain experience in these matters. . . . Such things can
be done quite discreetly. . . . No, of course not. . . . Yes, of
course that is true. . . . Certainly—certainly. I shall respect
your wishes in the matter."

He hung up the receiver thoughtfully.

"He does not know where she is," he said thoughtfully. "I
think that is quite genuine. The anxiety in his voice is unmistakable. He does not want to go to the police, that is understandable. Yes, I understand that. He does not want my assistance
either. That is, perhaps, not quite so understandable. . . . He
wants her found—but he does not want *me* to find her. . . . No,
definitely he does not want me to find her. . . . He seems
confident that he can manage the matter himself. He does not
think she can remain long hidden, for she has very little money
with her. Also she has the children. Yes, I fancy he will be able
to hunt her down before long. But, I think, Hastings, that we
shall be a little quicker than he is. It is important, I think, that we
should be."

"Do you think it's true that she is slightly batty?" I asked.

"I think that she is in a highly nervous, overwrought condition."

"But not to such a point that she ought to be in a mental
home?"

"That, very definitely, no."

"You know, Poirot, I don't quite understand all this."

"If you will pardon my saying so, Hastings, you do not
understand at all!"

"There seem so many—well—side issues."

"Naturally there are side issues. To separate the main issue
from the side issues is the first task of the orderly mind."

"Tell me, Poirot, have you realised all along that there were
eight possible suspects and not seven?"

Poirot replied dryly:

"I have taken that fact into consideration from the moment that
Theresa Arundell mentioned that the last time she saw Dr Donaldson was when he dined at Littlegreen House on April 14th."

"I can't quite see——" I broke off.

"What is it you cannot quite see?"

"Well if Donaldson had planned to do away with Miss Arundell by scientific means—by inoculation, that is to say—I can't see why he resorted to such a clumsy device as a string across the stairs."

"*En verité*, Hastings, there are moments when I lose patience with you! One method is a highly scientific one needing fully-specialised knowledge. That is so, is it not?"

"Yes."

"And the other is a homely simple method—'the kind that mother makes'—as the advertisements say. Is that not right?"

"Yes, exactly."

"Then think, Hastings—*think*. Lie back in your chair, close the eyes, employ the little grey cells."

I obeyed. That is to say, I leant back in the chair and closed my eyes and endeavoured to carry out the third part of Poirot's instructions. The result, however, did not seem to clarify matters much.

I opened my eyes to find Poirot regarding me with the kindly attention a nurse might display towards a childish charge.

"*Eh bien?*"

I made a desperate attempt to emulate Poirot's manner.

"Well," I said, "it seems to me that the kind of person who laid the original booby-trap is not the kind of person to plan out a scientific murder."

"Exactly."

"And I doubt if a mind trained to scientific complexities would think of anything so childish as the accident plan—it would be altogether too haphazard."

"Very clearly reasoned."

Emboldened, I went on:

"Therefore, the only logical solution seems to be this—the two attempts were planned by two different people. We have here to deal with murder attempted by two entirely different people."

"You do not think that is too much of a coincidence?"

"You said yourself once that one coincidence is nearly always found in a murder case."

"Yes, that is true. I have to admit it."

"Well, then."

"And who do you suggest for your villains?"

"Donaldson and Theresa Arundell. A doctor is clearly indicated for the final and successful murder. On the other hand we know that Theresa Arundell is concerned in the first attempt. I think it's possible that they acted quite independently of each other."

"You are so fond of saying, 'we know,' Hastings. I can assure you that no matter what *you* know, I do not know that Theresa was implicated."

"But Miss Lawson's story."

"Miss Lawson's story is Miss Lawson's story. Just that."

"But she says——"

"She says—she says. . . . Always you are so ready to take what people say for a proved and accepted fact. Now listen, *mon cher*, I told you at the time, did I not, that something struck me as wrong about Miss Lawson's story?"

"Yes, I remember your saying so. But you couldn't get hold of what it was."

"Well, I have done so now. A little moment and I will show you what I, imbecile that I am, ought to have seen at once."

He went over to the desk and opening a drawer took out a sheet of cardboard. He cut into this with a pair of scissors, motioning to me not to overlook what he was doing.

"Patience, Hastings, in a little moment we will proceed to our experiment."

I averted my eyes obligingly.

In a minute or two Poirot uttered an exclamation of satisfaction. He put away the scissors, dropped the fragments of cardboard into the waste-paper basket and came across the room to me.

"Now, do not look. Continue to avert the eyes while I pin something to the lapel of your coat."

I humoured him. Poirot completed the proceeding to his satisfaction, then, propelling me gently to my feet he drew me across the room, and into the adjoining bedroom.

"Now, Hastings, regard yourself in the glass. You are wearing, are you not, a fashionable brooch with your initials on it—only, *bien entendu*, the brooch is made not of chromium nor stainless steel, nor gold, nor platinum—but of humble cardboard!"

I looked at myself and smiled. Poirot is uncommonly neat with his fingers. I was wearing a very fair representation of Theresa Arundell's brooch—a circle cut out of cardboard and enclosing my initials. A.H. "*Eh bien*," said Poirot. "You are satisfied? You have there, have you not, a very smart brooch with your initials?"

"A most handsome affair," I agreed.

"It is true that it does not gleam and reflect the light, but all the same you are prepared to admit that that brooch could be seen plainly from some distance away?"

"I've never doubted it."

"Quite so. Doubt is not your strong point. Simple faith is more characteristic of you. And now, Hastings, be so good as to remove your coat."

Wondering a little, I did so. Poirot divested himself of his own coat and slipped on mine, turning away a little as he did so.

"And now," he said. "Regard how the brooch—the brooch with *your* initials—becomes me?"

He whisked round. I stared at him—for the moment uncomprehendingly. Then I saw the point.

"What a blithering fool I am! Of course. It's H.A. in the brooch, not A.H. at all."

Poirot beamed on me, as he reassumed his own clothes and handed me mine.

"Exactly—and now you see what struck me as wrong with Miss Lawson's story. She stated that she had seen Theresa's initials clearly on the brooch she was wearing. But she saw Theresa in the *glass*. So, *if she saw the initials at all*, she must have seen them *reversed*."

"Well," I argued, "perhaps she did, and realised that they were reversed."

"*Mon cher*, did that occur to you just now? Did you exclaim, 'Ha! Poirot, you've got it wrong. That's H.A. really—not A.H.' No, you did not. And yet you are a good deal more intelligent, I should say, than Miss Lawson. Do not tell me that a muddle-headed woman like that woke up suddenly, and still half-asleep, realised that A.T. was really T.A. No, that is not at all consistent with the mentality of Miss Lawson."

"She was determined it should be Theresa," I said slowly.

217

"You are getting nearer, my friend. You remember, I hint to her that she could not really see the face of any one on the stairs, and immediately—what does she do?"

"Remembers Theresa's brooch and lugs that in—forgetting that the mere fact of having seen it in the glass gave her own story the lie."

The telephone bell rang sharply. Poirot crossed to it.

He only spoke a few non-committal words.

"Yes? Yes . . . certainly. Yes, quite convenient. The afternoon, I think. Yes, two o'clock will do admirably."

He replaced the receiver and turned to me with a smile.

"Dr Donaldson is anxious to have a talk with me. He is coming here to-morrow afternoon at two o'clock. We progress, *mon ami*, we progress."

26. Mrs Tanios Refuses to Speak

WHEN I CAME round after breakfast the following morning I found Poirot busy at the writing-table.

He raised a hand in salutation, then proceeded with his task. Presently he gathered up the sheets, enclosed them in an envelope and sealed them up carefully.

"Well, old boy, what are you doing?" I asked facetiously. "Writing an account of the case to be placed in safe keeping in case some one bumps you off during the course of the day?"

"You know, Hastings, you are not so far wrong as you think." His manner was serious.

"Is our murderer really about to get dangerous?"

"A murderer is always dangerous" said Poirot gravely. "Astonishing how often that fact is overlooked."

"Any news?"

"Dr Tanios rang up."

"Still no trace of his wife?"

"No."

"Then that's all right."

"I wonder."

"Dash it all Poirot, you don't think she's been bumped off, do you?"

Poirot shook his head doubtfully.

"I confess," he murmured, "that I should like to know where she is."

"Oh, well," I said. "She'll turn up."

"Your cheerful optimism never fails to delight me, Hastings!"

"My goodness, Poirot, you don't think she'll turn up in parcels or dismembered in a trunk?"

Poirot said slowly:

"I find the anxiety of Dr Tanios somewhat excessive—but no more of that. The first thing to do is to interview Miss Lawson."

"Are you going to point out that little error over the brooch?"

"Certainly not. That little fact remains up my sleeve until the right moment comes."

"Then what are you going to say to her?"

"That, *mon ami*, you will hear in due course."

"More lies, I suppose?"

"You are really very offensive sometimes, Hastings. Anybody would think I enjoyed telling lies."

"I rather think you do. In fact, I'm sure of it."

"It is true that I sometimes compliment myself upon my ingenuity," Poirot confessed naïvely.

I could not help giving a shout of laughter. Poirot looked at me reproachfully and we set off for Clanroyden Mansions.

We were shown into the same crowded sitting-room and Miss Lawson came bustling in, her manner even more incoherent than usual.

"Oh, dear, M. Poirot, good-morning. Such a to do—rather untidy, I'm afraid. But then, everything is at sixes and sevens this morning. Ever since Bella arrived——"

"What is that you say? Bella?"

"Yes, Bella Tanios. She turned up half an hour ago—*and* the children—completely exhausted, poor soul! Really, I don't know what to do about it. You see, she's left her husband."

"Left him?"

"So she says. Of coures, I've no doubt she's fully *justified*, poor thing."

"She has confided in you?"

"Well—not exactly *that*. In fact, she won't say anything at all. Just repeats that she's left him and that nothing will induce her to go back to him!"

"That is a very serious step to take?"

"Of course it is! In fact, if he'd been an Englishman, I would have advised her—but there, he isn't an Englishman. . . . And she looks so peculiar, poor thing, so—well, so *scared*. What can he have been doing to her? I believe Turks are frightfully cruel sometimes."

"Dr Tanios is a Greek."

"Yes, of course, that's the other way about—I mean, they're usually the ones who get massacred by the Turks—or am I thinking of Armenians? But all the same, I don't like to think of it. I don't think she *ought* to go back to him, do you, M. Poirot? Anyway, I mean, she says she won't. . . . She doesn't even want him to know where she is."

"As bad as that?"

"Yes, you see it's the *children*. She's so afraid he could take them back to Smyrna. Poor soul, she really is in a terrible way. You see, she's got no money—no money at all. She doesn't know where to go or what to do. She wants to try and earn her living but really, you know, M. Poirot, that's not so easy as it sounds. I know that. It's not as though she were *trained* for anything."

"When did she leave her husband?"

"Yesterday. She spent last night in a little hotel near Paddington. She came to me because she couldn't think of any one else to go to, poor thing."

"And are you going to help her? That is very good of you."

"Well, you see, M. Poirot, I really feel it's my *duty*. But of course, it's all very difficult. This is a very small flat and there's no room—and what with one thing and another."

"You could send her to Littlegreen House?"

"I suppose I could—but you see, her husband might think of that. Just for the moment I've got her rooms at the Wellington Hotel in Queen's Road. She's staying there under the name of Mrs Peters."

"I see," said Poirot.

He paused for a minute, then said:

"I would like to see Mrs Tanios. You see, she called at my flat yesterday but I was out."

"Oh, did she? She didn't tell me that. I'll tell her, shall I?"

"If you would be so good."

Miss Lawson hurried out of the room. We could hear her voice.

"Bella—Bella—my dear, will you come and see M. Poirot?"

We did not hear Mrs Tanios' reply, but a minute or two later she came into the room.

I was really shocked at her appearance. There were dark circles under her eyes and her cheeks were completely destitute of colour, but what struck me far more than this was her obvious air of terror. She started at the least provocation, and she seemed to be continually listening.

Poirot greeted her in his most soothing manner. He came forward, shook hands, arranged a chair for her and handed her a cushion. He treated the pale, frightened woman as though she had been a queen.

"And now, madame, let us have a little chat. You came to see me yesterday, I believe?"

She nodded.

"I regret very much that I was away from home."

"Yes—yes, I wish you had been there."

"You came because you wanted to tell me something?"

"Yes, I—I meant to——"

"*Eh bien*, I am here, at your service."

Mrs Tanios did not respond. She sat quite still, twisting a ring round and round on her finger.

"Well, madame?"

Slowly, almost reluctantly, she shook her head.

"No," she said. "I daren't."

"You *daren't* madame?"

"No. I—if he knew—he'd——Oh, something would happen to me!"

"Come, come, madame—that is absurd."

"Oh, but it isn't absurd—it isn't absurd at all. You don't know him. . . ."

"By *him*, you mean your husband, madame?"

"Yes, of course."

Poirot was silent a minute or two, then he said:

"Your husband came to see me yesterday, madame."

A quick look of alarm sprang up in her face.

"Oh, no! You didn't tell him—but of course you didn't! you couldn't. You didn't know where I was. Did he—did he say I was *mad*?"

Poirot answered cautiously.

"He said that you were—highly nervous."

But she shook her head, undeceived.

"No, he said that I was mad—or that I was going mad! He wants to shut me up so that I shan't be able to tell any one ever."

"Tell any one—what?"

But she shook her head. Twisting her fingers nervously round and round, she muttered:

"I'm afraid. . . ."

"But madame, once you have *told* me—you are *safe*! The secret is out! That fact will protect you automatically."

But she did not reply. She went on twisting—twisting at her ring.

"You must see that yourself," said Poirot gently.

She gave a sort of gasp.

"How am I to know. . . . Oh, dear, it's terrible. He's *plausible!* And he's a doctor! People will believe him and not me. I know they will. I should myself. Nobody will believe me. How could they?"

"You will not even give me the chance?"

She shot a troubled glance at him.

"How do I know? You may be on his side."

"I am on no one's side, madame. I am—always—on the side of the truth."

"I don't know," said Mrs Tanios hopelessly. "Oh, I don't know."

She went on, her words gathering volume, tumbling over each other.

"It's been so awful for years now. I've seen things happening again and again. And I couldn't say anything or do anything. There have been the children. It's been like a long nightmare. And now this. . . . But I won't go back to him. I won't let him have the children! I'll go somewhere where he can't find me. Minnie Lawson will help me. She's been so kind—so wonderfully kind. Nobody could have been kinder." She stopped, then shot a quick look at Poirot and asked:

"What did he say about me? Did he say I had delusions?"

"He said, madame, that you had—changed towards him."

She nodded.

"And he said I had delusions. He *did* say that, didn't he?"

"Yes, madame, to be frank, he did."

"That's it, you see. That's what it will sound like. And I've no proof—no real proof."

Poirot leaned back in his chair. When he next spoke it was with an entire change of manner.

He spoke in a matter of fact, business-like voice with as little emotion as if he had been discussing some dry matter of business.

"Do you suspect your husband of doing away with Miss Emily Arundell?"

Her answer came quickly—a spontaneous flash.

"I don't suspect—I know."

"Then, madame, it is your duty to speak."

"Ah, but it isn't so easy—no, it isn't so easy."

"How did he kill her?"

"I don't know exactly—but he did kill her."

"But you don't know the method he employed?"

"No—it was something—something he did that last Sunday."

"The Sunday he went down to see her?"

"Yes."

"But you don't know what it was?"

"No."

"Then how, forgive me, madame, can you be so sure?"

"Because he——" she stopped and said slowly, "I *am* sure!"

"*Pardon*, madame, but there is something you are keeping back. Something you have not yet told me?"

"Yes."

"Come, then."

Bella Tanios got up suddenly.

"No. No. I can't do that. The children. Their father. I can't. I simply can't. . . ."

"But madame——"

"I can't, I tell you."

Her voice rose almost to a scream. The door opened and Miss Lawson came in, her head cocked on one side with a sort of pleasurable excitement.

"May I come in? Have you had your little talk. Bella, my dear, don't you think you ought to have a cup of tea, or some soup, or perhaps a little brandy even?"

Mrs Tanios shook her head.

"I'm quite all right." She gave a weak smile. "I must be getting back to the children. I have left them to unpack."

"Dear little things," said Miss Lawson. "I'm so fond of children."

Mrs Tanios turned to her suddenly.

224

"I don't know what I should do without you," she said. "You—you've been wonderfuly kind."

"There, there, my dear, don't cry. Everything's going to be all right. You shall come round and see my lawyer—such a nice man, so sympathetic, and he'll advise you the best way to get a divorce. Divorce is so simple nowadays, isn't it, everybody says so? Oh, dear, there's the bell. I wonder who that is."

She left the room hurriedly. There was a murmur of voices in the hall. Miss Lawson reappeared. She tiptoed in and shut the door carefully behind her. She spoke in an excited whisper, mouthing the words exaggeratedly.

"Oh, dear, Bella, it's your husband. I'm sure I don't know——"

Mrs Tanios gave one bound towards a door at the other end of the room. Miss Lawson nodded her head violently.

"That's right, dear, go in there, and then you can slip out when I've brought him in here."

Mrs Tanios whispered:

"Don't say I've been here. Don't say you've seen me."

"No, no, of course I won't."

Mrs Tanios slipped through the door. Poirot and I followed hastily. We found ourselves in a small dining-room.

Poirot crossed to the door into the hall, opened it a crack and listened. Then he beckoned.

"All is clear. Miss Lawson has taken him into the other room."

We crept through the hall and out by the front door. Poirot drew it to as noiselessly as possible after him.

Mrs Tanios began to run down the steps, stumbling and clutching at the bannisters. Poirot steadied her with a hand under her arm.

"*Du calme—du calme.* All is well."

We reached the entrance-hall.

"Come with me," said Mrs Tanios piteously. She looked as though she might be going to faint.

"Certainly I will come," said Poirot reassuringly.

We crossed the road, turned a corner, and found ourselves in the Queen's Road. The Wellington was a small, inconspicuous hotel of the boarding-house variety.

When we were inside Mrs Tanios sank down on a plush sofa. Her hand was on her beating heart.

Poirot patted her reassuringly on the shoulder.

"It was the narrow squeak—yes. Now, madame, you are to listen to me very carefully."

"I can't tell you anything more, M. Poirot. It wouldn't be *right*. You—you know what I think—what I believe. You—you must be satisfied with that."

"I asked you to listen, madame. Supposing—this is a supposition only—*that I already know the facts of the case.* Supposing that what you could tell me *I have already guessed*— that would make a difference, would it not?"

She looked at him doubtfully. Her eyes were painful in their intensity.

"Oh, believe me, madame, I am not trying to trap you into saying what you do not wish to. But it *would* make a difference —yes?"

"I—I suppose it would."

"Good. Then let me say this. *I, Hercule Poirot, know the truth.* I am not going to ask you to accept my word for it. Take this." He thrust upon her the bulky envelope I had seen him seal up that morning. "The facts are there. After you have read them, if they satisfy you, ring me up. My number is on the notepaper."

Almost reluctantly she accepted the envelope.

Poirot went on briskly:

"And now, one more point, you must leave this hotel at once."

"But why?"

"You will go to the Coniston Hotel near Euston. Tell no one where you are going."

"But surely—here—Minnie Lawson won't tell my husband where I am."

"You think not?"

"Oh, no—she's entirely on my side."

"Yes, but your husband, madame, is a very clever man. He will not find it difficult to turn a middle-aged lady inside out. It is essential—*essential*, you understand, that your husband should not know where you are."

She nodded dumbly.

Poirot held out a sheet of paper.

"Here is the address. Pack up and drive there with the children as soon as possible. You understand?"

She nodded.

"I understand."

"It is the children you must think of, madame, not yourself. You love your children."

He had touched the right note.

A little colour crept into her cheeks, her head went back. She looked, not a frightened drudge, but an arrogant, almost handsome woman.

"It is arranged, then," said Poirot.

He shook hands and he and I departed. But not far. From the shelter of a convenient café, we sipped coffee and watched the entrance of the hotel. In about five minutes we saw Dr Tanios walking down the street. He did not even glance up at the Wellington. He passed it, his head bowed in thought, then he turned into the Underground station.

About ten minutes later we saw Mrs Tanios and the children get into the taxi with their luggage and drive away.

"*Bien*," said Poirot, rising with the check in his hand. "We have done our part. Now it is on the knees of the gods."

27. Visit of Dr Donaldson

DONALDSON ARRIVED punctually at two o'clock. He was as calm and precise as ever.

The personality of Donaldson had begun to intrigue me. I had started by regarding him as a rather nondescript young man. I had wondered what a vivid, compelling creature like Theresa could see in him. But I now began to realise that Donaldson was anything but negligible. Behind that pedantic manner there was force.

After our preliminary greetings were over, Donaldson said:

"The reason for my visit is this. I am at a loss to understand exactly what your position is in this matter, M. Poirot?"

Poirot replied guardedly:

"You know my profession, I think?"

"Certainly. I may say that I have taken the trouble to make inquiries about you."

"You are a careful man, doctor."

Donaldson said dryly:

"I like to be sure of my facts."

"You have the scientific mind!"

"I may say that all reports on you are the same. You are obviously a very clever man in your profession. You have also the reputation of being a scrupulous and honest one."

"You are too flattering," murmured Poirot.

"That is why I am at a loss to explain your connection with this affair."

"And yet it is so simple!"

"Hardly that," said Donaldson. "You first present yourself as a writer of biographies."

"A pardonable deception, do you not think? One cannot go everywhere announcing the fact that one is a detective—though that, too, has its uses sometimes."

"So I should imagine." Again Donaldson's tone was dry. "Your next proceeding," he went on, "was to call on Miss Theresa Arundell and represent to her that her aunt's will might conceivably be set aside."

Poirot merely bowed his head in assent.

"That, of course, was ridiculous." Donaldson's voice was sharp. "You knew perfectly well that that will was valid in law and that nothing could be done about it."

"You think that is the case?"

"I am not a fool, M. Poirot——"

"No, Dr Donaldson, you are certainly not a fool."

"I know something—not very much, but enough—of the law. That will can certainly not be upset. Why did you pretend it could? Clearly for reasons of your own—reasons which Miss Theresa Arundell did not for a moment grasp."

"You seem very certain of her reactions."

A very faint smile passed across the young man's face.

He said unexpectedly:

"I know a good deal more about Theresa than she suspects. I have no doubt that she and Charles think they have enlisted your aid in some questionable business. Charles is almost completely amoral. Theresa has a bad heredity and her upbringing has been unfortunate."

"It is thus you speak of your fiancée—as though she was a guinea-pig?"

Donaldson peered at him through his pince-nez.

"I see no occasion to blink the truth. I love Theresa Arundell and I love her for what she is and not for any imagined qualities."

"Do you realise that Theresa Arundell is devoted to you and that her wish for money is mainly in order that your ambitions should be gratified?"

"Of course I realise it. I've already told you I'm not a fool. But I have no intention of allowing Theresa to embroil herself in any questionable situation on my account. In many ways Theresa is a child still. I am quite capable of furthering my career by my own efforts. I do not say that a substantial legacy would not have been acceptable. It would have been most acceptable. But it would merely have provided a short cut."

"You have, in fact, full confidence in your own abilities?"

"It probably sounds conceited, but I have," said Donaldson composedly.

"Let us proceed, then. I admit that I gained Miss Theresa's confidence by a trick. I let her think that I would be—shall we say, reasonably dishonest—for money. She believed that without the least difficulty."

"Theresa believes that any one would do anything for money," said the young doctor in the matter-of-fact tone one uses when stating a self-evident truth.

"True. That seems to be her attitude—her brother's also."

"Charles probably *would* do anything for money!"

"You have no illusions, I see, about your future brother-in-law."

"No. I find him quite an interesting study. There is, I think, some deep-seated neurosis—but that is talking shop. To return to what we are discussing. I have asked myself *why* you should act in the way you have done, and I have found only one answer. It is clear that you suspect either Theresa or Charles of having a hand in Miss Arundell's death. No, please don't bother to contradict me! Your mention of exhumation was, I think, a mere device to see what reaction you would get. Have you, in actual fact, taken any steps towards getting a Home Office order for exhumation?"

"I will be quite frank with you. As yet, I have not."

"So I thought. I suppose you have considered the possibility that Miss Arundell's death may turn out to be from natural causes?"

"I have considered the fact that it may appear to be so—yes."

"But your own mind is made up?"

"Very definitely. If you have a case of—say—tuberculosis that looks like tuberculosis, behaves like tuberculosis, and in which the blood gives a positive reaction—*eh bien*, you consider it *is* tuberculosis, do you not?"

"You look at it that way? I see. Then what exactly are you waiting for?"

"I am waiting for a final piece of evidence."

The telephone bell rang. At a gesture from Poirot I got up and answered it. I recognised the voice.

"Captain Hastings? This is Mrs Tanios speaking. Will you

tell M. Poirot that he is perfectly right. If he will come here to-morrow morning at ten o'clock, I will give him what he wants."

"At ten o'clock to-morrow?"

"Yes."

"Right, I'll tell him."

Poirot's eyes asked a question. I nodded.

He turned to Donaldson. His manner had changed. It was brisk—assured.

"Let me make myself clear," he said. "I have diagnosed this case of mine as a case of murder. It looked like murder, it gave all the characteristic reactions of murder—in fact, it *was* murder! Of that, there is not the least doubt."

"Where then, does the doubt—for I perceive there *is* a doubt—lie?"

"The doubt lay in *the identity of the murderer*—but that is a doubt no longer!"

"Really? You know?"

"Let us say that I shall have definite proof in my hands to-morrow."

Dr Donaldson's eyebrows rose in a slightly ironical fashion.

"Ah," he said. "To-morrow! Sometimes, M. Poirot, to-morrow is a long way off."

"On the contrary," said Poirot, "I always find that it succeeds to-day with monotonous regularity."

Donaldson smiled. He rose.

"I fear I have wasted your time, M. Poirot."

"Not at all. It is always as well to understand each other."

With a slight bow Dr Donaldson left the room.

28. Another Victim

"THAT IS A clever man," said Poirot thoughtfully.

"It's rather difficult to know what he is driving at."

"Yes. He is a little inhuman. But extremely perceptive."

"That telephone call was from Mrs Tanios."

"So I gathered."

I repeated the message. Poirot nodded approval.

"Good. All marches well. Twenty-four hours, Hastings, and I think we shall know exactly where we stand."

"I'm still a little fogged. Who exactly do we suspect?"

"I really could not say who *you* suspect, Hastings! Everybody in turn, I should imagine!"

"Sometimes I think you *like* to get me into that state!"

"No, no, I would not amuse myself in such a way."

"I wouldn't put it past you."

Poirot shook his head, but somewhat absently. I studied him.

"Is anything the matter?" I asked.

"My friend, I am always nervous towards the end of a case. If anything should go wrong——"

"Is anything likely to go wrong?"

"I do not think so." He paused—frowning. "I have, I think, provided against every contingency."

"Then, supposing that we forget crime and go to a show?"

"*Ma foi*, Hastings, that is a good idea!"

We passed a very pleasant evening, though I made the slight mistake of taking Poirot to a crook play. There is one piece of advice I offer to all my readers. Never take a soldier to a military play, a sailor to a naval play, a Scotsman to a Scottish play, a detective to a thriller—and an actor to any play, whatsoever! The shower of destructive criticism in each case is somewhat devastating. Poirot never ceased to complain of faulty psychology, and the hero detective's lack of order and method nearly drove him demented. We parted that night with Poirot still explaining how the whole business might have been laid bare in the first half of the first act.

"But in that case, Poirot, there would have been no play," I pointed out.

Poirot was forced to admit that perhaps that was so.

It was a few minutes past nine when I entered the sitting-room the next morning. Poirot was at the breakfast-table—as usual neatly slitting open his letters.

The telephone rang and I answered it.

A heavy-breathing female voice spoke:

"Is that M. Poirot? Oh, it's you, Captain Hatings."

There was a sort of gasp and a sob.

"Is that Miss Lawson?" I asked.

"Yes, yes, such a terrible thing has happened!"

I grasped the receiver tightly.

"What is it?"

"She left the Wellington, you know—Bella, I mean. I went there late in the afternoon yesterday and they said she'd left. Without a word to me, either! *Most* extraordinary! It makes me feel that perhaps after all, Dr Tanios was *right*. He spoke so *nicely* about her and seemed so *distressed*, and now it really looks as though he were right after all."

"But what's happened, Miss Lawson? Is it just that Mrs Tanios left the hotel without telling you?"

"Oh, no, it's not *that!* Oh, dear me, no. If that were all it would be *quite* all right. Though I do think it was *odd*, you know. Dr Tanios did say that he was afraid she wasn't quite—not *quite*—if you know what I mean. Persecution mania, he called it."

"Yes." (Damn the woman!) "But what's *happened?*"

"Oh, dear—it is terrible. Died in her sleep. An overdose of some sleeping stuff! And those *poor* little children! It all seems so dreadfully *sad*! I've done nothing but cry since I heard."

"How did you hear? Tell me all about it."

Out of the tail of my eye I noticed that Poirot had stopped opening his letters. He was listening to my side of the conversation. I did not like to cede my place to him. If I did it seemed highly probable that Miss Lawson would start with lamentations all over again.

233

"They rang me up. From the hotel. The Coniston it's called. It seems they found my name and address in her bag. Oh, dear, M. Poirot—Captain Hastings, I mean, *isn't it terrible?* Those poor little children left motherless."

"Look here," I said. "Are you sure it's an accident? They didn't think it could be suicide?"

"Oh, what a *dreadful* idea, Captain Hastings! Oh, dear, I don't know, I'm sure. Do you think it could be? That would be *dreadful!* Of course she *did* seem very depressed. But she needn't have been. I mean there wouldn't have been any difficulty about *money.* I was going to *share* with her—indeed I was! Dear Miss Arundell would have wished it. I'm sure of that! It seems so awful to think of her taking her own life—but perhaps she didn't. . . . The hotel people seemed to think it was an accident."

"What did she take?"

"One of those sleeping things. Veronal, I think. No, chloral. Yes, that was it. Chloral. Oh, dear, Captain Hastings, do you think——"

Unceremoniously I banged down the receiver. I turned to Poirot.

"Mrs Tanios——"

He raised a hand.

"Yes, yes, I know what you are going to say. She is dead, is she not?"

"Yes. Overdose of sleeping draught. Chloral."

Poirot got up.

"Come, Hastings, we must go there at once."

"Is this what you feared—last night? When you said you were always nervous towards the end of a case?"

"I feared another death—yes."

Poirot's face was set and stern. We said very little as we drove towards Euston. Once or twice Poirot shook his head.

I said timidly:

"You don't think——? Could it be an accident?"

"No, Hastings—no. It was not an accident."

"How on earth did he find out where she had gone?"

Poirot only shook his head without replying.

The Coniston was an unsavoury-looking place quite near

Euston station. Poirot, with his card, and a suddenly bullying manner, soon fought his way into the manager's office.

The facts were quite simple.

Mrs Peters as she had called herself and her two children had arrived about half-past twelve. They had had lunch at one o'clock.

At four o'clock a man had arrived with a note for Mrs Peters. The note had been sent up to her. A few minutes later she had come down with the two children and a suitcase. The children had then left with the visitor. Mrs Peters had gone to the office and explained that she should only want the one room after all.

She had not appeared exceptionally distressed or upset, indeed she had seemed quite calm and collected. She had had dinner about seven-thirty and had gone to her room soon afterwards.

On calling her in the morning the chambermaid had found her dead.

A doctor had been sent for and had pronounced her to have been dead for some hours. An empty glass was found on the table by the bed. It seemed fairly obvious that she had taken a sleeping-draught, and, by mistake, taken an overdose. Chloral hydrate, the doctor said, was a somewhat uncertain drug. There were no indications of suicide. No letter had been left. Searching for means of notifying her relations, Miss Lawson's name and address had been found and she had been communicated with by telephone.

Poirot asked if anything had been found in the way of letters or papers. The letter, for instance, brought by the man who had called for the children.

No papers of any kind had been found, the man said, but there was a pile of charred paper on the hearth.

Poirot nodded thoughtfully.

As far as any one could say, Mrs Peters had had no visitors and on one had come to her room—with the solitary exception of the man who had called for the two children.

I questioned the porter myself as to his appearance, but the man was very vague. A man of medium height—he thought fair-haired—rather military build—of somewhat nondescript appearance. No, he was positive the man had no beard.

"It wasn't Tanios," I murmured to Poirot.

"My dear Hastings! Do you really believe that Mrs Tanios, after all the trouble she was taking to get the children away from their father, would quite meekly hand them over to him without the least fuss or protest? Ah, that, no!"

"Then who was the man?"

"Clearly it was some one in whom Mrs Tanios had confidence or rather it was some one sent by a third person in whom Mrs Tanios had confidence."

"A man of medium height," I mused.

"You need hardly trouble yourself about his appearance, Hastings. I am quite sure that the man who actually called for the children was some quite unimportant personage. The real agent kept himself in the background!"

"And the note was from this third person?"

"Yes."

"Some one in whom Mrs Tanios had confidence?"

"Obviously."

"And the note is now burnt?"

"Yes, she was instructed to burn it."

"What about that resumé of the case that you gave her?"
Poirot's face looked unusually grim.

"That, too, is burned. But that does not matter!"

"No?"

"No. For you see—it is all in the head of Hercule Poirot."
He took me by the arm.

"Come, Hastings, let us leave here. Our concern is not with the dead but with the living. It is with them I have to deal."

29 . Inquest at Littlegreen House

IT WAS ELEVEN O'CLOCK the following morning.

Seven people were assembled at Littlegreen House.

Hercule Poirot stood by the mantelpiece. Charles and Theresa Arundell were on the sofa, Charles on the arm of it with his hand on Theresa's shoulder. Dr Tanios sat in a grandfather chair. His eyes were red-rimmed and he wore a black band round his arm.

On an upright chair by a round table sat the owner of the house, Miss Lawson. She, too, had red eyes. Her hair was even untidier than usual. Dr Donaldson sat directly facing Poirot. His face was quite expressionless.

My interest quickened as I looked at each face in turn.

In the course of my association with Poirot I had assisted at many such a scene. A little company of people, all outwardly composed with well-bred masks for faces. And I had seen Poirot strip the mask from one face and show it for what it was—*the face of a killer!*

Yes, there was no doubt of it. *One of these people was a murderer!* But which? Even now I was not *sure*.

Poirot cleared his throat—a little pompously as was his habit —and began to speak.

"We are assembled here, ladies and gentlemen, to inquire into the death of Emily Arundell on the first of May last. There are four possibilities—that she died naturally—that she died as the result of an accident—that she took her own life—or lastly that she met her death at the hands of some person known or unknown.

"No inquest was held at the time of her death, since it was assumed that she died from natural causes and a medical certificate to that effect was given by Dr Grainger.

"In a case where suspicion arises after burial has taken place it

237

is usual to exhume the body of the person in question. There are
reasons why I have not advocated that course. The chief of them
is that my client would not have liked it."

It was Dr Donaldson who interrupted. He said:

"Your client?"

Poirot turned to him.

"My client is Miss Emily Arundell. I am acting for her. Her
greatest desire was that there should be no scandal."

I will pass over the next ten minutes since it would involve
much needless repetition. Poirot told of the letter he had received, and producing it he read it aloud. He went on to explain
the steps he had taken on coming to Market Basing, and of his
discovery of the means taken to bring about the accident.

Then he paused, cleared his throat once more, and went on:

"I am now going to take you over the ground I travelled to get
at the truth. I am going to show you what I believe to be a true
reconstruction of the facts of the case.

"To begin with it is necessary to picture exactly what passed
in Miss Arundell's mind. That, I think, is fairly easy. She has a
fall, her fall is supposed to be occasioned by a dog's ball, but *she
herself knows better*. Lying there on her bed her active and
shrewd mind goes over the circumstances of her fall and she
comes to a very definite conclusion about it. Some one has
deliberately tried to injure—perhaps to kill her.

"From that conclusion she passes to a consideration of who
that person can be. There were *seven* people in the house—four
guests, her companion and two servants. Of these seven people
only one can be entirely exonerated—since to that one person no
advantage could accrue. She does not seriously suspect the two
servants, both of whom have been with her for many years and
whom she knows to be devoted to her. There remain then, *four*
persons, three of them members of her family, and one of them a
connection by marriage. *Each of those four persons benefit, three
directly, one indirectly, by her death.*

"She is in a difficult position since she is a woman with a
strong sense of family feeling. Essentially she is not one who
wishes to wash the dirty linen in public, as the saying goes. On
the other hand, she is not one to submit tamely to attempted
murder!

238

"She takes her decision and writes to me. She also takes a further step. That further step was, I believe, actuated by two motives. One, I think, was a distinct feeling of *spite* against her entire family! She suspected them all impartially, and she determined at all costs to score off them! The second and more reasoned motive was a wish to protect herself and a realisation of how this could be accomplished. As you know, she wrote to her lawyer, Mr Purvis, and directed him to draw up a will in favour of the one person in the house whom, she felt convinced, could have had no hand in her accident.

"Now I may say that, from the terms of her letter to me and from her subsequent actions, I am quite sure that Miss Arundell passed from *indefinite* suspicion of four people to *definite* suspicion of *one* of those four. The whole tenor of her letter to me is an insistence that this business must be kept strictly private since the honour of the family is involved.

"I think that, from a Victorian point of view, this means that a person of *her own name* was indicated—and preferably a *man*.

"If she had suspected Mrs Tanios she would have been quite as anxious to secure her own safety, but not quite as concerned for the family honour. She might have felt much the same about Theresa Arundell, but not nearly as intensely as she would feel about Charles.

"Charles was an *Arundell*. He bore the family *name!* Her reasons for suspecting him seem quite clear. To begin with, she had no illusions about Charles. He had come near to disgracing the family once before. That is, she knew him to be not only a *potential* but an *actual* criminal! He had already forged her name to a cheque. After forgery—a step further—murder!

"Also she had had a somewhat suggestive conversation with him only two days before her accident. He had asked her for money and she had refused and he had thereupon remarked— oh, lightly enough—that she was going the right way to get herself bumped off. To this she had responded that she could take care of herself! To this, we are told, her nephew responded, 'Don't be too sure.' *And two days later this sinister accident takes place.*

"It is hardly to be wondered at that lying there and brooding over the occurrence, Miss Arundell came definitely to the

239

conclusion that it was *Charles Arundell* who had made an attempt upon her life.

"The sequence of events is perfectly clear. The conversation with Charles. The accident. The letter written to me in great distress of mind. The letter to the lawyer. On the following Tuesday, the 21st, Mr Purvis brings the will and she signs it.

"Charles and Theresa Arundell come down the following week-end and Miss Arundell at once takes the necessary steps to safeguard herself. *She tells Charles about the will.* She not only *tells* him but she actually *shows* it to him! That, to my mind, is *absolutely conclusive. She is making it quite clear to a would-be murderer that murder would bring him nothing whatever!*

"She probably thought that Charles would pass on that information to his sister. But he did not do so. Why? I fancy that he had a very good reason—he felt guilty! He believed that it was *his* doing that the will had been made. But *why* did he feel guilty? Because he had really attempted murder? Or merely because he had helped himself to a small sum of ready cash? Either the serious crime or the petty one might account for his reluctance. He said nothing, hoping that his aunt would relent and change her mind.

"As far as Miss Arundell's state of mind was concerned I felt that I had reconstructed events with a fair amount of correctness. I had next to make up my mind if her suspicions were, in actual fact, justified.

"Just as she had done, I realised that my suspicions were limited to a narrow circle—seven people to be exact. Charles and Theresa Arundell, Dr Tanios and Mrs Tanios. The two servants, Miss Lawson. There was an eighth person who had to be taken into account—namely, Dr Donaldson, who dined there that night, but I did not learn of his presence until later.

"These seven persons that I was considering fell easily into two categories. Six of them stood to benefit in a greater or lesser degree by Miss Arundell's death. If any one of those six had committed the crime the reason was probably a plain matter of *gain*. The second category contained one person only—Miss Lawson. Miss Lawson did *not* stand to gain by Miss Arundell's death, but *as a result of the accident*, she did benefit considerably *later!*

"That meant that if Miss Lawson staged the so-called accident——"

"I never did anything of the kind!" Miss Lawson interrupted. "It's disgraceful! Standing up there and saying such things!"

"A little patience, mademoiselle. And be kind enough not to interrupt," said Poirot.

Miss Lawson tossed her head angrily.

"I insist on making my protest! Disgraceful, that's what it is! Disgraceful!"

Poirot went on unheeding.

"I was saying that *if* Miss Lawson staged that accident she did so for an entirely *different* reason—that is, she engineered it so that Miss Arundell *would naturally suspect her own family and become alienated from them.* That *was* a possibility! I searched to see if there were any confirmation or otherwise and I unearthed one very definite fact. If Miss Lawson wanted Miss Arundell to suspect her own family, she would have stressed the fact of the dog, Bob, being *out* that night. But on the contrary Miss Lawson took the utmost pains to *prevent* Miss Arundell hearing of that. Therefore, I argued, Miss Lawson *must* be innocent."

Miss Lawson said, sharply:

"I should hope so!"

"I next considered the problem of Miss Arundell's death. If one attempt to murder a person is made, a second attempt usually follows. It seemed to me significant that within a fortnight of the first attempt Miss Arundell should have died. I began to make inquiries.

"Dr Grainger did not seem to think there was anything unusual about his patient's death. That was a little damping to my theory. But, inquiring into the happenings of the last evening before she was taken ill, I came across a rather significant fact. Miss Isabel Tripp mentioned a halo of light that had appeared round Miss Arundell's head. Her sister confirmed her statement. They might, of course, be inventing—in a romantic spirit—but I did not think that the incident was quite a likely one to occur to them unprompted. When questioning Miss Lawson she also gave me an interesting piece of information. She referred to a luminous ribbon issuing from Miss Arundell's mouth and forming a luminous haze round her head.

241

"Obviously, though described somewhat differently by two different observers, the actual *fact* was the same. What it amounted to, shorn of spiritualistic significance, was this: *On the night in question Miss Arundell's breath was phosphorescent!*"

Dr Donaldson moved a little in his chair.

Poirot nodded to him.

"Yes, you begin to see. There are not very many phosphorescent substances. The first and most common one gave me exactly what I was looking for. I will read you a short extract from an article on phosphorus poisoning.

"*The person's breath may be phosphorescent before he feels in any way affected.* That is what Miss Lawson and the Misses Tripp saw in the dark—Miss Arundell's phosphorescent breath—'a luminous haze.' And here I will read you again. *The jaundice having thoroughly pronounced itself, the system may be considered as not only under the influence of the toxic action of phosphorus, but as suffering in addition from all the accidents incidental to the retention of the biliary secretion in the blood, nor is there from this point any special difference between phosphorus poisoning and certain affections of the liver—such for example as yellow atrophy.*

"You see the cleverness of that? Miss Arundell has suffered for years from liver trouble. The symptoms of phosphorus poisoning would only look like *another attack of the same complaint.* There will be nothing new, nothing startling about it.

"Oh! it was well-planned! Foreign matches—vermin paste? It is not difficult to get hold of phosphorus, and a very small dose will kill. The medicinal dose is from 1/100 to 1/30 grain.

"*Voilà.* How clear—how marvellously clear the whole business becomes! Naturally, the doctor is deceived—especially as I find his sense of smell is affected—the garlic odour of the breath is a distinct symptom of phosphorus poisoning. He had no suspicions—why should he have? There were no suspicious circumstances and the one thing that might have given him a hint was the one thing he would never hear—or if he did hear it he would only class it as spiritualistic nonsense.

"I was now sure (from the evidence of Miss Lawson and the Misses Tripp) that murder had been committed. The question still was by *whom?* I eliminated the servants—their mentality was obviously not adapted to such a crime. I eliminated Miss

Lawson since she would hardly have prattled on about luminous ectoplasm if she had been connected with the crime. I eliminated Charles Arundell *since he knew, having seen the will, that he would gain nothing by his aunt's death.*

"There remained his sister Theresa, Dr Tanios, Mrs Tanios and Dr Donaldson who I discovered to have been dining in the house on the evening of the dog's ball incident.

"At this point I had very little to help me. I had to fall back upon the psychology of the crime and the *personality* of the murderer! Both crimes had roughly *the same outline*. They were both *simple*. They were cunning, and carried out with efficiency. They required a certain amount of knowledge but not a great deal. The facts about phosphorus poisoning are easily learned, and the stuff itself, as I say, is quite easily obtained, especially abroad.

"I considered first the two men. Both of them were doctors, and both were clever men. Either of them might have thought of phosphorus and its suitability in this particular case, but the incident of the dog's ball did not seem to fit a masculine mind. The incident of the ball seemed to me essentially a *woman's* idea.

"I considered first of all Theresa Arundell. She had certain potentialities. She was bold, ruthless, and not over scrupulous. She had led a selfish and greedy life. She had always had everything she wanted and she had reached a point where she was desperate for money—both for herself and for the man she loved. Her manner, also, showed plainly that she knew her aunt had been murdered.

"There was an interesting little passage between her and her brother. I conceived the idea that *each suspected the other of the crime*. Charles endeavoured to make her say that *she knew of the existence of the new will*. Why? Clearly because if she knew of it she could not be suspected of the murder. She, on the other hand, clearly did not believe Charles' statement that Miss Arundell had shown it to him! She regarded it as a singularly clumsy attempt on his part to divert suspicion from himself.

"There was another significant point. Charles displayed a reluctance to use the word arsenic. Later I found that he had questioned the old gardener at length upon the strength of some weed-killer. It was clear what had been in his mind."

Charles Arundell shifted his position a little.

"I thought of it," he said. "But—well, I suppose I hadn't got the nerve."

Poirot nodded at him.

"Precisely, *it is not in your psychology*. Your crimes will always be the crimes of weakness. To steal, to forge—yes, it is the easiest way—but to kill—*no*! To kill one needs the type of mind that can be obsessed by an idea."

He resumed his lecturing manner.

"Theresa Arundell, I decided, had quite sufficient strength of mind to carry such a design through, but there were other facts to take into consideration. She had never been thwarted, she had lived fully and selfishly—but that type of person is *not the type that kills*—except perhaps in sudden anger. And yet—I felt sure—*it was Theresa Arundell who had taken the weed-killer from the tin*."

Theresa spoke suddenly:

"I'll tell you the truth. I thought of it. I actually took some weed-killer from a tin down at Littlegreen House. But I couldn't do it! I'm too fond of living—of being alive—I couldn't do that to any one—take life from them . . . I may be bad and selfish but there are things I can't do! I couldn't kill a living, breathing, human creature!"

Poirot nodded.

"No, that is true. And you are not as bad as you paint yourself, mademoiselle. You are only young—and reckless."

He went on:

"There remained Mrs Tanios. As soon as I saw her I realised that she was afraid. She saw that I realised that and she very quickly made capital out of that momentary betrayal. She gave a very convincing portrait of a woman *who is afraid for her husband*. A little later she changed her tactics. It was very cleverly done—but the change did not deceive me. A woman can be afraid *for* her husband or she can be afraid *of* her husband—but she can hardly be *both*. Mrs Tanios decided on the latter rôle—and she played her part cleverly—even to coming out after me into the hall of the hotel and pretending that there was something she wanted to tell me. When her husband followed her as she knew he would, she pretended that she could not speak before him.

"I realised at once, not that she feared her husband, but that she disliked him. And at once, summing the matter up, I felt convinced that here was the exact character I had been looking for. Here was—not a self-indulgent woman—but a thwarted one. A plain girl, leading a dull existence, unable to attract the men she would like to attract, finally accepting a man she did not care for rather than be left an old maid. I could trace her growing dissatisfaction with life, her life in Smyrna exiled from all she cared for in life. Then the birth of her children and her passionate attachment to them.

"Her husband was devoted to her but she came secretly to dislike him more and more. He had speculated with her money and lost it—another grudge against him.

"There was only one thing that illumined her drab life, the expectation of her Aunt Emily's death. Then she would have money, independence, the means to educate her children as she wished—and remember education meant a lot to her—she was a Professor's daughter!

"She may have already planned the crime, or had the idea of it in her mind, before she came to England. She had a certain knowledge of chemistry, having assisted her father in the laboratory. She knew the nature of Miss Arundell's complaint and she was well aware that phosphorus would be an ideal substance for her purpose.

"Then, when she came to Littlegreen House, a simpler method presented itself to her. The dog's ball—a thread or string across the top of the stairs. A simple, ingenious woman's idea.

"She made her attempt—and failed. I do not think that she had any idea that Miss Arundell was aware of the true facts of the matter. Miss Arundell's suspicions were directed entirely against Charles. I doubt if her manner to Bella showed any alteration. And so, quietly and determinedly, this self-contained, unhappy, ambitious woman put her original plan into execution. She found an excellent vehicle for the poison, some patent capsules that Miss Arundell was in the habit of taking after meals. To open a capsule, place the phosphorus inside and close it again, was child's play.

"The capsule was replaced among the others. Sooner or later

Miss Arundell would swallow it. Poison was not likely to be suspected. Even if, by some unlikely chance it was, she herself would be nowhere near Market Basing at the time.

"Yet she took one precaution. She obtained a double supply of chloral hydrate at the chemist's, forging her husband's name to the prescription. I have no doubt of what that was for—to keep by her in case anything went wrong.

"As I say, I was convinced from the first moment I saw her that Mrs Tanios was the person I was looking for, but I had absolutely no *proof* of the fact. I had to proceed carefully. If Mrs Tanios had any idea I suspected her, I was afraid that she might proceed to a further crime. Furthermore, I believed that the idea of that crime had already occurred to her. Her one wish in life was to shake herself free of her husband.

"Her original murder had proved a bitter disappointment. The money, the wonderful all-intoxicating money, had all gone to Miss Lawson! It was a blow, but she set to work most intelligently. She began to work on Miss Lawson's conscience which, I suspect, was already not too comfortable."

There was a sudden outburst of sobs. Miss Lawson took out her handkerchief and cried into it.

"It's been dreadful," she sobbed. "I've been wicked! Very wicked. You see, I was very curious about the will—why Miss Arundell had made a new one, I mean. And one day, when Miss Arundell was resting, I managed to unlock the drawer in the desk. And then I found she'd left it all to *me!* Of course, I never dreamed it was so *much*. Just a few thousands—that's all I thought it was. And why not? After all, her own relations didn't really *care* for her! But then, when she was so ill, she asked for the will. I could see—I felt sure—she was going to destroy it . . . And that's when I was so wicked. I told her she'd sent it back to Mr Purvis. Poor dear, she was so forgetful. She never remembered what she'd done with things. She believed me. Said I must write for it and I said I would.

"Oh, dear—Oh, dear—and then she got worse and couldn't think of anything. And she died. And when the will was read and it was all that money I felt *dreadful*. Three hundred and seventy-five thousand pounds. I'd never dreamed for a minute it was anything like that or I wouldn't have done it.

"I felt just as though I'd *embezzled* the money—and I didn't know what to do. The other day, when Bella came to me, I told her that she should have half of it. I felt sure that then I would feel happy again."

"You see?" said Poirot, "Mrs Tanios was succeeding in her object. That is why she was so averse to any attempt to contest the will. She had her own plans and the last thing she wanted to do was to antagonise Miss Lawson. She pretended, of course, to fall in at once with her husband's wishes, but she made it quite clear what her real feelings were.

"She had at that time two objects, to detach herself and her children from Dr Tanios and to obtain her share of the money. Then she would have what she wanted—a rich contented life in England with her children.

"As time went on she could no longer conceal her dislike from her husband. In fact, she did not try to. He, poor man, was seriously upset and distressed. Her actions must have seemed quite incomprehensible to him. Really, they were logical enough. She was playing the part of the terrorised woman. If I had suspicions—and she was fairly sure that that must be the case— she wished me to believe that her husband had committed the murder. And at any moment that second murder which I am convinced was already planned in her mind might occur. I knew that she had a lethal dose of chloral in her possession. I feared that she would stage a pretended suicide and confession on his part.

"And still I had no evidence against her! And then, when I was quite in despair, I got something at last! Miss Lawson told me that she had seen Theresa Arundell kneeling on the stairs on the night of Easter Monday. I soon discovered that Miss Lawson could not have seen Theresa at all clearly—not nearly clearly enough to recognise her *features*. Yet she was quite positive in her identification. On being pressed she mentioned a brooch with Theresa's initials—T.A.

"On my request Miss Thersa Arundell showed me the brooch in question. At the same time she absolutely denied having been on the stairs at the time stated. At first I fancied some one else had borrowed her brooch, but when I looked at the brooch in the glass the truth leaped at me. Miss Lawson waking up had seen a dim figure with the initials T.A. flashing in the light. She had leapt to the conclusion that it was Theresa.

"But if in the glass she had seen the intials T.A.—then the real initials must have been A.T. since the glass naturally reversed the order.

"Of course! Mrs Tanios' mother was Arabella Arundell. Bella is only a contraction. A.T. stood for Arabella Tanios. There was nothing odd in Mrs Tanios possessing a similar type of brooch. It had been exclusive last Christmas but by the spring they were all the rage, and I had already observed that Mrs Tanios copied her cousin Theresa's hats and clothes as far as she was able with her limited means.

"In my own mind, at anyrate, my case was proved.

"Now—what was I to do? Obtain a Home Office order for the exhumation of the body? That could doubtless be managed. I *might* prove that Miss Arundell had been poisoned with phosphorus though there was a little doubt about that. The body had been buried two months, and I understand that there have been cases of phosphorus poisoning where no lesions have been found and where the post mortem appearances are very indecisive. Even then, could I connect Mrs Tanios with the purchase or possession of phosphorus? Very doubtful, since she had probably obtained it abroad.

"At this juncture Mrs Tanios took a decisive action. She left her husband, throwing herself on the pity of Miss Lawson. She also definitely accused her husband of the murder.

"Unless I acted I felt convinced that he would be her next victim. I took steps to isolate them one from the other on the pretext that it was for her safety. She could not very well contradict that. Really, it was *his* safety I had in mind. And then—and then——"

He paused—a long pause. His face had gone rather white.

"But that was only a temporary measure. I had to make sure that the killer would kill no more. I had to assure the safety of the innocent.

"So I wrote out my construction of the case and gave it to Mrs Tanios."

There was a long silence.

Dr Tanios cried out:

248

"Oh, my God, so that's why she killed herself."

Poirot said gently:

"Was it not the best way? She thought so. There were, you see, the children to consider."

Dr Tanios buried his face in his hands.

Poirot came forward and laid a hand on his shoulder.

"It had to be. Believe me it was necessary. There would have been more deaths. First yours—then possibly, under certain circumstances, Miss Lawson's. And so it goes on."

He paused.

In a broken voice Tanios said:

"She wanted me—to take a sleeping draught one night. . . . There was something in her face—I threw it away. That was when I began to believe her mind was going. . . ."

"Think of it that way. It is indeed partly true. But not in the legal meaning of the term. She knew the meaning of her action. . . ."

Dr Tanios said wistfully:

"She was much too good for me—always."

A strange epitaph on a self-confessed murderess!

The Last Word

THERE is very little more to tell.

Theresa married her doctor shortly afterwards. I know them fairly well now and I have learnt to appreciate Donaldson—his clarity of vision and the deep, underlying force and humanity of the man. His manner I may say is just as dry and precise as ever, Theresa often mimics him to his face. She is, I think, amazingly happy and absolutely wrapped up in her husband's career. He is already making a big name for himself and is an authority on the functions of ductless glands.

Miss Lawson, in an acute attack of conscience, had to be restrained forcibly from denuding herself of every penny. A settlement agreeable to all parties was drawn up by Mr Purvis whereby Miss Arundell's fortune was shared out between Miss Lawson, the two Arundells and the Tanios children.

Charles went through his share in a little over a year and is now, I believe, in British Columbia.

Just two incidents.

"You're a downy fellow, ain't you?" said Miss Peabody, stopping us as we emerged from the gate of Littlegreen House one day. "Managed to hush everything up! No exhumation. Everything done decently."

"There seems to be no doubt that Miss Arundell died of yellow atrophy of the liver," said Poirot, gently.

"That's very satisfactory," said Miss Peabody. "Bella Tanios took an overdose of sleeping stuff, I hear."

"Yes, it was very sad."

"She was a miserable kind of woman—always wanting what she hadn't got. People go a bit queer sometimes when they're like that. Had a kitchenmaid once. Same thing. Plain girl. Felt it. Started writing anonymous letters. Queer kinks people get. Ah, well, I dare say it's all for the best."

"One hopes so, madame. One hopes so."

"Well," said Miss Peabody, preparing to resume her walk, "I'll say this for you. You've hushed things up nicely. Very nicely indeed." She walked on.

There was a plaintive "Wuff" behind me.

I turned and opened the gate.

"Come on, old man."

Bob bounced through. There was a ball in his mouth.

"You can't take that for a walk."

Bob sighed, turned and slowly ejected the ball inside the gate. He looked at it anxiously then passed through.

He looked up at me.

"If you say so, master, I suppose it's all right."

I drew a long breath.

"My word, Poirot, it's good to have a dog again."

"The spoils of war," said Poirot. "But I would remind you, my friend, that it was to *me* that Miss Lawson presented Bob, not to *you*."

"Possibly," I said. "But you're not really any good with a dog, Poirot. You don't understand dog psychology! Now Bob and I understand each other perfectly, don't we?"

'Woof," said Bob in energetic assent.

MURDER IN MESOPOTAMIA

Murder in
Mesopotamia

AGATHA
CHRISTIE

Contents

Foreword by Giles Reilly, M.D.

THE EVENTS chronicled in this narrative took place some four years ago. Circumstances have rendered it necessary, in my opinion, that a straightforward account of them should be given to the public. There have been the wildest and most ridiculous rumours suggesting that important evidence was suppressed and other nonsense of that kind. Those misconstructions have appeared more especially in the American press.

For obvious reasons it was desirable that the account should not come from the pen of one of the expedition staff, who might reasonably be supposed to be prejudiced.

I therefore suggested to Miss Amy Leatheran that she should undertake the task. She is obviously the person to do it. She has a professional character of the highest, she is not biased by having any previous connection with the University of Pitts-town Expedition to Iraq and she was an observant and intelligent eye-witness.

It was not very easy to persuade Miss Leatheran to undertake this task—in fact, persuading her was one of the hardest jobs of my professional career—and even after it was completed she displayed a curious reluctance to let me see the manuscript. I discovered that this was partly due to some critical remarks she had made concerning my daughter Sheila. I soon disposed of that, assuring her that as children criticise their parents freely in print nowadays, parents are only too delighted when their off-spring come in for their share of abuse! Her other objection was extreme modesty about her literary style. She hoped I would "put the grammar right and all that." I have, on the contrary, refused to alter so much as a single word. Miss Leatheran's style in my opinion is vigorous, individual and entirely apposite. If she calls Hercule Poirot 'Poirot' in one paragraph and "Mr Poirot" in the next, such a variation is both interesting and

9

suggestive. At one moment she is, so to speak, "remembering her manners" (and hospital nurses are great sticklers for etiquette) and at the next her interest in what she is telling is that of a pure human being—cap and cuffs forgotten!

The only thing I have done is to take the liberty of writing a first chapter—aided by a letter kindly supplied by one of Miss Leatheran's friends. It is intended to be in the nature of a frontispiece—that is, it gives a rough sketch of the narrator.

1. Frontispiece

IN THE HALL of the Tigris Palace Hotel in Baghdad a hospital nurse was finishing a letter. Her fountain-pen drove briskly over the paper.

". . . . Well dear, I think that's really all my news. I must say it's been nice to see a bit of the world—though England for me every time, thank you! The dirt and the mess in Baghdad you wouldn't believe—and not romantic at all like you'd think from the 'Arabian Nights!' Of course, it's pretty just on the river, but the town itself is just awful—and no proper shops at all. Major Kelsey took me through the bazaars, and of course there's no denying they're quaint—but just a lot of rubbish and hammering away at copper pans till they make your head ache—and not what I'd like to use myself unless I was sure about the cleaning. You've got to be so careful of verdigris with copper pans.

"I'll write and let you know if anything comes of the job that Dr Reilly spoke about. He said this American gentleman was in Baghdad now and might come and see me this afternoon. It's for his wife—she has 'fancies,' so Dr Reilly said. He didn't say any more than that, and of course, dear, one knows what that usually means (but I hope not actually D.T.'s!) Of course, Dr. Reilly didn't say anything—but he had a look—if you know what I mean. This Dr Leidner is an archæologist and is digging up a mound out in the desert somewhere for some American museum.

"Well, dear, I will close now. I thought what you told me about little Stubbins was simply killing! *Whatever did Matron say?*

"No more now.

> *"Yours ever,*
> *"Amy Leatheran."*

Enclosing the letter in an envelope, she addressed it to Sister Curshaw, St Christopher's Hospital, London.

As she put the cap on her fountain-pen, one of the native boys approached her.

"A gentleman come see you. Dr Leidner."

Nurse Leatheran turned. She saw a man of middle height with slightly stooping shoulders, a brown beard and gentle tired eyes.

Dr Leidner saw a woman of thirty-five of erect, confident bearing. He saw a good-humoured face with slightly prominent blue eyes and glossy brown hair. She looked, he thought, just what a hospital nurse for a nervous case ought to look. Cheerful, robust, shrewd and matter of fact.

Nurse Leatheran, he thought, would do.

2. Introducing Amy Leatheran

I DON'T PRETEND to be an author or to know anything about writing. I'm doing this simply because Dr Reilly asked me to, and somehow when Dr Reilly asks you to a thing you don't like to refuse.

"Oh, but, doctor," I said, "I'm not literary—not literary at all."

"Nonsense!" he said. "Treat it as case notes, if you like."

Well, of course, you *can* look at it that way.

Dr Reilly went on. He said that an unvarnished plain account of the Tell Yarimjah business was badly needed.

"If one of the interested parties writes it, it won't carry conviction. They'll say it's biased one way or another."

And of course that was true, too. I was in it all and yet an outsider, so to speak.

"Why don't you write it yourself, doctor?" I asked.

"I wasn't on the spot—you were. Besides," he added with a sigh, "my daughter won't let me."

The way he knuckles under to that chit of a girl of his is downright disgraceful. I had half a mind to say so, when I saw that his eyes were twinkling. That was the worst of Dr Reilly. You never knew whether he was joking or not. He always said things in the same slow melancholy way—but half the time there was a twinkle underneath it.

"Well," I said doubtfully. "I suppose I *could*."

"Of course you could."

"Only I don't quite know how to set about it."

"There's a good precedent for that. Begin at the beginning, go on to the end and then leave off."

"I don't even know quite where and what the beginning was," I said doubtfully.

"Believe me, nurse, the difficulty of beginning will be

nothing to the difficulty of knowing how to stop. At least that's the way it is with me when I have to make a speech. Some one's got to catch hold of my coat-tails and pull me down by main force."

"Oh, you're joking, doctor."

"It's profoundly serious I am. Now what about it?"

Another thing was worrying me. After hesitating a moment or two I said:

"You know, doctor, I'm afraid I might tend to be—well, a little *personal* sometimes."

"God bless my soul, woman, the more personal you are the better! This is a story of human beings—not dummies! Be personal—be prejudiced—be catty—be anything you please! Write the thing your own way. We can always prune out the bits that are libellous afterwards! You go ahead. You're a sensible woman, and you'll give a sensible common-sense account of the business."

So that was that, and I promised to do my best.

And here I am beginning, but as I said to the doctor, it's difficult to know just where to start.

I suppose I ought to say a word or two about myself. I'm thirty-two and my name is Amy Leatheran. I took my training at St Christopher's and after that did two years maternity. I did a certain amount of private work and I was for four years at Miss Bendix's Nursing Home in Devonshire Place. I came out to Iraq with a Mrs Kelsey. I'd attended her when her baby was born. She was coming out to Baghdad with her husband and had already got a children's nurse booked who had been for some years with friends of hers out there. Their children were coming home and going to school, and the nurse had agreed to go to Mrs Kelsey when they left. Mrs Kelsey was delicate and nervous about the journey out with so young a child, so Major Kelsey arranged that I should come out with her and look after her and the baby. They would pay my passage home unless we found some one needing a nurse for the return journey.

Well, there is no need to describe the Kelseys—the baby was a little love and Mrs Kelsey quite nice, though rather the fretting kind. I enjoyed the voyage very much. I'd never been a long trip on the sea before.

Dr Reilly was on board the boat. He was a black-haired, long-faced man who said all sorts of funny things in a low, sad voice. I think he enjoyed pulling my leg and used to make the most extraordinary statements to see if I would swallow them. He was the civil surgeon at a place called Hassanieh—a day and a half's journey from Baghdad.

I had been about a week in Baghdad when I ran across him and he asked when I was leaving the Kelseys. I said that it was funny his asking that because as a matter of fact the Wrights (the other people I mentioned) were going home earlier than they had meant to and their nurse was free to come straightaway.

He said that he had heard about the Wrights and that that was why he had asked me.

"As a matter of fact, nurse, I've got a possible job for you."

"A case?"

He screwed his face up as though considering.

"You could hardly call it a case. It's just a lady who has—shall we say—fancies?"

"Oh!" I said.

(One usually knows what *that* means—drink or drugs!)

Dr Reilly didn't explain further. He was very discreet.

"Yes," he said. "A Mrs Leidner. Husband's an American—an American Swede to be exact. He's the head of a large American dig."

And he explained how his expedition was excavating the site of a big Assyrian city something like Nineveh. The expedition house was not actually very far from Hassanieh, but it was a lonely spot and Dr Leidner had been worried for some time about his wife's health.

"He's not been very explicit about it, but it seems she has these fits of recurring nervous terrors."

"Is she left alone all day amongst natives?" I asked.

"Oh, no, there's quite a crowd—seven or eight. I don't fancy she's ever alone in the house. But there seems to be no doubt that she's worked herself up into a queer state. Leidner has any amount of work on his shoulders, but he's crazy about his wife and it worries him to know she's in this state. He felt he'd be happier if he knew that some responsible person with expert knowledge was keeping an eye on her."

"And what does Mrs Leidner herself think about it?"

Dr Reilly answered gravely.

"Mrs Leidner is a very lovely lady. She's seldom of the same mind about anything two days on end. But on the whole she favours the idea." He added, "She's an odd woman. A mass of affectation and, I should fancy, a champion liar—but Leidner seems honestly to believe that she is scared out of her life by something or other."

"What did she herself say to you, doctor?"

"Oh, she hasn't consulted me! She doesn't like me anyway— for several reasons. It was Leidner who came to me and propounded this plan. Well, nurse, what do you think of the idea? You'd see something of the country before you go home— they'll be digging for another two months. And excavation is quite interesting work."

After a moment's hesitation while I turned the matter over in my mind:

"Well," I said. "I really think I might try it."

"Splendid," said Dr Reilly, rising. "Leidner's in Baghdad now. I'll tell him to come round and see if he can fix things up with you."

Dr Leidner came to the hotel that afternoon. He was a middle-aged man with a rather nervous, hesitating manner. There was something gentle and kindly and rather helpless about him.

He sounded very devoted to his wife, but he was very vague about what was the matter with her.

"You see," he said, tugging at his beard in a rather perplexed manner that I later came to know to be characteristic of him, "my wife is really in a very nervous state. I—I'm quite worried about her."

"She is in good physical health?" I asked.

"Yes—oh, yes, I think so. No, I should not think there was anything the matter with her physically. But she—well— imagines things, you know."

"What kind of things?" I asked.

But he shied off from the point, merely murmuring perplexedly:

"She works herself up over nothing at all. . . . I really can see no foundations for these fears."

16

"Fears of what, Dr Leidner?"

He said vaguely, "Oh, just—nervous terrors, you know."

Ten to one, I thought to myself, it's drugs. And he doesn't realise it! Lots of men don't. Just wonder why their wives are so jumpy and have such extraordinary changes of mood.

I asked whether Mrs Leidner herself approved of the idea of my coming.

His face lighted up.

"Yes. I was surprised. Most pleasurably surprised. She said it was a very good idea. She said she would feel very much safer."

The word struck me oddly. *Safer*. A very queer word to use. I began to surmise that Mrs Leidner might be a mental case.

He went on with a kind of boyish eagerness.

"I'm sure you'll get on very well with her. She's really a very charming woman." He smiled disarmingly. "She feels you'll be the greatest comfort to her. I felt the same as soon as I saw you. You look, if you will allow me to say so, so splendidly healthy and full of common sense. I'm sure you're just the person for Louise."

"Well, we can but try, Dr Leidner," I said cheerfully. "I'm sure I hope I can be of use to your wife. Perhaps she's nervous of natives and coloured people?"

"Oh, dear me no." He shook his head, amused at the idea. "My wife likes Arabs very much—she appreciates their simplicity and their sense of humour. This is only her second season—we have been married less than two years—but she already speaks quite a fair amount of Arabic."

I was silent for a moment or two, then I had one more try.

"Can't you tell me at all what it is your wife is afraid of, Dr Leidner?" I asked.

He hesitated. Then he said slowly, "I hope—I believe—that she will tell you that herself."

And that's all I could get out of him.

3. Gossip

IT WAS ARRANGED that I should go to Tell Yarimjah the following week.

Mrs Kelsey was settling into her house at Alwiyah, and I was glad to be able to take a few things off her shoulders.

During that time I heard one or two allusions to the Leidner expedition. A friend of Mrs Kelsey's, a young squadron-leader, pursed his lips in surprise as he exclaimed:

"Lovely Louise. So that's her latest!" He turned to me. "That's our nickname for her, nurse. She's always known as Lovely Louise."

"Is she so very handsome then?" I asked.

"It's taking her at her own valuation. *She* thinks she is!"

"Now don't be spiteful, John," said Mrs Kelsey. "you know it's not only she who thinks so! Lots of people have been very smitten by her."

"Perhaps you're right. She's a bit long in the tooth, but she has a certain attraction."

"You were completely bowled over yourself," said Mrs Kelsey, laughing.

The squadron-leader blushed and admitted rather shame-facedly:

"Well, she has a way with her. As for Leidner himself, he worships the ground she walks on—and all the rest of the expedition has to worship too! It's expected of them!"

"How many are there altogether?" I asked

"All sorts and nationalities, nurse," said the squadron-leader cheerfully. "An English architect, a French Father from Carthage—he does the inscriptions—tablets and things, you know. And then there's Miss Johnson. She's English too—sort of general bottle-washer. And a little plump man who does the photography—he's an American. And the Mercados. Heaven knows what nationality they are—Dagos of some kind! She's

18

quite young—a snaky-looking creature—and oh! doesn't she hate Lovely Louise! And there are a couple of youngsters, and that's the lot. A few odd fish, but nice on the whole—don't you agree, Pennyman?"

He was appealing to an elderly man who was sitting thoughtfully twirling a pair of pince-nez.

The latter started and looked up.

"Yes—yes—very nice indeed. Taken individually, that is. Of course, Mercado is rather a queer fish——"

"He has such a very *odd* beard," put in Mrs Kelsey. "A queer limp kind."

Major Pennyman went on without noticing her interruption.

"The young 'uns are both nice. The American's rather silent, and the English boy talks a bit too much. Funny, it's usually the other way round. Leidner himself is a delightful fellow—so modest and unassuming. Yes, individually they are all pleasant people. But somehow or other, I may have been fanciful, but the last time I went to see them I got a queer impression of something being wrong. I don't know what it was exactly. . . . Nobody seemed quite natural. There was a queer atmosphere of tension. I can explain best what I mean by saying that they all passed the butter to each other too politely."

Blushing a little, because I don't like airing my own opinions too much, I said:

"If people are too much cooped up together it's got a way of getting on their nerves. I know that myself from experience in hospital."

"That's true," said Major Kelsey, "but it's early in the season, hardly time for that particular irritation to have set in."

"An expedition is probably like our life here in miniature," said Major Pennyman. "It has its cliques and rivalries and jealousies."

"It sounds as though they'd got a good many new-comers this year," said Major Kelsey.

"Let me see." The squadron-leader counted them off on his fingers. "Young Coleman is new, so is Reiter. Emmott was out last year and so were the Mercados. Father Lavigny is a new-comer. He's come in place of Dr Byrd, who was ill this year and couldn't come out. Carey, of course, is an old hand. He's been out ever since the beginning, five years ago. Miss Johnson's been out nearly as many years as Carey."

"I always thought they got on so well together at Tell Yarimjah," remarked Major Kelsey. "They seemed like a happy family—which is really surprising when one considers what human nature is! I'm sure Nurse Leatheran agrees with me."

"Well," I said. "I don't know that you're not right! The rows I've known in hospital and starting often from nothing more than a dispute about a pot of tea."

"Yes, one tends to get petty in close communities," said Major Pennyman. "All the same I feel there must be something more to it in this case. Leidner is such a gentle, unassuming man, with really a remarkable amount of tact. He's always managed to keep his expedition happy and on good terms with each other. And yet I *did* notice that feeling of tension the other day."

Mrs Kelsey laughed.

"And you don't see the explanation? Why, it leaps to the eye!"

"What do you mean?"

"*Mrs* Leidner, of course."

"Oh come, Mary," said her husband, "she's a charming woman—not at all the quarrelsome kind."

"I didn't say she was quarrelsome. She *causes* quarrels!"

"In what way? And why should she?"

"Why? Why? Because she's bored. She's not an archæologist, only the wife of one. She's bored shut away from any excitements and so she provides her own drama. She amuses herself by setting other people by the ears."

"Mary, you don't know in the least. You're merely imagining."

"Of course I'm imagining! But you'll find I'm right. Lovely Louise doesn't look like the Mona Lisa for nothing. She mayn't mean any harm, but she likes to see what will happen."

"She's devoted to Leidner."

"Oh! I dare say. I'm not suggesting vulgar intrigues. But she's an *allumeuse*, that woman."

"Woman are so sweet to each other," said Major Kelsey.

"I know. Cat, cat, cat, that's what you men say. But we're usually right about our own sex."

"All the same," said Major Pennyman thoughtfully, "assuming all Mrs Kelsey's uncharitable surmises to be true I don't think it would quite account for that curious sense of tension—rather like the feeling there is before a thunderstorm. I had the impression very strongly that the storm might break any minute."

"Now don't frighten nurse," said Mrs Kelsey. "She's going there in three days' time and you'll put her right off."

"Oh, you won't frighten me," I said, laughing.

All the same I thought a good deal about what had been said. Dr Leidner's curious use of the word "safer" recurred to me. Was it his wife's secret fear, unacknowledged or expressed perhaps, that was reacting on the rest of the party? Or was it the actual tension (or perhaps the unknown cause of it) that was reacting on *her* nerves?

I looked up the word "allumeuse" that Mrs Kelsey had used in a dictionary, but couldn't get any sense out of it.

"Well," I thought to myself, "I must wait and see."

4. I Arrive in Hassanieh

THREE DAYS LATER I left Baghdad.

I was sorry to leave Mrs Kelsey and the baby, who was a little love and was thriving splendidly, gaining her proper number of ounces every week. Major Kelsey took me to the station and saw me off. I should arrive at Kirkuk the following morning, and there some one was to meet me.

I slept badly. I never sleep very well in a train and I was troubled by dreams.

The next morning, however, when I looked out of the window it was a lovely day and I felt interested and curious about the people I was going to see.

As I stood on the platform hesitating and looking about me I saw a young man coming towards me. He had a round pink face, and really, in all my life, I have never seen any one who seemed so exactly like a young man out of one of Mr P. G. Wodehouse's books.

"Hallo, 'allo, 'allo," he said. "Are you Nurse Leatheran? Well, I mean you must be—I can see that. Ha ha! My name's Coleman. Dr Leidner sent me along. How are you feeling? Beastly journey and all that? Don't I know these trains! Well, here we are—had any breakfast? This your kit? I say, awfully modest, aren't you? Mrs Leidner has four suitcases and a trunk—to say nothing of a hat-box and a patent pillow, and this, that and the other. Am I talking too much? Come along to the old bus."

There was what I heard called later a station wagon waiting outside. It was a little like a wagonette, a little like a lorry and a little like a car. Mr Coleman helped me in, explaining that I had better sit next to the driver so as to get less jolting.

Jolting! I wonder the whole contraption didn't fall to pieces! And nothing like a road—just a sort of track all ruts and holes.

Glorious East indeed! When I thought of our splendid arterial roads in England it made me quite homesick.

Mr Coleman leaned forward from his seat behind me and yelled in my ear a good deal.

"Track's in pretty good condition," he shouted just after we had all been thrown up in our seats till we nearly touched the roof.

And apparently he was speaking quite seriously.

"Very good for you—jogs the liver," he said. "You ought to know that, nurse."

"A stimulated liver won't be much good to me if my head's split open," I observed tartly.

"You should come along here after it's rained! The skids are glorious. Most of the time one's going sideways."

To this I did not respond.

Presently we had to cross the river, which we did on the craziest ferry-boat you can imagine. To my mind it was a mercy we ever got across, but every one seemed to think it was quite usual.

It took us about four hours to get to Hassanieh, which, to my surprise, was quite a big place. Very pretty it looked, too, before we got there from the other side of the river—standing up quite white and fairy-like with minarets. It was a bit different, though, when one had crossed the bridge and come right into it. Such a smell, and everything ramshackle and tumble-down, and mud and mess everywhere.

Mr Coleman took me to Dr Reilly's house, where, he said, the doctor was expecting me to lunch.

Dr Reilly was just as nice as ever, and his house was nice too, with a bathroom and everything spick and span. I had a nice bath, and by the time I got back into my uniform and came down I was feeling fine.

Lunch was just ready and we went in, the doctor apologising for his daughter, whom he said was always late.

We'd just had a very good dish of eggs in sauce when she came in and Dr Reilly said, "Nurse, this is my daughter Sheila."

She shook hands, hoped I'd had a good journey, tossed off her hat, gave a cool nod to Mr Coleman and sat down.

"Well, Bill," she said. "How's everything?"

He began to talk to her about some party or other that was to come off at the club, and I took stock of her.

I can't say I took to her much. A thought too cool for my liking. An off-hand sort of girl, though good-looking. Black hair and blue eyes—a pale sort of face and the usual lip-sticked mouth. She'd a cool, sarcastic way of talking that rather annoyed me. I had a probationer like her under me once—a girl who worked well, I'll admit, but whose manner always riled me.

It looked to me rather as though Mr Coleman was gone on her. He stammered a bit, and his conversation became slightly more idiotic than it was before, if that was possible! He reminded me of a large stupid dog wagging its tail and trying to please.

After lunch Dr Reilly went off to the hospital, and Mr Coleman had some things to get in the town, and Miss Reilly asked me whether I'd like to see round the town a bit or whether I'd rather stop in the house. Mr Coleman, she said, would be back to fetch me in about an hour.

"Is there anything to see?" I asked.

"There are some picturesque corners," said Miss Reilly. "But I don't know that you'd care for them. They're extremely dirty."

The way she said it rather nettled me. I've never been able to see that picturesqueness excuses dirt.

In the end she took me to the club, which was pleasant enough, overlooking the river, and there were English papers and magazines there.

When we got back to the house Mr Coleman wasn't there yet, so we sat down and talked a bit. It wasn't easy somehow.

She asked me if I'd met Mrs Leidner yet.

"No," I said. "Only her husband."

"Oh," she said. "I wonder what you'll think of her?"

I didn't say anything to that. And she went on:

"I like Dr Leidner very much. Everybody likes him."

That's as good as saying, I thought, that you don't like his wife.

I still didn't say anything and presently she asked abruptly:

"What's the matter with her? Did Dr Leidner tell you?"

I wasn't going to start gossiping about a patient before I got there even, so I said evasively:

"I understand she's a bit run down and wants looking after."

She laughed—a nasty sort of laugh—hard and abrupt.

"Good God," she said. "Aren't nine people looking after her already enough?"

"I suppose they've all got their work to do," I said.

"Work to do? Of course they've got work to do. But Louise comes first—she sees to that all right."

"No," I said to myself. "You *don't* like her."

"All the same," went on Miss Reilly, "I don't see what she wants with a professional hospital nurse. I should have thought amateur assistance was more in her line; not some one who'll jam a thermometer in her mouth, and count her pulse and bring everything down to hard facts."

Well, I must admit it, I was curious.

"You think there's nothing the matter with her?" I asked.

"Of course there's nothing the matter with her! The woman's as strong as an ox. 'Dear Louise hasn't slept.' 'She's got black circles under her eyes.' Yes—put there with a blue pencil! Anything to get attention, to have everybody hovering round her, making a fuss of her!"

There was something in that, of course. I had (what nurse hasn't?) come across many cases of hypochondriacs whose delight it is to keep a whole household dancing attendance. And if a doctor or a nurse were to say to them "there's nothing on earth the matter with you!" Well, to begin with they wouldn't believe it, and their indignation would be as genuine as indignation can be.

Of course it was quite possible that Mrs Leidner might be a case of this kind. The husband, naturally, would be the first to be deceived. Husbands, I've found, are a credulous lot where illness is concerned. But all the same, it didn't quite square with what I'd heard. It did'nt, for instance, fit in with that word "safer."

Funny how that word had got kind of stuck in my mind.

Reflecting on it, I asked:

"Is Mrs Leidner a nervous woman? Is she nervous, for instance, of living out far from anywhere?"

"What is there to be nervous of? Good heavens, there are ten of them! And they've got guards too—because of the antiquities. Oh no, she's not nervous—at least——"

25

She seemed struck by some thought and stopped—going on slowly after a minute or two.

"It's odd your saying that."

"Why?"

"Flight-Lieutenant Jervis and I rode over the other day. It was in the morning. Most of them were up on the dig. She was sitting writing a letter and I suppose she didn't hear us coming. The boy who brings you in wasn't about for once, and we came straight up on to the verandah. Apparently she saw Flight-Lieutenant Jervis's shadow thrown on the wall—and she fairly screamed! Apologised, of course. Said she thought it was a strange man. A bit odd, that. I mean, even if it was a strange man, why get the wind up?"

I nodded thoughtfully.

Miss Reilly was silent, then burst out suddenly.

"I don't know what's the matter with them there this year. They've all got the jumps. Johnson goes about so glum she can't open her mouth. David never speaks if he can help it. Bill, of course, never stops, and somehow his chatter seems to make the others worse. Carey goes about looking as though something would snap any minute. And they all watch each other as though—as though— Oh, I don't know, but it's *queer*."

It was odd, I thought, that two such dissimilar people as Miss Reilly and Major Pennyman should have been struck in the same manner.

Just then Mr Coleman came bustling in. Bustling was just the word for it. If his tongue had hung out and he had suddenly produced a tail to wag you wouldn't have been surprised.

"Hallo-allo," he said. "Absolutely the world's best shopper—that's me. Have you shown nurse all the beauties of the town?"

"She wasn't impressed," said Miss Reilly dryly.

"I don't blame her," said Mr Coleman heartily. "Of all the one-horse tumble-down places!"

"Not a lover of the picturesque or the antique, are you, Bill? I can't think why you are an archæologist."

"Don't blame me for that. Blame my guardian. He's a learned bird—fellow of his college—browses among books in bedroom slippers—that kind of man. Bit of a shock for him to have a ward like me."

26

"I think it's frightfully stupid of you to be forced into a profession you don't care for," said the girl sharply.

"Not forced, Sheila, old girl, not forced. The old man asked if I had any special profession in mind, and I said I hadn't, and so he wangled a season out here for me."

"But haven't you any idea really what you'd *like* to do? You *must* have!"

"Of course I have. My idea would be to give work a miss altogether. What I'd like to do is to have plenty of money and go in for motor-racing."

"You're absurd!" said Miss Reilly.

She sounded quite angry.

"Oh, I realise that it's quite out of the question," said Mr Coleman cheerfully. "So, if I've got to do something, I don't much care what it is so long as it isn't mugging in an office all day long. I was quite agreeable to seeing a bit of the world. Here goes, I said, and along I came."

"And a fat lot of use you must be, I expect!"

"There you're wrong. I can stand up on the dig and shout '*Y'Allah*' with anybody! And as a matter of fact I'm not so dusty at drawing. Imitating handwriting used to be my speciality at school. I'd have made a first-class forger. Oh, well, I may come to that yet. If my Rolls-Royce splashes you with mud as you're waiting for a bus, you'll know that I've taken to crime."

Miss Reilly said coldly:

"Don't you think it's about time you started instead of talking so much?"

"Hospitable, aren't we, nurse?"

"I'm sure Nurse Leatheran is anxious to get settled in."

"You're always sure of everything," retorted Mr Coleman with a grin.

That was true enough, I thought. Cock-sure little minx.

I said dryly:

"Perhaps we'd better start, Mr Coleman."

"Right you are, nurse."

I shook hands with Miss Reilly and thanked her, and we set off.

"Damned attractive girl, Sheila," said Mr Coleman. "But always ticking a fellow off."

We drove out of the town and presently took a kind of track between green crops. It was very bumpy and full of ruts.

After about half an hour Mr Coleman pointed to a big mound by the river bank ahead of us and said:

"Tell Yarimjah."

I could see little black figures moving about it like ants.

As I was looking they suddenly began to run all together down the side of the mound.

"Fidos," said Mr Coleman. "Knocking-off-time. We knock off an hour before sunset."

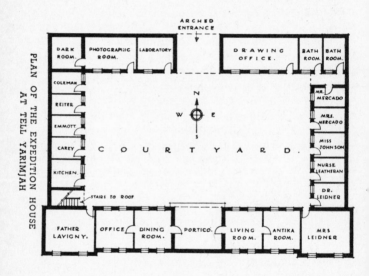

The expedition house lay a little back from the river.

The driver rounded a corner, bumped through an extremely narrow arch and there we were.

The house was built round a courtyard. Originally it had occupied only the south side of the courtyard with a few unimportant out-buildings on the east. The expedition had continued the building on the other two sides. As the plan of the

28

house was to prove of special interest later, I append a rough sketch of it here.

All the rooms opened on to the courtyard, and most of the windows—the exception being in the original south building where there were windows giving on the outside country as well. These windows, however, were barred on the outside. In the south-west corner a staircase ran up to a long flat roof with a parapet running the length of the south side of the building which was higher than the other three sides.

Mr Coleman led me along the east side of the courtyard and round to where a big open verandah occupied the centre of the south side. He pushed open a door at one side of it and we entered a room where several people were sitting round a tea-table.

"Toodle-oodle-oo!" said Mr Coleman. "Here's Sairey Gamp."

The lady who was sitting at the head of the table rose and came to greet me.

I had my first glimpse of Louise Leidner.

5. Tell Yarimjah

I DON'T mind admitting that my first impression on seeing Mrs Leidner was one of downright surprise. One gets into the way of imagining a person when one hears them talked about. I'd got it firmly into my head that Mrs Leidner was a dark, discontented kind of woman. The nervy kind, all on edge. And then, too, I'd expected her to be—well, to put it frankly—a bit vulgar.

She wasn't a bit like what I'd imagined her! To begin with, she was very fair. She wasn't a Swede, like her husband, but she might have been as far as looks went. She had that blonde Scandinavian fairness that you don't very often see. She wasn't a young woman. Midway between thirty and forty, I should say. Her face was rather haggard, and there was some grey hair mingled with the fairness. Her eyes, though, were lovely. They were the only eyes I've ever come across that you might truly describe as violet. They were very large, and there were faint shadows underneath them. She was very thin and fragile-looking, and if I say that she had an air of intense weariness and was at the same time very much alive, it sounds like nonsense—but that's the feeling I got. I felt, too, that she was a lady through and through. And that means something—even nowadays.

She put out her hand and smiled. Her voice was low and soft with an American drawl in it.

"I'm so glad you've come, nurse. Will you have some tea? Or would you like to go to your room first?"

I said I'd have tea, and she introduced me to the people sitting round the table.

"This is Miss Johnson—and Mr Reiter. Mrs Mercado. Mr Emmott. Father Lavigny. My husband will be in presently. Sit down here between Father Lavigny and Miss Johnson."

I did as I was bid and Miss Johnson began talking to me, asking about my journey and so on.

I liked her. She reminded me of a matron I'd had in my probationer days whom we had all admired and worked hard for.

She was getting on for fifty, I should judge, and rather mannish in appearance, with iron-grey hair cropped short. She had an abrupt, pleasant voice, rather deep in tone. She had an ugly rugged face with an almost laughably turned-up nose which she was in the habit of rubbing irritably when anything troubled or perplexed her. She wore a tweed coat and skirt made rather like a man's. She told me presently that she was a native of Yorkshire.

Father Lavigny I found just a bit alarming. He was a tall man with a great black beard and pince-nez. I had heard Mrs Kelsey say that there was a French monk there, and I now saw that Father Lavigny was wearing a monk's robe of some white woollen material. It surprised me rather, because I always understood that monks went into monasteries and didn't come out again.

Mrs Leidner talked to him mostly in French, but he spoke to me in quite fair English. I noticed that he had shrewd, observant eyes which darted about from face to face.

Opposite me were the other three. Mr Reiter was a stout, fair young man with glasses. His hair was rather long and curly, and he had very round blue eyes. I should think he must have been a lovely baby, but he wasn't much to look at now! In fact he was just a little like a pig. The other young man had very short hair cropped close to his head. He had a long, rather humorous face and very good teeth, and he looked very attractive when he smiled. He said very little, though, just nodded if spoken to or answered in monosyllables. He, like Mr Reiter, was an American. The last person was Mrs Mercado, and I couldn't have a good look at her because whenever I glanced in her direction I always found her staring at me with a kind of hungry stare that was a bit disconcerting to say the least of it. You might have thought a hospital nurse was a strange animal the way she was looking at me. No manners at all!

She was quite young—not more than about twenty-five—and sort of dark and slinky-looking, if you know what I mean. Quite nice-looking in a kind of way, but rather as though she might have what my mother used to call "a touch of the tarbrush." She had on a very vivid pullover and her nails matched it in colour. She had a thin bird-like eager face with big eyes and rather a tight, suspicious mouth.

The tea was very good—a nice strong blend—not like the weak China stuff that Mrs Kelsey always had and that had been a sore trial to me.

There was toast and jam and a plate of rock buns and a cutting cake. Mr Emmott was very polite passing me things. Quiet as he was he always seemed to notice when my plate was empty.

Presently Mr Coleman bustled in and took the place beyond Miss Johnson. There didn't seem to be anything the matter with *his* nerves. He talked away nineteen to the dozen.

Mrs Leidner sighed once and cast a wearied look in his direction but it didn't have any effect. Nor did the fact that Mrs Mercado, to whom he was addressing most of his conversation, was far too busy watching me to do more than make perfunctory replies.

Just as we were finishing, Dr Leidner and Mr Mercado came in from the dig.

Dr Leidner greeted me in his nice kind manner. I saw his eyes go quickly and anxiously to his wife's face and he seemed to be relieved by what he saw there. Then he sat down at the other end of the table and Mr Mercado sat down in the vacant place by Mrs Leidner. He was a tall, thin, melancholy man, a good deal older than his wife, with a sallow complexion and a queer, soft, shapeless-looking beard. I was glad when he came in, for his wife stopped staring at me and transferred her attention to him, watching him with a kind of anxious impatience that I found rather odd. He himself stirred his tea dreamily and said nothing at all. A piece of cake lay untasted on his plate.

There was still one vacant place, and presently the door opened and a man came in.

The moment I saw Richard Carey I felt he was one of the handsomest men I'd seen for a long time—and yet I doubt if that were really so. To say a man is handsome and at the same time to say he looks like a death's head sounds a rank contradiction, and yet it was true. His head gave the effect of having the skin stretched unusually tightly over the bones—but they were beautiful bones. The lean line of jaw and temple and forehead was so sharply outlined that he reminded me of a bronze statue. Out of this lean brown face looked two of the brightest and most intensely blue eyes I have ever seen. He stood about six foot and was, I should imagine, a little under forty years of age.

Dr Leidner said:

"This is Mr Carey, our architect, nurse."

He murmured something in a pleasant, inaudible English voice and sat down by Mrs Mercado.

Mrs Leidner said:

"I'm afraid the tea is a little cold, Mr Carey."

He said: "Oh, that's quite all right, Mrs Leidner. My fault for being late. I wanted to finish plotting those walls."

Mrs Mercado said, "Jam, Mr Carey?"

Mr Reiter pushed forward the toast.

And I remember Major Pennyman saying:

"I can explain best what I mean by saying that they all passed the butter to each other a shade too politely."

Yes, there was something a little odd about it. . . .

A shade formal. . . .

You'd have said it was a party of strangers—not people who had known each other—some of them—for quite a number of years.

6. First Evening

AFTER TEA Mrs Leidner took me to show me my room.

Perhaps here I had better give a short description of the arrangement of the rooms. This was very simple and can easily be understood by a reference to the plan.

On either side of the big open porch were doors leading into the two principal rooms. That on the right led into the dining-room, where we had had tea. The one on the other side led into an exactly similar room (I have called it the living-room) which was used as a sitting-room and kind of informal workroom— that is, a certain amount of drawing (other than the strictly architectural) was done there, and the more delicate pieces of pottery were brought there to be pieced together. Through the living-room one passed into the antiquities-room where all the finds from the dig were brought in and stored on shelves and in pigeon-holes, and also laid out on big benches and tables. From the antika-room there was no exit save through the living-room.

Beyond the antika-room, but reached through a door which gave on the courtyard, was Mrs Leidner's bedroom. This, like the other rooms on that side of the house, had a couple of barred windows looking out over the ploughed countryside. Round the corner next to Mrs Leidner's room, but with no actual communicating door, was Dr Leidner's room. This was the first of the rooms on the east side of the building. Next to it was the room that was to be mine. Next to me was Miss Johnson's, with Mr and Mrs Mercado's beyond. After that came two so-called bathrooms.

(When I once used that last term in the hearing of Dr Reilly he laughed at me and said a bathroom was either a bathroom or not a bathroom! All the same, when you've got used to taps and proper plumbing, it seems strange to call a couple of mud-rooms with a tin hip-bath in each of them, and muddy water brought in kerosene tins, *bathrooms*!)

34

All this side of the building had been added by Dr Leidner to the original Arab house. The bedrooms were all the same, each with a window and a door giving on to the courtyard.

Along the north side were the drawing office, the laboratory and the photographic rooms.

To return to the verandah, the arrangement of rooms was much the same on the other side. There was the dining-room leading into the office where the files were kept and the cataloguing and typing was done. Corresponding to Mrs Leidner's room was that of Father Lavigny, who was given the largest bedroom; he used it also for the decoding—or whatever you call it—of tablets.

In the south-west corner was the staircase running up to the roof. On the west side were first the kitchen quarters and then four small bedrooms used by the young men—Carey, Emmott, Reiter and Coleman.

At the north-west corner was the photographic-room with the dark-room leading out of it. Next to that the laboratory. Then came the only entrance—the big arched doorway through which we had entered. Outside were sleeping quarters for the native servants, the guard-house for the soldiers, and stables, etc., for the water horses. The drawing-office was to the right of the archway occupying the rest of the north side.

I have gone into the arrangements of the house rather fully here because I don't want to have to go over them again later.

As I say, Mrs Leidner herself took me round the building and finally established me in my bedroom, hoping that I should be comfortable and have everything I wanted.

The room was nicely though plainly furnished—a bed, a chest of drawers, a wash-stand and a chair.

"The boys will bring you hot water before lunch and dinner—and in the morning, of course. If you want it any other time, go outside and clap your hands, and when the boy comes say, *jib mai' har*. Do you think you can remember that?"

I said I thought so and repeated it a little haltingly.

"That's right. And be sure and shout it. Arabs don't understand anything said in an ordinary 'English' voice."

"Languages are funny things," I said. "It seems odd there should be such a lot of different ones."

Mrs Leidner smiled.

"There is a church in Palestine in which the Lord's Prayer is written up in—ninety, I think it is—different languages."

"Well!" I said, "I must write and tell my old aunt that. She *will* be interested."

Mrs Leidner fingered the jug and basin absently and shifted the soap-dish an inch or two.

"I do hope you'll be happy here," she said. "And not get too bored."

"I'm not often bored," I assured her. "Life's not long enough for that."

She did not answer. She continued to toy with the wash-stand as though abstractedly.

Suddenly she fixed her dark violet eyes on my face.

"What exactly did my husband tell you, nurse?"

Well, one usually says the same thing to a question of that kind.

"I gathered you were a bit run-down and all that, Mrs Leidner," I said glibly. "And that you just wanted some one to look after you and take any worries off your hands."

She bent her head slowly and thoughtfully.

"Yes," she said. "Yes—that will do very well."

That was just a little bit enigmatic, but I wasn't going to question it. Instead I said:

"I hope you'll let me help you with anything there is to do in the house. You mustn't let me be idle."

She smiled a little.

"Thank you, nurse."

Then she sat down on the bed and, rather to my surprise, began to cross-question me rather closely. I say rather to my surprise because, from the moment I set eyes on her, I felt sure that Mrs Leidner was a lady. And a lady, in my experience, very seldom displays curiosity about one's private affairs.

But Mrs Leidner seemed anxious to know everything there was to know about me. Where I'd trained and how long ago. What had brought me out to the East. How it had come about that Dr Reilly had recommended me. She even asked me if I had ever been in America or had any relations in America. One or two other questions she asked me that seemed quite purposeless at the time, but of which I saw the significance later.

Then, suddenly, her manner changed. She smiled—a warm sunny smile—and she said, very sweetly, that she was very glad I had come and that she was sure I was going to be a comfort to her.

She got up from the bed and said:

"Would you like to come up to the roof and see the sunset? It's usually very lovely about this time."

I agreed willingly.

As we went out of the room she asked:

"Were there many other people on the train from Baghdad? Any men?"

I said that I hadn't noticed anybody in particular. There had been two Frenchmen in the restaurant-car the night before. And a party of three men whom I gathered from their conversation had to do with the Pipe line.

She nodded and a faint sound escaped her. It sounded like a small sigh of relief.

We went up to the roof together.

Mrs Mercado was there, sitting on the parapet, and Dr Leidner was bending over looking at a lot of stones and broken pottery that were laid out in rows. There were big things he called querns, and pestles and celts and stone axes, and more broken bits of pottery with queer patterns on them than I've ever seen all at once.

"Come over here," called out Mrs Mercado. "Isn't it *too* too beautiful?"

It certainly was a beautiful sunset. Hassanieh in the distance looked quite fairy-like with the setting sun behind it, and the River Tigris flowing between its wide banks looked like a dream river rather than a real one.

"Isn't it lovely, Eric?" said Mrs Leidner.

The doctor looked up with abstracted eyes, murmured, "Lovely, lovely," perfunctorily and went on sorting potsherds.

Mrs. Leidner smiled and said:

"Archæologists only look at what lies beneath their feet. The sky and the heavens don't exist for them.

Mrs Mercado giggled.

"Oh, they're very queer people—you'll soon find *that* out, nurse," she said.

37

She paused and then added:

"We are all *so* glad you've come. We've been so very worried about our dear Mrs Leidner, haven't we, Louise?"

"Have you?"

Her voice was not encouraging.

"Oh, yes. She really has been *very* bad, nurse. All sorts of alarms and excursions. You know when anybody says to me of someone, 'It's just nerves,' I always say: but what could be *worse*? Nerves are the core and centre of one's being, aren't they?"

"Puss, puss," I thought to myself.

Mrs Leidner said dryly:

"Well, you needn't be worried about me any more, Marie. Nurse is going to look after me:

"Certainly I am," I said cheerfully.

"I'm sure that will make all the difference," said Mrs Mercado. "We've all felt that she ought to see a doctor or do *something*. Her nerves have really been all to pieces, haven't they, Louise dear?"

"So much so that I seem to have got on *your* nerves with them," said Mrs Leidner. "Shall we talk about something more interesting than my wretched ailments?"

I understood then that Mrs Leidner was the sort of woman who could easily make enemies. There was a cool rudeness in her tone (not that I blamed her for it) which brought a flush to Mrs Mercado's rather sallow cheeks. She stammered out something, but Mrs Leidner had risen and had joined her husband at the other end of the roof. I doubt if he heard her coming till she laid her hand on his shoulder, then he looked up quickly. There was affection and a kind of eager questioning in his face.

Mrs Leidner nodded her head gently. Presently, her arm through his, they wandered to the far parapet and finally down the steps together.

"He's devoted to her, isn't he?" said Mrs Mercado.

"Yes," I said. "It's very nice to see."

She was looking at me with a queer, rather eager sidelong glance.

"What do you think is really the matter with her, nurse?" she asked, lowering her voice a little.

"Oh, I don't suppose it's much," I said cheerfully. "Just a bit run-down, I expect."

38

Her eyes still bored into me as they had done at tea. She said abruptly:

"Are you a mental nurse?"

"Oh, dear no!" I said. "What made you think that?"

She was silent for a moment, then she said:

"Do you know how queer she's been? Did Dr Leidner tell you?"

I don't hold with gossiping about my cases. On the other hand, it's my experience that it's often very hard to get the truth out of the relatives, and until you know the truth you're often working in the dark and doing no good. Of course, when there's a doctor in charge, it's different. He tells you what it's necessary for you to know. But in this case there wasn't a doctor in charge. Dr Reilly had never been called in professionally. And in my own mind I wasn't at all sure that Dr Leidner had told me all he could have done. It's often the husband's instinct to be reticent— and more honour to him, I say. But all the same, the more I knew the better I could tell which line to take. Mrs Mercado (whom I put down in my own mind as a thoroughly spiteful little cat) was clearly dying to talk. And frankly, on the human side as well as the professional, I wanted to hear what she had to say. You can put it that I was just every-day curious if you like.

I said, "I gather Mrs Leidner's not been quite her normal self lately?"

Mrs Mercado laughed disagreeably.

"Normal? I should say not. Frightening us to death. One night it was fingers tapping on her window. And then it was a hand without an arm attached. But when it came to a yellow face pressed against the window—and when she rushed to the window there was nothing there—well, I ask you, it *is* a bit creepy for all of us."

"Perhaps somebody was playing a trick on her," I suggested.

"Oh, no, she fancied it all. And only three days ago at dinner they were firing off shots in the village—nearly a mile away— and she jumped up and screamed out—it scared us all to death. As for Dr Leidner, he rushed to her and behaved in the most ridiculous way. 'It's nothing, darling, it's nothing at all,' he kept saying. I think, you know, nurse, men sometimes *encourage* women in these hysterical fancies. It's a pity because it's a bad thing. Delusions shouldn't be encouraged."

"Not if they *are* delusions," I said dryly.

"What else could they be?"

I didn't answer because I didn't know what to say. It was a funny business. The shots and the screaming were natural enough—for any one in a nervous condition, that is. But this queer story of a spectral face and hand was different. It looked to me like one of two things—either Mrs Leidner had made the story up (exactly as a child shows off by telling lies about something that never happened in order to make herself the centre of attraction) or else it was, as I had suggested, a deliberate practical joke. It was the sort of thing, I reflected, that an unimaginative hearty sort of young fellow like Mr Coleman might think very funny. I decided to keep a close watch on him. Nervous patients can be scared nearly out of their minds by a silly joke.

Mrs Mercado said with a sideways glance at me:

"She's very romantic-looking, nurse, don't you think so? The sort of woman things *happen* to."

"Have many things happened to her?" I asked.

"Well, her first husband was killed in the war when she was only twenty. I think that's very pathetic and romantic, don't you?"

"It's one way of calling a goose a swan," I said dryly.

"Oh, nurse! What an extraordinary remark!"

It was really a very true one. The amount of women you hear say "If Donald—or Arthur—or whatever his name was—had *only* lived." And I sometimes think but if he had, he'd have been a stout, unromantic, short-tempered, middle-aged husband as likely as not.

It was getting dark and I suggested that we should go down. Mrs Mercado agreed and asked if I would like to see the laboratory. "My husband will be there—working."

I said I would like to very much and we made our way there. The place was lighted by a lamp but it was empty. Mrs Mercado showed me some of the apparatus and some copper ornaments that were being treated, and also some bones coated with wax.

"Where can Joseph be?" said Mrs Mercado.

She looked into the drawing-office, where Carey was at work. He hardly looked up as we entered, and I was struck by the extraordinary look of strain on his face. It came to me suddenly: "This man is at the end of his tether. Very soon, something will snap." And I remembered somebody else had noticed that same tenseness about him.

As we went out again I turned my head for one last look at him. He was bent over his paper, his lips pressed very closely together, and that "death's head" suggestion of his bones very strongly marked. Perhaps it was fanciful, but I thought that he looked like a knight of old who was going into battle and knew he was going to be killed.

And again I felt what an extraordinary and quite unconscious power of attraction he had.

We found Mr Mercado in the living-room. He was explaining the idea of some new process to Mrs Leidner. She was sitting on a straight wooden chair, embroidering flowers in fine silks, and I was struck anew by her strange, fragile, unearthly appearance. She looked a fairy creature more than flesh and blood.

Mrs Mercado said, her voice high and shrill:

"Oh, *there* you are, Joseph. We thought we'd find you in the lab."

He jumped up looking startled and confused, as though her entrance had broken a spell. He said stammeringly:

"I—I must go now. I'm in the middle of—the middle of——"

He didn't complete the sentence but turned towards the door.

Mrs Leidner said in her soft, drawling voice:

"You must finish telling me some other time. It was very interesting."

She looked up at us, smiled rather sweetly but in a far-away manner, and bent over her embroidery again.

In a minute or two she said:

"There are some books over there, nurse. We've got quite a good selection. Choose one and sit down."

I went over to the bookshelf. Mrs Mercado stayed for a minute or two, then, turning abruptly, she went out. As she passed me I saw her face and I didn't like the look of it. She looked wild with fury.

In spite of myself I remembered some of the things Mrs Kelsey had said and hinted about Mrs Leidner. I didn't like to think they were true because I liked Mrs Leidner, but I wondered, nevertheless, if there mightn't perhaps be a grain of truth behind them.

I didn't think it was all her fault, but the fact remained that dear ugly Miss Johnson, and that common little spitfire Mrs Mercado, couldn't hold a candle to her in looks or in attraction. And after all, men are men all over the world. You soon see a lot of that in my profession.

Mercado was a poor fish, and I don't suppose Mrs Leidner really cared two hoots for his admiration—but his wife cared. If I wasn't mistaken, she minded badly and would be quite willing to do Mrs Leidner a bad turn if she could.

I looked at Mrs Leidner sitting there and sewing at her pretty flowers, so remote and far away and aloof. I felt somehow I ought to warn her. I felt that perhaps she didn't know how stupid and unreasoning and violent jealousy and hate can be—and how little it takes to set them smouldering.

And then I said to myself, "Amy Leatheran, you're a fool. Mrs Leidner's no chicken. She's close on forty if she's a day, and she must know all about life there is to know."

But I felt that all the same perhaps she didn't.

She had such a queer untouched look.

I began to wonder what her life had been. I knew she'd only married Dr Leidner two years ago. And according to Mrs Mercado her first husband had died nearly twenty years ago.

I came and sat down near her with a book and presently I went and washed my hands for supper. It was a good meal—some really excellent curry. They all went to bed early and I was glad for I was tired.

Dr Leidner came with me to my room to see if had all I wanted.

He gave me a warm handclasp and said eagerly:

"She likes you, nurse. She's taken to you at once. I'm so glad. I feel everything's going to be all right now."

His eagerness was almost boyish.

I felt, too, that Mrs Leidner had taken a liking to me, and I was pleased it should be so.

But I didn't quite share his confidence. I felt, somehow, that there was more to it all than he himself might know.

There was *something*—something I couldn't get at. But I felt it in the air.

My bed was comfortable, but I didn't sleep well for all that. I dreamt too much.

The words of a poem by Keats, that I'd had to learn as a child, kept running through my head. I kept getting them wrong and it worried me. It was a poem I'd always hated—I suppose because I'd had to learn it whether I wanted to or not. But somehow when I woke up in the dark I saw a sort of beauty in it for the first time.

"Oh say what ails thee, knight at arms, alone—and (what was it?)*—palely loitering . . . ?* I saw the knight's face in my mind for the first time—and it was Mr Carey's face—a grim, tense, bronzed face like some of those poor young men I remembered as a girl during the war . . . and I felt sorry for him—and then I fell off to sleep again and I saw that the Belle Dame sans Merci was Mrs Leidner and she was leaning sideways on a horse with an embroidery of flowers in her hands—and then the horse stumbled and everywhere there were bones coated in wax, and I woke up all goose-flesh and shivering, and told myself that curry never *had* agreed with me at night.

7. The Man at the Window

I THINK I'd better make it clear right away that there isn't going to be any local colour in this story. I don't know anything about archæology and I don't know that I very much want to. Messing about with people and places that are buried and done with doesn't make sense to me. Mr Carey used to tell me that I hadn't got the archæological temperament and I've no doubt he was quite right.

The very first morning after my arrival Mr Carey asked if I'd like to come and see the palace he was—*planning* I think he called it. Though how you can plan for a thing that's happened long ago I'm sure I don't know! Well, I said I'd like to, and to tell the truth, I was a bit excited about it. Nearly three thousand years old that palace was, it appeared. I wondered what sort of palaces they had in those days, and if it would be like the pictures I'd seen of Tutankamen's tomb furniture. But would you believe it, there was nothing to see but *mud*! Dirty mud walls about two feet high—and that's all there was to it. Mr Carey took me here and there telling me things—how this was the great court, and there were some chambers here and an upper storey and various other rooms that opened off the central court. And all I thought was, "But how does he *know*?" though, of course, I was too polite to say so. I can tell you it *was* a disappointment! The whole excavation looked like nothing but mud to me—no marble or gold or anything handsome—my aunt's house in Cricklewood would have made a much more imposing ruin! And those old Assyrians or whatever they were, called themselves *kings*. When Mr Carey had shown me his old "palace," he handed me over to Father Lavigny, who showed me the rest of the mound. I was a little afraid of Father Lavigny, being a monk and a foreigner and having such a deep voice and all, but he was very kind—though rather vague. Sometimes I felt it wasn't much more real to him than it was to me.

Mrs Leidner explained that later. She said that Father Lavigny was only interested in "written documents"—as she called them. They wrote everything on clay, these people, queer heathenish-looking marks too, but quite sensible. There were even school tablets—the teacher's lesson on one side and the pupil's effort on the back of it. I confess that that did interest me rather—it seemed so human, if you know what I mean.

Father Lavigny walked round the work with me and showed me what were temples or palaces and what were private houses, and also a place which he said was an early Akkadian cemetery. He spoke in a funny jerky way, just throwing in a scrap of information and then reverting to other subjects.

He said:

"It is strange that you have come here. Is Mrs Leidner really ill, then?"

"Not exactly ill," I said cautiously.

He said:

"She is an odd woman. A dangerous woman, I think."

"Now what do you mean by that?" I said. "Dangerous? How dangerous?"

He shook his head thoughtfully.

"I think she is ruthless," he said. "Yes, I think she could be absolutely ruthless."

"If you'll excuse me," I said, "I think you're talking nonsense."

He shook his head.

"You do not know women as I do," he said.

And that was a funny thing, I thought, for a monk to say. But of course I suppose he might have heard a lot of things in confession. But that rather puzzled me, because I wasn't sure if monks heard confessions or if it was only priests. I supposed he *was* a monk with that long woollen robe—all sweeping up the dirt—and the rosary and all!

"Yes, she could be ruthless," he said musingly. "I am quite sure of that. And yet—though she is so hard—like stone, like marble—yet she is afraid. What is she afraid of?"

That, I thought, is what we should all like to know!

At least it was possible that her husband did know, but I didn't think any one else did.

He fixed me with a sudden bright, dark eye.

"It is odd here? You find it odd? Or quite natural?"

"Not quite natural," I said, considering. "It's comfortable enough as far as the arrangements go—but there isn't quite a comfortable feeling."

"It makes *me* uncomfortable. I have the idea," he became suddenly a little more foreign—"that something prepares itself. Dr Leidner, too, he is not quite himself. Something is worrying him also."

"His wife's health?"

"That perhaps. But there is more. There is—how shall I say it—an uneasiness."

And that was just it, there was an uneasiness.

We didn't say any more just then, for Dr Leidner came towards us. He showed me a child's grave that had just been uncovered. Rather pathetic it was—the little bones—and a pot or two and some little specks that Dr Leidner told me were a bead necklace.

It was the workmen that made me laugh. You never saw such a lot of scarecrows—all in long petticoats and rags, and their heads tied up as though they had toothache. And every now and then, as they went to and fro carrying away baskets of earth, they began to sing—at least I suppose it was meant to be singing—a queer sort of monotonous chant that went on and on over and over again. I noticed that most of their eyes were terrible—all covered with discharge, and one or two looked half blind. I was just thinking what a miserable lot they were when Dr Leidner said, "Rather a fine-looking lot of men, aren't they?" and I thought what a queer world it was and how two different people could see the same thing each of them the other way round. I haven't put that very well, but you can guess what I mean.

After a bit Dr Leidner said he was going back to the house for a mid-morning cup of tea. So he and I walked back together and he told me things. When *he* explained, it was all quite different. I sort of *saw* it all—how it used to be—the streets and the houses, and he showed me ovens where they baked bread and said the Arabs used much the same kind of ovens nowadays.

We got back to the house and found Mrs Leidner had got up. She was looking better to-day, not so thin and worn. Tea came in almost at once and Dr Leidner told her what had turned up during the morning on the dig. Then he went back to work and

46

Mrs Leidner asked me if I would like to see some of the finds they had made up to date. Of course I said "Yes," so she took me through into the antika-room. There was a lot of stuff lying about—mostly broken pots it seemed to me—or else ones that were all mended and stuck together. The whole lot might have been thrown away, I thought.

"Dear, dear," I said, "it's a pity they're all so broken, isn't it? Are they really worth keeping?"

Mrs Leidner smiled a little and she said:

"You mustn't let Eric hear you. Pots interest him more than anything else, and some of these are the oldest things we have—perhaps as much as seven thousand years old." And she explained how some of them came from a very deep cut on the mound down towards the bottom, and how, thousands of years ago, they had been broken and mended with bitumen, showing people prized their things just as much then as they do nowadays.

"And now," she said, "we'll show you something more exciting."

And she took down a box from the shelf and showed me a beautiful gold dagger with dark-blue stones in the handle.

I exclaimed with pleasure.

Mrs Leidner laughed.

"Yes, everybody likes gold! Except my husband."

"Why doesn't Dr Leidner like it?"

"Well, for one thing it comes expensive. You have to pay the workmen who find it the weight of the object in gold."

"Good gracious!" I exclaimed. "But why?"

"Oh, it's a custom. For one thing it prevents them from stealing. You see, if they *did* steal it wouldn't be for the archæological value but for the intrinsic value. They could melt it down. So we make it easy for them to be honest."

She took down another tray and showed me a really beautiful gold drinking-cup with a design of rams' heads on it.

Again I exclaimed.

"Yes, it is beautiful, isn't it? These came from a prince's grave. We found other royal graves but most of them had been plundered. This cup is our best find. It is one of the most lovely ever found anywhere. Early Akkadian. Unique."

Suddenly, with a frown, Mrs Leidner brought the cup up close to her eyes and scratched at it delicately with her nail.

"How extraordinary! There's actually wax on it. Some one must have been in here with a candle."

She detached the little flake and replaced the cup in its place.

After that she showed me some queer little terra-cotta figurines—but most of them were just rude. Nasty minds those old people had, I say.

When we went back to the porch Mrs Mercado was sitting polishing her nails. She was holding them out in front of her admiring the effect. I thought myself that anything more hideous than that orange red could hardly have been imagined.

Mrs Leidner had brought with her from the antika-room a very delicate little saucer broken in several pieces, and this she now proceeded to join together. I watched her for a minute or two and then asked if I could help.

"Oh yes, there are plenty more." She fetched quite a supply of broken pottery and we set to work. I soon got into the hang of it and she praised my ability. I suppose most nurses are handy with their fingers.

"How busy everybody is," said Mrs Mercado. "It makes me feel dreadfully idle. Of course I *am* idle."

"Why shouldn't you be if you like?" said Mrs Leidner.

Her voice was quite uninterested.

At twelve we had lunch. Afterwards Dr Leidner and Mr Mercado cleaned some pottery, pouring a solution of hydrochloric acid over it. One pot went a lovely plum colour and a pattern of bulls' horns came out on another one. It was really quite magical. All the dried mud that no washing would remove sort of foamed and boiled away.

Mr Carey and Mr Coleman went out on the dig and Mr Reiter went off to the photographic room.

"What will you do, Louise?" Dr Leidner asked his wife. "I suppose you'll rest for a bit?"

I gathered that Mrs Leidner usually lay down every afternoon.

"I'll rest for about an hour. Then perhaps I'll go out for a short stroll."

"Good. Nurse will go with you, won't you?"

"Of course," I said.

"No, no," said Mrs Leidner. "I like going alone. Nurse isn't to feel so much on duty that I'm not allowed out of her sight."

"Oh, but I'd like to come," I said.

"No, really, I'd rather you didn't." She was quite firm— almost peremptory. "I must be by myself every now and then. It's necessary to me."

I didn't insist, of course. But as I went off for a short sleep myself it struck me as odd that Mrs Leidner, with her nervous terrors, should be quite content to walk by herself without any kind of protection.

When I came out of my room at half-past three the courtyard was deserted save for a little boy with a large copper bath who was washing pottery, and Mr Emmott, who was sorting and arranging it. As I went towards them Mrs Leidner came in through the archway. She looked more alive than I had seen her yet. Her eyes shone and she looked uplifted and almost gay.

Dr Leidner came out from the laboratory and joined her. He was showing her a big dish with bull's horns on it.

"The prehistoric levels are being extraordinarily productive," he said. "It's been a good season so far. Finding that tomb right at the beginning was a real piece of luck. The only person who might complain is Father Lavigny. We've had hardly any tablets so far."

"He doesn't seem to have done very much with the few we have had," said Mrs. Leidner dryly. "He may be a very fine epigraphist but he's a remarkable lazy one. He spends all his afternoons sleeping."

"We miss Byrd," said Dr Leidner. "This man strikes me as slightly unorthodox—though, of course, I'm not competent to judge. But one or two of his translations have been surprising to say the least of it. I can hardly believe, for instance, that he's right about that inscribed brick, and yet he must know."

After tea Mrs Leidner asked me if I would like to stroll down to the river. I thought that perhaps she feared that her refusal to let me accompany her earlier in the afternoon might have hurt my feelings.

I wanted her to know that I wasn't the touchy kind, so I accepted at once.

It was a lovely evening. A path led between barley fields and then through some flowering fruit trees. Finally we came to the edge of the Tigris. Immediately on our left was the Tell with the workmen singing in their queer monotonous chant. A little to our right was a big water-wheel which made a queer groaning noise. It used to set my teeth on edge at first. But in the end I got fond of it and it had a queer soothing effect on me. Beyond the water-wheel was the village from which most of the workmen came.

"It's rather beautiful, isn't it?" said Mrs. Leidner.

"It's very peaceful," I said. "It seems funny to me to be so far away from everywhere."

"Far from everywhere," repeated Mrs Leidner. "Yes. Here at least one might expect to be safe."

I glanced at her sharply, but I think she was speaking more to herself than to me, and I don't think she realised that her words had been revealing.

We began to walk back to the house.

Suddenly Mrs Leidner clutched my arm so violently that I nearly cried out.

"Who's that, nurse? What's he doing?"

Some little distance ahead of us, just where the path ran near the expedition house, a man was standing. He wore European clothes and he seemed to be standing on tiptoe and trying to look in at one of the windows.

As we watched he glanced round, caught sight of us, and immediately continued on the path towards us. I felt Mrs Leidner's clutch tighten.

"Nurse," she whispered. "Nurse . . ."

"It's all right, my dear, it's all right," I said reassuringly.

The man came along and passed us. He was an Iraqi, and as soon as she saw him near to, Mrs Leidner relaxed with a sigh.

"He's only an Iraqi after all," she said.

We went on our way. I glanced up at the windows as I passed. Not only were they barred, but they were too high from the ground to permit of any one seeing in, for the level of the ground was lower here than on the inside of the courtyard.

"It must have been just curiosity," I said.

Mrs Leidner nodded.

"That's all. But just for a minute I thought——"

She broke off.

I thought to myself, "You thought *what*? That's what I'd like to know? *What* did you think?"

But I knew one thing now—that Mrs Leidner was afraid of a definite flesh and blood person.

8. Night Alarm

IT'S A LITTLE difficult to know exactly what to note in the week that followed my arrival at Tell Yarimjah.

Looking back as I do from my present standpoint of knowledge I can see a good many little signs and indications that I was quite blind to at the time.

To tell the story properly, however, I think I ought to try to recapture the point of view that I actually held—puzzled, uneasy, and increasingly conscious of *something* wrong.

For one thing *was* certain, the curious sense of strain and constraint was *not* imagined. It was genuine. Even Bill Coleman the insensitive commented upon it.

"This place gets under my skin," I heard him say. "Are they always such a glum lot?"

It was David Emmott to whom he spoke, the other assistant. I had taken rather a fancy to Mr Emmott, his taciturnity was not, I felt sure, unfriendly. There was something about him that seemed very steadfast and reassuring in an atmosphere where one was uncertain what any one was feeling or thinking.

"No," he said in answer to Mr Coleman. "It wasn't like this last year."

But he didn't enlarge on the theme, or say any more.

"What I can't make out is what it's all about," said Mr Coleman in an aggrieved voice.

Emmott shrugged his shoulders but didn't answer.

I had a rather enlightening conversation with Miss Johnson. I liked her very much. She was capable, practical and intelligent. She had, it was quite obvious, a distinct hero worship for Dr Leidner.

On this occasion she told me the story of his life since his young days. She knew every site he had dug, and the results of the dig. I would almost dare swear she could quote from every lecture he

52

had ever delivered. She considered him, she told me, quite the finest field archæologist living.

"And he's so simple. So completely unworldly. He doesn't know the meaning of the word conceit. Only a really great man could be so simple."

"That's true enough," I said. "Big people don't need to throw their weight about."

"And he's so light-hearted too. I can't tell you what fun we used to have—he and Richard Carey and I—the first years we were out here. We were such a happy party. Richard Carey worked with him in Palestine, of course. Theirs is a friendship of ten years or so. Oh, well, I've known him for seven."

"What a handsome man Mr Carey is," I said.

"Yes—I suppose he is."

She said it rather curtly.

"But he's just a little bit quiet, don't you think?"

"He usedn't to be like that," said Miss Johnson quickly. "It's only since——"

She stopped abruptly.

"Only since——?" I prompted.

"Oh, well." Miss Johnson gave a characteristic motion of her shoulders. "A good many things are changed nowadays."

I didn't answer. I hoped she would go on—and she did—prefacing her remarks with a little laugh as though to detract from their importance.

"I'm afraid I'm rather a conservative old fogy. I sometimes think that if an archæologist's wife isn't really interested, it would be wiser for her not to accompany the expedition. It often leads to friction."

"Mrs Mercado——" I suggested.

"Oh, her!" Miss Johnson brushed the suggestion aside. "I was really thinking of Mrs Leidner. She's a very charming woman—and one can quite understand why Dr Leidner 'fell for her'—to use a slang term. But I can't help feeling she's out of place here. She—it unsettles things."

So Miss Johnson agreed with Mrs Kelsey that it was Mrs Leidner who was responsible for the strained atmosphere. But then where did Mrs Leidner's own nervous fears come in?

"It unsettles *him*," said Miss Johnson earnestly. "Of course,

I'm—well, I'm like a faithful but jealous old dog. I don't like to see him so worn out and worried. His whole mind ought to be on the work—not taken up with his wife and her silly fears! If she's nervous of coming to out-of-the-way places, she ought to have stayed in America. I've no patience with people who come to a place and then do nothing but grouse about it!"

And then, a little fearful of having said more than she meant to say, she went on:

"Of course I admire her very much. She's a lovely woman and she's got great charm of manner when she chooses."

And there the subject dropped.

I thought to myself that it was always the same way—wherever women are cooped up together, there's bound to be jealousy. Miss Johnson clearly didn't like her chief's wife (that was perhaps natural) and unless I was much mistaken Mrs Mercado fairly hated her.

Another person who didn't like Mrs Leidner was Sheila Reilly. She came out once or twice to the dig, once in a car and twice with some young man on a horse—on two horses I mean, of course. It was at the back of my mind that she had a weakness for the silent young American, Emmott. When he was on duty at the dig she used to stay talking to him, and I thought, too, that *he* admired *her*.

One day, rather injudiciously, I thought, Mrs Leidner commented upon it at lunch.

"The Reilly girl is still hunting David down," she said with a little laugh. "Poor David, she chases you up on the dig even! How foolish girls are!"

Mr Emmott didn't answer, but under his tan his face got rather red. He raised his eyes and looked right into hers with a very curious expression—a straight, steady glance with something of a challenge in it.

She smiled very faintly and looked away.

I heard Father Lavigny murmur something, but when I said "Pardon?" he merely shook his head and did not repeat his remark.

That afternoon Mr Coleman said to me:

"Matter of fact I didn't like Mrs L. any too much at first. She used to jump down my throat every time I opened my mouth. But

54

I've begun to understand her better now. She's one of the kindest women I've ever met. You find yourself telling her all the foolish scrapes you ever got into before you know where you are. She's got her knife into Sheila Reilly, I know, but then Sheila's been damned rude to her once or twice. That's the worst of Sheila—she's got no manners. And a temper like the devil!"

That I could well believe. Dr Reilly spoilt her.

"Of course she's bound to get a bit full of herself, being the only woman in the place. But that doesn't excuse her talking to Mrs Leidner as though Mrs Leidner were her great-aunt. Mrs L's not exactly a chicken, but she's a damned good-looking woman. Rather like those fairy women who come out of marshes with lights and lure you away." He added bitterly, "You wouldn't find Sheila luring any one. All she does is to tick a fellow off."

I only remember two other incidents of any kind of significance.

One was when I went to the laboratory to fetch some acetone to get the stickiness off my fingers from mending the pottery. Mr Mercado was sitting in a corner, his head was laid down on his arms and I fancied he was asleep. I took the bottle I wanted and went off with it.

That evening, to my great surprise, Mrs Mercado tackled me.

"Did you take a bottle of acetone from the lab?"

"Yes," I said. "I did."

"You know perfectly well that there's a small bottle always kept in the antika-room."

She spoke quite angrily.

"Is there? I didn't know."

"I think you did! You just wanted to come spying round. I know what hospital nurses are."

I stared at her.

"I don't know what you're talking about, Mrs. Mercado," I said with dignity. "I'm sure I don't want to spy on any one."

"Oh, no! Of course not. Do you think I don't know what you're here for?"

Really, for a minute or two I thought she must have been drinking. I went away without saying any more. But I thought it was very odd.

The other thing was nothing very much. I was trying to entice a pi dog pup with a piece of bread. It was very timid, however, like all Arab dogs—and was convinced I meant no good. It slunk away and I followed it—out through the archway and round the corner of the house. I came round so sharply that before I knew I had cannoned into Father Lavigny and another man who were standing together—and in a minute I realised that the second man was the same one Mrs Leidner and I had noticed that day trying to peer through the window.

I apologised and Father Lavigny smiled, and with a word of farewell greeting to the other man he returned to the house with me.

"You know," he said, "I am very ashamed. I am a student of Oriental languages and none of the men on the work can understand me! It is humiliating, do you not think? I was trying my Arabic on that man, who is a townsman, to see if I got on better—but it still wasn't very successful. Leidner says my Arabic is too pure."

That was all. But it just passed through my head that it was odd the same man should still be hanging round the house.

That night we had a scare.

It must have been about two in the morning. I'm a light sleeper, as most nurses have to be. I was awake and sitting up in bed by the time that my door opened.

"Nurse, nurse!"

It was Mrs Leidner's voice, low and urgent.

I struck a match and lighted the candle.

She was standing by the door in a long blue dressing-gown. She was looking petrified with terror.

"There's some one—some one—in the room next to mine. . . . I heard him—scratching on the wall."

I jumped out of bed and came to her.

"It's all right," I said. "I'm here. Don't be afraid, my dear."

She whispered:

"Get Eric."

I nodded and ran out and knocked on his door. In a minute he was with us. Mrs Leidner was sitting on my bed, her breath coming in great gasps.

"I heard him," she said. "I heard him—scratching on the wall."

"Some one in the antika-room?" cried Dr Leidner.

56

He ran out quickly—and it just flashed across my mind how differently these two had reacted. Mrs Leidner's fear was entirely personal, but Dr Leidner's mind leaped at once to his precious treasures.

"The antika-room!" breathed Mrs Leider. "Of course! How stupid of me."

And rising and pulling her gown round her, she bade me come with her. All traces of her panic-stricken fear had vanished.

We arrived in the antika-room to find Dr Leidner and Father Lavigny. The latter had also heard a noise, had risen to investigate, and had fancied he saw a light in the antika-room. He had delayed to put on slippers and snatch up a torch and had found no one by the time he got there. The door, moreover, was duly locked, as it was supposed to be at night.

Whilst he was assuring himself that nothing had been taken, Dr Leidner had joined him.

Nothing more was to be learned. The outside archway door was locked. The guard swore nobody could have got in from outside, but as they had probably been fast asleep this was not conclusive. There were no marks or traces of an intruder and nothing had been taken.

It was possible that what had alarmed Mrs Leidner was the noise made by Father Lavigny taking down boxes from the shelves to assure himself that all was in order.

On the other hand, Father Lavigny himself was positive that he had (*a*) heard footsteps passing his window and (*b*) seen the flicker of a light, possibly a torch, in the antika-room.

Nobody else had heard or seen anything.

The incident is of value in my narrative because it led to Mrs Leidner's unburdening herself to me on the following day.

9. *Mrs Leidner's Story*

WE HAD JUST finished lunch. Mrs Leidner went to her room to rest as usual. I settled her on her bed with plenty of pillows and her book, and was leaving the room when she called me back.

"Don't go, nurse, there's something I want to say to you."

I came back into the room.

"Shut the door."

I obeyed.

She got up from the bed and began to walk up and down the room. I could see that she was making up her mind to something and I didn't like to interrupt her. She was clearly in great indecision of mind.

At last she seemed to have nerved herself to the required point. She turned to me and said abruptly:

"Sit down."

I sat down by the table very quietly. She began nervously:

"You must have wondered what all this is about?"

I nodded without saying anything.

"I've made up my mind to tell you—everything! I must tell some one or I shall go mad."

"Well," I said. "I think really it would be just as well. It's not easy to know the best thing to do when one's kept in the dark."

She stopped in her uneasy walk and faced me.

"Do you know what I'm frightened of?"

"Some man," I said.

"Yes—but I didn't say whom—I said what."

I waited.

She said:

"*I'm afraid of being killed!*"

Well, it was out now. I wasn't going to show any particular concern. She was near enough hysterics as it was.

"Dear me," I said. "So that's it, is it?"

58

Then she began to laugh. She laughed and she laughed—and the tears ran down her face.

"The way you said that!" she gasped. "The way you said it . . ."

"Now, now," I said. "This won't do." I spoke sharply. I pushed her into a chair, went over to the wash-stand and got a cold sponge and bathed her forehead and wrists.

"No more nonsense," I said. "Tell me calmly and sensibly all about it."

That stopped her. She sat up and spoke in her natural voice.

"You're a treasure, nurse," she said. "You make me feel as though I'm six. I'm going to tell you."

"That's right," I said. "Take your time and don't hurry."

She began to speak, slowly and deliberately.

"When I was a girl of twenty I married. A young man in one of our state departments. It was in 1918."

"I know," I said. "Mrs Mercado told me. He was killed in the war."

But Mrs Leidner shook her head.

"That's what she thinks. That's what everybody thinks. The truth is something quite different. I was a queer patriotic, enthusiastic girl, nurse, full of idealism. When I'd been married a few months I discovered—by a quite unforeseeable accident—that my husband was a spy in German pay. I learned that the information supplied by him had led directly to the sinking of an American transport and the loss of hundreds of lives. I don't know what most people would have done. . . . But I'll tell you what I did. I went straight to my father, who was in the War Department, and told him the truth. Frederick *was* killed in the war—but he was killed in America—shot as a spy."

"Oh dear, dear!" I ejaculated. "How terrible!"

"Yes," she said. "It was terrible. He was so kind, too—so gentle . . . And all the time . . . But I never hesitated. Perhaps I was wrong."

"It's difficult to say," I said. "I'm sure I don't know what one would do."

"What I'm telling you was never generally known outside the state departments. Ostensibly my husband had gone to the front and had been killed. I had a lot of sympathy and kindness shown me as a war widow."

Her voice was bitter and I nodded comprehendingly.

"Lots of people wanted to marry me, but I always refused. I'd had too bad a shock. I didn't feel I could ever *trust* any one again."

"Yes, I can imagine feeling like that."

"And then I became very fond of a certain young man. I wavered. An amazing thing happened! I got an anonymous letter—from Frederick—saying that if I ever married another man, he'd kill me!"

"From Frederick? From your dead husband?"

"Yes. Of course, I thought at first I was mad or dreaming. . . . At last I went to my father. He told me the truth. My husband hadn't been shot after all. He'd escaped—but his escape did him no good. He was involved in a train wreck a few weeks later and his dead body was found amongst others. My father had kept the fact of his escape from me, and since the man had died anyway he had seen no reason to tell me anything until now.

"But the letter I received opened up entirely new possibilities. Was it perhaps a fact that my husband was still alive?

"My father went into the matter as carefully as possible. And he declared that as far as one could humanly be sure the body that was buried as Frederick's *was* Frederick's. There had been a certain amount of disfiguration, so that he could not speak with absolute cast-iron certainty, but he reiterated his solemn belief that Frederick was dead and that this letter was a cruel and malicious hoax.

"The same thing happened more than once. If I seemed to be on intimate terms with any man, I would receive a threatening letter."

"In your husband's handwriting?"

She said slowly:

"That is difficult to say. I had no letters of his. I had only my memory to go by."

"There was no allusion or special form of words used that could make you sure?"

"No. There *were* certain terms—nicknames, for instance—private between us—if one of those had been used or quoted, then I should have been quite sure."

"Yes," I said thoughtfully. "That is odd. It looks as though it *wasn't* your husband. But is there any one else it could be?"

"There is a possibility. Frederick had a younger brother—a boy of ten or twelve at the time of our marriage. He worshipped Frederick and Frederick was devoted to him. What happened to this boy, William his name was, I don't know. It seems to me possible that, adoring his brother as fanatically as he did, he may have grown up regarding me as directly responsible for his death. He had always been jealous of me and may have invented this scheme by way of punishment."

"It's possible," I said. "It's amazing the way children do remember if they've had a shock."

"I know. This boy may have dedicated his life to revenge."

"Please go on."

"There isn't very much more to tell. I met Eric three years ago. I meant never to marry. Eric made me change my mind. Right up to our wedding day I waited for another threatening letter. None came. I decided that whoever the writer might be, he was either dead, or tired of his cruel sport. *Two days after our marriage I got this.*"

Drawing a small attaché-case which was on the table towards her, she unlocked it, took out a letter and handed it to me.

The ink was slightly faded. It was written in a rather womanish hand with a forward slant.

You have disobeyed. Now you cannot escape. You must be Frederick Bosner's wife only! You have to die.

"I was frightened—but not so much as I might have been to begin with. Being with Eric made me feel safe. Then, a month later, I got a second letter.

I have not forgotten. I am making my plans. You have got to die. Why did you disobey?

"Does your husband know about this?"

Mrs Leidner answered slowly.

"He knows that I am threatened. I showed him both letters when the second one came. He was inclined to think the whole thing was a hoax. He thought also that it might be some one who wanted to blackmail me by pretending my first husband was alive."

She paused and then went on.

61

"A few days after I received the second letter we had a narrow escape from death by gas poisoning. Somebody entered our apartment after we were asleep and turned on the gas. Luckily I woke and smelled the gas in time. Then I lost my nerve. I told Eric how I had been persecuted for years, and I told him that I was sure this madman, whoever he might be, did really mean to kill me. I think that for the first time I really did think it *was* Frederick. There was always something a little ruthless behind his gentleness.

"Eric was still, I think, less alarmed than I was. He wanted to go to the police. Naturally I wouldn't hear of that. In the end we agreed that I should accompany him here, and that it might be wise if I didn't return to America in the summer but stayed in London and Paris.

"We carried out our plan and all went well. I felt sure that now everything would be all right. After all, we had put half the globe between ourselves and my enemy.

"And then—a little over three weeks ago—I received a letter—with an Iraq stamp on it."

She handed me a third letter.

You thought you could escape. You were wrong. You shall not be false to me and live. I have always told you so. Death is coming very soon.

"And a week ago—*this*! Just lying on the table here. It had not even gone through the post."

I took the sheet of paper from her. There was just one phrase scrawled across it.

"*I have arrived.*"

She stared at me.

"You see? You understand? He's going to kill me. It may be Frederick—it may be little William—*but he's going to kill me.*"

Her voice rose shudderingly. I caught her wrist.

"Now—now," I said warningly. "Don't give way. We'll look after you. Have you got any sal volatile?"

She nodded towards the wash-stand and I gave her a good dose.

"That's better," I said, as the colour returned to her cheeks.

"Yes, I'm better now. But oh, nurse, do you see why I'm in this state? When I saw that man looking in through my window, I thought: *he's come*. . . . Even when *you* arrived I was suspicious. I thought you might be a man in disguise——"

"The idea!"

"Oh, I know it sounds absurd. But you might have been in league with him perhaps—not a hospital nurse at all."

"But that's nonsense!"

"Yes, perhaps. But I've got beyond sense."

Struck by a sudden idea, I said:

"You'd *recognise* your husband, I suppose?"

She answered slowly.

"I don't even know that. It's over fifteen years ago. I mightn't recognise his face."

Then she shivered.

"I saw it one night—but it was a *dead* face. There was a tap, tap on the window. And then I saw a face, a dead face, ghastly and grinning against the pane. I screamed and screamed. . . . And they said there wasn't anything there!"

I remembered Mrs Mercado's story.

"You don't think," I said hesitatingly, "that you *dreamt* that?"

"I'm sure I didn't!"

I wasn't so sure. It was the kind of nightmare that was quite likely under the circumstances and that easily might be taken for a waking occurrence. However, I never contradict a patient. I soothed Mrs Leidner as best I could and pointed out that if any stranger arrived in the neighbourhood it was pretty sure to be known.

I left her, I think, a little comforted, and I went in search of Dr Leidner and told him of our conversation.

"I'm glad she's told you," he said simply. "It has worried me dreadfully. I feel sure that all those faces and tappings on the window-pane have been sheer imagination on her part. I haven't known what to do for the best. What do you think of the whole thing?"

I didn't quite understand the tone in his voice, but I answered promptly enough.

"It's possible," I said, "that these letters may be just a cruel and malicious hoax."

"Yes, that is quite likely. But what are we to *do*? They are driving her mad. I don't know what to think."

I didn't either. It had occurred to me that possibly a woman might be concerned. Those letters had a feminine note about them. Mrs Mercado was at the back of my mind.

Supposing that by some chance she had learnt the facts of Mrs Leidner's first marriage? She might be indulging her spite by terrorising the other woman.

I didn't quite like to suggest such a thing to Dr Leidner. It's so difficult to know how people are going to take things.

"Oh," I said cheerfully, "we must hope for the best. I think Mrs Leidner seems happier already from just talking about it. That's always a help, you know. It's bottling things up that makes them get on your nerves."

"I'm very glad she has told you," he repeated. "It's a good sign. It shows she likes and trusts you. I've been at my wits end to know what to do for the best."

It was on the tip of my tongue to ask him whether he'd thought of giving a discreet hint to the local police, but afterwards I was glad I hadn't done so.

What happened was this. On the following day Mr Coleman was going in to Hassanieh to get the workmen's pay. He was also taking in all our letters to catch the air mail.

The letters, as written, were dropped into a wooden box on the dining-room window-sill. Last thing that night Mr Coleman took them out and was sorting them out into bundles and putting rubber-bands round them.

Suddenly he gave a shout.

"What is it?" I asked.

He held out a letter with a grin.

"It's our Lovely Louise—she really *is* going balmy. She's addressed a letter to some one at 42nd Street, Paris, France. I don't think that can be right, do you? Do you mind taking it to her and asking what she *does* mean? She's just gone off to bed."

I took it from him and ran off to Mrs Leidner with it and she amended the address.

It was the first time I had seen Mrs Leidner's handwriting, and I wondered idly where I had seen it before, for it was certainly quite familiar to me.

It wasn't till the middle of the night that it suddenly came to me.

Except that it was bigger and rather more straggling, *it was extraordinarily like the writing on the anonymous letters.*

New ideas flashed through my head.

Had Mrs Leidner conceivably written those letters *herself*?

And did Dr Leidner half-suspect the fact?

10. Saturday Afternoon

Mrs Leidner told me her story on a Friday.

On Saturday morning there was a feeling of slight anti-climax in the air.

Mrs Leidner, in particular, was inclined to be very off-hand with me and rather pointedly avoided any possibility of a *tête-à-tête*. Well, *that* didn't surprise me! I've had the same thing happen to me again and again. Ladies tell their nurses things in a sudden burst of confidence, and then, afterwards, they feel uncomfortable about it and wish they hadn't! It's only human nature.

I was very careful not to hint or remind her in any way of what she had told me. I purposely kept my conversation as matter-of-fact as possible.

Mr Coleman had started in to Hassanieh in the morning, driving himself in the lorry with the letters in a knapsack. He also had one or two commissions to do for the members of the expedition. It was pay-day for the men, and he would have to go to the bank and bring out the money in coins of small denominations. All this was a long business and he did not expect to be back until the afternoon. I rather suspected he might be lunching with Sheila Reilly.

Work on the dig was usually not very busy on the afternoon of pay-day as at three-thirty the paying-out began.

The little boy, Abdullah, whose business it was to wash pots, was established as usual in the centre of the courtyard, and again as usual, kept up his queer nasal chant. Dr Leidner and Mr Emmott were going to put in some work on the pottery until Mr Coleman returned, and Mr Carey went up to the dig.

Mrs Leidner went to her room to rest. I settled her as usual and then went to my own room, taking a book with me as I did not feel sleepy. It was then about a quarter to one, and a couple

66

of hours passed quite pleasantly. I was reading *Death in a Nursing Home*—really a most exciting story—though I don't think the author knew much about the way nursing homes are run! At any rate I've never known a nursing home like that! I really felt inclined to write to the author and put him right about a few points.

When I put the book down at last (it was the red-haired parlourmaid and I'd never suspected her once!) and looked at my watch I was quite surprised to find it was twenty minutes to three!

I got up, straightened my uniform, and came out into the courtyard.

Abdullah was still scrubbing and still singing his depressing chant, and David Emmott was standing by him sorting the scrubbed pots, and putting the ones that were broken into boxes to await mending. I strolled over towards them just as Dr Leidner came down the staircase from the roof.

"Not a bad afternoon," he said cheerfully. "I've made a bit of a clearance up there. Louise will be pleased. She's complained lately that there's not room to walk about. I'll go and tell her the good news."

He went over to his wife's door, tapped on it and went in.

It must, I suppose, have been about a minute and a half later that he came out again. I happened to be looking at the door when he did so. It was like a nightmare. He had gone in a brisk, cheerful man. He came out like a drunken one—reeling a little on his feet, and with a queer dazed expression on his face.

"Nurse——" he called in a queer, hoarse voice. "Nurse——"

I saw at once something was wrong and I ran across to him. He looked awful—his face was all grey and twitching, and I saw he might collapse any minute.

"My wife . . ." he said. "My wife . . . Oh, my God . . ."

I pushed past him into the room. Then I caught my breath.

Mrs Leidner was lying in a dreadful huddled heap by the bed.

I bent over her. She was quite dead—must have been dead an hour at least. The cause of death was perfectly plain—a terrific blow on the front of the head just over the right temple. She must have got up from the bed and been struck down where she stood.

I didn't handle her more than I could help.

I glanced round the room to see if there was anything that might give a clue, but nothing seemeed out of place or disturbed. The windows were closed and fastened, and there was no place where the murderer could have hidden. Obviously he had been and gone long ago.

I went out, closing the door behind me.

Dr Leidner had collapsed completely now. David Emmott was with him and turned a white, inquiring face to me.

In a few low words I told him what had happened.

As I had always suspected, he was a first-class person to rely on in trouble. He was perfectly calm and self-possessed. Those blue eyes of his opened very wide, but otherwise he gave no sign at all.

He considered for a moment and then said:

"I suppose we must notify the police as soon as possible. Bill ought to be back any minute. What shall we do with Leidner?"

"Help me to get him into his room."

He nodded.

"Better lock this door first, I suppose," he said.

He turned the key in the lock of Mrs Leidner's door, then drew it out and handed it to me.

"I guess you'd better keep this, nurse. Now then."

Together we lifted Dr Leidner and carried him into his own room and laid him on his bed. Mr Emmott went off in search of brandy. He returned, accompanied by Miss Johnson.

Her face was drawn and anxious, but she was calm and capable, and I felt satisfied to leave Dr Leidner in her charge.

I hurried out into the courtyard. The station wagon was just coming in through the archway. I think it gave us all a shock to see Bill's pink, cheerful face as he jumped out with his familiar "Hallo, allo, allo! Here's the oof!" He went on gaily, "No highway robberies——"

He came to a halt suddenly. "I say, is anything up? What's the matter with you all? You look as though the cat had killed your canary."

Mr Emmot said shortly:

"Mrs Leidner's dead—killed."

"*What?*" Bill's jolly face changed ludicrously. He stared, his eyes goggling. "Mother Leidner dead! You're pulling my leg."

"Dead?" It was a sharp cry. I turned to see Mrs Mercado behind me. "Did you say Mrs Leidner had been *killed*?"

"Yes," I said. "Murdered."

"No!" she gasped. "Oh, no! I won't believe it. Perhaps she's committed suicide."

"Suicides don't hit themselves on the head," I said dryly. "It's murder all right, Mrs Mercado."

She sat down suddenly on an upturned packing-case.

She said, "Oh, but this is horrible—*horrible* . . ."

Naturally it was horrible. We didn't need *her* to tell us so! I wondered if perhaps she was feeling a bit remorseful for the harsh feelings she had harboured against the dead woman, and all the spiteful things she had said.

After a minute or two she asked rather breathlessly:

"What are you going to do?"

Mr Emmott took charge in his quiet way.

"Bill, you'd better get in again to Hassanieh as quick as you can. I don't know much about the proper procedure. Better get hold of Captain Maitland, he's in charge of the police here, I think. Get Dr Reilly first. He'll know what to do."

Mr Coleman nodded. All the facetiousness was knocked out of him. He just looked young and frightened. Without a word he jumped into the station wagon and drove off.

Mr Emmott said rather uncertainly, "I suppose we ought to have a hunt round." He raised his voice and called:

"Ibrahim!"

"Na'am."

The house-boy came running. Mr Emmott spoke to him in Arabic. A vigorous colloquy passed between them. The boy seemed to be emphatically denying something.

At last Mr Emmott said in a perplexed voice:

"He says there's not been a soul here this afternoon. No stranger of any kind. I suppose the fellow must have slipped in without their seeing him."

"Of course he did," said Mrs Mercado. "He slunk in when the boys weren't looking."

"Yes," said Mr Emmott.

The slight uncertainty in his voice made me look at him inquiringly.

69

He turned and spoke to the little pot-boy, Abdullah, asking him a question.

The boy replied vehemently at length.

The puzzled frown on Mr Emmott's brow increased.

"I don't understand it," he murmured under his breath. "I don't understand it at all."

But he didn't tell me what he didn't understand.

11 . An Odd Business

I'M ADHERING as far as possible to telling only my personal part in the business. I pass over the events of the next two hours, the arrival of Captain Maitland and the police and Dr Reilly. There was a good deal of general confusion, questioning, all the routine business, I suppose.

In my opinion we began to get down to brass tacks about five o'clock when Dr Reilly asked me to come with him into the office.

He shut the door, sat down in Dr Leidner's chair, motioned me to sit down opposite him, and said briskly:

"Now, then, nurse, let's get down to it. There's something damned odd here."

I settled my cuffs and looked at him inquiringly.

He drew out a notebook.

"This is for my own satisfaction. Now, what time was it exactly when Dr Leidner found his wife's body?"

"I should say it was almost exactly a quarter to three," I said.

"And how do you know that?"

"Well, I looked at my watch when I got up. It was twenty to three then."

"Let's have a look at this watch of yours."

I slipped it off my wrist and held it out to him.

"Right to the minute. Excellent woman. Good, that's *that* fixed. Now did you form any opinion as to how long she'd been dead?"

"Oh, really, doctor," I said, "I shouldn't like to say."

"Don't be so professional. I want to see if your estimate agrees with mine."

"Well, I should say she'd been dead at least an hour."

"Quite so. I examined the body at half-past four and I'm inclined to put the time of death between 1.15 and 1.45. We'll say half-past one at a guess. That's near enough."

He stopped and drummed thoughtfully with his fingers on the table.

"Damned odd, this business," he said. "Can you tell me about it—you were resting, you say? Did you hear anything?"

"At half-past one? No, doctor. I didn't hear anything at half-past one or at any other time. I lay on my bed from a quarter to one until twenty to three and I didn't hear anything except that droning noise the Arab boy makes, and occasionally Mr Emmott shouting up to Dr Leidner on the roof."

"The Arab boy—yes."

He frowned.

At that moment the door opened and Dr Leidner and Captain Maitland came in. Captain Maitland was a fussy little man with a pair of shrewd grey eyes.

Dr Reilly rose and pushed Dr Leidner into his chair.

"Sit down, man. I'm glad you've come. We shall want you. There's something very queer about this business."

Dr Leidner bowed his head.

"I know." He looked at me. "My wife confided the truth to Nurse Leatheran. We mustn't keep anything back at this juncture, nurse, so please tell Captain Maitland and Dr Reilly just what passed between you and my wife yesterday."

As nearly as possible I gave our conversation verbatim.

Captain Maitland uttered an occasional ejaculation. When I had finished he turned to Dr Leidner.

"And this is all true Leidner—eh?"

"Every word Nurse Leatheran has told you is correct."

"What an extraordinary story," said Dr Reilly. "You can produce these letters?"

"I have no doubt they will be found amongst my wife's belongings."

"She took them out of the attaché-case on her table," I said.

"Then they are probably still there."

He turned to Captain Maitland and his usually gentle face grew hard and stern.

"There must be no question of hushing this story up, Captain Maitland. The one thing necessary is for this man to be caught and punished."

"You believe it actually is Mrs Leidner's former husband?" I asked.

"Don't you think so, nurse?" asked Captain Maitland.

"Well, I think it is open to doubt," I said hesitatingly.

"In any case," said Dr Leidner, "the man is a murderer—and I should say a dangerous lunatic also. He *must* be found, Captain Maitland. He must. It should not be difficult."

Dr Reilly said slowly:

"It may be more difficult than you think . . . eh, Maitland?"

Captain Maitland tugged at his moustache without replying. Suddenly I gave a start.

"Excuse me, I said, "but there's something perhaps I ought to mention."

I told my story of the Iraqi we had seen trying to peer through the window, and of how I had seen him hanging about the place two days ago trying to pump Father Lavigny.

"Good," said Captain Maitland, "we'll make a note of that. It will be something for the police to go on. The man may have some connection with the case."

"Probably paid to act as a spy," I suggested. "To find out when the coast was clear."

Dr Reilly rubbed his nose with a harassed gesture.

"That's the devil of it," he said. "Supposing the coast wasn't clear—eh?"

I stared at him in a puzzled fashion.

Captain Maitland turned to Dr Leidner.

"I want you to listen to me very carefully, Leidner. This is a review of the evidence we've got up to date. After lunch, which was served at twelve o'clock and was over by five and twenty to one, your wife went to her room accompanied by Nurse Leatheran, who settled her comfortably. You yourself went up to the roof, where you spent the next two hours, is that right?"

"Yes."

"Did you come down from the roof at all during that time?"

"No."

"Did any one come up to you?"

"Yes, Emmott did pretty frequently. He went to and fro between me and the boy, who was washing pottery down below."

"Did you yourself look over into the courtyard at all?"

"Once or twice—usually to call to Emmott about something."

"On each occasion the boy was sitting in the middle of the courtyard washing pots?"

"Yes."

"What was the longest period of time when Emmott was with you and absent from the courtyard?"

Dr Leidner considered.

"It's difficult to say—perhaps ten minutes. Personally I should say two or three minutes, but I know by experience that my sense of time is not very good when I am absorbed and interested in what I am doing."

Captain Maitland looked at Dr Reilly. The latter nodded. "We'd better get down to it," he said.

Captain Maitland took out a small notebook and opened it.

"Look here, Leidner, I'm going to read to you exactly what every member of your expedition was doing between one and two this afternoon."

"But surely——"

"Wait. You'll see what I'm driving at in a minute. First Mr and Mrs Mercado. Mr Mercado says he was working in his laboratory. Mrs Mercado says she was in her bedroom shampooing her hair. Miss Johnson says she was in the living-room taking impressions of cylinder seals. Mr Reiter says he was in the dark-room developing plates. Father Lavigny says he was working in his bedroom. As to the two remaining members of the expedition, Carey and Coleman, the former was up on the dig and Coleman was in Hassanieh. So much for the members of the expedition. Now for the servants. The cook—your Indian chap—was sitting immediately outside the archway chatting to the guard and plucking a couple of fowls. Ibrahim and Mansur, the house-boys, joined him there at about 1.15. They both remained there laughing and talking until 2.30—*by which time your wife was already dead*."

Dr Leidner leaned forward.

"I don't understand—you puzzle me. What are you hinting at?"

"Is there any means of access to your wife's room except by the door into the courtyard?"

"No. There are two windows, but they are heavily barred—
and besides, I think they were shut."

He looked at me questioningly.

"They were closed and latched on the inside," I said promptly.

"In any case," said Captain Maitland, "even if they had been
open, no one could have entered or left the room that way. My
fellows and I have assured ourselves of that. It is the same with
all the other windows giving on the open country. They all have
iron bars and all the bars are in good condition. To have got into
your wife's room, a stranger *must* have come through the arched
doorway into the courtyard. But we have the united assurances
of the guard, the cook and the house-boy that *nobody did so*."

Dr Leidner sprang up.

"What do you mean? What do you mean?"

"Pull yourself together, man," said Dr Reilly quietly. "I know
it's a shock, but it's got to be faced. *The murderer didn't come from
outside*—so he must have come from *inside*. It looks as though
Mrs Leidner must have been murdered *by a member of your own
expedition*."

12. 'I Didn't Believe . . .'

"No. No!"

Dr Leidner sprang up and walked up and down in an agitated manner.

"It's impossible what you say, Reilly. Absolutely impossible. One of *us*? Why, every single member of the expedition was devoted to Louise!"

A queer little expression pulled down the corners of Dr Reilly's mouth. Under the circumstances it was difficult for him to say anything, but if ever a man's silence was eloquent his was at that minute.

"Quite impossible," reiterated Dr Leidner. "They were all devoted to her. Louise had such wonderful charm. Every one felt it."

Dr Reilly coughed.

"Excuse me, Leidner, but after all that's only your opinion. If any member of the expedition had disliked your wife they would naturally not advertise the fact to you."

Dr Leidner looked distressed.

"True—quite true. But all the same, Reilly, I think you are wrong. I'm sure every one was fond of Louise."

He was silent for a moment or two and then burst out.

"This idea of yours is infamous. It's—it's frankly incredible."

"You can't get away from—er—the facts," said Captain Maitland.

"Facts? Facts? Lies told by an Indian cook and a couple of Arab house-boys. You know these fellows as well as I do, Reilly, so do you, Maitland. Truth as truth means nothing to them. They say what you want them to say as a mere matter of politeness."

"In this case," said Dr Reilly dryly, "they are saying what we *don't* want them to say. Besides, I know the habits of your

76

household fairly well. Just outside the gate is a kind of social club. Whenever I've been over here in the afternoon I've always found most of your staff there. It's the natural place for them to be."

"All the same I think you are assuming too much. Why shouldn't this man—this devil—have got in earlier and concealed himself somewhere?"

"I agree that that is not actually impossible," said Dr Reilly coolly. "Let us assume that a stranger *did* somehow gain admission unseen. He would have to remain concealed until the right moment (and he certainly couldn't have done so in Mrs Leidner's room, there is no cover there) and take the risk of being seen entering the room and leaving it—with Emmott and the boy in the courtyard most of the time."

"The boy. I'd forgotten the boy," said Dr Leidner. "A sharp little chap. But surely, Maitland, the boy *must* have seen the murderer go into my wife's room?"

"We've elucidated that. The boy was washing pots the whole afternoon with one exception. Somewhere around half-past one—Emmott can't put it closer than that—he went up to the roof and was with you for ten minutes—that's right, isn't it?"

"Yes. I couldn't have told you the exact time but it must have been about that."

"Very good. Well, during that ten minutes, the boy, seizing his chance to be idle, strolled out and joined the others outside the gate for a chat. When Emmott came down he found the boy absent and called him angrily, asking him what he meant by leaving his work. As far as I can see, *your wife must have been murdered during that ten minutes*."

With a groan Dr Leidner sat down and hid his face in his hands.

Dr Reilly took up the tale, his voice quiet and matter-of-fact.

"The time fits in with my evidence," he said. "She'd been dead about three hours when I examined her. The only question is—who did it?"

There was a silence. Dr Leidner sat up in his chair and passed a hand over his forehead.

"I admit the force of your reasoning, Reilly," he said quietly. "It certainly *seems* as though it were what people call 'an inside

77

job.' But I feel convinced that somewhere or other there is a mistake. It's plausible but there must be a flaw in it. To begin with, you are assuming that an amazing coincidence has occurred."

"Odd that you should use that word," said Dr Reilly.

Without paying any attention Dr Leidner went on:

"My wife receives threatening letters. She has reason to fear a certain person. Then she is—killed. And you ask me to believe that she is killed—not by that person—but by some one entirely different! I say that that is ridiculous."

"It seems so—yes," said Dr Reilly meditatively.

He looked at Captain Maitland. "Coincidence—eh? What do you say, Maitland? Are you in favour of the idea? Shall we put it up to Leidner?"

Captain Maitland gave a nod.

"Go ahead," he said shortly.

"Have you ever heard of a man called Hercúle Poirot, Leidner?"

Dr Leidner stared at him, puzzled.

"I think I have heard the name, yes," he said vaguely. "I once heard a Mr Van Aldin speak of him in very high terms. He is a private detective, is he not?"

"That's the man."

"But surely he lives in London, so how will that help us?"

"He lives in London, true," said Dr Reilly, "but this is where the coincidence comes in. He is now, not in London, but in Syria, and *he will actually pass through Hassanieh on his way to Baghdad to-morrow!*"

"Who told you this?"

"Jean Berat, the French consul. He dined with us last night and was talking about him. It seems he has been disentangling some military scandal in Syria. He's coming through here to visit Baghdad, and afterwards returning through Syria to London. How's that for a coincidence?"

Dr Leidner hesitated a moment and looked apologetically at Captain Maitland.

"What do you think, Captain Maitland?"

"Should welcome co-operation," said Captain Maitland promptly. "My fellows are good scouts at scouring the countryside and investigating Arab blood feuds, but frankly, Leidner, this business of your wife's seems to me rather out of my class. The whole thing looks confoundedly fishy. I'm more than willing to have the fellow take a look at the case."

"You suggest that I should appeal to this man Poirot to help us?" said Dr Leidner. "And suppose he refuses?"

"He won't refuse," said Dr Reilly.

"How do you know?"

"Because I'm a professional man myself. If a really intricate case of say—cerebro spinal meningitis comes my way and I'm invited to take a hand, I shouldn't be able to refuse. This isn't an ordinary crime, Leidner."

"No," said Dr Leidner. His lips twitched with sudden pain "Will you then, Reilly, approach this Hercule Poirot on my behalf?"

"I will."

Dr Leidner made a gesture of thanks.

"Even now," he said slowly, "I can't realise it—that Louise is really dead."

I could bear it no longer.

"Oh! Dr Leidner," I burst out, "I—I can't tell you how badly I feel about this. I've failed so badly in my duty. It was my job to watch over Mrs Leidner—to keep her from harm."

Dr Leidner shook his head gravely.

"No, no, nurse, you've nothing to reproach yourself with," he said slowly. "It's *I*, God forgive me, who am to blame. . . . *I didn't believe*—all along I didn't believe . . . I didn't dream for one moment that there was any *real* danger. . . ."

He got up. His face twitched.

"*I let her go to her death.* . . . Yes, I let her go to her death—*not believing*——"

He staggered out of the room.

Dr Reilly looked at me.

"I feel pretty culpable too," he said. "I thought the good lady was playing on his nerves."

"I didn't take it really seriously either," I confessed.

"We were all three wrong," said Dr Reilly gravely.

"So it seems," said Captain Maitland.

13. Hercule Poirot Arrives

I DON'T THINK I shall ever forget my first sight of Hercule Poirot. Of course, I got used to him later on, but to begin with it was a shock, and I think every one else must have felt the same!

I don't know what I'd imagined—something rather like Sherlock Holmes—long and lean with a keen, clever face. Of course, I knew he was a foreigner, but I hadn't expected him to be *quite* as foreign as he was, if you know what I mean.

When you saw him you just wanted to laugh! He was like something on the stage or at the pictures. To begin with, he wasn't above five-foot five, I should think—an odd plump little man, quite old, with an enormous moustache, and a head like an egg. He looked like a hairdresser in a comic play!

And this was the man who was going to find out who killed Mrs Leidner!

I suppose something of my disgust must have shown in my face, for almost straightaway he said to me with a queer kind of twinkle:

"You disapprove of me, *ma sœur*? Remember, the pudding proves itself only when you eat it."

The proof of the pudding's in the eating, I *suppose* he meant.

Well, that's a true enough saying, but I couldn't say I felt much confidence myself!

Dr Reilly brought him out in his car soon after lunch on Sunday, and his first procedure was to ask us all to assemble together.

We did so in the dining-room, all sitting round the table. Mr Poirot sat at the head of it with Dr Leidner one side and Dr Reilly the other.

When we were all assembled, Dr Leidner cleared his throat and spoke in his gentle, hesitating voice.

"I dare say you have all heard of M. Hercule Poirot. He was

passing through Hassanieh to-day, and has very kindly agreed to break his journey to help us. The Iraq police and Captain Maitland are, I am sure, doing their very best, but—but there are circumstances in the case"—he floundered and shot an appealing glance at Dr Reilly—"there may, it seems, be difficulties. . . ."

"It is not all the square and overboard—no?" said the little man at the top of the table. Why, he couldn't even speak English properly!

"Oh, he *must* be caught!" cried Mrs Mercado. "It would be unbearable if he got away!"

I noticed the little foreigner's eyes rest on her appraisingly.

"He? Who is *he*, madame?" he asked.

"Why, the murderer, of course."

"Ah! the murderer," said Hercule Poirot.

He spoke as though the murderer was of no consequence at all!

We stared at him. He looked from one face to another.

"It is likely, I think," he said, "that you have none of you been brought in contact with a case of murder before?"

There was a general murmur of assent.

Hercule Poirot smiled.

"It is clear, therefore, that you do not understand the A B C of the position. There are unpleasantnesses! Yes, there are a lot of unpleasantnesses. To begin with, there is *suspicion*."

"Suspicion?"

It was Miss Johnson who spoke. Mr Poirot looked at her thoughtfully. I had an idea that he regarded her with approval. He looked as though he were thinking, "Here is a sensible, intelligent person!"

"Yes, mademoiselle," he said. "Suspicion! Let us not make the bones about it. *You are all under suspicion here in this house.* The cook, the house-boy, the scullion, the pot-boy—yes, and all the members of the expedition too."

Mrs Mercado started up, her face working.

"How *dare* you? How dare you say such a thing! This is odious—unbearable! Dr Leidner—you can't sit here and let this man—and let this man——"

Dr Leidner said wearily:

"Please try and be calm, Marie."

Mr Mercado stood up too. His hands were shaking and his eyes were bloodshot.

"I agree. It is an outrage—an insult——"

"No, no," said Mr Poirot. "I do not insult you. I merely ask you all to face facts. *In a house where murder has been committed, every inmate comes in for a certain share of suspicion*. I ask you what evidence is there that the murderer came from outside at all?"

Mrs Mercado cried:

"But of course he did! it stands to reason! Why——" She stopped and said more slowly, "Anything else would be incredible!"

"You are doubtless correct, madame," said Poirot with a bow. "I explain to you only how the matter must be approached. First I assure myself of the fact that every one in this room is innocent. After that I seek the murderer elsewhere."

"Is it not possible that that may be a little late in the day?" asked Father Lavigny gravely.

"The tortoise, *mon père*, overtook the hare."

Father Lavigny shrugged his shoulders.

"We are in your hands," he said resignedly. "Convince yourself as soon as may be of our innocence in this terrible business."

"As rapidly as possible. It was my duty to make the position clear to you, so that you may not resent the impertinence of any questions I may have to ask. Perhaps, *mon père*, the Church will set an example?"

"Ask any questions you please of me," said Father Lavigny gravely.

"This is your first season out here?"

"Yes."

"And you arrived—when?"

"Three weeks ago almost to a day. That is, on the 27th of February."

"Coming from?"

"The Order of the *Pères Blancs* at Carthage."

"Thank you, *mon père*. Were you at any time acquainted with Mrs Leidner before coming here?"

"No, I had never seen the lady until I met her here."

"Will you tell me what you were doing at the time of the tragedy?"

"I was working on some cuneiform tablets in my own room."

I noticed that Poirot had at his elbow a rough plan of the building.

"That is the room at the south-west corner corresponding to that of Mrs Leidner on the opposite side?"

"Yes."

"At what time did you go to your room?"

"Immediately after lunch. I should say at about twenty minutes to one."

"And you remained there until—when?"

"Just before three o'clock. I had heard the station wagon come back—and then I heard it drive off again. I wondered why, and came out to see."

"During the time that you were there did you leave the room at all?"

"No, not once."

"And you heard or saw nothing that might have any bearing on the tragedy?"

"No."

"You have no window giving on the courtyard in your room?"

"No, both the windows give on the countryside."

"Could you hear at all what was happening in the courtyard?"

"Not very much. I heard Mr Emmott passing my room and going up to the roof. He did so once or twice."

"Can you remember at what time?"

"No, I'm afraid I can't. I was engrossed in my work, you see."

There was a pause and then Poirot said:

"Can you say or suggest anything at all that might throw light on this business? Did you, for instance, notice anything in the days preceding the murder?"

Father Lavigny looked slightly uncomfortable.

He shot a half-questioning look at Dr Leidner.

"That is rather a difficult question, monsieur," he said gravely. "If you ask me I must reply frankly that in my opinion Mrs Leidner was clearly in dread of some one or something. She was definitely nervous about strangers. I imagine she had a reason for this nervousness of hers—but I *know* nothing. She did not confide in me."

Poirot cleared his throat and consulted some notes that he held in his hand. "Two nights ago I understand there was a scare of burglary."

Father Lavigny replied in the affirmative and retailed his story of the light seen in the antika-room and the subsequent futile search.

"You believe, do you not, that some unauthorised person was on the premises at that time?"

"I don't know what to think," said Father Lavigny frankly. "Nothing was taken or disturbed in any way. It might have been one of the house-boys——"

"Or a member of the expedition?"

"Or a member of the expedition. But in that case there would be no reason for the person not admitting the fact."

"But it *might* equally have been a stranger from outside?"

"I suppose so."

"Supposing a stranger *had* been on the premises, could he have concealed himself successfully during the following day and until the afternoon of the day following that?"

He asked the question half of Father Lavigny and half of Dr Leidner. Both men considered the question carefully.

"I hardly think it would be possible," said Dr Leidner at last with some reluctance. "I don't see where he could possibly conceal himself, do you, Father Lavigny?"

"No—no—I don't."

Both men seemed reluctant to put the suggestion aside.

Poirot turned to Miss Johnson.

"And you, mademoiselle? Do you consider such a hypothesis feasible?"

After a moment's thought Miss Johnson shook her head.

"No," she said. "I don't. Where could any one hide? The bedrooms are all in use and, in any case, are sparsely furnished. The dark-room, the drawing-office and the laboratory were all in use the next day—so were all these rooms. There are no cupboards or corners. Perhaps, if the servants were in collusion——"

"That is possible, but unlikely," said Poirot.

He turned once more to Father Lavigny.

"There is another point. The other day Nurse Leatheran here

84

noticed you talking to a man outside. She had previously noticed that same man trying to peer in at one of the windows on the outside. It rather looks as though the man were hanging round the place deliberately."

"That is possible, of course," said Father Lavigny thoughtfully.

"Did you speak to this man first, or did he speak to you?"

Father Lavigny considered for a moment or two.

"I believe—yes, I am sure, that he spoke to me."

"What did he say?"

Father Lavigny made an effort of memory.

"He said, I think, something to the effect was this the American expedition house? And then something else about the Americans employing a lot of men on the work. I did not really understand him very well, but I endeavoured to keep up a conversation so as to improve my Arabic. I thought, perhaps, that being a townee he would understand me better than the men on the dig do."

"Did you converse about anything else?"

"As far as I remember, I said Hassanieh was a big town—and we then agreed that Baghdad was bigger—and I think he asked whether I was an Armenian or a Syrian Catholic—something of that kind."

Poirot nodded.

"Can you describe him?"

Again Father Lavigny frowned in thought.

"He was rather a short man," he said at last, "and squarely built. He had a very noticeable squint and was of fair complexion."

Mr Poirot turned to me.

"Does that agree with the way you would describe him?" he asked.

"Not exactly," I said hesitatingly. "I should have said he was tall rather than short, and very dark complexioned. He seemed to me of a rather slender build. I didn't notice any squint."

Mr Poirot gave a despairing shrug of the shoulders.

"It is always so! If you were the police how well you would know it! The description of the same man by two different people—never does it agree. Every detail is contradicted."

"I'm fairly sure about the squint," said Father Lavigny. "Nurse Leatheran may be right about the other points. By the way, when I said *fair*, I only meant fair for an *Iraqi*. I expect nurse would call that dark."

"Very dark," I said obstinately. "A dirty dark-yellow colour."

I saw Dr Reilly bite his lip and smile.

Poirot threw up his hands.

"*Passons!*" he said. "This stranger hanging about, he may be important—he may not. At any rate he must be found. Let us continue our inquiry."

He hesitated for a minute, studying the faces turned towards him round the table, then, with a quick nod, he singled out Mr Reiter.

"Come, my friend," he said. "Let us have your account of yesterday afternoon."

Mr Reiter's pink, plump face flushed scarlet.

"Me?" he said.

"Yes, you. To begin with, your name and your age?"

"Carl Reiter, twenty-eight."

"American—yes?"

"Yes, I come from Chicago."

"This is your first season?"

"Yes. I'm in charge of the photography."

"Ah, yes. And yesterday afternoon, how did you employ yourself?"

"Well—I was in the dark-room most of the time."

"*Most* of the time—eh?"

"Yes. I developed some plates first. Afterwards I was fixing up some objects to photograph."

"Outside?"

"Oh no, in the photographic room."

"The dark-room opens out of the photographic room?"

"Yes."

"And so you never came outside the photographic room?"

"No."

"Did you notice anything that went on in the courtyard?"

The young man shook his head.

"I wasn't noticing anything," he explained. "I was busy. I heard the car come back, and as soon as I could leave what I was doing I came out to see if there was any mail. It was then that I—heard."

"And you began your work in the photographic room—when?"

"At ten minutes to one."

"Were you acquainted with Mrs Leidner before you joined this expedition?"

The young man shook his head.

"No, sir. I never saw her till I actually got here."

"Can you think of *anything*—any incident—however small—that might help us?"

Carl Reiter shook his head.

He said helplessly:

"I guess I don't know anything at all, sir."

"Mr Emmott?"

David Emmott spoke clearly and concisely in his pleasant soft American voice.

"I was working with the pottery from a quarter to one till a quarter to three—overseeing the boy Abdullah, sorting it, and occasionally going up to the roof to help Dr Leidner."

"How often did you go up to the roof?"

"Four times, I think."

"For how long?"

"Usually a couple of minutes—not more. But on one occasion after I'd been working a little over half an hour I stayed as long as ten minutes—discussing what to keep and what to fling away."

"And I understand that when you came down you found the boy had left his place?"

"Yes. I called him angrily and he reappeared from outside the archway. He had gone out to gossip with the others."

"That was the only time he left his work?"

"Well, I sent him up once or twice to the roof with pottery."

Poirot said gravely:

"It is hardly necessary to ask you, Mr Emmott, whether you saw any one enter or leave Mrs Leidner's room during that time?"

Mr Emmott replied promptly.

"I saw no one at all. Nobody even came out into the courtyard during the two hours I was working."

"And to the best of your belief it was half-past one when both you and the boy were absent and the courtyard was empty?"

"It couldn't have been far off that time. Of course, I can't say *exactly*."

Poirot turned to Dr Reilly.

"That agrees with your estimate of the time of death, doctor?"

"It does," said Dr Reilly.

Mr Poirot stroked his great curled moustaches.

"I think we can take it," he said gravely, "that Mrs Leidner met her death during that ten minutes."

14. One of Us?

THERE was a little pause—and in it a wave of horror seemed to float round the room.

I think it was at that moment that I first believed Dr Reilly's theory to be right.

I *felt* that the murderer was in the room. Sitting with us—listening. *One of us.* . . .

Perhaps Mrs Mercado felt it too. For she suddenly gave a short sharp cry.

"I can't help it," she sobbed. "I—it's so *terrible!*"

"Courage, Marie," said her husband.

He looked at us apologetically.

"She is so sensitive. She feels things so much."

"I—I was so fond of Louise," sobbed Mrs Mercado.

I don't know whether something of what I felt showed in my face, but I suddenly found that Mr Poirot was looking at me, and that a slight smile hovered on his lips.

I gave him a cold glance, and at once he resumed his inquiry.

"Tell me, madame," he said, "of the way you spent yesterday afternoon?"

"I was washing my hair," sobbed Mrs Mercado. "It seems awful not to have known anything about it. I was quite happy and busy."

"You were in your room?"

"Yes."

"And you did not leave it?"

"No. Not till I heard the car. Then I came out and I heard what had happened. Oh, it was *awful!*"

"Did it surprise you?"

Mrs Mercado stopped crying. Her eyes opened resentfully.

"What do you mean, M. Poirot? Are you suggesting——?"

"What should I mean, madame? You have just told us how

fond you were of Mrs Leidner. She might, perhaps, have confided in you."

"Oh, I see. . . . No—no, dear Louise never told me anything—anything *definite*, that is. Of course, I could see she was terribly worried and nervous. And there were those strange occurrences—hands tapping on the window and all that."

"Fancies, I remember you said," I put in, unable to keep silent.

I was glad to see that she looked momentarily disconcerted.

Once again I was conscious of Mr Poirot's amused eye glancing in my direction.

He summed up in a business-like way.

"It comes to this, madame, you were washing your hair—you heard nothing and you saw nothing. Is there anything at all you can think of that would be a help to us in any way?"

Mrs Mercado took no time to think.

"No, indeed there isn't. It's the deepest mystery! But I should say there is no doubt—no doubt *at all* that the murderer came from outside. Why, it stands to reason."

Poirot turned to her husband.

"And you, monsieur, what have you to say?"

Mr Mercado started nervously. He pulled at his beard in an aimless fashion.

"Must have been. Must have been," he said. "Yet how could any one wish to harm her? She was so gentle—so kind—" He shook his head. "Whoever killed her must have been a fiend—yes, a fiend!"

"And you yourself, monsieur, how did you pass yesterday afternoon?"

"I?" he stared vaguely.

"You were in the laboratory, Joseph," his wife prompted him.

"Ah, yes, so I was—so I was. My usual tasks."

"At what time did you go there?"

Again he looked helplessly and inquiringly at Mrs Mercado.

"At ten minutes to one, Joseph."

"Ah, yes, at ten minutes to one."

"Did you come out in the courtyard at all?"

"No—I don't think so." He considered. "No, I am sure I didn't."

"When did you hear of the tragedy?"

"My wife came and told me. It was terrible—shocking. I could hardly believe it. Even now, I can hardly believe it is true."

Suddenly he began to tremble.

"It is horrible—horrible . . ."

Mrs Mercado came quickly to his side.

"Yes, yes, Joseph, we all feel that. But we mustn't give way. It makes it so much more difficult for poor Dr Leidner."

I saw a spasm of pain pass across Dr Leidner's face, and I guessed that this emotional atmosphere was not easy for him. He gave a half glance at Poirot as though in appeal. Poirot responded quickly.

"Miss Johnson?" he said.

"I'm afraid I can tell you very little," said Miss Johnson. Her cultured well-bred voice was soothing after Mrs Mercado's shrill treble. She went on:

"I was working in the living-room—taking impressions of some cylinder seals on plasticine."

"And you saw or noticed nothing?"

"No."

Poirot gave her a quick glance. His ear had caught what mine had—a faint note of indecision.

"Are you quite sure, mademoiselle? Is there something that comes back to you vaguely?"

"No—not really——"

"Something you saw, shall we say, out of the corner of your eye hardly knowing you saw it."

"No, certainly not," she replied positively.

"Something you *heard* then. Ah, yes, something you are not quite sure whether you heard or not?"

Miss Johnson gave a short vexed laugh.

"You press me very closely, M. Poirot. I'm afraid you are encouraging me to tell you what I am, perhaps, only imagining."

"Then there *was* something you—shall we say—imagined?"

Miss Johnson said slowly, weighing her words in a detached way:

"I have imagined—since—that at some time during the afternoon I heard a very faint cry. . . . What I mean is that I dare say I *did* hear a cry. All the windows in the living-room were open and one hears all sorts of sounds from people working in the barley fields. But you see—since—I've got the idea into my head that it was—that it was Mrs Leidner I heard. And that's made me rather unhappy. Because if I'd jumped up and run along to her room—well, who knows? I might have been in time . . ."

Dr Reilly interposed authoritatively.

"Now, don't start getting that into your head," he said. "I've no doubt but that Mrs Leidner (forgive me, Leidner) was struck down almost as soon as the man entered the room, and it was that blow that killed her. No second blow was struck. Otherwise she would have had time to call for help and make a real outcry."

"Still, I might have caught the murderer," said Miss Johnson.

"What time was this, mademoiselle?" asked Poirot. "In the neighbourhood of half-past one?"

"It must have been about that time—yes." She reflected a minute.

"That would fit in," said Poirot thoughtfully. "You heard nothing else—the opening or shutting of a door, for instance?"

Miss Johnson shook her head.

"No, I do not remember anything of that kind."

"You were sitting at a table, I presume. Which way were you facing? The courtyard? The antika-room? The verandah? Or the open countryside?"

"I was facing the courtyard."

"Could you see the boy Abdullah washing pots from where you were?"

"Oh, yes, if I looked up, but of course, I was very intent on what I was doing. All my attention was on that."

"If any one had passed the courtyard window, though, you would have noticed it?"

"Oh, yes, I am almost sure of that."

"And nobody did so?"

"No."

"But if any one had walked, say, across the middle of the courtyard, would you have noticed that?"

"I think—probably not—unless, as I say before, I had happened to look up and out of the window."

"You did not notice the boy Abdullah leave his work and go out to join the other servants?"

"No."

"Ten minutes," mused Poirot. "That fatal ten minutes."

There was a momentary silence.

Miss Johnson lifted her head suddenly and said:

"You know, M. Poirot, I think I have unintentionally misled you. On thinking it over, I do not believe that I could possibly have heard any cry uttered in Mrs Leidner's room from where I was. The antika-room lay between me and her—and I understand her windows were found closed."

"In any case, do not distress yourself, mademoiselle," said Poirot kindly. "It is not really of much importance."

"No, of course not. I understand that. But you see, it *is* of importance to me, because I feel I might have done something."

"Don't distress yourself, dear Anne," said Dr Leidner with affection. "You must be sensible. What you heard was probably one Arab bawling to another some distance away in the fields."

Miss Johnson flushed a little at the kindliness of his tone. I even saw tears spring to her eyes. She turned her head away and spoke even more gruffly than usual.

"Probably was. Usual thing after a tragedy—start imagining things that aren't so at all."

Poirot was once more consulting his notebook.

"I do not suppose there is much more to be said. Mr Carey?"

Richard Carey spoke slowly—in a wooden, mechanical manner.

"I'm afraid I can add nothing helpful. I was on duty at the dig. The news was brought to me there."

"And you know or can think of nothing helpful that occurred in the days immediately preceding the murder?"

"Nothing at all."

"Mr Coleman?"

"I was right out of the whole thing," said Mr Coleman with—was it just a shade of regret—in his tone. "I went into Hassanieh yesterday morning to get the money for the men's wages. When I came back Emmott told me what had happened and I went back in the bus to get the police and Dr Reilly."

"And beforehand?"

"Well, sir, things were a bit jumpy—but you know that already. There was the antika-room scare and one or two before that—hands and faces at the window—you remember, sir," he appealed to Dr Leidner, who bent his head in assent. "I think, you know, that you'll find some Johnny *did* get in from outside. Must have been an artful sort of beggar."

Poirot considered him for a minute or two in silence.

"You are an Englishman, Mr Coleman?" he asked at last.

"That's right, sir. All British. See the trade-mark. Guaranteed genuine."

"This is your first season?"

"Quite right."

"And you are passionately keen on archæology?"

This description of himself seemed to cause Mr Coleman some embarrassment. He got rather pink and shot the side look of a guilty schoolboy at Dr Leidner.

"Of course—it's all very interesting," he stammered. "I mean—I'm not exactly a brainy chap . . ."

He broke off rather lamely. Poirot did not insist.

He tapped thoughtfully on the table with the end of his pencil and carefully straightened an ink-pot that stood in front of him.

"It seems then," he said, "that that is as near as we can get for the moment. If any one of you thinks of something that has for the time being slipped his or her memory do not hesitate to come to me with it. It will be well now, I think, for me to have a few words alone with Dr Leidner and Dr Reilly."

It was the signal for a breaking up of the party. We all rose and filed out of the door. When I was half-way out, however, a voice recalled me.

"Perhaps," said M. Poirot, "Nurse Leatheran will be so kind as to remain. I think her assistance will be valuable to us."

I came back and resumed my seat at the table.

15. *Poirot Makes a Suggestion*

DR REILLY had risen from his seat. When every one had gone out he carefully closed the door. Then, with an inquiring glance at Poirot, he proceeded to shut the window giving on the court-yard. The others were already shut. Then he, too, resumed his seat at the table.

"*Bien!*" said Poirot. "We are now private and undisturbed. We can speak freely. We have heard what the members of the expedition have to tell us and—— But yes, *ma sœur*, what is it that you think?"

I got rather red. There was no denying that the queer little man had sharp eyes. He'd seen the thought passing through my mind—I suppose my face *had* shown a bit too clearly what I was thinking!

"Oh, it's nothing——" I said hesitating.

"Come on, nurse," said Dr Reilly. "Don't keep the specialist waiting."

"It's nothing really," I said hurriedly. "It only just passed through my mind, so to speak, that perhaps even if any one did know or suspect something it wouldn't be easy to bring it out in front of everybody else—or even, perhaps, in front of Dr Leidner."

Rather to my astonishment, M. Poirot nodded his head in vigorous agreement.

"Precisely. Precisely. It is very just what you say there. But I will explain. That little reunion we have just had—it served a purpose. In England before the races you have a parade of the horses, do you not? They go in front of the grandstand so that every one may have an opportunity of seeing and judging them. That is the purpose of my little assembly. In the sporting phrase, I run my eye over the possible starters."

Dr Leidner cried out violently, "I do not believe for one

minute that *any* member of my expedition is implicated in this crime!"

Then, turning to me, he said authoritatively:

"Nurse, I should be much obliged if you would tell M. Poirot here and now exactly what passed between my wife and you two days ago."

Thus urged, I plunged straight away into my story, trying as far as possible to recall the exact words and phrases Mrs Leidner had used.

When I had finished, M. Poirot said:

"Very good. Very good. You have the mind neat and orderly. You will be of great service to me here."

He turned to Dr Leidner.

"You have these letters?"

"I have them here. I thought that you would want to see them first thing."

Poirot took them from him, read them, and scrutinised them carefully as he did so. I was rather disappointed that he didn't dust powder over them or examine them with a microscope or anything like that—but I realised that he wasn't a very young man and that his methods were probably not very up to date. He just read them in the way that any one might read a letter.

Having read them he put them down and cleared his throat.

"Now," he said, "let us proceed to get our facts clear and in order. The first of these letters was received by your wife shortly after her marriage to you in America. There had been others but these she destroyed. The first letter was followed by a second. A very short time after the second arrived you both had a near escape from coal gas poisoning. You then came abroad and for nearly two years no further letters were received. They started again at the beginning of your season this year—that is to say within the last three weeks. That is correct?"

"Absolutely."

"Your wife displayed every sign of panic and, after consulting Dr Reilly, you engaged Nurse Leatheran here to keep your wife company and allay her fears?"

"Yes."

"Certain incidents occurred—hands tapping at the window—

a spectral face—noises in the antika-room. You did not witness any of these phenomena yourself?"

"No."

"In fact nobody did except Mrs Leidner?"

"Father Lavigny saw a light in the antika-room."

"Yes, I have not forgotten that."

He was silent for a minute or two, then he said:

"Had your wife made a will?"

"I do not think so."

"Why was that?"

"It did not seem worth it from her point of view."

"Is she not a wealthy woman?"

"Yes, during her lifetime. Her father left her a considerable sum of money in trust. She could not touch the principal. At her death it was to pass to any children she might have—and failing children to the Pittstown Museum."

Poirot drummed thoughtfully on the table.

"Then we can, I think," he said, "eliminate one motive from the case. It is, you comprehend, what I look for first. *Who benefits by the deceased's death?* In this case it is a museum. Had it been otherwise, had Mrs Leidner died intestate but possessed of a considerable fortune, I should imagine that it would prove an interesting question as to who inherited the money—you—or a former husband. But there would have been this difficulty, the former husband would have had to resurrect himself in order to claim it, and I should imagine that he would then be in danger of arrest, though I hardly fancy that the death penalty would be exacted so long after the war. However, these speculations need not arise. As I say, I settle first the question of money. For the next step I proceed always to suspect the husband or wife of the deceased! In this case, in the first place, you are proved never to have gone near your wife's room yesterday afternoon, in the second place, you lose instead of gain by your wife's death, and in the third place——"

He paused.

"Yes?" said Dr Leidner.

"In the third place," said Poirot slowly. "I can, I think, appreciate devotion when I see it. I believe, Dr Leidner, that your love for your wife was the ruling passion of your life. It is so, is it not?"

Dr Leidner answered quite simply:

"Yes."

Poirot nodded.

"Therefore," he said, "we can proceed."

"Hear, hear, let's get down to it," said Dr Reilly with some impatience.

Poirot gave him a reproving glance.

"My friend, do not be impatient. In a case like this everything must be approached with order and method. In fact, that is my rule in every case. Having disposed of certain possibilities, we now approach a very important point. It is vital that, as you say—all the cards should be on the table—there must be nothing kept back."

"Quite so," said Dr Reilly.

"That is why I demand the whole truth," went on Poirot.

Dr Leidner looked at him in surprise.

"I assure you, M. Poirot, that I have kept nothing back. I have told you everything that I know. There have been no reserves."

"*Tout de même,* you have not told me *everything.*"

"Yes, indeed. I cannot think of any detail that has escaped me."

He looked quite distressed.

Poirot shook his head gently.

"No," he said. "*You have not told me, for instance, why you installed Nurse Leatheran in the house.*"

Dr Leidner looked completely bewildered.

"But I have explained that. It is obvious. My wife's nervousness—her fears . . ."

Poirot leaned forward. Slowly and emphatically he wagged a finger up and down.

"No, no, no. There is something there that is not clear. Your wife is in danger, yes—she is threatened with death, yes. You send—*not for the police*—not for a private detective even—but for a *nurse*! It does not make the sense, that!"

"I—I——" Dr Leidner stopped. The colour rose in his cheeks. "I thought——" He came to a dead stop.

"Now we are coming to it," Poirot encouraged him. "You thought—what?"

Dr Leidner remained silent. He looked harassed and unwilling.

"See you," Poirot's tone became winning and appealing, "it all rings true what you have told me, *except for that*. Why a *nurse*? There is an answer—yes. In fact, there can be only one answer. *You did not believe yourself in your wife's danger.*"

And then with a cry Dr Leidner broke down.

"God help me," he groaned. "I didn't. I didn't."

Poirot watched him with the kind of attention a cat gives a mouse-hole—ready to pounce when the mouse shows itself.

"What *did* you think then?" he asked.

"I don't know. I don't know . . ."

"But you do know. You know perfectly. Perhaps I can help you—with a guess. *Did you, Dr Leidner, suspect that these letters were all written by your wife herself?*"

There wasn't any need for him to answer. The truth of Poirot's guess was only too apparent. The horrified hand he held up, as though begging for mercy, told its own tale.

I drew a deep breath. So I *had* been right in my half-formed guess! I recalled the curious tone in which Dr Leidner had asked me what I thought of it all. I nodded my head slowly and thoughtfully, and suddenly awoke to the fact that M. Poirot's eyes were on me.

"Did you think the same, nurse?"

"The idea did cross my mind," I said truthfully.

"For what reason?"

"I explained the similarity of the handwriting on the letter that Mr Coleman had shown me.

Poirot turned to Dr Leidner.

"Had you, too, noticed that similarity?"

Dr Leidner bowed his head.

"Yes, I did. The writing was small and cramped—not big and generous like Louise's, but several of the letters were formed the same way. I will show you."

From an inner breast pocket he took out some letters and finally selected a sheet from one which he handed to Poirot. It was part of a letter written to him by his wife. Poirot compared it carefully with the anonymous letters.

"Yes," he murmured. "Yes. There are several similarities—a curious way of forming the letter *s*, a distinctive *e*. I am not a handwriting expert—I cannot pronounce definitely (and for that matter, I have never found two handwriting experts who agree on any point whatsoever)—but one can at least say this—the similarity between the two handwritings is very marked. It seems highly probable that they were all written by the same person. But it is not *certain*. We must take all contingencies into mind.

He leaned back in his chair and said thoughtfully:

"There are three possibilities. First, the similarity of the handwriting is pure coincidence. Second, that these threatening letters were written by Mrs Leidner herself for some obscure reason. Third, that they were written by some one *who deliberately copied her handwriting*. Why? There seems no sense in it. One of these three possibilities must be the correct one."

He reflected for a minute or two and then, turning to Dr Leidner, he asked, with a resumal of his brisk manner.

"When the possibility that Mrs Leidner herself was the author of these letters first struck you, what theory did you form?"

Dr Leidner shook his head.

"I put the idea out of my head as quickly as possible. I felt it was monstrous."

"Did you search for no explanation?"

"Well," he hesitated, "I wondered if worrying and brooding over the past had perhaps affected my wife's brain slightly. I thought she might possibly have written those letters to herself without being conscious of having done so. That is possible, isn't it?" he added, turning to Dr Reilly.

Dr Reilly pursed up his lips.

"The human brain is capable of almost anything," he replied vaguely.

But he shot a lightning glance at Poirot, and as if in obedience to it, the latter abandoned the subject.

"The letters are an interesting point," he said. "But we must concentrate on the case as a whole. There are, as I see it, three possible solutions."

"Three?"

"Yes. Solution one: the simplest. Your wife's first husband is still alive. He first threatens her and then proceeds to carry out his threats. If we accept this solution, our problem is to discover how he got in or out without being seen.

"Solution two: Mrs Leidner, for reasons of her own (reasons probably more easily understood by a medical man than a layman), writes herself threatening letters. The gas business is staged by her (remember, it was she who roused you by telling you she smelt gas). But, *if Mrs Leidner wrote herself the letters, she cannot be in danger from the supposed writer*. We must, therefore, look elsewhere for the murderer. We must look, in fact, amongst the members of your staff. Yes," in answer to a murmur of protest from Dr Leidner, "that is the only logical conclusion. To satisfy a private grudge one of them killed her. That person, I may say, was probably aware of the letters—or was at any rate aware that Mrs Leidner feared or was pretending to fear some one. That fact, in the murderer's opinion, rendered the murder quite safe for him. He felt sure it would be put down to a mysterious outsider—the writer of the threatening letters.

"A variant of this solution is that the murderer actually wrote the letters himself, being aware of Mrs Leidner's past history. But in that case it is not quite clear *why* the criminal should have copied Mrs Leidner's own handwriting since, as far as we can see, it would be more to his or her advantage that they should appear to be written by an outsider.

"The third solution is the most interesting to my mind. I suggest that the letters are genuine. They are written by Mrs Leidner's first husband (or his younger brother), *who is actually one of the expedition staff*."

16. The Suspects

DR LEIDNER sprang to his feet.

"Impossible! Absolutely impossible! The idea is absurd!"

Mr Poirot looked at him quite calmly but said nothing.

"You mean to suggest that my wife's former husband is one of the expedition *and that she didn't recognise him?*"

"Exactly. Reflect a little on the facts. Nearly twenty years ago your wive lived with this man for a few months. Would she know him if she came across him after that lapse of time? I think not. His face will have changed, his build will have changed—his voice may not have changed so much, but that is a detail he can attend to himself. And remember, *she is not looking for him amongst her own household.* She visualises him as somewhere *outside*—a stranger. No, I do not think she would recognise him. And there is a second possibility. The young brother—the child of those days who was so passionately devoted to his elder brother. He is now a man. Will she recognise a child of ten or twelve years old in a man nearing thirty? Yes, there is young William Bosner to be reckoned with. Remember, his brother in his eyes may not loom as a traitor but as a patriot, a martyr for his own country—Germany. In his eyes *Mrs Leidner* is the traitor—the monster who sent his beloved brother to death! A susceptible child is capable of great hero worship, and a young mind can easily be obsessed by an idea which persists into adult life."

"Quite true," said Dr Reilly. "The popular view that a child forgets easily is not an accurate one. Many people go right through life in the grip of an idea which has been impressed on them in very tender years."

"*Bien.* You have these two possibilities. Frederick Bosner, a man by now of fifty odd, and William Bosner, whose age would be something short of thirty. Let us examine the members of your staff from these two points of view."

"This is fantastic," murmured Dr Leidner. "*My* staff! The members of my own expedition."

"And consequently considered above suspicion," said Poirot dryly. "A very useful point of view. *Commençons!* Who could emphatically *not* be Frederick or William?"

"The women."

"Naturally. Miss Johnson and Mrs Mercado are crossed off. Who else?"

"Carey. He and I have worked together for years before I even met Louise——"

"And also he is the wrong age. He is, I should judge, thirty-eight or nine, too young for Frederick, too old for William. Now for the rest. There is Father Lavigny and Mr Mercado. Either of them might be Frederick Bosner."

"But, my dear sir," cried Dr Leidner in a voice of mingled irritation and amusement, "Father Lavigny is known all over the world as an epigraphist and Mercado has worked for years in a well-known museum in New York. It is *impossible* that either of them should be the man you think!"

Poirot waved an airy hand.

"Impossible—impossible—I take no account of the word! The impossible, always I examine it very closely! But we will pass on for the moment. Who else have you? Carl Reiter, a young man with a German name, David Emmott——"

"He has been with me two seasons, remember."

"He is a young man with the gift of patience. *If* he committed a crime, it would not be in a hurry. All would be very well prepared."

Dr Leidner made a gesture of despair.

"And lastly, William Coleman," continued Poirot.

"He is an Englishman."

"*Pourquoi pas?* Did not Mrs Leidner say that the boy left America and could not be traced? He might easily have been brought up in England."

"You have an answer to everything," said Dr Leidner.

I was thinking hard. Right from the beginning I had thought Mr Coleman's manner rather more like a P. G. Wodehouse book than like a real live young man. Had he really been playing a part all the time?"

Poirot was writing in a little book.

"Let us proceed with order and method," he said. "On the first count we have two names. Father Lavigny and Mr Mercado. On the second we have Coleman, Emmott and Reiter.

"Now let us pass to the opposite aspect of the matter—means and opportunity. *Who amongst the expedition had the means and the opportunity of committing the crime?* Carey was on the dig, Coleman was in Hassanieh, you yourself were on the roof. That leaves us Father Lavigny, Mr Mercado, Mrs Mercado, David Emmott, Carl Reiter, Miss Johnson and Nurse Leatheran."

"Oh!" I exclaimed, and I bounded in my chair.

Mr Poirot looked at me with twinkling eyes.

"Yes, I'm afraid, *ma sœur*, that you have got to be included. It would have been quite easy for you to have gone along and killed Mrs Leidner while the courtyard was empty. You have plenty of muscle and strength, and she would have been quite unsuspicious until the moment the blow was struck."

I was so upset that I couldn't get a word out. Dr Reilly, I noticed, was looking highly amused.

"Interesting case of a nurse who murdered her patients one by one," he murmured.

Such a look as I gave him!

Dr Leidner's mind had been running on a different tack.

"Not Emmott, M. Poirot," he objected. "You can't include him. He was on the roof with me, remember, during that ten minutes."

"Nevertheless we cannot exclude him. He could have come down, gone straight to Mrs Leidner's room, killed her, and *then* called the boy back. Or he might have killed her on one of the occasions when he had *sent the boy up to you.*"

Dr Leidner shook his head, murmuring:

"What a nightmare! It's all so—fantastic."

To my surprise Poirot agreed.

"Yes, that is true. *This is a fantastic crime.* One does not often come across them. Usually murder is very sordid—very simple. But this is unusual murder . . . I suspect, Dr Leidner, that your wife was an unusual woman."

He had hit the nail on the head with such accuracy that I jumped.

"Is that true, nurse?" he asked.

Dr Leidner said quietly:

"Tell him what Louise was like, nurse. You are unprejudiced."

I spoke quite frankly.

"She was very lovely," I said. 'You couldn't help admiring her and wanting to do things for her. I've never met any one like her before."

"Thank you," said Dr Leidner and smiled at me.

"That is valuable testimony coming from an outsider," said Poirot politely. "Well, let us proceed. Under the heading of *means and opportunity* we have seven names. Nurse Leatheran, Miss Johnson, Mrs Mercado, Mr Mercado, Mr Reiter, Mr Emmott and Father Lavigny."

Once more he cleared his throat. I've always noticed that foreigners can make the oddest noises.

"Let us for the moment assume that our third theory is correct. That is that the murderer is Frederick or William Bosner, and that Frederick or William Bosner is a member of the expedition staff. By comparing both lists we can narrow down our suspects on this count to four. Father Lavigny, Mr Mercado, Carl Reiter and David Emmott."

"Father Lavigny is out of the question," said Dr Leidner with decision. "He is one of the *Pères Blancs* in Carthage."

"And his beard's quite real," I put in.

"*Ma sœur*," said Poirot, "a murderer of the first class *never* wears a false beard!"

"How do you know the murderer is of the first class?" I asked rebelliously.

"Because if he were not, the whole truth would be plain to me at this instant—and it is not."

That's pure conceit, I thought to myself.

"Anyway," I said, reverting to the beard, "it must have taken quite a time to grow."

"That is a practical observation," said Poirot.

Dr Leidner said irritably:

"But it's ridiculous—quite ridiculous. Both he and Mercado are well-known men. They've been known for years."

Poirot turned to him.

"You have not the true vision. You do not appreciate an

important point. *If Frederick Bosner is not dead—what has he been doing all these years?* He must have taken a different name. He must have built himself up a career."

"As a *Père Blanc*?" asked Dr Reilly sceptically.

"It is a little fantastic that, yes," confessed Poirot. "But we cannot put it right out of court. Besides, there are other possibilities."

"The young 'uns?" said Reilly. "If you want my opinion, on the face of it there's only one of your suspects that's even plausible."

"And that is?"

"Young Carl Reiter. There's nothing actually against him, but come down to it and you've got to admit a few things—he's the right age, he's got a German name, he's new this year and he had the opportunity all right. He'd only got to pop out of his photographic place, cross the courtyeard to do his dirty work and hare back again while the coast was clear. If any one were to have dropped into the photographic room while he was out of it, he can always say later that he was in the dark-room. I don't say he's your man but if you are going to suspect some one I say he's by far and away the most likely."

M. Poirot didn't seem very receptive. He nodded gravely but doubtfully.

"Yes," he said. "He is the most plausible, but it may not be so simple as all that."

Then he said:

"Let us say no more at present. I would like now if I may to examine the room where the crime took place."

"Certainly." Dr Leidner fumbled in his pockets then looked at Dr Reilly.

"Captain Maitland took it," he said.

"Maitland gave it to me," said Reilly. "He had to go off on that Kurdish business."

He produced the key.

Dr Leidner said hesitatingly:

"Do you mind—if I don't—— Perhaps, nurse——"

"Of course. Of course," said Poirot. "I quite understand. Never do I wish to cause you unnecessary pain. If you will be good enough to accompany me, *ma sœur*."

"Certainly," I said.

17. *The Stain by the Wash-stand*

MRS LEIDNER's body had been taken to Hassanieh for the post-mortem, but otherwise her room had been left exactly as it was. There was so little in it that it had not taken the police long to go over it.

To the right of the door as you entered was the bed. Opposite the door were the two barred windows giving on the country-side. Between them was a plain oak table with two drawers that served Mrs Leidner as a dressing-table. On the east wall there was a line of hooks with dresses hung up protected by cotton bags and a deal chest of drawers. Immediately to the left of the door was the wash-stand. In the middle of the room was a good-sized plain oak table with a blotter and inkstand and a small attaché-case. It was in the latter that Mrs Leidner had kept the anonymous letters. The curtains were short strips of native material—white striped with orange. The floor was of stone with some goatskin rugs on it, three narrow ones of brown striped with white in front of the two windows and the wash-stand, and a larger better quality one of white with brown stripes lying between the bed and the writing-table.

There were no cupboards or alcoves or long curtains—nowhere, in fact, where any one could have hidden. The bed was a plain iron one with a printed cotton quilt. The only trace of luxury in the room were three pillows all made of the best soft and billowy down. Nobody but Mrs Leidner had pillows like these.

In a few brief dry words Dr Reilly explained where Mrs Leidner's body had been found—in a heap on the rug beside the bed.

To illustrate his account, he beckoned me to come forward. "If you don't mind, nurse?" he said.

I'm not squeamish. I got down on the floor and arranged

myself as far as possible in the attitude in which Mrs Leidner's body had been found.

"Leidner lifted her head when he found her," said the doctor. "But I questioned him closely and it's obvious that he didn't actually change her position."

"It seems quite straightforward," said Poirot. "She was lying on the bed, asleep or resting—some one opens the door, she looks up, rises to her feet——"

"And he struck her down," finished the doctor. "The blow would produce unconsciousness and death would follow very shortly. You see——"

He explained the injury in technical language.

"Not much blood, then?" said Poirot.

"No, the blood escaped internally into the brain."

"*Eh bien,*" said Poirot, "that seems straightforward enough—except for one thing. *If* the man who entered was a stranger, why did not Mrs Leidner cry out at once for help? If she had screamed she would have been heard. Nurse Leatheran here would have heard her, and Emmott and the boy."

"That's easily answered," said Dr Reilly dryly. "*Because it wasn't a stranger.*"

Poirot nodded.

"Yes," he said meditatively. "She may have been *surprised* to see the person—but she was not *afraid*. Then, as he struck, she *may* have uttered a half cry—too late."

"The cry Miss Johnson heard?"

"Yes, if she *did* hear it. But on the whole I doubt it. These mud walls are thick and the windows were closed."

He stepped up to the bed.

"You left her actually lying down?" he asked me.

I explained exactly what I had done.

"Did she mean to sleep or was she going to read?"

"I gave her two books—a light one and a volume of memoirs. She usually read for a while and then sometimes dropped off for a short sleep."

"And she was—what shall I say—quite as usual?"

I considered.

"Yes. She seemed quite normal and in good spirits," I said. "Just a shade off-hand, perhaps, but I put that down to her

108

having confided in me the day before. It makes people a little uncomfortable sometimes."

Poirot's eyes twinkled.

"Ah, yes, indeed, me, I know that well."

He looked round the room.

"And when you came in here after the murder, was everything as you had seen it before?"

I looked round also.

"Yes, I think so. I don't remember anything being different."

"There was no sign of the weapon with which she was struck?"

"No."

Poirot looked at Dr Reilly.

"What was it in your opinion?"

The doctor replied promptly.

"Something pretty powerful of a fair size and without any sharp corners or edges. The rounded base of a statue, say—something like that. Mind you, I'm not suggesting that that *was* it. But that type of thing. The blow was delivered with great force."

"Struck by a strong arm? A man's arm?"

"Yes—unless——"

"Unless—what?"

Dr Reilly said slowly:

"It is just possible that Mrs Leidner might have been on her knees—in which case, the blow being delivered from above with a heavy implement, the force needed would not have been so great."

"*On her knees,*" mused Poirot. "It is an idea—that."

"It's only an idea, mind," the doctor hastened to point out. "There's absolutely nothing to indicate it."

"But it's possible."

"Yes. And after all, in view of the circumstances, it's not fantastic. Her fear might have led her to kneel in supplication rather than to scream when her instinct would tell her it was too late—that nobody could get there in time."

"Yes," said Poirot thoughtfully. "It is an idea . . ."

It was a very poor one, I thought. I couldn't for one moment imagine Mrs Leidner on her knees to any one.

Poirot made his way slowly round the room. He opened the windows, tested the bars, passed his head through and satisfied himself that by no means could his shoulders be made to follow his head.

"The windows were shut when you found her," he said. "Were they also shut when you left her at a quarter to one?"

"Yes, they were always shut in the afternoon. There is no gauze over these windows as there is in the living-room and dining-room. They are kept shut to keep out the flies."

"And in any case no one could get in that way," mused Poirot. "And the walls are of the most solid—mud-brick—and there are no trap-doors and no sky-lights. No, there is only one way into this room—*through the door*. And there is only one way to the door—*through the courtyard*. And there is only one entrance to the courtyard—*through the archway*. And outside the archway there were five people and they all tell the same story, and I do not think, me, that they are lying . . . No, they are not lying. They are not bribed to silence. The murderer was *here*. . . ."

I didn't say anything. Hadn't I felt the same thing just now when we were all cooped up around that table?

Slowly Poirot prowled round the room. He took up a photograph from the chest of drawers. It was of an elderly man with a white goatee beard. He looked inquiringly at me.

"Mrs Leidner's father," I said. "She told me so."

He put it down again and glanced over the articles on the dressing-table—all of plain tortoiseshell—simple but good. He looked up at a row of books in a shelf, repeating the titles aloud.

"*Who were the Greeks? Introduction to Relativity. Life of Lady Hester Stanhope. Crewe Train. Back to Methuselah. Linda Condon.* Yes, they tell us something, perhaps.

"She was not a fool, your Mrs Leidner. She had a mind."

"Oh! she was a *very* clever woman," I said eagerly. "Very well read and up in everything. She wasn't a bit ordinary."

He smiled as he looked over at me.

"No," he said. "I've already realised that."

He passed on. He stood for some moments at the wash-stand where there was a big array of bottles and toilet creams.

Then, suddenly, he dropped on his knees and examined the rug.

The Stain by the Wash-stand

Dr Reilly and I came quickly to join him. He was examining a small dark brown stain, almost invisible on the brown of the rug. In fact it was only just noticeable where it impinged on one of the white stripes.

"What do you say, doctor?" he said. "Is that blood?"

Dr Reilly knelt down.

"Might be," he said. "I'll make sure if you like?"

"If you would be so amiable."

Mr Poirot examined the jug and basin. The jug was standing on the side of the wash-stand. The basin was empty, but beside the wash-stand there was an empty kerosene tin containing slop water.

He turned to me.

"Do you remember, nurse? Was this jug *out* of the basin or *in* it when you left Mrs Leidner at a quarter to one?"

"I can't be sure," I said after a minute or two. "I rather think it was standing in the basin."

"Ah?"

"But you see," I said hastily. "I only think so because it usually was. The boys leave it like that after lunch. I just feel that if it hadn't been in I should have noticed it."

He nodded quite appreciatively.

"Yes, I understand that. It is your hospital training. If everything had not been just so in the room, you would quite unconsciously have set it to rights hardly noticing what you were doing. And after the murder? Was it like it is now?"

I shook my head.

"I didn't notice then," I said. "All I looked for was whether there was any place any one could be hidden or if there were anything the murderer had left behind him."

"It's blood all right," said Dr Reilly, rising from his knees. "Is it important?"

Poirot was frowning perplexedly. He flung out his hands with petulance.

"I cannot tell. How can I tell? It may mean nothing at all. I can say, if I like, that the murderer touched her—that there was blood on his hands—very little blood, but still blood—and so he came over here and washed them. Yes, it may have been like that. But I cannot jump to conclusions and say that it *was* so. That stain may be of no importance at all."

"There would have been very little blood," said Dr Reilly dubiously. "None would have spurted out or anything like that. It would have just oozed a little from the wound. Of course, if he'd probed it at all . . ."

I gave a shiver. A nasty sort of picture came up in my mind. The vision of somebody—perhaps that nice pig-faced photographic boy, striking down that lovely woman and then bending over her probing the wound with his finger in an awful gloating fashion and his face, perhaps, quite different . . . all fierce and mad . . .

Dr Reilly noticed my shiver.

"What's the matter, nurse?" he said.

"Nothing—just goose-flesh," I said. "A goose walking over my grave."

Mr Poirot turned round and looked at me.

"I know what you need," he said. "Presently when we have finished here and I go back with the doctor to Hassanieh we will take you with us. You will give Nurse Leatheran tea, will you not, doctor?"

"Delighted."

"Oh, no, doctor," I protested. "I couldn't think of such a thing."

M. Poirot gave me a little friendly tap on the shoulder. Quite an English tap, not a foreign one.

"You, *ma sœur*, will do as you are told," he said. "Besides, it will be of advantage to me. There is a good deal more that I want to discuss, and I cannot do it here where one must preserve the decencies. The good Dr Leidner he worshipped his wife and he is sure—oh, so sure—that everybody else felt the same about her! But that, in my opinion, would not be human nature! No, we want to discuss Mrs Leidner with—how do you say—the gloves removed? That is settled then. When we have finished here, we take you with us to Hassanieh."

"I suppose," I said doubtfully, "that I ought to be leaving anyway. It's rather awkward."

"Do nothing for a day or two," said Dr Reilly. "You can't very well go until after the funeral."

"That's all very well," I said. "And supposing *I* get murdered too, doctor?"

I said it half jokingly and Dr Reilly took it in the same fashion and would, I think, have made some jocular response.

But M. Poirot, to my astonishment, stood stock still in the middle of the floor and clasped his hands to his head.

"Ah! if that were possible," he murmured. "It is a danger— yes—a great danger—and what can one do? How can one guard against it?"

"Why, M. Poirot," I said, "I was only joking! Who'd want to murder me, I should like to know?"

"You—or another," he said, and I didn't like the way he said it at all. Positively creepy.

"But why?" I persisted.

He looked at me very straight then.

"I joke, mademoiselle," he said, "and I laugh. *But there are some things that are no joke.* There are things that my profession has taught me. And one of these things, the most terrible thing, is this:

"*Murder is a habit . . .*"

18. Tea at Dr Reilly's

Before leaving, Poirot made a round of the expedition house and the outbuildings. He also asked a few questions of the servants at second hand—that is to say, Dr Reilly translated the questions and answers from English into Arabic and vice versa.

These questions dealt mainly with the appearance of the stranger Mrs Leidner and I had seen looking through the window and to whom Father Lavigny had been talking on the following day.

"Do you really think that fellow had anything to do with it?" asked Dr Reilly when we were bumping along in his car on our way to Hassanieh.

"I like all the information there is," was Poirot's reply.

And really, that described his methods very well. I found later that there wasn't anything—no small scrap of insignificant gossip—in which he wasn't interested. Men aren't usually so gossipy.

I must confess I was glad of my cup of tea when we got to Dr Reilly's house. M. Poirot, I noticed, put five lumps of sugar in his.

Stirring it carefully with his teaspoon he said:

"And now we can talk, can we not? We can make up our minds who is likely to have committed the crime."

"Lavigny, Mercado, Emmott or Reiter?" asked Dr Reilly.

"No, no—that was theory number three. I wish to concentrate now on theory number two—leaving aside all question of a mysterious husband or brother-in-law turning up from the past. Let us discuss now quite simply which member of the expedition had the means and opportunity to kill Mrs Leidner, and who is likely to have done so."

"I thought you didn't think much of that theory."

"Not at all. But I have some natural delicacy," said Poirot

reproachfully. "Can I discuss in the presence of Dr Leidner the motives likely to lead to the murder of his wife by a member of the expedition? That would not have been delicate at all. I had to sustain the fiction that his wife was adorable and that every one adored her!

"But naturally it was not like that at all. Now we can be brutal and impersonal and say what we think. We have no longer to consider people's feelings. And that is where Nurse Leatheran is going to help us. She is, I am sure, a very good observer."

"Oh, I don't know about that," I said.

Dr Reilly handed me a plate of hot scones—"to fortify yourself," he said. They were very good scones.

"Come now," said M. Poirot in a friendly, chatty way. "You shall tell me, *ma sœur*, exactly what each member of the expedition felt towards Mrs Leidner."

"I was only there a week, M. Poirot," I said.

"Quite long enough for one of your intelligence. A nurse sums up quickly. She makes her judgments and abides by them. Come, let us make a beginning. Father Lavigny, for instance?"

"Well, there now, I really couldn't say. He and Mrs Leidner seemed to like talking together. But they usually spoke French and I'm not very good at French myself though I learnt it as a girl at school. I've an idea they talked mainly about books."

"They were, as you might say, companionable together—yes?"

"Well, yes, you might put it that way. But all the same, I think Father Lavigny was puzzled by her and—well—almost annoyed by being puzzled, if you know what I mean."

And I told him of the conversation I had had with him out on the dig that first day when he had called Mrs Leidner a "dangerous woman."

"Now that is very interesting," M. Poirot said. "And she—what do you think she thought of him?"

"That's rather difficult to say, too. It wasn't easy to know what Mrs Leidner thought of people. Sometimes, I fancy, *he* puzzled *her*. I remember her saying to Dr Leidner that he was unlike any priest she had ever known."

"A length of hemp to be ordered for Father Lavigny," said Dr Reilly facetiously.

"My dear friend," said Poirot. "Have you not, perhaps, some patients to attend? I would not for the world detain you from your professional duties."

"I've got a whole hospital of them," said Dr Reilly.

And he got up and said a wink was as good as a nod to a blind horse, and went out laughing.

"That is better," said Poirot. "We will have now an interesting conversation *tête-à-tête*. But you must not forget to eat your tea."

He passed me a plate of sandwiches and suggested my having a second cup of tea. He really had very pleasant, attentive manners.

"And now," he said, "let us continue with your impressions. Who was there who in your opinion did *not* like Mrs Leidner?"

"Well," I said, "it's only my opinion and I don't want it repeated as coming from me."

"Naturally not."

"But in my opinion little Mrs Mercado fairly hated her!"

"Ah! And Mr Mercado?"

"He was a bit soft on her," I said. "I shouldn't think women, apart from his wife, had ever taken much notice of him. And Mrs Leidner had a nice kind way of being interested in people and the things they told her. It rather went to the poor man's head, I fancy."

"And Mrs Mercado—she was not pleased?"

"She was just plain jealous—that's the truth of it. You've got to be very careful when there's a husband and wife about, and that's a fact. I could tell you some surprising things. You've no idea the extraordinary things women get into their heads when it's a question of their husbands."

"I do not doubt the truth of what you say. So Mrs Mercado was jealous? And she hated Mrs Leidner?"

"I've seen her look at her as though she'd have liked to kill her—oh, gracious!" I pulled myself up. "Indeed, M. Poirot, I didn't mean to say—I mean that is, not for one moment——"

"No, no. I quite understand. The phrase slipped out. A very convenient one. And Mrs Leidner, was she worried by this animosity of Mrs Mercado's?"

"Well," I said reflecting, "I don't really think she was

worried at all. In fact, I don't even know whether she noticed it. I thought once of just giving her a hint—but I didn't like to. Least said soonest mended. That's what I say."

"You are doubtless wise. Can you give me any instances of how Mrs Mercado showed her feelings?"

I told him about our conversation on the roof.

"So she mentioned Mrs Leidner's first marriage," said Poirot thoughtfuly. "Can you remember—in mentioning it—did she look at you as though she wondered whether you had heard a different version?"

"You think she may have known the truth about it?"

"It is a possibility. She may have written those letters—and engineered a tapping hand and all the rest of it."

"I wondered something of the same kind myself. It seemed the kind of petty revengeful thing she might do."

"Yes. A cruel streak, I should say. But hardly the temperament for cold-blooded brutal murder unless, of course——"

He paused and then said:

"It is odd, that curious thing she said to you. '*I know why you are here.*' What did she mean by it?"

"I can't imagine," I said frankly.

"She thought you were there for some ulterior reason apart from the declared one. What reason? And why should she be so concerned in the matter. Odd, too, the way you tell me she stared at you all through tea the day you arrived."

"Well, she's not a lady, M. Poirot," I said primly.

"That, *ma sœur*, is an excuse but not an explanation."

I wasn't quite sure for the minute what he meant. But he went on quickly.

"And the other members of the staff?"

I considered.

"I don't think Miss Johnson liked Mrs Leidner either very much. But she was quite open and above-board about it. She as good as admitted she was prejudiced. You see, she's very devoted to Dr Leidner and had worked with him for years. And of course, marriage does change things—there's no denying it."

"Yes," said Poirot. "And from Miss Johnson's point of view it would be an unsuitable marriage. It would really have been much more suitable if Dr Leidner had married *her*."

"It would really," I agreed. "But there, that's a man all over. Not one in a hundred considers suitability. And one can't really blame Dr Leidner. Miss Johnson, poor soul, isn't so much to look at. Now Mrs Leidner was really beautiful—not young, of course—but oh! I wish you'd known her. There was something about her. . . . I remember Mr Coleman saying she was like a thingummyjig that came to lure people into marshes. That wasn't a very good way of putting it, but—oh, well—you'll laugh at me, but there *was* something about her that was—well—unearthly."

"She could cast a spell—yes, I understand," said Poirot.

"Then I don't think she and Mr Carey got on very well either," I went on. "I've an idea *he* was jealous just like Miss Johnson. He was always very stiff with her and so was she with him. You know—she passed him things and was very polite and called him Mr Carey rather formally. He was an old friend of her husband's, of course, and some women can't stand their husband's old friends. They don't like to think that any one knew them before they did—at least that's rather a muddled way of putting it——"

"I quite understand. And the three young men? Coleman, you say, was inclined to be poetic about her."

I couldn't help laughing.

"It was funny, M. Poirot," I said. "He's such a matter-of-fact young man."

"And the other two?"

"I don't really know about Mr Emmott. He's always so quiet and never says much. She was very nice to him always. You know—friendly—called him David and used to tease him about Miss Reilly and things like that."

"Ah, really? And did he enjoy that?"

"I don't quite know," I said doubtfully. "He'd just look at her. Rather funnily. You couldn't tell what he was thinking."

"And Mr Reiter?"

"She wasn't always very kind to him," I said slowly. "I think he got on her nerves. She used to say quite sarcastic things to him."

"And did he mind?"

"He used to get very pink, poor boy. Of course, she didn't *mean* to be unkind."

And then suddenly, from feeling a little sorry for the boy, it came over me that he was very likely a cold-blooded murderer and had been playing a part all the time.

"Oh, M. Poirot," I exclaimed. "What do you think *really* happened?"

He shook his head slowly and thoughtfully.

"Tell me," he said. "You are not afraid to go back there to-night?"

"Oh *no*," I said. "Of course, I remember what you said, but who would want to murder *me*?"

"I do not think that any one could," he said slowly. "That is partly why I have been so anxious to hear all you could tell me. No, I think—I am sure—you are quite safe."

"If any one had told me in Baghdad——" I began and stopped.

"Did you hear any gossip about the Leidners and the expedition before you came here?" he asked.

I told him about Mrs Leidner's nickname and just a little of what Mrs Kelsey had said about her.

In the middle of it the door opened and Miss Reilly came in. She had been playing tennis and had her racquet in her hand.

I gathered Poirot had already met her when he arrived in Hassanieh.

She said how do you do to me in her usual off-hand manner and picked up a sandwich.

"Well, M. Poirot," she said. "How are you getting on with our local mystery?"

"Not very fast, mademoiselle."

"I see you've rescued nurse from the wreck."

"Nurse Leatheran has been giving me valuable information about the various members of the expedition. Incidentally I have learnt a good deal—about the victim. And the victim, mademoiselle, is very often the clue to the mystery."

Miss Reilly said:

"That's rather clever of you, M. Poirot. It's certainly true that if ever a woman deserved to be murdered Mrs Leidner was that woman!"

"Miss Reilly!" I cried scandalised.

She laughed, a short, nasty laugh.

"Ah!" she said. "I thought you hadn't been hearing quite the truth. Nurse Leatheran, I'm afraid, was quite taken in, like many other people. Do you know, M. Poirot, I rather hope that this case isn't going to be one of your successes. I'd quite like the murderer of Louise Leidner to get away with it. In fact, I wouldn't much have objected to putting her out of the way myself."

I was simply disgusted with the girl. M. Poirot, I must say, didn't turn a hair. He just bowed and said quite pleasantly:

"I hope, then, that you have an alibi for yesterday afternoon?"

There was a moment's silence and Miss Reilly's racquet went clattering down on to the floor. She didn't bother to pick it up. Slack and untidy like all her sort! She said in a rather breathless voice:

"Oh, yes, I was playing tennis at the club. But, seriously, M. Poirot, I wonder if you know anything at all about Mrs Leidner and the kind of woman she was?"

Again he made a funny little bow and said:

"You shall inform me, mademoiselle."

She hesitated a minute and then spoke with a callousness and lack of decency that really sickened me.

"There's a convention that one doesn't speak ill of the dead. That's stupid, I think. The truth's always the truth. On the whole it's better to keep your mouth shut about living people. You might conceivably injure them. The dead are past that. But the harm they've done lives after them sometimes. Not quite a quotation from Shakespeare but very nearly! Has nurse told you of the queer atmosphere there was at Tell Yarimjah? Has she told you how jumpy they all were? And how they all used to glare at each other like enemies? That was Louise Leidner's doing. When I was a kid out here three years ago they were the happiest, jolliest lot imaginable. Even last year they were pretty well all right. But this year there was a blight over them—and it was *her* doing. She was the kind of woman who won't let anybody else be happy! There *are* women like that and she was one of them! She wanted to break up things always. Just for fun—or for the sense of power—or perhaps just because she was made that way. And she was the kind of woman who had to get hold of every male creature within reach!"

"Miss Reilly," I cried, "I don't think that's true. In fact I *know* it isn't."

She went on without taking the least notice of me.

"It wasn't enough for her to have her husband adore her. She had to make a fool of that long-legged shambling idiot of a Mercado. Then she got hold of Bill. Bill's a sensible cove, but she was getting him all mazed and bewildered. Carl Reiter she just amused herself by tormenting. It was easy. He's a sensitive boy. And she had a jolly good go at David.

"David was better sport to her because he put up a fight. He felt her charm—but he wasn't having any. I think because he'd got sense enough to know that she didn't really care a damn. And that's why I hate her so. She's not sensual. She doesn't *want* affairs. It's just cold-blooded experiment on her part and the fun of stirring people up and setting them against each other. She dabbled in that too. She's the sort of woman who's never had a row with any one in her life—but rows always happen where she is! She *makes* them happen. She's a kind of female Iago. She *must* have drama. But she doesn't want to be involved *herself*. She's always outside pulling strings—looking on—enjoying it. Oh, do you see *at all* what I mean?"

"I see, perhaps, more than you know, mademoiselle," said Poirot.

I couldn't make his voice out. He didn't sound indignant. He sounded—oh, well, I can't explain it.

Sheila Reilly seemed to understand for she flushed all over her face.

"You can think what you choose," she said. 'But I'm right about her. She was a clever woman and she was bored and she experimented—with people—like other people experiment with chemicals. She enjoyed working on poor old Johnson's feelings and seeing her bite on the bullet and control herself like the old sport she is. She liked goading little Mercado into a white-hot frenzy. She liked flicking *me* on the raw—and she could do it too, every time! She liked finding out things about people and holding it over them. Oh, I don't mean crude blackmail—I mean just letting them know that she *knew*—and leaving them uncertain what she meant to do about it. My God, though, that woman was an artist! There was nothing crude about *her* methods!"

"And her husband?" asked Poirot.

"She never wanted to hurt him," said Miss Reilly slowly. "I've never known her anything but sweet to him. I suppose she was fond of him. He's a dear—wrapped up in his own world—his digging and his theories. And he worshipped her and thought her perfection. That might have annoyed some women. It didn't annoy her. In a sense he lived in a fool's paradise—and yet it wasn't a fool's paradise because to him she was what he thought her. Though it's hard to reconcile that with——"

She stopped.

"Go on, mademoiselle," said Poirot.

She turned suddenly on me.

"What have you said about Richard Carey?"

"About Mr Carey?" I asked astonished.

"About her and Carey?"

"Well," I said, "I've mentioned that they didn't hit it off very well——"

To my surprise she broke into a fit of laughter.

"Didn't hit it off very well! You fool! He's head over ears in love with her. And it's tearing him to pieces—because he worships Leidner too. He's been his friend for years. That would be enough for her, of course. She's made it her business to come between them. But all the same I've fancied——"

"*Eh, bien?*"

She was frowning, absorbed in thought.

"I've fancied that she'd gone too far for once—that she was not only biter but bit! Carey's attractive. He's as attractive as hell. . . . She was a cold devil—but I believe she could have lost her coldness with him. . . ."

"I think it's scandalous what you're saying," I cried. "Why, they hardly spoke to each other!"

"Oh, didn't they?" She turned on me. "A hell of a lot you know about it. It was 'Mr Carey' and 'Mrs Leidner' in the house, but they used to meet outside. She'd walk down the path to the river. And he'd leave the dig for an hour at a time. They used to meet among the fruit trees.

"I saw him once just leaving her, striding back to the dig, and she was standing looking after him. I was a female cad, I suppose. I had some glasses with me and I took them out and had a good look at her face. If you ask me I believe she cared like hell for Richard Carey. . . ."

She broke off and looked at Poirot.

"Excuse my butting in on your case," she said with a sudden rather twisted grin, "but I thought you'd like to have the local colour correct."

And she marched out of the room.

"M. Poirot," I cried. "I don't believe one word of it all!"

He looked at me and he smiled, and he said (very queerly I thought):

"You can't deny, nurse, that Miss Reilly has shed a certain— illumination on the case."

19. *A New Suspicion*

WE COULDN'T SAY any more just then because Dr Reilly came in, saying jokingly that he'd killed off the most tiresome of his patients.

He and M. Poirot settled down to a more or less medical discussion of the psychology and mental state of an anonymous letter-writer. The doctor cited cases that he had known professionally, and M. Poirot told various stories from his own experience.

"It is not so simple as it seems," he ended. "There is the desire for power and very often a strong inferiority complex."

Dr Reilly nodded.

"That's why you often find that the author of anonymous letters is the last person in the place to be suspected. Some quiet inoffensive little soul who apparently can't say Bo to a goose— all sweetness and Christian meekness on the outside—and seething with all the fury of hell underneath!"

Poirot said thoughtfully:

"Should you say Mrs Leidner had any tendency to an inferiority complex?"

Dr Reilly scraped out his pipe with a chuckle.

"Last woman on earth I'd describe that way. No repressions about her. Life, life and more life—that's what she wanted— and got, too!"

"Do you consider it a possibility, psychologically speaking, that she wrote those letters?"

"Yes, I do. But if she did, the reason arose out of her instinct to dramatise herself. Mrs Leidner was a bit of a film star in private life! She *had* to be the centre of things—in the limelight. By the law of opposites she married Leidner who's about the most retiring and modest man I know. He adored her—but adoration by the fireside wasn't enough for her. She had to be the persecuted heroine as well."

"In fact," said Poirot smiling, "you don't subscribe to his theory that she wrote them and retained no memory of her act?"

"No, I don't. I didn't turn down the idea in front of him. You can't very well say to a man who's just lost a dearly loved wife that that same wife was a shameless exhibitionist, and that she drove him nearly crazy with anxiety to satisfy her sense of the dramatic. As a matter of fact it wouldn't be safe to tell any man the truth about his wife! Funnily enough, I'd trust most women with the truth about their husbands. Women can accept the fact that a man is a rotter, a swindler, a drug-taker, a confirmed liar, and a general swine without batting an eyelash and without its impairing their affection for the brute in the least! Women are wonderful realists."

"Frankly, Dr Reilly, what *was* your exact opinion of Mrs Leidner?"

Dr Reilly lay back in his chair and puffed slowly at his pipe.

"Frankly—it's hard to say! I didn't know her well enough. She'd got charm—any amount of it. Brains, sympathy . . . What else? She hadn't any of the ordinary unpleasant vices. She wasn't sensual or lazy or even particularly vain. She was, I've always thought (but I've no proofs of it), a most accomplished liar. What I don't know (and what I'd like to know) is whether she lied to herself or only to other people. I'm rather partial to liars myself. A woman who doesn't lie is a woman without imagination and without sympathy. I don't think she was really a man-hunter—she just liked the sport of bringing them down 'with my bow and arrow.' If you get my daughter on the subject——"

"We have had that pleasure," said Poirot with a slight smile.

"H'm," said Dr Reilly. "She hasn't wasted much time! Shoved her knife into her pretty thoroughly, I should imagine! The younger generation has no sentiment towards the dead. It's a pity all young people are prigs! They condemn the 'old morality' and then proceed to set up a much more hard and fast code of their own. If Mrs Leidner had had half a dozen affairs Sheila would probably have approved of her as 'living her life fully'— or 'obeying her blood instincts.' What she doesn't see is that Mrs Leidner was acting true to type—*her* type. The cat *is* obeying its blood instinct when it plays with the mouse! It's made that way.

Men aren't little boys to be shielded and protected. They've got to meet cat women—and faithful spaniel, yours-till-death adoring women, and hen-pecking nagging bird women—and all the rest of it! Life's a battlefield—not a picnic! I'd like to see Sheila honest enough to come off her high horse and admit that she hated Mrs Leidner for good old thorough-going personal reasons. Sheila's about the only young girl in this place and she naturally assumes that she ought to have it all her own way with the young things in trousers. Naturally it annoys her when a woman, who in her view is middle-aged and who has already two husbands to her credit, comes along and licks her on her own ground. Sheila's a nice child, healthy and reasonably good-looking and attractive to the other sex as she should be. But Mrs Leidner was something out of the ordinary in that line. She'd got just that sort of calamitous magic that plays the deuce with things—a kind of Belle Dame sans Merci."

I jumped in my chair. What a coincidence his saying that!

"Your daughter—I am not indiscreet—she has perhaps a *tendresse* for one of the young men out there?"

"Oh, I don't suppose so. She's had Emmott and Coleman dancing attendance on her as a matter of course. I don't know that she cares for one more than the other. There are a couple of young Air Force chaps too. I fancy all's fish that comes to her net at present. No, I think it's age daring to defeat youth that annoys her so much! She doesn't know as much of the world as I do. It's when you get to my age that you really appreciate a schoolgirl complexion and a clear eye and a firmly knit young body. But a woman over thirty can listen with rapt attention and throw in a word here and there to show the talker what a fine fellow he is—and few young men can resist that! Sheila's a pretty girl—but Louise Leidner was beautiful. Glorious eyes and that amazing golden fairness. Yes, she was a beautiful woman."

Yes, I thought to myself, he's right. Beauty's a wonderful thing. She *had* been beautiful. It wasn't the kind of looks you were jealous of—you just sat back and admired. I felt that first day I met her that I'd do *anything* for Mrs Leidner!

All the same, that night as I was being driven back to the Tell Yarimjah (Dr Reilly made me stay for an early dinner) one or two things came back to my mind and made me rather uncomfortable. At the time I hadn't believed a word of all Sheila Reilly's outpouring. I'd taken it for sheer spite and malice.

But now I suddenly remembered the way Mrs Leidner had insisted on going for a stroll by herself that afternoon and wouldn't hear of me coming with her. I couldn't help wondering if perhaps, after all, she *had* been going to meet Mr Carey . . . And of course, it *was* a little odd, really, the way he and she spoke to each other so formally. Most of the others she called by their Christian names.

He never seemed to look at her, I remembered. That might be because he disliked her—or it might be just the opposite . . .

I gave myself a little shake. Here I was fancying and imagining all sorts of things—all because of a girl's spiteful outburst! It just showed how unkind and dangerous it was to go about saying that kind of thing.

Mrs Leidner *hadn't* been like that at all. . . .

Of course, *she* hadn't liked Sheila Reilly. She'd really been—almost catty about her that day at lunch to Mr Emmott.

Funny, the way he'd looked at her. The sort of way that you couldn't possibly tell what he was thinking. You never could tell what Mr Emmott was thinking. He was so quiet. But very nice. A nice dependable person.

Now Mr Coleman was a foolish young man if there ever was one!

I'd got to that point in my meditations when we arrived. It was just on nine o'clock and the big door was closed and barred.

Ibrahim came running with his great key to let me in.

We all went to bed early at Tell Yarimjah. There weren't any lights showing in the living-room. There was a light in the drawing-office and one in Dr Leidner's office, but nearly all the other windows were dark. Every one must have gone to bed even earlier than usual.

As I passed the drawing-office to go to my room I looked in. Mr Carey was in his shirt sleeves working over his big plan.

Terribly ill, he looked, I thought. So strained and worn. It gave me quite a pang. I don't know what there was about Mr Carey—it wasn't what he *said* because he hardly said anything—and that of the most ordinary nature, and it wasn't what he *did*, for that didn't amount to much either—and yet you just couldn't help noticing him, and everything about him seemed to matter more than it would have about any one else. He just *counted*, if you know what I mean.

He turned his head and saw me. He removed his pipe from his mouth and said:

"Well, nurse, back from Hassanieh?"

"Yes, Mr Carey. You're up working late. Everybody else seems to have gone to bed."

"I thought I might as well get on with things," he said. "I was a bit behind-hand. And I shall be out on the dig all to-morrow. We're starting digging again."

"Already?" I asked, shocked.

He looked at me rather queerly.

"It's the best thing, I think. I put it up to Leidner. He'll be in Hassanieh most of to-morrow seeing to things. But the rest of us will carry on here. You know it's not too easy all sitting round and looking at each other as things are."

He was right there, of course. Especially in the nervy, jumpy state every one was in.

"Well, of course you're right in a way," I said. "It takes one's mind off if one's got something to do."

The funeral, I knew, was to be the day after to-morrow.

He had bent over his plan again. I don't know why, but my heart just ached for him. I felt certain that he wasn't going to get any sleep."

"If you'd like a sleeping draught, Mr Carey?" I said hesitatingly.

He shook his head with a smile.

"I'll carry on, nurse. Bad habit, sleeping draughts."

"Well, good-night, Mr Carey," I said. "If there's anything I can do——"

"Don't think so, thank you, nurse. Good-night."

"I'm terribly sorry," I said, rather too impulsively I suppose.

"Sorry?" He looked surprised.

"For—for everybody. It's all so dreadful. But especially for you."

"For me? Why for me?"

"Well, you're such an old friend of them both."

"I'm an old friend of Leidner's. I wasn't a friend of hers particularly."

He spoke as though he had actually disliked her. Really, I wished Miss Reilly could have heard him!

"Well, good-night," I said and hurried along to my room.

I fussed around a bit in my room before undressing. Washed out some handkerchiefs and a pair of wash-leather gloves and wrote up my diary. I just looked out of my door again before I really started to get ready for bed. The lights were still on in the drawing-office and in the south building.

I supposed Dr Leidner was still up and working in his office. I wondered whether I ought to go and say good-night to him. I hesitated about it—I didn't want to seem officious. He might be busy and not want to be disturbed. In the end, however, a sort of uneasiness drove me on. After all, it couldn't do any harm. I'd just say good-night, ask if there was anything I could do and come away.

But Dr Leidner wasn't there. The office itself was lit up but there was no one in it except Miss Johnson. She had her head down on the table and was crying as though her heart would break.

It gave me quite a turn. She was such a quiet, self-controlled woman. It was pitiful to see her.

"Whatever is it, my dear?" I cried. I put my arm round her and patted her. "Now, now, this won't do at all . . . You mustn't sit here crying all by yourself."

She didn't answer and I felt the dreadful shuddering sobs that were racking her.

"Don't, my dear, don't," I said. "Take a hold on yourself. I'll go and make you a cup of nice hot tea."

She raised her head and said:

"No, no, it's all right, nurse. I'm being a fool."

"What's upset you, my dear?" I asked.

She didn't answer at once, then she said:

"It's all too awful. . . ."

"Now don't start thinking of it," I told her. "What's happened has happened and can't be mended. It's no use fretting."

She sat up straight and began to pat her hair.

"I'm making rather a fool of myself," she said in her gruff voice. "I've been clearing up and tidying the office. Thought it was best to *do* something. And then—it all came over me suddenly——"

129

"Yes, yes," I said hastily. "I know. A nice strong cup of tea and a hot-water bottle in your bed is what you want," I said.

And she had them too. I didn't listen to any protests.

"Thank you, nurse," she said when I'd settled her in bed, and she was sipping her tea and the hot-water bottle was in. "You're a nice kind sensible woman. It's not often I make such a fool of myself."

"Oh, anybody's liable to do that at a time like this," I said. "What with one thing and another. The strain and the shock and the police here, there and everywhere. Why, I'm quite jumpy myself."

She said slowly in rather a queer voice:

"What you said in there is true. What's happened has happened and can't be mended. . . ."

She was silent for a minute or two and then said—rather oddly, I thought:

"She was never a nice woman!"

Well, I didn't argue the point. I'd always felt it was quite natural for Miss Johnson and Mrs Leidner not to hit it off.

I wondered if, perhaps, Miss Johnson had secretly had a feeling that she was pleased Mrs Leidner was dead, and had then been ashamed of herself for the thought.

I said:

"Now you go to sleep and don't worry about anything."

I just picked up a few things and set the room to rights. Stockings over the back of the chair and coat and skirt on a hanger. There was a little ball of crumpled paper on the floor where it must have fallen out of a pocket.

I was just smoothing it out to see whether I could safely throw it away when she quite startled me.

"Give that to me!"

I did so—rather taken aback. She'd called out so peremptorily. She snatched it from me—fairly snatched it—and then held it in the candle flame till it was burnt to ashes.

As I say, I was startled—and I just stared at her.

I hadn't had time to see what the paper was—she'd snatched it so quick. But funnily enough, as it burned it curled over towards me and I just saw that there were words written in ink on the paper.

It wasn't till I was getting into bed that I realised why they'd looked sort of familiar to me.

It was the same handwriting as that of the anonymous letters.

Was *that* why Miss Johnson had given way to a fit of remorse? Had it been her all along who had written those anonymous letters?

20. Miss Johnson, Mrs Mercado, Mr Reiter

I DON'T MIND confessing that the idea came as a complete shock to me. I'd never thought of associating *Miss Johnson* with the letters. Mrs Mercado, perhaps. But Miss Johnson was a real lady, and so self-controlled and sensible.

But I reflected, remembering the conversation I had listened to that evening between M. Poirot and Dr Reilly, that that might be just *why*.

If it were Miss Johnson who had written the letters it explained a lot. Mind you, I didn't think for a minute Miss Johnson had had anything to do with the murder. But I *did* see that her dislike of Mrs Leidner might have made her succumb to the temptation of well—putting the wind up her—to put it vulgarly.

She might have hoped to frighten away Mrs Leidner from the dig.

But then Mrs Leidner had been murdered and Miss Johnson had felt terrible pangs of remorse—first for her cruel trick and also, perhaps, because she realised that those letters were acting as a very good shield to the actual murderer. No wonder she had broken down so utterly. She was, I was sure, a decent soul at heart. And it explained, too, why she had caught so eagerly at my consolation of "what's happened's happened and can't be mended."

And then her cryptic remark—her vindication of herself— "she was never a nice woman!"

The question was, what was *I* to do about it?

I tossed and turned for a while and in the end decided I'd let M. Poirot know about it at the first opportunity.

He came out next day but I didn't get a chance of speaking to him what you might call privately.

We had just a minute alone together and before I could collect myself to know how to begin, he had come close to me and was whispering instructions in my ear.

"Me, I shall talk to Miss Johnson—and others, perhaps, in the living-room. You have the key of Mrs Leidner's room still?"

"Yes," I said.

"*Très bien*. Go there, shut the door behind you and give a cry—not a scream—a cry. You understand what I mean—it is alarm—surprise that I want you to express—not mad terror. As for the excuse if you are heard—I leave that to you—the stepped toe or what you will."

At that moment Miss Johnson came out into the courtyard and there was not time for more.

I understood well enough what M. Poirot was after. As soon as he and Miss Johnson had gone into the living-room I went across to Mrs Leidner's room and, unlocking the door, went in and pulled the door to behind me.

I can't say I didn't feel a bit of a fool standing up in an empty room and giving a yelp all for nothing at all. Besides, it wasn't so easy to know just how loud to do it. I gave a pretty loud "Oh" and then tried it a bit higher and a bit lower.

Then I came out again and prepared my excuse of a stepped (stubbed I *suppose* he meant!) toe.

But it soon appeared that no excuse would be needed. Poirot and Miss Johnson were talking together earnestly and there had clearly been no interruption.

"Well," I thought, "that settles that. Either Miss Johnson imagined that cry she heard or else it was something quite different."

I didn't like to go in and interrupt them. There was a deck-chair on the porch so I sat down there. Their voices floated out to me.

"The position is delicate, you understand," Poirot was saying. "Dr Leidner—obviously he adored his wife——"

"He worshipped her," said Miss Johnson.

"He tells me, naturally, how fond all his staff was of her! As for them, what can they say? Naturally they say the same thing. It is politeness. It is decency. It *may* also be the truth! But also it may *not*! And I am convinced, mademoiselle, that the key to this enigma lies in a complete understanding of Mrs Leidner's character. If I could get the opinion—the honest opinion—of every member of the staff, I might, from the whole, build up a picture. Frankly, that is why I am here to-day. I knew Dr Leidner would be in Hassanieh. That makes it easy for me to have an interview with each of you here in turn, and beg your help."

"That's all very well," began Miss Johnson and stopped.

"Do not make me the British *clichés*," Poirot begged. "Do not say it is not the cricket or the football, that to speak anything but well of the dead is not done—that—*enfin*—there is loyalty! Loyalty it is a pestilential thing in crime. Again and again it obscures the truth."

"I've no particular loyalty to Mrs Leidner," said Miss Johnson dryly. There was indeed a sharp and acid tone in her voice. "Dr Leidner's a different matter. And, after all, she was his wife."

"Precisely—precisely. I understand that you would not wish to speak against your chief's wife. But this is not a question of testimonial. It is a question of sudden and mysterious death. If I am to believe that it is a martyred angel who has been killed it does not add to the easiness of my task."

"I certainly shouldn't call her an angel," said Miss Johnson and the acid tone was even more in evidence.

"Tell me your opinion, frankly, of Mrs Leidner—as a woman."

"H'm! To begin with, M. Poirot, I'll give you this warning. I'm prejudiced. I am—we all were—devoted to Dr Leidner. And, I suppose, when Mrs Leidner came along, we were jealous. We resented the demands she made on his time and attention. The devotion he showed her irritated us. I'm being truthful, M. Poirot, and it isn't very pleasant for me. I resented her presence here—yes, I did, though, of course, I tried never to show it. It made a difference to us, you see."

"Us? You say us?"

"I mean Mr Carey and myself. We're the two old-timers, you see. And we didn't much care for the new order of things. I suppose that's natural, though perhaps it was rather petty of us. But it *did* make a difference."

"What kind of a difference?"

"Oh! to everything. We used to have such a happy time. A good deal of fun, you know, and rather silly jokes, like people do who work together. Dr Leidner was quite light-hearted—just like a boy."

"And when Mrs Leidner came she changed all that?"

"Well, I suppose it wasn't her *fault*. It wasn't so bad last year. And please believe, M. Poirot, that it wasn't anything she *did*. She's always been charming to me—quite charming. That's why I've felt ashamed sometimes. It wasn't her fault that little things she said and did seemed to rub me up the wrong way. Really nobody could be nicer than she was."

"But nevertheless things were changed this season? There was a different atmosphere."

"Oh, entirely. Really, I don't know what it was. Everything seemed to go wrong—not with the work—I mean with us—our tempers and our nerves. All on edge. Almost the sort of feeling you get when there is a thunderstorm coming."

"And you put that down to Mrs Leidner's influence?"

"Well, it was never like that before she came," said Miss Johnson dryly. "Oh! I'm a cross-grained, complaining old dog. Conservative—liking things always the same. You really mustn't take any notice of me, M. Poirot."

"How would you describe to me Mrs Leidner's character and temperament?"

Miss Johnson hesitated for a moment. Then she said slowly:

"Well, of course, she was temperamental. A lot of ups and downs. Nice to people one day and perhaps wouldn't speak to them the next. She was very kind, I think. And very thoughtful for others. All the same you could see she had been thoroughly spoilt all her life. She took Dr Leidner's waiting on her hand and foot as perfectly natural. And I don't think she ever really appreciated what a very remarkable—what a really great—man she had married. That used to annoy me sometimes. And of course she was terribly highly strung and nervous. The things she used to imagine and the states she used to get into! I was thankful when Dr Leidner brought Nurse Leatheran here. It was too much for him having to cope both with his work and with his wife's fears."

"What is your own opinion of these anonymous letters she received?"

I had to do it. I leaned forward in my chair till I could just catch sight of Miss Johnson's profile turned to Poirot in answer to his question.

She was looking perfectly cool and collected.

"I think some one in America had a spite against her and was trying to frighten or annoy her."

"*Pas plus serieux que ça?*"

"That's my opinion. She was a very handsome woman, you know, and might easily have had enemies. I think those letters were written by some spiteful woman. Mrs Leidner being of a nervous temperament took them seriously."

"She certainly did that," said Poirot. "But remember—the last of them arrived by hand."

"Well, I suppose that *could* have been managed if any one had given their minds to it. Women will take a lot of trouble to gratify their spite, M. Poirot."

They will indeed, I thought to myself!

"Perhaps you are right, mademoiselle. As you say, Mrs Leidner was handsome. By the way, you know Miss Reilly, the doctor's daughter?"

"Sheila Reilly? Yes, of course,"

Poirot adopted a very confidential, gossipy tone.

"I have heard a rumour (naturally I do not like to ask the doctor) that there was a *tendresse* between her and one of the members of Dr Leidner's staff. Is that so, do you know?"

Miss Johnson appeared rather amused.

"Oh, young Coleman and David Emmott were both inclined to dance attendance. I believe there was some rivalry as to who was to be her partner in some event at the club. Both the boys went in on Saturday evenings to the club as a general rule. But I don't know that there was anything in it on her side. She's the only young creature in the place, you know, and so she's by way of being the belle of it. She's got the Air Force dancing attendance on her as well."

"So you think there is nothing in it?"

"Well—I don't know." Miss Johnson became thoughtful. "It is true that she comes out this way fairly often. Up to the dig and all that. In fact, Mrs Leidner was chaffing David Emmott about it the other day—saying the girl was running after him. Which was rather a catty thing to say, I thought, and I don't

think he liked it. . . . Yes, she was here a good deal. I saw her
riding towards the dig on that awful afternoon." She nodded
her head towards the open window. "But neither David
Emmott nor Coleman were on duty that afternoon. Richard
Carey was in charge. Yes, perhaps she *is* attracted to one of
the boys—but she's such a modern unsentimental young
woman that one doesn't know quite how seriously to take her.
I'm sure I don't know which of them it is. Bill's a nice boy,
and not nearly such a fool as he pretends to be. David
Emmott is a dear—and there's a lot to him. He is the deep,
quiet kind."

Then she looked quizzically at Poirot and said:

"But has this any bearing on the crime, M. Poirot?"

M. Poirot threw up his hands in a very French fashion.

"You make me blush, mademoiselle," he said. "You expose
me as a mere gossip. But what will you, I am interested always in
the love affairs of young people."

"Yes," said Miss Johnson with a little sigh. "It's nice when
the course of true love runs smooth."

Poirot gave an answering sigh. I wondered if Miss Johnson
was thinking of some love affair of her own when she was a girl.
And I wondered if M. Poirot had a wife, and if he went on in the
way you always hear foreigners do, with mistresses and things
like that. He looks so comic I couldn't imagine it.

"Sheila Reilly has a lot of character," said Miss Johnson.
"She's young and she's crude, but she's the right sort."

"I take your word for it, mademoiselle," said Poirot.

He got up and said, "Are there any other members of the staff
in the house?"

"Marie Mercado is somewhere about. All the men are up on
the dig to-day. I think they wanted to get out of the house. I
don't blame them. If you'd like to go up to the dig——"

She came out on the verandah and said, smiling to me:

"Nurse Leatheran won't mind taking you, I dare say."

"Oh certainly, Miss Johnson," I said.

"And you'll come back to lunch, won't you, M. Poirot?"

"Enchanted, mademoiselle."

Miss Johnson went back into the living-room where she was
engaged in cataloguing.

"Mrs Mercado's on the roof," I said. "Do you want to see her first?"

"It would be as well, I think. Let us go up."

As we went up the stairs I said:

"I did what you told me. Did you hear anything?"

"Not a sound."

"That will be a weight off Miss Johnson's mind at any rate," I said. "She's been worrying that she might have done something about it."

Mrs Mercado was sitting on the parapet, her head bent down, and she was so deep in thought that she never heard us till Poirot halted opposite her and bade her good-morning.

Then she looked up with a start.

She looked ill this morning, I thought, her small face pinched and wizened and great dark circles under her eyes.

"*Encore moi*," said Poirot. "I come to-day with a special object."

And he went on much in the same way as he had done to Miss Johnson, explaining how necessary it was that he should get a true picture of Mrs Leidner.

Mrs Mercado, however, wasn't as honest as Miss Johnson had been. She burst into fulsome praise which, I was pretty sure, was quite far removed from her real feelings.

"Dear, *dear* Louise! It's so hard to explain her to some one who didn't know her. She was such an *exotic* creature. Quite different from any one else. You felt that, I'm sure, nurse? A martyr to nerves, of course, and full of fancies, but one put up with things in her, one wouldn't from any one else. And she was so *sweet* to us all, wasn't she nurse? And so *humble* about herself—I mean she didn't know anything about archæology, and she was so eager to learn. Always asking my husband about the chemical processes for treating the metal objects and helping Miss Johnson to mend pottery. Oh, we were all *devoted* to her."

"Then it is not true, madame, what I have heard, that there was a certain tenseness—an uncomfortable atmosphere— here?"

Mrs Mercado opened her opaque black eyes very wide.

"Oh! who *can* have been telling you that? Nurse? Dr Leidner? I'm sure *he* would never notice anything, poor man."

And she shot a thoroughly unfriendly glance at me.

Poirot smiled easily.

"I have my spies, madame," he declared gaily. And just for a minute I saw her eyelids quiver and blink.

"Don't you think," asked Mrs Mercado with an air of great sweetness, "that after an event of this kind, every one always pretends a lot of things that never were? You know—tension, atmosphere, a 'feeling that something was going to happen?' I think people just *make up* these things afterwards."

"There is a lot in what you say, madame," said Poirot.

"And it really *wasn't* true! We were a thoroughly happy family here."

"That woman is one of the most utter liars I've ever known," I said indignantly, when M. Poirot and I were clear of the house and walking along the path to the dig. "I'm sure she simply hated Mrs Leidner really!"

"She is hardly the type to whom one would go for the truth," Poirot agreed.

"Waste of time talking to her," I snapped.

"Hardly that—hardly that. If a person tells you lies with her lips she is sometimes telling you truth with her eyes. What is she afraid of, little Madame Mercado? I saw fear in her eyes. Yes—decidedly she is afraid of something. It is very interesting."

"I've got something to tell you, M. Poirot," I said.

Then I told him all about my return the night before and my strong belief that Miss Johnson was the writer of the anonymous letters.

"So *she's* a liar too!" I said. "The cool way she answered you this morning about these same letters!"

"Yes," said Poirot. "It was interesting, that. *For she let out the fact that she knew all about those letters.* So far they have not been spoken of in the presence of the staff. Of course, it is quite possible that Dr Leidner told her about them yesterday. They are old friends, he and she. But if he did not—well—then it is curious and interesting, is it not?"

My respect for him went up. It was clever the way he had tricked her into mentioning the letters.

"Are you going to tackle her about them?" I asked.

M. Poirot seemed quite shocked by the idea.

"No, no, indeed. Always it is unwise to parade one's knowledge. Until the last minute I keep everything here," he tapped his forehead. "At the right moment—I make the spring—like the panther—and, *mon Dieu*! the consternation!"

I couldn't help laughing to myself at little M. Poirot in the rôle of a panther.

We had just reached the dig. The first person we saw was Mr Reiter, who was busy photographing some walling.

It's my opinion that the men who were digging just hacked out walls wherever they wanted them. That's what it looked like anyway. Carey explained to me that you could feel the difference at once with a pick, and he tried to show me—but I never saw. When the man said *"Libn"*—mud brick—it was just ordinary dirt and mud as far as I could see.

Mr Reiter finished his photographs and handed over the camera and the plates to his boy and told him to take them back to the house.

Poirot asked him one or two questions about exposures and film packs and so on which he answered very readily. He seemed pleased to be asked about his work.

He was just tendering his excuses for leaving us when Poirot plunged once more into his set speech. As a matter of fact it wasn't quite a set speech because he varied it a little each time to suit the person he was talking to. But I'm not going to write it all down every time. With sensible people like Miss Johnson he went straight to the point, and with some of the others he had to beat about the bush a bit more. But it came to the same in the end.

"Yes, yes, I see what you mean," said Mr Reiter. "But indeed, I do not see that I can be much help to you. I am new here this season and I did not speak much with Mrs Leidner. I regret, but indeed I can tell you nothing."

There was something a little stiff and foreign in the way he spoke, though, of course, he hadn't got any accent—except an American one, I mean.

"You can at least tell me whether you liked or disliked her?" said Poirot with a smile.

Mr Reiter got quite red and stammered:

"She was a charming person—most charming. And intellectual. She had a very fine brain—yes."

"*Bien!* You liked her. And she liked you?"

Mr Reiter got redder still.

"Oh, I—I don't know that she noticed me much. And I was unfortunate once or twice. I was always unlucky when I tried to do anything for her. I'm afraid I annoyed her by my clumsiness. It was quite unintentional . . . I would have done *any*thing——"

Poirot took pity on his flounderings.

"Perfectly—perfectly. Let us pass to another matter. Was it a happy atmosphere in the house?"

"Please."

"Were you all happy together? Did you laugh and talk?"

"No—no, not exactly that. There was a little—stiffness."

He paused, struggling with himself, and then said:

"You see, I am not very good in company. I am clumsy. I am shy. Dr Leidner always he has been most kind to me. But—it is stupid—I cannot overcome my shyness. I say always the wrong thing. I upset water jugs. I am unlucky."

He really looked like a large awkward child.

"We all do these things when we are young," said Poirot, smiling. "The poise, the *savoir faire*, it comes later."

Then with a word of farewell we walked on.

He said:

"That, *ma sœur*, is either an extremely simple young man or a very remarkable actor."

I didn't answer. I was caught up once more by the fantastic notion that one of these people was a dangerous and cold-blooded murderer. Somehow, on this beautiful, still, sunny morning, it seemed impossible.

21. Mr Mercado, Richard Carey

"THEY WORK in two separate places, I see," said Poirot halting.

Mr Reiter had been doing his photography on an outlying portion of the main excavation. A little distance away from us a second swarm of men were coming and going with baskets.

"That's what they call the deep cut," I explained. "They don't find much there, nothing but rubbishy broken pottery, but Dr Leidner always says it's very interesting, so I suppose it must be."

"Let us go there."

We walked together slowly for the sun was hot.

Mr Mercado was in command. We saw him below us talking to the foreman, an old man like a tortoise who wore a tweed coat over his long striped cotton gown.

It was a little difficult to get down to them as there was only a narrow path or stair and basket boys were going up and down it constantly, and they always seemed to be as blind as bats and never to think of getting out of the way.

As I followed Poirot down he said suddenly over his shoulder:

"Is Mr Mercado right-handed or left-handed?"

Now that was an extraordinary question if you like!

I thought a minute, then:

"Right-handed," I said decisively.

Poirot didn't condescend to explain. He just went on and I followed him.

Mr Mercado seemed rather pleased to see us.

His long melancholy face lit up.

M. Poirot pretended to an interest in archæology that I'm sure he couldn't have really felt, but Mr Mercado responded at once.

He explained that they had already cut down through twelve levels of house occupation.

"We are now definitely in the fourth millennium," he said with enthusiasm.

I always thought a millennium was in the future—the time when everything comes right.

Mr Mercado pointed out belts of ashes (how his hand did shake! I wondered if he might possibly have malaria) and he explained how the pottery changed in character, and about burials—and how they had had one level almost entirely composed of infant burials—poor little things—and about flexed position and orientation, which seemed to mean the way the bones were lying.

And then suddenly, just as he was stooping down to pick up a kind of flint knife that was lying with some pots in a corner, he leapt into the air with a wild yell.

He spun round to find me and Poirot staring at him in astonishment.

He clapped his hand to his left arm.

"Something stung me—like a red-hot needle."

Immediately Poirot was galvanised into energy.

"Quick, *mon cher*, let us see. Nurse Leatheran!"

I came forward.

He seized Mr Mercado's arm and deftly rolled back the sleeve of his khaki shirt to the shoulder.

"There," said Mr Mercado, pointing.

About three inches below the shoulder there was a minute prick from which the blood was oozing.

"Curious," said Poirot. He peered into the rolled-up sleeve. "I can see nothing. It was an ant, perhaps?"

"Better put on a little iodine," I said.

I always carry an iodine pencil with me, and I whipped it out and applied it. But I was a little absent-minded as I did so, for my attention had been caught by something quite different. Mr Mercado's arm, all the way up the forearm to the elbow, was marked all over by tiny punctures. I knew well enough what *they* were—*the marks of a hypodermic needle*.

Mr Mercado rolled down his sleeve again and recommenced his explanations. Mr Poirot listened, but didn't try to bring the conversation round to the Leidners. In fact he didn't ask Mr Mercado anything at all.

Presently we said good-bye to Mr Mercado and climbed up the path again.

"It was neat that, did you not think so?" my companion asked.

"Neat?" I asked.

M. Poirot took something from behind the lapel of his coat and surveyed it affectionately. To my surprise I saw that it was a long sharp darning needle with a blob of sealing wax making it into a pin.

"M. Poirot," I cried, "did *you* do that?"

"I was the stinging insect—yes. And very neatly I did it, too, do you not think so? You did not see me."

That was true enough. *I* never saw him do it. And I'm sure Mr Mercado hadn't suspected. He must have been quick as lightning.

"But, M. Poirot, why?" I asked.

He answered me by another question.

"Did you notice anything, sister?" he asked.

I nodded my head slowly.

"Hypodermic marks," I said.

"So now we know something about Mr Mercado," said Poirot. "I suspected—but I did not *know*. It is always necessary to *know*."

"And you don't care how you set about it!" I thought, but didn't say.

Poirot suddenly clapped his hand to his pocket.

"Alas, I have dropped my handkerchief down there. I concealed the pin in it."

"I'll get it for you," I said and hurried back.

I'd got the feeling, you see, by this time, that M. Poirot and I were the doctor and nurse in charge of a case. At least, it was more like an operation and he was the surgeon. Perhaps I oughtn't to say so, but in a queer way I was beginning to enjoy myself.

I remember just after I'd finished my training, I went to a case in a private house and the need for an immediate operation arose, and the patient's husband was cranky about nursing homes. He just wouldn't hear of his wife being taken to one. Said it had to be done in the house.

Well, of course it was just splendid for me! Nobody else to have a look in! I was in charge of everything. Of course, I was terribly nervous—I thought of everything conceivable that

144

doctor could want, but even then I was afraid I might have forgotten something. You never know with doctors. They ask for absolutely anything sometimes! But everything went splendidly! I had each thing ready as he asked for it, and he actually told me I'd done first-rate after it was over—and that's a thing most doctors wouldn't bother to do! The G.P. was very nice too. And I ran the whole thing myself!

The patient recovered, too, so everybody was happy.

Well, I felt rather the same now. In a way M. Poirot reminded me of that surgeon. *He* was a little man, too. Ugly little man with a face like a monkey, but a wonderful surgeon. He knew instinctively just where to go. I've seen a lot of surgeons and I know what a lot of difference there is.

Gradually I'd been growing a kind of confidence in M. Poirot. I felt that he, too, knew exactly what he was doing. And I was getting to feel that it was my job to help him—as you might say—to have the forceps and the swabs and all handy just when he wanted them. That's why it seemed just as natural for me to run off and look for his handkerchief as it would have been to pick up a towel that a doctor had thrown on the floor.

When I'd found it and got back I couldn't see him at first. But at last I caught sight of him. He was sitting a little way from the mound talking to Mr Carey. Mr Carey's boy was standing near with that great big rod thing with metres marked on it, but just at that moment he said something to the boy and the boy took it away. It seemed he had finished with it for the time being.

I'd like to get this next bit clear. You see, I wasn't quite sure what M. Poirot did or didn't want me to do. He might, I mean, have sent me back for that handkerchief *on purpose*. To get me out of the way.

It was just like an operation over again. You've got to be careful to hand the doctor just what he wants and not what he *doesn't* want. I mean, suppose you gave him the artery forceps at the wrong moment, and were late with them at the right moment! Thank goodness I know my work in the theatre well enough. I'm not likely to make mistakes there. But in this business I was really the rawest of raw little probationers. And so I had to be particularly careful not to make any silly mistakes.

Of course, I didn't for one moment imagine that M. Poirot

didn't want me to hear what he and Mr Carey were saying. But he might have thought he'd get Mr Carey to talk better if I wasn't there.

Now I don't want anybody to get it into their heads that I'm the kind of woman who goes about eavesdropping on private conversations. I wouldn't do such a thing. Not for a moment. Not however much I wanted to.

And what I mean is if it *had* been a private conversation I wouldn't for a moment have done what, as a matter of fact, I actually did do.

As I looked at it I was in a privileged position. After all, you hear many a thing when a patient's coming round after an anæsthetic. The patient wouldn't want you to hear it—and usually has no idea you *have* heard it—but the fact remains you *do* hear it. I just took it that Mr Carey was the patient. He'd be none the worse for what he didn't know about. And if you think that I was just curious, well, I'll admit that I *was* curious. I didn't want to miss anything I could help.

All this is just leading up to the fact that I turned aside and went by a roundabout way up behind the big dump until I was a foot from where they were, but concealed from them by the corner of the dump. And if any one says it was dishonourable I just beg to disagree. *Nothing* ought to be hidden from the nurse in charge of the case, though, of course, it's for the doctor to say what shall be *done*.

I don't know, of course, what M. Poirot's line of approach had been, but by the time I'd got there he was aiming straight for the bull's eye, so to speak.

"Nobody appreciates Dr Leidner's devotion to his wife more than I do," he was saying. "But it is often the case that one learns more about a person from their enemies than from their friends."

"You suggest that their faults are more important than their virtues?" said Mr Carey. His tone was dry and ironic.

"Undoubtedly—when it comes to murder. It seems odd that as far as I know nobody has yet been murdered for having too perfect a character! And yet perfection is undoubtedly an irritating thing."

"I'm afraid I'm hardly the right person to help you," said Mr

Carey. "To be perfectly honest, Mrs Leidner and I didn't hit it off particularly well. I don't mean that we were in any sense of the word enemies, but we were not exactly friends. Mrs Leidner was, perhaps, a shade jealous of my old friendship with her husband. I, for my part, although I admired her very much and thought she was an extremely attractive woman, was just a shade resentful of her influence over Leidner. As a result we were quite polite to each other, but not intimate."

"Admirably explained," said Poirot.

I could just see their heads, and I saw Mr Carey's turn sharply as though something in M. Poirot's detached tone struck him disagreeably.

M. Poirot went on:

"Was not Dr Leidner distressed that you and his wife did not get on together better?"

Carey hesitated a minute before saying:

"Really—I'm not sure. He never said anything. I always hoped he didn't notice it. He was very wrapped up in his work, you know."

"So the truth, according to you, is that you did not really like Mrs Leidner?"

Carey shrugged his shoulders.

"I should probably have liked her very much if she hadn't been Leidner's wife."

He laughed as though amused by his own statement.

Poirot was arranging a little heap of broken potsherds. He said in a dreamy, far-away voice:

"I talked to Miss Johnson this morning. She admitted that she was prejudiced against Mrs Leidner and did not like her very much, although she hastened to add that Mrs Leidner had always been charming to her."

"All quite true, I should say," said Carey.

"So I believed. Then I had a conversation with Mrs Mercado. She told me at great length how devoted she had been to Mrs Leidner and how much she had admired her."

Carey made no answer to this, and after waiting a minute or two Poirot went on:

"That—I did not believe! Then I come to you and that which you tell me—well, again—*I do not believe* . . ."

Carey stiffened. I could hear the anger—repressed anger—in his voice.

"I really cannot help your beliefs—or your disbeliefs, M. Poirot. You've heard the truth and you can take it or leave it as far as I am concerned."

Poirot did not grow angry. Instead he sounded particularly meek and depressed.

"Is it my fault what I do—or do not believe? I have a sensitive ear, you know. And then—there are always plenty of stories going about—rumours floating in the air. One listens—and perhaps—one learns something! Yes, there *are* stories . . ."

Carey sprang to his feet. I could see clearly a little pulse that beat in his temple. He looked simply splendid! So lean and so brown—and that wonderful jaw, hard and square. I don't wonder women fell for that man.

"What stories?" he asked savagely.

Poirot looked sideways at him.

"Perhaps you can guess. The usual sort of story—about you and Mrs Leidner."

"What foul minds people have!"

"*N'est ce pas?* They are like dogs. However deep you bury an unpleasantness a dog will always root it up again."

"And you believe these stories?"

"I am willing to be convinced—of the truth," said Poirot gravely.

"I doubt if you'd know the truth if you heard it," Carey laughed rudely.

"Try me and see," said Poirot, watching him.

"I will then! You shall have the truth! I hated Louise Leidner—there's the truth for you! I hated her like hell!"

22. David Emmott, Father Lavigny and a Discovery

Turning abruptly away, Carey strode off with long angry strides.

Poirot sat looking after him and presently he murmured:

"Yes—I see . . ."

Without turning his head he said in a slightly louder voice:

"Do not come round the corner for a minute, nurse. In case he turns his head. Now it is all right. You have my handkerchief? Many thanks. You are most amiable."

He didn't say anything at all about my having been listening—and how he knew I *was* listening I can't think. He'd never once looked in that direction. I was rather relieved he didn't say anything. I mean, I felt all right with *myself* about it, but it might have been a little awkward explaining to him. So it was a good thing he didn't seem to want explanations.

"Do you think he did hate her, M. Poirot?" I asked.

Nodding his head slowly with a curious expression on his face, Poirot answered.

"Yes—I think he did."

Then he got up briskly and began to walk to where the men were working on the top of the mound. I followed him. We couldn't see any one but Arabs at first, but we finally found Mr Emmott lying face downwards blowing dust off a skeleton that had just been uncovered.

He gave his pleasant grave smile when he saw us.

"Have you come to see round?" he asked. "I'll be free in a minute."

He sat up, took his knife and began daintily cutting the earth away from round the bones, stopping every now and then to use either a bellows or his own breath. A very insanitary proceeding the latter, I thought.

"You'll get all sorts of nasty germs in your mouth, Mr Emmott," I protested.

"Nasty germs are my daily diet, nurse," he said gravely. "Germs can't do anything to an archæologist—they just get naturally discouraged trying."

He scraped a little more away round the thigh bone. Then he spoke to the foreman at his side, directing him exactly what he wanted done.

"There," he said, rising to his feet. "That's ready for Reiter to photograph after lunch. Rather nice stuff she had in with her."

He showed us a little verdigrissy copper bowl and some pins. And a lot of gold and blue things that had been her necklace of beads.

The bones and all the objects were brushed and cleaned with a knife and kept in position ready to be photographed.

"Who is she?" asked Poirot.

"First millenium. A lady of some consequence perhaps. Skull looks rather odd—I must get Mercado to look at it. It suggests death by foul play."

"A Mrs Leidner of two thousand odd years ago?" said Poirot.

"Perhaps," said Mr Emmott.

Bill Coleman was doing something with a pick to a wall face.

David Emmott called something to him which I didn't catch and then started showing M. Poirot round.

When the short explanatory tour was over Emmott looked at his watch.

"We knock off in ten minutes," he said. "Shall we walk back to the house?"

"That will suit me excellently," said Poirot.

We walked slowly along the well-worn path.

"I expect you are all glad to get back to work again," said Poirot.

Emmott replied gravely:

"Yes, it's much the best thing. It's not been any too easy loafing about the house and making conversation."

"Knowing all the time *that one of you was a murderer*."

Emmott did not answer. He made no gesture of dissent. I knew now that he had had a suspicion of the truth from the very first when he had questioned the house-boys.

After a few minutes he asked quietly:

"Are you getting anywhere, M. Poirot?"

Poirot said gravely:

"Will you help me to get somewhere?"

"Why, naturally."

Watching him closely, Poirot said:

"The hub of the case is Mrs Leidner. I want to know about Mrs Leidner."

David Emmott said slowly:

"What do you mean by knowing about her?"

"I do not mean where she came from and what her maiden name was. I do not mean the shape of her face and the colour of her eyes. I mean her—herself."

"You think that counts in the case?"

"I am quite sure of it."

Emmott was silent for a moment or two, then he said:

"Maybe you're right."

"And that is where you can help me. You can tell me what sort of a woman she was."

"Can I? I've often wondered about it myself."

"Didn't you make up your mind on the subject?"

"I think I did in the end."

"Eh bien?"

But Mr Emmott was silent for some minutes, then he said:

"What did nurse think of her? Women are said to sum up other women quickly enough, and a nurse has a wide experience of types."

Poirot didn't give me any chance of speaking even if I had wanted to. He said quickly:

"What I want to know is what a *man* thought of her?"

Emmott smiled a little.

"I expect they'd all be much the same." He paused and said, "She wasn't young, but I think she was about the most beautiful woman I've ever come across."

"That's hardly an answer, Mr Emmott."

"It's not so far off one, M. Poirot."

He was silent a minute or two and then he went on:

"There used to be a fairy story I read when I was a kid. A Northern fairy story about the Snow Queen and Little Kay. I guess Mrs Leidner was rather like that—always taking Little Kay for a ride."

"Ah, yes, a tale of Hans Andersen, is it not? And there was a girl in it. Little Gerda, was that her name?"

"Maybe. I don't remember much of it."

"Can't you go a little further, Mr Emmott?"

David Emmott shook his head.

"I don't even know if I've summed her up correctly. She wasn't easy to read. She'd do a devilish thing one day, and a really fine one the next. But I think you're about right when you say that she's the hub of the case. That's what she always wanted to be—*at the centre of things*. And she liked to get *at* other people—I mean, she wasn't just satisfied with being passed the toast and the peanut butter, she wanted you to turn your mind and soul inside out for her to look at it."

"And if one did not give her that satisfaction?" asked Poirot.

"Then she could turn ugly!"

I saw his lips close resolutely and his jaw set.

"I suppose, Mr Emmott, you would not care to express a plain unofficial opinion as to who murdered her?"

"I don't know," said Emmott. "I really haven't the slightest idea. I rather think that, if I'd been Carl—Carl Reiter, I mean—I would have had a shot at murdering her. She was a pretty fair devil to him. But, of course, he asks for it by being so darned sensitive. Just invites you to give him a kick in the pants."

"And did Mrs Leidner give him—a kick in the pants?" inquired Poirot.

Emmott gave a sudden grin.

"No. Pretty little jabs with an embroidery needle—that was her method. He *was* irritating, of course. Just like some blubbering, poor-spirited kid. But a needle's a painful weapon."

I stole a glance at Poirot and thought I detected a slight quiver of his lips.

"But you don't really believe that Carl Reiter killed her?" he asked.

"No. I don't believe you'd kill a woman because she persistently made you look a fool at every meal."

Poirot shook his head thoughtfully.

152

David Emmott, Father Lavigny and a Discovery

Of course, Mr Emmott made Mrs Leidner sound quite inhuman. There was something to be said on the other side too.

There had been something terribly irritating about Mr Reiter's attitude. He jumped when she spoke to him, and did idiotic things like passing her the marmalade again and again when he knew she never ate it. I'd have felt inclined to snap at him a bit myself.

Men don't understand how their mannerisms can get on women's nerves so that you feel you just have to snap.

I thought I'd just mention that to Mr Poirot some time.

We had arrived back by now and Mr Emmott offered Poirot a wash and took him into his room.

I hurried across the courtyard to mine.

I came out again about the same time they did and we were all making for the dining-room when Father Lavigny appeared in the doorway of his room and invited Poirot in.

Mr Emmott came on round and he and I went into the dining-room together. Miss Johnson and Mrs Mercado were there already, and after a few minutes Mr Mercado, Mr Reiter and Bill Coleman joined us.

We were just sitting down and Mercado had told the Arab boy to tell Father Lavigny lunch was ready when we were all startled by a faint, muffled cry.

I suppose our nerves weren't very good yet, for we all jumped, and Miss Johnson got quite pale and said:

"*What was that?* What's happened?"

Mrs Mercado stared at her and said:

"My dear, what *is* the matter with you? It's some noise outside in the fields."

But at that minute Poirot and Father Lavigny came in.

"We thought some one was hurt," Miss Johnson said.

"A thousand pardons, mademoiselle," cried Poirot. "The fault is mine. Father Lavigny, he explains to me some tablets, and I take one to the window to see better—and, *ma foi*, not looking where I was going, I steb the toe, and the pain is sharp for the moment and I cry out."

"We thought it was another murder," said Mrs Mercado, laughing.

"Marie!" said her husband.

His tone was reproachful and she flushed and bit her lip.

Miss Johnson hastily turned the conversation to the dig and what objects of interest had turned up that morning. Conversation all through lunch was sternly archæological.

I think we all felt it was the safest thing.

After we had had coffee we adjourned to the living-room. Then the men, with the exception of Father Lavigny, went off to the dig again.

Father Lavigny took Poirot through into the antika-room and I went with them. I was getting to know the things pretty well by now and I felt a thrill of pride—almost as though it were my own property—when Father Lavigny took down the gold cup and I heard Poirot's exclamation of admiration and pleasure.

"How beautiful! What a work of art!"

Father Lavigny agreed eagerly and began to point out its beauties with real enthusiasm and knowledge.

"No wax on it to-day," I said.

"Wax?" Poirot stared at me.

"Wax?" So did Father Lavigny.

I explained my remark.

"Ah, *je comprends*," said Father Lavigny. "Yes, yes, candle grease."

That led direct to the subject of the midnight visitor. Forgetting my presence they both dropped into French and I left them together and went back into the living-room.

Mrs Mercado was darning her husband's socks and Miss Johnson was reading a book. Rather an unusual thing for her. She usually seemed to have something to work at.

After a while Father Lavigny and Poirot came out, and the former excused himself on the score of work. Poirot sat down with us.

"A most interesting man," he said, and asked how much work there had been for Father Lavigny to do so far.

Miss Johnson explained that tablets had been scarce and that there had been very few inscribed bricks or cylinder seals. Father Lavigny, however, had done his share of work on the dig and was picking up colloquial Arabic very fast.

That led the talk to cylinder seals, and presently Miss Johnson fetched from a cupboard a sheet of impressions made by rolling them out on plasticine.

I realised as we bent over them, admiring the spirited designs, that these must be what she had been working at on that fatal afternoon.

As we talked I noticed that Poirot was rolling and kneading a little ball of plasticine between his fingers.

"You use a lot of plasticine, mademoiselle?" he asked.

"A fair amount. We seem to have got through a lot already this year—though I can't imagine how. But half our supply seems to have gone."

"Where is it kept, mademoiselle?"

"Here—in this cupboard."

As she replaced the sheet of impressions she showed him the shelf with rolls of plasticine, Durofix, photographic paste and other stationery supplies.

Poirot stooped down.

"And this—what is this, mademoiselle?"

He had slipped his hand right to the back and had brought out a curious crumpled object.

As he straightened it out we could see that it was a kind of mask, with eyes and mouth crudely painted on in Indian ink and the whole thing roughly smeared with plasticine.

"How perfectly extraordinary," cried Miss Johnson. "I've never seen it before. How did it get there? And what is it?"

"As to how it got there, well one hiding-place is as good as another, and I presume that this cupboard would not have been turned out till the end of the season. As to what it *is*—that, too, I think, is not difficult to say. *We have here the face that Mrs Leidner described*. The ghostly face seen in the semi-dusk outside her window—without body attached."

Mrs Mercado gave a little shriek.

Miss Johnson was white to the lips. She murmured:

"Then it was *not* fancy. It was a trick—a wicked trick! But who played it?"

"Yes," cried Mrs Mercado. "Who could have done such a wicked, wicked thing?"

Poirot did not attempt a reply. His face was very grim as he went into the next room, returned with an empty cardboard box in his hand and put the crumpled mask into it.

"The police must see this," he explained.

"It's horrible," said Miss Johnson in a low voice. "Horrible!"

"Do you think everything's hidden here somewhere?" cried Mrs Mercado shrilly. "Do you think perhaps the weapon—the club she was killed with—all covered with blood still, perhaps. . . . Oh! I'm frightened—I'm frightened . . ."

Miss Johnson gripped her by the shoulder.

"Be quiet," she said fiercely. "Here's Dr Leidner. We mustn't upset him."

Indeed, at that very moment the car had driven into the courtyard. Dr Leidner got out of it and came straight across and in at the living-room door. His face was set in lines of fatigue and he looked twice the age he had three days ago.

He said in a quiet voice:

"The funeral will be at eleven o'clock to-morrow. Major Deane will read the service."

Mrs Mercado faltered something, then slipped out of the room.

Dr Leidner said to Miss Johnson:

"You'll come, Anne?"

And she answered.

"Of course, my dear, we'll all come. Naturally."

She didn't say anything else, but her face must have expressed what her tongue was powerless to do, for his face lightened up with affection and a momentary ease.

"Dear Anne," he said. "You are such a wonderful comfort and help to me. My dear old friend."

He laid his hand on her arm and I saw the red colour creep up in her face as she muttered, gruff as ever:

"That's all right."

But I just caught a glimpse of her expression and knew that, for one short moment, Anne Johnson was a perfectly happy woman.

And another idea flashed across my mind. Perhaps soon, in the natural course of things, turning to his old friend for sympathy, a new and happy state of things might come about.

Not that I'm really a matchmaker, and of course it was indecent to think of such a thing before the funeral even. But after all, it *would* be a happy solution. He was very fond of her, and there was no doubt she was absolutely devoted to him and would be perfectly happy devoting the rest of her life to him. That is, if she could bear to hear Louise's perfections sung all the time. But women can put up with a lot when they've got what they want.

Dr Leidner then greeted Poirot, asking him if he had made any progress.

Miss Johnson was standing behind Dr Leidner and she looked hard at the box in Poirot's hand and shook her head, and I realised that she was pleading with Poirot not to tell him about the mask. She felt, I was sure, that he had enough to bear for one day.

Poirot fell in with her wish.

"These things march slowly, monsieur," he said.

Then, after a few desultory words, he took his leave.

I accompanied him out to his car.

There were half a dozen things I wanted to ask him, but somehow, when he turned and looked at me, I didn't ask anything at all. I'd as soon have asked a surgeon if he thought he'd made a good job of an operation. I just stood meekly waiting for instructions.

Rather to my surprise he said:

"Take care of yourself, my child."

And then he added:

"I wonder if it is well for you to remain here?"

"I must speak to Dr Leidner about leaving," I said. "But I thought I'd wait until after the funeral."

He nodded in approval.

"In the meantime," he said, "do not try to find out too much. You understand, I do not want you to be clever!" And he added with a smile, "It is for you to hold the swabs and for me to do the operation."

Wasn't it funny, his actually saying that?

Then he said quite irrelevantly:

"An interesting man, that Father Lavigny."

"A monk being an archæologist seems odd to me," I said.

"Ah, yes, you are a Protestant. Me, I am a good Catholic. I know something of priests and monks."

He frowned, seemed to hesitate, then said:

"Remember, he is quite clever enough to turn you inside out if he likes."

If he was warning me against gossiping I felt that I didn't need any such warning!

It annoyed me, and though I didn't like to ask him any of the things I really wanted to know, I didn't see why I shouldn't at any rate say one thing.

"You'll excuse me, M. Poirot," I said. "But it's 'stubbed your toe,' not *stepped* or stebbed."

"Ah? Thank you, *ma sœur*."

"Don't mention it. But it's just as well to get a phrase right."

"I will remember," he said—quite meekly for him.

And he got in the car and was driven away, and I went slowly back across the courtyard wondering about a lot of things.

About the hypodermic marks on Mr Mercado's arm, and what drug it was he took. And about that horrid yellow smeared mask. And how odd it was that Poirot and Miss Johnson hadn't heard my cry in the living-room that morning, whereas we had all heard Poirot perfectly well in the dining-room at lunch time—and yet Father Lavigny's room and Mrs Leidner's were just the same distance from the living-room and the dining-room respectively.

And then I felt rather pleased that I'd taught *Doctor* Poirot one English phrase correctly!

Even if he *was* a great detective he'd realise he *didn't* know *everything!*

23. I Go Psychic

THE FUNERAL WAS, I thought, a very affecting affair. As well as ourselves, all the English people in Hassanieh attended it. Even Sheila Reilly was there, looking quiet and subdued in a dark coat and skirt. I hoped that she was feeling a little remorseful for all the unkind things she had said.

When we got back to the house I followed Dr Leidner into the office and broached the subject of my departure. He was very nice about it, thanked me for what I had done (Done! I had been worse than useless) and insisted on my accepting an extra week's salary.

I protested because really I felt I'd done nothing to earn it.

"Indeed, Dr Leidner, I'd rather not have any salary at all. If you'd just refund me my travelling expenses that's all I want."

But he wouldn't hear of that.

"You see," I said, "I don't feel I deserve it, Dr Leidner. I mean, I've—well, I've failed. She—my coming didn't save her."

"Now don't get that idea into your head, nurse," he said earnestly. "After all, I didn't engage you as a female detective. I never dreamt my wife's life was in danger. I was convinced it was all nerves and that she'd worked herself up into a rather curious mental state. You did all any one could do. She liked and trusted you. And I think in her last days she felt happier and safer because of your being here. There's nothing for you to reproach yourself with."

His voice quivered a little and I knew what he was thinking. *He* was the one to blame for not having taken Mrs Leidner's fears seriously.

"Dr Leidner," I said curiously. "Have you ever come to any conclusion about those anonymous letters?"

He said with a sigh:

159

"I don't know what to believe. Has M. Poirot come to any definite conclusion?"

"He hadn't yesterday," I said, steering rather neatly, I thought, between truth and fiction. After all, he hadn't until I told him about Miss Johnson.

It was on my mind that I'd like to give Dr Leidner a hint and see if he reacted. In the pleasure of seeing him and Miss Johnson together the day before, and his affection and reliance on her, I'd forgotten all about the letters. Even now I felt it was perhaps rather mean of me to bring it up. Even if she had written them, she had had a bad time after Mrs Leidner's death. Yet I did want to see whether that particular possibility had ever entered Dr Leidner's head.

"Anonymous letters are usually the work of a woman," I said. I wanted to see how he'd take it.

"I suppose they are," he said with a sigh. "But you seem to forget, nurse, that these may be genuine. They may actually be written by Frederick Bosner."

"No, I haven't forgotten," I said. "But I can't believe somehow that that's the real explanation."

"I do," he said. "It's all nonsense his being one of the expedition staff. That is just an ingenious theory of M. Poirot's. I believe that the truth is much simpler. The man is a madman, of course. He's been hanging round the place—perhaps in disguise of some kind. And somehow or other he got in on that fatal afternoon. The servants may be lying—they may have been bribed."

"I suppose it's possible," I said doubtfully.

Dr Leidner went on with a trace of irritability.

"It is all very well for M. Poirot to suspect the members of my expedition. I am perfectly certain *none* of them have anything to do with it! I have worked with them. I *know* them!"

He stopped suddenly, then he said:

"Is that your experience, nurse? That anonymous letters are usually written by women?"

"It isn't always the case," I said. "But there's a certain type of feminine spitefulness that finds relief that way."

"I suppose you are thinking of Mrs Mercado?" he said.

Then he shook his head.

"Even if she were malicious enough to wish to hurt Louise she would hardly have the necessary knowledge," he said.

I remembered the earlier letters in the attaché-case.

If Mrs Leidner had left that unlocked and Mrs Mercado had been alone in the house one day pottering about, she might easily have found them and read them. Men never seem to think of the simplest possibilities!

"And apart from her there is only Miss Johnson," I said, watching him.

"That would be quite ridiculous!"

The little smile with which he said it was quite conclusive. The idea of Miss Johnson being the author of the letters had never entered his head! I hesitated just for a minute—but I didn't say anything. One doesn't like giving away a fellow woman, and besides, I had been a witness of Miss Johnson's genuine and moving remorse. What was done was done. Why expose Dr Leidner to a fresh disillusion on top of all his other troubles?

It was arranged that I should leave on the following day, and I had arranged through Dr Reilly to stay for a day or two with the matron of the hospital whilst I made arrangements for returning to England either via Baghdad or direct via Nissibin by car and train.

Dr Leidner was kind enough to say that he would like me to choose a memento from amongst his wife's things.

"Oh, no, really, Dr Leidner," I said. "I couldn't. It's much too kind of you."

He insisted.

"But I should like you to have something. And Louise, I am sure, would have wished it."

Then he went on to suggest that I should have her tortoise-shell toilet set!

"Oh, no, Dr Leidner! Why, that's a most *expensive* set. I couldn't, really."

"She had no sisters, you know—no one who wants these things. There is no one else to have them."

I could quite imagine that he wouldn't want them to fall into Mrs Mercado's greedy little hands. And I didn't think he'd want to offer them to Miss Johnson.

He went on kindly:

"You just think it over. By the way, here is the key of Louise's jewel case. Perhaps you will find something there you would rather have. And I should be very grateful if you would pack up—all—all her clothes. I dare say Reilly can find a use for them amongst some of the poor Christian families in Hassanieh."

I was very glad to be able to do that for him, and I expressed my willingness.

I set about it at once.

Mrs Leidner had only had a very simple wardrobe with her and it was soon sorted and packed up into a couple of suitcases. All her papers had been in the small attaché-case. The jewel case contained a few simple trinkets—a pearl ring, a diamond brooch, a small string of pearls and one or two plain gold bar brooches of the safety-pin type, and a string of large amber beads.

Naturally I wasn't going to take the pearls or the diamonds, but I hesitated a bit between the amber beads and the toilet set. In the end, however, I didn't see why I shouldn't take the latter. It was a kindly thought on Dr Leidner's part, and I was sure there wasn't any patronage about it. I'd take it in the spirit it had been offered without any false pride. After all, I *had* been fond of her.

Well, that was all done and finished with. The suitcases packed, the jewel case locked up again and put separate to give to Dr Leidner with the photograph of Mrs Leidner's father and one or two other personal little odds and ends.

The room looked bare and forlorn emptied of all its accoutrements, when I'd finished. There was nothing more for me to do—and yet somehow or other I shrank from leaving the room. It seemed as though there were something still to do there—something I ought to *see*—or something I ought to have *known*.

I'm not superstitious, but the idea *did* pop into my head that perhaps Mrs Leidner's spirit was hanging about the room and trying to get in touch with me.

I remember once at the hospital some of us girls got a planchette and really it wrote some very remarkable things.

Perhaps, although I'd never thought of such a thing, I might be mediumistic.

As I say, one gets all worked up to imagine all sorts of foolishness sometimes.

I prowled round the room uneasily, touching this and that. But, of course, there wasn't anything in the room but bare furniture. There was nothing slipped behind drawers or tucked away. I couldn't hope for anything of that kind.

In the end (it sounds rather batty, but as I say, one gets worked up) I did rather a queer thing.

I went and lay down on the bed and closed my eyes.

I deliberately tried to forget who and what I was. I tried to think myself back to that fatal afternoon. I was Mrs Leidner lying here resting, peaceful and unsuspicious.

It's extraordinary how you *can* work yourself up.

I'm a perfectly normal matter-of-fact individual—not the least little bit spooky, but I tell you that after I'd lain there about five minutes I began to *feel* spooky.

I didn't try to resist. I deliberately encouraged the feeling.

I said to myself:

"I'm Mrs Leidner. I'm Mrs Leidner. I'm lying here—half asleep. Presently—very soon now—the door's going to open."

I kept on saying that—as though I were hypnotising myself.

"It's just about half-past one . . . it's just about the time . . . The door is going to open . . . *the door is going to open* . . . . I shall see who comes in. . . ."

I kept my eyes glued on that door. Presently it was going to open. I should *see* it open. And I should see *the person who opened it*.

I must have been a little over-wrought that afternoon to imagine I could solve the mystery that way.

But I did believe it. A sort of chill passed down my back and settled in my legs. They felt numb—paralysed.

"You're going into a trance," I said. "And in that trance you'll see . . ."

And once again I repeated monotonously again and again:

"The door is going to open—the door is going to open . . ."

The cold numbed feeling grew more intense.

And then, slowly, *I saw the door just beginning to open*.

It was horrible.

I've never known anything so horrible before or since.

I was paralysed—chilled through and through. I couldn't move. For the life of me I couldn't have moved.

And I was terrified. Sick and blind and dumb with terror.

That slowly opening door.

So noiseless.

In a minute I should see . . .

Slowly—slowly—wider and wider.

Bill Coleman came quietly in.

He must have had the shock of his life!

I bounded off the bed with a scream of terror and hurled myself across the room.

He stood stock still, his blunt pink face pinker and his mouth opened wide with surprise.

"Hallo-allo-allo," he said. "What's up, nurse?"

I came back to reality with a crash.

"Goodness, Mr Coleman," I said. "How you startled me!"

"Sorry," he said with a momentary grin.

I saw then that he was holding a little bunch of scarlet ranunculus in his hand. They were pretty little flowers and they grew wild on the sides of the Tell. Mrs Leidner had been very fond of them.

He blushed and got rather red as he said:

"One can't get any flowers or things in Hassanieh. Seemed rather rotten not to have any flowers for the grave. I thought I'd nip in here and put a little posy in that little pot thing she always had flowers in on her table. Sort of show she wasn't forgotten—eh? A bit asinine, I know, but—well—I mean to say."

I thought it was very nice of him. He was all pink with embarrassment like Englishmen are when they've done anything sentimental. I thought it was a very sweet thought.

"Why, I think that's a very nice idea, Mr Coleman," I said.

And I picked up the little pot and went and got some water in it and we put the flowers in.

I really thought much more of Coleman for this idea of his. It showed he had a heart and nice feelings about things.

He didn't ask me again what made me let out such a squeal and I'm thankful he didn't. I should have felt a fool explaining.

"Stick to common sense in future, woman," I said to myself as I settled my cuffs and smoothed my apron. "You're not cut out for this psychic stuff."

I bustled about doing my own packing and kept myself busy for the rest of the day.

I Go Psychic

Father Lavigny was kind enough to express great distress at my leaving. He said my cheerfulness and common sense had been such a help to everybody. Common sense! I'm glad he didn't know about my idiotic behaviour in Mrs Leidner's room.

"We have not seen M. Poirot to-day," he remarked.

I told him that Poirot had said he was going to be busy all day sending off telegrams.

Father Lavigny raised his eyebrows.

"Telegrams? To America?"

"I suppose so. He said 'All over the world!' but I think that was rather a foreign exaggeration."

And then I got rather red, remembering that Father Lavigny was a foreigner himself.

He didn't seem offended though, just laughed quite pleasantly and asked me if there were any news of the man with the squint.

I said I didn't know but I hadn't heard of any.

Father Lavigny asked me again about the time Mrs Leidner and I had noticed the man and how he had seemed to be standing on tiptoe and peering through the window.

"It seems clear the man had some overwhelming interest in Mrs Leidner," he said thoughtfully. "I have wondered since whether the man could possibly have been a European got up to look like an Iraqi?"

That was a new idea to me and I considered it carefully. I had taken it for granted that the man was a native, but of course, when I came to think of it, I was really going by the cut of his clothes and the yellowness of his skin.

Father Lavigny declared his intention of going round outside the house to the place where Mrs Leidner and I had seen the man standing.

"You never know, he might have dropped something. In the detective stories the criminal always does."

"I expect in real life criminals are more careful," I said.

I fetched some socks I had just finished darning and put them on the table in the living-room for the men to sort out when they came in, and then, as there was nothing much more to do, I went up on the roof.

Miss Johnson was standing there but she didn't hear me. I got right up to her before she noticed me.

But long before that I'd seen that there was something very wrong.

She was standing in the middle of the roof staring straight in front of her, and there was the most awful look on her face. As though she'd seen something she couldn't possibly believe.

It gave me quite a shock.

Mind you, I'd seen her upset the other evening, but this was quite different.

"My dear," I said, hurrying to her, "whatever's the matter?"

She turned her head at that and stood looking at me—almost as if she didn't see me.

"What is it?" I persisted.

She made a queer sort of grimace—as though she were trying to swallow but her throat was too dry. She said hoarsely:

"I've just seen something."

"What have you seen? Tell me. Whatever can it be? You look all in."

She gave an effort to pull herself together, but she still looked pretty dreadful.

She said, still in that same dreadful choked voice:

"I've seen how some one could come in from outside—and no one would ever guess."

I followed the direction of her eyes but I couldn't see anything.

Mr Reiter was standing in the door of the photographic room and Father Lavigny was just crossing the courtyard—but there was nothing else.

I turned back puzzled and found her eyes fixed on mine with the strangest expression in them.

"Really," I said, "I don't see what you mean. Won't you explain?"

But she shook her head.

"Not now. Later. We *ought* to have seen. Oh, we ought to have seen!"

"If you'd only tell me——"

But she shook her head.

"I've got to think it out first."

And pushing past me, she went stumbling down the stairs.

I didn't follow her as she obviously didn't want me with her.

Instead I sat down on the parapet and tried to puzzle things out. But I didn't get anywhere. There was only the one way into the courtyard—through the big arch. Just outside it I could see the water-boy and his horse and the Indian cook talking to him. Nobody could have passed them and come in without their seeing him.

I shook my head in perplexity and went downstairs again.

24. *Murder is a Habit*

WE ALL WENT to bed early that night. Miss Johnson had appeared at dinner and had behaved more or less as usual. She had, however, a sort of dazed look, and once or twice quite failed to take in what other people said to her.

It wasn't somehow a very comfortable sort of meal. You'd say, I suppose, that that was natural enough in a house where there'd been a funeral that day. But I know what I mean.

Lately our meals had been hushed and subdued, but for all that there had been a feeling of comradeship. There had been sympathy with Dr Leidner in his grief and a fellow feeling of being all in the same boat amongst the others.

But to-night I was reminded of my first meal there—when Mrs Mercado had wathed me and there had been that curious feeling as though something might snap any minute.

I'd felt the same thing—only very much intensified—when we'd sat round the dining-room table with Poirot at the head of it.

To-night it was particularly strong. Every one was on edge— jumpy—on tenterhooks. If any one had dropped something I'm sure somebody would have screamed.

As I say, we all separated early afterwards. I went to bed almost at once. The last thing I heard as I was dropping off to sleep was Mrs Mercado's voice saying good-night to Miss Johnson just outside my door.

I dropped off to sleep at once—tired by my exertions and even more by my silly experience in Mrs Leidner's room. I slept heavily and dreamlessly for several hours.

I awoke when I did awake with a start and a feeling of impending catastrophe. Some sound had woken me, and as I sat up in bed listening I heard it again.

An awful sort of agonised choking groan.

I had lit my candle and was out of bed in a twinkling. I snatched up a torch, too, in case the candle should blow out. I came out of my door and stood listening. I knew the sound wasn't far away. It came again—from the room immediately next to mine—Miss Johnson's room.

I hurried in. Miss Johnson was lying in bed, her whole body contorted in agony. As I set down the candle and bent over her, her lips moved and she tried to speak—but only an awful hoarse whisper came. I saw that the corners of her mouth and the skin of her chin were burnt a kind of greyish white.

Her eyes went from me to a glass that lay on the floor evidently where it had dropped from her hand. The light rug was stained a bright red where it had fallen. I picked it up and ran a finger over the inside, drawing back my hand with a sharp exclamation. Then I examined the inside of the poor woman's mouth.

There wasn't the least doubt what was the matter. Somehow or other, intentionally or otherwise, she'd swallowed a quantity of corrosive acid—oxalic or hydrochloric, I suspected.

I ran out and called to Dr Leidner and he woke the others, and we worked over her for all we were worth, but all the time I had an awful feeling it was no good. We tried a strong solution of carbonate of soda—and followed it with olive oil. To ease the pain I gave her a hypodermic of morphine sulphate.

David Emmott had gone off to Hassanieh to fetch Dr Reilly, but before he came it was over.

I won't dwell on the details. Poisoning by a strong solution of hydrochloric acid (which is what it proved to be) is one of the most painful deaths possible.

It was when I was bending over her to give her the morphia that she made one ghastly effort to speak. It was only a horrible strangled whisper when it came.

"*The window* . . ." she said. "*Nurse* . . . the window . . ."

But that was all—she couldn't go on. She collapsed completely.

I shall never forget that night. The arrival of Dr Reilly. The arrival of Captain Maitland. And finally with the dawn, Hercule Poirot.

He it was who took me gently by the arm and steered me into the dining-room where he made me sit down and have a cup of good strong tea.

"There, *mon enfant*," he said, "that is better. You are worn out."

Upon that, I burst into tears.

"It's too awful," I sobbed. "It's been like a nightmare. Such awful suffering. And her eyes . . . Oh, M. Poirot—her eyes . . ."

He patted me on the shoulder. A woman couldn't have been kinder.

"Yes, yes—do not think of it. You did all you could."

"It was one of the corrosive acids."

"It was a strong solution of hydrochloric acid."

"The stuff they use on the pots?"

"Yes. Miss Johnson probably drank it off before she was fully awake. That is—unless she took it on purpose."

"Oh, M. Poirot, what an awful idea!"

"It is a possibility, after all. What do you think?"

I considered for a moment and then shook my head decisively.

"I don't believe it. No, I don't believe it for a moment." I hesitated and then said, "I think she found out something yesterday afternoon."

"What is that you say? She found out something?"

I repeated to him the curious conversation we had had together.

Poirot gave a low soft whistle.

"*La pauvre femme!*" he said. "She said she wanted to think it over—eh? That is what signed her death warrant. If she had only spoken out—then—at once."

He said:

"Tell me again her exact words?"

I repeated them.

"She saw how some one could have come in from outside without any of you knowing? Come, *ma sœur*, let us go up to the roof and you shall show me just where she was standing."

We went up to the roof together and I showed Poirot the exact spot where Miss Johnson had stood.

"Like this?" said Poirot. "Now what do I see? I see half the courtyard—and the archway—and the doors of the drawing-office and the photographic room and the laboratory. Was there any one in the courtyard?"

"Father Lavigny was just going towards the archway and Mr Reiter was standing in the door of the photographic room."

"And still I do not see in the least how any one could come in from outside and none of you know about it. . . . But *she* saw . . ."

He gave it up at last, shaking his head.

"*Sacré nom d'un chien—va!* What *did* she see?"

The sun was just rising. The whole eastern sky was a riot of rose and orange and pale, pearly grey.

"What a beautiful sunrise," said Poirot gently.

The river wound away to our left and the Tell stood up outlined in gold colour. To the south were the blossoming trees and the peaceful cultivation. The water-wheel groaned in the distance—a faint unearthly sound. In the north were the slender minarets and the clustering fairy whiteness of Hassanieh.

It was all incredibly beautiful.

And then, close at my elbow, I heard Poirot give a long deep sigh.

"Fool that I have been," he murmured. "When the truth is so clear—so clear."

25. Suicide or Murder?

I HADN'T TIME to ask Poirot what he meant, for Captain Maitland was calling up to us and asking us to come down.

We hurried down the stairs.

"Look here, Poirot," he said. "Here's another complication. The monk fellow is missing."

"Father Lavigny?"

"Yes. Nobody noticed it till just now. Then it dawned on somebody that he was the only one of the party not around, and we went to his room. His bed's not been slept in and there's no sign of him."

The whole thing was like a bad dream. First Miss Johnson's death and then the disappearance of Father Lavigny.

The servants were called and questioned, but they couldn't throw any light on the mystery. He had last been seen at about eight o'clock the night before. Then he had said he was going out for a stroll before going to bed.

Nobody had seen him come back from that stroll.

The big doors had been closed and barred at nine o'clock as usual. Nobody, however, remembered unbarring them in the morning. The two house-boys each thought the other one must have done the unfastening.

Had Father Lavigny ever returned the night before? Had he, in the course of his earlier walk, discovered anything of a suspicious nature, gone out to investigate it later, and perhaps fallen a third victim?

Captain Maitland swung round as Dr Reilly came up with Mr Mercado behind him.

"Hallo, Reilly. Got anything?"

"Yes. The stuff came from the laboratory here. I've just been checking up the quantities with Mercado. It's H.C.L. from the lab."

"The laboratory—eh? Was it locked up?"

Mr Mercado shook his head. His hands were shaking and his face was twitching. He looked a wreck of a man.

"It's never been the custom," he stammered. "You see—just now—we're using it all the time. I—nobody ever dreamt——"

"Is the place locked up at night?"

"Yes—all the rooms are locked. The keys are hung up just inside the living-room."

"So if any one had a key to that they could get the lot."

"Yes."

"And it's a perfectly ordinary key, I suppose?"

"Oh, yes."

"Nothing to show whether she took it herself from the laboratory?" asked Captain Maitland.

"She didn't," I said loudly and positively.

I felt a warning touch on my arm. Poirot was standing close behind me.

And then something rather ghastly happened.

Not ghastly in itself—in fact it was just the incongruousness that made it seem worse than anything else.

A car drove into the courtyard and a little man jumped out. He was wearing a sun helmet and a short thick trench coat.

He came straight to Dr Leidner, who was standing by Dr Reilly, and shook him warmly by the hand.

"*Vous voilà, mon cher,*" he cried. "Delighted to see you. I passed this way on Saturday afternoon—en route to the Italians at Fugima. I went to the dig but there wasn't a single European about and alas! I cannot speak Arabic. I had not time to come to the house. This morning I leave Fugima at five—two hours here with you—and then I catch the convoy on. *Eh bien*, and how is the season going?"

It was ghastly.

The cheery voice, the matter-of-fact manner, all the pleasant sanity of an everyday world now left far behind. He just bustled in, knowing nothing and noticing nothing—full of cheerful bonhomie.

No wonder Dr Leidner gave an inarticulate gasp and looked in mute appeal at Dr Reilly.

The doctor rose to the occasion.

173

He took the little man (he was a French archæologist called Verrier who dug in the Greek islands, I heard later) aside and explained to him what had occurred.

Verrier was horrified. He himself had been staying at an Italian dig right away from civilisation for the last few days and had heard nothing.

He was profuse in condolences and apologies, finally striding over to Dr Leidner and clasping him warmly by both hands.

"What a tragedy! My God, what a tragedy! I have no words. *Mon pauvre collègue.*"

And shaking his head in one last ineffectual effort to express his feelings, the little man climbed into his car and left us.

As I say, that momentary introduction of comic relief into tragedy seemed really more gruesome than anything else that had happened.

"The next thing," said Dr Reilly firmly, "is breakfast. Yes, I insist. Come, Leidner, you must eat."

Poor Dr Leidner was almost a complete wreck. He came with us to the dining-room and there a funereal meal was served. I think the hot coffee and fried eggs did us all good, though no one actually felt they wanted to eat. Dr Leidner drank some coffee and sat twiddling his bread. His face was grey, drawn with pain and bewilderment.

After breakfast, Captain Maitland got down to things.

I explained how I had woken up, heard a queer sound and had gone into Miss Johnson's room.

"You say there was a glass on the floor?"

"Yes. She must have dropped it after drinking."

"Was it broken?"

"No, it had fallen on the rug. (I'm afraid the acid's ruined the rug, by the way.) I picked the glass up and put it back on the table."

"I'm glad you've told us that. There are only two sets of fingerprints on it, and one set is certainly Miss Johnson's own. The other must be yours."

He was silent for a moment, then he said:

"Please go on."

I described carefully what I'd done and the methods I had tried, looking rather anxiously at Dr Reilly for approval. He gave it with a nod.

"You tried everything that could possibly have done any good," he said. And though I was pretty sure I had done so, it was a relief to have my belief confirmed.

"Did you know exactly what she had taken?" Captain Maitland asked.

"No—but I could see, of course, that it was a corrosive acid."

Captain Maitland asked gravely:

"Is it your opinion, nurse, that Miss Johnson deliberately administered this stuff to herself?"

"Oh, no," I exclaimed. "I never thought of such a thing!"

I don't know why I was so sure. Partly, I think, because of M. Poirot's hints. His "murder is a habit" had impressed itself on my mind. And then one doesn't readily believe that any one's going to commit suicide in such a terribly painful way.

I said as much and Captain Maitland nodded thoughtfully.

"I agree that it isn't what one would choose," he said. "But if any one were in great distress of mind and this stuff were easily available it might be taken for that reason."

"*Was* she in great distress of mind?" I asked doubtfully.

"Mrs Mercado says so. She says that Miss Johnson was quite unlike herself at dinner last night—that she hardly replied to anything that was said to her. Mrs Mercado is quite sure that Miss Johnson was in terrible distress over something and that the idea of making away with herself had already occurred to her."

"Well, I don't believe it for a moment," I said bluntly.

Mrs Mercado indeed! Nasty slinking little cat!

"Then what *do* you think?"

"I think she was murdered," I said bluntly.

He rapped out his next question sharply. I felt rather that I was in the orderly room.

"Any reasons?"

"It seems to me by far and away the most possible solution."

"That's just your private opinion. There was no reason why the lady should be murdered?"

"Excuse me," I said, "there was. She found out something."

"Found out something? What did she find out?"

I repeated our conversation on the roof word for word.

"She refused to tell you what her discovery was?"

"Yes. She said she must have time to think it over."

"But she was very excited by it?"

"Yes."

"*A way of getting in from outside*," Captain Maitland puzzled over it, his brows knit. "Had you no idea at all of what she was driving at?"

"Not in the least. I puzzled and puzzled over it but I couldn't even get a glimmering."

Captain Maitland said:

"What do you think, M. Poirot?"

Poirot said:

"I think you have there a possible motive."

"For murder?"

"For murder."

Captain Maitland frowned.

"She wasn't able to speak before she died?"

."Yes, she just managed to get out two words."

"What were they?"

"*The window* . . ."

"The window?" repeated Captain Maitland. "Did you understand to what she was referring?"

I shook my head.

"How many windows were there in her bedroom?"

"Just the one."

"Giving on the courtyard?"

"Yes."

"Was it open or shut? Open, I seem to remember. But perhaps one of you opened it?"

"No, it was open all the time. I wondered——"

I stopped.

"Go on, nurse."

"I examined the window, of course, but I couldn't see anything unusual about it. I wondered whether, perhaps, somebody changed the glasses that way."

"Changed the glasses?"

"Yes. You see, Miss Johnson always takes a glass of water to bed with her. I think that glass must have been tampered with and a glass of acid put there in its place."

"What do you say, Reilly?"

"If it's murder, that was probably the way it was done," said Dr Reilly promptly. "No ordinary moderately observant human being would drink a glass of acid in mistake for one of water—if they were in full possession of their waking faculties. But if any one's accustomed to drinking off a glass of water in the middle of the night, that person might easily stretch out an arm, find the glass in the accustomed place, and still half asleep, toss off enough of the stuff to be fatal before realising what had happened."

Captain Maitland reflected a minute.

"I'll have to go back and look at that window. How far is it from the head of the bed?"

I thought.

"With a very long stretch you could just reach the little table that stands by the head of the bed."

"The table on which the glass of water was?"

"Yes."

"Was the door locked?"

"No."

"So whoever it was could have come in that way and made the substitution?"

"Oh, yes."

"There would be more risk that way," said Dr Reilly. "A person who is sleeping quite soundly will often wake up at the sound of a footfall. If the table could be reached from the window it would be the safer way."

"I'm not only thinking of the glass," said Captain Maitland absent-mindedly.

Rousing himself, he addressed me once again.

"It's your opinion that when the poor lady felt she was dying she was anxious to let you know that somebody had substituted acid for water through the open window? Surely the person's *name* would have been more to the point?"

"She mayn't have known the name," I pointed out.

"Or it would have been more to the point if she'd managed to hint what it was that she had discovered the day before?"

Dr Reilly said:

"When you're dying, Maitland, you haven't always got a sense of proportion. One particular fact very likely obsesses your mind. That a murderous hand had come through the window may have been the principal fact obsessing her at the minute. It may have seemed to her important that she should let people know that. In my opinion she wasn't far wrong either. It was important! She probably jumped to the fact that you'd think it was suicide. If she could have used her tongue freely, she'd probably have said 'It wasn't suicide. I didn't take it myself. Somebody else must have put it near my bed *through the window*.'"

Captain Maitland drummed with his fingers for a minute or two without replying. Then he said:

"There are certainly two ways of looking at it. It's either suicide or murder. Which do you think, Dr Leidner?"

Dr Leidner was silent for a minute or two, then he said quietly and decisively:

"Murder. Anne Johnson wasn't the sort of woman to kill herself."

"No," allowed Captain Maitland. "Not in the normal run of things. But there might be circumstances in which it would be quite a natural thing to do."

"Such as?"

Captain Maitland stooped to a bundle which I had previously noticed him place by the side of his chair. He swung it on to the table with something of an effort.

"There's something here that none of you know about," he said. "We found it under her bed."

He fumbled with the knot of the covering, then threw it back revealing a heavy great quern or grinder.

That was nothing in itself—there were a dozen or so already found in the course of the excavations.

What riveted our attention on this particular specimen was a dull, dark stain and a fragment of something that looked like hair.

"That'll be your job, Reilly," said Captain Maitland. "But I shouldn't say that there's much doubt about this being the instrument with which Mrs Leidner was killed!"

26. Next it Will be Me!

IT WAS RATHER horrible. Dr Leidner looked as though he were going to faint and I felt a bit sick myself.

Dr Reilly examined it with professional gusto.

"No fingerprints, I presume?" he threw out.

"No fingerprints."

Dr Reilly took out a pair of forceps and investigated delicately.

"H'm—a fragment of human tissue—and hair—fair blonde hair. That's the unofficial verdict. Of course, I'll have to make a proper test, blood group, etc., but there's not much doubt. Found under Miss Johnson's bed? Well, well—so *that's* the big idea. She did the murder, and then, God rest her, remorse came to her and she finished herself off. It's a theory—a pretty theory."

Dr Leidner could only shake his head helplessly.

"Not Anne—not Anne," he murmured.

"I don't know where she hid this to begin with," said Captain Maitland. "Every room was searched after the first crime."

Something jumped into my mind and I thought, "in the stationery cupboard," but I didn't say anything.

"Wherever it was, she became dissatisfied with its hiding-place and took it into her own room, which had been searched with all the rest. Or perhaps she did that after making up her mind to commit suicide."

"I don't believe it," I said aloud.

And I couldn't somehow believe that kind nice Miss Johnson had battered out Mrs Leidner's brains. I just couldn't *see* it happening! And yet it *did* fit in with some things—her fit of weeping that night, for instance. After all, I'd said "remorse" myself—only I'd never thought it was remorse for anything but the smaller, more insignificant crime.

"I don't know what to believe," said Captain Maitland.

"There's the French Father's disappearance to be cleared up too. My men are out hunting around in case he's been knocked on the head and his body rolled into a convenient irrigation ditch."

"Oh! I remember now——" I began.

Every one looked towards me inquiringly.

"It was yesterday afternoon," I said. "He'd been cross-questioning me about the man with a squint who was looking in at the window that day. He asked me just where he'd stood on the path and then he said he was going out to have a look round. He said in detective stories the criminal always dropped a convenient clue."

"Damned if any of my criminals ever do," said Captain Maitland. "So that's what he was after, was it? By jove, I wonder if he *did* find anything. A bit of a coincidence if both he and Miss Johnson discovered a clue to the identity of the murderer at practically the same time."

He added irritably, "Man with a squint? Man with a squint? There's more in this tale of that fellow with a squint than meets the eye. I don't know why the devil my fellows can't lay hold of him?"

"Probably because he hasn't got a squint," said Poirot quietly.

"Do you mean he faked it? Didn't know you could fake an actual squint."

Poirot merely said:

"A squint can be a very useful thing."

"The devil it can! I'd give a lot to know where that fellow is now, squint or no squint!"

"At a guess," said Poirot, "he has already passed the Syrian frontier."

"We've warned Tell Kotchek and Abu Kemal—all the frontier posts, in fact."

"I should imagine that he took the route through the hills. The route lorries sometimes take when running contraband."

Captain Maitland grunted.

"Then we'd better telegraph Deir ez Zor?"

"I did so yesterday—warning them to look out for a car with two men in it whose passports will be in the most impeccable order."

Captain Maitland favoured him with a stare.

"*You* did, did you? Two men—eh?"

Poirot nodded.

"There are two men in this."

"It strikes me, M. Poirot, that you've been keeping quite a lot of things up your sleeve."

Poirot shook his head.

"No," he said. "Not really. The truth came to me only this morning when I was watching the sun rise. A very beautiful sunrise."

I don't think that any of us had noticed that Mrs Mercado was in the room. She must have crept in when we were all taken aback by the production of that horrible great bloodstained stone.

But now, without the least warning, she set up a noise like a pig having its throat cut.

"Oh, my God!" she cried. "I see it all. I see it all now. *It was Father Lavigny*. He's mad—religious mania. He thinks women are sinful. *He's killing them all*. First Mrs Leidner—then Miss Johnson. And next it will be *me*. . . ."

With a scream of frenzy she flung herself across the room and clutched at Dr Reilly's coat.

"I won't stay here, I tell you! I won't stay here a day longer. There's danger. There's danger all round. He's hiding some-where—waiting his time. He'll spring out on me!"

Her mouth opened and she began screaming again.

I hurried over to Dr Reilly, who had caught her by the wrists. I gave her a sharp slap on each cheek and with Dr Reilly's help I sat her down in a chair.

"Nobody's going to kill you," I said. "We'll see to that. Sit down and behave yourself."

She didn't scream any more. Her mouth closed and she sat looking at me with startled, stupid eyes.

Then there was another interruption. The door opened and Sheila Reilly came in.

Her face was pale and serious. She came straight to Poirot.

"I was at the post office early, M. Poirot," she said, "and there was a telegram there for you—so I brought it along."

"Thank you, mademoiselle."

He took it from her and tore it open while she watched his face.

It did not change, that face. He read the telegram, smoothed it out, folded it up neatly and put it in his pocket.

Mrs Mercado was watching him. She said in a choked voice: "Is that—from America?"

He shook his head.

"No, madame," he said. "It is from Tunis."

She stared at him for a moment as though she did not understand, then with a long sigh, she leánt back in her seat.

"Father Lavigny," she said. "I *was* right. I've always thought there was something queer about him. He said things to me once . . . I suppose he's mad. . . ." She paused and then said, "I'll be quiet. But I *must* leave this place. Joseph and I can go in and sleep at the Rest House."

"Patience, madame," said Poirot. "I will explain everything."

Captain Maitland was looking at him curiously.

"Do you consider you've definitely got the hang of this business?" he demanded.

Poirot bowed.

It was a most theatrical bow. I think it rather annoyed Captain Maitland.

"Well," he barked. "Out with it, man."

But that wasn't the way Hercule Poirot did things. I saw perfectly well that he meant to make a song and dance of it. I wondered if he really *did* know the truth, or if he was just showing off.

He turned to Dr Reilly.

"Will you be so good, Dr Reilly, as to summon the others?"

Dr Reilly jumped up and went off obligingly. In a minute or two the other members of the expedition began to file into the room. First Reiter and Emmott. Then Bill Coleman. Then Richard Carey and finally Mr Mercado.

Poor man, he really looked like death. I suppose he was mortally afraid that he'd get hauled over the coals for carelessness in leaving dangerous chemicals about.

Every one seated themselves round the table very much as we had done on the day M. Poirot arrived. Both Bill Coleman and David Emmott hesitated before they sat down, glancing towards

Sheila Reilly. She had her back to them and was standing looking out of the window.

"Chair, Sheila?" said Bill.

David Emmott said in his low pleasant drawl, "Won't you sit down?"

She turned then and stood for a minute looking at them. Each was indicating a chair, pushing it forward. I wondered whose chair she would accept.

In the end she accepted neither.

"I'll sit here," she said brusquely. And she sat down on the edge of a table quite close to the window.

"That is," she added, "if Captain Maitland doesn't mind my staying?"

I'm not quite sure what Captain Maitland would have said. Poirot forestalled him.

"Stay by all means, mademoiselle," he said. "It is, indeed, necessary that you should."

She raised her eyebrows.

"Necessary?"

"That is the word I used, mademoiselle. There are some questions I shall have to ask you."

Again her eyebrows went up but she said nothing further. She turned her face to the window as though determined to ignore what went on in the room behind her.

"And now," said Captain Maitland, "perhaps we shall get at the truth!"

He spoke rather impatiently. He was essentially a man of action. At this very moment I feel sure that he was fretting to be out and doing things—directing the search for Father Lavigny's body, or alternatively sending out parties for his capture and arrest.

He looked at Poirot with something akin to dislike.

"If the beggar's got anything to say, why doesn't he say it?"

I could see the words on the tip of his tongue.

Poirot gave a slow appraising glance at us all, then rose to his feet.

I don't know what I expected him to say—something dramatic certainly. He was that kind of person.

But I certainly didn't expect him to start off with a phrase in Arabic.

Yet that is what happened. He said the words slowly and solemnly—and really quite religiously, if you know what I mean.

"*Bismillahi ar rahman ar rahim.*"

And then he gave the translation in English.

"In the name of Allah, the Merciful, the Compassionate."

27. *Beginning of a Journey*

"BISMILLAHI AR RAHMAN AR RAHIM. That is the Arab phrase used before starting out on a journey. *Eh bien*, we too, start on a journey. A journey into the past. A journey into the strange places of the human soul."

I don't think that up till that moment I'd ever felt any of the so-called "glamour of the East." Frankly, what had struck me was the *mess* everywhere. But suddenly, with M. Poirot's words, a queer sort of vision seemed to grow up before my eyes. I thought of words like Samarkand and Ispahan—and of merchants with long beards—and kneeling camels—and staggering porters carrying great bales on their backs held by a rope round the forehead—and women with henna-stained hair and tattooed faces kneeling by the Tigris and washing clothes, and I heard their queer, wailing chants and the far-off groaning of the water-wheel. . . .

They were mostly things I'd seen and heard and thought nothing much of. But now, somehow they seemed *different*— like a piece of fusty old stuff you take into the light and suddenly see the rich colours of an old embroidery. . . .

Then I looked round the room we were sitting in and I got a queer feeling that what M. Poirot said was true—we *were* all starting on a journey. We were here together now, but we were all going our different ways.

And I looked at every one as though, in a sort of way, I were seeing them for the first time—*and* for the last time—which sounds stupid, but it was what I felt all the same.

Mr Mercado was twisting his fingers nervously—his queer light eyes with their dilated pupils were staring at Poirot. Mrs Mercado was looking at her husband. She had a strange watchful look like a tigress waiting to spring. Dr Leidner seemed to have shrunk in some curious fashion. This last blow had just crumpled him up. You might almost say he wasn't in the room at all. He was somewhat far away in a place of his own. Mr Coleman was looking straight at Poirot. His mouth was slightly open and his eyes protruded. He looked almost idiotic. Mr Emmott was looking down at his feet and I couldn't see his face properly. Mr Reiter looked bewildered. His mouth was pushed out in a pout and that made him look more like a nice clean pig than ever. Miss Reilly was looking steadily out of the window. I don't know what she was thinking or feeling. Then I looked at Mr Carey, and somehow his face hurt me and I looked away. There we were, all of us. And somehow I felt that when M. Poirot had finished we'd all be somewhere quite different. . . .

It was a queer feeling. . . .

Poirot's voice went quietly on. It was like a river running evenly between its banks . . . running to the sea. . . .

"From the very beginning, I have felt that to understand this case one must seek not for external signs or clues, but for the truer clues of the clash of personalities and the secrets of the heart.

"And I may say that though I have now arrived at what I believe to be the true solution of the case, *I have no material proof of it*. I *know* it is so, because it *must* be so, because *in no other way* can every single fact fit into its ordered and recognised place.

"And that, to my mind, is the most satisfying solution there can be."

He paused and then went on:

"I will start my journey at the moment when I myself was brought into the case—when I had it presented to me as an accomplished happening. Now, every case, in my opinion, has a definite *shape* and *form*. The pattern of this case, to my mind, all revolved round the personality of Mrs Leidner. Until I knew *exactly what kind of a woman Mrs Leidner was* I should not be able to know why she was murdered and who murdered her.

"That, then, was my starting point—the personality of Mrs Leidner.

"There was also one other psychological point of interest—the curious state of tension described as existing amongst the members of the expedition. This was attested to by several different witnesses—some of them outsiders—and I made a note that although hardly a starting point, it should nevertheless be borne in mind during my investigations.

"The accepted idea seemed to be that it was directly the result of Mrs Leidner's influence on the members of the expedition, but for reasons which I will outline to you later this did not seem to me entirely acceptable.

"To start with, as I say I concentrated solely and entirely on the personality of Mrs Leidner. I had various means of assessing that personality. There were the reactions she produced in a number of people, all varying widely in character and temperament, and there was what I could glean by my own observation. The scope of the latter was naturally limited. But I *did* learn certain facts.

"Mrs Leidner's tastes were simple and even on the austere side. She was clearly not a luxurious woman. On the other hand, some embroidery she had been doing was of an extreme fineness and beauty. That indicated a woman of fastidious and artistic taste. From the observation of the books in her bedroom I formed a further estimate. She had brains, and I also fancied that she was, essentially, an egoist.

"It had been suggested to me that Mrs Leidner was a woman whose main preoccupation was to attract the opposite sex—that she was, in fact, a sensual woman. This I did not believe to be the case.

"In her bedroom I noticed the following books on a shelf: *Who Were the Greeks? Introduction to Relativity, Life of Lady Hester Stanhope, Back to Methuselah, Linda Condon, Crewe Train*.

"She had, to begin with, an interest in culture and in modern science—that is, a distinct intellectual side. Of the novels *Linda Condon*, and in a lesser degree *Crewe Train*, seemed to show that Mrs Leidner had a sympathy and interest in the independent woman—unencumbered or entrapped by man. She was also obviously interested by the personality of Lady Hester Stanhope. *Linda Condon* is an exquisite study of the worship of her own beauty by a woman. *Crewe Train* is a study of a passionate individualist. *Back to Methuselah* is in sympathy with the intellectual rather than the emotional attitude to life. I felt that I was beginning to understand the dead woman.

"I next studied the reactions of those who had formed Mrs Leidner's immediate circle—and my picture of the dead woman grew more and more complete.

"It was quite clear to me from the accounts of Dr Reilly and others that Mrs Leidner was one of those women who are endowed by Nature not only with beauty but with the kind of calamitous magic which sometimes accompanies beauty and can, indeed, exist independently of it. Such women usually leave a trail of violent happenings behind them. They bring disaster—sometimes on others—sometimes on themselves.

"I was convinced that Mrs Leidner was a woman who essentially worshipped *herself* and who enjoyed more than anything else the sense of *power*. Wherever she was, she *must* be the centre of the universe. And every one round her, man or woman, had got to acknowledge her sway. With some people that was easy. Nurse Leatheran, for instance, a generous-natured woman with a romantic imagination, was captured instantly and gave in un-grudging manner full appreciation. But there was a second way in which Mrs Leidner exercised her sway—the way of fear. Where conquest was too easy she indulged a more cruel side to her nature—but I wish to reiterate emphatically that it was not what you might call *conscious* cruelty. It was as natural and unthinking as is the conduct of a cat with a mouse. Where consciousness came in, she was essentially kind and would often go out of her way to do kind and thoughtful actions for other people.

"Now of course the first and most important problem to solve was the problem of the anonymous letters. Who had written them and why? I asked myself: Had Mrs Leidner written them *herself?*

"To answer this problem it was necessary to go back a long way—to go back, in fact, to the date of Mrs Leidner's first marriage. It is here we start on our journey proper. The journey of Mrs Leidner's life.

"First of all we must realise that the Louise Leidner of all those years ago is essentially the same Louise Leidner of the present time.

"She was young then, of remarkable beauty—that same haunting beauty that affects a man's spirit and senses as no mere material beauty can—and she was already essentially an egoist.

"Such women naturally revolt from the idea of marriage. They may be attracted by men, but they prefer to belong to themselves. They are truly *La Belle Dame sans Merci* of the legend. Nevertheless Mrs Leidner *did* marry—and we can assume, I think, that her husband must have been a man of a certain force of character.

"Then the revelation of his traitorous activities occurs and Mrs Leidner acts in the way she told Nurse Leatheran. She gave information to the Government.

"Now I submit that there was a psychological significance in her action. She told Nurse Leatheran that she was a very patriotic idealistic girl and that that feeling was the cause of her action. But it is a well-known fact that we all tend to deceive ourselves as to the motives for our own actions. Instinctively we select the best-sounding motive! Mrs Leidner may have believed herself that it was patriotism that inspired her action, but I believe myself that it was really the outcome of an unacknowledged desire to get rid of her husband! She disliked domination—she disliked the feeling of belonging to some one else—in fact she disliked playing second fiddle. She took a patriotic way of regaining her freedom.

"But underneath her consciousness was a gnawing sense of guilt which was to play its part in her future destiny.

"We now come directly to the question of the letters. Mrs Leidner was highly attractive to the male sex. On several occasions she was attracted by them—but in each case a threatening letter played its part and the affair came to nothing.

"Who wrote those letters? Frederick Bosner or his brother William or *Mrs Leidner herself*?

"There is a perfectly good case for either theory. It seems clear to me that Mrs Leidner was one of those women who do inspire devouring devotions in men, the type of devotion which can become an obsession. I find it quite possible to believe in a Frederick Bosner to whom Louise, his wife, mattered more than anything in the world! She had betrayed him once and he dared not approach her openly, but he was determined at least that she should be his or no one's. He preferred her death to her belonging to another man.

"On the other hand, if Mrs Leidner had, deep down, a dislike

189

of entering into the marriage bond, it is possible that she took this way of extricating herself from difficult positions. She was a huntress who, the prey once attained, had no further use for it! Craving drama in her life, she invented a highly satisfactory drama—a resurrected husband forbidding the banns! It satisfied her deepest instincts. It made her a romantic figure, a tragic heroine, and it enabled her not to marry again.

"This state of affairs continued over a number of years. Every time there was any likelihood of marriage—a threatening letter arrived.

"*But now we come to a really interesting point*. Dr Leidner came upon the scene—and no forbidding letter arrived! Nothing stood in the way of her becoming Mrs Leidner. Not until *after* her marriage did a letter arrive.

"At once we ask ourselves—why?

"Let us take each theory in turn.

"*If* Mrs Leidner wrote the letters herself the problem is easily explained. Mrs Leidner really *wanted* to marry Dr Leidner. And so she *did* marry him. But in that case, *why did she write herself a letter afterwards*? Was her craving for drama too strong to be suppressed? And why only those two letters? After that no other letter was received until a year and a half later.

"Now take the other theory, that the letters were written by her first husband, Frederick Bosner (or his brother). Why did the threatening letter arrive *after* the marriage? Presumably Frederick could not have *wanted* her to marry Leidner. Why, then, did he not stop the marriage? He had done so successfully on former occasions. And why, *having waited till the marriage had taken place*, did he then resume his threats?

"The answer, an unsatisfactory one, is that he was somehow or other unable to protest sooner. He may have been in prison or he may have been abroad.

"There is next the attempted gas poisoning to consider. It seems extremely unlikely that it was brought about by an outside agency. The likely persons to have staged it were Dr and Mrs Leidner themselves. There seems no conceivable reason why *Dr* Leidner should do such a thing, so we are brought to the conclusion that *Mrs* Leidner planned and carried it out herself.

"Why? More drama?

"After that Dr and Mrs Leidner go abroad and for eighteen months they lead a happy, peaceful life with no threats of death to disturb it. They put that down to having successfully covered their traces, but such an explanation is quite absurd. In these days going abroad is quite inadequate for that purpose. And especially was that so in the case of the Leidners. He was the director of a museum expedition. By inquiry at the museum, Frederick Bosner could at once have obtained his correct address. Even granting that he was in too reduced circumstances to pursue the couple himself, there would be no bar to his continuing his threatening letters. And it seems to me that a man with his obsession would certainly have done so.

"Instead nothing is heard of him until nearly two years later when the letters are resumed.

"*Why* were the letters resumed?

"A very difficult question—most easily answered by saying that Mrs Leidner was bored and wanted more drama. But I was not quite satisfied with that. This particular form of drama seemed to me a shade too vulgar and too crude to accord well with her fastidious personality.

"The only thing to do was to keep an open mind on the question.

"There were three definite possibilities: (1) the letters were written by Mrs Leidner herself; (2) they were written by Frederick Bosner (or young William Bosner); (3) they might have been written *originally* by either Mrs Leidner or her first husband, but they were now *forgeries*—that is, they were being written by a *third* person who was aware of the earlier letters.

"I now come to direct consideration of Mrs Leidner's entourage.

"I examined first the actual opportunities that each member of the staff had had for committing the murder.

"Roughly, on the face of it, *any one* might have committed it (as far as opportunity went), with the exception of three persons.

"Dr Leidner, by overwhelming testimony, had never left the roof. Mr Carey was on duty at the mound. Mr Coleman was in Hassanieh.

"But those alibis, my friends, were not *quite* as good as they looked. I except Dr Leidner's. There is absolutely no doubt that he was on the roof all the time and did not come down until quite an hour and a quarter after the murder had happened.

"But was it *quite* certain that Mr Carey was on the mound all the time?

"And had Mr Coleman *actually been in Hassanieh* at the time the murder took place?"

Bill Coleman reddened, opened his mouth, shut it and looked round uneasily.

Mr Carey's expression did not change.

Poirot went on smoothly.

"I also considered one other person who, I satisfied myself, would be perfectly capable of committing murder *if she felt strongly enough*. Miss Reilly has courage and brains and a certain quality of ruthlessness. When Miss Reilly was speaking to me on the subject of the dead woman, I said to her, jokingly, that I hoped she had an alibi. I think Miss Reilly was conscious then that she had had in her heart the desire, at least, to kill. At any rate she immediately uttered a very silly and purposeless lie. She said she had been playing tennis on that afternoon. The next day I learned from a casual conversation with Miss Johnson that far from playing tennis, Miss Reilly *had actually been near this house at the time of the murder*. It occurred to me that Miss Reilly, if not guilty of the crime, might be able to tell me something useful."

He stopped and then said quietly:

"Will you tell us, Miss Reilly, what you *did* see that afternoon?"

The girl did not answer at once. She still looked out of the window without turning her head, and when she spoke it was in a detached and measured voice.

"I rode out to the dig after lunch. It must have been about a quarter to two when I got there."

"Did you find any of your friends on the dig?"

"No, there seemed to be no one there but the Arab foreman."

"You did not see Mr Carey?"

"No."

"Curious," said Poirot. "No more did M. Verrier when he went there that same afternoon."

He looked invitingly at Carey, but the latter neither moved nor spoke.

"Have you any explanation, Mr Carey?"

"I went for a walk. There was nothing of interest turning up."

"In which direction did you go for a walk?"

"Down by the river."

"Not back towards the house?"

"No."

"I suppose," said Miss Reilly, "that you were waiting for some one who didn't come."

He looked at her but didn't answer.

Poirot did not press the point. He spoke once more to the girl.

"Did you see anything else, mademoiselle?"

"Yes. I was not far from the expedition house when I noticed the expedition lorry drawn up in a wadi. I thought it was rather queer. Then I saw Mr Coleman. He was walking along with his head down as though he were searching for something."

"Look here," burst out Mr Coleman, "I——"

Poirot stopped him with an authoritative gesture.

"Wait. Did you speak to him, Miss Reilly?"

"No, I didn't."

"Why?"

The girl said slowly:

"Because, from time to time, he started and looked round with an extraordinary furtive look. It—gave me an unpleasant feeling. I turned my horse's head and rode away. I don't think he saw me. I was not very near and he was absorbed in what he was doing."

"Look here," Mr Coleman was not to be hushed any longer. "I've got a perfectly good explanation for what—I admit—looks a bit fishy. As a matter of fact, the day before I had slipped a jolly fine cylinder seal into my coat pocket instead of putting it in the antika-room—forgot all about it. And then I discovered I'd been and lost it out of my pocket—dropped it somewhere. I didn't want to get into a row about it so I decided I'd have a jolly good search on the quiet. I was pretty sure I'd dropped it on the way to or from the dig. I rushed over my business in Hassanieh. Sent a walad to do some of the shopping and got back early. I stuck the bus where it wouldn't show and had a jolly good hunt for over an hour. And didn't find the damned thing at that! Then I got into the bus and drove on to the house. Naturally, every one thought I'd just got back."

"And you did not undeceive them?" asked Poirot sweetly.

"Well, that was pretty natural under the circumstances, don't you think?"

"I hardly agree," said Poirot.

"Oh, come now—don't go looking for trouble—that's *my* motto! But you can't fasten anything on me. I never went into the courtyard, and you can't find any one who'll say I did."

"That, of course, has been the difficulty," said Poirot. "The evidence of the servants that *no one entered the courtyard from outside*. But it occurred to me, upon reflection, that that was really *not* what they had said. They had sworn that *no stranger* had entered the premises. They had not been asked *if a member of the expedition* had done so."

"Well, you ask them," said Coleman. "I'll eat my hat if they saw me or Carey either."

"Ah! but that raises rather an interesting question. They would notice *a stranger* undoubtedly—but would they have even *noticed* a member of the expedition? The members of the staff are passing in and out all day. The servants would hardly notice their going and coming. It is possible, I think, that either Mr Carey or Mr Coleman *might* have entered and the servants' minds would have no remembrance of such an event."

"Bunkum!" said Mr Coleman.

Poirot went on calmly:

"Of the two, I think Mr Carey was the least likely to be noticed going or coming. Mr Coleman had started to Hassanieh in the car that morning and he would be expected to return in it. His arrival on foot would therefore be noticeable."

"Of course it would!" said Coleman.

Richard Carey raised his head. His deep-blue eyes looked straight at Poirot.

"Are you accusing me of murder, M. Poirot?" he asked.

His manner was quite quiet but his voice had a dangerous undertone.

Poirot bowed to him.

"As yet I am only taking you all on a journey—my journey towards the truth. I had now established one fact—that all the members of the expedition staff, and also Nurse Leatheran, could in actual *fact* have committed the murder. That there was very little likelihood of some of them having committed it was a secondary matter.

"I had examined *means* and *opportunity*. I next passed to *motive*. I discovered that *one and all of you could be credited with a motive!*"

"Oh! M. Poirot," I cried. "Not *me*! Why, I was a stranger. I'd only just come."

"*Eh bien, ma sœur*, and was not that *just what Mrs Leidner had been fearing*? A *stranger* from *outside*?"

"But—but—— Why, Dr Reilly knew all about me! He suggested my coming!"

"How much did he really know about you? *Mostly what you yourself had told him*. Impostors have passed themselves off as hospital nurses before now."

"You can write to St Christopher's," I began.

"For the moment will you silence yourself. Impossible to proceed while you conduct this argument. I do not say I suspect you *now*. All I say is that, keeping the open mind, you might quite easily be some one other than you pretended to be. There are many successful female impersonators, you know. Young William Bosner might be something of that kind."

I was about to give him a further piece of my mind. Female impersonator indeed! But he raised his voice and hurried on with such an air of determination that I thought better of it.

"I am going now to be frank—brutally so. It is necessary. I am going to lay bare the underlying structure of this place.

"I examined and considered every single soul here. To begin with Dr Leidner, I soon convinced myself that his love for his wife was the mainspring of his existence. He was a man torn and ravaged with grief. Nurse Leatheran I have already mentioned. If she were a female impersonator she was a most amazingly successful one, and I inclined to the belief that she was exactly what she said she was—a thoroughly competent hospital nurse."

"Thank you for nothing," I interposed.

"My attention was immediately attracted towards Mr and Mrs Mercado, who were both of them clearly in a state of great agitation and unrest. I considered first Mrs Mercado. Was she capable of murder and if so for what reasons?

"Mrs Mercado's physique was frail. At first sight it did not seem possible that she could have had the physical strength to strike down a woman like Mrs Leidner with a heavy stone implement. If, however, Mrs Leidner had been on her knees at the time, the thing would at least be *physically possible*. There are ways in which one woman can induce another to go down on her knees. Oh! not emotional ways! For instance, a woman might be turning up the hem of a skirt and ask another woman to put in the pins for her. The second woman would kneel on the ground quite unsuspectingly.

"But the motive? Nurse Leatheran had told me of the angry glances she had seen Mrs Mercado direct at Mrs Leidner. Mr Mercado had evidently succumbed easily to Mrs Leidner's spell. But I did not think the solution was to be found in mere jealousy. I was sure Mrs Leidner was not in the least interested really in Mr Mercado—and doubtless Mrs Mercado was aware of the fact. She might be furious with her for the moment, but for *murder* there would have to be greater provocation. But Mrs Mercado was essentially a fiercely maternal type. From the way she looked at her husband I realised, not only that she loved him, but that she would fight for him tooth and nail—and more than that—*that she envisaged the possibility of having to do so*. She was constantly on her guard and uneasy. The uneasiness was for him—not for herself. And when I studied Mr Mercado I could make a fairly easy guess at what the trouble was. I took means to assure myself of the truth of my guess. Mr Mercado was a drug addict—in an advanced stage of the craving.

"Now I need probably not tell you all that the taking of drugs over a long period has the result of considerably blunting the moral sense.

"Under the influence of drugs a man commits actions that he would not have dreamed of committing a few years earlier before he began the practice. In some cases a man has committed murder—and it has been difficult to say whether he was wholly responsible for his actions or not. The law of different countries varies slightly on that point. The chief characteristic of the drug-fiend criminal is overweening confidence in his own cleverness.

"I thought it possible that there was some discreditable incident, perhaps a criminal incident, in Mr Mercado's past which his wife had somehow or other succeeded in hushing up. Nevertheless his career hung on a thread. If anything of this past incident were bruited about, Mr Mercado would be ruined. His wife was always on the watch. But there was Mrs Leidner to be reckoned with. She had a sharp intelligence and a love of power. She might even induce the wretched man to confide in her. It would just have suited her peculiar temperament to feel she knew a secret which she could reveal at any minute with disastrous effects.

"Here, then, was a possible motive for murder on the part of the Mercados. To protect her mate, Mrs Mercado, I felt sure, would stick at nothing! Both she and her husband had had the opportunity—during that ten minutes when the courtyard was empty."

Mrs Mercado cried out, "It's not *true*!"

Poirot paid no attention.

"I next considered Miss Johnson. Was *she* capable of murder?

"I thought she was. She was a person of strong will and iron self-control. Such people are constantly repressing themselves— and one day the dam bursts! But if Miss Johnson had committed the crime it could only be for some reason connected with Dr Leidner. If in any way she felt convinced that Mrs Leidner was spoiling her husband's life, then the deep unacknowledged jealousy far down in her would leap at the chance of a plausible motive and give itself full rein.

"Yes, Miss Johnson was distinctly a possibility.

"Then there were the three young men.

"First Carl Reiter. If, by any chance, one of the expedition staff was William Bosner, then Reiter was by far the most likely person. But if he *was* William Bosner, then he was certainly a most accomplished actor! If he were merely *himself*, had he any reason for murder?

"Regarded from Mrs Leidner's point of view, Carl Reiter was far too easy a victim for good sport. He was prepared to fall on his face and worship immediately. Mrs Leidner despised undiscriminating adoration—and the door-mat attitude nearly always brings out the worst side of a woman. In her treatment of Carl Reiter Mrs Leidner displayed really deliberate cruelty. She inserted a gibe here—a prick there. She made the poor young man's life a hell to him.''

Poirot broke off suddenly and addressed the young man in a personal, highly confidential manner.

"*Mon ami*, let this be a lesson to you. You are a *man*. Behave, then, like a *man*! It is against Nature for a man to grovel. Women and Nature have almost exactly the same reactions! Remember it is better to take the largest plate within reach and fling it at a woman's head than it is to wriggle like a worm whenever she looks at you!''

He dropped his private manner and reverted to his lecture style.

"Could Carl Reiter have been goaded to such a pitch of torment that he turned on his tormentor and killed her? Suffering does queer things to a man. I could not be *sure* that it was *not* so!

"Next, William Coleman. His behaviour, as reported by Miss Reilly, is certainly suspicious. If he was the criminal it could only be because his cheerful personality concealed the hidden one of William Bosner. I do not think William Coleman, as William Coleman, has the temperament of a murderer. His faults might lie in another direction. Ah! perhaps Nurse Leatheran can guess what they would be?''

How *did* the man do it? I'm sure I didn't look as though I was thinking anything at all.

"It's nothing really,'' I said, hesitating. "Only if it's to be all truth, Mr Coleman *did* say once himself that he would have made a good forger.''

"A good point,'' said Poirot. "Therefore if he had come across some of the old threatening letters, he could have copied them without difficulty.''

"Oy, oy, oy!'' called out Mr Coleman. "This is what they call a frame up.''

Poirot swept on.

"As to his being or not being William Bosner such a matter is difficult of verification. But Mr Coleman has spoken of a *guardian*—not of a father—and there is nothing definitely to veto the idea.''

"Tommyrot,'' said Mr Coleman. "Why all of you listen to this chap beats me.''

"Of the three young men there remains Mr Emmott," went on Poirot. "He again might be a possible shield for the identity of William Bosner. Whatever *personal* reasons he might have for the removal of Mrs Leidner I soon realised that I should have no means of learning them from him. He could keep his own counsel remarkably well, and there was not the least chance of provoking him nor of tricking him into betraying himself on any point. Of all the expedition he seemed to be the best and most dispassionate judge of Mrs Leidner's personality. I think that he always knew her for exactly what she was—but what impression her personality made on him I was unable to discover. I fancy that Mrs Leidner herself must have been provoked and angered by his attitude.

"I may say that of all the expedition, *as far as character and capability were concerned*, Mr Emmott seemed to me the most fitted to bring a clever and well-timed crime off satisfactorily."

For the first time Mr Emmott raised his eyes from the toes of his boots.

"Thank you," he said.

There seemed to be just a trace of amusement in his voice.

"The last two people on my list were Richard Carey and Father Lavigny.

"According to the testimony of Nurse Leatheran and others, Mr Carey and Mrs Leidner disliked each other. They were both civil with an effort. Another person, Miss Reilly, propounded a totally different theory to account for their attitude of frigid politeness.

"I soon had very little doubt that Miss Reilly's explanation was the correct one. I acquired my certitude by the simple expedient of provoking Mr Carey into reckless and unguarded speech. It was not difficult. As I soon saw, he was in a state of high nervous tension. In fact he was—and is—very near a complete nervous breakdown. A man who is suffering up to the limit of his capacity can seldom put up much of a fight.

"Mr Carey's barriers came down almost immediately. He told me, with a sincerity that I did not for a moment doubt, that he hated Mrs Leidner.

"And he was undoubtedly speaking the truth. He *did* hate Mrs Leidner. But *why* did he hate her?

"I have spoken of women who have a calamitous magic. But men have that magic too. There are men who are able without the least effort to attract women. What they call in these days *le sex appeal*! Mr Carey had this quality very strongly. He was to begin with devoted to his friend and employer, and indifferent to his employer's wife. That did not suit Mrs Leidner. She *must* dominate—and she set herself out to capture Richard Carey. But here, I believe, something entirely unforeseen took place. She herself, for perhaps the first time in her life, fell a victim to an overmastering passion. She fell in love—really in love—with Richard Carey.

"And he—was unable to resist her. Here is the truth of the terrible state of nervous tension that he has been enduring. He has been a man torn by two opposing passions. He loved Louise Leidner—yes, but he also hated her. He hated her for undermining his loyalty to his friend. There is no hatred so great as that of a man who has been made to love a woman against his will.

"I had here all the motive that I needed. I was convinced that *at certain moments* the most natural thing for Richard Carey to do would have been to strike with all the force of his arm at the beautiful face that had cast a spell over him.

"All along I had felt sure that the murder of Louise Leidner was a *crime passionnel*. In Mr Carey I had found an ideal murderer for that type of crime.

"There remains one other candidate for the title of murderer—Father Lavigny. My attention was attracted to the good Father straight away by a certain discrepancy between his description of the strange man who had been seen peering in at the window and the one given by Nurse Leatheran. In all accounts given by different witnesses there is usually *some* discrepancy, but this was absolutely glaring. Moreover, Father Lavigny insisted on a certain characteristic—a squint—which ought to make identification much easier.

"But very soon it became apparent that *while Nurse Leatheran's description was substantially accurate*, Father Lavigny's was *nothing of the kind*. It looked almost as though Father Lavigny was deliberately misleading us—as though he did *not want the man caught*.

"But in that case *he must know something about this curious person*. He had been seen talking to the man but we had only his word for what they had been talking about.

"What had the Iraqi been doing when Nurse Leatheran and Mrs Leidner saw him? Trying to peer through the window—Mrs Leidner's window, so they thought, but I realised when I went and stood where they had been, that it might equally have been *the antika-room window*.

"The night after that an alarm was given. Some one was in the antika-room. Nothing proved to have been taken, however. The interesting point to me is that when Dr Leidner got there he found *Father Lavigny there before him*. Father Lavigny tells his story of seeing a light. *But again we have only his word for it*.

"I begin to get curious about Father Lavigny. The other day when I make the suggestion that Father Lavigny may be Frederick Bosner Dr Leidner pooh-poohs the suggestion. He says Father Lavigny is a well-known man. I advance the supposition that Fredrick Bosner, who has had nearly twenty years to make a career for himself, under a new name, may very possibly *be* a well-known man by this time! All the same, I do not think that he has spent the intervening time in a religious community. A very much simpler solution presents itself.

"Did any one at the expedition know Father Lavigny by sight before he came? Apparently not. Why then should not it be *some one impersonating the good Father*? I found out that a telegram had been sent to Carthage on the sudden illness of Dr Byrd, who was to have accompanied the expedition. To intercept a telegram, what could be easier? As to the work, there was no other epigraphist attached to the expedition. With a smattering of knowledge a clever man *might* bluff his way through. There had been very few tablets and inscriptions so far, and already I gathered that Father Lavigny's pronouncements had been felt to be somewhat unusual.

"It looked very much as though Father Lavigny were an *impostor*.

"But was he Frederick Bosner?

"Somehow affairs did not seem to be shaping themselves that way. The truth seemed likely to lie in quite a different direction.

"I had a lengthy conversation with Father Lavigny. I am a

201

practising Catholic and I know many priests and members of religious communities. Father Lavigny struck me as not ringing quite true to his rôle. But he struck me, on the other hand, as familiar in quite a different capacity. I *had* met men of his type quite frequently—but they were not members of a religious community. Far from it!

"I began to send off telegrams.

"And then, unwittingly, Nurse Leatheran gave me a valuable clue. We were examining the gold ornaments in the antika-room and she mentioned a trace of wax having been found adhering to a gold cup. Me, I say, 'Wax?' and Father Lavigny, he said 'Wax?' and his tone was enough! I knew in a flash exactly what he was doing here."

Poirot paused and addressed himself directly to Dr Leidner.

"I regret to tell you, monsieur, that the gold cup in the antika-room, the gold dagger, the hair ornaments and several other things *are not the genuine articles found by you*. They are very clever electro-types. Father Lavigny, I have just learned by this last answer to my telegrams, is none other than Raoul Menier, one of the cleverest thieves known to the French police. He specialises in thefts from museums of *objets d'art* and such like. Associated with him is Ali Yusuf, a semi-Turk, who is a first-class working jeweller. Our first knowledge of Menier was when certain objects in the Louvre were found not to be genuine—in every case it was discovered that a distinguished archæologist *not known previously by sight to the director* had recently had the handling of the spurious articles when paying a visit to the Louvre. On inquiry all these distinguished gentlemen denied having paid a visit to the Louvre at the times stated!

"I have learned that Menier was in Tunis preparing the way for a theft from the Holy Fathers when your telegram arrived. Father Lavigny, who was in ill-health, was forced to refuse, but Menier managed to get hold of the telegram and substitute one of acceptance. He was quite safe in doing so. Even if the monks should read in some paper (in itself an unlikely thing) that Father Lavigny was in Iraq they would only think that the newspapers had got hold of a half truth as so often happens.

"Menier and his accomplice arrived. The latter is seen when he is reconnoitring the antika-room from outside. The plan is for Father Lavigny to take wax impressions. Ali then makes clever duplicates. There are always certain collectors who are willing to pay a good price for genuine antiques and will ask no embarrassing questions. Father Lavigny will effect the substitution of the fake for the genuine article—preferably at night.

"And that is doubtless what he was doing when Mrs Leidner heard him and gave the alarm. What can he do? He hurriedly makes up a story of having seen a light in the antika-room.

"That 'went down,' as you say, very well. But Mrs Leidner was no fool. She may have remembered the trace of wax she had noticed and then put two and two together. And if she did, what will she do then? Would it not be *dans son caractère* to do nothing at once, but to enjoy herself by letting hints slip to the discomfiture of Father Lavigny. She will let him see that she suspects—but not that she *knows*. It is, perhaps, a dangerous game, but she enjoys a dangerous game.

"And perhaps she plays that game too long. Father Lavigny sees the truth, and strikes before she realises what he means to do.

"Father Lavigny is Raoul Menier—a thief. Is he also—a *murderer*?"

Poirot paced the room. He took out a handkerchief, wiped his forehead and went on:

"That was my position this morning. There were eight distinct possibilities and I did not know which of these possibilities was the right one. I still did not know *who was the murderer*.

"But murder is a habit. The man or woman who kills once will kill again.

"And by the second murder, the murderer was delivered into my hands.

"All along it was ever present in the back of my mind that some one of these people might have knowledge that they had kept back—knowledge incriminating the murderer.

"If so, that person would be in danger.

"My solicitude was mainly on account of Nurse Leatheran. She had an energetic personality and a brisk inquisitive mind. I was terrified of her finding out more than it was safe for her to know.

"As you all know, a second murder did take place. But the victim was not Nurse Leatheran—it was Miss Johnson.

"I like to think that I should have reached the correct solution anyway by pure reasoning, but it is certain that Miss Johnson's murder helped me to it much quicker.

"To begin with, one suspect was eliminated—Miss Johnson herself—for I did not for a moment entertain the theory of suicide.

"Let us examine now the facts of this second murder.

"Fact One: On Sunday evening Nurse Leatheran finds Miss Johnson in tears, and that same evening Miss Johnson burns a fragment of a letter which nurse believes to be in the same handwriting as that of the anonymous letters.

"Fact two: The evening before her death Miss Johnson is found by Nurse Leatheran standing on the roof in a state that nurse describes as one of incredulous horror. When nurse questions her she says, 'I've seen how some one could come in from outside—and no one would ever guess.' She won't say any more. Father Lavigny is crossing the courtyard and Mr Reiter is at the door of the photographic-room.

"Fact three: Miss Johnson is found dying. The only words she can manage to articulate are 'the window—the window——'

"Those are the facts, and these are the problems with which we are faced:

"What is the truth of the letters?

"What did Miss Johnson see from the roof?

"What did she mean by 'the window—the window?'

"*Eh bien*, let us take the second problem first as the easiest of solution. I went up with Nurse Leatheran and I stood where Miss Johnson had stood. From there she could see the courtyard and the archway and the north side of the building and two members of the staff. Had her words anything to do with either Mr Reiter or Father Lavigny?

"Almost at once a possible explanation leaped to my brain. If a stranger came in from *outside* he could only do so in *disguise*. And there was only *one* person whose general appearance lent itself to such an impersonation. Father Lavigny! With a sun helmet, sun glasses, black beard and a monk's long woollen robe, a stranger could pass in without the servants *realising* that a stranger had entered.

"Was *that* Miss Johnson's meaning? Or had she gone further?

Did she realise that Father Lavigny's whole *personality* was a disguise. That he was some one other than he pretended to be?

"Knowing what I did know about Father Lavigny I was inclined to call the mystery solved. Raoul Menier was the murderer. He had killed Mrs Leidner to silence her before she could give him away. Now *another person lets him see that she has penetrated his secret*. She, too, must be removed.

"And so everything is explained! The second murder. Father Lavigny's flight—minus robe and beard. (He and his friend are doubtless careering through Syria with excellent passports as two commercial travellers.) His action in placing the blood-stained quern under Miss Johnson's bed.

"As I say, I was almost satisfied—but not quite. For the perfect solution must explain *everything*—and this does not do so.

"It does not explain, for instance, why Miss Johnson should say 'the window—the window,' as she was dying. It does not explain her fit of weeping over the letter. It does not explain her mental attitude on the roof—her incredulous horror and her refusal to tell Nurse Leatheran what it was that *she now suspected or knew*.

"It was a solution that fitted the *outer* facts, but it did not satisfy the *psychological* requirements.

"And then, as I stood on the roof, going over in my mind those three points: the letters, the roof, the window, I *saw*—just as Miss Johnson had seen!

"*And this time what I saw explained everything!*"

28. Journey's End

POIROT LOOKED ROUND. Every eye was now fixed upon him. There had been a certain relaxation—a slackening of tension. Now the tension suddenly returned.

There was something coming . . . something . . .

Poirot's voice, quiet and unimpassioned, went on:

"The letters, the roof, 'the window' . . . Yes, everything was explained—everything fell into place.

"I said just now that three men had alibis for the time of the crime. Two of those alibis I have shown to be worthless. I saw now my great—my amazing mistake. The third alibi was worthless too. Not only *could* Dr Leidner have committed the murder—but I was convinced that he *had* committed it."

There was a silence, a bewildered uncomprehending silence. Dr Leidner said nothing. He seemed lost in his far-away world still. David Emmott, however, stirred uneasily and spoke.

"I don't know what you mean to imply, M. Poirot. I told you that Dr Leidner never left the roof until at least a quarter to three. That is the absolute truth. I swear it solemnly. I am not lying. And it would have been quite impossible for him to have done so without my seeing him."

Poirot nodded.

"Oh, I believe you. *Dr Leidner did not leave the roof.* That is an undisputed fact. But what I saw—and what Miss Johnson had seen—was *that Dr Leidner could murder his wife from the roof without leaving it.*"

We all stared.

"The *window*," cried Poirot. "*Her* window! That is what I realised—just as Miss Johnson realised it. Her window was directly underneath, on the side away from the courtyard. And Dr Leidner was alone up there with no one to witness his actions. And those heavy stone querns and grinders were up

206

there all ready to his hand. So simple, so very simply, granted one thing—*that the murderer had the opportunity to move the body before any one else saw it.* . . . Oh, it is beautiful—of an unbelievable simplicity!

"Listen—it went like this:

"Dr Leidner is on the roof working with the pottery. He calls you up, Mr Emmott, and while he holds you in talk he notices that, as usually happens, the small boy takes advantage of your absence to leave his work and go outside the courtyard. He keeps you with him ten minutes, then he lets you go and as soon as you are down below shouting to the boy he sets his plan in operation.

"He takes from his pocket the plasticine smeared mask with which he has already scared his wife on a former occasion and dangles it over the edge of the parapet till it taps on his wife's window.

"That, remember, is the window giving on the countryside facing the opposite direction to the courtyard.

"Mrs Leidner is lying on her bed half asleep. She is peaceful and happy. Suddenly the mask begins tapping on the window and attracts her-attention. But it is not dusk now—it is broad daylight—there is nothing terrifying about it. She recognises it for what it is—a crude form of trickery! She is not frightened but indignant. She does what any other woman would do in her place. Jumps off the bed, opens the window, passes her head through the bars and turns her face upwards to see who is playing the trick on her.

"Dr Leidner is waiting. He has in his hands, poised and ready, a heavy quern. At the psychological moment *he drops it*. . . .

"With a faint cry (heard by Miss Johnson) Mrs Leidner collapses on the rug underneath the window.

"Now there is a hole in this quern, and through that Dr Leidner had previously passed a cord. He has now only to haul in the cord and bring up the quern. He replaces the latter neatly, bloodstained side down, amongst the other objects of that kind on the roof.

"Then he continues his work for an hour or more till he judges the moment has come for the second act. He descends the stairs, speaks to Mr Emmott and Nurse Leatheran, crosses the courtyard and enters his wife's room. This is the explanation he himself gives of his movements there.

"*'I saw my wife's body in a heap by the bed. For a moment or two I felt paralysed as though I couldn't move. Then at last I went and knelt down by her and lifted up her head. I saw she was dead. . . . At last I got up. I felt dazed and as though I were drunk. I managed to get to the door and call out.'*

"A perfectly possible account of the actions of a grief-dazed man. Now listen to what I believe to be the truth. Dr Leidner enters the room, hurries to the window, and having pulled on a pair of gloves, closes and fastens it, then picks up his wife's body and transports it to a position between the bed and the door. Then he notices a slight stain on the window-side rug. He cannot change it with the other rug, they are a different size, but he does the next best thing. He puts the stained rug in front of the wash-stand and the rug from the wash-stand under the window. *If* the stain is noticed, it will be connected with the *wash-stand*— not with the *window*—a very important point. There must be no suggestion that the window played any part in the business. Then he comes to the door and acts the part of the overcome husband, and that, I imagine, is not difficult. For he *did* love his wife."

"My good man," cried Dr Reilly impatiently, "if he loved her why did he kill her? Where's the motive? Can't you speak, Leidner? Tell him he's mad."

Dr Leidner neither spoke nor moved.

Poirot said:

"Did I not tell you all along that this was a *crime passionnel*? Why did her first husband, Frederick Bosner, threaten to kill her? Because he loved her. . . . And in the end, you see, he made his boast good. . . .

"*Mais oui—mais oui—once I realise that it is Dr Leidner who did the killing* everything falls into place. . . .

"For the second time I recommence my journey from the beginning—Mrs Leidner's first marriage—the threatening letters—her second marriage. The letters prevented her marrying any other man—but they did not prevent her marrying Dr Leidner. How simple that is—*if Dr Leidner is actually Frederick Bosner*.

"Once more let us start our journey—from the point of view this time of young Frederick Bosner.

"To begin with he loves his wife Louise with an overpowering passion such as only a woman of her kind can evoke. She betrays him. He is sentenced to death. He escapes. He is involved in a railway accident but he manages to emerge with a second personality—*that of a young Swedish archæologist, Eric Leidner*, whose body is badly disfigured and who will be conveniently buried as Frederick Bosner.

"What is the new Eric Leidner's attitude to the woman who was willing to send him to his death? First and most important, *he still loves her*. He sets to work to build up his new life. He is a man of great ability, his profession is congenial to him and he makes a success of it. *But he never forgets the ruling passion of his life*. He keeps himself informed of his wife's movements. Of one thing he is cold-bloodedly determined (remember Mrs Leidner's own description of him to Nurse Leatheran—gentle and kind but ruthless), *she shall belong to no other man*. Whenever he judges it necessary he despatches a letter. He imitates some of the peculiarities of her handwriting in case she should think of taking his letters to the police. Women who write sensational anonymous letters to themselves are such a common pheno-menon that the police will be sure to jump to that solution given the likeness of the handwriting. At the same time he leaves her in doubt as to whether he is really alive or not.

"At last, after many years, he judges that the time has arrived; he re-enters her life. All goes well. His wife never dreams of his real identity. He is a well-known man. The upstanding, good-looking young fellow is now a middle-aged man with a beard and stooping shoulders. And so we see history repeating itself. As before, Frederick is able to dominate Louise. For the second time she consents to marry him. *And no letter comes to forbid the banns*.

"But *afterwards* a letter *does* come. Why?

"I think that Dr Leidner was taking no chances. The intimacy of marriage *might* awaken a memory. He wishes to impress on his wife, once and for all, *that Eric Leidner and Frederick Bosner are two* different people. So much so that a threatening letter comes from the former on account of the latter. The rather puerile gas poisoning business follows—arranged by Dr Leidner, of course. Still with the same object in view.

"After that he is satisfied. No more letters need come. They can settle down to happy married life together.

"And then, after nearly two years, *the letters recommence*.

"*Why? Eh bien*, I think I know. *Because the threat underlying the letters was always a genuine threat.* (That is why Mrs Leidner has always been frightened. She *knew* her Frederick's gentle but ruthless nature.) *If she belongs to any other man but him he would kill her. And she has given herself to Richard Carey.*

"And so, having discovered this, cold-bloodedly, calmly, Dr Leidner prepares the scene for murder.

"You see now the important part played by Nurse Leatheran? Dr Leidner's rather curious conduct (it puzzled me at the very first) in securing her services for his wife is explained. It was vital that a reliable professional witness should be able to state incontrovertibly that Mrs Leidner had been dead *over an hour* when her body was found—that is that she had been killed at a time when *everybody could swear her husband was on the roof*. A suspicion *might* have arisen that he had killed her when he entered the room and found the body—but that was out of the question when a trained hospital nurse would assert positively that she had already been dead an hour.

"Another thing that is explained is the curious state of tension and strain that had come over the expedition this year. I never from the first thought that that could be attributed solely to *Mrs.* Leidner's influence. For several years this particular expedition had had a reputation for happy good-fellowship. In my opinion the state of mind of a community is always directly due to the influence of the man at the top. Dr Leidner, quiet though he was, was a man of great personality. It was due to his tact, to his judgment, to his sympathetic manipulation of human beings that the atmosphere had always been such a happy one.

"If there was a change, therefore, the change must be due to the man at the top—in other words to Dr Leidner. It was *Dr* Leidner, not Mrs Leidner, who was responsible for the tension and uneasiness. No wonder the staff felt the change without understanding it. The kindly genial Dr Leidner, outwardly the same, was only playing the part of himself. The real man was an obsessed fanatic plotting to kill.

"And now we will pass on to the second murder—that of Miss Johnson. In tidying up Dr Leidner's papers in the office (a job she took on herself unasked, craving for something to do) she must have come on some unfinished draft of one of the anonymous letters.

"It must have been both incomprehensible and extremely upsetting to her! Dr Leidner has been deliberately terrorising his wife! She cannot understand it—but it upsets her badly. It is in this mood that Nurse Leatheran discovers her crying.

"I do not think at the moment that she suspected Dr Leidner of being the murderer, but my experiments with sounds in Mrs Leidner's and Father Lavigny's rooms are not lost upon her. She realises that if it *was* Mrs Leidner's cry she heard, *the window in her room must have been open, not shut*. At the moment that conveys nothing vital to her, *but she remembers it*.

"Her mind goes on working—ferreting its way towards the truth. Perhaps she makes some reference to the letters which Dr Leidner understands and his manner changes. She may see that he is, suddenly, afraid.

"But Dr Leidner *cannot* have killed his wife! He was on the *roof* all the time.

"And then, one evening, as she herself is on the roof puzzling about it, the truth comes to her in a flash. Mrs Leidner has been killed from up *here*, through the open window.

"It was at that minute that Nurse Leatheran found her.

"And immediately, her old affection reasserting itself, she puts up a quick camouflage. Nurse Leatheran must not guess the horrifying discovery she has just made.

"She looks deliberately in the opposite direction (towards the courtyard) and makes a remark suggested to her by Father Lavigny's appearance as he crosses the courtyard.

"She refuses to say more. She has got to 'think things out.'

"And Dr Leidner, who has been watching her anxiously, *realises that she knows the truth*. She is not the kind of woman to conceal her horror and distress from him.

"It is true that as yet she has not given him away—but how long can he depend upon her?

"Murder is a habit. That night he substitutes a glass of acid for her glass of water. There is just a chance she may be believed to have deliberately poisoned herself. There is even a chance she may be considered to have done the first murder and has now been overcome with remorse. To strengthen the latter idea he takes the quern from the roof and puts it under her bed.

"No wonder that poor Miss Johnson, in her death agony, could only try desperately to impart her hard-won information. Through 'the window,' *that* is how Mrs Leidner was killed, *not* through the door—through the *window*. . . .

"And so thus, everything is explained, everything falls into place. . . . Psychologically perfect.

"But there is no proof. . . . No proof at all. . . ."

None of us spoke. We were lost in a sea of horror. . . . Yes, and not only horror. Pity, too.

Dr Leidner had neither moved nor spoken. He sat just as he had done all along. A tired, worn elderly man.

At last he stirred slightly and looked at Poirot with gentle tired eyes.

"No," he said, "there is no proof. But that does not matter. You knew that I would not deny truth. . . . I have never denied truth . . . I think—really—I am rather glad . . . I'm so tired . . ."

Then he said simply:

"I'm sorry about Anne. That was bad—senseless—it wasn't *me*! And she suffered, too, poor soul. Yes, that wasn't me. It was fear. . . ."

A little smile just hovered on his pain-twisted lips.

"You would have made a good archæologist, M. Poirot. You have the gift of re-creating the past.

"It was all very much as you said.

"I loved Louise and I killed her . . . If you'd known Louise you'd have understood. . . . No, I think you understand anyway. . . ."

29. *L'envoi*

THERE ISN'T REALLY any more to say about things.

They got "Father" Lavigny and the other man just as they were going on board a steamer at Beyrouth.

Sheila Reilly married young Emmott. I think that will be good for her. He's no door-mat—he'll keep her in her place. She'd have ridden roughshod over poor Bill Coleman.

I nursed him, by the way, when he had appendicitis a year ago. I got quite fond of him. His people were sending him out to farm in South Africa.

I've never been out East again. It's funny—sometimes I wish I could. I think of the noise the water-wheel made and the women washing, and that queer haughty look that camels give you—and I get quite a homesick feeling. After all, perhaps dirt isn't really so unhealthy as one is brought up to believe!

Dr Reilly usually looks me up when he's in England, and as I said, it's he who's got me into this. "Take it or leave it," I said to him. "I know the grammar's all wrong and it's not properly written or anything like that—but there it is."

And he took it. Made no bones about it. It will give me a queer feeling if it's ever printed.

M. Poirot went back to Syria and about a week later he went home on the Orient Express and got himself mixed up in another murder. He was clever, I don't deny it, but I shan't forgive him in a hurry for pulling my leg the way he did. Pretending to think I might be mixed up in the crime and not a real hospital nurse at all!

Doctors are like that sometimes. Will have their joke, some of them will, and never think of *your* feelings!

I've thought and thought about Mrs Leidner and what she was really like. . . . Sometimes it seems to me she was just a terrible woman—and other times I remember how nice she was

213

to me and how soft her voice was—and her lovely fair hair and everything—and I feel that perhaps, after all, she was more to be pitied than blamed. . . .

And I can't help but pity Dr Leidner. I know he was a murderer twice over, but it doesn't seem to make any difference. He was so dreadfully fond of her. It's awful to be fond of any one like that.

Somehow, the more I get older, and the more I see of people and sadness and illness and everything, the sorrier I get for every one. Sometimes, I declare, I don't know what's become of the good strict principles my aunt brought me up with. A very religious woman she was, and most particular. There wasn't one of our neighbours whose faults she didn't know backwards and forwards. . . .

Oh, dear, it's quite true what Dr Reilly said. How does one stop writing? If I could find a really good telling phrase.

I must ask Dr Reilly for some Arab one.

Like the one M. Poirot used.

In the name of Allah, the Merciful, the Compassionate . . .

Something like that.

Mrs McGinty's Dead

AGATHA
CHRISTIE

MRS McGINTY'S DEAD

I

HERCULE POIROT came out of the *Vieille Grand'mère* restaurant into Soho. He turned up the collar of his overcoat through prudence, rather than necessity, since the night was not cold. "But at my age, one takes no risks," Poirot was wont to declare.

His eyes held a reflective sleepy pleasure. The *Escargots de la Vieille Grand'mère* had been delicious. A real find, this dingy little restaurant. Meditatively, like a well fed dog, Hercule Poirot curled his tongue round his lips. Drawing his handkerchief from his pocket, he dabbed his luxuriant moustaches.

Yes, he had dined well . . . And now what?

A taxi, passing him, slowed down invitingly. Poirot hesitated for a moment, but made no sign. Why take a taxi? He would in any case reach home too early to go to bed.

"Alas," murmured Poirot to his moustaches, "that one can only eat three times a day . . ."

For afternoon tea was a meal to which he had never become acclimatised. "If one partakes of the five o'clock, one does not," he explained, "approach the dinner with the proper quality of expectant gastric juices. And the dinner let us remember, is the supreme meal of the day!"

Not for him, either, the mid-morning coffee. No, chocolate and *croissants* for breakfast, *Déjeuner* at twelve-thirty if possible but certainly not later than one o'clock, and finally the climax: *Le Dîner*!

These were the peak periods of Hercule Poirot's day. Always a man who had taken his stomach seriously, he was reaping his reward in old age. Eating was now not only a physical pleasure, it was also an intellectual research. For in between meals he spent quite a lot of time searching out and marking down possible sources of new and delicious food. *La Vieille Grand'mère* had just received the seal of Hercule Poirot's gastronomic approval.

7

But now, unfortunately, there was the evening to put in.

Hercule Poirot sighed.

"If only," he thought, *"ce cher Hastings* were available . . ."

He dwelt with pleasure on his remembrances of his old friend.

"My first friend in this country—and still to me the dearest friend I have. True, often and often did he enrage me. But do I remember that now? No. I remember only his incredulous wonder, his open-mouthed appreciation of my talents—the ease with which I misled him without uttering an untrue word, his bafflement, his stupendous astonishment when he at last perceived the truth that had been clear to me all along. *Ce cher, cher ami!* It is my weakness, it has always been my weakness, to desire to show off. That weakness, Hastings could never understand. But indeed it is very necessary for a man of my abilities to admire himself—and for that one needs stimulation from outside. I cannot, truly I cannot, sit in a chair all day reflecting how truly admirable I am. One needs the human touch. One needs— as they say nowadays—the *stooge.*"

Hercule Poirot sighed. He turned into Shaftesbury Avenue.

Should he cross it and go on to Leicester Square and spend the evening at a cinema? Frowning slightly, he shook his head. The cinema, more often than not, enraged him by the looseness of its plots—the lack of logical continuity in the argument—even the photography which, raved over by some, to Hercule Poirot seemed often no more than the portrayal of scenes and objects so as to make them appear totally different from what they were in reality.

Everything, Hercule Poirot decided, was too artistic nowadays. Nowhere was there the love of order and method that he himself prized so highly. And seldom was there any appreciation of subtlety. Scenes of violence and crude brutality were the fashion, and as a former police officer, Poirot was bored by brutality. In his early days, he had seen plenty of crude brutality. It had been more the rule than the exception. He found it fatiguing, and unintelligent.

"The truth is," Poirot reflected as he turned his steps homeward, "I am not in tune with the modern world. And I am, in a superior way, a slave as other men are slaves. My work has enslaved me just as their work enslaves them. When the hour of leisure arrives, they have nothing with which to fill their leisure. The retired financier takes up golf, the little merchant puts bulbs in the garden, me, I eat. But there it is, I come round to it again. *One can only eat three times a day.* And in between are the gaps."

He passed a newspaper-seller and scanned the bill.

"Result of McGinty Trial. Verdict."

It stirred no interest in him. He recalled vaguely a small paragraph in the papers. It had not been an interesting murder. Some wretched old woman knocked on the head for a few pounds. All part of the senseless crude brutality of these days.

Poirot turned into the courtyard of his block of flats. As always his heart swelled in approval. He was proud of his home. A splendid symmetrical building. The lift took him up to the third floor where he had a large luxury flat with impeccable chromium fittings, square armchairs, and severely rectangular ornaments. There could truly be said not to be a curve in the place.

As he opened the door with his latchkey and stepped into the square, white lobby, his manservant, George, stepped softly to meet him.

"Good evening, sir. There is a—gentleman waiting to see you."

He relieved Poirot deftly of his overcoat.

"Indeed?" Poirot was aware of that very slight pause before the word *gentleman*. As a social snob, George was an expert.

"What is his name?"

"A Mr Spence, sir."

"Spence." The name, for the moment, meant nothing to Poirot. Yet he knew that it should do so.

Pausing for a moment before the mirror to adjust his moustaches to a state of perfection, Poirot opened the door of the sitting-room and entered. The man sitting in one of the big square armchairs got up.

"Hallo, M. Poirot, hope you remember me. It's a long time . . . Superintendent Spence."

"But of course." Poirot shook him warmly by the hand.

Superintendent Spence of the Kilchester Police. A very interesting case that had been . . . As Spence had said, a long time ago now . . .

Poirot pressed his guest with refreshments. *A grenadine? Crème de Menthe? Benedictine? Crème de Cacao? . . .*

At this moment George entered with a tray on which was a whisky bottle and a siphon. "Or beer if you prefer it, sir?" he murmured to the visitor.

Superintendent Spence's large red face lightened.

"Beer for me," he said.

Poirot was left to wonder once more at the accomplishments of George. He himself had had no idea that there was beer in the flat and it seemed incomprehensible to him that it could be preferred to a sweet liqueur.

When Spence had his foaming tankard, Poirot poured himself out a tiny glass of gleaming green *crème de menthe*.

"But it is charming of you to look me up," he said. "Charming. You have come up from——?"

"Kilchester. I'll be retired in about six months. Actually, I was due for retirement eighteen months ago. They asked me to stop on and I did."

"You were wise," said Poirot with feeling. "You were very wise . . ."

"Was I? I wonder. I'm not so sure."

"Yes, yes, you were wise," Poirot insisted. "The long hours of *ennui*, you have no conception of them."

"Oh, I'll have plenty to do when I retire. Moved into a new house last year, we did. Quite a bit of garden and shamefully neglected. I haven't been able to get down to it properly yet."

"Ah yes, you are one of those who garden. Me, once, I decided to live in the country and grow vegetable marrows. It did not succeed. I have not the temperament."

"You should have seen one of my marrows last year," said Spence with enthusiasm. "Colossal! And my roses. I'm keen on roses. I'm going to have——"

He broke off.

"That's not what I came to talk about."

"No, no, you came to see an old acquaintance—it was kind. I appreciate it."

"There's more to it than that, I'm afraid, M. Poirot. I'll be honest. I want something."

Poirot murmured delicately:

"There is a mortgage, possibly, on your house? You would like a loan——"

Spence interrupted in a horrified voice:

"Oh, good lord, it's not *money*! Nothing of that kind."

Poirot waved his hands in graceful apology.

"I demand your pardon."

"I'll tell you straight out—it's damned cheek what I've come for. If you send me away with a flea in my ear I shan't be surprised."

"There will be no flea," said Poirot. "But continue."

"It's the McGinty case. You've read about it, perhaps?"

Poirot shook his head.

"Not with attention. Mrs McGinty—an old woman in a shop or a house. She is dead, yes. How did she die?"

Spence stared at him.

"Lord!" he said. "That takes me back. Extraordinary. And I never thought of it until now."

"I beg your pardon?"

"Nothing. Just a game. Child's game. We used to play it when we were kids. A lot of us in a row. Question and answer all down the line. '*Mrs McGinty' dead!*' '*How did she die?*' '*Down on one knee just like I.*' And then the next question, '*Mrs McGinty's dead.*' '*How did she die?*' '*Holding her hand out just like I.*' And there we'd be, all kneeling and our right arms held out stiff. And then you *got* it! '*Mrs McGinty's dead.*' '*How did she die?*' '*Like THIS!*' Smack, the top of the row would fall sideways and down we all went like a pack of ninepins!'' Spence laughed uproariously at the remembrance. "Takes me back, it does!"

Poirot waited politely. This was one of the moments when, even after half a lifetime in the country, he found the English incomprehensible. He himself had played at *Cache Cache* in his childhood, but he felt no desire to talk about it or even to think about it.

When Spence had overcome his own amusement, Poirot repeated with some slight weariness, "How *did* she die?"

The laughter was wiped off Spence's face. He was suddenly himself again.

"She was hit on the back of her head with some sharp, heavy implement. Her savings, about thirty pounds in cash, were taken after her room had been ransacked. She lived alone in a small cottage except for a lodger. Man of the name of Bentley. James Bentley."

"Ah yes, Bentley."

"The place wasn't broken into. No signs of any tampering with the windows or locks. Bentley was hard up, had lost his job, and owed two months' rent. The money was found hidden under a loose stone at the back of the cottage. Bentley's coat sleeve had blood on it and hair—same blood group and the right hair. According to his first statement he was never near the body—so it couldn't have come there by accident."

"Who found her?"

"The baker called with bread. It was the day he got paid. James Bentley opened the door to him and said he'd knocked at Mrs McGinty's bedroom door, but couldn't get an answer. The baker suggested she might have been taken bad. They got the woman from next door to go up and see. Mrs McGinty wasn't in the bedroom, and hadn't slept in the bed, but the room had been ransacked and the floorboards had been prised up. Then they thought of looking in the parlour. She was there, lying on the floor, and the neighbour fairly screamed her head off. Then they got the police, of course."

"And Bentley was eventually arrested and tried?"

"Yes. The case came on at the Assizes. Yesterday. Open and shut case. The jury were only out twenty minutes this morning. Verdict: Guilty. Condemned to death."

Poirot nodded.

"And then, after the verdict, you got in a train and came to London and came here to see me. Why?"

Superintendent Spence was looking into his beer glass. He ran his finger slowly round and round the rim.

"Because," he said, "I don't think he did it. . . ."

2

THERE WAS a moment or two of silence.

"You came to me——"

Poirot did not finish the sentence.

Superintendent Spence looked up. The colour in his face was deeper than it had been. It was a typical countryman's face, unexpressive, self-contained, with shrewd but honest eyes. It was the face of a man with definite standards who would never be bothered by doubts of himself or by doubts of what constituted right and wrong.

"I've been a long time in the Force," he said. "I've had a good deal of experience of this, that and the other. I can judge a man as well as any other could do. I've had cases of murder during my service—some of them straightforward enough, some of them not so straightforward. One case *you* know of, M. Poirot——"

Poirot nodded.

"Tricky, that was. But for you, we mightn't have seen clear. But we did see clear—and there wasn't any doubt. The same with the others you don't know about. There was Whistler, he got his—*and* deserved it. There were those chaps who shot old Guterman. There was Verall and his arsenic. Tranter got off—but he did it all right. Mrs Courtland—she was lucky—her husband was a nasty perverted bit of work, and the jury acquitted her accordingly. Not justice—just sentiment. You've to allow for that happening now and again. Sometimes there isn't enough evidence—sometimes there's sentiment, sometimes a murderer manages to put it across the jury—that last doesn't happen often, but it can happen. Sometimes it's a clever bit of work by defending counsel—or a prosecuting counsel takes the wrong tack. Oh yes, I've seen a lot of things like that. But—but——"

Spence wagged a heavy forefinger.

"I haven't seen—in *my* experience—an innocent man hanged for something he didn't do. It's a thing, M. Poirot, that I don't *want* to see."

"Not," added Spence, "in *this* country!"

Poirot gazed back at him.

"And you think you are going to see it now. But why——"

Spence interrupted him.

"I know some of the things you're going to say. I'll answer them without you having to ask them. I was put on this case. I was put on to get evidence of what happened. I went into the whole business very carefully. I got the facts, all the facts I could. All those facts pointed one way—pointed to one person. When I'd got all the facts I took them to my superior officer. After that it was out of my hands. The case went to the Public Prosecutor and it was up to him. He decided to prosecute—he couldn't have done anything else—not on the evidence. And so James Bentley was arrested and committed for trial, and was duly tried and has been found guilty. They couldn't have found him anything else, not on the evidence. And evidence is what a jury have to consider. Didn't have any qualms about it either, I should say. No, I should say they were all quite satisfied he *was* guilty."

"But you—are not?"

"No."

"Why?"

Superintendent Spence sighed. He rubbed his chin thoughtfully with his big hand.

"I don't know. What I mean is, I can't give a reason—a concrete reason. To the jury I dare say he looked like a murderer—to me he didn't—and I know a lot more about murderers than they do."

"Yes, yes, you are an expert."

"For one thing, you know, he wasn't *cocky*. Not cocky at all. And in my experience they usually are. Always so damned pleased with themselves. Always think they're stringing you along. Always sure they've been so clever about the whole thing. And even when they're in the dock and must know they're for it, they're still in a queer sort of way getting a kick out of it all. They're in the limelight. They're the central figure. Playing the star part—perhaps for the first time in their lives. They're—well—you know—*cocky!*"

Spence brought out the word with an air of finality.

"You'll understand what I mean by that, M. Poirot."

"I understand very well. And this James Bentley—he was not like that?"

"No. He was—well, just scared stiff. Scared stiff from the start. And to some people that would square in with his being guilty. But not to me."

"No, I agree with you. What is he like, this James Bentley?"

"Thirty-three, medium height, sallow complexion, wears glasses——"

Poirot arrested the flow.

"No, I do not mean his physical characteristics. What sort of a personality?"

"Oh—that." Superintendent Spence considered. "Unprepossessing sort of fellow. Nervous manner. Can't look you straight in the face. Has a sly sideways way of peering at you. Worst possible sort of manner for a jury. Sometimes cringing and sometimes truculent. Blusters in an inefficient kind of way."

He paused and added in a conversational tone:

"Really a shy kind of chap. Had a cousin rather like that. If anything's awkward they go and tell some silly lie that hasn't a chance of being believed."

"He does not sound attractive, your James Bentley."

"Oh, he isn't. Nobody could *like* him. But I don't want to see him hanged for all that."

"And you think he will be hanged?"

"I don't see why not. His counsel may lodge an appeal—but if so it will be on very flimsy grounds—a technicality of some kind, and I don't see that it will have a chance of success."

"Did he have a good counsel?"

"Young Graybrook was allotted to him under the Poor Persons' Defence Act. I'd say he was thoroughly conscientious and put up the best show he could."

"So the man had a fair trial and was condemned by a jury of his fellow-men."

"That's right. A good average jury. Seven men, five women—

15

all decent reasonable souls. Judge was old Stanisdale. Scrupulously fair—no bias."

"So—according to the law of the land—James Bentley has nothing to complain of?"

"If he's hanged for something he didn't do, he's got something to complain of!"

"A very just observation."

"And the case against him was *my* case—*I* collected the facts and put them together—and it's on that case and those facts that he's been condemned. And I don't like it, M. Poirot, I don't like it."

Hercule Poirot looked for a long time at the red agitated face of Superintendent Spence.

"*Eh bien*," he said. "What do you suggest?"

Spence looked acutely embarrassed.

"I expect you've got a pretty good idea of what's coming. The Bentley case is closed. I'm on another case already—embezzlement. Got to go up to Scotland to-night. I'm not a free man."

"And I—am?"

Spence nodded in a shame-faced sort of way.

"You've got it. Awful cheek, you'll think. But I can't think of anything else—of any other way. I did all I could at the time, I examined every possibility I could. And I didn't get anywhere. I don't believe I ever would get anywhere. But who knows, it may be different for you. You look at things in—if you'll pardon me for saying so—in a funny sort of way. Maybe that's the way you've got to look at them in this case. Because if James Bentley didn't kill her, then somebody else did. She didn't chop the back of her head in herself. You may be able to find something that I missed. There's no reason why you should do anything about this business. It's infernal cheek my even suggesting such a thing. But there it is. I came to you because it was the only thing I could think of. But if you don't want to put yourself out—and why should you——"

Poirot interrupted him.

"Oh, but indeed there are reasons. I have leisure—too much leisure. And you have intrigued me—yes, you have intrigued me very much. It is a challenge—to the little grey cells of my brain. And then, I have a regard for you. I see you, in your garden in six months' time, planting, perhaps, the rose bushes—and as you plant them it is not with the happiness you should be feeling, because behind everything there is an unpleasantness in your brain, a recollection that you try to push away, and I would not have you feel that, my friend. And finally——" Poirot sat upright and nodded his head vigorously, "there is the principle of the thing. If a man has not committed murder, he should not be hanged." He paused and then added, "But supposing that after all, he did kill her?"

"In that case I'd be only too thankful to be convinced of it."

"And two heads are better than one? *Voilà*, everything is settled. I precipitate myself upon the business. There is, that is clear, no time to be lost. Already the scent is cold. Mrs McGinty was killed—when?"

"Last November, 22nd."

"Then let us at once get down to the brass tacks."

"I've got my notes on the case which I'll pass over to you."

"Good. For the moment, we need only the bare outline. If James Bentley did not kill Mrs McGinty, who did?"

Spence shrugged his shoulders and said heavily:

"There's nobody, so far as I can see."

"But that answer we do not accept. Now, since for every murder there must be a motive, what, in the case of Mrs McGinty, could the motive be? Envy, revenge, jealousy, fear, money? Let us take the last and the simplest? Who profited by her death?"

"Nobody very much. She had two hundred pounds in the Savings Bank. Her niece gets that."

"Two hundred pounds is not very much—but in certain circumstances it could be enough. So let us consider the niece. I apologise, my friend, for treading in your footsteps. You too, I know, must have considered all this. But I have to go over with you the ground already traversed."

Spence nodded his large head.

"We considered the niece, of course. She's thirty-eight, married. Husband is employed in the building and decorating trade—a painter. He's got a good character, steady employment, sharp sort of fellow, no fool. She's a pleasant young woman, a bit talkative, seemed fond of her aunt in a mild sort of way. Neither of them had any urgent need for two hundred pounds, though quite pleased to have it, I dare say."

"What about her cottage? Do they get that?"

"It was rented. Of course, under the Rent Restriction Act the landlord couldn't get the old woman out. But now she's dead, I don't think the niece could have taken over—anyway she and her husband didn't want to. They've got a small modern council house of their own of which they are extremely proud." Spence sighed. "I went into the niece and her husband pretty closely— they seemed the best bet, as you'll understand. But I couldn't get hold of anything."

"*Bien.* Now let us talk about Mrs McGinty herself. Describe her to me—and not only in physical terms, if you please."

Spence grinned.

"Don't want a police description? Well, she was sixty-four. Widow. Husband had been employed in the drapery department of Hodges in Kilchester. He died about seven years ago. Pneumonia. Since then, Mrs McGinty has been going out daily to various houses round about. Domestic chores. Broadhinny's a small village which has lately become residential. One or two retired people, one of the partners in an engineering works, a doctor, that sort of thing. There's quite a good bus and train service to Kilchester, and Cullenquay which, as I expect you know, is quite a large summer resort, is only eight miles away, but Broadhinny itself is still quite pretty and rural—about a quarter of a mile off the main Drymouth and Kilchester road."

Poirot nodded.

"Mrs McGinty's cottage was one of four that form the village proper. There is the post office and village shop, and agricultural labourers live in the others."

"And she took in a lodger?"

"Yes. Before her husband died, it used to be summer visitors, but after his death she just took one regular. James Bentley had been there for some months."

"So we come to—James Bentley?"

"Bentley's last job was with a house agent's in Kilchester. Before that, he lived with his mother in Cullenquay. She was an invalid and he looked after her and never went out much. Then she died, and an annuity she had died with her. He sold the little

18

house and found a job. Well educated man, but no special qualifications or aptitudes, and, as I say, an unprepossessing manner. Didn't find it easy to get anything. Anyway, they took him on at Breather & Scuttle's. Rather a second-rate firm. I don't think he was particularly efficient or successful. They cut down staff and he was the one to go. He couldn't get another job, and his money ran out. He usually paid Mrs McGinty every month for his room. She gave him breakfast and supper and charged him three pounds a week—quite reasonable, all things considered. He was two months behind in paying her, and he was nearly at the end of his resources. He hadn't got another job and she was pressing him for what he owed her."

"And he knew that she had thirty pounds in the house? Why did she have thirty pounds in the house, by the way, since she had a Savings Bank account?"

"Because she didn't trust the Government. Said they'd got two hundred pounds of her money, but they wouldn't get any more. She'd keep that where she could lay her hand on it any minute. She said that to one or two people. It was under a loose board in her bedroom floor—a very obvious place. James Bentley admitted he knew it was there."

"Very obliging of him. And did niece and husband know that too?"

"Oh yes."

"Then we have now arrived back at my first question to you. How did Mrs McGinty die?"

"She died on the night of November 22nd. Police surgeon put the time of death as being between 7 and 10 p.m. She'd had her supper—a kipper and bread and margarine, and according to all accounts, she usually had that about half-past six. If she adhered to that on the night in question, then by the evidence of digestion she was killed about eight-thirty or nine o'clock. James Bentley, by his own account, was out walking that evening from seven-fifteen to about nine. He went out and walked most evenings after dark. According to his own story he came in at about nine o'clock (he had his own key) and went straight upstairs to his room. Mrs McGinty had had wash-basins fixed in the bedrooms because of summer visitors. He read for about half an hour and then went to bed. He heard and noticed nothing out of the way. Next morning he came downstairs and looked into the kitchen, but there was no one there and no signs of breakfast being prepared. He says he hesitated a bit and then knocked on Mrs McGinty's door, but got no reply.

"He thought she must have overslept, but didn't like to go on knocking. Then the baker came and James Bentley went up and knocked again, and after that, as I told you, the baker went next door and fetched in a Mrs Elliot, who eventually found the body and went off the deep end. Mrs McGinty was lying on the parlour floor. She'd been hit on the back of the head with something rather in the nature of a meat chopper with a very sharp edge. She'd been killed instantaneously. Drawers were pulled open and things strewn about, and the loose board in the floor in her bedroom had been prised up and the *cache* was empty. All the windows were closed and shuttered on the inside. No signs of anything being tampered with or of being broken into from outside."

"Therefore," said Poirot, "either James Bentley must have killed her, or else she must have admitted her killer herself whilst Bentley was out?"

"Exactly. It wasn't any hold-up or burglar. Now who would she be likely to let in? One of the neighbours, or her niece, or her niece's husband. It boils down to that. We eliminated the neighbours. Niece and her husband were at the pictures that night. It is possible—just possible, that one or other of them left the cinema unobserved, bicycled three miles, killed the old woman, hid the money outside the house, and got back into the cinema unnoticed. We looked into that possibility, but we didn't find any confirmation of it. And why hide the money outside McGinty's house if so? Difficult place to pick it up later. Why not somewhere along the three miles back? No, the only reason for hiding it where it was hidden——"

Poirot finished the sentence for him.

"Would be because you were living in that house, but didn't want to hide it in your room or anywhere inside. In fact: James Bentley."

"That's right. Everywhere, every time, you came up against Bentley. Finally there was the blood on his cuff."

20

"How did he account for that?"

"Said he remembered brushing up against a butcher's shop the previous day. Baloney! It wasn't animal blood."

"And he stuck to that story?"

"Not likely. At the trial he told a completely different tale. You see, there was a hair on the cuff as well—a blood-stained hair, and the hair was identical with Mrs McGinty's hair. That had got to be explained away. He admitted then that he had gone into the room the night before when he came back from his walk. He'd gone in, he said, after knocking, and found her there, on the floor, dead. He'd bent over and touched her, he said, to make sure. And then he'd lost his head. He'd always been very much affected by the sight of blood, he said. He went to his room in a state of collapse and more or less fainted. In the morning he couldn't bring himself to admit he knew what had happened."

"A very fishy story," commented Poirot.

"Yes, indeed. And yet, you know," said Spence thoughtfully, "it might well be true. It's not the sort of thing that an ordinary man—or a jury—can believe. But I've come across people like that. I don't mean the collapse story. I mean people who are confronted by a demand for responsible action and who simply can't face up to it. Shy people. He goes in, say, and finds her. He knows that he ought to do something—get the police—go to a neighbour—do the right thing whatever it is. And he funks it. He thinks 'I don't need to know anything about it. I needn't have come in here to-night. I'll go to bed just as if I hadn't come in here at all. . . .' Behind it, of course, there's fear—fear that he may be suspected of having a hand in it. He thinks he'll keep himself out of it as long as possible, and so the silly juggins goes and puts himself into it—up to his neck."

Spence paused.

"It *could* have been that way."

"It could," said Poirot thoughtfully.

"Or again, it may have been just the best story his counsel could think up for him. But I don't know. The waitress in the café in Kilchester where he usually had lunch said that he always chose a table where he could look into a wall or a corner and not see people. He was that kind of a chap—just a bit screwy. But not screwy enough to be a killer. He'd no persecution complex or anything of that kind."

Spence looked hopefully at Poirot—but Poirot did not respond—he was frowning.

The two men sat silent for a while.

3

AT LAST Poirot roused himself with a sigh.

"*Eh bien*," he said. "We have exhausted the motive of money. Let us pass to other theories. Had Mrs McGinty an enemy? Was she afraid of anyone?"

"No evidence of it."

"What did her neighbours have to say?"

"Not very much. They wouldn't to the police, perhaps, but I don't think they were holding anything back. She kept herself to herself, they said. But that's regarded as natural enough. Our villages, you know, M. Poirot, aren't friendly. Evacuees found that during the war. Mrs McGinty passed the time of the day with the neighbours but they weren't intimate."

"How long had she lived there?"

"Matter of eighteen or twenty years, I think."

"And the forty years before that?"

"There's no mystery about her. Farmer's daughter from North Devon. She and her husband lived near Ilfracombe for a time, and then moved to Kilchester. Had a cottage the other side of it—but found it damp, so they moved to Broadhinny. Husband seems to have been a quiet, decent man, delicate— didn't go to the pub much. All very respectable and aboveboard. No mysteries anywhere, nothing to hide."

"And yet she was killed?"

"And yet she was killed."

"The niece didn't know of anyone who had a grudge against her aunt?"

"She says not."

Poirot rubbed his nose in an exasperated fashion.

"You comprehend, my dear friend, it would be so much easier if Mrs McGinty was *not* Mrs McGinty, so to speak. If she could be what is called a Mystery Woman—a woman with a past."

"Well, she wasn't," said Spence stolidly. "She was just Mrs McGinty, a more or less uneducated woman, who let rooms and went out charring. Thousands of them all over England."

"But they do not all get murdered."

"No. I grant you that."

"So why should Mrs McGinty get murdered? The obvious answer we do not accept. What remains? A shadowy and improbable niece. An even more shadowy and improbable stranger. Facts? Let us stick to facts. What are the facts? An elderly charwoman is murdered. A shy and uncouth young man is arrested and convicted of the murder. Why was James Bentley arrested?"

"The evidence against him. I've told you——"

"Yes. Evidence. But tell me, my Spence, was it real evidence or was it contrived?"

"Contrived?"

"Yes. Granted the premise that James Bentley is innocent two possibilities remain. The evidence was manufactured, deliberately, to throw suspicion upon him. Or else he was just the unfortunate victim of circumstances."

Spence considered.

"Yes. I see what you're driving at."

"There is nothing to show that the former was the case. But again there is nothing to show that it was not so. The money was taken and hidden outside the house in a place easily found. To have actually hidden it in his room would have been a little too much for the police to swallow. The murder was committed at a time when Bentley was taking a lonely walk, as he often did. Did the bloodstain come on his sleeve as he said it did at his trial, or was that, too, contrived? Did someone brush against him in the darkness and smear tell-tale evidence on his sleeve?"

"I think that's going a bit far, M. Poirot."

"Perhaps, perhaps. But we have got to go far. I think that in this case we have got to go so far that the imagination cannot as yet see the path clearly. . . . For, you see, *mon cher Spence*, if Mrs McGinty is just an ordinary charwoman—it is the *murderer* who must be extraordinary. Yes—that follows clearly. It is in the murderer and not the murdered that the interest of this case lies. That is not the case in most crimes. Usually it is in the personality of the murdered person that the crux of the situation lies. It is the silent dead in whom I am usually interested. Their hates, their loves, their actions. And when you really know the murdered victim, then the victim speaks, and those dead lips utter a name—the name you want to know."

Spence looked rather uncomfortable.

"These foreigners!" he seemed to be saying to himself.

"But here," continued Poirot, "it is the opposite. Here we guess at a veiled personality—a figure still hidden in darkness. How did Mrs McGinty die? Why did she die? The answer is not to be found in studying the life of Mrs McGinty. The answer is to be found in the personality of the murderer. You agree with me there?"

"I suppose so," said Superintendent Spence cautiously.

"Someone who wanted—what? To strike down Mrs McGinty? *Or to strike down James Bentley?*"

The Superintendent gave a doubtful "H'm!"

"Yes—yes, that is one of the first points to be decided. Who is the real victim? Who was intended to be the victim?"

Spence said incredulously: "You really think someone would bump off a perfectly inoffensive old woman in order to get someone else hanged for murder?"

"One cannot make an omelette, they say, without breaking eggs. Mrs McGinty, then, may be the egg, and James Bentley is the omelette. So let me hear, now, what you know of James Bentley."

"Nothing much. Father was a doctor—died when Bentley was nine years old. He went to one of the smaller public schools, unfit for the Army, had a weak chest, was in one of the Ministries during the war and lived with a possessive mother."

"Well," said Poirot, "there are certain possibilities there . . . More than there are in the life history of Mrs McGinty."

"Do you seriously believe what you are suggesting?"

"No, I do not believe anything as yet. But I say that there are two distinct lines of research, and that we have to decide, very soon, which is the right one to follow."

"How are you going to set about things, M. Poirot? Is there anything I can do?"

"First, I should like an interview with James Bentley."

"That can be managed. I'll get on to his solicitors."

"After that and subject, of course, to the result, if any—I am not hopeful—of that interview, I shall go to Broadhinny. There, aided by your notes, I shall, as quickly as possible, go over that same ground where you have passed before me."

"In case I've missed anything," said Spence with a wry smile.

"In case, I would prefer to say, that some circumstance should strike me in a different light to the one in which it struck you. Human reactions vary and so does human experience. The resemblance of a rich financier to a soap boiler whom I had known in Liége once brought about a most satisfactory result. But no need to go into that. What I should like to do is to eliminate one or other of the trails I indicated just now. And to eliminate the Mrs McGinty trail—trail No. 1—will obviously be quicker and easier than to attack trail No. 2. Where, now, can I stay in Broadhinny? Is there an inn of moderate comfort?"

"There's the Three Ducks—but it doesn't put people up. There's the Lamb in Cullavon three miles away—or there is a kind of a Guest House in Broadhinny itself. It's not really a Guest House, just a rather decrepit country house where the young couple who own it take in paying guests. I don't think," said Spence dubiously, "that it's very comfortable."

Hercule Poirot closed his eyes in agony.

"If I suffer, I suffer," he said. "It has to be."

"I don't know what you'll go there as," continued Spence doubtfully as he eyed Poirot. "You might be some kind of an opera singer. Voice broken down. Got to rest. That might do."

"I shall go," said Hercule Poirot, speaking with accents of royal blood, "as myself."

Spence received this pronouncement with pursed lips.

"D'you think that's advisable?"

"I think it is *essential*! But yes, essential. Consider, *cher ami*, it is *time* we are up against. What do we know? Nothing. So the hope, the best hope, is to go pretending that I know a great deal. I am Hercule Poirot. I am the great, the unique Hercule Poirot. And I, Hercule Poirot, am not satisfied about the verdict in the McGinty case. I, Hercule Poirot, have a very shrewd suspicion of *what really happened*. There is a circumstance that I, alone, estimate at its true value. You see?"

"And then?"

"And then, having made my effect, I observe the reactions. For there should be reactions. Very definitely, there should be reactions."

Superintendent Spence looked uneasily at the little man.

"Look here, M. Poirot," he said. "Don't go sticking out your neck. I don't want anything to happen to you."

"But if it does, you would be proved right beyond the shadow of doubt, is it not so?"

"I don't want it proved the hard way," said Superintendent Spence.

4

WITH GREAT DISTASTE, Hercule Poirot looked round the room in which he stood. It was a room of gracious proportions but there its attraction ended. Poirot made an eloquent grimace as he drew a suspicious finger along the top of a book case. As he had suspected—dust! He sat down gingerly on a sofa and its broken springs sagged depressingly under him. The two faded arm-chairs were, as he knew, little better. A large fierce-looking dog whom Poirot suspected of having mange growled from his position on a moderately comfortable fourth chair.

The room was large, and had a faded Morris wallpaper. Steel engravings of unpleasant subjects hung crookedly on the walls with one or two good oil paintings. The chair-covers were both faded and dirty, the carpet had holes in it and had never been of a pleasant design. A good deal of miscellaneous bric-a-brac was scattered haphazard here and there. Tables rocked dangerously owing to absence of castors. One window was open, and no power on earth could, apparently, shut it again. The door, temporarily shut, was not likely to remain so. The latch did not hold, and with every gust of wind it burst open and whirling gusts of cold wind eddied round the room.

"I suffer," said Hercule Poirot to himself in acute self-pity. "Yes, I suffer."

The door burst open and the wind and Mrs Summerhayes came in together. She looked round the room, shouted "What?" to someone in the distance and went out again.

Mrs Summerhayes had red hair and an attractively freckled face and was usually in a distracted state of putting things down, or else looking for them.

Hercule Poirot sprang to his feet and shut the door.

A moment or two later it opened again and Mrs Summerhayes

28

eappeared. This time she was carrying a large enamel basin and
a knife.

A man's voice from some way away called out:

"Maureen, that cat's been sick again. What shall I do?"

Mrs Summerhayes called: "I'm coming, darling. Hold everything."

She dropped the basin and the knife and went out again.

Poirot got up again and shut the door. He said:

"Decidedly, I suffer."

A car drove up, the large dog leaped from the chair and raised
ts voice in a crescendo of barking. He jumped on a small table
by the window and the table collapsed with a crash.

"*Enfin,*" said Hercule Poirot. "*C'est insupportable!*"

The door burst open, the wind surged round the room, the
dog rushed out, still barking. Maureen's voice came, upraised
oud and clear.

"Johnnie, why the hell did you leave the back door open!
Those bloody hens are in the larder."

"And for this," said Hercule Poirot with feeling, "I pay seven
guineas a week!"

The door banged to with a crash. Through the window came
he loud squawking of irate hens.

Then the door opened again and Maureen Summerhayes
came in and fell upon the basin with a cry of joy.

"Couldn't think where I'd left it. Would you mind frightfully, Mr Er—hum—I mean, would it bother you if I sliced the
beans in here? The smell in the kitchen is too frightful."

"Madame, I should be enchanted."

It was not, perhaps, the exact phrase, but it was near enough.
It was the first time in twenty-four hours that Poirot had seen
any chance of a conversation of more than six seconds' duration.

Mrs Summerhayes flung herself down in a chair and began
slicing beans with frenzied energy and considerable awkward-
ness.

"I do hope," she said, "that you're not too frightfully uncomfortable? If there's anything you want altered, do say so."

Poirot had already come to the opinion that the only thing in
Long Meadows he could even tolerate was his hostess.

"You are too kind, madame," he replied politely. "I only

wish it were within my powers to provide you with suitabl
domestics."

"Domestics!" Mrs Summerhayes gave a squeal. "What
hope! Can't even get hold of a *daily*. Our really good one wa
murdered. Just my luck."

"That would be Mrs McGinty," said Poirot quickly.

"Mrs McGinty it was. God, how I miss that woman! O
course it was all a big thrill at the time. First murder we've eve
had right in the family, so to speak, but as I told Johnnie, it wa
a downright bit of bad luck for us. Without McGinty I just can'
cope."

"You were attached to her?"

"My dear man, she was *reliable*. She *came*. Monday after
noons and Thursday mornings—just like a clock. Now I hav
that Burp woman from up by the station. Five children and
husband. Naturally she's never here. Either the husband'
taken queer, or the old mother, or the children have some fou
disease or other. With old McGinty, at least it was only sh
herself who came over queer, and I must say she hardly eve
did."

"And you found her always reliable and honest? You ha
trust in her?"

"Oh, she'd never pinch anything—not even food. Of cours
she snooped a bit. Had a look at one's letters and all that. Bu
one expects that sort of thing. I mean they must live suc
awfully drab lives, mustn't they?"

"Had Mrs McGinty had a drab life?"

"Ghastly, I expect," said Mrs Summerhayes vaguely. "Alway
on your knees scrubbing. And then piles of other people'
washing up waiting for you on the sink when you arrive in th
morning. If I had to face that every day, I'd be positivel
relieved to be murdered. I really would."

The face of Major Summerhayes appeared at the window
Mrs Summerhayes sprang up, upsetting the beans, and rushe
across to the window, which she opened to the fullest extent.

"That damned dog's eaten the hens' food again, Maureen.'

"Oh damn, now *he*'ll be sick!"

"Look here," John Summerhayes displayed a colander full o
greenery, "is this enough spinach?"

"Of course not."

"Seems a colossal amount to me."

"It'll be about a teaspoonful when it's cooked. Don't you know by now what spinach is like?"

"Oh lord!"

"Has the fish come?"

"Not a sign of it."

"Hell, we'll have to open a tin of something. You might do that, Johnnie. One of the ones in the corner cupboard. That one we thought was a bit bulged. I expect it's quite all right really."

"What about the spinach?"

"I'll get that."

She leaped through the window, and husband and wife moved away together.

"Nom d'un nom d'un nom!" said Hercule Poirot. He crossed the room and closed the window as nearly as he could. The voice of Major Summerhayes came to him borne on the wind.

"What about this new fellow, Maureen? Looks a bit peculiar to me. What's his name again?"

"I couldn't remember it just now when I was talking to him. Had to say Mr Er-um. Poirot—that's what it is. He's French."

"You know, Maureen, I seem to have seen that name some-where."

"Home Perm, perhaps. He looks like a hairdresser." Poirot winced.

"N-no. Perhaps it's pickles. I don't know. I'm sure it's familiar. Better get the first seven guineas out of him, quick."

The voices died away.

Hercule Poirot picked up the beans from the floor where they had scattered far and wide. Just as he finished doing so, Mrs Summerhayes came in again through the door.

He presented them to her politely:

"Voici, madame."

"Oh thanks awfully. I say, these beans look a bit black. We store them, you know, in crocks, salted down. But these seem to have gone wrong. I'm afraid they won't be very nice."

"I, too, fear that . . . You permit that I shut the door? There is a decided draught."

"Oh yes, do. I'm afraid I always leave doors open."

"So I have noticed."

"Anyway, that door never stays shut. This house is practically falling to pieces. Johnnie's father and mother lived here and they were very badly off, poor dears, and they never did a thing to it. And then when we came home from India to live here, we couldn't afford to do anything either. It's fun for the children in the holidays, though, lots of room to run wild in, and the garden and everything. Having paying guests here just enables us to keep going, though I must say we've had a few rude shocks."

"Am I your only guest at present?"

"We've got an old lady upstairs. Took to her bed the day she came and has been there ever since. Nothing the matter with her that I can see. But there she is, and I carry up four trays a day. Nothing wrong with her appetite. Anyway, she's going tomorrow to some niece or other."

Mrs Summerhayes paused for a moment before resuming in a slightly artificial voice.

"The fisherman will be here in a minute. I wonder if you'd mind—er—forking out the first week's rent. You are staying a week, aren't you?"

"Perhaps longer."

"Sorry to bother you. But I've not got any cash in the house and you know what these people are like—always dunning you."

"Pray do not apologise, madame." Poirot took out seven pound notes and added seven shillings. Mrs Summerhayes gathered the money up with avidity.

"Thanks a lot."

"I should, perhaps, madame, tell you a little more about myself. *I am Hercule Poirot.*"

The revelation left Mrs Summerhayes unmoved.

"What a lovely name," she said kindly. "Greek, isn't it?"

"I am, as you may know," said Poirot, "a detective." He tapped his chest. "Perhaps the most famous detective there is."

Mrs Summerhayes screamed with amusement.

"I see you're a great practical joker, M. Poirot. What are you detecting? Cigarette ash and footprints?"

"I am investigating the murder of Mrs McGinty," said Poirot. "And I do not joke."

"Ouch," said Mrs Summerhayes. "I've cut my hand."

She raised a finger and inspected it.

Then she stared at Poirot.

"Look here," she said. "Do you mean it? What I mean is, it's over, all that. They arrested that poor half-wit who lodged there and he's tried and convicted and everything. He's probably been hanged by now."

"No, madame," said Poirot. "He has not been hanged—yet. And it is not 'over'—the case of Mrs McGinty. I will remind you of the line from one of your poets. 'A question is never settled until it is settled—right.'"

"Oo," said Mrs Summerhayes, her attention diverted from Poirot to the basin in her lap. "I'm bleeding over the beans. Not too good as we've got to have them for lunch. Still it won't matter really because they'll go into boiling water. Things are always all right if you boil them, aren't they? Even tins."

"I think," said Hercule Poirot quietly, "that I shall not be in for lunch."

5

"I DON'T KNOW, I'm sure," said Mrs Burch.

She had said that three times already. Her natural distrust of foreign-looking gentlemen with black moustaches, wearing large fur-lined coats was not to be easily overcome.

"Very unpleasant it's been," she went on. "Having poor auntie murdered and the police and all that. Tramping round everywhere, and ferreting about, and asking questions. With the neighbours all agog. I didn't feel at first we'd ever live it down. And my husband's mother's been downright nasty about it. Nothing of that kind ever happened in *her* family, she kept saying. And 'poor Joe' and all that. What about poor me? She was *my* aunt, wasn't she? But really I did think it was all over now."

"And supposing that James Bentley is innocent, after all?"

"Nonsense," snapped Mrs Burch. "Of course he isn't innocent. He did it all right. I never did like the looks of him. Wandering about muttering to himself. Said to auntie, I did: 'You oughtn't to have a man like that in the house. Might go off his head,' I said. But she said he was quiet and obliging and didn't give trouble. No drinking, she said, and he didn't even smoke. Well, she knows better now, poor soul."

Poirot looked thoughtfully at her. She was a big, plump woman with a healthy colour and a good-humoured mouth. The small house was neat and clean and smelt of furniture polish and brasso. A faint appetising smell came from the direction of the kitchen.

A good wife who kept her house clean and took the trouble to cook for her man. He approved. She was prejudiced and obstinate but, after all, why not? Most decidedly, she was not the kind of woman one could imagine using a meat chopper on her aunt, or conniving at her husband's doing so. Spence had not thought her that kind of woman, and rather reluctantly, Hercule Poirot agreed with him. Spence had gone into the financial background of the Burches and had found no motive there for murder, and Spence was a very thorough man.

He sighed, and persevered with his task, which was the breaking down of Mrs Burch's suspicion of foreigners. He led the conversation away from murder and focused on the victim of it. He asked questions about "poor auntie," her health, her habits, her preferences in food and drink, her politics, her late husband, her attitude to life, to sex, to sin, to religion, to children, to animals.

Whether any of this irrelevant matter would be of use, he had no idea. He was looking through a haystack to find a needle. But, incidentally, he was learning something about Bessie Burch.

Bessie did not really know very much about her aunt. It had been a family tie, honoured as such, but without intimacy. Now and again, once a month or so, she and Joe had gone over on a Sunday to have midday dinner with auntie, and more rarely, auntie had come over to see them. They had exchanged presents at Christmas. They'd known that auntie had a little somthing put by, and that they'd get it when she died.

"But that's not to say we were needing it," Mrs Burch explained with rising colour. "We've got something put by ourselves. And we buried her beautiful. A real nice funeral it was. Flowers and everything."

Auntie had been fond of knitting. She didn't like dogs, they messed up a place, but she used to have a cat—a ginger. It strayed away and she hadn't had one since, but the woman at the post office had been going to give her a kitten. Kept her house very neat and didn't like litter. Kept brass a treat and washed down the kitchen floor every day. She made quite a nice thing of going out to work. One shilling and tenpence an hour—two shillings from Holmeleigh, that was Mr Carpenter's of the Works' house. Rolling in money, the Carpenters were. Tried to get auntie to come more days in the week, but auntie wouldn't disappoint her other ladies because she'd gone to them before she went to Mr Carpenter's, and it wouldn't have been right.

Poirot mentioned Mrs Summerhayes at Long Meadows.

Oh yes, auntie went to her—two days a week. They'd come back from India where they'd had a lot of native servants and Mrs

Summerhayes didn't know a thing about a house. They tried to market-garden, but they didn't know anything about that, either. When the children came home for the holidays, the house was just pandemonium. But Mrs Summerhayes was a nice lady and auntie liked her.

So the portrait grew. Mrs McGinty knitted, and scrubbed floors and polished brass, she liked cats and didn't like dogs. She liked children, but not very much. She kept herself to herself.

She attended church on Sunday, but didn't take part in any church activities. Sometimes, but rarely, she went to the pictures. She didn't hold with goings on—and had given up working for an artist and his wife when she had discovered they weren't properly married. She didn't read books, but she enjoyed the Sunday paper and she liked old magazines when her ladies gave them to her. Although she didn't go much to the pictures, she was interested in hearing about film stars and their doings. She wasn't interested in politics, but voted Conservative like her husband had always done. Never spent much on clothes, but got quite a lot given her from her ladies, and was of a saving disposition.

Mrs McGinty was, in fact, very much the Mrs McGinty that Poirot had imagined she would be. And Bessie Burch, her niece, was the Bessie Burch of Superintendent Spence's notes.

Before Poirot took his leave, Joe Burch came home for the lunch hour. A small, shrewd man, less easy to be sure about than his wife. There was a faint nervousness in his manner. He showed less signs of suspicion and hostility than his wife. Indeed he seemed anxious to appear cooperative. And that, Poirot reflected, was very faintly out of character. For why should Joe Burch be anxious to placate an importunate foreign stranger? The reason could only be that that stranger had brought with him a letter from Superintendent Spence of the County Police.

So Joe Burch was anxious to stand in well with the police? Was it that he couldn't afford, as his wife could, to be critical of the police?

A man, perhaps, with an uneasy conscience. Why was that conscience uneasy? There could be so many reasons—none of them connected with Mrs McGinty's death. Or was it that, somehow or other, the cinema alibi had been cleverly faked, and that it was Joe Burch who had knocked on the door of the cottage, had been admitted by auntie and who had struck down the unsuspecting old woman. He would pull out the drawers and ransack the rooms to give the appearance of robbery, he might hide the money outside, cunningly, to incriminate James Bentley, the money that was in the Savings Bank was what he was after. Two hundred pounds coming to his wife which, for some reason unknown, he badly needed. The weapon, Poirot remembered, had never been found. Why had that not also been left on the scene of the crime? Any moron knew enough to wear gloves or rub off fingerprints. Why then had the weapon, which must have been a heavy one with a sharp edge, been removed? Was it because it could easily be identified as belonging to the Burch ménage? Was that same weapon, washed and polished, here in the house now? Something in the nature of a meat chopper, the police surgeon had said—but not, it seemed, actually a meat chopper. Something, perhaps a little unusual . . . a little out of the ordinary, easily identified. The police had hunted for it, but not found it. They had searched woods, dragged ponds. There was nothing missing from Mrs McGinty's kitchen, and nobody could say that James Bentley had had anything of that kind in his possession. They had never traced any purchase of a meat chopper or any such implement to him. A small, but negative point in his favour. Ignored in the weight of other evidence. But still a point . . .

Poirot cast a swift glance round the rather overcrowded little sitting-room in which he was sitting.

Was the weapon here, somewhere, in this house? Was that why Joe Burch was uneasy and conciliatory?

Poirot did not know. He did not really think so. But he was not absolutely sure. . . .

6

In the offices of Messrs. Breather & Scuttle, Poirot was shown, after some demur, into the room of Mr Scuttle himself.

Mr Scuttle was a brisk, bustling man, with a hearty manner.

"Good morning. Good morning." He rubbed his hands. "Now, what can we do for you?"

His professional eye shot over Poirot, trying to place him, making, as it were, a series of marginal notes.

Foreign. Good quality clothes. Probably rich. Restaurant proprietor? Hotel manager? Films?

"I hope not to trespass on your time unduly. I wanted to talk to you about your former employee, James Bentley."

Mr Scuttle's expressive eyebrows shot up an inch and dropped.

"James Bentley. James Bentley?" He shot out a question. "Press?"

"No."

"And you wouldn't be police?"

"No. At least—not of this country."

"Not of this country." Mr Scuttle filed this away rapidly as though for future reference. "What's it all about?"

Poirot, never hindered by a pedantic regard for truth, launched out into speech.

"I am opening a further inquiry into James Bentley's case—at the request of certain relatives of his."

"Didn't know he had any. Anyway, he's been found guilty, you know, and condemned to death."

"But not yet executed."

"While there's life, there's hope, eh?" Mr Scuttle shook his head. "Should doubt it, though. Evidence was strong. Who are these relations of his?"

"I can tell you only this, they are both rich and powerful. Immensely rich."

"You surprise me." Mr Scuttle was unable to help thawing slightly. The words "immensely rich" had an attractive and hypnotic quality. "Yes, you really do surprise me."

"Bentley's mother, the late Mrs Bentley," explained Poirot, "cut herself and her son off completely from her family."

"One of these family feuds, eh? Well, well. And young Bentley without a farthing to bless himself with. Pity these relations didn't come to the rescue before."

"They have only just become aware of the facts," explained Poirot. "They have engaged me to come with all speed to this country and do everything possible."

Mr Scuttle leaned back, relaxing his business manner.

"Don't know what you can do. I suppose there's insanity? A bit late in the day—but if you got hold of the big medicos. Of course I'm not up in these things myself."

Poirot leaned forward.

"Monsieur, James Bentley worked here. You can tell me about him."

"Precious little to tell—precious little. He was one of our junior clerks. Nothing against him. Seemed a perfectly decent young fellow, quite conscientious and all that. But no idea of salesmanship. He just couldn't put a project over. That's no good in this job. If a client comes to us with a house he wants to sell, we're there to sell it for him. And if a client wants a house, we find him one. If it's a house in a lonely place with no amenities, we stress its antiquity, call it a period piece—and don't mention the plumbing! And if a house looks straight into the gasworks, we talk about amenities and facilities and don't mention the view. Hustle your client into it—that's what you're here to do. All sorts of little tricks there are. 'We advise you, madam, to make an immediate offer. There's a Member of Parliament who's very keen on it—very keen indeed. Going out to see it again this afternoon.' They fall for that every time—a Member of Parliament is always a good touch. Can't think why! No member ever lives away from his constituency. It's just the good solid sound of it." He laughed suddenly, displayed gleaming dentures. "Psychology—that's what it is—just psychology."

Poirot leaped at the word.

"Psychology. How right you are. I see that you are a judge of men."

"Not too bad. Not too bad," said Mr Scuttle modestly.

"So I ask you again what was your impression of James Bentley? Between ourselves—strictly between ourselves—you think he killed the old woman?"

Scuttle stared.

"Of course."

"And you think, too, that it was a likely thing for him to do—psychologically speaking?"

"Well—if you put it like that—no, not really. Shouldn't have thought he had the guts. Tell you what, if you ask me, he was barmy. Put it that way, and it works. Always a bit soft in the head, and what with being out of a job and worrying and all that, he just went right over the edge."

"You had no special reason for discharging him?"

Scuttle shook his head.

"Bad time of year. Staff hadn't enough to do. We sacked the one who was least competent. That was Bentley. Always would be, I expect. Gave him a good reference and all that. He didn't get another job, though. No pep. Made a bad impression on people."

It always came back to that, Poirot thought, as he left the office. James Bentley made a bad impression on people. He took comfort in considering various murderers he had known whom most people had found full of charm.

ii

"Excuse me, do you mind if I sit down here and talk to you for a moment?"

Poirot, ensconced at a small table in the Blue Cat, looked up from the menu he was studying with a start. It was rather dark in the Blue Cat, which specialised in an old-world effect of oak and leaded panes, but the young woman who had just sat down opposite to him stood out brightly from her dark background.

She had determinedly golden hair, and was wearing an electric

40

blue jumper suit. Moreover, Hercule Poirot was conscious of having noticed her somewhere only a short time previously.

She went on:

"I couldn't help, you see, hearing something of what you were saying to Mr Scuttle."

Poirot nodded. He had realised that the partitions in the offices of Breather & Scuttle were made for convenience rather than privacy. That had not worried him, since it was chiefly publicity that he desired.

"You were typing," he said, "to the right of the back window."

She nodded. Her teeth shone white in an acquiescing smile. A very healthy young woman, with a full buxom figure that Poirot approved. About thirty-three or four, he judged, and by nature dark-haired, but not one to be dictated to by nature.

"About Mr Bentley," she said.

"What about Mr Bentley?"

"Is he going to appeal? Does it mean that there's new evidence? Oh, I'm so glad. I couldn't—I just couldn't believe he did it."

Poirot's eyebrows rose.

"So you never thought he did it," he said slowly.

"Well, not at first. I thought it must be a mistake. But then the evidence——" she stopped.

"Yes, the evidence," said Poirot.

"There just didn't seem anyone else who could have done it. I thought perhaps he'd gone a little mad."

"Did he ever seem to you a little—what shall I say—queer?"

"Oh no. Not queer in that way. He was just shy and awkward as anyone might be. The truth was, he didn't make the best of himself. He hadn't confidence in himself."

Poirot looked at her. She certainly had confidence in herself. Possibly she had enough confidence for two.

"You liked him?" he asked.

She flushed.

"Yes, I did. Amy—that's the other girl in the office—used to laugh at him and call him a drip, but I liked him very much. He was gentle and polite—and he knew a lot really. Things out of books, I mean."

"Ah yes, things out of books."

"He missed his mother. She'd been ill for years, you know. At

41

least, not really ill, but not strong, and he'd done everything for her."

Poirot nodded. He knew those mothers.

"And of course she'd looked after him, too. I mean taken care of his health and his chest in winter and what he ate and all that."

Again he nodded. He asked:

"You and he were friends?"

"I don't know—not exactly. We used to talk sometimes. But after he left here, he—I—I didn't see much of him. I wrote to him once in a friendly way, but he didn't answer."

Poirot said gently:

"But you like him?"

She said rather defiantly:

"Yes, I do . . ."

"That is excellent," said Poirot.

His mind switched back to the day of his interview with the condemned prisoner. . . . He saw James Bentley clearly. The mouse-coloured hair, the thin awkward body, the hands with their big knuckles and wrists, the Adam's apple in the lean neck. He saw the furtive, embarrassed—almost sly glance. Not straightforward, not a man whose word could be trusted—a secretive, sly deceitful fellow with an ungracious, muttering way of talking. . . . That was the impression James Bentley would give to most superficial observers. It was the impression he had given in the dock. The sort of fellow who would tell lies, and steal money, and hit an old woman over the head. . . .

But on Superintendent Spence, who knew men, he had not made that impression. Nor on Hercule Poirot. . . . And now here was this girl.

"What is your name, mademoiselle?" he asked.

"Maude Williams. Is there anything I could do—to help?"

"I think there is. There are people who believe, Miss Williams, that James Bentley is innocent. They are working to prove that fact. I am the person charged with that investigation, and I may tell you that I have already made considerable progress—yes, considerable progress."

He uttered that lie without a blush. To his mind it was a very necessary lie. Someone, somewhere, had got to be made uneasy.

42

Maude Williams would talk, and talk was like a stone in a pond, it made a ripple that went on spreading outwards.

He said: "You tell me that you and James Bentley talked together. He told you about his mother and his home life. Did he ever mention anyone with whom he, or perhaps his mother, was on bad terms?"

Maude Williams reflected.

"No—not what you'd call bad terms. His mother didn't like young women much, I gather."

"Mothers of devoted sons never like young women. No, I mean more than that. Some family feud, some enmity. Someone with a grudge?"

She shook her head.

"He never mentioned anything of that kind."

"Did he ever speak of his landlady, Mrs McGinty?"

She shivered slightly.

"Not by name. He said once that she gave him kippers much too often—and once he said his landlady was upset because she had lost her cat."

"Did he ever—you must be honest, please—mention that he knew where she kept her money?"

Some of the colour went out of the girl's face, but she threw up her chin defiantly.

"Actually, he did. We were talking about people being distrustful of banks—and he said his old landlady kept her spare money under a floorboard. He said: 'I could help myself any day to it when she's out.' Not quite as a joke, he didn't joke, more as though he were really worried by her carelessness."

"Ah," said Poirot. "That is good. From my point of view, I mean. When James Bentley thinks of stealing, it presents itself to him as an action that is done behind someone's back. He might have said, you see, 'Some day someone will knock her on the head for it.'"

"But either way, he wouldn't be meaning it."

"Oh no. But talk, however light, however idle, gives away, inevitably, the sort of person you are. The wise criminal would never open his mouth, but criminals are seldom wise and usually vain and they talk a good deal—and so most criminals are caught."

Maude Williams said abruptly:

"But *someone* must have killed the old woman."

"Naturally."

"Who did? Do you know? Have you any idea?"

"Yes," said Hercule Poirot mendaciously. "I think I have a very good idea. But we are only at the beginning of the road."

The girl glanced at her watch.

"I must get back. We're only supposed to take half an hour. One-horse place, Kilchester—I've always had jobs in London before. You'll let me know if there's anything I can do—really *do*, I mean?"

Poirot took out one of his cards. On it he wrote Long Meadows and the telephone number.

"That is where I am staying."

His name, he noted with chagrin, made no particular impression on her. The younger generation, he could not but feel, were singularly lacking in knowledge of notable celebrities.

iii

Hercule Poirot caught a bus back to Broadhinny feeling slightly more cheerful. At any rate there was one person who shared his belief in James Bentley's innocence. Bentley was not so friendless as he had made himself out to be.

His mind went back again to Bentley in prison. What a dispiriting interview it had been. There had been no hope aroused, hardly a stirring of interest.

"Thank you," Bentley had said dully, "but I don't suppose there is anything anyone can do."

No, he was sure he had not got any enemies.

"When people barely notice you're alive, you're not likely to have any enemies."

"Your mother? Did she have an enemy?"

"Certainly not. Everyone liked and respected her."

There was a faint indignation in his tone.

"What about your friends?"

And James Bentley had said, or rather muttered, "I haven't any friends . . ."

44

But that had not been quite true. For Maude Williams was a friend.

"What a wonderful dispensation it is of Nature's," thought Hercule Poirot, "that every man, however superficially unattractive, should be some woman's choice."

For all Miss Williams's sexy appearance, he had a shrewd suspicion that she was really the maternal type.

She had the qualities that James Bentley lacked, the energy, the drive, the refusal to be beaten, the determination to succeed.

He sighed.

What monstrous lies he had told that day! Never mind—they were necessary.

"For somewhere," said Poirot to himself, indulging in an absolute riot of mixed metaphors, "there is in the hay a needle, and among the sleeping dogs there is one on whom I shall put my foot, and by shooting the arrows into the air, one will come down and hit a glass-house!"

7

i

THE COTTAGE WHERE Mrs McGinty had lived was only a few
steps from the bus stop. Two children were playing on the
doorstep. One was eating a rather wormy-looking apple and the
other was shouting and beating on the door with a tin tray. They
appeared quite happy. Poirot added to the noise by beating hard
on the door himself.

A woman looked round the corner of the house. She had on a
coloured overall and her hair was untidy.

"Stop it, Ernie," she said.

"Sha'n't," said Ernie and continued.

Poirot deserted the doorstep and made for the corner of the
house.

"Can't do anything with children, can you?" the woman said.

Poirot thought you could, but forbore to say so.

He was beckoned round to the back door.

"I keep the front bolted up, sir. Come in, won't you?"

Poirot passed through a very dirty scullery into an almost
more dirty kitchen.

"She wasn't killed here," said the woman. "In the parlour."

Poirot blinked slightly.

"That's what you're down about, isn't it? You're the foreign
gentleman from up at Summerhayes?"

"So you know all about me?" said Poirot. He beamed. "Yes,
indeed, Mrs——"

"Kiddle. My husband's a plasterer. Moved in four months
ago, we did. Been living with Bert's mother before . . . Some
folks said: 'You'd never go into a house where there's been a
murder, surely?'—but what I said was, a house is a house,
and better than a back sitting-room and sleeping on two

46

chairs. Awful, this 'ousing shortage, isn't it? And anyway *we*'ve never been troubled 'ere. Always say they *walk* if they've been murdered, but she doesn't! Like to see where it happened?"

Feeling like a tourist being taken on a conducted tour, Poirot assented.

Mrs Kiddle led him into a small room over-burdened with a heavy Jacobean suite. Unlike the rest of the house, it showed no signs of ever having been occupied.

"Down on the floor she was and the back of her head split open. Didn't half give Mrs Elliot a turn. She's the one what found her—she and Larkin who comes from the Co-op with the bread. But the money was took from upstairs. Come along up and I'll show you where."

Mrs Kiddle led the way up the staircase and into a bedroom which contained a large chest of drawers, a big brass bed, some chairs, and a fine assembly of baby clothes, wet and dry.

"Right here it was," said Mrs Kiddle proudly.

Poirot looked round him. Hard to visualise that this rampant stronghold of haphazard fecundity was once the well-scrubbed domain of an elderly woman who was house-proud. Here Mrs McGinty had lived and slept.

"I suppose this isn't her furniture?"

"Oh no. Her niece over in Cullavon took away all that."

There was nothing left here of Mrs McGinty. The Kiddles had come and conquered. Life was stronger than death.

From downstairs the loud fierce wail of a baby arose.

"That's the baby woken up," said Mrs Kiddle unnecessarily.

She plunged down the stairs and Poirot followed her.

There was nothing here for him.

He went next door.

ii

"Yes, sir, it was me found her."

Mrs Elliot was dramatic. A neat house, this, neat and prim. The only drama in it was Mrs Elliot's, a tall gaunt dark-haired woman, recounting her one moment of glorious living.

"Larkin, the baker, he came and knocked at the door. 'It's Mrs McGinty,' he said, 'we can't make her hear. Seems she might have been taken bad.' And indeed I thought she might. She wasn't a young woman, not by any means. And palpitations she'd had, to my certain knowledge. I thought she might have had a stroke. So I hurried over, seeing as there were only the two men, and naturally they wouldn't like to go into the bedroom."

Poirot accepted this piece of propriety with an assenting murmur.

"Hurried up the stairs, I did. *He* was on the landing, pale as death he was. Not that I ever thought at the time—well, of course, then I didn't know what had happened. I knocked on the door loud and there wasn't any answer, so I turned the handle and I went in. The whole place messed about—and the board in the floor up. 'It's robbery,' I said. 'But where's the poor soul herself?' And then we thought to look in the sitting-room. *And there she was* . . . Down on the floor with her poor head stove in. Murder! I saw at once what it was—murder! Couldn't be anything else! Robbery and murder! Here in Broadhinny. I screamed and I screamed! Quite a job they had with me. Came over all faint, I did. They had to go and get me brandy from the Three Ducks. And even then I was all of a shiver for hours and hours. 'Don't you take on so, mother,' that's what the sergeant said to me when he came. 'Don't you take on so. You go home and make yourself a nice cup of tea.' And so I did. And when Elliot came home, 'Why, whatever's happened?' he says, staring at me. Still all of a tremble I was. Always was sensitive from a child."

Poirot dexterously interrupted this thrilling personal narrative.

"Yes, yes, one can see that. And when was the last time you had seen poor Mrs McGinty?"

"Must have been the day before, when she'd stepped out into the back garden to pick a bit of mint. I was just feeding the chickens."

"Did she say anything to you?"

"Just good afternoon and were they laying any better."

"And that's the last time you saw her? You didn't see her on the day she died?"

"No. I saw *Him* though." Mrs Elliot lowered her voice.

"About eleven o'clock in the morning. Just walking along the road. Shuffling his feet the way he always did."

Poirot waited, but it seemed that there was nothing to add. He asked:

"Were you surprised when the police arrested him?"

"Well, I was and I wasn't. Mind you, I'd always thought he was a bit daft. And no doubt about it, these daft ones do turn nasty, sometimes. My uncle had a feeble-minded boy, and he could go very nasty sometimes—as he grew up, that was. Didn't know his strength. Yes, that Bentley was daft all right, and I shouldn't be surprised if they don't hang him when it comes to it, but sends him to the asylum instead. Why, look at the place he hid the money. No one would hide money in a place like that unless he wanted it to be found. Just silly and simple like, that's what he was."

"Unless he wanted it found," murmured Poirot. "You did not, by any chance, miss a chopper—or an axe?"

"No, sir, I did *not*. The police asked me that. Asked all of us in the cottages here. It's a mystery still what he killed her with."

iii

Hercule Poirot walked towards the post office.

The murderer had wanted the money found, but he had not wanted the weapon to be found. For the money would point to James Bentley and the weapon would point to—whom?

He shook his head. He had visited the other two cottages. They had been less exuberant than Mrs Kiddle and less dramatic than Mrs Elliot. They had said in effect that Mrs McGinty was a very respectable woman who kept herself to herself, that she had a niece over at Cullavon, that nobody but the said niece ever came to see her, that nobody, so far as they knew, disliked her or bore a grudge against her, that was it true that there was a petition being got up for James Bentley and would they be asked to sign it?

"I get nowhere—nowhere," said Poirot to himself. "There is nothing—no little gleam. I can well understand the despair of

49

Superintendent Spence. But it should be different for *me*. Superintendent Spence, he is a very good and painstaking police officer, but me, I am Hercule Poirot. For *me*, there should be illumination!"

One of his patent leather shoes slopped into a puddle and he winced.

He was the great, the unique Hercule Poirot, but he was also a very old man and his shoes were tight.

He entered the post office.

The right-hand side was given to the business of His Majesty's mails. The left-hand side displayed a rich assortment of varied merchandise, comprising sweets, groceries, toys, hardware, stationery, birthday cards, knitting wool and children's under-clothes.

Poirot proceeded to a leisurely purchase of stamps.

The woman who bustled forward to attend to him was middle-aged with sharp, bright eyes.

"Here," said Poirot to himself, "is undoubtedly the brains of the village of Broadhinny."

Her name, not inappropriately, was Mrs Sweetiman.

"And twelve pennies," said Mrs Sweetiman, deftly extracting them from a large book. "That's four and tenpence altogether. Will there be anything more, sir?"

She fixed a bright eager glance on him. Through the door at the back a girl's head showed listening avidly. She had untidy hair and a cold in the head.

"I am by way of being a stranger in these parts," said Poirot solemnly.

"That's right, sir," agreed Mrs Sweetiman. "Come down from London, haven't you?"

"I expect you know my business here as well as I do," said Poirot with a slight smile.

"Oh no, sir, I've really no idea," said Mrs Sweetiman in a wholly perfunctory manner.

"Mrs McGinty," said Poirot.

Mrs Sweetiman shook her head.

"That was a sad business—a shocking business."

"I expect you knew her well?"

"Oh I did. As well as anyone in Broadhinny, I should say.

She'd always pass the time of day with me when she came in here for any little thing. Yes, it was a terrible tragedy. And not settled yet, or so I've heard people say."

"There is a doubt—in some quarters—as to James Bentley's guilt."

"Well," said Mrs Sweetiman, "it wouldn't be the first time the police got hold of the wrong man—though I wouldn't say they had in this case. Not that I should have thought it of him really. A shy awkward sort of fellow, but not dangerous or so you'd think. But there, you never know, do you?"

Poirot hazarded a request for notepaper.

"Of course, sir. Just come across the other side, will you?"

Mrs Sweetiman bustled round to take her place behind the left-hand counter.

"What's difficult to imagine is, who it could have been if it wasn't Mr Bentley," she remarked as she stretched up to a top shelf for notepaper and envelopes. "We do get some nasty tramps along here sometimes, and it's possible one of these might have found a window unfastened and got in that way. But he wouldn't go leaving the money behind him, would he? Not after doing murder to get it—and pound notes anyway, nothing with numbers or marked. Here you are, sir, that's a nice blue Bond, and envelopes to match."

Poirot made his purchase.

"Mrs McGinty never spoke of being nervous of anyone, or afraid, did she?" he asked.

"Not to me, she didn't. She wasn't a nervous woman. She'd stay late sometimes at Mr Carpenter's—that's Homeleigh at the top of the hill. They often have people to dinner and stopping with them, and Mrs McGinty would go there in the evening sometimes to help wash up, and she'd come down the hill in the dark, and that's more than I'd like to do. Very dark it is—coming down that hill."

"Do you know her niece at all—Mrs Burch?"

"I know her just to speak to. She and her husband come over sometimes."

"They inherited a little money when Mrs McGinty died."

The piercing dark eyes looked at him severely.

"Well, that's natural enough, isn't it, sir? You can't take it

51

with you, and it's only right your own flesh and blood should get it."

"Oh yes, oh yes, I am entirely in agreement. Was Mrs McGinty fond of her niece?"

"Very fond of her, I think, sir. In a quiet way."

"And her niece's husband?"

An evasive look appeared in Mrs Sweetiman's face.

"As far as I know."

"When did you see Mrs McGinty last?"

Mrs Sweetiman considered, casting her mind back.

"Now let me see, when was it, Edna?" Edna, in the doorway, sniffed unhelpfully. "Was it the day she died? No, it was the day before—or the day before that again? Yes, it was a Monday. That's right. She was killed on the Wednesday. Yes, it was Monday. She came in to buy a bottle of ink."

"She wanted a bottle of ink?"

"Expect she wanted to write a letter," said Mrs Sweetiman brightly.

"That seems probable. And she was quite her usual self, then? She did not seem different in any way?"

"N-no, I don't think so."

The sniffing Edna shuffled through the door into the shop and suddenly joined in the conversation.

"She was different," she asserted. "Pleased about something—well—not pleased quite—excited."

"Perhaps you're right," said Mrs Sweetiman. "Not that I noticed it at the time. But now that you say so—sort of spry, she was."

"Do you remember anything she said on that day?"

"I wouldn't ordinarily. But what with her being murdered and the police and everything, it makes things stand out. She didn't say anything about James Bentley, that I'm quite sure. Talked about the Carpenters a bit and Mrs Upward—places where she worked, you know."

"Oh yes, I was going to ask you whom exactly she worked for here."

Mrs Sweetiman replied promptly:

"Mondays and Thursdays she went to Mrs Summerhayes at Long Meadow. That's where you are staying, isn't it?"

52

"Yes." Poirot sighed. "I suppose there is not anywhere else to stay?"

"Not right in Broadhinny, there isn't. I suppose you aren't very comfortable at Long Meadows? Mrs Summerhayes is a nice lady but she doesn't know the first thing about a house. These ladies don't who come back from foreign parts. Terrible mess there always was there to clean up, or so Mrs McGinty used to say. Yes, Monday afternoons and Thursday mornings Mrs Summerhayes, then Tuesday mornings Dr Rendell's and afternoons Mrs Upward at Laburnums. Wednesday was Mrs Wetherby at Hunter's Close and Friday Mrs Selkirk—Mrs Carpenter she is now. Mrs Upward's an elderly lady who lives with her son. They've got a maid, but she's getting on, and Mrs McGinty used to go once a week to give things a good turn out. Mr and Mrs Wetherby never seem to keep any help long—she's rather an invalid. Mr and Mrs Carpenter have a beautiful home and do a lot of entertaining. They're all very nice people."

It was with this final pronouncement on the population of Broadhinny that Poirot went out into the street again.

He walked slowly up the hill towards Long Meadows. He hoped devoutly that the contents of the bulged tin and the bloodstained beans had been duly eaten for lunch and had not been saved for a supper treat for him. But possibly there were other doubtful tins. Life at Long Meadows certainly had its dangers.

It had been, on the whole, a disappointing day.

What had he learned?

That James Bentley had a friend. That neither he nor Mrs McGinty had had any enemies. That Mrs McGinty had looked excited two days before her death and had bought a bottle of ink——

Poirot stopped dead . . . Was that a fact, a tiny fact at last?

He had asked idly, what Mrs McGinty should want with a bottle of ink, and Mrs Sweetiman had replied, quite seriously, that she supposed she wanted to write a letter.

There was significance there—a significance that had nearly escaped him because to him, as to most people, writing a letter was a common everyday occurrence.

But it was not so to Mrs McGinty. Writing a letter was to Mrs

McGinty such an uncommon occurrence that she had to go out and buy a bottle of ink if she wanted to do so.

Mrs McGinty, then, hardly ever wrote letters. Mrs Sweetiman, who was the postmistress, was thoroughly cognisant of that fact. But Mrs McGinty had written a letter two days before her death. To whom had she written and why?

It might be quite unimportant. She might have written to her niece—to an absent friend. Absurd to lay such stress on a simple thing like a bottle of ink.

But it was all he had got and he was going to follow it up.

A bottle of ink . . .

8

i

"A LETTER?" Bessie Burch shook her head. "No, I didn't get any letter from auntie. What should she write to me about?"

Poirot suggested: "There might have been something she wanted to tell you."

"Auntie wasn't much of a one for writing. She was getting on for seventy, you know, and when she was young they didn't get much schooling."

"But she could read and write?"

"Oh, of course. Not much of a one for reading, though she liked her *News of the World* and her *Sunday Comet*. But writing came a bit difficult always. If she'd anything to let me know about, like putting us off from coming to see her, or saying she couldn't come to us, she'd usually ring up Mr Benson, the chemist next door, and he'd send the message in. Very obliging that way, he is. You see, we're in the area, so it only cost twopence. There's a call-box at the post ofice in Broadhinny."

Poirot nodded. He appreciated the fact that twopence was better than twopence ha'penny. He already had a picture of Mrs McGinty as the spare and saving kind. She has been, he thought, very fond of money.

He persisted gently:

"But your aunt did write to you sometimes, I suppose?"

"Well, there were cards at 'Xmas."

"And perhaps she had friends in other parts of England to whom she wrote?"

"I don't know about that. There was her sister-in-law, but she died two years ago and there was a Mrs Birdlip—but she's dead too."

"So, if she wrote to someone, it would be most likely in answer to a letter she had received?"

Again Bessie Burch looked doubtful.

"I don't know who'd be writing to her, I'm sure. . . . Of course," her face brightened, "there's the Government."

Poirot agreed that in these days, communications from what Bessie loosely referred to as "The Government" were the rule, rather than the exception.

"And a lot of fandangle it usually is," said Mrs Burch. "Forms to fill in, and a lot of impertinent questions as shouldn't be asked of any decent body."

"So Mrs McGinty might have got some Government communication that she had to answer?"

"If she had, she'd have brought it along to Joe, so as he could help her with it. Those sort of things fussed her and she always brought them to Joe."

"Can you remember if there were any letters among her personal possessions?"

"I couldn't rightly say. I don't remember anything. But then the police took over at first. It wasn't for quite a while they let me pack her things and take them away."

"What happened to those things?"

"That chest over there is hers—good solid mahogany, and there's a wardrobe upstairs, and some good kitchen stuff. The rest we sold because we'd no room for them."

"I meant her own personal things." He added: "Such things as brushes and combs, photographs, toilet things, clothes . . ."

"Oh, them. Well, tell you the truth, I packed them in a suitcase and it's still upstairs. Didn't rightly know what to do with them. Thought I'd take the clothes to the jumble sale at 'Xmas, but I forgot. Didn't seem nice to take them to one of those nasty second-hand clothes people."

"I wonder—might I see the contents of that suitcase?"

"Welcome, I'm sure. Though I don't think you'll find anything to help you. The police went through it all, you know."

"Oh I know. But, all the same——"

Mrs Burch led him briskly into a minute back bedroom, used, Poirot judged, mainly for home dressmaking. She pulled out a suitcase from under the bed and said:

"Well, here you are, and you'll excuse me stopping, but I've got the stew to see to."

Poirot gratefully excused her, and heard her thumping downstairs again. He drew the suitcase towards him and opened it.

A waft of mothballs came out to greet him.

With a feeling of pity, he lifted out the contents, so eloquent in their revelation of a woman who was dead. A rather worn long black coat. Two woollen jumpers. A coat and skirt. Stockings. No underwear (presumably Bessie Burch had taken those for her own wear). Two pairs of shoes wrapped up in newspaper. A brush and comb, worn but clean. An old dented silver-backed mirror. A photograph in a leather frame of a wedding pair dressed in the style of thirty years ago—a picture of Mrs McGinty and her husband presumably. Two picture post-cards of Margate. A china dog. A recipe torn out of a paper for making vegetable marrow jam. Another piece dealing with "Flying Saucers" on a sensational note. A third clipping dealt with Mother Shipton's prophecies. There was also a Bible and a Prayer Book.

There were no handbags, or gloves. Presumably Bessie Burch had taken these, or given them away. The clothes here, Poirot judged, would have been too small for the buxom Bessie. Mrs McGinty had been a thin, spare woman.

He unwrapped one of the pairs of shoes. They were of quite good quality and not much worn. Decidedly on the small side for Bessie Burch.

He was just about to wrap them up neatly again when his eye was caught by the heading on the piece of newspaper.

It was the *Sunday Comet* and the date was November 19th.

Mrs McGinty had been killed on November 22nd.

This then was the paper she had bought on the Sunday preceding her death. It had been lying in her room and Bessie Burch had used it in due course to wrap up her aunt's things.

Sunday, November 19th. And on *Monday* Mrs McGinty had gone into the post ofice to buy a bottle of ink. . . .

Could that be because of something she had seen in Sunday's newspaper?

He unwrapped the other pair of shoes. They were wrapped in the *News of the World* of the same date.

He smoothed out both papers and took them over to a chair where he sat down to read them. And at once he made a discovery. On one page of the *Sunday Comet*, something had been cut out. It was a rectangular piece out of the middle page. The space was too big for any of the clippings he had found.

He looked through both newspapers, but could find nothing else of interest. He wrapped them round the shoes again and packed the suitcase tidily.

Then he went downstairs.

Mrs Burch was busy in the kitchen.

"Don't suppose you found anything?" she said.

"Alas, no." He added in a casual voice: "You do not remember if there was a cutting from a newspaper in your aunt's purse or in her handbag, was there?"

"Can't remember any. Perhaps the police took it."

But the police had not taken it. That Poirot knew from his study of Spence's notes. The contents of the dead woman's handbag had been listed, no newspaper cutting was among them.

"*Eh bien*," said Hercule Poirot to himself. "The next step is easy. It will be either the wash-out—or else, at last, I advance."

ii

Sitting very still, with the dusty files of newspaper in front of him, Poirot told himself that his recognition of the significance of the bottle of ink had not played him false.

The *Sunday Comet* was given to romantic dramatisations of past events.

The paper at which Poirot was looking was the *Sunday Comet* of Sunday, November 19th.

At the top of the middle page were these words in big type:

WOMEN VICTIMS OF BYGONE TRAGEDIES

WHERE ARE THESE WOMEN NOW?

Below the caption were four very blurred reproductions of photographs clearly taken many years ago.

The subjects of them did not look tragic. They looked, actually, rather ridiculous, since nearly all of them were dressed in the style of a bygone day, and nothing is more ridiculous than the fashions of yesterday—though in another thirty years or so their charm may have reappeared, or at any rate be once more apparent.

Under each photo was a name.

Eva Kane, the "other woman" in the famous Craig case.

Janice Courtland, the "tragic wife" whose husband was a fiend in human form.

Little Lily Gamboll, tragic child product of our overcrowded age.

Vera Blake, unsuspecting wife of a killer.

And then came the question in bold type again:

WHERE ARE THESE WOMEN NOW?

Poirot blinked and set himself to read meticulously the somewhat romantic prose which gave the life stories of these dim and blurry heroines.

The name of Eva Kane he rememberd, for the Craig Case had been a very celebrated one. Alfred Craig had been Town Clerk of Parminster, a conscientious, rather nondescript little man, correct and pleasant in his behaviour. He had had the misfortune to marry a tiresome and temperamental wife. Mrs Craig ran him into debt, bullied him, nagged him, and suffered from nervous maladies that unkind friends said were entirely imaginary. Eva Kane was the young nursery governess in the house. She was nineteen, pretty, helpless and rather simple. She fell desperately in love with Craig and he with her. Then one day the neighbours heard that Mrs. Craig had been "ordered abroad" for her health. That had been Craig's story. He took her up to London, the first stage of the journey, by car late one evening, and "saw her off" to the South of France. Then he returned to Parminster and at intervals mentioned how his wife's health was no better by her accounts of it in letters. Eva Kane remained behind to house-keep for him, and tongues soon started wagging. Finally, Craig received news of his wife's death abroad. He went away and returned a week later, with an account of the funeral.

In some ways, Craig was a simple man. He made the mistake

of mentioning where his wife had died, a moderately well-known resort on the French Riviera. It only remained for someone who had a relative or friend living there to write to them, discover that there had been no death or funeral of anyone of that name and, after a period of rank gossip, to communicate with the police.

Subsequent events can be briefly summarised.

Mrs Craig had not left for the Riviera. She had been cut in neat pieces and buried in the Craig cellar. And the autopsy of the remains showed poisoning by a vegetable alkaloid.

Craig was arrested and sent for trial. Eva Kane was originally charged as an accessory, but the charge was dropped, since it appeared clear that she had throughout been completely ignorant of what had occurred. Craig in the end made a full confession and was sentenced and executed.

Eva Kane, who was expecting a child, left Parminster and, in the words of the *Sunday Comet: Kindly relatives in the New World offered her a home. Changing her name, the pitiful young girl, seduced in her trusting youth by a cold-blooded murderer, left these shores for ever, to begin a new life and to keep for ever locked in her heart and concealed from her daughter the name of her father.*

"My daughter shall grow up happy and innocent. Her life shall not be tainted by the cruel past. That I have sworn. My tragic memories shall remain mine alone."

Poor frail trusting Eva Kane. To learn, so young, the villainy and infamy of man. Where is she now? Is there, in some Mid-western town, an elderly woman, quiet and respected by her neighbours, who has, perhaps, sad eyes . . . And does a young woman, happy and cheerful, with children, perhaps, of her own, come and see "Momma," telling her of all the little rubs and grievances of daily life—with no idea of what past sufferings her mother has endured?

"Oh la la!" said Hercule Poirot. And passed on to the next Tragic Victim.

Janice Courtland, the "tragic wife," had certainly been unfortunate in her husband. His peculiar practices, referred to in such a guarded way as to rouse instant curiosity, had been suffered by her for eight years. Eight years of martyrdom, the *Sunday Comet* said firmly. Then Janice made a friend. An idealistic and unworldly young man who, horrified by a scene between husband and wife that he had witnessed by accident, had thereupon assaulted the husband with such vigour that the latter had crashed in his skull on a sharply-edged marble fire surround. The jury had found that provocation had been intense, that the young idealist had no intention of killing, and a sentence of five years for manslaughter was given.

The suffering Janice, horrified by all the publicity the case had brought her, had gone abroad "to forget."

Has she forgotten? asked the *Sunday Comet. We hope so. Somewhere, perhaps, is a happy wife and mother to whom those years of nightmare suffering silently endured, seem now only like a dream. . . .*

"Well, well," said Hercule Poirot and passed on to Lily Gamboll, the tragic child product of our overcrowded age.

Lily Gamboll had, it seemed, been removed from her overcrowded home. An aunt had assumed responsibility for Lily's life. Lily had wanted to go to the pictures, aunt had said "No." Lily Gamboll had picked up the meat chopper which was lying conveniently on the table and had aimed a blow at her aunt with it. The aunt, though autocratic, was small and frail. The blow killed her. Lily was a well-developed and muscular child for her twelve years. An approved school had opened its doors and Lily had disappeared from the everyday scene.

By now she is a woman, free again to take her place in our civilisation. Her conduct, during her years of confinement and probation, is said to have been exemplary. Does not this show that it is not the child, but the system, that we must blame? Brought up in ignorance, in slum conditions, little Lily was the victim of her environment.

Now, having atoned for her tragic lapse, she lives somewhere, happily, we hope, a good citizen and a good wife and mother. Poor little Lily Gamboll.

Poirot shook his head. A child of twelve who took a swing at her aunt with a meat chopper and hit her hard enough to kill her was not, in his opinion, a nice child. His sympathies were, in this case, with the aunt.

He passed on to Vera Blake.

Vera Blake was clearly one of those women with whom everything goes wrong. She had first taken up with a boy-friend who turned out to be a gangster wanted by the police for killing a bank watchman. She had then married a respectable tradesman who turned out to be a receiver of stolen goods. Her two children had likewise, in due course, attracted the attention of the police. They went with mamma to department stores and did a pretty line in shoplifting. Finally, however, a "good man" had appeared on the scene. He had offered tragic Vera a home in the Dominions. She and her children should leave this effete country.

From henceforward a New Life awaited them. At last, after long years of repeated blows from Fate, Vera's troubles are over.

"I wonder," said Poirot sceptically. "Very possibly she will find she has married a confidence trickster who works the liners!"

He leant back and studied the four photographs. Eva Kane with tousled curly hair over her ears and an enormous hat, held a bunch of roses up to her ear like a telephone receiver. Janice Courtland had a cloche hat pushed down over her ears and a waist round her hips. Lily Gamboll was a plain child with an adenoidal appearance of open mouth, hard breathing and thick spectacles. Vera Blake was so tragically black and white that no features showed.

For some reason Mrs McGinty had torn out this feature, photographs and all. Why? Just to keep because the stories interested her? He thought not. Mrs McGinty had kept very few things during her sixty-odd years of life. Poirot knew that from the police reports of her belongings.

She had torn this out on the Sunday and on the Mondy she had bought a bottle of ink and the inference was that she, who never wrote letters, was about to write a letter. If it had been a business letter, she would probably have asked Joe Burch to help her. So it had not been business. It had been—what?

Poirot's eyes looked over the four photographs once again.

Where, the *Sunday Comet* asked, *are these women now?*

One of them, Poirot thought, might have been in Broadhinny last November.

iii

It was not until the following day that Poirot found himself *tête à tête* with Miss Pamela Horsefall.

Miss Horsefall couldn't give him long, because she had to rush away to Sheffield, she explained.

Miss Horsefall was tall, manly-looking, a hard drinker and smoker, and it would seem, looking at her, highly improbable that it was her pen which had dropped such treacly sentiment in the *Sunday Comet*. Nevertheless it was so.

"Cough it up, cough it up," said Miss Horsefall impatiently to Poirot. "I've got to be going."

"It is about your article in the *Sunday Comet*. Last November. The series about Tragic Women."

"Oh, *that* series. Pretty lousy, weren't they?"

Poirot did not express an opinion on that point. He said:

"I refer in particular to the article on Women Associated with Crime that appeared on November 19th. It concerned Eva Kane, Vera Blake, Janice Courtland and Lily Gamboll."

Miss Horsefall grinned.

"Where are these tragic women now? I remember."

"I suppose you sometimes get letters after the appearance of these articles?"

"You bet I do! Some people seem to have nothing better to do than write letters. Somebody 'once saw the murderer Craig walking down the street.' Somebody would like to tell me 'the story of her life, far more tragic than anything I could ever imagine.'"

"Did you get a letter after the appearance of that article from a Mrs McGinty of Broadhinny?"

"My dear man, how on earth should I know? I get buckets of letters. How should I remember one particular name?"

"I thought you might remember," said Poirot, "because a few days later Mrs McGinty was murdered."

"Now you're talking." Miss Horsefall forgot to be impatient to get to Sheffield, and sat down astride a chair. "McGinty—McGinty . . . I do remember the name. Conked on the head by her lodger. Not a very exciting crime from the point of view of the public. No sex appeal about it. You say the woman wrote to me?"

"She wrote to the *Sunday Comet*, I think."

"Same thing. It would come on to me. And with the murder—and her name being in the news—surely I should remember——"

She stopped. "Look here—it wasn't from Broadhinny. It was from Broadway."

"So you do remember?"

"Well, I'm not sure . . . But the name . . . Comic name, isn't it? McGinty! Yes—atrocious writing and quite illiterate. If I'd only realised . . . But I'm sure it came from Broadway."

Poirot said: "You say yourself the writing was bad. Broadway and Broadhinny—they could look alike."

"Yes—might be so. After all, one wouldn't be likely to know these queer rural names. McGinty—yes. I do remember definitely. Perhaps the murder fixed the name for me."

"Can you remember what she said in her letter?"

"Something about a photograph. She knew where there was a photograph like in the paper—and would we pay her anything for it and how much?"

"And you answered?"

"My dear man, we don't want anything of that kind. We sent back the standard reply. Polite thanks but nothing doing. But as we sent it to Broadway—I don't suppose she'd ever get it."

"*She knew where there was a photograph. . . .*"

Into Poirot's mind there came back a remembrance. Maureen Summerhayes' careless voice saying, "Of course she snooped round a bit."

Mrs McGinty had snooped. She was honest, but she liked to know about things. And people kept things—foolish, meaningless things from the past. Kept them for sentimental reasons, or just overlooked them and didn't remember they were there.

Mrs McGinty had seen an old photograph and later she had recognised it reproduced in the *Sunday Comet*. And she had wondered if there was any money in it. . . .

He rose briskly. "Thank you, Miss Horsefall. You will pardon me, but those notes on the cases that you wrote, were they accurate? I notice, for instance, that the year of the Craig trial is given wrongly—it was actually a year later than you say. And in the Courtland case, the husband's name was Herbert, I seem to remember, not Hubert. Lily Gamboll's aunt lived in Buckinghamshire, not Berkshire."

Miss Horsefall waved a cigarette.

"My dear man. No point in accuracy. Whole thing was a

64

romantic farrago from beginning to end. I just mugged up the facts a bit and then let fly with a lot of hou ha."

"What I am trying to say is that even the characters of your heroines are not, perhaps, quite as represented."

Pamela let out a neighing sound like a horse.

"Course they weren't. What do *you* think? I've no doubt that Eva Kane was a thorough little bitch, and not an injured innocent at all. And as for the Courtland woman, why did she suffer in silence for eight years with a sadistic pervert? Because he was rolling in money, and the romantic boy-friend hadn't any."

"And the tragic child, Lily Gamboll?"

"I wouldn't care to have her gambolling about *me* with a meat chopper."

Poirot ticked off on his fingers.

"They left the country—they went to the New World—abroad—'to the Dominions'—'to start a New Life.' And there is nothing to show, is there, that they did not, subsequently, come back to this country?"

"Not a thing," agreed Miss Horsefall. "And now—I really must fly——"

Later that night Poirot rang up Spence.

"I've been wondering about you, Poirot. Have you got anything? Anything at all?"

"I have made my inquiries," said Poirot grimly.

"Yes?"

"And the result of them is this: *The people who live in Broadhinny are all very nice people.*"

"What do you mean by that, M. Poirot?"

"Oh, my friend, consider. 'Very nice people.' That has been, before now, a motive for murder."

9

i

"ALL VERY nice people," murmured Poirot as he turned in at the gate of Crossways, near the station.

A brass plate in the doorpost announced that Dr Rendell, M.D., lived there.

Dr Rendell was a large cheerful man of forty. He greeted his guest with definite *empressement*.

"Our quiet little village is honoured," he said, "by the presence of the great Hercule Poirot."

"Ah," said Poirot. He was gratified. "*You* have, then, heard of me?"

"Of course we have heard of you. Who hasn't?"

The answer to that would have been damaging to Poirot's self-esteem. He merely said politely: "I am fortunate to find you at home."

It was not particularly fortunate. It was, on the contrary, astute timing. But Dr Rendell replied heartily:

"Yes. Just caught me. Surgery in a quarter of an hour. Now what can I do for you? I'm devoured with curiosity to know what you're doing down here. A rest cure? Or have we crime in our midst?"

"In the past tense—not the present."

"Past? I don't remember——"

"Mrs McGinty."

"Of course. Of course. I was forgetting. But don't say you're concerned with that—at this late date?"

"If I may mention this to you in confidence, I am employed by the defence. Fresh evidence on which to lodge an appeal."

Dr Rendell said sharply: "But what fresh evidence can there be?"

"That, alas, I am not at liberty to state——"

"Oh, quite—please forgive me."

"But I have come across certain things which are, I may say—very curious—very—very—how shall I put it?—suggestive? I came to you, Dr Rendell, because I understand that Mrs McGinty occasionally was employed here."

"Oh yes, yes—she was—— What about a drink? Sherry? Whisky? You prefer sherry? So do I." He brought two glasses and, sitting down by Poirot, he went on: "She used to come once a week to do extra cleaning. I've got a very good housekeeper—excellent—but the brasses—and scrubbing the kitchen floor—well, my Mrs Scott can't get down on her knees very well. Mrs McGinty was an excellent worker."

"Do you think that she was a truthful person?"

"Truthful? Well, that's an odd question. I don't think I could say—no opportunity of knowing. As far as I know she was quite truthful."

"If then she made a statement to anyone, you think that statement would probably be true?"

Dr Rendell looked faintly disturbed.

"Oh, I wouldn't like to go as far as that. I really know so little about her. I could ask Mrs Scott. She'd know better."

"No, no. It would be better not to do that."

"You're arousing my curiosity," said Dr Rendell genially. "What was it she was going around saying? Something a bit libellous, was it? Slanderous, I suppose I mean."

Poirot merely shook his head. He said: "You understand, all this is extremely hush hush at present. I am only at the very commencement of my investigation."

Dr Rendell said rather dryly:

"You'll have to hurry a bit, won't you?"

"You are right. The time at my disposal is short."

"I must say you surprise me . . . We've all been quite sure down here that Bentley did it. There didn't seem any doubt possible."

"It seemed an ordinary sordid crime—not very interesting. That is what you would say?"

"Yes—yes, that sums it up very fairly."

"You knew James Bentley?"

"He came to see me professionally once or twice. He was nervous about his own health. Coddled by his mother, I fancy. One sees that so often. We've another case in point here."

"Ah, indeed?"

"Yes. Mrs Upward. Laura Upward. Dotes upon that son of hers. She keeps him well tied to her apron-strings. He's a clever fellow—not quite as clever as he thinks himself, between you and me—but still definitely talented. By way of being a budding playwright is our Robin."

"They have been here long?"

"Three or four years. Nobody has been in Broadhinny very long. The original village was only a handful of cottages, grouped round Long Meadows. You're staying there, I understand?"

"I am," said Poirot without undue elation.

Dr Rendell appeared amused.

"Guest House indeed," he said. "What that young woman knows about running a Guest House is just nothing at all. She's lived in India all her married life with servants running round all over the place. I bet you're uncomfortable. Nobody ever stays long. As for poor old Summerhayes, he'll never make anything of this market gardening stunt he's trying to run. Nice fellow—but not an idea of the commercial life—and the commercial life it's got to be nowadays if you want to keep your head above water. Don't run away with the idea that I heal the sick. I'm just a glorified form-filler and signer of certificates. I like the Summerhayes, though. She's a charming creature, and though Summerhayes has a devilish temper and is inclined to be moody, he's one of the old gang. Out of the top drawer all right. You should have known old Colonel Summerhayes, a regular tartar, proud as the devil."

"That was Major Summerhayes' father?"

"Yes. There wasn't much money when the old boy died and of course there have been death duties to cripple these people, but they're determined to stick to the old place. One doesn't know whether to admire them, or whether to say 'Silly fools.'"

He looked at his watch.

"I must not keep you," said Poirot.

"I've got a few minutes still. Besides, I'd like you to meet my wife. I can't think where she is. She was immensely interested to hear you were down here. We're both very crime-minded. Read a lot about it."

"Criminology, fiction, or the Sunday papers?" asked Poirot smiling.

"All three."

"Do you descend as low as the *Sunday Comet*?"

Rendell laughd.

"What would Sunday be without it?"

"They had some interesting articles about five months ago. One in particular about women who had been involved in murder cases and the tragedy of their lives."

"Yes, I remember the one you mean. All a lot of hooey, though."

"Ah, you think that?"

"Well of course the Craig case I only know from reading about it, but one of the others—Courtland case, I can tell you *that* woman was no tragic innocent. Regular vicious bit of goods. I know because an uncle of mine attended the husband. He was certainly no beauty, but his wife wasn't much better. She got hold of that young greenhorn and egged him on to murder. Then he goes to prison for manslaughter and she goes off, a rich widow, and marries someone else."

"The *Sunday Comet* did not mention that. Do you remember whom she married?"

Rendell shook his head.

"Don't think I ever heard the name, but someone told me that she'd done pretty well for herself."

"One wondered in reading the article where those four women were now," mused Poirot.

"I know. One may have met one of them at a party last week. I bet they all keep their past pretty dark. You'd certainly never recognise any of 'em from those photographs. My word, they looked a plain lot."

The clock chimed and Poirot rose to his feet. "I must detain you no longer. You have been most kind."

"Not much help, I'm afraid. The mere man barely knows what his charlady looks like. But half a second, you must meet the wife. She'd never forgive me."

He preceded Poirot out into the hall, calling loudly:

"Shelagh—Shelagh——"

A faint answer came from upstairs.

"Come down here. I've got something for you."

A thin fair-haired pale woman ran lightly down the stairs.

"Here's M. Hercule Poirot, Shelagh. What do you think of that?"

"Oh," Mrs Rendell appeared to be startled out of speaking. Her very pale blue eyes stared at Poirot apprehensively.

"Madame," said Poirot, bowing over her hand in his most foreign manner.

"We heard that you were here," said Shelagh Rendell. "But we didn't know——" She broke off. Her light eyes went quickly to her husband's face.

"It is from him she takes the Greenwich time," said Poirot to himself.

He uttered a few florid phrases and took his leave.

An impression remained with him of a genial Dr Rendell and a tongue-tied, apprehensive Mrs Rendell.

So much for the Rendells, where Mrs McGinty had gone to work on Tuesday mornings.

ii

Hunter's Close was a solidly built Victorian house approached by a long untidy drive overgrown with weeds. It had not originally been considered a big house, but was now big enough to be inconvenient domestically.

Poirot inquired of the foreign young woman who opened the door for Mrs Wetherby.

She stared at him and then said: "I do not know. Please to come. Miss Henderson perhaps?"

She left him standing in the hall. It was in an estate agent's phrase "'fully furnished"—with a good many curios from various parts of the world. Nothing looked very clean or well dusted.

Presently the foreign girl reappeared. She said: "Please to come," and showed him into a chilly little room with a large desk. On the mantelpiece was a big and rather evil-looking copper coffee pot with an enormous hooked spout like a large hooked nose.

The door opened behind Poirot and a girl came into the room.

"My mother is lying down," she said. "Can I do anything for you?"

"You are Miss Wetherby?"

"Henderson. Mr Wetherby is my stepfather."

She was a plain girl of about thirty, large and awkward. She had watchful eyes.

"I was anxious to hear what you could tell me about a Mrs McGinty who used to work here."

She stared at him.

"Mrs McGinty? But she's dead."

"I know that," said Poirot gently. "Nevertheless, I would like to hear about her."

"Oh. Is it for insurance or something?"

"Not for insurance. It is a question of fresh evidence."

"Fresh evidence. You mean—her death?"

"I am engaged," said Poirot, "by the solicitors for the defence to make an inquiry on James Bentley's behalf."

Staring at him, she asked: "But didn't he do it?"

"The jury thought he did. But juries have been known to make a mistake."

"Then it was really somebody else who killed her?"

"It may have been."

She asked abruptly: "Who?"

"That," said Poirot softly, "is the question."

"I don't understand at all."

"No? But you can tell me something about Mrs McGinty, can't you?"

She said rather reluctantly:

"I suppose so. . . . What do you want to know?"

"Well—to begin with—what did you think of her?"

"Why—nothing in particular. She was just like anybody else."

"Talkative or silent? Curious or reserved? Pleasant or morose? A nice woman, or—not a very nice woman?"

Miss Henderson reflected.

"She worked well—but she talked a lot. Sometimes she said rather funny things. . . . I didn't—really—like her very much."

The door opened and the foreign help said:

"Miss Deirdre, your mother say: please to bring."

71

"My mother wants me to take this gentleman upstairs to her?"

"Yes please, thank you."

Deirdre Henderson looked at Poirot doubtfully.

"Will you come up to my mother?"

"But certainly."

Deirdre led the way across the hall and up the stairs. She said inconsequently: "One does get so very tired of foreigners."

Since her mind was clearly running on her domestic help and not on the visitor, Poirot did not take offence. He reflected that Deirdre Henderson seemed a rather simple young woman—simple to the point of gaucheness.

The room upstairs was crowded with knick-knacks. It was the room of a woman who had travelled a good deal and who had been determined wherever she went to have a souvenir of the place. Most of the souvenirs were clearly made for the delight and exploitation of tourists. There were too many sofas and tables and chairs in the room, too little air and too many draperies—and in the midst of it all was Mrs Wetherby.

Mrs Wetherby seemed a small woman—a pathetic small woman in a large room. That was the effect. But she was not really quite so small as she had decided to appear. The "poor little me" type can achieve its result quite well, even if really of medium height.

She was reclining very comfortably on a sofa and near her were books and some knitting and a glass of orange juice and a box of chocolates. She said brightly:

"You *must* forgive me not getting up, but the doctor does so insist on my resting every day, and everyone scolds me if I don't do what I'm told."

Poirot took her extended hand and bowed over it with the proper murmur of homage.

Behind him, uncompromising, Deirdre said: "He wants to know about Mrs McGinty."

The delicate hand that had lain passively in his tightened and he was reminded for a moment of the talon of a bird. Not really a piece of delicate Dresden china—a scratchy predatory claw . . .

Laughing slightly, Mrs Wetherby said:

"How ridiculous you are, Deirdre darling. Who is Mrs McGinty?"

"Oh, Mummy—you do remember really. She worked for us. You know, the one who was murdered."

Mrs Wetherby closed her eyes, and shivered.

"Don't, darling. It was all so horrid. I felt nervous for weeks afterwards. Poor old woman, but so *stupid* to keep money under the floor. She ought to have put it in the bank. Of course I remember all that—I'd just forgotten her *name*."

Deirdre said stolidly:

"He wants to know about her."

"Now do sit down, M. Poirot. I'm quite devoured by curiosity. Mrs Rendell just rang up and she said we had a very famous criminologist down here, and she described you. And then, when that idiot Frieda described a visitor, I felt sure it must be you, and I sent down word for you to come up. Now tell me, what *is* all this?"

"It is as your daughter says, I want to know about Mrs McGinty. She worked here. She came to you, I understand, on Wednesdays. And it was on a Wednesday she died. So she had been here that day, had she not?"

"I suppose so. Yes, I suppose so. I can't really tell now. It's so long ago."

"Yes. Several months. And she did not say anything that day—anything special?"

"That class of person always talks a lot," said Mrs Wetherby with distaste. "One doesn't really listen. And anyway she couldn't tell she was going to be robbed and killed that night, could she?"

"There is cause and effect," said Poirot.

Mrs Wetherby wrinkled her forehead.

"I don't see what you mean."

"Perhaps I do not see myself—not yet. One works through darkness towards light. . . . Do you take in the Sunday papers, Mrs Wetherby?"

Her blue eyes opened very wide.

"Oh yes. Of course. We have the *Observer* and the *Sunday Times*. Why?"

"I wondered. Mrs McGinty took the *Sunday Comet* and the *News of the World*."

He paused but nobody said anything. Mrs Wetherby sighed and half closed her eyes. She said:

"It was all very upsetting. That horrible lodger of hers. I don't think really he can have been quite right in the head. Apparently he was quite an educated man, too. That makes it worse, doesn't it?"

"Does it?"

"Oh yes—I do think so. Such a brutal crime. A meat chopper. Ugh!"

"The police never found the weapon," said Poirot.

"I expect he threw it in a pond or something."

"They dragged the ponds," said Deirdre. "I saw them."

"Darling," her mother sighed, "don't be morbid. You know how I hate thinking of things like that. My head."

Fiercely the girl turned on Poirot.

"You mustn't go on about it," she said. "It's bad for her. She's frightfully sensitive. She can't even read detective stories."

"My apologies," said Poirot. He rose to his feet. "I have only one excuse. A man is to be hanged in three weeks' time. If he did not do it——"

Mrs Wetherby raised herself on her elbow. Her voice was shrill.

"But of course he did it," she cried. "Of course he did."

Poirot shook his head.

"I am not so sure."

He left the room quickly. As he went down the stairs, the girl came after him. She caught up with him in the hall.

"What do you mean?" she asked.

"What I said, mademoiselle."

"Yes, but——" She stopped.

Poirot said nothing.

Deirdre Henderson said slowly:

"You've upset my mother. She hates things like that—robberies and murders and—and violence."

"It must, then, have been a great shock to her when a woman who had actually worked here was killed."

"Oh yes—oh yes, it was."

"She was prostrated—yes?"

"She wouldn't hear anything about it. . . . We—I—we try to—to spare her things. All the beastliness."

"What about the war?"

"Luckily we never had any bombs near here."

"What was your part in the war, mademoiselle?"

"Oh, I did V.A.D. work in Kilchester. And some driving for the W.V.S. I couldn't have left home, of course. Mother needed me. As it was, she minded my being out so much. It was all very difficult. And then servants—naturally mother's never done any housework—she's not strong enough. And it was so difficult to get anyone at all. That's why Mrs McGinty was such a blessing. That's when she began coming to us. She was a splendid worker. But of course nothing—anywhere—is like it used to be."

"And do you mind that so much, mademoiselle?"

"I? Oh no." She seemed surprised. "But it's different for mother. She—she lives in the past a lot."

"Some people do," said Poirot. His visual memory conjured up the room he had been in a short time before. There had been a bureau drawer half pulled out. A drawer full of odds and ends—a silk pin-cushion, a broken fan, a silver coffee pot—some old magazines. The drawer had been too full to shut. He said softly: "And they keep things—memories of old days—the dance pro-gramme, the fan, the photographs of bygone friends, even the menu cards and the theatre programmes because, looking at these things, old memories revive."

"I suppose that's it," said Deirdre. "I can't understand it myself. I never keep anything."

"You look forwards, not back?"

Deirdre said slowly:

"I don't know that I look anywhere . . . I mean, to-day's usually enough, isn't it?"

The front door opened and a tall, spare, elderly man came into the hall. He stopped dead as he saw Poirot.

He glanced at Deirdre and his eyebrows rose in interrogation.

"This is my stepfather," said Deirdre. "I—I don't know your name?"

"I am Hercule Poirot," said Poirot with his usual embarrassed air of announcing a royal title.

Mr Wetherby seemed unimpressed.

He said "Ah," and turned to hang up his coat.

Deirdre said:

"He came to ask about Mrs McGinty."

75

Mr Wetherby remained still for a second, then he finished his adjustment of the coat on the peg.

"That seems to me rather remarkable," he said. "The woman met her death some months ago and, although she worked here, we have no information concerning her or her family. If we had done we should already have given it to the police."

There was finality in his tone. He glanced at his watch.

"Lunch, I presume, will be ready in a quarter of an hour." . . .

"I'm afraid it may be rather late to-day."

Mr Wetherby's eyebrows rose again.

"Indeed? Why, may I ask?"

"Frieda has been rather busy."

"My dear Deirdre, I hate to remind you, but the task of running the household devolves on you. I should appreciate a little more punctuality."

Poirot opened the front door and let himself out. He glanced over his shoulder.

There was cold dislike in the gaze that Mr Wetherby gave his stepdaughter. There was something very like hate in the eyes that looked back at him.

10

Poirot left his third call until after luncheon. Luncheon was under-stewed oxtail, watery potatoes, and what Maureen hoped optimistically might turn out to be pancakes. They were very peculiar.

Poirot walked slowly up the hill. Presently, on his right, he would come to Laburnums, two cottages knocked into one and remodelled to modern taste. Here lived Mrs Upward and that promising young playwright, Robin Upward.

Poirot paused a moment at the gate to pass a hand over his moustaches. As he did so a car came twisting slowly down the hill and an apple core directed with force struck him on the cheek.

Startled, Poirot let out a yelp of protest. The car halted and a head came through the window.

"I'm so sorry. Did I hit you?"

Poirot paused in the act of replying. He looked at the rather noble face, the massive brow, the untidy billows of grey hair and a chord of memory stirred. The apple core, too, assisted his memory.

"But surely," he exclaimed, "it is Mrs Oliver."

It was indeed that celebrated detective-story writer.

Exclaiming "Why, it's M. Poirot," the authoress attempted to extract herself from the car. It was a small car and Mrs Oliver was a large woman. Poirot hastened to assist.

Murmuring in an explanatory voice, "Stiff after the long drive," Mrs Oliver suddenly arrived out on the road, rather in the manner of a volcanic eruption.

Large quantities of apples came, too, and rolled merrily down the hill.

"Bag's burst," explained Mrs Oliver.

She brushed a few stray pieces of half-consumed apple from the jutting shelf of her bust and then shook herself rather like a large

77

Newfoundland dog. A last apple, concealed in the recesses of her person, joined its brothers and sisters.

"Pity the bag burst," said Mrs Oliver. "They were Cox's. Still I suppose there will be lots of apples down here in the country. Or aren't there? Perhaps they all get sent away. Things are so odd nowadays, I find. Well, how are you, M. Poirot? You don't live here, do you? No, I'm sure you don't. Then I suppose it's murder? Not my hostess, I hope?"

"Who is your hostess?"

"In there," said Mrs Oliver, nodding her head. "That's to say if that's a house called Laburnums, half-way down the hill on the left after you pass the church. Yes, that must be it. What's she like?"

"You do not know her?"

"No, I've come down professionally, so to speak. A book of mine is being dramatised—by Robin Upward. We're supposed to sort of get together over it."

"My felicitations, madame."

"It's not like that at all," said Mrs Oliver. "So far it's pure *agony*. Why I ever let myself in for it I don't know. My books bring me in quite enough money—that is to say the blood-suckers take most of it, and if I made more, they'd take more, so I don't overstrain myself. But you've no idea of the agony of having your characters taken and made to say things that they never would have said, and do things that they never would have done. And if you protest, all they say is that it's 'good theatre.' That's all Robin Upward thinks of. Everyone says he's very clever. If he's so clever I don't see why he doesn't write a play of his own and leave my poor unfortunate Finn alone. He's not even a Finn any longer. He's become a member of the Norwegian Resistance movement." She ran her hands through her hair. "What have I done with my hat?"

Poirot looked into the car.

"I think madame, that you must have been sitting on it."

"It does look like it," agreed Mrs Oliver, surveying the wreckage. "Oh well," she continued cheerfully, "I never liked it much. But I thought I might have to go to church on Sunday, and although the Archbishop has said one needn't, I still thank that the more old-fashioned clergy expect one to wear a hat. But tell me about your murder or whatever it is. Do you remember *our* murder?"

"Very well indeed."

"Rather fun, wasn't it? Not the actual murder—I didn't like that at all. But afterwards. Who is it this time?"

"Not so picuresque a person as Mr Shaitana. An elderly charwoman who was robbed and murdered five months ago. You may have read about it. Mrs McGinty. A young man was convicted and sentenced to death——"

"And he didn't do it, but you know who did, and you're going to prove it," said Mrs Oliver rapidly. "Splendid."

"You go too fast," said Poirot with a sigh. "I do not yet know who did it—and from there it will be a long way to prove it."

"Men are so slow," said Mrs Oliver disparagingly. "I'll soon tell you who did it. Someone down here, I suppose? Give me a day or two to look round, and I'll spot the murderer. A woman's intuition—that's what you need. I was quite right over the Shaitana case, wasn't I?"

Poirot gallantly forbore to remind Mrs Oliver of her rapid changes of suspicion on that occasion.

"You men," said Mrs Oliver indulgently. "Now if a woman were the head of Scotland Yard——"

She left this well worn theme hanging in the air as a voice hailed them from the door of the cottage.

"Hallo," said the voice, an agreeable light tenor. "Is that Mrs Oliver?"

"Here I am," called Mrs Oliver. To Poirot she murmured: "Don't worry. I'll be very discreet."

"No, no, madame. I do not want you to be discreet. *On the contrary*."

Robin Upward came down the path and through the gate. He was bareheaded and wore very old grey flannel trousers and a disreputable sports coat. But for a tendency to embonpoint, he would have been good looking.

"Ariadne, my precious!" he exclaimed and embraced her warmly.

He stood away, his hands on her shoulders.

"My dear, I've had the most marvellous idea for the second act."

"Have you?" said Mrs Oliver without enthusiasm. "This is M. Hercule Poirot."

"Splendid," said Robin. "Have you got any luggage?"

"Yes, it's in the back."

Robin hauled out a couple of suitcases.

"Such a bore," he said. "We've no proper servants. Only old Janet. And we have to spare her all the time. That's such a nuisance don't you think? How heavy your cases are. Have you got bombs in them?"

He staggered up the path, calling out over his shoulder:

"Come in and have a drink."

"He means you," said Mrs Oliver, removing her handbag, a book, and a pair of old shoes from the front seat. "Did you actually say just now that you wanted me to be *indiscreet*?"

"The more indiscreet the better."

"I shouldn't tackle it that way myself," said Mrs Oliver, "but it's *your* murder. I'll help all I can."

Robin reappeared at the front door.

"Come in, come in," he called. "We'll see about the car later. Madre is dying to meet you."

Mrs Oliver swept up the path and Hercule Poirot followed her.

The interior of Laburnums was charming. Poirot guessed that a very large sum of money had been spent on it, but the result was an expensive and charming simplicity. Each small piece of cottage oak was a genuine piece.

In a wheeled chair by the fireplace of the living-room Laura Upward smiled a welcome. She was a vigorous-looking woman of sixty-odd, with iron-grey hair and a determined chin.

"I'm delighted to meet you, Mrs Oliver," she said. "I expect you hate people talking to you about your books, but they've been an enormous solace to me for years—and especially since I've been such a cripple."

"That's very nice of you," said Mrs Oliver, looking uncomfortable and twisting her hands in a schoolgirlish way. "Oh, this is M. Poirot, an old friend of mine. We met by chance just outside here. Actually I hit him with an apple core. Like William Tell—only the other way about."

"How d'you do, M. Poirot. Robin."

"Yes, Madre?"

"Get some drinks. Where are the cigarettes?"

"On the table."

Mrs Upward asked: "Are you a writer, too, M. Poirot?"

"Oh, no," said Mrs Oliver. "He's a detective. You know. The Sherlock Holmes kind—deerstalkers and violins and all that. And he's come here to solve a murder."

There was a faint tinkle of broken glass. Mrs Upward said sharply: "Robin, do be careful." To Poirot she said: "That's very interesting, M. Poirot."

"So Maureen Summerhayes was right," exclaimed Robin. "She told me some long rigmarole about having a detective on the premises. She seemed to think it was frightfully funny. But it's really quite serious, isn't it?"

"Of course it's serious," said Mrs Oliver. "You've got a criminal in your midst."

"Yes, but look here, who's been murdered? Or is it someone that's been dug up and it's all frightfully hush hush?"

"It is not hush hush," said Poirot. "The murder, you know about it already."

"Mrs Mc—something—a charwoman—last autumn," said Mrs Oliver.

"Oh!" Robin Upward sounded disappointed. "But that's all over."

"It's not over at all," said Mrs Oliver. "They arrested the wrong man, and he'll be hanged if M. Poirot doesn't find the real murderer in time. It's all frightfully exciting."

Robin apportioned the drinks.

"White Lady for you, Madre."

"Thank you, my dear boy."

Poirot frowned slightly. Robin handed drinks to Mrs Oliver and to him.

"Well," said Robin, "here's to crime."

He drank.

"She used to work here," he said.

"Mrs McGinty?" asked Mrs Oliver.

"Yes. Didn't she, Madre?"

"When you say work here, she came one day a week."

"And odd afternoons sometimes."

81

"What was she like?" asked Mrs Oliver.

"Terribly respectable," said Robin. "And maddeningly tidy. She had a ghastly way of tidying up everything and putting things into drawers so that you simply couldn't guess where they were."

Mrs Upward said with a certain grim humour:

"If somebody didn't tidy things away at least one day a week, you soon wouldn't be able to move in this small house."

"I know, Madre, I know. But unless things are left where I put them, I simply can't work at all. My notes get all disarranged."

"It's annoying to be as helpless as I am," said Mrs Upward. "We have a faithful old maid, but it's all she can manage just to do a little simple cooking."

"What is it?" asked Mrs Oliver. "Arthritis?"

"Some form of it. I shall have to have a permanent nurse-companion soon, I'm afraid. Such a bore. I like being independent."

"Now, darling," said Robin. "Don't work yourself up."

He patted her arm.

She smiled at him with sudden tenderness.

"Robin's as good as a daughter to me," she said. "He does everything—and thinks of everything. No one could be more considerate."

They smiled at each other.

Hercule Poirot rose.

"Alas," he said. "I must go. I have another call to make and then a train to catch. Madame, I thank you for your hospitality. Mr Upward, I wish all success to the play."

"And all success to you with your murder," said Mrs Oliver.

"Is this really serious, M. Poirot?" asked Robin Upward. "Or is it a terrific hoax?"

"Of course it isn't a hoax," said Mrs Oliver. "It's deadly serious. He won't tell me who the murderer is, but he knows, don't you?"

"No, no, madame," Poirot's protest was just sufficiently unconvincing. "I told you that as yet, no, I do not know."

"That's what you said, but I think you do know really. . . . But you're so frightfully secretive, aren't you?"

Mrs Upward said sharply:

"Is this really true? It's not a joke?"

"It is not a joke, madame," said Poirot.

He bowed and departed.

As he went down the path he heard Robin Upward's clear tenor voice:

— "But Ariadne, darling," he said, "it's all very well, but with that moustache and everything, how *can* one take him seriously? Do you really mean he's *good*?"

Poirot smiled to himself. Good indeed!

About to cross the narrow lane, he jumped back just in time.

The Summerhayes' station wagon, lurching and bumping, came racing past him. Summerhayes was driving.

"Sorry," he called. "Got to catch train." And faintly from the distance: "Covent Garden . . ."

Poirot also intended to take a train—the local train to Kilchester, where he had arranged a conference with Superintendent Spence.

He had time, before catching it, for just one last call.

He went to the top of the hill and through gates and up a well-kept drive to a modern house of frosted concrete with a square roof and a good deal of window. This was the home of Mr and Mrs Carpenter. Guy Carpenter was a partner in the big Carpenter Engineering Works—a very rich man who had recently taken to politics. He and his wife had only been married a short time.

The Carpenters' front door was not opened by foreign help, or an aged faithful. An imperturbable manservant opened the door and was loath to admit Hercule Poirot. In his view Hercule Poirot was the kind of caller who is left outside. He clearly suspected that Hercule Poirot had come to sell something.

"Mr and Mrs Carpenter are not at home."

"Perhaps, then, I might wait?"

"I couldn't say when they will be in."

He closed the door.

Poirot did not go down the drive. Instead he walked round the corner of the house and almost collided with a tall young woman in a mink coat.

"Hallo," she said. "What the hell do you want?"

Poirot raised his hat with gallantry.

"I was hoping," he said, "that I could see Mr or Mrs Carpenter. Have I the pleasure of seeing Mrs Carpenter?"

"I'm Mrs Carpenter."

She spoke ungraciously, but there was a faint suggestion of appeasement behind her manner.

"My name is Hercule Poirot."

Nothing registered. Not only was the great, the unique name unknown to her, but he thought that she did not even identify him as Maureen Summerhayes' latest guest. Here, then, the local grape vine did not operate. A small but significant fact, perhaps.

"Yes?"

"I demand to see either Mr or Mrs Carpenter, but you, madame, will be the best for my purpose. For what I have to ask is of domestic matters."

"We've got a Hoover," said Mrs Carpenter suspiciously.

Poirot laughed.

"No, no, you misunderstand. It is only a few questions that I ask about a domestic matter."

"Oh, you mean one of these domestic questionnaires. I do think it's absolutely idiotic——" She broke off. "Perhaps you'd better come inside."

Poirot smiled faintly. She had just stopped herself from uttering a derogatory comment. With her husband's political activities, caution in criticising Government activities was indicated.

She led the way through the hall and into a good-sized room giving on to a very carefully tended garden. It was a very new-looking room, a large brocaded suite of sofa and two wing-chairs, three or four reproductions of Chippendale chairs, a bureau, a writing desk. No expense had been spared, the best firms had been employed, and there was absolutely no sign of individual taste. The bride, Poirot thought, had been what? Indifferent? Careful?

He looked at her appraisingly as she turned. An expensive and good-looking young woman. Platinum blonde hair, carefully applied make-up, but something more—wide corn-flower blue eyes—eyes with a wide frozen stare in them—beautiful drowned eyes.

She said—graciously now, but concealing boredom:

"Do sit down."

He sat. He said:

"You are most amiable, madame. These questions now that I wish to ask you. They relate to a Mrs McGinty who died—was killed that is to say—last November?"

"Mrs McGinty? I don't know what you mean?"

She was glaring at him. Her eyes hard and suspicious.

"You remember Mrs McGinty?"

"No, I don't. I don't know anything about her."

"You remember her murder? Or is murder so common here that you do not even notice it?"

"Oh, the *murder*? Yes, of course. I'd forgotten what the old woman's name was."

"Although she worked for you in this house?"

"She didn't. I wasn't living here then. Mr Carpenter and I were only married three months ago."

"But she did work for you. On Friday mornings, I think it was. You were then Mrs Selkirk and you lived in Rose Cottage."

She said sulkily:

"If you know the answers to everything I don't see why you need to ask questions. Anyway, what's it all about?"

"I am making an investigation into the circumstances of the murder."

"Why? What on earth for? Anyway, why come to me?"

"You might know something—that would help me."

"I don't know anything at all. Why should I? She was only a stupid old charwoman. She kept her money under the floor and somebody robbed and murdered her for it. It was quite disgusting—beastly, the whole thing. Like things you read in the Sunday papers."

Poirot took that up quickly.

"Like the Sunday papers, yes. Like the *Sunday Comet*. You read, perhaps, the *Sunday Comet*?"

She jumped up, and made her way, blunderingly, towards the opened french windows. So uncertainly did she go that she actually collided with the window frame. Poirot was reminded of a beautiful big moth, fluttering blindly against a lamp shade.

She called: "Guy—Guy!"

A man's voice a little way away answered:

"Eve?"

"Come here quickly."

A tall man of about thirty-five came into sight. He quickened his pace and came across the terrace to the window. Eve Carpenter said vehemently:

"There's a man here—a foreigner. He's asking me all sorts of questions about that horrid murder last year. Some old char-woman—you remember? I *hate* things like that. You know I do."

Guy Carpenter frowned and came into the drawing-room through the window. He had a long face like a horse, he was pale and looked rather supercilious. His manner was pompous.

Hercule Poirot found him unattractive.

"May I ask what all this is about?" he asked. "Have you been annoying my wife?"

Hercule Poirot spread out his hands.

"The last thing I should wish is to annoy so charming a lady. I hoped only that, the deceased woman having worked for her, she might be able to aid me in the investigations I am making."

"But—what are these investigations?"

"Yes, ask him that," urged his wife.

"A fresh inquiry is being made into the circumstances of Mrs McGinty's death."

"Nonsense—the case is over."

"No, no, there you are in error. It is not over."

"A fresh inquiry, you say?" Guy Carpenter frowned. He said suspiciously: "By the police? Nonsense—you're nothing to do with the police."

"That is correct. I am working independently of the police."

"It's the Press," Eve Crpenter broke in. "Some horrid Sunday newspaper. He said so."

A gleam of caution came into Guy Carpenter's eye. In his position he was not anxious to antagonise the Press. He said, more amicably:

"My wife is very sensitive. Murders and things like that upset her. I'm sure it can't be necessary for you to bother her. She hardly knew this woman."

Eve said vehemently:

"She was only a stupid old charwoman. I told him so."

She added:

"And she was a frightful liar, too."

"Ah, that is interesting." Poirot turned a beaming face from one to the other of them. "So she told lies. That may give us a very valuable lead."

"I don't see how," said Eve sulkily.

"The establishment of motive," said Poirot. "That is the line I am following up."

"She was robbed of her savings," said Carpenter sharply. "That was the motive of the crime."

"Ah," said Poirot softly. "But was it?"

He rose like an actor who had just spoken a telling line.

"I regret if I have caused madame any pain," he said politely. "These affairs are always rather unpleasant."

"The whole business was distressing," said Carpenter quickly. "Naturally my wife didn't like being reminded of it. I'm sorry we can't help you with any information."

"Oh, but you have."

"I beg your pardon?"

Poirot said softly:

"*Mrs McGinty told lies*. A valuable fact. What lies, exactly, did she tell, madame?"

He waited politely for Eve Carpenter to speak. She said at last:

"Oh, nothing particular. I mean—I can't remember."

Conscious perhaps, that both men were looking at her expectantly, she said:

"Stupid things—about people. Things that couldn't be true."

Still there was a silence, then Poirot said:

"I see—she had a dangerous tongue."

Eve Carpenter made a quick movement.

"Oh no—I didn't mean as much as that. She was just a gossip, that was all."

"Just a gossip," said Poirot softly.

He made a gesture of farewell.

Guy Carpenter accompanied him out into the hall.

"This paper of yours—this Sunday paper—which is it?"

"The paper I mentioned to madame," replied Poirot carefully, "was the *Sunday Comet*."

He paused. Guy Carpenter repeated thoughtfully:

"The *Sunday Comet*. I don't very often see that, I'm afraid."

"It has interesting articles sometimes. And interesting illustrations. . . ."

Before the pause could be too long, he bowed, and said quickly:

"Au revoir, Mr Carpenter. I am sorry if I have—disturbed you."

Outside the gate, he looked back at the house.

"I wonder," he said. "Yes, I wonder . . ."

II

SUPERINTENDENT SPENCE sat opposite Hercule Poirot and sighed.

"I'm not saying you haven't got anything, M. Poirot," he said slowly. "Personally, I think you have. But it's thin. It's terribly thin!"

Poirot nodded.

"By itself it will not do. There must be more."

"My sergeant or I ought to have spotted that news-paper."

"No, no, you cannot blame yourself. The crime was so obvious. Robbery with violence. The room all pulled about, the money missing. Why should there be significance to you in a torn newspaper amongst the other confusion."

Spence repeated obstinately:

"I should have got that. And the bottle of ink——"

"I heard of that by the merest chance."

"Yet it meant something to you—why?"

"Only because of that chance phrase about writing a letter. You and I, Spence, we write so many letters—to us it is such a matter of course."

Superintendent Spence sighed. Then he laid out on the table four photographs.

"These are the photos you asked me to get—the original photos that the *Sunday Comet* used. At any rate they're a little clearer than the reproductions. But upon my word, they're not much to go upon. Old, faded—and with women the hair-do makes a difference. There's nothing definite in any of them to go upon like ears or a profile. That *cloche* hat and that arty hair and the roses! Doesn't give you a chance."

"You agree with me that we can discard Vera Blake?"

"I should think so. If Vera Blake was in Broadhinny,

everyone would know it—telling the sad story of her life seems to have been her speciality."

"What can you tell me about the others?"

"I've got what I could for you in the time. Eva Kane left the country after Craig was sentenced. And I can tell you the name she took. It was Hope. Symbolic, perhaps?"

Poirot murmured:

"Yes, yes—the romantic aproach. '*Beautiful Evelyn Hope is dead.*' A line from one of your poets. I dare say she thought of that. Was her name Evelyn, by the way?"

"Yes, I believe it was. But Eva was what she was known as always. And by the way, M. Poirot, now that we're on the subject, the police opinion of Eva Kane doesn't quite square with this article here. Very far from it."

Poirot smiled.

"What the police think—it is not evidence. But it is usually a sound guide. What did the police think of Eva Kane?"

"That she was by no means the innocent victim that the public thought her. I was quite a young chap at the time and remember hearing it discussed by my old Chief and Inspector Traill who was in charge of the case. Traill believed (no evidence, mind you) that the pretty little idea of putting Mrs Craig out of the way was all Eva Kane's idea—and that she not only thought of it, but she did it. Craig came home one day and found his little friend had taken a short cut. She thought it would all pass off as natural death, I dare say. But Craig knew better. He got the wind up and disposed of the body in the cellar and elaborated the plan of having Mrs Craig die abroad. Then, when the whole thing came out, he was frantic in his asseverations that he'd done it alone, that Eva Kane had known nothing about it. Well," Superintendent Spence shrugged his shoulders, "nobody could prove anything else. The stuff was in the house. Either of them could have used it. Pretty Eva Kane was all innocence and horror. Very well she did it, too: a clever little actress. Inspector Traill had his doubts—but there was nothing to go upon. I'm giving you that for what it's worth, M. Poirot. It's not evidence."

"But it suggests the possibility that one, at least, of these 'tragic women' was something more than a tragic woman—that she was a murderess and that, if the incentive was strong enough, she might murder again . . . And now the next one, Janice Courtland, what can you tell me about her?"

"I've looked up the files. A nasty bit of goods. If we hanged Edith Thompson we certainly ought to have hanged Janice Courtland. An unpleasant pair, she and her husband, nothing to choose between them, and she worked on that young man until she had him all up in arms. But all the time, mark you, there was a rich man in the background, and it was to marry him she wanted her husband out of the way."

"Did she marry him?"

Spence shook his head.

"No idea."

"She went abroad—and then?"

Spence shook his head.

"She was a free woman. She'd not been charged with anything. Whether she married, or what happened to her, we don't know."

"One might meet her at a cocktail party any day," said Poirot, thinking of Dr Rendell's remark.

"Exactly."

Poirot shifted his gaze to the last photograph.

"And the child? Lily Gamboll?"

"Too young to be charged with murder. She was sent to an approved school. Good record there. Was taught shorthand and typing and was found a job under probation. Did well. Last heard of in Ireland. I think we could wash her out, you know, M. Poirot, same as Vera Blake. After all, she'd made good, and people don't hold it against a kid of twelve for doing something in a fit of temper. What about washing her out?"

"I might," said Poirot, "if it were not for the chopper. It is undeniable that Lily Gamboll used a chopper on her aunt, and the unknown killer of Mrs McGinty used something that was said to be like a chopper."

"Perhaps you're right. Now, M. Poirot, let's have your side of things. Nobody's tried to do you in, I'm glad to see."

"N-no," said Poirot, with a momentary hesitation.

"I don't mind telling you I've had the wind up about you once or twice since that evening in London. Now what are the possibilities amongst the residents of Broadhinny?"

Poirot opened his little notebook.

"Eva Kane, if she is still alive, would be now approaching sixty. Her daughter, of whose adult life our *Sunday Comet* paints such a touching picture, would be now in the thirties. Lily Gamboll would also be about that age. Janice Courtland would now be not far short of fifty."

Spence nodded agreement.

"So we come to the residents of Broadhinny, with especial reference to those for whom Mrs McGinty worked."

"That last is a fair assumption, I think."

"Yes, it is complicated by the fact that Mrs McGinty did occasional odd work here and there, but we will assume for the time being that she saw whatever she did see, presumably a photograph, at one of her regular 'houses.'"

"Agreed."

"Then as far as age goes, that gives us as possibles—first the Wetherbys where Mrs McGinty worked on the day of her death. Mrs Wetherby is the right age for Eva Kane and she has a daughter of the right age to be Eva Kane's daughter—a daughter said to be by a previous marriage."

"And as regards the photograph?"

"*Mon cher*, no positive identification from that is possible. Too much time has passed, too much water, as you say, has flowed from the waterworks. One can but say this: Mrs Wetherby has been, decidedly, a pretty woman. She has all the mannerisms of one. She seems much too fragile and helpless to do murder, but then that was, I understand, the popular belief about Eva Kane. How much actual physical strength would have been needed to kill Mrs McGinty is difficult to say without knowing exactly what weapon was used, its handle, the ease with which it could be swung, the sharpness of its cutting edge, etcetera."

"Yes, yes. Why we never managed to find that—but go on."

"The only other remarks I have to make about the Wetherby household are that Mr Wetherby could make himself, and I fancy does make himself, very unpleasant if he likes. The daughter is fanatically devoted to her mother. She hates her stepfather. I do not remark on these facts. I present them, only, for consideration. Daughter might kill to prevent mother's past coming to stepfather's ears. Mother might kill for same reason. Father might kill to prevent 'scandal' coming out. More murders have been committed for respectability than one would believe possible! The Wetherbys are 'nice people.'"

Spence nodded.

"If—I say if—there is anything in this *Sunday Comet* business, then the Wetherbys are clearly the best bet," he said.

"Exactly. The only other person in Broadhinny who would fit in age with Eva Kane is Mrs Upward. There are two arguments against Mrs Upward, as Eva Kane, having killed Mrs McGinty. First, she suffers from arthritis, and spends most of her time in a wheeled chair——"

"In a book," said Spence enviously, "that wheeled chair business would be phony, but in real life it's probably all according to Cocker."

"Secondly," continued Poirot, "Mrs Upward seems of a dogmatic and forceful disposition, more inclined to bully than to coax, which does not agree with the accounts of our young Eva. On the other hand, people's characters do develop and self-assertiveness is a quality that often comes with age."

"That's true enough," conceded Spence. "Mrs Upward— not impossible but unlikely. Now the other possibilities. Janice Courtland?"

"Can, I think, be ruled out. There is no one in Broadhinny the right age."

"Unless one of the young women is Janice Courtland with her face lifted. Don't mind me—just my little joke."

"There are three women of thirty-odd. There is Deirdre Henderson. There is Dr Rendell's wife, and there is Mrs Guy Carpenter. That is to say, any one of these *could* be Lily Gamboll or alternatively Eva Kane's daughter as far as age goes."

"And as far as possibility goes?"

Poirot sighed.

"Eva Kane's daughter may be tall or short, dark or fair—we have no guide to what she looks like. We have considered Deirdre Henderson in that role. Now for the other two. First of all I will tell you this: Mrs Rendell is afraid of something."

"Afraid of you?"

"I think so."

"That might be significant," said Spence slowly. "you're suggesting that Mrs Rendell might be Eva Kane's daughter *or* Lily Gamboll. Is she fair or dark?"

"Fair."

"Lily Gamboll was a fair-haired child."

"Mrs Carpenter is also fair-haired. A most expensively made-up young woman. Whether she is actually good-looking or not, she has very remarkable eyes. Lovely wide-open dark-blue eyes."

"Now, Poirot——" Spence shook his head at his friend.

"Do you know what she looked like as she ran out of the room to call her husband? I was reminded of a lovely fluttering moth. She blundered into the furniture and stretched her hands out like a blind thing."

Spence looked at him indulgently.

"Romantic, that's what you are, M. Poirot," he said. "You and your lovely fluttering moths and wide-open blue eyes."

"Not at all," said Poirot. "My friend Hastings, *he* was romantic and sentimental, me never! Me, I am severely practical. What I am telling you is that if a girl's claims to beauty depend principally on the loveliness of her eyes, then, no matter how short-sighted she is, she will take off her spectacles and learn to feel her way round even if outlines are blurred and distances hard to judge."

And gently, with his forefinger, he tapped the photograph of the child Lily Gamboll in her thick disfiguring spectacles.

"So that's what you think? Lily Gamboll?"

"No, I speak only of what might be. At the time Mrs McGinty died Mrs Carpenter was not yet Mrs Carpenter. She was a young war widow, very badly off, living in a labourer's cottage. She was engaged to be married to the rich man of the neighbourhood— a man with political ambitions and a great sense of his own importance. If Guy Carpenter had found out that he was about to marry, say, a child of low origin who had attained notoriety by hitting her aunt on the head with a chopper, or alternatively the daughter of Craig, one of the most notorious criminals of the century—prominently placed in your Chamber of Horrors— well, one asks would he have gone through with it? You say

94

perhaps, if he loved the girl, *yes*! But he is not quite that kind of man. I would put him down as selfish, ambitious, and a man very nice in the manner of his reputation. I think that if young Mrs Selkirk, as she was then, was anxious to achieve the match she would have been very very anxious that no hint of an unfortunate nature got to her fiancé's ears."

"I see, you think it's her, do you?"

"I tell you again, *mon cher*, *I do not know*. I examine only possibilities. Mrs Carpenter was on her guard against me, watchful, alarmed."

"That looks bad."

"Yes, yes, but it is all very difficult. Once I stayed with some friends in the country and they went out to do the shooting. You know the way it goes? One walks with the dogs and the guns, and the dogs, they put up the game—it flies out of the woods, up into the air and you go bang bang. That is like us. It is not only one bird we put up, perhaps, there are other birds in the covert. Birds, perhaps, with which we have nothing to do. But the birds themselves do not know that. We must make very sure, *cher ami*, which is *our* bird. During Mrs Carpenter's widowhood, there may have been indiscretions—no worse than that, but still inconvenient. Certainly there must be some reason why she says to me quickly that Mrs McGinty was a liar!"

Superintendent Spence rubbed his nose.

"Let's get this clear, Poirot. What *do* you really think?"

"What I think does not matter. I must *know*. And as yet, the dogs have only just gone into the covert."

Spence murmured: "If we could get anything at all definite. One really suspicious circumstance. As it is, it's all theory and rather far-fetched theory at that. The whole thing's thin, you know, as I said. *Does* anyone really murder for the reasons we've been considering?"

"That depends," said Poirot. "It depends on a lot of family circumstances we do not know. But the passion for respectability is very strong. These are not artists or Bohemians. Very nice people live in Broadhinny. My post-mistress said so. And nice people like to preserve their niceness. Years of happy married life, maybe, no suspicion that you were once a notorious figure in one of the most sensational murder trials, no suspicion that your child is the child of a famous murderer. One might say 'I would rather die than have my husband know!' Or 'I would rather die than have my daughter discover who she is!' And then you would go on to reflect that it would be better, perhaps, if Mrs McGinty died. . . ."

Spence said quietly:

"So you think it's the Wetherbys."

"No. They fit the best, perhaps, but that is all. In actual character, Mrs Upward is a more *likely* killer than Mrs Wetherby. She has determination and willpower and she fairly dotes on her son. To prevent his learning of what happened before she married his father and settled down to respectable married bliss, I think she might go far."

"Would it upset him so much?"

"Personally I do not think so. Young Robin has a modern sceptical point of view, is thoroughly selfish, and in any case is less devoted, I should say, to his mother than she to him. He is not another James Bentley."

"Granting Mrs Upward *was* Eva Kane, her son Robin wouldn't kill Mrs McGinty to prevent that fact coming out?"

"Not for a moment, I should say. He would probably capitalise it. Use the fact for publicity for his plays! I can't see Robin Upward committing a murder for respectability, or devotion, or in fact for anything but a good solid gain to Robin Upward."

Spence sighed. He said: "It's a wide field. We may be able to get something on the past history of these people. But it will take time. The war has complicated things. Records destroyed— endless opportunities for people who want to cover their traces doing so by means of other people's identity cards, etc., especially after 'incidents' when nobody could know which corpse was which! If we could concentrate on just *one* lot, but you've got so many possibles, M. Poirot."

"We may be able to cut them down soon."

Poirot left the superintendent's office with less cheerfulness in his heart than he had shown in his manner. He was obsessed as Spence was, by the urge of time. If only he could have *time* . . .

And further back still was the one teasing doubt—was the

edifice he and Spence had built up really sound? Supposing, after all, that James Bentley *was* guilty. . . .

He did not give in to that doubt, but it worried him.

Again and again he had gone over in his mind the interview he had had with James Bentley. He thought of it now whilst he waited on the platform of Kilchester for his train to come in. It had been market day and the platform was crowded. More crowds were coming in through the barriers.

Poirot leaned forward to look. Yes, the train was coming at last. Before he could right himself he felt a sudden hard purposeful shove in the small of his back. It was so violent and so unexpected that he was taken completely unawares. In another second he would have fallen on the line under the incoming train, but a man beside him on the platform caught hold of him in the nick of time, pulling him back.

"Why, whatever came over you?" he demanded. He was a big burly Army sergeant. "Taken queer? Man, you were nearly under the train."

"I thank you. I thank you a thousand times." Already the crowd was milling round them, boarding the train, others leaving it.

"All right now? I'll help you in."

Shaken, Poirot subsided on to a seat.

Useless to say "I was pushed," but he *had* been pushed. Up till that very evening he had gone about consciously on his guard, on the alert for danger. But after talking with Spence, after Spence's bantering inquiry as to whether any attempt on his life had been made, he had insensibly regarded the danger as over or unlikely to materialise.

But how wrong he had been! Amongst those he had interviewed in Broadhinny one interview had achieved a result. Somebody had been afraid. Somebody had sought to put an end to his dangerous resuscitation of a losed case.

From a call-box in the station at Broadhinny, Poirot rang up Superintendent Spence.

"It is you, *mon aimi*? Attend, I pray. I have news for you. Splendid news. *Somebody has tried to kill me.* . . ."

He listened with satisfaction to the flow of remarks from the other end.

"No, I am not hurt. But it was a very near thing. . . . Yes, under a train. No, I did not see who did it. But be assured, my friend, *I shall find out*. We know now—that we are on the right track."

12

i

THE MAN WHO was testing the electric meter passed the time of day with Guy Carpenter's superior manservant, who was watching him.

"Electricity's going to operate on a new basis," he explained. "Graded flat rate according to occupancy."

The superior butler remarked sceptically:

"What you mean is it's going to cost more like everything else."

"That depends. Fair shares for all, that's what I say. Did you go in to the meeting at Kilchester last night?"

"No."

"Your boss, Mr Carpenter, spoke very well, they say. Think he'll get in?"

"It was a near shave last time, I believe."

"Yes. A hundred and twenty-five majority, something like that. Do you drive him in to these meetings, or does he drive himself?"

"Usually drives himself. Likes driving. He's got a Rolls Bentley."

"Does himself well. Mrs Carpenter drive too?"

"Yes. Drives a lot too fast, in my opinion."

"Women usually do. Was she at the meeting last night too? Or isn't she interested in politics?"

The superior butler grinned.

"Pretends she is, anyway. However, she didn't stick it out last night. Had a headache or something and left in the middle of the speeches."

"Ah!" The electrician peered into the fuse boxes. "Nearly done now," he remarked. He put a few more desultory questions as he collected his tools and prepared to depart.

He walked briskly down the drive, but round the corner from the gateway he stopped and made an entry in his pocket book.

"C. drove home alone last night. Reached home 10.30 (approx.). Could have been at Kilchester Central Station time indicated. Mrs C. left meeting early. Got home only ten minutes before C. Said to have come home by train."

It was the second entry in the electrician's book. The first ran:

"Dr R. called out on case last night. Direction of Kilchester. Could have been at Kilchester Central Station at time indicated. Mrs R. alone all evening in house (?) After taking coffee in, Mrs Scott, housekeeper, did not see her again that night. Has small car of her own."

ii

At Laburnums, collaboration was in process.

Robin Upward was saying earnestly:

"You do see, don't you, what a wonderful line that is? And if we really get a feeling of sex antagonism between the chap and the girl it'll pep the whole thing up enormously!"

Sadly, Mrs Oliver ran her hands through her windswept grey hair, causing it to look as though swept not by wind but by a tornado.

"You do see what I mean, don't you, Ariadne darling?"

"Oh, I see what you *mean*," said Mrs Oliver gloomily.

"But the main thing is for you to feel really happy about it."

Nobody but a really determined self-deceiver could have thought that Mrs Oliver looked happy.

Robin continued blithely:

"What I feel is, here's that wonderful young man, parachuted down——"

Mrs Oliver interrupted:

"He's sixty."

"Oh *no*!"

"He is."

"I don't *see* him like that. Thirty-five—not a day older."

"But I've been writing books about him for thirty years, and he was at least thirty-five in the first one."

"But, darling, if he's sixty, you can't have the tension between him and the girl—what's her name? Ingrid. I mean, it would make him just a nasty old man!"

"It certainly would."

"So you see, he *must* be thirty-five," said Robin triumphantly.

"Then he can't be Sven Hjerson. Just make him a Norwegian young man who's in the Resistance Movement."

"But darling Ariadne, the whole *point* of the play is Sven Hjerson. You've got an enormous public who simply *adore* Sven Hjerson, and who'll flock to see Sven Hjerson. He's *box office*, darling!"

"But people who read my books *know* what he's like! You can't invent an entirely new young man in the Norwegian Resistance Movement and just *call* him Sven Hjerson."

"Ariadne darling, I *did* explain all that. It's not a *book*, darling, it's a *play*. And we've just got to have glamour! And if we get this tension, this antagonism between Sven Hjerson and this—what's-her-name?—Karen—you know, all against each other and yet really frightfully attracted——"

"Sven Hjerson never cared for women," said Mrs Oliver coldly.

"But you *can't* have him a *pansy*, darling! Not for *this* sort of play. I mean it's not green bay trees or anything like *that*. It's thrills and murders and clean open-air fun."

The mention of open air had its effect.

"I think I'm going out," said Mrs Oliver abruptly. "I need air. I need air *badly*."

"Shall I come with you?" asked Robin tenderly.

"No, I'd rather go alone."

"Just as you like, darling. Perhaps you're right. I'd better go and whip up an egg nog for Madre. The poor sweet is feeling just a teeny weeny bit left out of things. She *does* like attention, you know. And you'll think about that scene in the cellar, won't you? The whole thing is coming really wonderfully well. It's going to be the most tremendous success. I *know* it is!"

Mrs Oliver sighed.

"But the main thing," continued Robin, "is for you to feel happy about it!"

Casting a cold look at him, Mrs Oliver threw a showy military cape which she had once bought in Italy about her ample shoulders and went out into Broadhinny.

She would forget her troubles, she decided, by turning her mind to the elucidation of real crime. Hercule Poirot needed help. She would take a look at the inhabitants of Broadhinny, exercise her woman's intuition which had never failed, and tell Poirot who the murderer was. Then he would only have to get the necessary evidence.

Mrs Oliver started her quest by going down the hill to the post office and buying two pounds of apples. During the purchase, she entered into amicable conversation with Mrs Sweetiman.

Having agreed that the weather was very warm for the time of year, Mrs Oliver remarked that she was staying with Mrs Upward at Laburnums.

"Yes, I know. You'll be the lady from London that writes the murder books? Three of them I've got here now in Penguins."

Mrs Oliver cast a glance over the Penguin display. It was slightly overlaid by children's waders.

"The Affair of the Second Goldfish," she mused, "that's quite a good one. *The Cat it was Who Died*—that's where I made a blowpipe a foot long and it's really *six* feet. Ridiculous that a blowpipe should be that size, but someone wrote from a museum to tell me so. Sometimes I think there are people who only read books in the hope of finding mistakes in them. What's the other one of them? Oh! *Death of a Débutante*—that's frightful tripe! I made sulphonal soluble in water and it isn't, and the whole thing is wildly impossible from start to finish. At least eight people die before Sven Hjerson gets his brainwave."

"Very popular they are," said Mrs Sweetiman, unmoved by this interesting self-criticism. "You wouldn't believe! I've never read any myself, because I don't really get time for reading."

"You had a murder of your own down here, didn't you?" said Mrs Oliver.

"Yes, last November that was. Almost next door here, as you might say."

"I hear there's a detective down here, looking into it?"

"Ah, you mean the little foreign gentleman up at Long Meadows? He was in here only yesterday and——"

Mrs Sweetiman broke off as another customer entered for stamps.

She bustled round to the post office side.

"Good morning, Miss Henderson. Warm for the time of year, to-day."

"Yes, it is."

Mrs Oliver stared hard at the tall girl's back. She had a Sealyham with her on a lead.

"Means the fruit blossom will get nipped later!" said Mrs Sweetiman, with gloomy relish. "How's Mrs Wetherby keeping?"

"Fairly well, thank you. She hasn't been out much. There's been such an east wind lately."

"There's a very good picture on at Kilchester this week, Miss Henderson. You ought to go."

"I thought of going last night, but I couldn't really bother."

"It's Betty Grable next week—I'm out of 5*s.* books of stamps. Will two 2*s.* 6*d.* ones do you?"

As the girl went out, Mrs Oliver said:

"Mrs Wetherby's an invalid, isn't she?"

"That's as may be," Mrs Sweetiman replied rather acidly. "There's *some* of us as hasn't the time to lay by."

"I do so agree with you," said Mrs Oliver. "I tell Mrs Upward that if she'd only make more of an effort to use her legs it would be better for her."

Mrs Sweetiman looked amused.

"She gets about when she wants to—or so I've heard."

"Does she now?"

Mrs Oliver considered the source of information.

"Janet?" she hazarded.

"Janet Groom grumbles a bit," said Mrs Sweetiman. "And you can hardly wonder, can you? Miss Groom's not so young herself and she has the rheumatism cruel bad when the wind's in the east. But archititis, it's called, when it's the gentry has it, *and* invalid chairs and what not. Ah well, I wouldn't risk losing the use of my legs, I wouldn't. But there, nowadays even if you've got a chilblain you run to the doctor with it so as to get your money's worth out of the National Health. Too much of this health business we've got. Never did you any good thinking how bad you feel."

"I expect you're right," said Mrs Oliver.

She picked up her apples and went out in pursuit of Deirdre Henderson. This was not difficult, since the Sealyham was old and fat and was enjoying a leisurely examination of tufts of grass and pleasant smells.

Dogs, Mrs Oliver considered, were always a means of introduction.

"What a darling!" she exclaimed.

The big young woman with the plain face looked gratified.

"He *is* rather attractive," she said. "Aren't you, Ben?"

Ben looked up, gave a slight wiggle of his sausage-like body, resumed his nasal inspection of a tuft of thistles, approved it and proceeded to register approval in the usual manner.

"Does he fight?" asked Mrs Oliver. "Sealyhams do very often."

"Yes, he's an awful fighter. That's why I keep him on the lead."

"I thought so."

Both women considered the Sealyham.

Then Deirdre Henderson said with a kind of rush:

"You're—you're Ariadne Oliver, aren't you?"

"Yes. I'm staying with the Upwards."

"I know. Robin told us you were coming. I must tell you how much I enjoy your books."

Mrs Oliver, as usual, went purple with embarrassment.

"Oh," she murmured unhappily. "I'm very glad," she added gloomily.

"I haven't read as many of them as I'd like to, because we get books sent down from the Times Book Club and Mother doesn't like detective stories. She's frightfully sensitive and they keep her awake at night. But I adore them."

"You've had a real crime down here, haven't you?" said Mrs Oliver. "Which house was it? One of these cottages?"

"That one there."

Deirdre Henderson spoke in a rather choked voice.

Mrs Oliver directed her gaze on Mrs McGinty's former dwelling, the front doorstep of which was at present occupied by two unpleasant little Kiddles who were happily torturing a cat. As Mrs Oliver stepped forward to remonstrate, the cat escaped by a firm use of its claws.

The eldest Kiddle, who had been severely scratched, set up a howl.

"Serves you right," said Mrs Oliver, adding to Deirdre Henderson: "It doesn't *look* like a house where there's been a murder, does it?"

"No, it doesn't."

Both women seemed to be in accord about that.

Mrs Oliver continued:

"An old charwoman, wasn't it, and somebody robbed her?"

"Her lodger. She had some money—under the floor."

"I see."

Deirdre Henderson said suddenly:

"But perhaps it wasn't him after all. There's a funny little man down here—a foreigner. His name's Hercule Poirot——"

"Hercule Poirot? Oh yes, I know all about him."

"Is he really a detective?"

"My dear, he's frightfully celebrated. And terribly clever."

"Then perhaps he'll find out that he didn't do it after all."

"Who?"

"The—the lodger. James Bentley. Oh, I do hope he'll get off."

"Do you? Why?"

"Because I don't want it to be him. I never wanted it to be him."

Mrs Oliver looked at her curiously, startled by the passion in her voice.

"Did you know him?"

"No," said Deirdre slowly, "I didn't *know* him. But once Ben got his foot caught in a trap and he helped me to get him free. And we talked a little. . . ."

"What was he like?"

"He was dreadfully lonely. His mother had just died. He was frightfully fond of his mother."

"And you are very fond of yours?" said Mrs Oliver acutely.

"Yes. That made me understand. Understand what he felt, I mean. Mother and I—we've just got each other, you see."

"I thought Robin told me that you had a stepfather."

Deirdre said bitterly: "Oh, yes, I've got a *step*father."

Mrs Oliver said vaguely: "It's not the same thing, is it, as one's own father. Do you remember your own father?"

"No, he died before I was born. Mother married Mr Wetherby when I was four years old. I—I've always hated him. And Mother——" She paused before saying: "Mother's had a very sad life. She's had no sympathy or understanding. My stepfather is a most unfeeling man, hard and cold."

Mrs Oliver nodded, and then murmured:

"This James Bentley doesn't sound at all like a criminal."

"I never thought the police would arrest *him*. I'm sure it must have been some tramp. There are horrid tramps along this road sometimes. It must have been one of them."

Mrs Oliver said consolingly:

"Perhaps Hercule Poirot will find out the truth."

"Yes, perhaps——"

She turned off abruptly into the gateway of Hunter's Close.

Mrs Oliver looked after her for a moment or two, then drew a small notebook from her handbag. In it she wrote: "*Not* Deirdre Henderson," and underlined the *not* so firmly that the pencil broke.

iii

Half-way up the hill she met Robin Upward coming down it with a handsome platinum-haired young woman.

Robin introduced them.

"This is the wonderful Ariadne Oliver, Eve," he said. 'My dear, I don't know *how* she does it. Looks so benevolent, too, doesn't she? Not at all as though she wallowed in crime. This is Eve Carpenter. Her husband is going to be our next Member. The present one, Sir George Cartwright, is quite gaga, poor old man. He jumps out at young girls from behind doors."

"Robin, you mustn't invent such terrible lies. You'll discredit the Party."

"Well, why should *I* care? It isn't my Party. I'm a Liberal. That's the only Party it's possible to belong to nowadays, really small and select, and without a chance of getting in. I adore lost causes."

He added to Mrs Oliver:

"Eve wants us to come in for drinks this evening. A sort of

party for you, Ariadne. You know, meet the lion. We're all terribly terribly thrilled to have you here. Can't you put the scene of your next murder in Broadhinny?"

"Oh do, Mrs Oliver," said Eve Carpenter.

"You can easily get Sven Hjerson down here," said Robin. "He can be like Hercule Poirot, staying at the Summerhayes' Guest House. We're just going there now because I told Eve Hercule Poirot is just as much a celebrity in his line as you are in yours, and she says she was rather rude to him yesterday, so she's going to ask him to the party too. But seriously dear, do make your next murder happen in Broadhinny. We'd all be so thrilled."

"Oh do, Mrs Oliver. It would be such fun," said Eve Carpenter.

"Who shall we have as murderer and who as victim?" asked Robin.

"Who's your present charwoman?" asked Mrs Oliver.

"Oh my dear, not *that* kind of murder. So dull. No, I think Eve here would make rather a nice victim. Strangled, perhaps, with her own nylon stockings. No, that's been done."

"I think *you'd* better be murdered, Robin," said Eve. "The coming playwright, stabbed in country cottage."

"We haven't settled on a murderer yet," said Robin. "What about my Mamma? Using her wheeled chair so that there wouldn't be footprints. I think that would be lovely."

"She wouldn't want to stab you, though, Robin."

Robin considered.

"No, perhaps not. As a matter of fact I was considering her strangling *you*. She wouldn't mind doing that half as much."

"But I want *you* to be the victim. And the person who kills you can be Deirdre Henderson. The repressed plain girl whom nobody notices."

"There you are, Ariadne," said Robin. "The whole plot of your next novel presented to you. All you'll have to do is work in a few false clues, and—of course—do the actual writing. Oh, goodness, what terrible dogs Maureen does have."

They had turned in at the gate of Long Meadows, and two Irish wolfhounds had rushed forward, barking.

Maureen Summerhayes came out into the stableyard with a bucket in her hand.

"Down, Flyn. Come here, Cormic. Hallo. I'm just cleaning out Piggy's stable."

"We know that, darling," said Robin. "We can smell you from here. How's Piggy getting along?"

"We had a terrible fright about him yesterday. He was lying down and he didn't want his breakfast. Johnnie and I read up all the diseases in the Pig Book and couldn't sleep for worrying about him, but this morning he was frightfully well and gay and absolutely charged Johnnie when Johnnie came in with his food. Knocked him flat, as a matter of fact. Johnnie had to go and have a bath."

"What exciting lives you and Johnnie lead," said Robin.

Eve said: "Will you and Johnnie come in and have drinks with us this evening, Maureen?"

"Love to."

"To meet Mrs Oliver," said Robin, "but actually you can meet her now. This is she."

"Are you really?" said Maureen. "How thrilling? You and Robin are doing a play together, aren't you?"

"It's coming along splendidly," said Robin. "By the way, Ariadne, I had a brainwave after you went out this morning. About casting."

"Oh, casting," said Mrs Oliver in a relieved voice.

"I know just the right person to play Eric. Cecil Leech—he's playing in the Little Rep at Cullenquay. We'll run over and see the show one evening."

"We want your P.G.," said Eve to Maureen. "Is he about? I want to ask him to-night too."

"We'll bring him along," said Maureen.

"I think I'd better ask him myself. As a matter of fact I was a bit rude to him yesterday."

"Oh! Well, he's somewhere about," said Maureen vaguely. "In the garden, I think—Cormic—Flynn—those damned dogs——" She dropped the bucket with a clatter and ran in the direction of the duck pond, whence a furious quacking had arisen.

13

MRS OLIVER, glass in hand, approached Hercule Poirot towards the end of the Carpenters' party. Up till that moment they had each of them been the centre of an admiring circle. Now that a good deal of gin had been consumed, and the party was going well, there was a tendency for old friends to get together and retail local scandal, and the two outsiders were able to talk to each other.

"Come out on the terrace," said Mrs Oliver, in a conspirator's whisper.

At the same time she pressed into his hand a small piece of paper.

Together they stepped out through the french windows and walked along the terrace. Poirot unfolded the piece of paper.

"Dr Rendell," he read.

He looked questioningly at Mrs Oliver. Mrs Oliver nodded vigorously, a large plume of grey hair falling across her face as she did so.

"He's the murderer," said Mrs Oliver.

"You think so? Why?"

"I just know it," said Mrs Oliver. "He's the *type*. Hearty and genial, and all that."

"Perhaps."

Poirot sounded unconvinced.

"But what would you say was his motive?"

"Unprofessional conduct," said Mrs Oliver. "And Mrs McGinty knew about it. But whatever the reason was, you can be quite sure it was him. I've looked at all the others, and he's the one."

In reply, Poirot remarked conversationally:

"Last night somebody tried to push me on to the railway line at Kilchester station."

"Good gracious. To kill you, do you mean?"

"I have no doubt that was the idea."

"And Dr Rendell was out on a case, I know he was."

"I understand—yes—that Dr Rendell *was* out on a case."

"Then that settles it," said Mrs Oliver with satisfaction.

"Not quite," said Poirot. "Both Mr and Mrs Carpenter were in Kilchester last night and came home separately. Mrs Rendell may have sat at home all the evening listening to her wireless or she may not—no one can say. Miss Henderson often goes to the pictures in Kilchester."

"She didn't last night. She was at home. She told me so."

"You cannot believe all you are told," said Poirot reprovingly. "Families hang together. The foreign maid, Frieda, on the other hand, *was* at the pictures last night, so she cannot tell us who was or was not at home at Hunter's Close! You see, it is not so easy to narrow things down."

"I can probably vouch for our lot," said Mrs Oliver. "What time did you say this happened?"

"At nine thirty-five exactly."

"Then at any rate Laburnums has got a clean bill of health. From eight o'clock to half-past ten, Robin, his mother, and I were playing poker patience."

"I thought possibly that you and he were closeted together doing the collaboration?"

"Leaving Mamma to leap on a motor bicycle concealed in the shrubbery?" Mrs Oliver laughed. "No, Mamma was under our eye." She sighed as sadder thoughts came to her. "Collaboration," she said bitterly. "The whole thing's a nightmare! How would *you* like to see a big black moustache stuck on to Superintendent Battle and be told it was *you*."

Poirot blinked a little.

"But it is a nightmare, that suggestion!"

"Now you know what I suffer."

"I, too, I suffer," said Poirot. "The cooking of Madame Summerhayes, it is beyond description. It is not cooking at all. And the draughts, the cold winds, the upset stomachs of the cats, the long hairs of the dogs, the broken legs of the chairs, the terrible, terrible bed in which I sleep"—he shut his eyes in remembrance of agonies—"the tepid water in the bathroom, the holes in the stair carpet, and the coffee—words cannot describe to you the fluid which they serve to you as coffee. It is an affront to the stomach."

"Dear me," said Mrs Oliver. "And yet, you know, she's awfully nice."

"Mrs Summerhayes? She is charming. She is quite charming. That makes it much more difficult."

"Here she comes now," said Mrs Oliver.

Maureen Summerhayes was approaching them.

There was an ecstatic look on her freckled face. She carried a glass in her hand. She smiled at them both with affection.

"I think I'm a bit tiddly," she announced. "Such lots of lovely gin. I do like parties! We don't often have one in Broadhinny. It's because of you both being so celebrated. I wish *I* could write books. The trouble with me is, I can't do *anything* properly."

"You are a good wife and mother, madame," said Poirot primly.

Maureen's eyes opened wide. Attractive hazel eyes in a small freckled face. Mrs Oliver wondered how old she was. Not much more than thirty, she guessed.

"Am I?" said Maureen. "I wonder. I love them all terribly, but is that enough?"

Poirot coughed.

"If you will not think me presumptuous, madame. A wife who truly loves her husband should take great care of his stomach. It is important, the stomach."

Maureen looked slightly affronted.

"Johnnie's got a wonderful stomach," she said indignantly. "Absolutely flat. Practically not a stomach at all."

"I was referring to what is put inside it."

"You mean my cooking," said Maureen. "I never think it matters much *what* one eats."

Poirot groaned.

"Or what one wears," said Maureen dreamily. "Or what one does. I don't think *things* matter—not really."

She was silent for a moment or two, her eyes alcoholically hazy, as though she was looking into the far distance.

"There was a woman writing in the paper the other day," she said suddenly. "A really stupid letter. Asking what was best to do—to let your child be adopted by someone who could give it every advantage—*every advantage*, that's what she said—and she meant a good education, and clothes and comfortable surroundings—or whether to keep it when you couldn't give it advantages of any kind. I think that's stupid—*really* stupid. If you can just give a child enough to eat—that's all that matters."

She stared down into her empty glass as though it were a crystal.

"*I* ought to know," she said. "I was an adopted child. My mother parted with me and I had every advantage, as they call it. And it's always hurt—always—always—to know that you weren't really wanted, that your mother could let you go."

"It was a sacrifice for your good, perhaps," said Poirot.

Her clear eyes met his.

"I don't think that's ever true. It's the way they put it to themselves. But what it boils down to is that they can, really, get on without you. . . . And it hurts. I wouldn't give up *my* children—not for all the advantages in the world!"

"I think you're quite right," said Mrs Oliver.

"And I, too, agree," said Poirot.

"Then that's all right," said Maureen cheerfully. "What are we arguing about?"

Robin, who had come along the terrace to join them, said:

"Yes, what are you arguing about?"

"Adoption," said Maureen. "I don't like being adopted, do you?"

"Well, it's much better than being an orphan, don't you think so, darling? I think we ought to go now, don't you? Ariadne?"

The guests left in a body. Dr Rendell had already had to hurry away. They walked down the hill together talking gaily with that extra hilarity that a series of cocktails induces.

When they reached the gate of Laburnums, Robin insisted that they should all come in.

"Just to tell Madre all about the party. So boring for her, poor sweet, not to have been able to go because her leg was playing her up. But she so hates being left out of things."

They surged in cheerfully and Mrs Upward seemed pleased to see them.

"Who else was there?" she asked. "The Wetherbys?"

"No, Mrs Wetherby didn't feel well enough, and that dim Henderson girl wouldn't come without her."

"She's really rather pathetic, isn't she?" said Shelagh Rendell.

"I think almost pathological, don't you?" said Robin.

"It's that mother of hers," said Maureen. "Some mothers really do almost eat their young, don't they?"

She flushed suddenly as she met Mrs Upward's quizzical eye.

"Do I devour you, Robin?" Mrs Upward asked.

"Madre! Of course not!"

To cover her confusion Maureen hastily plunged into an account of her breeding experiences with Irish wolfhounds. The conversation became technical.

Mrs Upward said decisively:

"You can't get away from heredity—in people as well as dogs."

Shelagh Rendell murmured:

"Don't you think it's environment?"

Mrs Upward cut her short.

"No, my dear, I don't. Environment can give a veneer—no more. It's what's bred in people that counts."

Hercule Poirot's eyes rested curiously on Shelagh Rendell's flushed face. She said with what seemed unnecessary passion:

"But that's cruel—unfair."

Mrs Upward said: "Life is unfair."

The slow lazy voice of Johnnie Summerhayes joined in.

"I agree with Mrs Upward. Breeding tells. That's been my creed always."

Mrs Oliver said questioningly: "You mean things are handed down. Unto the third or fourth generation——"

Maureen Summerhayes said suddenly in her sweet high voice:

"But that quotation goes on: 'And show mercy unto thousands.'"

Once again everybody seemed a little embarrassed, perhaps at the serious note that had crept into the conversation.

They made a diversion by attacking Poirot.

"Tell us all about Mrs McGinty, M. Poirot. Why didn't the dreary lodger kill her?"

"He used to mutter, you know," said Robin. "Walking about

in the lanes. I've often met him. And really, definitely, he looked frightfully queer."

"You must have some reason for thinking he didn't kill her, M. Poirot. Do tell us."

Poirot smiled at them. He twirled his moustache.

"If he didn't kill her, who did?"

"Yes, who did?"

Mrs Upward said drily: "Don't embarrass the man. He probably suspects one of us."

"One of us? Oo!"

In the clamour Poirot's eyes met those of Mrs Upward. They were amused and—something else—challenging?

"He suspects one of us," said Robin delightedly. "Now then, Maureen," he assumed the manner of a bullying K.C., "Where were you on the night of the—what night *was* it?"

"November 22nd," said Poirot.

"On the night of the 22nd?"

"Gracious, I don't know," said Maureen.

"Nobody could know after all this time," said Mrs Rendell.

"Well, I can," said Robin. "Because I was broadcasting that night. I drove to Coalport to give a talk on Some Aspects of the Theatre. I remember because I discussed Galsworthy's charwoman in the Silver Box at great length and the next day Mrs McGinty was killed and I wondered if the charwoman in the play had been like her."

"That's right," said Shelagh Rendell suddenly. "And I remember now because you said your mother would be all alone because it was Janet's night off, and I came down here after dinner to keep her company. Only unfortunately I couldn't make her hear."

"Let me think," said Mrs Upward. "Oh! yes, of course. I'd gone to bed with a headache and my bedroom faces the back garden."

"And next day," said Shelagh, "when I heard Mrs McGinty had been killed, I thought 'Oo! I might have passed the murderer in the dark'—because at first we all thought it must have been some tramp who broke in."

"Well, I still don't remember what I was doing," said Maureen. "But I do remember the next morning. It was the baker told us. 'Old Mrs McGinty's been done in,' he said. And there I was, wondering why she hadn't turned up as usual."

She gave a shiver.

"It's horrible really, isn't it?" she said.

Mrs Upward was still watching Poirot.

He thought to himself: "She is a very intelligent woman—and a ruthless one. Also selfish. In whatever she did, she would have no qualms and no remorse. . . ."

A thin voice was speaking—urging, querulous.

"Haven't you got *any* clues, M. Poirot?"

It was Shelagh Rendell.

Johnnie Summerhayes' long dark face lit up enthusiastically.

"That's it, clues," he said. "That's what I like in detective stories. Clues that mean everything to the detective—and nothing to you—until the end when you fairly kick yourself. Can't you give us one little clue, M. Poirot?"

Laughing, pleading faces turned to him. A game to them all (or perhaps not to one of them?). But murder wasn't a game—murder was dangerous. You never knew.

With a sudden brusque movement, Poirot pulled out four photographs from his pocket.

"You want a clue?" he said. "*Voilà!*"

And with a dramatic gesture he tossed them down on the table.

They clustered round, bending over, and uttering ejaculations.

"*Look!*"

"What frightful frumps!"

"Just look at the roses. '*Rowses, rowses, all the way!*'"

"My dear, that *hat!*"

"What a frightful child!"

"But who are they?"

"Aren't fashions ridiculous?"

"That woman must really have been rather good-looking once."

"But why are they clues?"

"Who are they?"

Poirot looked slowly round at the circle of faces.

He saw nothing other than he might have expected to see.

"You do not recognise any of them?"

"Recognise?"

"You do not, shall I say, remember having seen any of those photographs before? But yes—Mrs Upward? You recognise something, do you not?"

Mrs Upward hesitated.

"Yes—I think——"

"Which one?"

Her forefinger went out and rested on the spectacled childlike face of Lily Gamboll.

"You have seen that photograph—when?"

"Quite recently. . . . Now where—no, I can't remember. But I'm sure I've seen a photograph just like that."

She sat frowning, her brows drawn together.

She came out of her abstraction as Mrs Rendell came to her.

"Good-bye, Mrs Upward. I do hope you'll come to tea with me one day if you feel up to it."

"Thank you, my dear. If Robin pushes me up the hill."

"Of course, Madre. I've developed the most tremendous muscles pushing that chair. Do you remember the day we went to the Wetherbys and it was so muddy——"

"Ah!" said Mrs Upward suddenly.

"What is it, Madre?"

"Nothing. Go on."

"Getting you up the hill again. First the chair skidded and then I skidded. I thought we'd never get home."

Laughing, they took their leave and trooped out.

Alcohol, Poirot thought, certainly loosens the tongue.

Had he been wise or foolish to display those photographs? Had that gesture also been the result of alcohol?

He wasn't sure.

But, murmuring an excuse, he turned back.

He pushed open the gate and walked up to the house. Through the open window on his left he heard the murmur of two voices. They were the voices of Robin and Mrs Oliver. Very little of Mrs Oliver and a good deal of Robin.

Poirot pushed the door open and went through the right-hand door into the room he had left a few moments before. Mrs Upward was sitting before the fire. There was a rather grim look on her face. She had been so deep in thought that his entry startled her.

At the sound of the apologetic little cough he gave, she looked up sharply, with a start.

"Oh," she said. "It's you. You startled me."

"I am sorry, madame. Did you think it was someone else? Who did you think it was?"

She did not answer that, merely said:

"Did you leave something behind?"

"What I feared I had left was danger."

"Danger?"

"Danger, perhaps, to you. Because you recognised one of those photographs just now."

"I wouldn't say recognised. All old photographs look exactly alike."

"Listen, madame. Mrs McGinty also, or so I believe, recognised one of those photographs. *And Mrs McGinty is dead.*"

With an unexpected glint of humour in her eye, Mrs Upward said:

"*Mrs McGinty's dead. How did she die? Sticking her neck out just like I.* Is that what you mean?"

"Yes. If you know anything—anything at all, tell it to me now. It will be safer so."

"My dear man, it's not nearly so simple as that. I'm not at all sure that I do know anything—certainly nothing as definite as a *fact*. Vague recollections are very tricky things. One would have to have some idea of how and where and when, if you follow what I mean."

"But it seems to me that you already have that idea."

"There is more to it than that. There are various factors to be taken into consideration. Now it's no good your rushing me, M. Poirot. I'm not the kind of person who rushes into decisions. I've a mind of my own, and I take time to make it up. When I come to a decision, I act. But not till I'm ready."

"You are in many ways a secretive woman, madame."

"Perhaps—up to a point. Knowledge is power. Power must only be used for the right ends. You will excuse my saying that you don't perhaps appreciate the pattern of our English country life."

"In other words you say to me, 'You are only a damned foreigner.'"

Mrs Upward smiled slightly.

"I shouldn't be as rude as that."

"If you do not want to talk to me, there is Superintendent Spence."

"My dear M. Poirot. Not the police. Not at this stage."

He shrugged his shoulders.

"I have warned you," he said.

For he was sure that by now Mrs Upward remembered quite well exactly when and where she had seen the photograph of Lily Gamboll.

14

i

"DECIDEDLY," said Hercule Poirot to himself the following morning, "the spring is here."

His apprehensions of the night before seemed singularly groundless.

Mrs Upward was a sensible woman who could take good care of herself.

Nevertheless in some curious way, she intrigued him. He did not at all understand her reactions. Clearly she did not want him to. She had recognised the photograph of Lily Gamboll and she was determined to play a lone hand.

Poirot, pacing a garden path while he pursued these reflections, was startled by a voice behind him.

"M. Poirot."

Mrs Rendell had come up so quietly that he had not heard her. Since yesterday he had felt extremely nervous.

"*Pardon*, madame. You made me jump."

Mrs Rendell smiled mechanically. If he were nervous, Mrs Rendell, he thought, was even more so. There was a twitching in one of her eyelids and her hands worked restlessly together.

"I—I hope I'm not interrupting you. Perhaps you're busy."

"But no, I am not busy. The day it is fine. I enjoy the feeling of spring. It is good to be outdoors. In the house of Mrs Summerhayes there is always, but always, the current of air."

"The current——"

"What in England you call a draught."

"Yes. Yes, I suppose there is."

"The windows, they will not shut and the doors they fly open all the time."

"It's rather a ramshackle house. And of course, the

Summerhayes are so badly off they can't afford to do much to it. I'd let it go if I were them. I know it's been in their family for hundreds of years, but nowadays you just can't cling on to things for sentiment's sake."

"No, we are not sentimental nowadays."

There was a silence. Out of the corner of his eye, Poirot watched those nervous white hands. He waited for her to take the initiative. When she did speak it was abruptly.

"I suppose," she said, "that when you are, well, investigating a thing, you'd always have to have a pretext?"

Poirot considered the question. Though he did not look at her, he was perfectly well aware of her eager sideways glance fixed on him.

"As you say, madame," he replied non-committally. "It is a convenience."

"To explain your being there, and—and asking things."

"It might be expedient."

"Why—why are you really here in Broadhinny, M. Poirot?"

He turned a mild surprised gaze on her.

"But, my dear lady, I told you—to inquire into the death of Mrs McGinty."

Mrs Rendell said sharply:

"I know that's what you say. But it's ridiculous."

Poirot raised his eyebrows.

"Is it?"

"Of course it is. Nobody believes it."

"And yet I assure you, it is simple fact."

Her pale blue eyes blinked and she looked away.

"You won't tell me."

"Tell you—what, madame?"

She changed the subject abruptly again, it seemed.

"I wanted to ask you—about anonymous letters."

"Yes," said Poirot encouragingly as she stopped.

"They're really always lies, aren't they?"

"They are sometimes lies," said Poirot cautiously.

"Usually," she persisted.

"I don't know that I would go as far as saying that."

Shelagh Rendell said vehemently:

"They're cowardly, treacherous, *mean* things!"

"All that, yes, I would agree."

"And you wouldn't ever believe what was said in one, would you?"

"That is a very difficult question," said Poirot gravely.

"I wouldn't. I wouldn't believe anything of that kind."

She added vehemently:

"I know why you're down here. And it isn't true, I tell you, it isn't true."

She turned sharply and walked away.

Hercule Poirot raised his eyebrows in an interested fashion.

"And now what?" he demanded of himself. "Am I being taken up the garden walk? Or is this the bird of a different colour?"

It was all, he felt, very confusing.

Mrs Rendell professed to believe that he was down here for a reason other than that of inquiring into Mrs McGinty's death. She had suggested that that was only a pretext.

Did she really believe that? Or was she, as he had just said to himself, leading him up the garden walk?

What had anonymous letters got to do with it?

Was Mrs Rendell the original of the photograph that Mrs Upward had said she had "seen recently"?

In other words, was Mrs Rendell Lily Gamboll? Lily Gamboll, a rehabilitated member of society, had been last heard of in Eire. Had Dr Rendell met and married his wife there, in ignorance of her history? Lily Gamboll had been trained as a stenographer. Her path and the doctor's might easily have crossed.

Poirot shook his head and sighed.

It was all perfectly possible. But he had to be sure.

A chilly wind sprang up suddenly and the sun went in.

Poirot shivered and retraced his steps to the house.

Yes, he had to be sure. If he could find the actual weapon of the murder——

And at that moment, with a strange feeling of certainty—he *saw it*.

ii

Afterwards he wondered whether, subconsciously, he had seen and noted it much earlier. It had stood there, presumably, ever since he had come to Long Meadows . . .

There on the littered top of the bookcase near the window. He thought: "Why did I never notice that before?"

He picked it up, weighed it in his hands, examined it, balanced it, raised it to strike—— Maureen came in through the door with her usual rush, two dogs accompanying her. Her voice, light and friendly, said:

"Hallo, are you playing with the sugar cutter?"

"Is that what it is? A sugar cutter?"

"Yes. A sugar cutter—or a sugar hammer—I don't know what exactly is the right term. It's rather fun, isn't it? So childish with the little bird on top."

Poirot turned the implement carefully in his hands. Made of much ornamented brass, it was shaped like an adze, heavy, with a sharp cutting edge. It was studded here and there with coloured stones, pale blue and red. On top of it was a frivolous little bird with turquoise eyes.

"Lovely thing for killing anyone, wouldn't it be?" said Maureen conversationally.

She took it from him and aimed a murderous blow on a point in space.

"Frightfully easy," she said. "What's that bit in the Idylls of the King? '*"Mark's way," he said, and clove him to the brain.*' I should think you could cleave anyone to the brain with this all right, don't you?"

Poirot looked at her. Her freckled face was serene and cheerful. She said:

"I've told Johnnie what's coming to him if I get fed up with him. I call it the wife's best friend!"

She laughed, put the sugar hammer down and turned towards the door.

"What did I come in here for?" she mused. "I can't remember . . . Bother! I'd better go and see if that pudding needs more water in the saucepan."

Poirot's voice stopped her before she got to the door.

"You brought this back with you from India, perhaps?"

"Oh no," said Maureen. "I got it at the B. and B. at Christmas."

"B. and B.?" Poirot was puzzled.

"Bring and Buy," explained Maureen glibly. "At the

Vicarage. You bring things you don't want, and you buy something. Something not too frightful if you can find it. Of course there's practically never anything you really want. I got this and that coffee pot. I like the coffee pot's nose and I liked the little bird on the hammer."

The coffee pot was a small one of beaten copper. It had a big curving spout that struck a familiar note to Poirot.

"I think they come from Baghdad," said Maureen. "At least I think that's what the Wetherbys said. Or it may have been Persia."

"It was from the Wetherbys' house, then, that these came?"

"Yes. They've got a most frightful lot of junk. I *must* go. That pudding."

She went out. The door banged. Poirot picked up the sugar cutter again and took it to the window.

On the cutting edge were faint, very faint, discolourations.

Poirot nodded his head.

He hesitated for a moment, then he carried the sugar hammer out of the room and up to his bedroom. There he packed it carefully in a box, did the whole thing up neatly in paper and string, and going downstairs again, left the house.

He did not think that anyone would notice the disappearance of the sugar cutter. It was not a tidy household.

iii

At Laburnums, collaboration was pursuing its difficult course.

"But I really don't feel it's right making him a vegetarian, darling," Robin was objecting. "Too faddy. And definitely not glamorous."

"I can't help it," said Mrs Oliver obstinately. "He's *always* been a vegetarian. He takes round a little machine for grating raw carrots and turnips."

"But, Ariadne, precious, *why*?"

"How do I know?" said Mrs Oliver crossly. "How do I know why I ever thought of the revolting man? I must have been mad! Why a Finn when I know nothing about Finland? Why a vegetarian? Why all the idiotic mannerisms he's got? These things just *happen*. You try something—and people seem to like it—and then you go on—and before you know where you are, you've got someone like that maddening Sven Hjerson tied to you for life. And people even write and say how fond you must be of him. Fond of him? If I met that bony, gangling, vegetable-eating Finn in real life, I'd do a better murder than any I've ever invented."

Robin Upward gazed at her with reverence.

"You know, Ariadne, that might be rather a marvellous idea. A real Sven Hjerson—and *you* murder him. You might make a Swan Song book of it—to be published after your death."

"No fear!" said Mrs Oliver. "What about the money? Any money to be made out of murders I want now."

"Yes. Yes. There I couldn't agree with you more."

The harassed playwright strode up and down.

"This Ingrid creature is getting rather tiresome," he said. "And after the cellar scene which is really going to be marvellous, I don't quite see how we're going to prevent the next scene from being rather an anti-climax."

Mrs Oliver was silent. Scenes, she felt, were Robin Upward's headache.

Robin shot a dissatisfied glance at her.

That morning, in one of her frequent changes of mood, Mrs Oliver had disliked her windswept coiffure. With a brush dipped in water she had plastered her grey locks close to her skull. With her high forehead, her massive glasses, and her stern air, she was reminding Robin more and more of a school teacher who had awed his early youth. He found it more and more difficult to address her as darling, and even flinched at "Ariadne."

He said fretfully:

"You know, I don't feel a bit in the mood to-day. All that gin yesterday, perhaps. Let's scrap work and go into the question of casting. If we can get Denis Callory, of course it will be too marvellous, but he's tied up in films at the moment. And Jean Bellews for Ingrid would be just right—and she *wants* to play it which is so nice. Eric—as I say, I've had a brainwave for Eric. We'll go over to the Little Rep to-night, shall we? And you'll tell me what you think of Cecil for the part."

Mrs Oliver agreed hopefully to this project and Robin went off to telephone.

"There," he said returning. "That's all fixed."

iv

The fine morning had not lived up to its promise. Clouds had gathered and the day was oppressive with a threat of rain. As Poirot walked through the dense shrubberies to the front door of Hunter's Close, he decided that he would not like to live in this hollow valley at the foot of the hill. The house itself was closed in by trees and its walls suffocated in ivy. It needed, he thought, the woodman's axe.

(The *axe*. The sugar cutter?)

He rang the bell and after getting no response, rang it again.

It was Deirdre Henderson who opened the door to him. She seemed surprised.

"Oh," she said, "it's you."

"May I come in and speak to you?"

"I—well, yes, I suppose so."

She led him into the small dark sitting-room where he had waited before. On the mantelpiece he recognised the big brother of the small coffee pot on Maureen's shelf. Its vast hooked nose seemed to dominate the small Western room with a hint of Eastern ferocity.

"I'm afraid," said Deirdre in an apologetic tone, "that we're rather upset to-day. Our help, the German girl—she's going. She's only been here a month. Actually it seems she just took this post to get over to this country because there was someone she wanted to marry. And now they've fixed it up, and she's going straight off to-night."

Poirot clicked his tongue.

"Most inconsiderate."

"It is, isn't it? My stepfather says it isn't legal. But even if it isn't legal, if she just goes off and gets married, I don't see what one can do about it. We shouldn't even have known she *was* going if I hadn't found her packing her clothes. She would just have walked out of the house without a word."

"It is, alas, not an age of consideration."

"No," said Deirdre dully. "I suppose it's not."

She rubbed her forehead with the back of her hand.

"I'm tired," she said. "I'm very tired."

"Yes," said Poirot gently. "I think you may be very tired."

"What was it you wanted, M. Poirot?"

"I wanted to ask you about a sugar hammer."

"A sugar hammer?"

Her face was blank, uncomprehending.

"An instrument of brass, with a bird on it, and inlaid with blue and red and green stones." Poirot enunciated the description carefully.

"Oh yes, I know."

Her voice showed no interest or animation.

"I understand it came from this house?"

"Yes. My mother bought it in the bazaar at Baghdad. It's one of the things we took to the Vicarage sale."

"The Bring and Buy sale, that is right?"

"Yes. We have a lot of them here. It's difficult to get people to give money, but there's usually something you can rake up and send."

"So it was here, in this house, until Christmas, and then you sent it to the Bring and Buy sale? Is that right?"

Deirdre frowned.

"Not the Christmas Bring and Buy. It was the one before. The Harvest Festival one."

"The Harvest Festival—that would be—when? October? September?"

"The end of September."

It was very quiet in the little room. Poirot looked at the girl and she looked back at him. Her face was mild, expressionless, uninterested. Behind the blank wall of her apathy, he tried to guess what was going on. Nothing, perhaps. Perhaps she was, as she had said, just tired. . . .

He said, quietly, urgently:

"You are quite sure it was the Harvest Festival Sale? Not the Christmas one?"

"Quite sure."

Her eyes were steady, unblinking.

Hercule Poirot waited. He continued to wait. . . .

But what he was waiting for did not come.

He said formally:

"I must not keep you any longer, mademoiselle."

She went with him to the front door.

Presently he was walking down the drive again.

Two divergent statements—statements that could not possibly be reconciled.

Who was right? Maureen Summerhayes or Deirdre Henderson?

If the sugar cutter had been used as he believed it had been used, the point was vital. The Harvest Festival had been the end of September. Between then and Christmas, on November 22nd, Mrs McGinty had been killed. Whose property had the sugar cutter been at that time?

He went to the post office. Mrs Sweetiman was always helpful and she did her best. She's been to both sales, she said. She always went. You picked up many a nice bit there. She helped, too, to arrange things beforehand. Though most people brought things with them and didn't send them beforehand.

A brass hammer, rather like an axe, with coloured stones and a little bird? No, she couldn't rightly remember. There was such a lot of things, and so much confusion and some things snatched up at once. Well, perhaps she did remember something like that—priced at five shillings it had been, and with a copper coffee pot, but the pot had got a hole in the bottom—you couldn't use it, only for ornament. But she couldn't remember when it was—some time ago. Might have been Christmas, might have been before. She hadn't been noticing. . . .

She accepted Poirot's parcel. Registered? Yes.

She copied down the address; he noticed just a sharp flicker of interest in her keen black eyes as she handed him the receipt.

Hercule Poirot walked slowly up the hill, wondering to himself.

Of the two, Maureen Summerhayes, scatter-brained, cheerful, inaccurate, was the more likely to be wrong. Harvest or Christmas, it would be all one to her.

Deirdre Henderson, slow, awkward, was far more likely to be accurate in her identification of times and dates.

Yet there remained that irking question.

Why, after his questions, hadn't she asked him *why he wanted to know?* Surely a natural, an almost inevitable, question?

But Deirdre Henderson hadn't asked it.

"SOMEONE RANG you up," called Maureen from the kitchen as Poirot entered the house.

"Rang me up? Who was that?"

He was slightly surprised.

"Don't know. But I jotted the number down on my ration book."

"Thank you, Madame".

He went into the dining-room and over to the desk. Amongst the litter of papers he found the ration book lying near the telephone and the words—Kilchester 350.

Raising the receiver of the telephone, he dialled the number.

Immediately a woman's voice said:

"Breather & Scuttle."

Poirot made a quick guess.

"Can I speak to Miss Maude Williams?"

There was a moment's interval and then a contralto voice said:

"Miss Williams speaking."

"This is Hercule Poirot. I think you rang me."

"Yes—yes, I did. It's about the property you were asking me about the other day."

"The property?" For a moment Poirot was puzzled. Then he realised that Maude's conversation was being overheard. Probably she had telephoned him before when she was alone in the office.

"I understand you, I think. It is the affair of James Bentley and Mrs McGinty's murder."

"That's right. Can we do anything in the matter for you?"

"You want to help. You are not private where you are?"

"That's right."

"I understand. Listen carefully. You really want to help James Bentley?"

"Yes."

"Would you resign your present post?"

There was no hesitation.

"Yes."

"Would you be willing to take a domestic post? Possibly with not very congenial people."

"Yes."

"Could you get away at once? By to-morrow, for instance."

"Oh yes, M. Poirot. I think that could be managed."

"You understand what I want you to do. You would be a domestic help—to live in. You can cook?"

A faint amusement tinged the voice.

"Very well."

"*Bon Dieu*, what a rarity! Now listen, I am coming into Kilchester at once. I will meet you in the same café where I met you before, at lunch time."

"Yes, certainly."

Poirot rang off.

"An admirable young woman," he reflected. "Quick-witted, knows her own mind—perhaps, even, she can cook. . . ."

With some difficulty he disinterred the local telephone directory from under a treatise on pigkeeping and looked up the Wetherbys number.

The voice that answered him was that of Mrs Wetherby.

"'Allo'? 'Allo? It is M. Poirot—you remember, madame——"

"I don't think I——"

"M. Hercule Poirot."

"Oh yes—of course—do forgive me. Rather a domestic upset to-day——"

"It is for that reason exactly I rang you up. I am desolated to learn of your difficulties."

"So ungrateful—these foreign girls. Her fare paid over here, and everything. I do so hate ingratitude."

"Yes, yes. I do indeed sympathise. It is monstrous—that is why I hasten to tell you that I have, perhaps, a solution. By the merest chance I know of a young woman wanting a domestic post. Not, I fear, fully trained."

"Oh, there's no such thing as training nowadays. Will she cook—so many of them won't cook."

"Yes—yes—she cooks. Shall I then send her to you—at least on trial? Her name is Maude Williams."

"Oh, please do, M. Poirot. It's most kind of you. Anything would be better than nothing. My husband is so particular and gets so annoyed with dear Deirdre when the household doesn't go smoothly. One can't expect men to understand how difficult everything is nowadays—I————"

There was an interruption. Mrs Wetherby spoke to someone entering the room, and though she had placed her hand over the receiver Poirot could hear her slightly muffled words.

"It's that little detective man—knows of someone to come in to replace Frieda. No, not foreign—English, thank goodness. Very kind of him, really, he seems quite concerned about me. Oh, darling, don't make objections. What does it *matter?* You know the absurd way Roger goes on. Well, I think it's very kind—and I don't suppose she's too awful."

The asides over, Mrs Wetherby spoke with the utmost graciousness.

"Thank you very much, M. Poirot. We are most grateful."

Poirot replaced the receiver and glanced at his watch.

He went to the kitchen.

"Madame, I shall not be in to lunch. I have to go to Kilchester."

"Thank goodness," said Maureen. "I didn't get to that pudding in time. It had boiled dry. I think it's really all right—just a little scorched perhaps. In case it tasted rather nasty I thought I would open a bottle of those raspberries I put up last summer. They seem to have a bit of mould on top but they say nowadays that that doesn't matter. It's really rather good for you—practically penicillin."

Poirot left the house, glad that scorched pudding and near-penicillin were not to be his portion to-day. Better—far better—eat macaroni and custard and plums at the Blue Cat than the improvisations of Maureen Summerhayes.

ii

At Laburnums a little friction had arisen.

"Of course, Robin, you never seem to remember anything when you are working on a play."

Robin was contrite.

"Madre, I am most terribly sorry. I'd forgotten all about its being Janet's night out.'"

"It doesn't matter at all," said Mrs Upward coldly.

"Of course it matters. I'll ring up the Rep and tell them we'll go to-morrow night instead."

"You'll do nothing of the sort. You've arranged to go to-night and you'll go."

"But really——"

"That's settled."

"Shall I ask Janet to go out another night?"

"Certainly *not*. She hates to have her plans disarranged."

"I'm sure she wouldn't really mind. Not if I put it to her——"

"You'll do nothing of the sort, Robin. Please don't go up-setting Janet. And don't go on about it. I don't care to feel I'm a tiresome old woman spoiling other people's pleasure."

"Madre—sweetest——"

"That's enough—you go and enjoy yourselves. I know who I'll ask to keep me company."

"Who?"

"That's my secret," said Mrs Upward, her good humour restored. "Now stop fussing, Robin."

"I'll ring up Shelagh Rendell——"

"I'll do my own ringing up, thank you. It's all settled. Make the coffee before you go, and leave it by me in the percolator ready to switch on. Oh, and you might as well put out an extra cup—in case I have a visitor."

16

Sitting at lunch in the Blue Cat, Poirot finished outlining his instructions to Maude Williams.

"So you understand what it is you have to look for?"

Maude Williams nodded.

"You have arranged matters with your office?"

She laughed.

"My auntie's dangerously ill! I sent myself a telegram."

"Good. I have one more thing to say. Somewhere, in that village, we have a murderer at large. That is not a very safe thing to have."

"Warning me?"

"Yes."

"I can take care of myself," said Maude Williams.

"That," said Hercule Poirot, "might be classed under the heading of Famous Last Words."

She laughed again, a frank amused laugh. One or two heads at near tables turned round to look at her.

Poirot found himself appraising her carefully. A strong, confident young woman, full of vitality, keyed up and eager to attempt a dangerous task. Why? He thought again of James Bentley, his gentle defeated voice, his lifeless apathy. Nature was indeed curious and interesting.

Maude said:

"You're *asking* me to do it, aren't you? Why suddenly try to put me off?"

"Because if one offers a mission, one must be exact about what it involves."

"I don't think I'm in any danger," said Maude confidently.

"I do not think so at the moment. You are unknown in Broadhinny?"

Maude considered.

"Ye-es. Yes, I should say so."

"You have been there?"

"Once or twice—for the firm, of course—only once recently— that was about five months ago."

"Who did you see? Where did you go?"

"I went to see an old lady—Mrs Carstairs—or Carlisle—I can't remember her name for sure. She was buying a small property near here, and I went over to see her with some papers and some queries and a surveyor's report which we'd got for her. She was staying at that Guest House sort of place where you are."

"Long Meadows?"

"That was it. Uncomfortable-looking house with a lot of dogs."

Poirot nodded.

"Did you see Mrs Summerhayes, or Major Summerhayes?"

"I saw Mrs Summerhayes, I suppose it was. She took me up to the bedroom. The old pussy was in bed."

"Would Mrs Summerhayes remember you?"

"Don't suppose so. Even if she did, it wouldn't matter, would it? After all, one changes one's job quite often these days. But I don't suppose she even looked at me. Her sort don't."

There was a faint bitterness in Maude Williams' voice.

"Did you see anyone else in Broadhinny?"

Maud said rather awkwardly:

"Well, I saw Mr Bentley."

"Ah, you saw Mr Bentley. By accident."

Maude wriggled a little in her chair.

"No, as a matter of fact, I'd sent him a p.c. Telling him I was coming that day. Asked him if he'd meet me as a matter of fact. Not that there was anywhere to go. Dead little hole. No café or cinema or anything. 'S a matter of fact we just talked in the bus stop. While I was waiting for my bus back."

"That was before the death of Mrs McGinty?"

"Oh yes. But not much before, though. Because it was only a few days later that it was all in the newspapers."

"Did Mr Bentley speak to you at all of his landlady?"

"I don't think so."

"And you spoke to no one else in Broadhinny?"

"Well—only Mr Robin Upward. I've heard him talk on the wireless. I saw him coming out of his cottage and I recognised him from his pictures and I did ask him for his autograph."

"And he gave it you?"

"Oh yes, he was ever so nice about it. I hadn't my book with me, but I'd got an odd sheet of notepaper, and he whipped out his fountain pen and wrote it at once."

"Do you know any of the other people in Broadhinny by sight?"

"Well, I know the Carpenters, of course. They're in Kilchester a lot. Lovely car they've got, and she wears lovely clothes. She opened a Bazaar about a month ago. They say he's going to be our next M.P."

Poirot nodded. Then he took from his pocket the envelope that he always carried about with him. He spread the four photographs on the table.

"Do you recognise any of—what's the matter?"

"It was Mr Scuttle. Just going out of the door. I hope he didn't see you with me. It might seem a bit odd. People are talking about you, you know. Saying you've been sent over from Paris—from the Sooretay or some name like that."

"I am Belgian, not French, but no matter."

"What's this about these photographs?" She bent over, studying them closely. "Rather on the old-fashioned side, aren't they?"

"The oldest is thirty years ago."

"Awfully silly, old fashioned clothes look. Makes the women look such fools."

"Have you seen any of them before?"

"D'you mean do I recognise any of the women, or do you mean have I seen the pictures?"

"Either."

"I've an idea I've seen that one." Her finger rested against Janice Courtland in her cloche hat. "In some paper or other, but I can't remember when. That kid looks a bit familiar, too. But I can't remember when I saw them; some time ago."

"All those photographs appeared in the *Sunday Comet* on the Sunday before Mrs McGinty died."

Maude looked at him sharply.

"And they've got something to do with it? That's why you want me to——"

She did not finish the sentence.

"Yes," said Hercule Poirot. "That is why."

He took something else from his pocket and showed it to her. It was the cutting from the *Sunday Comet*.

"You had better read that," he said.

She read it carefully. Her bright golden head bent over the flimsy bit of newsprint.

Then she looked up.

"So that's who they are? And reading this has given you ideas?"

"You could not express it more justly."

"But all the same I don't see——" She was silent a moment, thinking. Poirot did not speak. However pleased he might be with his own ideas, he was always ready to hear other people's ideas too.

"You think one or other of these people is in Broadhinny?"

"It might be, might it not?"

"Of course. Anyone may be anywhere . . ." She went on, placing her finger on Eva Kane's pretty simpering face: "She'd be quite old now—about Mrs Upward's age."

"About that."

"What I was thinking was—the sort of woman she was— there must be several people who'd have it in for her."

"That is a point of view," said Poirot slowly. "Yes, it is a point of view." He added: "You remember the Craig case?"

"Who doesn't?" said Maude Williams. "Why, he's in Madame Tussaud's! I was only a kid at the time, but the newspapers are always bringing him up and comparing the case with other cases. I don't suppose it will ever be forgotten, do you?"

Poirot raised his head sharply.

He wondered what brought that sudden note of bitterness into her voice.

17

FEELING COMPLETELY bewildered, Mrs Oliver was endeavouring to cower in the corner of a very minute theatrical dressing-
room. Not being the figure to cower, she only succeeded in
bulging. Bright young men, removing grease paint with towels,
surrounded her and at intervals pressed warm beer upon her.

Mrs Upward, her good humour completely restored, had
speeded their departure with good wishes. Robin had been
assiduous in making all arrangements for her comfort before
departure, running back a couple of times after they were in the
car to see that all was as it should be.

On the last occasion he came back grinning.

"Madre was just ringing off on the telephone, and the wicked
old thing still won't tell me who she was ringing up. But I bet I
know."

"I know, too," said Mrs Oliver.

"Well, who do you say?"

"Hercule Poirot."

"Yes, that's my guess, too. She's going to pump him. Madre
does like having her little secrets, doesn't she? Now darling,
about the play to-night. It's very important that you tell me
honestly just what you think of Cecil—and whether he's your
idea of Eric . . ."

Needless to say, Cecil Leech had not been at all Mrs Oliver's
idea of Eric. Nobody, indeed, could have been more unlike.
The play itself she had enjoyed, but the ordeal of "going round
afterwards" was fraught with its usual terrors.

Robin, of course, was in his element. He had Cecil (at least
Mrs Oliver supposed it was Cecil) pinned against the wall and
was talking nineteen to the dozen. Mrs Oliver had been terrified
of Cecil and much preferred somebody called Michael who was
talking to her kindly at the moment. Michael, at least, did not

expect her to reciprocate, in fact Michael seemed to prefer a monologue. Somebody called Peter made occasional incursions on the conversation, but on the whole it resolved itself into a thin stream of faintly amusing malice by Michael.

"——too sweet of Robin," he was saying. "We've been urging him to come and see the show. But of course he's completely under that terrible woman's thumb, isn't he? Dancing attendance. And really Robin is brilliant, don't you think so? Quite quite brilliant. He shouldn't be sacrificed on a Matriarchal altar. Women can be awful, can't they? You know what she did to poor Alex Roscoff? All over him for nearly a year then discovered that he wasn't a Russian émigré at all. Of course he had been telling her some very tall stories, but quite amusing, and we all knew it wasn't true, but after all why should one care?—and then when she found out he was just a little East End tailor's son, she dropped him, my dear. I mean, I do hate a snob, don't you? Really Alex was thankful to get away from her. He said she could be quite frightening sometimes—a little queer in the head, he thought. Her rages! Robin dear, we're talking about your wonderful Madre. Such a shame she couldn't come to-night. But it's marvellous to have Mrs Oliver. All those delicious murders."

An elderly man with a deep bass voice grasped Mrs Oliver's hand and held it in a hot, sticky grasp.

"How can I ever thank you?" he said in tones of deep melancholy. "You've saved my life—saved my life many a time."

Then they all came out into the fresh night air and went across to the Pony's Head, where there were more drinks and more stage conversation.

By the time Mrs Oliver and Robin were driving homeward, Mrs Oliver was quite exhausted. She leaned back and closed her eyes. Robin, on the other hand, talked without stopping.

"——and you do think that might be an idea, don't you?" he finally ended.

"What?"

Mrs Oliver jerked open her eyes.

She had been lost in a nostalgic dream of home. Walls covered with exotic birds and foliage. A deal table, her typewriter, black coffee, apples everywhere . . . What bliss, what glorious and solitary bliss! What a mistake for an author to emerge from her secret fastness. Authors were shy, unsociable creatures, atoning for their lack of social aptitude by inventing their own companions and conversations.

"I'm afraid you're tired," said Robin.

"Not really. The truth is I'm not very good with people."

"I adore people, don't you?" said Robin happily.

"No," said Mrs Oliver firmly.

"But you must. Look at all the people in your books."

"That's different. I think trees are much nicer than people, more restful."

"I need people," said Robin, stating an obvious fact. "They stimulate me."

He drew up at the gate of Laburnums.

"You go in," he said. "I'll put the car away."

Mrs Oliver extracted herself with the usual difficulty and walked up the path.

"The door's not locked," Robin called.

It wasn't. Mrs Oliver pushed it open and entered. There were no lights on, and that struck her as rather ungracious on her hostess's part. Or was it perhaps economy? Rich people were so often economical. There was a smell of scent in the hall, something rather exotic and expensive. For a moment Mrs Oliver wondered if she were in the right house, then she found the light switch and pressed it down.

The light sprang up in the low oak-beamed square hall. The door into the sitting-room was ajar and she caught sight of a foot and leg. Mrs Upward, after all, had not gone to bed. She must have fallen asleep in her chair, and since no lights were on, she must have been asleep a long time.

Mrs Oliver went to the door and switched on the lights in the sitting-room.

"We're back——" she began and then stopped.

Her hand went up to her throat. She felt a tight knot there, a desire to scream that she could not put into operation.

Her voice came out in a whisper:

"Robin—Robin . . ."

It was some time before she heard him coming up the path, whistling, and then she turned quickly and ran to meet him in the hall.

"Don't go in there—don't go in. Your mother—she—she's dead—I think—she's been killed . . ."

18

"Quite a neat bit of work," said Superintendent Spence.

His red countryman's face was angry. He looked across to where Hercule Poirot sat gravely listening.

"Neat and ugly," he said. "She was strangled," he went on. "Silk scarf—one of her own silk scarves, one she'd been wearing that day—just passed around the neck and the ends crossed—and pulled. Neat, quick, efficient. The thugs did it that way in India. The victim doesn't struggle or cry out—pressure on the carotid artery."

"Special knowledge?"

"Could be—need not. If you were thinking of doing it, you could read up the subject. There's no practical difficulty. Especially with the victim quite unsuspicious—and she *was* unsuspicious."

Poirot nodded.

"Someone she knew."

"Yes. They'd had coffee together—a cup opposite her and one opposite the—guest. Prints had been wiped off the guest's cup very carefully but lipstick is more difficult—there were still faint traces of lipstick."

"A woman, then?"

"You expected a woman, didn't you?"

"Oh yes. Yes, that was indicated."

Spence went on:

"Mrs Upward recognised one of those photographs—the photograph of Lily Gamboll. So it ties up with the McGinty murder."

"Yes," said Poirot. "It ties up with the McGinty murder."

He remembered Mrs Upward's slightly amused expression as she had said:

> *"Mrs McGinty's dead. How did she die?*
> *Sticking her neck out, just like I."*

Spence was going on:

"She took an opportunity that seemed good to her—her son and Mrs Oliver were going off to the theatre. She rang up the person concerned and asked that person to come and see her. Is that how you figure it out? She was playing detective."

"Something like that. Curiosity. She kept her knowledge to herself, but she wanted to find out more. She didn't in the least realise what she was doing might be dangerous." Poirot sighed. "So many people think of murder as a game. It is not a game. I told her so. But she would not listen."

"No, we know that. Well, that fits in fairly well. When young Robin started off with Mrs Oliver and ran back into the house his mother had just finished telephoning to someone. She wouldn't say who to. Played it mysterious. Robin and Mrs Oliver thought it might be *you*."

"I wish it had been," said Hercule Poirot. "You have no idea to whom it was that she telephoned?"

"None whatever. It's all automatic round here, you know."

"The maid couldn't help you in any way?"

"No. She came in about half-past ten—she has a key to the back door. She went straight into her own room which leads off the kitchen and went to bed. The house was dark and she assumed that Mrs Upward had gone to bed and that the others had not yet returned."

Spence added:

"She's deaf and pretty crotchety as well. Takes very little notice of what goes on—and I imagine does as little work as she can with as much grumbling as possible."

"Not really an old faithful?"

"Oh no! She's only been with the Upwards a couple of years."

A constable put his head round the door.

"There's a young lady to see you, sir," he said. "Says there's something perhaps you ought to know. About last night."

"About last night? Send her in."

Deirdre Henderson came in. She looked pale and strained and, as usual, rather awkward.

"I thought perhaps I'd better come," she said. "If I'm not interrupting you or anything," she added apologetically.

"Not at all, Miss Henderson."

Spence rose and pushed forward a chair. She sat down on it squarely in an ungainly schoolgirlish sort of way.

"Something about last night?" said Spence encouragingly. "About Mrs Upward, you mean?"

"Yes, it's true, isn't it, that she was murdered? I mean the post said so and the baker. Mother said of course it couldn't be true——" She stopped.

"I'm afraid your mother isn't quite right there. It's true enough. Now, you wanted to make a—to tell us something?"

Deirdre nodded.

"Yes," she said. "You see, *I* was there."

A difference crept into Spence's manner. It was, perhaps, even more gentle, but an official hardness underlay it.

"You were there," he said. "At Laburnums. At what time?"

"I don't know exactly," said Deirdre. "Between half-past eight and nine, I suppose. Probably nearly nine. After dinner, anyway. You see, she telephoned to me."

"Mrs Upward telephoned to you?"

"Yes. She said Robin and Mrs Oliver were going to the theatre in Cullenquay and that she would be all alone and would I come along and have coffee with her."

"And you went?"

"Yes?"

"And you—had coffee with her?"

Deirdre shook her head.

"No, I got there—and I knocked. But there wasn't any answer. So I opened the door and went into the hall. It was quite dark and I'd seen from outside that there was no light in the sitting-room. So I was puzzled. I called 'Mrs Upward' once or twice but there was no answer. So I thought there must be some mistake."

"What mistake did you think there could have been?"

"I thought perhaps she'd gone to the theatre with them after all."

"Without letting you know?"

"That did seem queer."

"You couldn't think of any other explanation?"

"Well, I thought perhaps Frieda might have bungled the original message. She does get things wrong sometimes. She's a foreigner. She was excited herself last night because she was leaving."

"What did you do, Miss Henderson?"

"I just went away."

"Back home?"

"Yes—that is, I went for a little walk first. It was quite fine."

Spence was silent for a moment or two, looking at her. He was looking, Poirot noticed, at her mouth.

Presently he roused himself and said briskly:

"Well, thank you, Miss Henderson. You were quite right to come and tell us this. We're much obliged to you."

He got up and shook hands with her.

"I thought I ought to," said Deirdre. "Mother didn't want me to."

"Didn't she now?"

"But I thought I'd better."

"Quite right."

He showed her out and came back.

He sat down, drummed on the table and looked at Poirot.

"No lipstick," he said. "Or is that only this morning?"

"No, it is not only this morning. She never uses it."

"That's odd, nowadays, isn't it?"

"She is rather an odd kind of girl—undeveloped."

"And no scent, either, as far as I could smell. That Mrs Oliver says there was a distinct smell of scent—expensive scent, she says—in the house last night. Robin Upward confirms that. It wasn't any scent his mother uses."

"This girl would not use scent, I think," said Poirot.

"I shouldn't think so either," said Spence. "Looks rather like the hockey captain from an old-fashioned girls' school—but she must be every bit of thirty, I should say."

"Quite that."

"Arrested development, would you say?"

Poirot considered. Then he said it was not quite so simple as that.

"It doesn't fit," said Spence frowning. "No lipstick, no scent. And since she's got a perfectly good mother, and Lily Gamboll's mother was done in in a drunken brawl in Cardiff when Lily Gamboll was nine years old, I don't see how she can be Lily

Gamboll. *But*—Mrs Upward telephoned her to come there last night—you can't get away from that." He rubbed his nose. "It isn't straightforward going."

"What about the medical evidence?"

"Not much help there. All the police surgeon will say definitely is that she was probably dead by half-past nine."

"So she may have been dead when Deirdre Henderson came to Laburnums?"

"Probably was if the girl is speaking the truth. Either she *is* speaking the truth—or else she's a deep one. Mother didn't want her to come to us, she said. Anything there?"

Poirot considered.

"Not particularly. It is what mother would say. She is the type, you comprehend, that avoids unpleasantness."

Spence sighed.

"So we've got Deirdre Henderson—on the spot. Or else someone who came there before Deirdre Henderson. A woman. A woman who uses lipstick and expensive scent."

Poirot murmured: "You will inquire——"

Spence broke in.

"I'm inquiring! Just tactfully for the moment. We don't want to alarm anyone. What was Eve Carpenter doing last night? What was Shelagh Rendell doing last night? Ten to one they were just sitting at home. Carpenter, I know, had a political meeting."

"Eve," said Poirot thoughtfully. "The fashions in names change, do they not? Hardly ever, nowadays, do you hear of an Eva. It has gone out. But Eve, it is popular."

"She can afford expensive scent," said Spence, pursuing his own train of thought.

He sighed.

"We've got to get at more of her background. It's so convenient to be a war widow. You can turn up anywhere looking pathetic and mourning some brave young airman. Nobody likes to ask you questions."

He turned to another subject.

"That sugar hammer or what-not you sent along—I think you've hit the bull's-eye. It's the weapon used in the McGinty murder. Doctor agrees it's exactly suitable for the type of blow.

And there has been blood on it. It was washed, of course—but they don't realise nowadays that a microscopic amount of blood will give a reaction with the latest reagents. Yes, it's human blood all right. And that again ties up with the Wetherbys and the Henderson girl. Or doesn't it?"

"Deirdre Henderson was quite definite that the sugar hammer went to the Harvest Festival Bring and Buy."

"And Mrs Summerhayes was equally positive it was the Christmas one?"

"Mrs Summerhayes is never positive about anything," said Poirot gloomily. "She is a charming person, but she has no order or method in her composition. But I will tell you this—I who have lived at Long Meadows—the doors and the windows they are always open. Anyone—anyone at all, could come and take something away and later come and put it back and neither Major Summerhayes nor Mrs Summerhayes would notice. If it is not there one day, she thinks that her husband has taken it to joint a rabbit or to chop wood—and he, he would think she had taken it to chop dogmeat. In that house nobody uses the right implements—they just seize what is at hand and leave it in the wrong place. And nobody remembers anything. If I were to live like that I should be in a continual state of anxiety—but they—they do not seem to mind."

Spence sighed.

"Well—there's one good thing about all this—they won't execute James Bentley until this business is all cleared up. We've forwarded a letter to the Home Secretary's office. It gives us what we've been wanting—time."

"I think," said Poirot, "that I would like to see Bentley again—now that we know a little more."

ii

There was little change in James Bentley. He was, perhaps, rather thinner, his hands were more restless—otherwise he was the same quiet, hopeless creature.

Hercule Poirot spoke carefully. There had been some fresh evidence. The police were re-opening the case. There was, therefore, hope . . .

But James Bentley was not attracted by hope.

He said:

"It will be all no good. What more can they find out?"

"Your friends," said Hercule Poirot, "are working very hard."

"My friends?" He shrugged his shoulders. "I have no friends."

"You should not say that. You have, at the very least, two friends."

"Two friends? I should like to know who they are."

His tone expressed no wish for the information, merely a weary disbelief.

"First, there is Superintendent Spence——"

"Spence? Spence? The police superintendent who worked up the case against me? That's almost funny."

"It is not funny. It is fortunate. Spence is a very shrewd and conscientious police officer. He likes to be very sure that he has got the right man."

"He's sure enough of that."

"Oddly enough, he is not. That is why, as I said, he is your friend."

"That kind of a friend!"

Hercule Poirot waited. Even James Bentley, he thought, must have some human attributes. Even James Bentley could not be completely devoid of ordinary human curiosity.

And true enough, presently James Bentley said:

"Well, who's the other?"

"The other is Maude Williams."

Bentley did not appear to react.

"Maude Williams? Who is she?"

"She worked in the office of Breather & Scuttle."

"Oh—that Miss Williams."

"*Précisément*, that Miss Williams."

"But what's it got to do with her?"

There were moments when Hercule Poirot found the personality of James Bentley so irritating that he heartily wished that he could believe Bentley guilty of Mrs McGinty's murder. Unfortunately the more Bentley annoyed him, the more he came round to Spence's way of thinking. He found it more and

147

more difficult to envisage Bentley's murdering anybody. James Bentley's attitude to murder would have been, Poirot felt sure, that it wouldn't be much good anyway. If cockiness, as Spence insisted, was a characteristic of murderers, Bentley was certainly no murderer.

Containing himself, Poirot said:

"Miss Williams interests herself in this affair. She is convinced you are innocent."

"I don't see what she can know about it."

"She knows *you*."

James Bentley blinked. He said, grudgingly:

"I suppose she does, in a way, but not well."

"You worked together in the office, did you not? You had, sometimes, meals together?"

"Well—yes—once or twice. The Blue Cat Café, it's very convenient—just across the street."

"Did you never go for walks with her?"

"As a matter of fact we did, once. We walked up on the downs."

Hercule Poirot exploded.

"*Ma foi*, is it a crime that I seek to drag from you? To keep the company with a pretty girl, is it not natural? Is it not enjoyable? Can you not be pleased with yourself about it?"

"I don't see why," said James Bentley.

"At your age it is natural and right to enjoy the company of girls."

"I don't know many girls."

"*Ca se voit!* But you should be ashamed of that, not smug! You knew Miss Williams. You worked with her and talked with her and sometimes had meals with her, and once went for a walk on the downs. And when I mention her, you do not even remember her name!"

James Bentley flushed.

"Well, you see—I've never had much to do with girls. And she isn't quite what you'd call a lady, is she? Oh very nice—and all that—but I can't help feeling that Mother would have thought her common."

"It is what *you* think that matters."

Again James Bentley flushed.

148

"Her hair," he said. "And the kind of clothes she wears—
Mother, of course, was old-fashioned——"

He broke off.

"But you found Miss Williams—what shall I say—
sympathetic?"

"She was always very kind," said James Bentley slowly. "But
she didn't—really—*understand*. Her mother died when she was
only a child, you see."

"And then you lost your job," said Poirot. "You couldn't get
another. Miss Williams met you once at Broadhinny, I understand?"

James Bentley looked distressed.

"Yes—yes. She was coming over there on business and she
sent me a post-card. Asked me to meet her. I can't think why. It
isn't as if I knew her at all well."

"But you did meet her?"

"Yes. I didn't want to be rude."

"And you took her to the pictures or a meal?"

James Bentley looked scandalised.

"Oh no. Nothing of that kind. We—er—just talked whilst
she was waiting for her bus."

"Ah, how amusing that must have been for the poor girl!"

James Bentley said sharply:

"I hadn't got any money. You must remember that. I hadn't
any money at all."

"Of course. It was a few days before Mrs McGinty was killed,
wasn't it?"

James Bentley nodded. He said unexpectedly:

"Yes, it was on the Monday. She was killed on Wednesday."

"I'm going to ask you something else, Mr Bentley. Mrs
McGinty took the *Sunday Comet*."

"Yes, she did."

"Did you ever see her *Sunday Comet*?"

"She used to offer it sometimes, but I didn't often accept.
Mother didn't care for that kind of paper."

"So you didn't see that week's *Sunday Comet*?"

"No."

"And Mrs McGinty didn't speak about it, or about anything
in it?"

149

"Oh yes, she did," said James Bentley unexpectedly. "She was full of it!"

"Ah la la. So she was full of it. And what did she say? Be careful. This is important."

"I don't remember very well now. It was all about some old murder case. Craig, I think it was—no, perhaps it wasn't Craig. Anyway, she said somebody connected with the case was living in Broadhinny now. Full of it, she was. I couldn't see why it mattered to her."

"Did she say who it was—in Broadhinny?"

James Bentley said vaguely:

"I think it was that woman whose son writes plays."

"She mentioned her by name?"

"No—I—really it's so long ago——"

"I implore you—try to think. You want to be free again, do you not?"

"Free?" Bentley sounded surprised.

"Yes, free."

"I—yes—I suppose I do——"

"Then *think! What did Mrs McGinty say?*"

"Well—something like—'so pleased with herself as she is and so proud. Not so much to be proud of if all's known.' And then, 'You'd never think it was the same woman to look at the photograph.' But of course it had been taken years ago."

"But what made you sure that it was Mrs Upward of whom she was speaking?"

"I really don't know. . . . I just formed the impression. She had been speaking of Mrs Upward—and then I lost interest and didn't listen, and afterwards—well, now I come to think of it, I don't really know who she was speaking about. She talked a lot, you know."

Poirot sighed.

He said: "I do not think myself that it was Mrs Upward of whom she spoke. I think it was somebody else. It is preposterous to reflect that if you are hanged it will be because you do not pay proper attention to the people with whom you converse. . . . Did Mrs McGinty speak much to you of the houses where she worked, or the ladies of those houses?"

"Yes, in a way—but it's no good asking me. You don't seem

to realise, M. Poirot, that I had my own life to think of at that time I was in very serious anxiety."

"Not in so much serious anxiety as you are now! Did Mrs McGinty speak of Mrs Carpenter—Mrs Selkirk she was then— or of Mrs Rendell?"

"Carpenter has that new house at the top of the hill and a big car, hasn't he? He was engaged to Mrs Selkirk—Mrs McGinty was always very down on Mrs Selkirk. I don't know why. 'Jumped up,' that's what she used to call her. I don't know what she meant by it."

"And the Rendells?"

"He's the doctor, isn't he? I don't remember her saying anything particular about them."

"And the Wetherbys?"

"I do remember what she said about them." James Bentley looked pleased with himself. " 'No patience with her fusses and her fancies,' that's what she said. And about him, 'Never a word, good or bad, out of him.' " He paused. "She said—it was an unhappy house."

Hercule Poirot looked up. For a second James Bentley's voice had held something that Poirot had not heard in it before. He was not repeating obediently what he could recall. His mind, for a very brief space, had moved out of its apathy. James Bentley was thinking of Hunter's Close, of the life that went on there, of whether or not it was an unhappy house. James Bentley was thinking objectively.

Poirot said softly:

"You knew them? The mother? The father? The daughter?"

"Not really. It was the dog. A Sealyham. It got caught in a trap. She couldn't get it undone. I helped her."

There was again something new in Bentley's tone. "I helped her," he had said, and in those words was a faint echo of pride.

Poirot remembered what Mrs Oliver had told him of her conversation with Deirdre Henderson.

He said gently:

"You talked together?"

"Yes. She—her mother suffered a lot, she told me. She was very fond of her mother."

"And you told her about yours?"

151

"Yes," said James Bentley simply.

Poirot said nothing. He waited.

"Life is very cruel," said James Bentley. "Very unfair. Some people never seem to get any happiness."

"It is possible," said Hercule Poirot.

"I don't think she had had much. Miss Wetherby."

"Henderson."

"Oh yes. She told me she had a stepfather."

"Deirdre Henderson," said Poirot. "Deirdre of the Sorrows. A pretty name—but not a pretty girl, I understand?"

James Bentley flushed.

"*I* thought," he said, "she was rather good-looking . . ."

19

"Now just you listen to me," said Mrs Sweetiman.

Edna sniffed. She had been listening to Mrs Sweetiman for some time. It had been a hopeless conversation, going round in circles. Mrs Sweetiman had said the same things several times, varying the phraseology a little, but even that not much. Edna had sniffed and occasionally blubbered and had reiterated her own two contributions to the discussion: first, that she couldn't ever! Second, that Dad would skin her alive, he would.

"That's as may be," said Mrs Sweetiman, "but murder's murder, and what you saw you saw, and you can't get away from it."

Edna sniffed.

"And what you did ought to do——"

Mrs Sweetiman broke off and attended to Mrs Wetherby, who had come in for some knitting pins and another ounce of wool.

"Haven't seen you about for some time, m'am," said Mrs Sweetiman brightly.

"No, I've been very far from well lately," said Mrs Wetherby. "My heart, you know." She sighed deeply. 'I have to lie up a great deal."

"I heard as you've got some help at last," said Mrs Sweetiman. "You'll want dark needles for this light wool."

"Yes. Quite capable as far as she goes, and cooks not at all badly. But her manners! And her appearance! Dyed hair and the most unsuitable tight jumpers."

"Ah," said Mrs Sweetiman. "Girls aren't trained proper to service nowadays. My mother, she started at thirteen and she got up at a quarter to five every morning. Head housemaid she was when she finished, and three maids under her. And she trained them proper, too. But there's none of that nowadays— girls aren't trained nowadays, they're just educated, like Edna."

Both women looked at Edna, who leant against the post office counter, sniffing and sucking a peppermint, and looking particularly vacant. As an example of education, she hardly did the educational system credit.

"Terrible about Mrs Upward, wasn't it?" continued Mrs Sweetiman conversationally, as Mrs Wetherby sorted through various coloured needles.

"Dreadful," said Mrs Wetherby. "They hardly dared tell me. And when they did, I had the most frightful palpitations. I'm so sensitive."

"Shock to all of us, it was," said Mrs Sweetiman. "As for young Mr Upward, he took on something terrible. Had her hands full with him, the authoress lady did, until the doctor came and give him a seddytiff or something. He's gone up to Long Meadows now as a paying guest, felt he couldn't stay in the cottage—and I don't know as I blame him. Janet Groom, she's gone home to her niece and the police have got the key. The lady what writes the murder books has gone back to London, but she'll come down for the inquest."

Mrs Sweetiman imparted all this information with relish. She prided herself on being well informed. Mrs Wetherby, whose desire for knittng needles had perhaps been prompted by a desire to know what was going on, paid for her purchase.

"It's most upsetting," she said. "It makes the whole village so *dangerous*. There must be a maniac about. When I think that my own dear daughter was out that night, that she herself might have been attacked, perhaps killed." Mrs Wetherby closed both eyes and swayed on her feet. Mrs Sweetiman watched her with interest, but without alarm. Mrs Wetherby opened her eyes again, and said with dignity:

"This place should be patrolled. No young people should go about after dark. And all doors should be locked and bolted. You know that up at Long Meadows, Mrs Summerhayes never locks *any* of her doors. Not even at *night*. She leaves the back door and the drawing-room window open so that the dogs and cats can get in and out. I myself consider that is absolute madness, but she says they've always done it and that if burglars want to get in, they always can."

Mrs McGinty's Dead

"Reckon there wouldn't be much for a burglar to take up at Long Meadows," said Mrs Sweetiman.

Mrs Wetherby shook her head sadly and departed with her purchase.

Mrs Sweetiman and Edna resumed their argument.

"It's no good your setting yourself up to know best," said Mrs Sweetiman. "Right's right and murder's murder. Tell the truth and shame the devil. That's what I say."

"Dad would skin me alive, he would, for sure," said Edna.

"I'd talk to your Dad," said Mrs Sweetiman.

"I couldn't ever," said Edna.

"Mrs Upward's dead," said Mrs Sweetiman. "And you saw something the police don't know about. You're employed in the post office, aren't you? You're a Government servant. You've got to do your duty. You've got to go along to Bert Hayling——"

Edna's sobs burst out anew.

"Not to Bert, I couldn't. However could I go to Bert? It'd be all over the place."

Mrs Sweetiman said rather hesitantly:

"There's that foreign gentleman——"

"Not a foreigner, I couldn't. Not a foreigner."

"No, maybe you're right there."

A car drew up outside the post office with a squealing of brakes.

Mrs Sweetiman's face lit up.

"That's Major Summerhayes, that is. You tell it all to him and he'll advise you what to do."

"I couldn't ever," said Edna, but with less conviction.

Johnnie Summerhayes came into the post office, staggering under the burden of three cardboard boxes.

"Good morning, Mrs Sweetiman," he said cheerfully. "Hope these aren't overweight?"

Mrs Sweetiman attended to the parcels in her official capacity. As Summerhayes was licking the stamps, she spoke.

"Excuse me, sir, I'd like your advice about something."

"Yes, Mrs Sweetiman?"

"Seeing as you belong here, sir, and will know best what to do."

Summerhayes nodded. He was always curiously touched by

155

the lingering feudal spirit of English villages. The villagers knew little of him personally, but because his father and his grandfather and many great-great-grandfathers had lived at Long Meadows, they regarded it as natural that he should advise and direct when asked so to do.

"It's about Edna here," said Mrs Sweetiman.

Edna sniffed.

Johnnie Summerhayes looked at Edna doubtfully. Never, he thought, had he seen a more unprepossessing girl. Exactly like a skinned rabbit. Seemed half-witted too. Surely she couldn't be in what was known officially as "trouble." But no, Mrs Sweetiman would not have come to him for advice in that case.

"Well," he said kindly, "what's the difficulty?"

"It's about the murder, sir. The night of the murder. Edna saw something."

Johnnie Summerhayes transferred his quick dark gaze from Edna to Mrs Sweetiman and back again to Edna.

"What did you see, Edna?" he said.

Edna began to sob. Mrs Sweetiman took over.

"Of course we've been hearing this and that. Some's rumour and some's true. But it's said definite as that there were a lady there that night who drank coffee with Mrs Upward. That's so, isn't it, sir?"

"Yes, I believe so."

"I know as that's true, because we had it from Bert Hayling."

Albert Hayling was the local constable whom Summerhayes knew well. A slow-speaking man with a sense of his own importance.

"I see," said Summerhayes.

"But they don't know, do they, who the lady is? Well, Edna here *saw* her."

Johnnie Summerhayes looked at Edna. He pursed his lips as though to whistle.

"You saw her, did you, Edna? Going in—or coming out?"

"Going in," said Edna. A faint sense of importance loosened her tongue. "Across the road I was, under the trees. Just by the turn of the lane where it's dark. I saw her. She went in at the gate and up to the door and she stood there a bit, and then—and then she went in."

Johnnie Summerhayes' brow cleared.

"That's all right," he said. "It was Miss Henderson. The police know all about that. She went and told them."

Edna shook her head.

"It wasn't Miss Henderson," she said.

"It wasn't—then who was it?"

"I dunno. I didn't see her face. Had her back to me, she had, going up the path and standing there. But it wasn't Miss Henderson."

"But how do you know it wasn't Miss Henderson if you didn't see her face?"

"Because she had fair hair. Miss Henderson's is dark."

Johnnie Summerhayes looked disbelieving.

"It was a very dark night. You'd hardly be able to see the colour of anyone's hair."

"But I did, though. That light was on over the porch. Left like that, it was, because Mr Robin and the detective lady had gone out together to the theatre. And she was standing right under it. A dark coat she had on, and no hat, and her hair was shining fair as could be. I saw it."

Johnnie gave a low whistle. His eyes were serious now.

"What time was it?" he asked.

Edna sniffed.

"I don't rightly know."

"You know about what time," said Mrs Sweetiman.

"It wasn't nine o'clock. I'd have heard the church. And it was after half-past eight."

"Between half-past eight and nine. How long did she stop?"

"I dunno, sir. Because I didn't wait no longer. And I didn't hear nothing. No groans or cries or nothing like that."

Edna sounded slightly aggrieved.

But there would have been no groans and no cries. Johnnie Summerhayes knew that. He said gravely:

"Well, there's only one thing to be done. The police have got to hear about this."

Edna burst into long sniffling sobs.

"Dad'll skin me alive," she whimpered. "He will, for sure."

She cast an imploring look at Mrs Sweetiman and bolted into the back room. Mrs Sweetiman took over with competence.

"It's like this, sir," she said in answer to Summerhayes' inquiring glance. "Edna's been behaving very foolish like. Very strict her Dad is, maybe a bit over strict, but it's hard to say what's best nowadays. There's a nice young fellow over to Cullavon and he and Edna have been going together nice and steady, and her Dad was quite pleased about it, but Reg he's on the slow side, and you know what girls are. Edna's taken up lately with Charlie Masters."

"Masters? One of Farmer Cole's men, isn't he?"

"That's right, sir. Farm labourer. And a married man with two children. Always after the girls, he is, and a bad fellow in every way. Edna hasn't got any sense, and her Dad, he put a stop to it. Quite right. So, you see, Edna was going into Cullavon that night to go to the pictures with Reg—at least that's what she told her Dad. But really she went out to meet this Masters. Waited for him, she did, at the turn of the lane where it seems they used to meet. Well, he didn't come. Maybe his wife kept him at home, or maybe he's after another girl, but there it is. Edna waited but at last she gave up. But it's awkward for her, as you can see, explaining what she was doing here, when she ought to have taken the bus into Cullavon."

Johnnie Summerhayes nodded. Suppressing an irrelevant feeling of wonder that the unprepossessing Edna could have sufficient sex appeal to attract the attention of two men, he dealt with the practical aspect of the situation.

"She doesn't want to go to Bert Hayling about it," he said with quick comprehension.

"That's right, sir."

Summerhayes reflected rapidly.

"I'm afraid the police have got to know," he said gently.

"That's what I told her, sir," said Mrs Sweetiman.

"But they will probably be quite tactful about—er—the circumstances. Possibly she mayn't have to give evidence. And what she tells them, they'll keep to themselves. I could ring up Spence and ask him to come over here—no, better still, I'll take young Edna into Kilchester with me in my car. If she goes to the police station there, nobody here need know anything about it. I'll just ring them up first and warn them we're coming."

And so, after a brief telephone call, the sniffing Edna, buttoned firmly into her coat and encouraged by a pat on the back from Mrs Sweetiman, stepped into the station wagon and was driven rapidly away in the direction of Kilchester.

20

HERCULE POIROT was in Superintendent Spence's office in Kilchester. He was leaning back in a chair, his eyes closed and the tips of his fingers just touching each other in front of him.

The superintendent received some reports, gave instructions to a sergeant, and finally looked across at the other man.

"Getting a brainwave, M. Poirot?" he demanded.

"I reflect," said Poirot. "I review."

"I forgot to ask you. Did you get anything useful from James Bentley when you saw him?"

Poirot shook his head. He frowned.

It was indeed of James Bentley he had been thinking.

It was annoying, thought Poirot with exasperation, that on a case such as this where he had offered his services without reward, solely out of friendship and respect for an upright police officer, that the victim of circumstances should so lack any romantic appeal. A lovely young girl, now, bewildered and innocent, or a fine upstanding young man, also bewildered, but whose "head is bloody but unbowed," thought Poirot, who had been reading a good deal of English poetry in an anthology lately. Instead, he had James Bentley, a pathological case if there ever was one, a self-centred creature who had never thought much of anyone but himself. A man ungrateful for the efforts that were being made to save him—almost, one might say, uninterested in them.

Really, thought Poirot, one might as well let him be hanged since he does not seem to care. . . .

No, he would not go quite as far as that.

Superintendent Spence's voice broke into these reflections.

"Our interview," said Poirot, "was, if I might say so, singularly unproductive. Anything useful that Bentley might have remembered he did not remember—what he did remember is so vague and uncertain that one cannot build upon it. But at any rate it seems fairly certain that Mrs McGinty was excited by the article in the *Sunday Comet* and spoke about it to Bentley with special reference to 'someone connected with the case,' living in Broadhinny.''

"With which case?" asked Superintendent Spence sharply.

"Our friend could not be sure," said Poirot. "He said, rather doubtfully, the Craig case—but the Craig case being the only one he had ever heard of, it would, presumably, be the only one he could remember. But the 'someone' was a woman. He even quoted Mrs McGinty's words. Somebody who had 'not so much to be proud of if all's known.'"

"Proud?"

"Mais oui," Poirot nodded his appreciation. "A suggestive word, is it not?"

"No clue as to who the proud lady was?"

"Bentley suggested Mrs Upward—but as far as I can see for no real reason!"

Spence shook his head.

"Probably because she was a proud masterful sort of woman— outstandingly so, I should say. But it couldn't have been Mrs Upward, because Mrs Upward's dead, and dead for the same reason as Mrs McGinty died—because she recognised a photograph."

Poirot said sadly: "I warned her."

Spence murmured irritably:

"Lily Gamboll! So far as age goes, there are only two possibilities, Mrs Rendell and Mrs Carpenter. I don't count the Henderson girl—she's got a background."

"And the others have not?"

Spence sighed.

"You know what things are nowadays. The war stirred up everyone and everything. The approved school where Lily Gamboll was, and all its records, were destroyed by a direct hit. Then take people. It's the hardest thing in the world to check on people. Take Broadhinny—the only people in Broadhinny we know anything about are the Summerhayes family, who have been there for three hundred years, and Guy Carpenter, who's one of the engineering Carpenters. All the others are—what shall I say—fluid? Dr Rendell's on the Medical Register and we know where he trained and where he's practised, but we don't know his home background. His wife came from near Dublin. Eve Selkirk, as she was before she married Guy Carpenter, was a pretty young war widow. Anyone can be a pretty young war widow. Take the Wetherbys—they seem to have floated round the world, here, there and everywhere. Why? Is there a reason? Did he embezzle from a bank? Or did they occasion a scandal? I don't say we can't dig up about people. We can—but it takes time. The people themselves won't help you."

"Because they have something to conceal—but it need not be murder," said Poirot.

"Exactly. It may be trouble with the law, or it may be a humble origin, or it may be common or garden scandal. But whatever it is, they've taken a lot of pains to cover up—and that makes it difficult to uncover."

"But not impossible."

"Oh no. Not impossible. It just takes time. As I say, if Lily Gamboll is in Broadhinny, she's *either* Eve Carpenter or Shelagh Rendell. I've questioned them—just routine—that's the way I put it. They say they were both at home—alone. Mrs Carpenter was the wide-eyed innocent, Mrs Rendell was nervous—but then she's a nervous type, you can't go by that."

"Yes," said Poirot thoughtfully. "She is a nervous type."

He was thinking of Mrs Rendell in the garden at Long Meadows. Mrs Rendell had received an anonymous letter, or so she said. He wondered, as he had wondered before, about that statement.

Spence went on:

"And we have to be careful—because even if one of them *is* guilty, the other is innocent."

"And Guy Carpenter is a prospective Member of Parliament and an important local figure."

"That wouldn't help him if he was guilty of murder or accessory to it," said Spence grimly.

"I know that. But you have, have you not, to be *sure*?"

"That's right. Anyway you'll agree, won't you, that it lies between the two of them?"

Poirot sighed.

"No—no—I would not say that. There are other possibilities."

"Such as?"

Poirot was silent for a moment, then he said in a different, almost casual tone of voice:

"Why do people keep photographs?"

"Why? Goodness knows! Why do people keep all sorts of things—junk—trash, bits and pieces. They do—that's all there is to it!"

"Up to a point I agree with you. Some people keep things. Some people throw everything away as soon as they have done with it. That, yes, it is a matter of temperament. But I speak now especially of photographs. Why do people keep, in particular, *photographs*?"

"As I say, because they just don't throw things away. Or else because it reminds them——"

Poirot pounced on the words.

"Exactly. *It reminds them*. Now again we ask—why? *Why* does a woman keep a photograph of herself when young? And I say that the first reason is, essentially, vanity. She has been a pretty girl and she keeps a photograph of herself to remind her of what a pretty girl she was. It encourages her when her mirror tells her unpalatable things. She says, perhaps, to a friend, 'That was me when I was eighteen . . .' and she sighs. . . . You agree?"

"Yes—yes, I should say that's true enough."

"Then that is reason No. 1. Vanity. Now reason No. 2. Sentiment."

"That's the same thing?"

"No, no, not quite. Because this leads you to preserve not only your own photograph but that of someone else. . . . A picture of your married daughter—when she was a child sitting on a hearthrug with tulle round her."

"I've seen some of those," Spence grinned.

"Yes. Very embarrassing to the subject sometimes, but mothers like to do it. And sons and daughters often keep pictures of their mothers, especially, say, if their mother died young. 'This was my mother as a girl.'"

"I'm beginning to see what you're driving at, Poirot."

"And there is, possibly, a *third* category. Not vanity, not sentiment, not love—perhaps *hate*—what do you say?"

"Hate?"

"Yes. To keep a desire for revenge alive. Someone who has injured you—you might keep a photograph to remind you, might you not?"

"But surely that doesn't apply in this case?"

"Does it not?"

"What are you thinking of?"

Poirot murmured:

"Newspaper reports are often inaccurate. The *Sunday Comet* stated that Eva Kane was employed by the Craigs as a nursery governess. Was that actually the case?"

"Yes, it was. But we're working on the assumption that it's Lily Gamboll we're looking for."

Poirot sat up suddenly very straight in his chair. He wagged an imperative forefinger at Spence.

"Look. Look at the photograph of Lily Gamboll. She is not pretty—no! Frankly, with those teeth and those spectacles she is hideously ugly. Then nobody has kept that photograph for the first of our reasons. No woman would keep that photo out of vanity. If Eve Carpenter or Shelagh Rendell, who are both good-looking women, especially Eve Carpenter, had this photograph of themselves, they would tear it in pieces quickly in case somebody should see it!"

"Well, there is something in that."

"So reason No. 1 is out. Now take sentiment. Did anybody love Lily Gamboll at that age? The whole point of Lily Gamboll is that they did not. She was an unwanted and unloved child. The person who liked her best was her aunt, and her aunt died under the chopper. So it was not sentiment that kept this picture. And revenge? Nobody hated her either. Her murdered aunt was a lonely woman without a husband and with no close friends. Nobody had hate for the little slum child—only pity."

"Look here, M. Poirot, what you're saying is that *nobody* would have kept that photo."

"Exactly—that is the result of my reflections."

"But somebody did. Because Mrs Upward had seen it."

"*Had she?*"

"Dash it all. It was you who told me. She said so herself."

"Yes, she said so," said Poirot. "But the late Mrs Upward

was, in some ways, a secretive woman. She liked to manage things her own way. I showed the photographs, and she recognised one of them. But then, for some reason, she wanted to keep the identification to herself. She wanted, let us say, to deal with a certain situation in the way she fancied. And so, being very quick-witted, she deliberately pointed to the *wrong* picture. Thereby keeping her knowledge to herself."

"But why?"

"Because, as I say, she wanted to play a lone hand."

"It wouldn't be blackmail? She was an extremely wealthy woman, you know, widow of a North Country manufacturer."

"Oh no, not blackmail. More likely beneficence. We'll say that she quite liked the person in question, and that she didn't want to give their secret away. But nevertheless she was *curious*. She intended to have a private talk with that person. And whilst doing so, to make up her mind whether or not that person had had anything to do with the death of Mrs McGinty. Something like that."

"Then that leaves the other three photos in?"

"Precisely. Mrs Upward meant to get in touch with the person in question at the first opportunity. That came when her son and Mrs Oliver went over to the Repertory Theatre at Cullenquay."

"*And she telephoned to Deirdre Henderson.* That puts Deirdre Henderson right back in the picture. *And* her mother!"

Superintendent Spence shook his head sadly at Poirot.

"You do like to make it difficult, don't you, M. Poirot?" he said.

21

MRS WETHERBY walked back home from the post office with a gait surprisingly spry in one habitually reported to be an invalid.

Only when she had entered the front door did she once more shuffle feebly into the drawing-room and collapse on the sofa.

The bell was within reach of her hand and she rang it.

Since nothing happened she rang it again, this time keeping her finger on it for some time.

In due course Maude Williams appeared. She was wearing a flowered overall and had a duster in her hand.

"Did you ring, madam?"

"I rang twice. When I ring I expect someone to come at once. I might be dangerously ill."

"I'm sorry, madam. I was upstairs."

"I know you were. You were in my room. I heard you overhead. And you were pulling the drawers in and out. I can't think why. It's no part of your job to go prying into my things."

"I wasn't prying. I was putting some of the things you left lying about away tidily."

"Nonsense. All you people snoop. And I won't have it. I'm feeling very faint. Is Miss Deirdre in?"

"She took the dog for a walk."

"How stupid. She might know I would need her. Bring me an egg beaten up in milk and add a little brandy. The brandy is on the sideboard in the dining-room."

"There are only just the three eggs for breakfast tomorrow."

"Then someone will have to go without. Hurry, will you? Don't stand there looking at me. And you're wearing far too much make-up. It isn't suitable."

There was a bark in the hall and Deirdre and her Sealyham came in as Maude went out.

"I heard your voice," said Deirdre breathlessly. "What have you been saying to her?"

"Nothing."

"She looked like thunder."

"I put her in her place. Impertinent girl."

"Oh, Mummy darling, must you? It's so difficult to get anyone. And she does cook well."

"I suppose it's of no importance that she's insolent to *me*! Oh well, I shan't be with you much longer." Mrs Wetherby rolled up her eyes and took some fluttering breaths. "I walked too far," she murmured.

"You oughtn't to have gone out, darling. Why didn't you tell me you were going?"

"I thought some air would do me good. It's so stuffy. It doesn't matter. One doesn't really want to live—not if one's only a trouble to people."

"You're not a trouble, darling. I'd die without you."

"You're a good girl—but I can see how I weary you and get on your nerves."

"You don't—you don't," said Deirdre passionately.

Mrs Wetherby sighed and let her eyelids fall.

"I—can't talk much," she murmured. "I must just lie still."

"I'll hurry up Maude with the egg nog."

Deirdre ran out of the room. In her hurry she caught her elbow on a table and a bronze god bumped on the ground.

"So clumsy," murmured Mrs Wetherby to herself, wincing.

The door opened and Mr Wetherby came in. He stood there for a moment. Mrs Wetherby opened her eyes.

"Oh, it's you, Roger?"

"I wondered what all the noise was in here. It's impossible to read quietly in this house."

"It was just Deirdre, dear. She came in with the dog."

Mr Wetherby stooped and picked up the bronze monstrosity from the floor.

"Surely Deirdre's old enough not to knock things down the whole time."

"She's just rather awkward."

"Well, it's absurd to be awkward at her age. And can't she keep that dog from barking?"

"I'll speak to her, Roger."

"If she makes her home here, she must consider our wishes and not behave as though the house belonged to her."

"Perhaps you'd rather she went away," murmured Mrs Wetherby. Through half-closed eyes she watched her husband.

"No, of course not. Of course not. Naturally her home is with us. I only ask for a little more good sense and good manners." He added: "You've been out, Edith?"

"Yes. I just went down to the post office."

"No fresh news about poor Mrs Upward?"

"The police still don't know who it was."

"They seem to be quite hopeless. Any motive? Who gets her money?"

"The son, I suppose."

"Yes—yes, then it really seems as though it must have been one of these tramps. You should tell this girl she's got to be careful about keeping the front door locked. And only to open it on the chain when it gets near dusk. These men are very daring and brutal nowadays."

"Nothing seems to have been taken from Mrs Upward's."

"Odd."

"Not like Mrs McGinty," said Mrs Wetherby.

"Mrs McGinty? Oh! the charwoman. What's Mrs McGinty got to do with Mrs Upward?"

"She did work for her, Roger."

"Don't be silly, Edith."

Mrs Wetherby closed her eyes again. As Mr Wetherby went out of the room she smiled to herself.

She opened her eyes with a start to find Maude standing over her, holding a glass.

"Your egg nog, madam," said Maude.

Her voice was loud and clear. It echoed too resonantly in the deadened house.

Mrs Wetherby looked up with a vague feeling of alarm.

How tall and unbending the girl was. She stood over Mrs Wetherby like—"like a figure of doom," Mrs Wetherby thought to herself—and then wondered why such extraordinary words had come into her head.

She raised herself on her elbow and took the glass.

"Thank you, Maude," she said.

Maude turned and went out of the room.

Mrs Wetherby still felt vaguely upset.

22

i

HERCULE POIROT took a hired car back to Broadhinny.

He was tired because he had been thinking. Thinking was always exhausting. And his thinking had not been entirely satisfactory. It was as though a pattern, perfectly visible, was woven into a piece of material and yet, although he was holding the piece of material, he could not see what the pattern was.

But it was all there. That was the point. It was all there. Only it was one of those patterns, self-coloured and subtle, that are not easy to perceive.

A little way out of Kilchester his car encountered the Summerhayes' station wagon coming in the opposite direction. Johnnie was driving and he had a passenger. Poirot hardly noticed them. He was still absorbed in thought.

When he got back to Long Meadows, he went into the drawing-room. He removed a colander full of spinach from the most comfortable chair in the room and sat down. From overhead come the faint drumming of a typewriter. It was Robin Upward, struggling with a play. Three versions he had already torn up, so he told Poirot. Somehow, he couldn't concentrate.

Robin might feel his mother's death quite sincerely, but he remained Robin Upward, chiefly interested in himself.

"Madre," he said solemnly, "would have wished me to go on with my work."

Hercule Poirot had heard many people say much the same thing. It was one of the most convenient assumptions, this knowledge of what the dead would wish. The bereaved had never any doubt about their dear ones' wishes and those wishes usually squared with their own inclinations.

In this case it was probably true. Mrs Upward had had great faith in Robin's work and had been extremely proud of him.

Poirot leaned back and closed his eyes.

He thought of Mrs Upward. He considered what Mrs Upward had really been like. He remembered a phrase that he had once heard used by a police officer.

"We'll take him apart and see what makes him tick."

What had made Mrs Upward tick?

There was a crash, and Maureen Summerhayes came in. Her hair was flapping madly.

"I can't think what's happened to Johnnie," she said. "He just went down to the post office with those special orders. He ought to have been back hours ago. I want him to fix the henhouse door."

A true gentleman, Poirot feared, would have gallantly offered to fix the henhouse door himself. Poirot did not. He wanted to go on thinking about two murders and about the character of Mrs Upward.

"And I can't find that Ministry of Agriculture form," continued Maureen. "I've looked everywhere."

"The spinach is on the sofa," Poirot offered helpfully.

Maureen was not worried about spinach.

"The form came last week," she mused. "And I must have put it somewhere. Perhaps it was when I was darning that pullover of Johnnie's."

She swept over to the bureau and started pulling out the drawers. Most of the contents she swept on to the floor ruthlessly. It was agony to Hercule Poirot to watch her.

Suddenly she uttered a cry of triumph.

"Got it!"

Delightedly she rushed from the room.

Hercule Poirot sighed and resumed meditation.

To arrange, with order and precision——

He frowned. The untidy heap of objects on the floor by the bureau distracted his mind. What a way to look for things!

Order and method. That was the thing. Order and method.

Though he had turned sideways in his chair, he could still see the confusion on the floor. Sewing things, a pile of socks, letters, knitting wool, magazines, sealing wax, photographs, a pullover——

It was insupportable!

Poirot rose, went across to the bureau and with quick deft movements began to return the objects to the open drawers.

The pullover, the socks, the knitting wool. Then, in the next drawer, the sealing wax, the photographs, the letters.

The telephone rang.

The sharpness of the bell made him jump.

He went across to the telephone and lifted the receiver.

"'Allo, 'allo, 'allo," he said.

The voice that spoke to him was the voice of Superintendent Spence.

"Ah! it's you, M. Poirot. Just the man I want."

Spence's voice was almost unrecognisable. A very worried man had given place to a confident one.

"Filling me up with a lot of fandangle about the wrong photograph," he said with reproachful indulgence. "We've got some new evidence. Girl at the post office in Broadhinny. Major Summerhayes just brought her in. It seems she was standing practically opposite the cottage that night and she saw a woman go in. Sometime after eight-thirty and before nine o'clock. And it wasn't Deirdre Henderson. It was a woman with fair hair. That puts us right back where we were—it's definitely between the two of them—Eve Carpenter and Shelagh Rendell. The only question is—which?"

Poirot opened his mouth but did not speak. Carefully, deliberately, he replaced the receiver on the stand.

He stood there staring unseeingly in front of him.

The telephone rang again.

"'Allo! 'Allo! 'Allo!"

"Can I speak to M. Poirot, please?"

"Hercule Poirot speaking."

"Thought so. Maude Williams here. Post office in a quarter of an hour?"

"I will be there."

He replaced the receiver.

He looked down at his feet. Should he change his shoes? His feet ached a little. Ah well—no matter.

Resolutely Poirot clapped on his hat and left the house.

On his way down the hill he was hailed by one of Superintendent Spence's men just emerging from Laburnums.

"Morning, M. Poirot."

Poirot responded politely. He noticed that Sergeant Fletcher was looking excited.

"The Super sent me over to have a thorough check up," he explained. "You know—any little thing we might have missed. Never know, do you? We'd been over the desk, of course, but the Super got the idea there might be a secret drawer—must have been reading spy stuff. Well, there wasn't a secret drawer. But after that I got on to the books. Sometimes people slip a letter into a book they're reading. You know?"

Poirot said that he knew. "And you found something?" he asked politely.

"Not a letter or anything of that sort, no. But I found something interesting—at least *I* think it's interesting. Look here."

He unwrapped from a piece of newspaper an old and rather decrepit book.

"In one of the bookshelves it was. Old book, published years ago. But look here." He opened it and showed the flyleaf. Pencilled across it were the words: *Evelyn Hope*.

"Interesting, don't you think? That's the name, in case you don't remember——"

"The name that Eva Kane took when she left England. I do remember," said Poirot.

"Looks as though when Mrs McGinty spotted one of those photos here in Broadhinny, it was our Mrs Upward. Makes it kind of complicated, doesn't it?"

"It does," said Poirot with feeling. "I can assure you that when you go back to Superintendent Spence with this piece of information he will pull out his hair by the roots—yes, assuredly by the roots."

"I hope it won't be as bad as that," said Sergeant Fletcher.

Poirot did not reply. He went on down the hill. He had ceased to think. Nothing anywhere made sense.

He went into the post office. Maude Williams was there looking at knitting patterns. Poirot did not speak to her. He went to the stamp counter. When Maude had made her purchase,

Mrs Sweetiman came over to him and he bought some stamps. Maude went out of the shop.

Mrs Sweetiman seemed preoccupied and not talkative. Poirot was able to follow Maude out fairly quickly. He caught her up a short distance along the road and fell into step beside her.

Mrs Sweetiman, looking out of the post office window, exclaimed to herself disapprovingly. "Those foreigners! All the same, every manjack of 'em. Old enough to be her grandfather, he is!"

ii

"*Eh bien*," said Poirot, "you have something to tell me?"

"I don't know that it's important. There was somebody trying to get in at the window of Mrs Wetherby's room."

"When?"

"This morning. *She'd* gone out, and the girl was out with the dog. Old frozen fish was shut up in his study as usual. I'd have been in the kitchen normally—it faces the other way like the study—but actually it seemed a good opportunity to—you understand?"

Poirot nodded.

"So I nipped upstairs and into Her Acidity's bedroom. There was a ladder against the window and a man was fumbling with the window catch. She's had everything locked and barred since the murder. Never a bit of fresh air. When the man saw me he scuttled down and made off. The ladder was the gardener's—he'd been cutting back the ivy and had gone to have his elevenses."

"Who was the man? Can you describe him?"

"I only got the merest glimpse. By the time I got to the window he was down the ladder and gone, and when I first saw him he was against the sun, so I couldn't see his face."

"You are sure it *was* a man?"

Maude considered.

"Dressed as a man—an old felt hat on. It *might* have been a woman, of course. . . ."

"It is interesting," said Poirot. "It is very interesting. . . . Nothing else?"

"Not yet. The junk that old woman keeps! Must be dotty! She came in without me hearing this morning and bawled me out for snooping. I shall be murdering her next. If anyone asks to be murdered that woman does. A really nasty bit of goods."

Poirot murmured softly:

"Evelyn Hope . . ."

"What's that?" She spun round on him.

"So you know that name?"

"Why—yes . . . It's the name Eva Whatsername took when she went to Australia. It—it was in the paper—the *Sunday Comet*."

"The *Sunday Comet* said many things, but it did not say that. The police found the name written in a book in Mrs Upward's house."

Maude exclaimed:

"Then it *was* her—and she *didn't* die out there . . . Michael was right."

"Michael?"

Maude said abruptly:

"I can't stop. I'll be late serving lunch. I've got it all in the oven, but it will be getting dried up."

She started off at a run. Poirot stood looking after her.

At the post office window, Mrs Sweetiman, her nose glued to the pane, wondered if that old foreigner had been making suggestions of a certain character. . . .

iii

Back at Long Meadows, Poirot removed his shoes, and put on a pair of bedroom slippers. They were not *chic*, not in his opinion *comme il faut*—but there must be relief.

He sat down on the easy-chair again and began once more to think. He had by now a lot to think about.

There were things he had missed—little things.

The pattern was all there. It only needed cohesion.

Maureen, glass in hand, talking in a dreamy voice—asking a question. . . . Mrs Oliver's account of her evening at the

Rep. Cecil? Michael? He was almost sure that she had mentioned a Michael—Eva Kane, nursery governess to the Craigs——

Evelyn Hope . . .

Of course! Evelyn Hope!

23

i

EVE CARPENTER came into the Summerhayes' house in the casual way that most people did, using any door or window that was convenient.

She was looking for Hercule Poirot and when she found him she did not beat about the bush.

"Look here," she said. "You're a detective and you're supposed to be good. All right, I'll hire you."

"Suppose I am not for hire. *Mon Dieu*, I am not a taxicab!"

"You're a private detective and private detectives get paid, don't they?"

"It is the custom."

"Well, that's what I'm saying. I'll pay you. I'll pay you well."

"For what? What do you want me to do."

Eve Carpenter said sharply:

"Protect me against the police. They're crazy. They seem to think I killed the Upward woman. And they're nosing round, asking me all sorts of questions—ferreting out things. I don't like it. It's driving me mental."

Poirot looked at her. Something of what she said was true. She looked many years older than when he had first seen her a few weeks ago. Circles under her eyes spoke of sleepless nights. There were lines from her mouth to her chin, and her hand, when she lit a cigarette, shook badly.

"You've got to stop it," she said. "You've got to."

"Madame, what can I do?"

"Fend them off somehow or other. Damned cheek! If Guy was a man he'd stop all this. He wouldn't let them persecute me."

"And—he does nothing?"

She said sullenly:

"I've not told him. He just talks pompously about giving the police all the assistance possible. It's all right for *him*. He was at some ghastly political meeting that night."

"And you?"

"I was just sitting at home. Listening to the radio actually."

"But, if you can prove that——"

"How can I prove it? I offered the Crofts a fabulous sum to say they'd been in and out and seen me there—the damned swine refused."

"That was a very unwise move on your part."

"I don't see why. It would have settled the business."

"You have probably convinced your servants that you did commit the murder."

"Well—I'd paid Croft anyway for——"

"For what?"

"Nothing."

"Remember—you want my help."

"Oh! it was nothing that matters. But Croft took the message from her."

"From Mrs Upward?"

"Yes. Asking me to go down and see her that night."

"And you say you didn't go?"

"Why should I go? Damned dreary old woman. Why should I go and hold her hand? I never dreamed of going for a moment."

"When did this message come?"

"When I was out. I don't know exactly when—between five and six, I think. Croft took it."

"And you gave him money to forget he had taken that message. Why?"

"Don't be idiotic. I didn't want to get mixed up in it all."

"And then you offer him money to give you an alibi? What do you suppose he and his wife think?"

"Who cares what they think!"

"A jury may care," said Poirot gravely.

She stared at him.

"You're not serious?"

"I am serious."

"They'd listen to servants—and not to me?"

Poirot looked at her.

Such crass rudeness and stupidity! Antagonising the people who might have been helpful. A short-sighted stupid policy. Short-sighted——

Such lovely wide blue eyes.

He said quietly:

"Why don't you wear glasses, madame? You need them."

"What? Oh, I do sometimes. I did as a child."

"And you had then a plate for your teeth."

She stared.

"I did, as a matter of fact. Why all this?"

"The ugly duckling becomes the swan?"

"I was certainly ugly enough."

"Did your mother think so?"

She said sharply:

"I don't remember my mother. What the hell are we talking about anyway? Will you take on the job?"

"I regret I cannot."

"Why can't you?"

"Because in this affair I act for James Bentley."

"James Bentley? Oh, you mean that half-wit who killed the charwoman. What's he got to do with the Upwards?"

"Perhaps—nothing."

"Well, then! Is it a question of money? How much?"

"That is your great mistake, madame. You think always in terms of money. You have money and you think that only money counts."

"I haven't always had money," said Eve Carpenter.

"No," said Poirot. "I thought not." He nodded his head gently. "That explains a good deal. It excuses some things. . . ."

ii

Eve Carpenter went out the way she had come, blundering a little in the light as Poirot remembered her doing before.

Poirot said softly to himself: "Evelyn Hope . . ."

So Mrs Upward had rung up both Deirdre Henderson *and*

Evelyn Carpenter. Perhaps she had rung up someone else.
Perhaps——

With a crash Maureen came in.

"It's my scissors now. Sorry lunch is late. I've got three pairs
and I can't find one of them."

She rushed over to the bureau and the process with which Poirot
was well acquainted was repeated. This time, the objective was
attained rather sooner. With a cry of joy, Maureen departed.

Almost automatically, Poirot stepped over and began to replace the things in the drawer. Sealing wax, notepaper, a work
basket, photographs——

Photographs . . .

He stood staring at the photograph he held in his hand.

Footsteps rushed back along the passage.

Poirot could move quickly in spite of his age. He had dropped
the photograph on the sofa, put a cushion on it, and had himself
sat on the cushion, by the time that Maureen re-entered.

"Where the hell I've put a colander full of spinach——"

"But it is there, madame."

He indicated the colander as it reposed beside him on the sofa.

"So that's where I left it." She snatched it up. "Everything's
behindhand to-day . . ." Her glance took in Hercule Poirot
sitting bolt upright.

"What on earth do you want to sit there for? Even on a
cushion, it's the most uncomfortable seat in the room. All the
springs are broken."

"I know, madame. But I am—I am admiring that picture on
the wall."

Maureen glanced up at the oil painting of a naval officer
complete with telescope.

"Yes—it's good. About the only good thing in the house.
We're not sure that it isn't a Gainsborough." She sighed. "Johnnie
won't sell it, though. It's his great-great and I think a few more
greats, grandfather and he went down with his ship or did
something frightfully gallant. Johnnie's terribly proud of it."

"Yes," said Poirot gently. "Yes, he has something to be
proud about, your husband!"

iii

It was three o'clock when Poirot arrived at Dr Rendell's house.

He had eaten rabbit stew and spinach and hard potatoes and a rather peculiar pudding, not scorched this time. Instead, "The water got in," Maureen had explained. He had drunk half a cup of muddy coffee. He did not feel well.

The door was opened by the elderly housekeeper Mrs Scott, and he asked for Mrs Rendell.

She was in the drawing-room with the radio on and started up when he was announced.

He had the same impression of her that he had had the first time he saw her. Wary, on her guard, frightened of him, or frightened of what he represented.

She seemed paler and more shadowy than she had done. He was almost certain that she was thinner.

"I want to ask you a question, madame."

"A question? Oh? Oh yes?"

"Did Mrs Upward telephone to you on the day of her death?"

She stared at him. She nodded.

"At what time?"

"Mrs Scott took the message. It was about six o'clock, I think."

"What was the message? To ask you to go there that evening?"

"Yes. She said that Mrs Oliver and Robin were going into Kilchester and she would be all alone as it was Janet's night out. Could I come down and keep her company."

"Was any time suggested?"

"Nine o'clock or after."

"And you went?"

"I meant to. I really meant to. But I don't know how it was, I fell fast asleep after dinner that night. It was after ten when I woke up. I thought it was too late."

"You did not tell the police about Mrs Upward's call?"

Her eyes widened. They had a rather innocent childlike stare.

"Ought I to have done? Since I didn't go, I thought it didn't matter. Perhaps, even, I felt rather guilty. If I'd gone, she might

have been alive now." She caught her breath suddenly. "Oh, I
hope it wasn't like that."

"Not quite like that," said Poirot.

He paused and then said:

"*What are you afraid of, madame?*"

She caught her breath sharply.

"Afraid? I'm not afraid."

"But you are."

"What nonsense. What—what should I be afraid of?"

Poirot paused for a moment before speaking.

"I thought perhaps you might be afraid of *me* . . ."

She didn't answer. But her eyes widened. Slowly, defiantly,
she shook her head.

24

i

"This way to Bedlam," said Spence.

"It is not as bad as that," said Poirot soothingly.

"That's what you say. Every single bit of information that comes in makes things more difficult. Now you tell me that Mrs Upward rang up *three* women. Asked them to come that evening. Why three? Didn't she know herself which of them was Lily Gamboll? Or isn't it a case of Lily Gamboll at all? Take that book with the name of Evelyn Hope in it. It suggests, doesn't it, that Mrs Upward and Eva Kane are one and the same."

"Which agrees exactly with James Bentley's impression of what Mrs McGinty said to him."

"I thought he wasn't sure."

"He was not sure. It would be impossible for James Bentley to be sure of anything. He did not listen properly to what Mrs McGinty was saying. Nevertheless, if James Bentley had an impression that Mrs McGinty was talking about Mrs Upward, it may very well be true. Impressions often are."

"Our latest information from Australia (it was Australia she went to, by the way, not America) seems to be to the effect that the 'Mrs Hope' in question died out there twenty years ago."

"I have already been told that," said Poirot.

"You always know everything, don't you, Poirot?"

Poirot took no notice of this gibe. He said:

"At the one end we have 'Mrs Hope' deceased in Australia—and at the other?"

"At the other end we have Mrs Upward, the widow of a rich North Country manufacturer. She lived with him near Leeds, and had a son. Soon after the son's birth, her husband died. The boy was inclined to be tubercular and since her husband's death she lived mostly abroad."

"And when does this saga begin?"

"The saga begins four years after Eva Kane left England. Upward met his wife somewhere abroad and brought her home after the marriage."

"So actually Mrs Upward *could* be Eva Kane. What was her maiden name?"

"Hargraves, I understand. But what's in a name?"

"What indeed. Eva Kane, or Evelyn Hope, may have died in Australia—but she may have arranged a convenient decease and resuscitated herself as Hargraves and made a wealthy match."

"It's all a long time ago," said Spence. "But supposing that it's true. Supposing she kept a picture of herself and supposing that Mrs McGinty saw it—then one can only assume that *she* killed Mrs McGinty."

"That could be, could it not? Robin Upward was broadcasting that night. Mrs Rendell mentions going to the cottage that evening, remember, and not being able to make herself heard. According to Mrs Sweetiman, Janet Groom told her that Mrs Upward was not really as crippled as she made out."

"That's all very well, Poirot, but the fact remains that *she herself* was killed—after recognising a photograph. Now you want to make out that the two deaths are not connected."

"No, no. I do not say that. They are connected all right."

"I give it up."

"Evelyn Hope. There is the key to the problem."

"Evelyn Carpenter? Is that your idea? *Not* Lily Gamboll— but Eva Kane's daughter! But surely she wouldn't kill her own mother."

"No, no. This is not matricide."

"What an irritating devil you are, Poirot. You'll be saying next that Eva Kane and Lily Gamboll, and Janice Courtland *and* Vera Blake are *all* living in Broadhinny. All four suspects."

"We have more than four. Eva Kane was the Craigs' nursery governess, remember."

"What's that got to do with it?"

"Where there is a nursery governess, there must be children— or at least a child. What happened to the Craig children?"

"There was a girl and a boy, I believe. Some relative took them."

"So there are two more people to take into account. Two people who might have kept a photograph for the third reason I mentioned—revenge."

"I don't believe it," said Spence.

Poirot sighed.

"It has to be considered, all the same. I think I know the truth—though there is one fact that baffles me utterly."

"I'm glad something baffles you," said Spence.

"Confirm one thing for me, *mon cher* Spence. Eva Kane left the country before Craig's execution, that is right?"

"Quite right."

"And she was, at that time, expecting a child?"

"Quite right."

"*Bon Dieu*, how stupid I have been," said Hercule Poirot. "The whole thing is simple, is it not?"

It was after that remark that there was very nearly a third murder—the murder of Hercule Poirot by Superintendent Spence in Kilchester Police Headquarters.

ii

"I want," said Hercule Poirot, "a personal call. To Mrs Ariadne Oliver."

A personal call to Mrs Oliver was not achieved without difficulties. Mrs Oliver was working and could not be disturbed. Poirot, however, disregarded all denials. Presently he heard the authoress's voice.

It was cross and rather breathless.

"Well, what is it?" said Mrs 'Oliver. "Have you got to ring me up just now? I've thought of a most wonderful idea for a murder in a draper's shop. You know, the old-fashioned kind that sells combinations and funny vests with long sleeves."

"I do not know," said Poirot. "And anyway what I have to say to you is far more important."

"It couldn't be," said Mrs Oliver. "Not to *me*, I mean. Unless I get a rough sketch of my idea jotted down, it will *go*!"

Hercule Poirot paid no attention to this creative agony. He asked sharp imperative questions to which Mrs Oliver replied somewhat vaguely.

"Yes—yes—it's a little Repertory Theatre—I don't know its name. . . . Well, one of them was Cecil Something, and the one I was talking to was Michael."

"Admirable. That is all I need to know."

"But why Cecil and Michael?"

"Return to the combinations and the long-sleeved vests, madame."

"I can't think why you don't arrest Dr Rendell," said Mrs Oliver. "I would, if I were the Head of Scotland Yard."

"Very possibly. I wish you luck with the murder in the draper's shop."

"The whole idea has gone now," said Mrs Oliver. "You've ruined it."

Poirot apologised handsomely.

He put down the receiver and smiled at Spence.

"We go now—or at least I will go—to interview a young actor whose Christian name is Michael and who plays the less important parts in the Cullenquay Repertory Theatre. I pray only that he is the right Michael."

"Why on earth——"

Poirot dexterously averted the rising wrath of Superintendent Spence.

"Do you know, *cher ami*, what is a *secret de Polichinelle*?"

"Is this a French lesson?" demanded the superintendent wrathfully.

"A *secret de Polichinelle* is a secret that everyone can know. For this reason the people who do not know it never hear about it—for if everyone thinks you know a thing, nobody tells you."

"How I manage to keep my hands off you I don't know," said Superintendent Spence.

25

THE INQUEST was over—a verdict had been returned of murder by a person or persons unknown.

After the inquest, at the invitation of Hercule Poirot, those who had attended it came to Long Meadows.

Working diligently, Poirot had induced some semblance of order in the long drawing-room. Chairs had been arranged in a neat semi-circle, Maureen's dogs had been excluded with difficulty, and Hercule Poirot, a self-appointed lecturer, took up his position at the end of the room and initiated proceedings with a slightly self-conscious clearing of the throat.

"Messieurs et Mesdames——"

He paused. His next words were unexpected and seemed almost farcical.

> "Mrs McGinty's dead. How did she die?
> *Down on her knees just like I.*
> Mrs McGinty's dead. How did she die?
> *Holding her hand out just like I.*
> Mrs McGinty's dead. How did she die?
> *Like this . .*"

Seeing their expressions, he went on:

"No, I am not mad. Because I repeat to you the childish rhyme of a childish game, it does not mean that I am in my second childhood. Some of you may have played that game as children. Mrs Upward had played it. Indeed she repeated it to me—with a difference. She said: '*Mrs McGinty's dead. How did she die? Sticking her neck out just like I.*' That is what she said— and that is what she did. She stuck her neck out—and so she also, like Mrs McGinty, died. . . .

"For our purpose we must go back to the beginning—to Mrs

McGinty—down on her knees scrubbing other people's houses. Mrs McGinty was killed, and a man, James Bentley, was arrested, tried and convicted. For certain reasons, Superintendent Spence, the officer in charge of the case, was not convinced of Bentley's guilt, strong though the evidence was. I agreed with him. I came down here to answer a question. 'How did Mrs McGinty die? *Why* did she die?'

"I will not make you the long and complicated histories. I will say only that as simple a thing as a bottle of ink gave me a clue. In the *Sunday Comet*, read by Mrs McGinty on the Sunday before her death, four photographs were published. You know all about those photographs by now, so I will only say that Mrs McGinty recognised one of those photographs as a photograph she had seen in one of the houses where she worked.

"She spoke of this to James Bentley though he attached no importance to the matter at the time, nor indeed afterwards. Actually he barely listened. But he had the impression that Mrs McGinty had seen the photograph in Mrs Upward's house and that when she referred to a woman who need not be so proud if all was known, she was referring to Mrs Upward. We cannot depend on that statement of his, but she certainly used that phrase about pride and there is no doubt that Mrs Upward *was* a proud and imperious woman.

"As you all know—some of you were present and the others will have heard—I produced those four photographs at Mrs Upward's house. I caught a flicker of surprise and recognition in Mrs Upward's expression and taxed her with it. She had to admit it. She said that she 'had seen one of the photographs somewhere but she couldn't remember where.' When asked which photograph, she pointed to a photograph of the child Lily Gamboll. But that, let me tell you, *was not the truth*. For reasons of her own, Mrs Upward wanted to keep her recognition to herself. She pointed to the wrong photograph to put me off.

"But one person was not deceived—the *murderer*. One person *knew* which photograph Mrs Upward had recognised. And here I will not beat to and fro about the bush—the photograph in question was that of Eva Kane—a woman who was accomplice, victim or possibly leading spirit in the famous Craig Murder Case.

"On the next evening Mrs Upward was killed. She was killed for the same reason that Mrs McGinty was killed. Mrs McGinty stuck her hand out, Mrs Upward stuck her neck out—the result was the same.

"Now before Mrs Upward died, three women received telephone calls. Mrs Carpenter, Mrs Rendell, and Miss Henderson. All three calls were a message from Mrs Upward asking the person in question to come and see her that evening. It was her servant's night out and her son and Mrs Oliver were going into Cullenquay. It would seem, therefore, that she wanted a private conversation with each of these three women.

"Now why *three* women? Did Mrs. Upward know *where* she had seen the photograph of Eva Kane? Or did she know she had seen it but could not remember where? Had these three women anything in common? Nothing, it would seem, but their *age*. They were all, roughly, in the neighbourhood of thirty.

"You have, perhaps, read the article of the *Sunday Comet*. There is a truly sentimental picture in it of Eva Kane's daughter in years to come. The women asked by Mrs Upward to come and see her were all of the right age to be Eva Kane's daughter.

"So it would seem that living in Broadhinny was a young woman who was the daughter of the celebrated murderer Craig and of his mistress Eva Kane, and it would also seem that that young woman would go to any lengths to prevent that fact being known. Would go, indeed, to the length of twice committing murder. For when Mrs Upward was found dead, there were two coffee cups on the table, both used, and on the visitor's cup faint traces of lipstick.

"Now let us go back to the three women who received telephone messages. Mrs Carpenter got the message but says she did not go to Laburnums that nights. Mrs Rendell meant to go, but fell asleep in her chair. Miss Henderson *did* go to Laburnums but the house was dark and she could not make anyone hear and she came away again.

"That is the story these three women tell—but there is conflicting evidence. There is that second coffee cup with lipstick on it, and an outside witness, the girl Edna, states positively that she saw a fair-haired woman go *in* to the house. There is also the

189

evidence of scent—an expensive and exotic scent which Mrs Carpenter uses alone of those concerned."

There was an interruption. Eve Carpenter cried out:

"It's a lie. It's a wicked cruel lie. It wasn't me! I never went there! I never went near the place. Guy, can't you do something about these lies?"

Guy Carpenter was white with anger.

"Let me inform you, M Poirot, that there is a law of slander and all these people present are witnesses."

"Is it slander to say that your wife uses a certain scent—and also, let me tell you, a certain lipstick?"

"It's ridiculous," cried Eve. "Absolutely ridiculous! *Anyone* could go splashing my scent about."

Unexpectedly Poirot beamed on her.

"*Mais oui*, exactly! Anyone could. An obvious, not very subtle thing to do. Clumsy and crude. So clumsy that, as far as I was concerned, it defeated its object. It did more. It gave me, as the phrase goes, ideas. Yes, it gave me ideas.

"Scent—and traces of lipstick on a cup. But it is so easy to remove lipstick from a cup—I assure you every trace can be wiped off quite easily. Or the cups themselves could be removed and washed. Why not? There was no one in the house. But that was not done. I asked myself why? And the answer seemed to be a deliberate stress on femininity, an underlining of the fact that it was a *woman's* murder. I reflected on the telephone calls to those three women—all of them had been *messages*. In no case had the recipient herself spoken to Mrs Upward. So perhaps it was *not* Mrs Upward who had telephoned. It was someone who was anxious to involve a *woman*—any woman—in the crime. Again I asked why? And there can be only one answer—that it was not a woman who killed Mrs Upward—but a *man*."

He looked round on his audience. They were all very still. Only two people responded.

Eve Carpenter said with a sigh: "Now you're talking sense!"

Mrs Oliver, nodding her head vigorously, said: "Of course."

"So I have arrived at this point—a *man* killed Mrs Upward and a *man* killed Mrs McGinty! What man? The reason for the murder must still be the same—it all hinges on a photograph. In whose possession was that photograph? That is the first question? And why was it kept?

"Well, that is perhaps not so difficult. Say that it was kept originally for sentimental reasons. Once Mrs McGinty is— removed, the photograph need not be destroyed. But after the second murder, it is different. This time the photograph has definitely been connected with the murder. The photograph is now a dangerous thing to keep. Therefore you will all agree, it is sure to be destroyed."

He looked round at the heads that nodded agreement.

"But, for all that, the photograph was *not* destroyed! No, it was not destroyed! I know that—because I found it. I found it a few days ago. I found it in this house. In the drawer of the bureau that you see standing against the wall. I have it here."

He held out the faded photograph of a simpering girl with roses.

"Yes," said Poirot. "It is Eva Kane. And on the back of it are written two words in pencil. Shall I tell you what they are? '*My mother*' . . ."

His eyes, grave and accusing, rested on Maureen Summerhayes. She pushed back the hair from her face and stared at him with wide bewildered eyes.

"I don't understand. I never——"

"No, Mrs Summerhayes, you do not understand. There can be only two reasons for keeping this photograph after the second murder. The first of them is an innocent sentimentality. *You* had no feeling of guilt and so you could keep the photograph. You told us yourself, at Mrs Carpenter's house one day, that you were an adopted child. I doubt whether you have ever known what your real mother's name was. But somebody else knew. Somebody who has all the pride of family—a pride that makes him cling to his ancestral home, a pride in his ancestors and his lineage. That man would rather die than have the world—and his children—know that Maureen Summerhayes is the daughter of the murderer Craig and of Eva Kane. That man, I have said, would rather die. But that would not help, would it? So instead let us say that we have here a man who is prepared to kill."

Johnnie Summerhayes got up from his seat. His voice, when he spoke, was quiet, almost friendly.

"Rather a lot of nonsense you're talkin', aren't you? Enjoying yourself spouting out a lot of theories? Theories, that's all they are! Saying things about my wife——"

His anger broke suddenly in a furious tide.

"You damned filthy swine——"

The swiftness of his rush across the floor took the room unawares. Poirot skipped back nimbly and Superintendent Spence was suddenly between Poirot and Summerhayes.

"Now, now, Major Summerhayes, take it easy—take it easy——"

Summerhayes recovered himself, shrugged, said:

"Sorry. Ridiculous really! After all—*anyone* can stick a photograph in a drawer."

"Precisely," said Poirot. "And the interesting thing about this photograph is that it has no fingerprints on it."

He paused, then nodded his head gently.

"But it should have had," he said. "If Mrs Summerhayes kept it, she would have kept it innocently, and so her fingerprints *should* have been on it."

Maureen exclaimed:

"I think you're mad. I've never seen that photograph in my life—except at Mrs Upward's that day."

"It is fortunate for you," said Poirot, "that I know that you are speaking the truth. The photograph was put into that drawer *only a few minutes before I found it there*. Twice that morning the contents of that drawer were tumbled on to the ground, twice I replaced them; the first time the photograph was *not* in the drawer, the second time it *was*. It had been placed there during that interval—*and I know by whom*."

A new note crept into his voice. He was no longer a ridiculous little man with an absurd moustache and dyed hair, he was a hunter very close to his quarry.

"The crimes were committed by a *man*—they were committed for the simplest of all reasons—for money. In Mrs Upward's house there was a book found and on the flyleaf of that book is written *Evelyn Hope*. Hope was the name Eva Kane took when she left England. If her real name was Evelyn then in all probability she gave the name of Evelyn to her child when it was born. *But Evelyn is a man's name as well as a woman's*. Why had we assumed that Eva Kane's child was a girl? Roughly because the *Sunday Comet* said so! But actually the *Sunday Comet* had not said so in so many words, it had assumed it because of a romantic interview with Eva Kane. But Eva Kane left England *before* her child was born—so nobody could say what the sex of the child would be.

"That is where I let myself be misled. By the romantic inaccuracy of the Press.

"Evelyn Hope, Eva Kane's *son*, comes to England. He is talented and he attracts the attention of a very rich woman who knows nothing about his origin—only the romantic story he chooses to tell her. (A very pretty little story it was—all about a tragic young ballerina dying of tuberculosis in Paris!)

"She is a lonely woman who has recently lost her own son. The talented young playwright takes her name by deed poll.

"But your real name is Evelyn Hope isn't it, Mr Upward?"

Robin Upward cried out shrilly:

"Of course it isn't! I don't know what you're talking about."

"You really cannot hope to deny it. There are people who know you under that name. The name Evelyn Hope, written in the book, is in your handwriting—the same handwriting as the words 'my mother' on the back of this photograph. Mrs McGinty saw the photograph and the writing on it when she was tidying your things away. She spoke to you about it after reading the *Sunday Comet*. Mrs McGinty assumed that it was a photograph of *Mrs Upward* when young, since she had no idea Mrs Upward was not your real mother. But you knew that if once she mentioned the matter so that it came to Mrs Upward's ears, it would be the end. Mrs Upward had quite fanatical views on the subject of heredity. She would not tolerate for a moment an adopted son who was the son of a famous murderer. Nor would she forgive your lies on the subject.

"So Mrs McGinty had at all costs to be silenced. You promised her a little present, perhaps, for being discreet. You called on her the next evening on your way to broadcast—and you killed her! *Like this . . ."*

With a sudden movement, Poirot seized the sugar hammer from the shelf and whirled it round and down as though to bring it crashing down on Robin's head.

So menacing was the gesture that several of the circle cried out.

Robin Upward screamed. A high terrified scream.

He yelled: "Don't . . . don't . . . It was an accident. I swear it was an accident. I didn't mean to kill her. I lost my head. I swear I did."

"You washed off the blood and put the sugar hammer back in this room where you had found it. But there are new scientific methods of determining blood stains—and of bringing up latent fingerprints."

"I tell you I never meant to kill her. . . . It was all a mistake. . . . And anyway it isn't my fault. . . . I'm not responsible. It's in my blood. I can't help it. You can't hang me for something that isn't my fault. . . ."

Under his breath Spence muttered: "Can't we? You see if we don't!"

Aloud he spoke in a grave official voice:

"I must warn you, Mr Upward, that anything you say . . ."

26

"I REALLY DON'T see, M Poirot, how ever you came to suspect Robin Upward."

Poirot looked complacently at the faces turned towards him. He always enjoyed explanations.

"I ought to have suspected him much sooner. The clue, such a simple clue, was the sentence uttered by Mrs Summerhayes at the cocktail party that day. She said to Robin Upward: 'I don't like being adopted, do you?' Those were the revealing two words. *Do you?* They meant—they could only mean—that Mrs Upward was not Robin's own mother.

"Mrs Upward was morbidly anxious herself that no one should know that Robin was not her own son. She had probably heard too many ribald comments on brilliant young men who live with and upon elderly women. And very few people did know—only the small theatrical *coterie* where she had first come across Robin. She had few intimate friends in this country, having lived abroad so long, and she chose in any case to come and settle down here far away from her own Yorkshire. Even when she met friends of the old days, she did not enlighten them when they assumed that this Robin was the same Robin they had known as a little boy.

"But from the very first something had struck me as not quite natural in the household at Laburnums. Robin's attitude to Mrs Upward was not that of either a spoiled child, or of a devoted son. It was the attitude of a protégé to a *patron*. The rather fanciful title of Madre had a theatrical touch. And Mrs Upward, though she was clearly very fond of Robin, nevertheless unconsciously treated him as a prized possession that she had bought and paid for.

"So there is Robin Upward, comfortably established, with 'Madre's' purse to back his ventures, and then into his assured world comes Mrs McGinty who has recognised the photograph that he keeps in a drawer—the photograph with 'my mother' written on the back of it. His mother, whom he has told Mrs Upward was a talented young ballet dancer who died of tuberculosis! Mrs McGinty, of course, thinks that the photograph is of Mrs Upward when young, since she assumes as a matter of course that Mrs Upward is Robin's own mother. I do not think that actual blackmail ever entered Mrs McGinty's mind, but she did hope, perhaps, for a 'nice little present,' as a reward for holding her tongue about a piece of bygone gossip which would not have been pleasant for a 'proud' woman like Mrs Upward.

"But Robin Upward was taking no chances. He purloins the sugar hammer, laughingly referred to as a perfect weapon for murder by Mrs Summerhayes, and on the following evening, he stops at Mrs McGinty's cottage on his way to broadcast. She takes him into the parlour, quite unsuspicious, and he kills her. He knows where she keeps her savings—everyone in Broadhinny seems to know—and he fakes a burglary, hiding the money outside the house. Bentley is suspected and arrested. Everything is now safe for clever Robin Upward.

"But then, suddenly, I produce four photographs, and Mrs Upward recognises the one of Eva Kane as being identical with a photograph of Robin's ballerina mother! She needs a little time to think things out. Murder is involved. Can it be possible that Robin——? No, she refuses to believe it.

"What action she would have taken in the end we do not know. But Robin was taking no chances. He plans the whole *mise en scène*. The visit to the Rep on Janet's night out, the telephone calls, the coffee cup carefully smeared with lipstick taken from Eve Carpenter's bag, he even buys a bottle of her distinctive perfume. The whole thing was a theatrical scene setting with prepared props. Whilst Mrs Oliver waited in the car, Robin ran back twice into the house. The murder was a matter of seconds. After that there was only the swift distribution of the 'props.' And with Mrs Upward dead, he inherited a large fortune by the terms of her will, and no suspicion could attach to him since it would seem quite certain that a *woman* had committed the crime. With three women visiting the cottage that night, one of them was almost sure to be suspected. And that, indeed, was so.

"But Robin, like all criminals, was careless and over confident. Not only was there a book in the cottage with his original name scribbled in it, but he also kept, for purposes of his own, the fatal photograph. It would have been much safer for him if he had destroyed it, but he clung to the belief that he could use it to incriminate someone else at the right moment.

"He probably thought then of Mrs Summerhayes. That may be the reason he moved out of the cottage and into Long Meadows. After all, the sugar hammer was hers, and Mrs Summerhayes was, he knew, an adopted child and might find it hard to prove she was not Eva Kane's daughter.

"However, when Deirdre Henderson admitted having been on the scene of the crime, he conceived the idea of planting the photograph amongst *her* possessions. He tried to do so, using a ladder that the gardener had left against the window. But Mrs Wetherby was nervous and had insisted on all the windows being kept locked, so Robin did not succeed in his purpose. He came straight back here and put the photograph in a drawer which, unfortunately for him, I had searched only a short time before.

"I knew, therefore, that the photograph had been planted, and I knew by whom—by the only other person in the house—that person who was typing industriously over my head.

"Since the name Evelyn Hope had been written on the flyleaf of the book from the cottage, Evelyn Hope must be either Mrs. Upward—or Robin Upward. . . .

"The name Evelyn had led me astray—I had connected it with Mrs Carpenter since her name was Eve. *But Evelyn was a man's name as well as a woman's.*

"I remembered the conversation Mrs Oliver had told me about at the Little Rep in Cullenquay. The young actor who had been talking to her was the person I wanted to confirm my theory—the theory that Robin was not Mrs Upward's own son. For by the way he had talked, it seemed clear that he knew the real facts. And his story of Mrs Upward's swift retribution on a young man who had deceived her as to his origins was suggestive.

"The truth is that I ought to have seen the whole thing very much sooner. I was handicapped by a serious error. I believed that I had been deliberately pushed with the intention of sending me on to a railway line—and that the person who had done so was the murderer of Mrs McGinty. Now Robin Upward was practically the only person in Broadhinny who could *not* have been at Kilchester station at that time."

There was a sudden chuckle from Johnnie Summerhayes.

"Probably some old market woman with a basket. They do shove."

Poirot said:

"Actually, Robin Upward was far too conceited to fear me at all. It is a characteristic of murderers. Fortunately, perhaps. For in this case there was very little evidence."

Mrs Oliver stirred.

"Do you mean to say," she demanded incredulously, "that Robin murdered his mother whilst I sat outside in the car, and that I hadn't the least idea of it? There wouldn't have been time!"

"Oh yes, there would. People's ideas of time are usually ludicrously wrong. Just notice some time how swiftly a stage can be reset. In this case it was mostly a matter of props."

"Good theatre," murmured Mrs Oliver mechanically.

"Yes, it was pre-eminently a theatrical murder. All very much contrived."

"And I sat there in the car—and hadn't the least idea!"

"I am afraid," murmured Poirot, "that your woman's intuition was taking a day off. . . ."

27

"I'M NOT going back to Breather & Scuttle," said Maude Williams. "They're a lousy firm anyway."

"And they have served their purpose."

"What do you mean by that, M. Poirot?"

"Why did you come to this part of the world?"

"I suppose being Mr Knowall, you think you know?"

"I have a little idea."

"And what is this famous idea?"

Poirot was looking meditatively at Maude's hair.

"I have been very discreet," he said. "It has been assumed that the woman who went into Mrs Upward's house, the fair-haired woman that Edna saw, was Mrs Carpenter, and that she has denied being there simply out of fright. Since it was Robin Upward who killed Mrs Upward, her presence has no more significance than that of Miss Henderson. But all the same I do not think she *was* there. I think, Miss Williams, that the woman Edna saw was *you*."

"Why me?"

Her voice was hard.

Poirot countered with another question.

"Why were you so interested in Broadhinny? Why, when you went over there, did you ask Robin Upward for an autograph—you are not the autograph-hunting type. What did you know about the Upwards? Why did you come to this part of the world in the first place? How did you know that Eva Kane died in Australia and the name she took when she left England?"

"Good at guessing, aren't you? Well, I've nothing to hide, not really."

She opened her handbag. From a worn notecase she pulled out a small newspaper cutting frayed with age. It showed the face that Poirot by now knew so well, the simpering face of Eva Kane.

Written across it were the words, *She killed my mother*.
Poirot handed it back to her.

"Yes, I thought so. Your real name is Craig?"

Maude nodded.

"I was brought up by some cousins—very decent they were. But I was old enough when it all happened not to forget. I used to think about it a good deal. About *her*. She was a nasty bit of goods all right—children know! My father was just—weak. And besotted by her. But he took the rap. For something, I've always believed, that *she* did. Oh yes, I know he's an accessory after the fact—but it's not quite the same thing, is it? I always meant to find out what had become of *her*. When I was grown up, I got detectives on to it. They traced her to Australia and finally reported that she was dead. She'd left a son—Evelyn Hope he called himself.

"Well, that seemed to close the account. But then I got pally with a young actor chap. He mentioned someone called Evelyn Hope who'd come from Australia, but who now called himself Robin Upward and who wrote plays. I was interested. One night Robin Upward was pointed out to me—and he was with his *mother*. So I thought that, after all, Eva Kane *wasn't* dead. Instead, she was queening it about with a packet of money.

"I got myself a job down here. I was curious—and a bit more than curious. All right, I'll admit it, I thought I'd like to get even with her in some way. . . . When you brought up all this business about James Bentley, I jumped to the conclusion that it was Mrs Upward who'd killed Mrs McGinty. Eva Kane up to her tricks again. I happened to hear from Michael West that Robin Upward and Mrs Oliver were coming over to this show at the Cullenquay Rep. I decided to go to Broadhinny and beard the woman. I meant—I don't quite know what I meant. I'm telling you everything—I took a little pistol I had in the war with me. To frighten her? Or more? Honestly, I don't know . . .

"Well, I got there. There was no sound in the house. The door was unlocked. I went in. You know how I found her. Sitting here dead, her face all purple and swollen. All the things I'd been thinking seemed silly and melodramatic. I knew that I'd never, really, want to kill anyone when it came to it. . . . But I did realise that it might be awkward to explain what I'd been doing in the house. It was a cold night and I'd got gloves on, so I knew I hadn't left any fingerprints, and I didn't think for a moment anyone had seen me. That's all." She paused and added abruptly: "What are you going to do about it?"

"Nothing," said Hercule Poirot. "I wish you good luck in life, that is all."

Epilogue

HERCULE POIROT and Superintendent Spence were celebrating at the *La Vieille Grand'mère*.

As coffee was served Spence leaned back in his chair and gave a deep sigh of repletion.

"Not at all bad grub here," he said approvingly. "A bit frenchified, perhaps, but after all where *can* you get a decent steak and chips nowadays?"

"I had been dining here on the evening you first came to me," said Poirot reminiscently.

"Ah, a lot of water under the bridge since then. I've got to hand it to you, M. Poirot. You did the trick all right." A slight smile creased his wooden countenance. "Lucky that young man didn't realise how very little evidence we'd really got. Why, a clever counsel would have made mincemeat of it! But he lost his head completely, and gave the show away. Spilt the beans and incriminated himself up to the hilt. Lucky for us!"

"It was not entirely luck," said Poirot reprovingly. "I played him, as you play the big fish! He thinks I take the evidence against Mrs Summerhayes seriously—when it is not so, he suffers the reaction and goes to pieces. And besides, he is a coward. I whirl the sugar hammer and he thinks I mean to hit him. Acute fear always produces the truth."

"Lucky you didn't suffer from Major Summerhayes' re-action," said Spence with a grin. "Got a temper, he has, *and* quick on his feet. I only got between you just in time. Has he forgiven you yet?"

"Oh yes, we are the firmest friends. And I have given Mrs Summerhayes a cookery book and have also taught her personally how to make an omelette. *Bon Dieu*, what I suffered in that house!"

He closed his eyes.

"Complicated business, the whole thing," ruminated Spence, uninterested in Poirot's agonised memories. "Just shows how true the old saying is that everyone's got something to hide. Mrs Carpenter, now, had a narrow squeak of being arrested for murder. If ever a woman acted guilty, she did, and all for what?"

"*Eh bien*, what?" asked Poirot curiously.

"Just the usual business of a rather unsavoury past. She had been a taxi dancer—and a bright girl with plenty of men friends! She wasn't a war widow when she came and settled down in Broadhinny. Only what they call nowadays an 'unofficial wife.' Well, of course all that wouldn't do for a stuffed shirt like Guy Carpenter, so she'd spun him a very different sort of tale. And she was frantic lest the whole thing would come out once we started poking round into people's origins."

He sipped his coffee, and then gave a low chuckle.

"Then take the Wetherbys. Sinister sort of house. Hate and malice. Awkward frustrated sort of girl. And what's behind that? Nothing sinister. Just money! Plain £.s.d."

"As simple as that!"

"The girl has the money—quite a lot of it. Left her by an aunt. So mother keeps tight hold of her in case she should want to marry. And stepfather loathes her because *she* has the dibs and pays the bills. I gather he himself has been a failure at anything he's tried. A mean cuss—and as for Mrs W., she's pure poison dissolved in sugar."

"I agree with you." Poirot nodded his head in a satisfied fashion. "It is fortunate that the girl has money. It makes her marriage to James Bentley much more easy to arrange."

Superintendent Spence looked surprised.

"Going to marry James Bentley? Deirdre Henderson? Who says so?"

"I say so," said Poirot. "I occupy myself with the affair. I have, now that our little problem is over, too much time on my hands. I shall employ myself in forwarding this marriage. As yet, the two concerned have no idea of such a thing. But they are attracted. Left to themselves, nothing would happen—but they have to reckon with Hercule Poirot. You will see! The affair will march."

Spence grinned.

"Don't mind sticking your fingers in other people's pies, do you?"

"*Mon cher*, that does not come well from you," said Poirot reproachfully.

"Ah, you've got me there. All the same, James Bentley is a poor stick."

"Certainly he is a poor stick! At the moment he is positively aggrieved because he is not going to be hanged."

"He ought to be down on his knees with gratitude to you," said Spence.

"Say, rather, to you. But apparently he does not think so."

"Queer cuss."

"As you say, and yet at least two women have been prepared to take an interest in him. Nature is very unexpected."

"I thought it was Maude Williams you were going to pair off with him."

"He shall make his choice," said Poirot. "He shall—how do you say it?—award the apple. But I think that it is Deirdre Henderson that he will choose. Maude Williams has too much energy and vitality. With her he would retire even farther into his shell."

"Can't think why either of them should want him!"

"The ways of Nature are indeed inscrutable."

"All the same, you'll have your work cut out. First bringing him up to the scratch—and then prising the girl loose from poison puss mother—she'll fight you tooth and claw!"

"Success is on the side of the big battalions."

"On the side of the big moustaches, I suppose you mean."

Spence roared. Poirot stroked his moustache complacently and suggested a brandy.

"I don't mind if I do, M. Poirot."

Poirot gave the order.

"Ah," said Spence, "I knew there was something else I had to tell you. You remember the Rendells?"

"Naturally."

"Well, when were were checking up on him, something rather odd came to light. It seems that when his first wife died in Leeds where his practice was at that time, the police there got some rather nasty anonymous letters about him. Saying, in effect, that he'd poisoned her. Of course people do say that sort of thing. She'd been attended by an outside doctor, reputable man, and he seemed to think her death was quite above board. There was nothing to go upon except the fact that they'd mutually insured their lives in each other's favour, and people do do that. . . . Nothing for us to go upon, as I say, and yet—I wonder? What do *you* think?"

Poirot remembered Mrs Rendell's frightened air. Her mention of anonymous letters, and her insistence that she did not believe anything they said. He remembered, too, her certainty that his inquiry about Mrs McGinty was only a pretext.

He said, "I would imagine that it was not only the police who got anonymous letters."

"Sent them to her, too?"

"I think so. When I appeared in Broadhinny, she thought I was on her husband's track, and that the McGinty business was a pretext. Yes—and he thought so, too. . . . That explains it! It was Dr Rendell who tried to push me under the train that night!"

"Think he'll have a shot at doing this wife in, too?"

"I think she would be wise not to insure her life in his favour," said Poirot dryly. "But if he believes we have an eye on him he will probably be prudent."

"We'll do what we can. We'll keep an eye on our genial doctor, and make it clear we're doing so."

Poirot raised his brandy glass.

"To Mrs Oliver," he said.

"What put her into your head suddenly?"

"Woman's intuition," said Poirot.

There was silence for a moment, then Spence said slowly: "Robin Upward is coming up for trial next week. You know, Poirot, I can't help feeling doubtful——"

Poirot interrupted him with horror.

"*Mon Dieu!* You are not now doubtful about Robin Upward's guilt, are you? Do not say you want to start over again."

Superintendent Spence grinned reassuringly.

"Good lord, no. *He's* a murderer all right!" He added: "Cocky enough for anything!"